STREET BOYS

LORENZO CARCATERRA

STREET BOYS

SIMON & SCHUSTER

London · New York · Sydney · Tokyo · Singapore · Toronto · Dublin

A VIACOM COMPANY

First published in Great Britain by Simon & Schuster UK Ltd, 2002
A Viacom company

1 3 5 7 9 10 8 6 4 2

Simon & Schuster UK Ltd
Africa House
64–78 Kingsway
London WC2B 6AH

www.simonsays.co.uk

Simon & Schuster Australia
Sydney

A CIP catalogue record for this book is available from the British Library

Hardback ISBN 0-7432-3208-9
Trade paperback ISBN 0-7432-3132-5

Printed and bound in Great Britain by
The Bath Press, Bath

This one's for Kate.

ACKNOWLEDGMENTS

I've always wanted to write a novel about the war and the brave young men and women of Naples. There are many who have helped make that possible. I would like to thank my mother, Raffaela, and my Nonna Maria for sharing their stories of pain and loss. And to my family and friends in Italy (especially Paolo Murino and Vincent Cerbone) who opened their hearts and showed me the city of Naples and its people in ways I would never have been able to see on my own. *Ai sempre un posto nel mio cuoro.*

Warm thanks must also be sent to Peter Gethers, hands down the best editor in the book business, and to Gina Centrello, a terrific publisher whose energy and enthusiasm help fuel each of my stories. And to the rest of the Ballantine posse—Ed, Ann, Kim, Marie, Leyla, Claudia and the best sales force on the planet—thank you.

A writer is only as good as the team around him, and I have the best. Owen, Joni, Rob, Suzanne and Tracy at William Morris cover me like a warm blanket. Lou Pitt puts up with the phone calls and the complaints, all the while making sure that what needs to be done gets done. Robert Offer delivers comfort and hard work and always has the right answer. And the great Jake Bloom has never wavered in his love and care. He's the father I wish I had and the friend I will always have.

To Lorenzo Di Bonaventura, thanks for the trust and the friendship. This novel is yours as much as it is mine. To Courtenay Valenti and Steve Reuther for loving this story as much as I do, and to Paula Weinstein and Barry Levinson for their help.

To my friends who put up with the calls and always leave me with a smile—Hank Gallo, Dr. George, Mr. G., Steve Allie, William Diehl,

Bobby G., Captain Joe, Eric and Peggy, Ida and Anthony, Peter Giuliano, Rocco, Fast Freddie, Sonny, Adriana, Rabbi Liz, Sister K, Michael C., Judge Leslie Crocker Snyder—a heartfelt thank you. Uncle Robert and Aunt Jane have earned a special place in my heart. And it is always a pleasure to spend time in the company of Caroline Shea, Dustin Fleischman and Peter Paleokrassas.

To my wife, Susan Toepfer, who endured a turbulent year and showed everyone around her how to handle it with both class and quiet dignity. I end up with her by my side. The other guys end up with each other. I win.

To my daughter, Kate, now old enough to teach me a few life lessons of her own, keep reaching for your dreams. You'll figure out a way to get there. And to my son, Nick, the smiles, the hugs and the wise cracks help a lot more than you can ever know.

And to Big Jack Sanders—we all miss you every day.

AUTHOR'S NOTE

During a four-day period, starting on September 28 and ending on October 1, 1943, a band of Italian street orphans, numbering less than three hundred, took on an advancing German Panzer Division that had been sent to finish the destruction of their home city of Naples. The boys and a handful of girls, armed only with primitive weapons and an arsenal of street cunning, fought with bravery and distinction.

It is a story I have heard many times. My mother always told it to me on the nights when I had trouble sleeping. She had lost a six-month-old son to the bombing of Salerno in 1943, and her story, told in her native Neapolitan dialect, always ended in tears for both of us.

As I got older and spent many months across many years in southern Italy, I heard different versions of the same story from people who had suffered through that war and through those days, many of them relatives. I have been a close friend for nearly twenty years with one of the boys who was part of that battle. For him, the victory was cruel: he lost a mother and two sisters in the rubble that was Naples.

I am not a historian and this book is not factual. All the characters are fictional, as are the details of the battles. The dialogue and settings can be found nowhere but on these pages. But at the very heart of this novel, at its deepest center, there is a simple truth: that a band of children, stripped of all that mattered to their lives, stood up against the most powerful army ever to invade their soil.

This novel stands as a testament to the courage of the *scugnizzi* of Naples. And to the blood they spilled.

—LORENZO CARCATERRA
FEBRUARY 2002

We talk just like lions
But we sacrifice like lambs

—"Round Here,"
Counting Crows

PREFACE

The German tank stopped in front of the small stone house, its tracks grinding the quarter-acre vegetable garden into pockets of dust. A German officer, young and in full battle gear, stood alongside, a bullhorn in one hand, a lit cigarette in the other. He raised the bullhorn to his lips, staring out with crystal blue eyes at the alarmed faces, young and old.

"You must leave now," he commanded, his voice echoing through the funnel of the horn. "Take no possessions, take no food. This is no longer your home and this is no longer your property. The city is now under our rule. There is always a price to be paid for betrayal. This is yours."

He saw the old woman out of the corner of his right eye.

She walked with a hobble as she rushed out of the back of the house, her arms wrapped around a three-foot statue of the Virgin Mary. She was dressed in black, with a hand-knit black shawl draped across her shoulders, her long strands of hair, white as an afternoon cloud, rolled and held in place by rows of thick pins. The war had cost her all she had once called her own—a husband she loved, sons and daughters who doted on her, grandchildren she cuddled in her arms, singing them to sleep in the silence of the Neapolitan night. Her home, where she was born, the place where she had made a life for herself and her husband, was now in enemy hands. All she had left was the statue that had been in her family for three generations. Gianna Mazella, seventy-eight years old, riddled with the pains of advancing age and the weight of a broken heart, would rather be found dead than let it fall into someone else's hands. So she ran with her head down and her lips pursed against the sculptured edges of the statue, murmuring words of prayer as she moved over strips of parched land in search of safety. Her old heart was beating hard and fast, heavy patches of sweat forming on her back and chest, rivulets of perspiration running down the sides of her olive-skinned face. *"Madanna Mia, famme arrivera in tempo,"* the old woman mumbled into the cool marble, her arms gripping the statue as if it were a life preserver. *"Ti prego, famme arrivera."*

The German officer turned to his left, looking down at an infantry-man with his rifle at his side. The officer nodded and the soldier dropped to one knee and brought his rifle up against the base of his shoulder. His right eye squinted shut, his left searched for the old woman in his scope. "Do you have her in range?" the officer asked.

"Yes, sir," the soldier answered without a shift in position. "I can graze her in the arm or leg. That will bring her to a stop."

"We are not here to waste bullets," the officer said. "Nor are we here to stop escaping prisoners. We are here to kill them."

The soldier closed both eyes for a brief moment and rubbed the fingers of his hands together, looking to free them of sweat. "I have the head shot, sir," he said softly.

"Then take it," the officer told him.

The young soldier gave the trigger a gentle squeeze, the mild recoil jolting him slightly. He opened both eyes and brought the rifle back against his chest. He saw the old woman spread out, facedown across a dry patch of dirt, lower limbs still twitching, blood oozing out of a large gaping wound in her temple, the religious statue next to her, inches beyond her grasp.

"Well done," the officer said, turning away from the soldier. "Perhaps now the rest of these Italians will realize it doesn't pay to ignore our orders."

In the late summer of 1943, Naples was a city under siege.

Italy was once the third and weakest spoke in the Axis wheel forged by Germany and Japan as each nation sought to grab a piece of the world. Now the country and its citizens found themselves the victims of an abrupt switch in gears. Their once beloved leader, Benito Mussolini, in power since 1922, had been ousted from office by the anti-Fascists and was on the run in northern Italy, turning futilely to his last remaining ally, Adolf Hitler, for help. This left the Italians, for the most part, leaderless and stripped of any hope for a reasonable peace.

For the first fifteen years of Il Duce's reign, from 1922 to 1937, Italy had thrived.

Roads long abandoned and unfit for use were dug up and repaved. Factory doors once bolted were opened wide and the businesses running at full capacity. Museum works were refurbished and the train stations modernized. Crime that was once rampant, claiming thousands of victims a day, was shut down, the criminals either behind bars or beneath freshly turned ground. A once starving populace pranced around with full stomachs and pockets crammed with cash. The Italians, who for decades had been treated as the adorable doormats of Europe, reveled in their fresh avenues of strength. "We are the new America," Italians would brag in long letters sent to relatives living and struggling in the States. "We no longer need to leave our land to find fortune."

The Italians, especially those in the more impoverished southern regions of the country, took to heart Mussolini's words and beliefs. "It is better to live one day as a lion than a thousand years as a lamb" was a credo that even the youngest schoolboy could recite. Mussolini promised his people riches and glory not seen since the days of the Roman Empire, and for many years they believed in all that he said and all that he did. The Italians would follow him in any quest and answer his call to conquer any land.

The arrival of World War II brought a vicious and brutal halt to those dreams of power and respect, and forced Italians to awaken to a national nightmare.

The once rebuilt and redesigned infrastructures were blown to shreds by the onslaught of Allied bombing raids. Relics and artifacts that had withstood the battering of centuries now caved and shattered to the tumult of war. Mussolini's government bolted and the people's mood turned from adoration to rage as they saw their lands destroyed and the bodies of loved ones, young and old, in uniform and out, dead for reasons no one could fathom. The dictator's once-mighty government shattered into tiny glass particles and was dispersed throughout Italy, its officers seeking solace in any port that would have them. The new government, led by a weak puppet named Marshal Pietro Badoglio, failed to rally the spirits of his people, who were short of food and fuel and living in a cauldron of destruction and upheaval. One hundred and ten thousand Italian soldiers lay dead in the frozen tundra of the Russian front, sent there by Mussolini to aid Hitler in his maniacal quest. An equal number of bodies were scattered throughout the Italian countryside and in North Africa, all of them victims of their leader's thirst for world domination.

The years of victory were quickly erased from Italian memories.

By the summer of 1943, Italy was being attacked on two fronts, turning the country into one large battle zone. The combined Allied forces of American and British troops occupied lands and islands to the south. Sicily, Salerno and Paestum all fell in quick succession. At the same time, what had been an uneasy German friendship now turned into full-blown Nazi rage. Suddenly, Hitler's air attacks and tank divisions throttled the Italian seacoast, Naples taking the hardest of the hits.

The Nazi high command had deemed Naples a port city that could not be left intact or it would become a stronghold for the Allied forces, giving them a clear path to the open sea. They knew it was inevitable that an American/British takeover of the city would occur, so a sinister three-step program was set in motion to ensure that miles of burning buildings, downed electrical wires, blown water systems and bombed-out roads would form a welcoming committee. Phase one was to evacuate anyone with the strength to walk out of the city. Phase two involved nighttime aerial attacks, aimed at destroying any structure that could be used by the enemy as housing or as a place to store arms. The final phase involved the complete and total destruction of Naples, a city that had withered but never fallen to the onslaught of dozens of conquerors over a handful of centuries. "If the city cannot belong to Hitler," one German commander fumed, "then it will belong to no one."

Any Neapolitan who resisted evacuation would be subject to the whim of the commanding officer in the sector. The few members of the growing Italian resistance fled to the surrounding hillside to await orders that were expected to come from the north. The Neapolitans were not sure of their future, but neither were they foolish enough to believe that the Germans planned to bring them out of Naples and usher them into a safe environment. They understood that they were being led to slaughter. It is why all resources were used to hide their children from Nazi eyes. The majority of those children were boys. Such thinking reflected a belief that boys would be best able to survive and cope on their own, which easily fed into the southern Italian reluctance to ever leave an unmarried daughter behind, regardless of circumstances. "Our families walked to a death sentence," said Fabrizio Serra, who turned eighteen the day the Germans came into the city. "The lines started forming early in the morning, men and women marching side by side, leaving behind the only place they had ever lived. None of them turned around. No one could stand to see their homes burned, their animals killed, their furniture destroyed. I was hiding in a corner of a church steeple, looking down at the long lines stretched throughout the city. The only voices I heard were German, yelling out orders, setting fires, shooting anyone who refused to listen or who moved too slowly. My mother, father and aunt Julia left that day. They had accepted their fate. As he passed by the church, my father glanced up at me, one hand over his heart. It was his way of saying good-bye."

They were piled onto the backs of flatbed trucks and herded into empty cargo trains at the main terminal. They walked with the slow gait of the defeated, tattered shoes leaving behind small mounds of dust, arms heavy by their sides, heads too weak to gaze at anything other than the dirt and cobblestones in front of them. The people of Naples had handed their destinies to a dictator who had promised them a piece of paradise on their ride to world rule. In its stead, there was now a land of darkness and upheaval, sadness and loss at every turn.

The boy's name was Vincenzo Scolardi and he ran down the narrow streets, dodging cracks in the pavement and shattered stones, an early morning mist resting like a large quilt over the length of the city. He had

a round, brown-crusted loaf of bread jammed under one arm and a string
of rosary beads wrapped around the fingers of his left hand. He kept his
head down, his thin-soled shoes landing softly on small puddles of brown
water and hard edges of broken glass. The boy was tall for sixteen, with
rich, curly brown hair, olive eyes and a casual manner. He had been both
a gifted student and a superb soccer player prior to the eruption of the
war. But neither school nor sports were what inspired the boy now. He
loved and lived for a life in the military, eager to carry on a family tradition begun by his great-grandfather Giovanni, who held high the banner
of a unified Naples, fighting alongside the legendary Giuseppe Garibaldi
during his march into the city on September 7, 1860. Vincenzo devoured
books on military history and tactics, envisioning the day when he would
lead his own troops into the firestorm of battle.

He had spent the night sleeping under an old cot topped by a soiled mattress in a deserted apartment off Via Toledo, waiting out the bombing attacks that greeted Naples each night. His mother had sent him out earlier in
the day in search of black market bread, which arrived nightly, carted in by
flatbed trucks and sold in the darkness of quiet alleys. The war had stripped
Neapolitans of even the most basic necessities, and they were forced to dole
out small ransoms for what had once been inexpensive staples.

The trucks had been late.

They usually drove into the alleys at nine, but were delayed by mines
and German checkpoints. The boy waited on a long, quiet line until
nearly midnight for the round loaf that would serve as that day's meal for
his mother and two sisters. The air-raid alarms sounded seconds after the
boy paid for the bread. He dropped his lira into the hands of a black mar-
keter he had come to know, nodded and turned to leave. "Don't go home,
Vincenzo," the man whispered from the emptiness of the dark truck.

"My mother's waiting for this," Vincenzo said. "My sisters haven't
eaten all day."

"Forget about tonight," the man said. "Let them have their bread in
the morning."

"I'm not worried about the bombs," Vincenzo said. "I've run through
them before."

"It's not the bombs you need to be concerned about," the man said. "It's the thieves who wait to steal the bread you buy. They haven't eaten all day, either. And they never pay for what goes in their mouths."

Vincenzo stared at the man, not sure whether to trust his own instincts or the word of a seller who profited from the hunger of his own people. "I'm not afraid," Vincenzo said, looking around him at the now empty alley.

"Nor are you foolish," the man said. "Find a warm place and wait out the night. You can make your run in the morning. Feed your family a good meal then. It's a better choice than arriving home with empty hands."

The first of the bombs fell in the piazza off the alley, sending debris and dust flying into the night air, the area now lit with flames. The truck's engine kicked over and the man stood away from Vincenzo and let the cover drop over the back of the truck. "Save yourself," the man said as he disappeared from view. "And the bread, too."

Vincenzo waited until dawn before he braved the run back home.

He turned the final corner and skidded to a stop. He stood across from where his house had once been and stared at the crumpled mass of pink stucco, cement and wood. He dropped the bread and fell to his knees, head bowed, hands spread down the length of his face. He began to moan, moving back and forth in painful rhythms of agony, his body lifeless, his muscles weak. He lowered his head to the top of his knees and shook with rage and remorse. He didn't need to look, didn't need to search through rubble to find what he already knew to be true—they were dead.

His mother, who had born the weight of the war with stoic strength and love, was gone from his life. His younger sister, always quick to tease him and who loved to hear him laugh, lay crushed under the weight of stones that had once kept her safe. His older sister, who sang and rocked him to sleep when he was a toddler, reached out to her mother one final time before the bomb tore apart their lives.

Vincenzo lifted his head, his face rich with tears and sorrow, and looked to the sky, searching through morning mist for the faces he loved. He let out a series of loud screams, his hands held tight, pounding at the ground around him. No one heard. No one saw. No one came. He was a lost boy now, adrift without a home or a family to fill it. He was a victim of the war, joining the ranks of so many Italians who had been stripped of all they held close to their hearts. He was still only a child, but now he would be forced to set aside such thoughts, to think and fend like a man, responsible to no one other than himself. And he was in pain; sharp, agonizing jolts jarred his every movement. At that moment, empty of all feeling, ripped away from all that he loved, the boy wanted nothing more than to die. Instead, Vincenzo faced the long and grueling process of burying his family.

"You want a marker for the graves?" his friend Franco asked. Franco was fourteen, with a muscular frame, crisp dark eyes and a thick head of hair that he hated to have cut, long locks ruffled by the slightest wind.

The boy shook his head. "I'm the only one who needs to know where they are," he said.

"I'm sorry, Vincenzo," Franco said. "They did not deserve to die like this."

Vincenzo stared at the graves and nodded. "No one does," he said.

"Maybe if they had left along with the others," Franco said. He stood next to Vincenzo, his right foot resting against a crumpled stone wall that had once been the older boy's home. "Left when the Germans told them to leave. Maybe today they would still be alive."

"My mother said that if we were to die, we had earned the right to die in our own city," Vincenzo said.

"You heard the soldiers with the bullhorns," Franco said. "You read the leaflets they dropped. They're coming back. This time with tanks and many more soldiers. They're not going to stop until they destroy all of it."

"I heard them," Vincenzo said. "And I believe them. What they can't have, they want no one else to have."

"These graves we made won't last very long," Franco said. "The bombs will see to that."

Vincenzo looked past Franco and out across the smoke and ruin of Naples. "The bombs can't hurt them anymore," he said.

BOOK ONE

. . . We are but warriors for the working day.

—*HENRY V*,
WILLIAM SHAKESPEARE

1

Captain Edward Anders leaned under the warm shade of a fig tree, a lit Lucky Strike hanging from his lips, and stared down at the beachhead below. His troops had been in the first wave of the attack to capture a city whose name he had never heard before the war. It took the combined forces of American and British troops nine days to advance past the beach and up the side of the sloping mountain where he now stood, smoking the last cigarette in his pack. Behind him, a command post had been set up inside a long series of brown tents. Inside the main tent, there were 3,500 sets of dog tags scattered in four wooden boxes, waiting to be mailed Stateside for eventual delivery to the relatives of the men who had been lost in a fight for sand and rock. Anders stared at the mountains above him, up toward Cassino, then back down toward the city of Naples, and knew there was still a lot of hard fighting left.

"Hey, Cap," a voice behind him said. "Word is you want to see me."

"It was more like an order," Captain Anders said. "But let's not stand on formalities."

Captain Anders turned to look at Corporal Steve Connors as he stood at attention and held his salute, the Gulf of Salerno at his back. Anders brushed away the salute. "From what I've seen, you have as little patience for that shit as I do. Which probably means neither one of us is going to get far in this army."

"I just want to get far enough to go home, Cap," Connors said.

"Will Naples do you in the meantime?" Anders asked.

"What's in Naples?"

"Most likely nothing. From the reports I've seen, the city's already nothing more than a ghost town."

"But still, you want me to go," Connors said.

He removed his helmet and wiped the sweat from his brow with the sleeve of his uniform. Steve Connors was twenty-five years old, a college graduate and second-year law student from Covington, Kentucky. He was just shy of six feet tall with a middleweight fighter's rugged build, topped by thick strands of dark hair, brown eyes and a wide smile that balanced out a hard edge. He had fought under Anders's command for fourteen months, pounding and slashing his way from one blood-drenched beachhead to the next, always the first in line, always the first to fire. He had a street fighter's instincts for battle and survival and was, as far as Captain Ed Anders was concerned, the best soldier for the task at hand.

"It might just be a ghost town with two of our men in it," Anders said. "We had a handful of G.I.s helping the Italian resistance—or whatever the hell was left of it. Most of them slipped out before the evacuation. Two didn't. They could be dead. They could be hiding. They could be back in the States for all I know. But we've got to find out."

"I go in alone?" Connors asked.

"You'd like that, wouldn't you?" Anders said.

"Very much, sir."

"I'd like a bowl of my wife's white bean soup," Anders said. "But that's not going to happen, either. You'll be part of a three-man team. You go in, as quiet as you can, check out the city and see if you can find our guys."

"Who else is on the team, sir?"

"If our soldiers are still in there, they might be hurt. So you'll take one of the medics, Willis. And then another good rifle to cover your back. That'll be Scott Taylor."

Connors winced at the sound of Taylor's name. "Every man out here has a rifle, sir," he said. "Not just Taylor."

"But not every man's going," Anders said, raising his voice. "Taylor is. I know you two rub each other the hard way, but this ain't the senior prom. If it gets tight, he's somebody good to have on your side. Neither one of you has to like it. You just have to do it."

"Yes, sir," Connors said. "Anything else I need to know?"

"Not a damn thing." Anders reached into the front flap of the younger soldier's shirt and pulled a loose cigarette from his open pack. "Just radio back what you see. We'll do the rest."

"And if we don't find our men?" Connors asked. "What then, Cap?"

"Enjoy your stay in Naples," Captain Anders said as he turned and headed back up to his command post.

2

16TH PANZER DIVISION HEADQUARTERS
FIFTEEN MILES OUTSIDE ROME, ITALY. SEPTEMBER 25, 1943

The eighty Mark IV tanks sat in long silent rows. German soldiers were scattered about, searching out shade and a cool place to doze. Colonel Rudolph Von Klaus stood in the open pit of his tank and stared at the note in his hands. The words on the paper had been passed down directly from Adolf Hitler himself. They were as simple and direct as any order he had received in his twenty-five-year military career. "Allow no stone in Naples to stand" was all it said.

To a precise and proud officer, the order read as nothing more than a complete waste—of a city once bold and beautiful, of a Panzer division that had fought too hard for too long to be reduced to a mop-up unit, and of time, of which there was precious little left before this wretched war would reach its ruinous conclusion. Naples had already been contained, its streets emptied. Aerial bombings had destroyed any buildings that could possibly be of future use to the enemy. It was a mission of madness. Just one more foolish request springing from the unhinged mind of a leader he found lacking in military logic.

Von Klaus folded the order into sections and shoved it into his pant pocket. He gazed around at his troops and took some comfort from the fact that as inane as the order was, its simplicity would at least guarantee that he would not have to leave behind any more of his men, lying dead or wounded on a battlefield. After the Naples mission, Von Klaus was scheduled to head back home, to a wife he had not seen in two years, a daughter who would now be eight and a son too young to remember the last time his father cradled him in his arms. Von Klaus was only forty-six years old, but felt decades past that. Nothing, he believed, aged a man more than having to face the reality of inevitable defeat.

"The tanks are repaired and fueled, sir." The young soldier stood several feet across from Von Klaus, half-hidden by the shadows of dangling tree limbs. He looked to be months removed from his teenage years.

"Good," Von Klaus said. "And the mules have been fed as well?"

"Yes, sir," the soldier said. "Earlier this morning."

"Check on them again tomorrow," Von Klaus told him. "Until then, enjoy this warm Italian sun."

"Sir, if I may, some of the men were wondering when we would be moving on," the soldier said.

"Do you have a girl back home that you care about, Kunnalt?" Von Klaus asked him.

"Yes, sir," Kunnalt said, surprised at the question. "We plan to marry once the war is over."

"Then go and find a large rock, sit down and write her a letter," Von Klaus said. "Make it a long one and take your time doing it. I'm in no rush to leave. The empty buildings of Naples will wait for us."

3

Two hundred boys and girls were spread out around a large fire, the flames licking the thick, crusty wood, sending sparks and smoke into the starlit sky. Their clothes were dirty and shredded at the sleeves and cuffs, shoes held together by cardboard and string. All their memories had been scarred by the frightful cries of war and the loss that always followed. The youngest members of the group, between five and seven years old, stood with their backs to the others, tossing small pebbles into the oil-soaked Bay of Naples. The rest, their tired faces filled with hunger and sadness, the glow from the fire illuminating their plight, huddled around Vincenzo and Franco. They were children without a future, marked for an unknown destiny.

Vincenzo stepped closer to the fire and glanced up at the sky, enjoying the rare evening silence. He looked down and smiled at two small boys, Giancarlo and Antonio, playing quietly by the edge of the pier, their thin legs dangling several feet above the water below. He glanced past them at a girl slowly making her way toward him, squeezing past a cluster of boys standing idle and silent. She was tall, about fifteen, with rich brown hair rolled up and buried under a cap two sizes too large. Her tan face was marred by streaks of soot and dirt. She stepped between Vincenzo and the two boys, her arms by her side, an angry look to her soft eyes.

"Where do we go from here?" she asked.

"The hills," Vincenzo said with a slight shrug. "It seems the safest place. At least for now."

"And after that?" she asked in a voice younger than her years.

"What's your name?" Vincenzo asked, the flames from the fire warming his face.

"Angela," she said. "I lived in Forcella with my family. Now I live there alone."

Forcella was the roughest neighborhood in Naples, a tight space of only a few blocks that historically had been the breeding ground for thieves and killers and the prime recruitment territory for the Camorra, the Neapolitan Mafia. "Forcella?" Vincenzo said to her. "Not even a Nazi would be brave enough to set foot on those streets."

"Especially after dark," Franco said, laughing.

"But they did," Angela said, lowering her eyes for a brief moment.

"What do you want me to do?" Vincenzo said. "Where do you think we should go? Look around you. This is all that's left of us."

"So we run," she said, words laced with sarcasm. "Like always."

Vincenzo stepped closer to her, his face red from both the fire and his rising anger. "There is nothing else to do," he said. "You can help us with some of the little ones. A lot of them are too sick to walk."

Angela glared at Vincenzo for several moments, lowered her head and then turned back into the mouth of the crowd.

Vincenzo walked in silence around the edges of the fire, the sounds of the crackling wood mixing with the murmurs of the gathered teens. They were all children forced to bear the burden of adults, surviving on the barest essentials, living like cornered animals in need of shelter and a home. They had been scattered throughout the city, gutter rats in soiled clothing, enduring the daily thrashings of a war started by strangers in uniforms who spoke of worlds to conquer.

They had been born under the reign of Benito Mussolini and his fascist regime. As the United States suffered through the pangs of a Great Depression, Italy lived under the warmth of economic prosperity. Its fields were flush with crops and its factories filled to capacity with products that brought the country headfirst into the modern age. Now, the fields were burned and barren, the factories bombed and bare. Where there was once hope, there now rested only hunger. Where once visions of great victories filled Italian hearts, there was now nothing more than the somber acceptance of a humiliating defeat.

"Naples has always been ruled by outsiders," Vincenzo said, stopping alongside Franco and tossing two more planks of old wood onto the fire. "We've always been someone's prisoner. But in all that time, the people have never surrendered the streets without a fight. This war, against this enemy, would be the first time that has ever happened."

"Who are we to stop it?" Franco said, staring into his friend's eyes.

Vincenzo stood in front of the flames, his shirt and arms stained with sweat, light gray smoke filling his lungs. He then turned and walked away, disappearing into the darkness of the Neapolitan night.

4

A HIGHWAY ROAD, TWENTY-FIVE MILES OUTSIDE OF SALERNO
SEPTEMBER 26, 1943

Steve Connors shifted gears on the jeep and eased it gently past a large hole in the dirt road and onto a long patch of brown grass. He killed the engine, grabbed a newspaper off the passenger seat and stepped out of the jeep. He lit a cigarette as he walked and folded a four-week-old edition of the *Cincinnati Enquirer* over to the sports section. He scanned past the headlines, searching for the baseball standings and the box scores.

"Why we stopping?" Scott Taylor asked, sitting in the front seat of the jeep. Taylor was twenty-four, a year younger than Connors. He was tall and muscular with short blond hair and pale skin that was quick to redden under the Italian sun, a high school football star back in his hometown of Pittsburgh. The two had known each other since basic training and shared a mutual respect for their respective battle skills and a dislike toward one another for almost everything else.

Connors flopped down under the shade of an old fig tree, leaning his head against its rugged bark. "Germans mine everything," he said. "A road leading into Naples is one they wouldn't miss. Which means we have to drive on grass. Which means before I start, I need a break."

"I don't need convincing," Willis, the medic, said, jumping out of the backseat of the jeep and walking toward Connors and the shade. Willis was still a teenager, even though he tried to act older. He was the only child of a single mother who worked as a schoolteacher back in Davenport, Iowa. Willis was slight, had thin brown hair and walked with a farmer's gait. He was a good medic and never panicked under the rush of battle. "Besides, you can only ride in these jeeps for so long. Makes your whole body numb."

"I'll wait here," Taylor said, stretching his legs out and lighting a cigarette.

"That's a good idea, Taylor," Connors said, his eyes still shut. "I'd hate to have some sheepherder come along and drive off with the jeep."

Connors tipped his helmet down across his face and allowed his mind to drift back to the many lazy afternoons he had spent across the river from Covington, sitting in the cheap seats at Crosley Field. With a youthful and still innocent exuberance, Connors would cheer the Cincinnati Reds to victory, savoring the win even more if it was brought about by the exploits of his favorite player, first baseman Frank McCormick.

Connors didn't have much nostalgia for home, other than the normal longing for family and familiar faces and places. But not even the brutal events of a war could diminish his love for baseball. He longed for a game that was at once so simple yet so strict with its traditions and its rules. He loved the finality that embraced the two teams at the completion of nine innings, only to see each one grasp a new beginning with the start of the very next game. He lifted his helmet and gazed out at his surroundings, craters and rubble dotting a landscape once rich with vineyards and villas, and knew that such simplicity never could be applied to the much harsher rules of war.

After each Reds home game, Connors and a small pack of friends would drive over to Bob's Restaurant, a twelve-mile run off the flat-road highway connecting Cincinnati to Cleveland, and order up a tableful of onion-smeared cheeseburgers and a platter of gravy fries, the entire greasy meal washed down with long-neck bottles of root beer and cream soda. Those days seemed so far removed from him now, distant memories from an orderly world.

The months he had spent in Europe, fighting battles in places he used to read about in schoolbooks and novels, had changed both his outlook on life and the direction he envisioned for his future. If America had been able to steer itself clear of war, Connors would have finished off his years of law school, settled down with a local girl and carved out a life as a tax attorney working for a Cincinnati firm, walking a similar life path as his father. And, much like his father, Steve Connors knew he would have lived out his days a happy man. But now, after all that he had seen and all that he had done as a soldier, he realized he would never be able to accept such a set-in-stone existence. He wasn't quite sure what his new course would turn out to be or what events would enable him to give it shape and substance, and for now he didn't feel any urgent need to know. For the moment, Connors was content with the knowledge that he had not only survived the rugged call of battle but thrived under its constant, daily pressure.

None of his combat moments, he honestly believed, required bravery or defiant acts of courage, and none contributed to his abilities as a soldier. He simply was a young man incapable of accepting defeat from anyone, at any time, and that is what helped fuel his desire not only to fight but to survive. It was a character trait that had followed him from early childhood and one he had never taken the time to notice. Especially since his unwillingness to concede a loss usually occurred over such unimportant events as a Little League baseball game, friendly nights of poker or a drag race in a remodified Chevy down dusty Graves Road outside Batavia, Ohio. But in war, such a trait looms large enough to gain attention and change the course of a man's life.

Connors rested the sports section on his legs and looked out at the silent countryside. The area between Rome and Naples had been shelled hard, destroying most of the standing structures and turning Mussolini's modern roadways into a graveyard for busted tires and broken axles. Yet despite all the damage, the region still retained the core of its stunning beauty and hard-to-resist charm. It was a stubborn land, much like the people who had lived off it. He lit a fresh cigarette, rubbed at the back of his neck and stared over at Willis, stretched out under the tree across from his. He glanced over at Taylor, stubbornly stewing in the front of the jeep, the sun turning his cheeks and forehead the color of beets, and shook his head.

In many ways, Connors feared for his future back home in America more than he feared any battle he would face here in Europe. He was a less complicated man living in Covington. There, he had understood his place and his standing, all the pieces of his life evenly and conveniently sorted and wrapped. But all that had changed, starting in those first weeks at basic, going right up to the final bullet he had fired during last week's taking of the Salerno beachhead.

It often startled him to discover how calm he was in the midst of battle, how in check his emotions stayed and how he was able to rein in his fear and use its energy to his advantage, even as all around him the faces of the familiar fell dead. He thrived on the confrontation with the enemy and seemed impenetrable to their vicious and steady assault. No one in Covington would ever have envisioned him to be the soldier he had turned out to be. Back home he was the guy who was always quick with a sharp answer, ready and eager to make light of any situation. On European soil, he proved to be even quicker with a rifle, finding peace in the hard moments of a tense fight. He knew he would never find such peace back home, sitting in a quiet corner of a tax attorney's office. He wondered if all that would change for him yet again, once he got back Stateside and lived among the surroundings he had always called his own. Part of him hoped so.

And, strangely, part of him didn't.

The dog's growl forced open his eyes.

Connors turned his head and saw a cream-colored bullmastiff stand-ing a few feet to his left, its thick jowls curled in anger, a wide blotch of blood staining its massive left hind leg. He stared at the dog for several seconds, trying to decide if it was looking for a fight or just on a break from one. He lowered a hand off his leg and stretched out his fingers, reaching for a pack of Necco wafers wedged in the center of his K ra-tions. The dog caught the hand motion and took two steps forward, heavy paws digging into the soft, dark dirt. Connors pulled the wafers from his pack and tossed them toward the dog, watching as the animal's eyes shifted away from him and toward the food. He sniffed at the wafers, small lines of foam forming at the edges of his jaw, and then raised his right front paw and kicked the package back under the shade of the tree. Connors slapped his hand against the dirt and laughed. "I can't even get a starving dog to eat this shit," he muttered.

Willis turned his head and looked over his shoulder at the dog. "Cars in my town ain't as big as that dog," he said.

"He's as scared as he is big," Connors said. "So if you're going to move, do it slow."

He heard the rifle click and turned to see Taylor standing in the front seat of the jeep, his weapon pointed down at the dog. "So long as that dog stays in place, you do the same," Connors told him.

"We're here to find two soldiers," Taylor said. "I didn't hear anything about any dog."

"Pull that trigger and you're going to have to deal with me."

Connors stood and, with one hand held out, fingers curled inward, took several slow steps toward the mastiff. The dog lifted his head and crouched down even more, his growl holding steady. "I'm gonna check your wound," Connors said in a soft voice. "See how bad it is and if there's anything I can do about it." The dog began to sniff at his knuck-les. "All I ask is you don't take a chunk of my ass."

The dog licked at Connors's hand, the snout of his nose rubbing against the side of the soldier's leg. He gently patted the dog's massive neck, searching for a collar. "Looks like you're out here on your own," he said. "Like us."

Connors squatted down and looked at the wound. The bleeding had slowed, but the cut was still open and raw. "He looks like he might need some stitches," Connors said to Willis. "You up for that?"

Willis walked on hands and knees toward the mastiff, stopping at eye level across from the wound. "Don't see how I can botch it up any worse than I do on you guys," he said.

The mastiff turned his massive head and stared at Connors. "You're just going to have to trust us," he said to the dog. "Same as we're doing with you."

Connors turned to Willis. "What do you need?" he asked.

"Get me some water from out of that stream," Willis said.

Connors walked over to a small stream, pith helmet in his right hand. He lowered the helmet into the still waters and brought it back to the surface, thin lines slipping down its sides and onto his wrists. He came up behind the dog, still holding his place, and kneeled in front of the wound, pith helmet cradled between his legs. "Okay," he said to Willis. "Now what?"

"I'll get my pack and bring back the supplies I need," Willis said. "You run water over the cut. Do it about two or three times if you have to, just enough to wash off the dried blood. Then I'm going to dab at it with some wet gauze, clean up the area around the wound. Then I'll either tape him up or stitch him."

"You ever have a dog, Willis?" Connors asked, watching the mastiff flinch as the water fell down the sides of his wound, turning the dirt around his back paws into small puddles of red soil.

"Grew up on a farm," Willis said. "Don't think there was an animal we *didn't* have. How about you?"

"Always wanted one," Connors said. "But my folks didn't need another mouth to feed."

Connors made four trips to the meadow and back, clearing enough blood away for Willis to get a good look at the cut. "He took a hit of shrapnel," the medic said. "Nothing too heavy, just enough to slice him. I'll put some medicine on it and then bandage it up. And if he can stop chasing rabbits for a few days, he should be good as new."

Connors stood in front of the dog, watching Willis work on his wounds, his back to Taylor's rifle. "What was the plan?" he asked Taylor. "Shoot me and then the dog?"

"Only if I had to," Taylor said. "And believe me, I wouldn't lose much sleep over either of you."

"He for real?" Willis asked, gazing over Connors's shoulder at Taylor.

"We run into trouble, we'll be glad he's with us," Connors said. "The rest of the time he's like having a rotting tooth."

Connors watched Willis work on the mastiff's wound for the better part of the next hour. He was careful not to hurt the animal, dabbing at the cut, never pushing or prodding. He ripped open a powder pack and poured its contents over the cut, patting the thicker parts into the open edge with a palm full of wadded-up Waldorf toilet paper. Then he triple-wrapped thin slabs of gauze around the edges of the cut and tied them into place under the dog's stomach. For his part, the dog never barked nor growled, content to let the young stranger go about his business. The overhead sun was hot and bright, the branches of the trees wilting under its steady gaze.

When he was finished, Willis paused to wipe his forehead and take a long drink from his canteen. He passed a hand across his mouth and looked over at the dog. "He's probably thirsty, too," he said to Connors.

Connors nodded, bent down and patted the dog's head. "I suppose we could be rubes and have you drink from the stream over there, but you've been pretty good about all this, so some fresh water isn't all that much to ask in return." Connors bent down, cupped his hand, poured canteen water into it and held it up to the mastiff's mouth. He smiled as the dog lapped up four handfuls, the large tongue slurping his fingers dry each time. "Okay, bud," Connors said, capping his canteen. "That'll do you until your next fight."

Connors walked back toward the tree, folded his newspaper and shoved it into his pack, picked up his gear and rifle and then headed for the parked jeep. He turned to look at the dog, the animal's eyes aware of his every move. Willis stood across from him, his gear already on his back. Behind them, Taylor, his rifle at ease, sat back down in the front of the jeep, wiping the sweat from his face and neck with a white cloth. "You be good," Connors said to the dog. "If you see any Germans, bite them."

Connors and Willis walked together toward the jeep, the dog following slowly behind them. "Thanks for doing that," he said to Willis.

"He's the first patient I've had since I've been out here who hasn't bitched and moaned about my medical abilities," Willis said.

"You two ready?" Taylor asked. "Or do you want to see if any birds need their wings mended?"

Connors tossed his gear into the jeep and jumped in behind the wheel. He turned the ignition key and started the engine, shifting gears from neutral to first. Then, for the only time that day, the bullmastiff barked, loud and often, running toward the jeep as he did, staring up at Connors with round, pasta-bowl eyes. Connors kept both hands on the steering wheel, his own eyes fixed on the empty road leading into Naples. He took one hand off the wheel, reached into his shirt pocket and pulled out a piece of gum. He unfolded the wrapper and shoved the slice deep into a corner of his mouth. He turned to look at the bullmastiff, now sitting alongside the jeep. They stared at one another for several moments, the sun bearing down hard.

"Get in," Connors said, reaching back to pat the rear seat. "Take you as far as Naples. After that, you're back on your own."

"Are you nuts?" Taylor asked. "We can't take a dog with us. It's against any orders anybody would ever give."

"He could be a help," Willis said.

"Another wilted mind heard from," Taylor said, turning to glare at Willis in the backseat. "How the hell is a dog going to be any help? Wounded one to boot."

"He might know his way around the city," Connors said. "Sure to know it better than we do. Besides, it'll give Willis something else to look at other than the back of your scrawny neck."

"Which, I should mention, if it gets any redder I could heat my lunch on it," Willis said.

"Give him some space," Connors said. "He'll need room to drool."

Connors watched as the mastiff jumped into the backseat, his 140-pound girth taking up a solid portion of the rear, and nestled alongside Willis. "They grow dogs big around here," he said, looking toward the road, turning the wheel to the left, grinding the clutch into gear, scattering patches of dry grass and dust in his wake, riding along the tree lines. "I hope the same isn't true about the women."

5

SANTA CATERINA A FORMIELLO, NAPLES
SEPTEMBER 26, 1943

The two boys knelt before the main altar of the old church, their heads bowed in prayer. The church, with its tilted dome and boxlike design, was a cherished remnant of the Renaissance, built in 1593 by Romolo Balsimelli, an obscure architect who never planned on his work standing for centuries, defiant in the face of war and neglect. The church was cool, dark and silent, the whispers of the two boys echoing off the stone walls and shattered windows.

"I can still smell the bowls of Mama's lentils," said Giancarlo Bardini, at twelve, the older by two years, sitting in a straw chair facing the main altar. "Me eating them with a spoon and you with bread."

"Is Uncle Mario with us, too?" Antonio asked. He was shivering, huddled close to his brother, back of his head leaning against the top rung of his chair.

"Always," Giancarlo said to him with a smile.

"And Nonna Maria?"

"In her chair, fanning herself," Giancarlo said.

The older boy stood and looked around the empty, dust-filled church. "We need to go and join the others," he said. "We don't want to be left behind."

"Just one more prayer," Antonio said. "The one I always save for Mama."

Giancarlo nodded, watching his brother walk the three steps up to the altar. "You say more prayers than a priest," he whispered.

Antonio stretched his small frame across the base of the altar, stretching to reach the large cross resting in the center. His small hands gripped the base of the heavy cross, bedded down with jewels and sparkling stones. He slid it closer toward him, easing it across the smooth surface of the cold marble, and tilted it toward his face. As he reached up to kiss the crucified body of Christ, he saw the wires attached to the base of the cross and heard the click of the mechanism that snapped the fuse of the mine. Antonio let go of the cross, stepped back and turned to look at Giancarlo for one final time, his wide and frightened eyes telling him what they both already knew.

The explosion rocked the church to its foundation. Thick shards of marble and wood flew through the air, mixing in a violent dance with the shattered columns and broken glass hurtling toward the ceiling that was lined with a painting of Saint Catherine, her arms spread wide, surrounded by angels riding on puffs of clouds. Below her, buried under the collapsed altar and the mounds of destruction set off by the blast of a German mine, the bodies of Antonio and Giancarlo Bardini lay facedown and still, the darkened remains of the cross resting between them.

Their war had finally found its end.

6

Vincenzo and Franco lead a slow-moving contingent of two hundred or so boys and girls through the empty streets of Naples. They walked with their heads down and in silence, the few belongings they had left bundled up inside of old shirts and flung over their shoulders. "When do you think we can come back?" Franco asked, wiping sweat from his brow with a torn rag.

"Maybe never," Vincenzo said.

The front door of the church blasted open. Shards of marble, wood and shattered glass embraced the street. Vincenzo and Franco scattered to the ground, covering their heads against the force of the fiery blast. Behind them, the other children scampered for any visible signs of cover, thick streams of smoke covering them like a warm brown blanket. A large marble statue of Saint Catherine was knocked off its pedestal and fell facedown across the front of the church entryway, splintering into two large chunks.

Vincenzo got to his feet and waded through the burning smoke, making his way to the front entrance, now nothing more than a small wall of silent flames. He stood there for several long seconds, the smoke washing past him, the fire licking at his legs and arms, before stepping into the remains of the church. He walked past the crumpled piles of wood and stone, rays of sunlight slicing in through the cracks in the stained-glass windows from above. He stopped in front of the main altar, its thick marble split in two, one side resting at a slant, its sharp ends imbedded against a side wall. A thin river of smoke floated past his legs and his eyes were tinged red from the heat and flames. He shifted his feet and brushed against a rolled-up set of rosary beads. Vincenzo bent down, dropped his hand into the clouds of smoke and picked them up. He stared at them, letting the beads rest against the sides of his fingers.

He closed his hands around them, bowed his head, turned and walked out of the church.

He stepped through the charred opening and walked past Franco and Angela, ignoring the faces of the boys and girls who stood in a large huddle around the front entrance and walked back toward the center of the city. "Where are you going?" Franco asked.

"I'm staying," Vincenzo said, not bothering to turn or lift his head.

"And do what?" Franco asked.

Vincenzo stopped, gazed at the faces that surrounded him, frightened and confused, all grouped together on an empty street across from a burning church. He took a deep breath, the smoke still burning his lungs, and looked at Franco. "Kill as many of them who come back as I can. Until they kill me."

"You walk into a grave if you do that," Franco said, stepping closer to him, Angela by his side.

"If I'm going to die, I'll die here," Vincenzo said. "In my city. On my streets."

Vincenzo looked up at the black smoke billowing from the church and then into the eyes of the faces surrounding him. He lowered his head, turned slowly and walked back down the center of the street.

Franco and Angela watched him go. They stood in silence, their breath coming in spurts, their faces and necks tinged with sweat. They looked at each other and nodded, then started to walk toward Vincenzo, following him back into the heart of the city. The crowd of more than two hundred milled nervously about, mumbling in low tones or exchanging furtive glances, apprehension and indecision the rule of the moment. Then, the wave back began. Three boys broke from the pack and followed Franco and Angela. Soon, five more trailed them. And then another five. Then, eight others gathered their belongings and shifted direction.

In all, it took less than fifteen minutes for the entire band of street boys and girls to turn and begin a slow walk back to nowhere.

7

PALAZZO CESARINO, NAPLES
SEPTEMBER 26, 1943

Carlo Maldini stood against the side of a broken window and stared down at the street below. He took a long drink from a half-empty bottle of wine. He watched the flames bring down the walls of what had once been his favorite church, too used to violence to be moved by what he saw, unaware that two boys had perished in the blast, all in the quest for a silent prayer. Maldini was fifty-six years old, dark hair tinged white at the sides, face speckled with the remnants of a three-day growth. He was thin but muscular, bones built solid after many years spent running a railroad engine for the Italian National Service. His clothes were old, torn and in need of a cleaning. On most days, Maldini was too deep into his wine to notice.

The burdens of war had turned Carlo Maldini into a weathered man with a sad face. Benito Mussolini's dream of an Italian empire spanning continents had cost Carlo a wife and two sons and filled him with an anger and frustration that bordered on madness. He rubbed a soot-smeared hand across his forehead and gulped down another mouthful of wine. He had spent many a Sunday in that church, walking side by side with his family, their heads bowed in solemn prayer, listening to soft words of peace spoken by a priest too young to comprehend the eventual price of war.

He gazed up the street and watched the large group of children march back down the main road, their final destination unknown to him. He turned his head and stared across at the young woman standing with her arms folded and her eyes focused on the activity below. She looked so beautiful in the early-morning sunlight that filtered in through the huge holes in what was left of their home. From where he stood, staring at her through the glazed effect of one too many bottles of wine, the woman looked exactly like her mother. She had long dark strands of hair gently brushing the tops of her shoulders, a round, unlined face filled with the power and passion of her youth, and olive-shaped eyes that could easily burn a hole through the very soul of a man. Her name was Nunzia. She was twenty years old and his daughter, the only child he had left to lose.

Maldini could not leave Naples when the Germans had ordered the evacuation of the city. He was too drunk and too crammed with rage even to move. He cowered in the basement of his building, hiding behind long-discarded bureaus, his Nunzia at his side.

"We must go," she had said to him. "We'll hide in the mountains and then make our way north, up toward the Americans."

Maldini could only mumble senseless words about a family he no longer had and happier days he would no longer see. He tried pushing his daughter away, struggling to free himself of her grip. "I won't leave you here," Nunzia said, her tender voice filled with defiance.

"There's nothing left for me, little angel," Maldini said to her, a sad smile crossing his lips, one hand gently caressing his daughter's hair. "I have my wine and my memories. That's all a man like me needs."

"I'm staying by your side, Papa," Nunzia said.

"Your mother was stubborn," Maldini said, a rush of madness in his voice. "She wouldn't leave either, not when I asked her to. *Begged* her to. And now she's dead. They're all dead. And those that aren't will soon join them."

"Then we will die here, Papa," Nunzia said. "In Naples, where you belong. Where we *both* belong."

"You don't belong with a drunk," Maldini said.

"I belong with my father," Nunzia replied.

Maldini swallowed a long drink of wine and rubbed the visions from his eyes. He stared at his daughter as she turned her look toward him.

"What will they do?" Nunzia asked.

"Something foolish, no doubt," Maldini said.

"I heard a rumor in the piazza yesterday," Nunzia said. "From Signora Matturano. She told me while we were pulling up water from the well."

Maldini rested his head against a cracked wall and snickered. "Americans are in Salerno fighting," he said. "Nazi soldiers are spread throughout Italy. And what are the Italians doing? Spreading rumors. If medals were given out for gossip and rumors, Italy would be crowned champion every year."

"She said the Nazis were coming back," Nunzia said, ignoring her father's sarcasm.

"Let them come," Maldini said with an indifferent shrug. "There's nothing left for them to take."

Maldini took a long swig of the wine and rested the bottle on the wooden sill. He stared out the window as the caravan of children began to disappear from view. "And how does Signora Matturano know all this?" he asked. "Did the Nazis call and tell her?"

"She said there were leaflets dropped from planes," Nunzia said. "Her grandson, Franco, showed her one. He's in that group of children down there. I can take you to meet them. I know where they'll sleep tonight."

Maldini looked away from the window and stared at his daughter. "Why would I want to do something so crazy?" he asked.

"To help them, Papa," she said. "In case the Nazis come back."

"Help them get *killed*!" Maldini shouted, his voice echoing off the barren walls. "Have I not seen enough of my own blood lost? Now you ask me to put the lives of strangers on my head, too. Leave it as it is, little one. Each to his own destiny."

"If they're staying and the Germans are coming back, they'll be forced to fight," Nunzia said, not backing down. "With your help or without. If that happens, most of them will die."

"That's a decision for them to make," Maldini said. "Not for me. Take a good look at me, Nunzia. Open your eyes and look beyond your father and see instead the madman who sits in his place. Then tell me, what help can that be to any man or boy?"

"You can tell them what they don't know, Papa," Nunzia said, stepping closer to her father.

"And what is it you think this old drunk knows, little girl?" Maldini asked.

"You know about the guns," Nunzia said.

8

Vincenzo stood in the center of the largest square in Naples, surrounded by the Palazzo Royale and the church of San Francisco di
Paola. Hundreds of children were spread throughout the square, waiting for some direction, some voice to tell them what to do. Franco and
Angela walked past the crowd and stood across from Vincenzo, their
backs cooled by the shadows of a large statue.

"I counted twenty-three knives and four handguns," Franco said.
"One of them looks like it works."

"A map of the city would be a good thing to have," Vincenzo said.

"So would more guns," Angela said.

"We need to keep the youngest children out of sight," Vincenzo said.
"We don't know what's coming and when, but we have to keep them
safe. They should have gone to the hills."

"We can use them as messengers if we need to," Franco said. "Nothing more than that."

Vincenzo walked around the large square, staring at the ground, gazing under piles of rubble, looking down at shattered cobblestones. "Not
every bomb the Nazis dropped on us exploded. There are at least a
dozen here in the square."

"If we can find some carts, we can gather them up," Franco said.

"How do you know the bombs will be of any use?" Angela asked.
"They didn't explode when they were dropped from a plane. What are
we going to do? *Slide* them toward the Germans?"

"I have no idea," Vincenzo said, with a voice filled with weary irritation. "All I know is they are bombs and that they do explode."

Angela turned and sat under the shadow of the bronze statue of
King Ferdinand I, leaning her back against the cold marble. "You
haven't said anything about me being a girl," she said.

"What's there to say?" Vincenzo said with a slight shrug. "You want to stay, you can stay. Girl or not."

"Would you turn me away if you could?" she asked.

"You're not the first girl to fight for Naples," Vincenzo said. "Eleonora Fonseca fought in the rebellion in 1799. Did pretty well, too, at least from what I read about her. She helped in the victory that made the city a republic."

Angela nodded her head. "What else do you know about her?"

Vincenzo walked closer to Angela, a sparkle in his eyes. "She had her moments," he said. "When the Cardinal came to power, he had the leaders of the uprising punished. He ordered Fonseca taken to the Piazza Mercato. She was put on a scaffold and executed."

Vincenzo glanced over Angela's shoulder and winked at Franco. "Cheer up," he said to her. "Nazis don't use scaffolds."

"How many of them will there be?" Angela asked, a slight trace of fear creeping into her diffident manner.

"We won't know until they're back in the city," Vincenzo said. "If they really do come back."

Angela looked around her, at the boys and girls spread throughout the square, sitting under the warmth of a loving sun. "How do we keep them alive?" she asked.

Vincenzo stayed silent for several minutes before answering. "The streets are our best weapon," he said. "We use what they give us. The dark alleys and the paths under the sewers. Hidden walkways inside churches and museums. Tunnels outside the railroad station, guard towers of Saint Efremo, castle grottos that lead out to sea. If we use all that, we can fight and never be seen. We'll be an invisible army. One that can beat the Nazis."

"*Beat* them!" Franco said with an air of frustration. "Entire *armies* couldn't beat them. They've killed over four hundred thousand Neapolitans and none of us has even *seen* a German soldier except from a distance. But you can talk about beating them with an invisible army of children. The words of one lunatic put us in this place, Vincenzo. I'm not ready for the words of another."

"It's been tried before," Vincenzo said. "Against an army just as formidable."

"When?" Franco asked.

"The sixteen hundreds, during the Spanish rule," Vincenzo said, "a young fishseller named Aniello led a band of rebels against Ponce De Leon. They were short on weapons, but used what they had and fought well. Not very different from what faces us."

"What happened to them?" Angela asked.

"They were betrayed," Vincenzo said, jamming his hands in his pockets. "And Aniello was captured. The Spanish cut up his body and tossed it on top of a large pile of cow shit."

Franco looked at Vincenzo and grinned. Angela leaned her head down and covered her mouth.

"What?" Vincenzo asked.

"If you're going to keep telling us these stories of yours," Angela said, "it might be nice if one of them, just one, ended on a happy note."

9

16TH PANZER DIVISION, FIFTY MILES OUTSIDE OF ROME
SEPTEMBER 26, 1943

Colonel Rudolph Von Klaus raised his head up to the warm sun, helmet resting on the edge of the tank, goggles loose around his neck. He found the ride down the coastline, dotted with farmlands and vineyards, a peaceful one and a welcome break from the toils of war. His troops seemed equally invigorated, each soldier eager to complete his mission in Naples and head home for some promised relief. He wondered what they would find back in Germany. Would their cities and towns be as battered as those they had crushed in Italy? Would their people be as withered and beaten down, as weary as the Italians he encountered, who seemed to have surrendered their very souls to a lost cause? No one, Von Klaus believed, could comprehend the cost of war more than a military man, and no one bore its damaging effects more than an innocent civilian. He was relieved it would all soon be at an end.

He caught the movement behind the large bush out of a corner of his eye.

Von Klaus tapped one hand on the inside lid of the tank and reached for his revolver with the other. The machine-gun unit shifted under him, moving slowly to its right, the bush in its target sites. "Draw him out," Von Klaus said in a calm voice.

Six machine-gun rounds pelted at the dirt around the bush, kicking up small armies of dust and rocks. Within seconds, two small, thin arms were raised up, barely visible beyond the lush leaves of the bush. "Hold fire," Von Klaus ordered.

Von Klaus watched as a barefoot boy in shorts and a dirty white T-shirt stepped out from behind the bush and walked toward his tank, arms still raised. The boy stopped at the edge of a dirt patch, his round face looking up at the colonel. Von Klaus stared down at the boy, momentarily flashing on an image of his own son, and hoped his child would never have to endure such conditions. "How old are you?" Von Klaus asked him. He spoke in a fluent Italian he had quickly mastered during a year spent as a student in Florence.

"Seven," the boy answered. He spoke without either hesitation or fear.

"And what were you doing back there?" Von Klaus asked.

"Hiding," the boy said.

The soldiers surrounding him erupted into chuckles and laughter. Von Klaus looked around at his men and then back to the boy. "You're not very good at it," he said.

The boy nodded and wiped at the sweat forming along his upper lip with the front of his shoulder, his arms still held high. "Are you a soldier in the Italian army?" Von Klaus asked him.

"No, signor," the boy said. "I'm too young to be a soldier."

"Then you're too young for me to take as prisoner," Von Klaus said. "So bring your arms to rest."

The boy did as he was told, his eyes darting around at the soldiers next to him, rifles by their side. "My brother Marco was a soldier," the boy said, looking back at Von Klaus. "He was in the war in Africa, fighting the English. He was killed there."

"Who looks after you?" Von Klaus asked.

The boy hesitated, reluctant to reply. He stared at Von Klaus and shook his head. "I don't need anyone," he said.

"Your leader would be proud of you," Von Klaus said, his voice soft and sad. "If he were still in charge. Have you heard the news? About Mussolini?"

"Is he dead?" the boy asked.

"Not yet, but it won't be much longer," Von Klaus said. "He's signed over his command to the Fascist Grand Council. He's no longer in power. And you no longer need to fight."

"Are you going to kill me?" the boy asked, the first hint of fear etched in his voice.

"What's your name?" Von Klaus asked.

"Massimo," the boy said.

"Why would you ask such a question, Massimo?"

"You're a Nazi," Massimo said, his lower lip starting to tremble. "And Nazis killed my mother and father."

Von Klaus shook his head. "No," he said. "I'm not going to kill you, Massimo. But I am going to give you an order and I expect it to be followed."

"What kind of an order?"

"I want you to go up deeper into the hills," Von Klaus said to him. "Find a bigger bush to hide behind. And this time, stay low enough to the ground that you will not be seen from the road. You never know. There might be more Nazis behind me. Can I count on you to follow such an order?"

"Yes," Massimo said.

"Good," Von Klaus said. "Spoken like a true soldier."

The colonel nodded as he and Massimo exchanged a final glance. Then the boy turned and ran back up the sloping hillside, higher and deeper into the coverage than when he had first been found. Von Klaus looked away once the boy was out of sight and caught a disapproving glance from his second-in-command, Sergeant Albert Hartz, standing alongside his tank, arms folded across his massive chest.

"Would you have preferred I shot him dead?" Von Klaus asked.

"He'll run and tell others our position and where we're heading," Hartz said.

"What others? All the other seven-year-olds?" Von Klaus said with a smile. "Nonetheless, inform high command. Let them know there may still be children hiding in the area. That should satisfy any of your concerns."

"It is still a risk I would not have taken, sir."

"Then you can take a measure of pride in knowing that you are a better Nazi that I am," Von Klaus said.

The colonel turned away from Sergeant Hartz, rapped on the side of his tank and looked back up at the hillside as his Division continued its slow descent into Naples.

10

CASTEL DELL'OVO, NAPLES
SEPTEMBER 26, 1943

One hundred boys and girls sat around the castle's edge. Carlo Maldini stood to the side, the back of his wool shirt soaked with the sweat brought on by the early-morning heat. Nunzia was off to his left, her eyes studying the faces of Vincenzo, Franco and Angela.

"Are you the leader?" Maldini asked Vincenzo.

"I don't lead anybody," Vincenzo said. "They followed me."

"That means they're looking for you to lead." Maldini eased himself past Nunzia and stood towering above Vincenzo. "Except in many cases, the good Lord sends bread to those who can't chew."

"What's that supposed to mean?" Franco asked, looking over at Vincenzo and Angela.

"It means your friend here acts like a leader, even talks like one," Maldini said. "But he doesn't think like one."

"I told you, I'm not anyone's leader," Vincenzo said.

"Then why are you here?" Maldini asked. "And why do they follow you? It's because they heard you talk. But that only gets you so far. Now they need to see you think."

"We're making a plan," Angela said. "Just in case the Nazis do come."

"Does this plan call for weapons?" Maldini asked. "Or are you just going to stare at the Nazis until they leave?"

"Many of us have knives and a few have handguns," Vincenzo said. "It's not much, but it's a start."

Maldini turned away from Vincenzo and stared out at the glimmering waters of the bay. "Think back," he said. "Think to when the Nazis first came to Naples. What is the first thing they did?"

"They took away the guns and rifles our fathers kept," Franco said.

"That's right," Maldini said, glancing over Franco's shoulder as twenty more boys hustled to join the group. "And they took them where?"

Vincenzo stepped away from Maldini and looked down at the water splashing against the sides of the pier.

"That's right," Maldini whispered. "They threw them in the bay."

"How deep?" Vincenzo asked.

"Fifty feet," Maldini said. "Seventy-five at the most."

"Can they still be used?" Angela asked.

"Once they're dried, cleaned and oiled, they'll be good as new," Maldini said. "Maybe a bit rusty, but nothing worse than that."

"And we get them out how?" Vincenzo asked. "It would take every free hand we have a full day to dive down and bring up each gun. And that's assuming we were good enough even to do something like that. Then you would need another full day to dry them out. The Nazis might be in the center of the city before one of us would be able to fire off a single shot."

"You're not thinking!" Maldini said, between clenched teeth, his index finger jabbing against the side of his temple. "You're ready to fight any Nazi who might come into Naples, but you don't even know how to pull guns from still waters."

Maldini stepped away from the edge of the pier and walked in a tight circle around Vincenzo. "My daughter tells me you are a student of history," he said to him. "You should know your religion as well."

Vincenzo glared into Maldini's eyes, the older man's harsh words a chilling challenge to the boy, forcing him to look beyond the words and pictures of old schoolbooks and confront the reality of his situation. If the leaflets were right and the Nazis were returning to Naples, it would not be words that would force them to take a step back, but the actions of the children that stood in a circle around them. Vincenzo looked away and glanced at the long row of fishing boats moored to the dock, their oars spread out on the hot ground to dry. "The boats," he said.

"That's right," Maldini said, smiling. "The boats. You will do as the apostles once did. You take the boats out and let the waters fill your nets. Only in place of fish, you pull up guns."

"Will you stay and help us?" Franco asked.

"It is no longer my war," Maldini said.

"I will help you," Nunzia said, arms at her sides, her eyes hard. "And so will my father. It is better for him to drink his wine in the middle of the bay than behind the window of an empty building."

Maldini stared at his daughter for several moments, then looked at Vincenzo and shrugged. "It is easier to fight a Nazi than go against the wishes of a Neapolitan woman," he said.

11

Steve Connors lay prone in the warm grass and looked down at Naples. He rested his binoculars by his side and turned to gaze out across the bay, toward the islands of Ischia and Capri in the distance, and then back down to what had once been a city. The bullmastiff lay head first next to him, his face buried between two large legs, asleep. Taylor and Willis sat behind him, each picking at the contents of a small can of hash with the edges of a cracker.

Connors ran a hand across the stubble of his chin, his eyes burning from the hot sun and the difficult drive. He had come to Naples expecting to see ruin, the same as he had come across at every one of his stops in Europe. But he had not been prepared for the level of destruction that stretched out before him.

He lay there and stared at the devastation for nearly an hour. He had seen men die and had buried soldiers who had become friends in a short span of time. But those were losses sustained in the fiery heat of battle. What he saw now was affixed to a larger, even more frightening plateau. On that bluff, surrounded by pristine waters and lush islands, Steve Connors was made a witness to the price of war. There, during those long moments under the blazing Italian heat, the history of the most conquered city in Europe played itself out through the eyes of a tough young corporal from the small town of Covington, Kentucky.

Naples has known neither peace nor prosperity in its centuries by the sea.

It began as a Greek settlement, a port of rest for seamen coming in from Asia Minor, sometime in the fifth century. The Greeks named the town Neapolis, which translates to New City. Under their rule, Naples began to develop. An extensive roadway system modernized access into and out of the city, and its citizens were taught and encouraged to speak Latin. Soon, the Greeks were ousted and the remnants of the Roman Empire took their place, only to be supplanted by the Byzantines.

From that point on, Naples became the lethargic host to a revolving door of nations quick to conquer and just as eager to leave behind snatches of their culture and flee at the approach of the next enemy. The Normans were followed by the rule of the Swabians, who then fell to Charles of Anjou, who quickly branded the area surrounding the city as his own, crowning it the Kingdom of Naples. The Aragonese period, which began in 1441 and lasted until 1503, brought about cultural upheaval and the building of the great works of architecture, a few of which Steve Connors could still see from his post. Then came the arrival of the Spaniards, who ruled until the Austrian takeover in 1707, who then ceded the city to the Bourbons in 1734.

By the eighteenth century, Naples had grown into the most populated city in Europe, one to which other national leaders would point to as the urban ideal. This moment of glory was not to last, however, as the city was brought to its knees by two blood-drenched and bitter revolutions. The Parthenopean Revolt began as a battle between intellectuals and ended with the cream of Neapolitan culture hanging by their necks. The French arrived with yet another revolution, this one led by Napolean's brother, Joseph Bonaparte. After the Bonapartes were handed their European walking papers, the city was delivered back into the hands of the Bourbons. It was under their rule that the Camorra, the Neapolitan Mafia, first began to organize, initially giving themselves the less-sinister-sounding name of the Fine Reformed Society. They built a steady network, one that would never relinquish its power, maintaining an iron grip on the city through every passing decade, regardless of what foreign powers entered its gates, bending only slightly to Mussolini's rule. To this very day, the members of the Camorra remain the undeclared kings of Naples, immune even to the outbreak of war and the evacuation of its people.

Finally, on September 7, 1860, Giuseppe Garibaldi took control of the city, the first Italian to do so since the time of the Romans. It was to

remain under the unsteady reign of Italian hands until the first of the
Nazi bombs came crashing down.

The turbulence of its history has contributed to the complexity of
the Neapolitan character. The men are, by nature, cynical and have little respect for authority. A close-knit group, they are distrustful of
strangers. They look with dubious eyes at even the most benign acts,
knowing that behind each kind gesture lurks the potential for betrayal.
Within their own country they are disliked, dismissed as shiftless, lazy
and brimming with criminal intent. They wear the stripes of national
hatred as a badge of civic honor.

The women are fiery and loud, ruling over their children and
younger siblings with tightfisted control. They are passionate in both
love and anger and are not afraid to display their emotions in public, unlike their more educated counterparts to the north. They love to sing;
fine, textured voices bellowing out mournful words to typically sad,
Neapolitan ballads from "Soli, Soli Nella Notte" to "Un Giorno Ti
Diro." Most of the songs are tearful reminders of loves lost and lives
burdened by the weight of poverty and illness. Neapolitan women are
stubborn, religious and superstitious, believing in the magical healing
powers of both saints and sinners. They attend church and lay down a
gypsy's curse with equal abandon.

The complex genetic mix of so many different countries invading
their city has given the women a distinct look, one that makes it possible
for them to blend together as one on the streets of Naples and to stand
out in a crowded marketplace in Milan. Their hair is dark and usually
kept long, their eyes almond-shaped and the color of Greek olives.
Their smile is wide and expressive and their laughter is as rich and textured as the red wine they are not shy about consuming. They grow old
with comfort, wearing their age with as much pride as they would a rare
new dress. Advancing years bring a firmer grip on their family rule, and
they hold on to this control with dictatorial force. Their only known enemy is the one who blocks the path they have chosen.

Connors stepped back from the bluff and stuffed the small binoculars into the rear of his pack. "Never seen churches so big," he said to

Willis and Taylor, glancing over at the sleeping mastiff. "You could fit half of Covington inside any one of them. And there are so many. The people who lived on those streets must have given a lot of hours over to prayer." He turned to take one more look down through the smoldering smoke and misty haze of the broken buildings below. "Didn't seem to do them all that much good though, did it?"

"I never used to pray," Willis said. "Not until I started eating army rations. Now I pray before every meal."

"You think we'll ever get a taste of that Italian food we hear the Dagos in our unit talk about?" Taylor asked, holding up his can of hash. "Or is this as good as it's going to get?"

"I wouldn't mind a nice cool glass of wine myself," Connors said. "All we got in Covington is moonshine and watered-down beer."

"From the looks of what's left of that city down there," Taylor said, "the only wine bottles we're going to find are broken ones."

The first shot rang out and bounced off a rock, missing Connors's leg by less than an inch. The second one clipped the back of the tree where Taylor and Willis were eating their hash, sending both men scurrying for cover. "You see anything?" Taylor shouted out, rifle at the ready, as he braced himself against the side of a large boulder.

Connors looked at the mastiff and watched as the dog stood, his eyes staring up into the clearing to his right. "In the thick bushes," he said. "About two o'clock."

"How many you figure?" Willis asked. He was laying flat down, the tree his only cover.

Connors ran from the edge of the bluff and threw himself to the ground, seeking cover behind a small stone wall. Two bullets rang out, each nicking off a piece of rock. "So far, I figure it's just the one," he said. "But the others could be out there waiting for us to make a move."

Taylor raised his rifle above the boulder and fired off two quick rounds into the bushes overhead. "Save your ammo," Connors said. "Count on seeing him, not on luck."

"If he's in there, I'll bring him out," Taylor said, checking his ammo belt. "When I do, you take him."

Connors nodded. "Willis, you any good with a gun?" he asked the medic.

"I'm better with wounds," Willis said, his head still down.

"You figure Krauts or Dagos?" Taylor asked, his knees bent, waiting to make his move.

"Italians have no reason to shoot at us now," Connors said. "My guess is a Nazi scout team."

The mastiff's bark forced Connors to turn to his left and he fired off two rounds as soon as he saw the glint of a rifle. The second bullet found its mark as he heard a loud grunt and saw a German soldier fall forward into a row of hedges. Taylor looked over his shoulder and then waved across to Connors. "The medic covers me," he said. "And you take out the other German."

"He's got the sun to his back," Connors said. "You're going to be shooting into glare. He'll have clear sight on you. None of us will have it on him."

"We can't wait," Taylor said. "There might be more than two or there might be more coming. Or he can radio back for help. I'm moving and I'm moving now. Back me."

Connors took a deep breath and nodded. "Go," he said.

Willis and Connors fired into the hedges above them as Taylor made his way up the bluff, running from tree to tree, looking to gain leverage on the hidden soldier. The mastiff stood next to Connors, protected by the row of stones. "I'm just shooting blind rounds here," Willis said. "I'm going to move to that tree to the right."

"Stay put," Connors said. "Let Taylor get to the top of the hill, then we both move."

"Got an aunt back home like you," Willis said. "All worries and no smiles. I'll meet you at the jeep."

Willis jumped to his feet and ran for a large tree covered by a thick circle of shrubs. "Willis!" Connors shouted, watching as the medic stepped into the green patch, the area below his feet too dense for him to see the hidden mine. The explosion sent Willis flying back, his chest and face blown away. He lay there, still and dead, a young boy from Iowa who had promised his mother he would make it back home.

Connors lowered his head and took in several slow, deep breaths. "Damn it," he said. "Goddamn it!"

He looked back up and saw that Taylor was now directly across from the German's position. Taylor was well-hidden by the trees and took careful aim with his rifle, looking to shoot low and hit at the ground cover. He fired off three quick rounds and popped out an empty ammo clip. He reached behind him for a new eight-bullet clip, the smoke from his rifle drifting into the air and giving away his position.

Connors saw the German move away from his coverage and raised his rifle.

He had him in his scope lines when he saw Taylor move toward the soldier, firing off a steady stream of bullets. Connors held his aim until he had a sure shot and then both he and the German soldier squeezed their triggers at the same time. They both hit their target.

It took Scott Taylor the rest of that afternoon to die.

Connors lay there and held him in his arms. It was all that was left for him to do. He couldn't radio back to headquarters for help, not that it would have been able to save Taylor's life. The transmitter had been blown to bits along with Willis, but even if he still had it, he couldn't risk giving away his position to any other Germans who were in the area. So, instead, Connors just sat and listened to a soldier he had never liked gasp and wheeze his final words. Taylor told him as much as he could about his life in the short hours he had left. Connors nodded and smiled when the words called for it, wiping the younger soldier's brow and promising to let his family back home know how brave he had been.

"I never did want to come to Italy," Taylor said, blood running in a thin line out of his mouth and down his neck. "Now I guess I'll never leave."

"You shouldn't have moved," Connors said. "I had him. All you needed to do was hold your position."

"Can't let you be the hero every time," Taylor said, managing a snicker.

"It wouldn't have killed you," Connors said.

"Thanks for staying with me," Taylor said.

"You'd have done the same," Connors said.

"Don't bet your life on it," Taylor said, his eyes closing for a final time.

12

PORTO DI SANTA LUCIA, NAPLES
SEPTEMBER 26, 1943

Twelve rowboats, in rows of two with four to a boat, slowly made their way out from the shore of the bay.

Maldini and Vincenzo rode in the lead boat, the older man pulling on a set of wooden oars, gliding them through the calm waters. The boats were weighed down with massive fishing nets curled up and running along their centers. The hot sun was now at full boil, its scalding rays browning the backs of the rowers. They slapped hands full of seawater on their shoulders and arms, seeking a mild dose of relief.

"How will you know when to stop?" Vincenzo asked.

"My father fished these waters most of his life," Maldini said. "He made sure his children knew the ways of the sea. The tide moves at its own pace, affected only by time and weather."

"Which means what?" Vincenzo asked with unmasked impatience.

Maldini pulled his oars out of the water and rested them inside the boat. "Which means," he said, "that we are here. Floating above the guns."

"Should we drop the nets?" Vincenzo asked, standing on unsteady legs in the center of the boat.

"It's what I would do," Maldini said. "But then, I'm not the one in charge."

Vincenzo cupped his hands around his mouth, balancing himself against the bumps of the small waves. "Lift your nets," he shouted to the boys in the other boats. "And hold them above your heads. Stand as steady as you can."

The boys grunted and grimaced as they went about a task that normally required the girth and strength of grown men. They struggled with the nets as a few of the younger kids fell over the sides of the boats and one nearly capsized his small vessel. "Have them bend their legs," Maldini told Vincenzo. "It will help steady their weight."

Vincenzo shouted out the new instructions and then looked back at Maldini. "How far do the nets need to be tossed?" he asked.

"Enough to stretch them out," Maldini said. "Fifteen feet would be a decent throw. Even ten feet would be acceptable. Anything less, we would pull up nothing but sand and shells."

"They're not strong enough to make that long a throw," Vincenzo said, sitting back down in the boat, his hands resting on Maldini's knees.

Maldini stared at Vincenzo, the stubble on his face glistening from the spray mist of the waves. He then turned to look back at the boys struggling with the nets. "Grab that rope from the bow," he ordered. "Run it through the ring behind me and then go boat to boat and link them together. It will keep us in tight formation. I'll meet up with you and Franco in the last boat."

Vincenzo tore off his shirt, ran the thick chord through the circular ring at the nose of the boat and dove into the sea. He swam with one hand, holding the rope above his head with the other, pulling it toward the extended arms of a curly-haired twelve-year-old. "Give it back to me at the other end," Vincenzo told him, "then jump into the water. It will be easier for you to empty the nets from there."

Maldini was in the water, swimming toward the last boat on the line. He stopped and turned back toward Vincenzo. "Have the youngest child swim to shore," he called out. "We need more boys. As many as can be found. It will take many hands to lift the nets from the bottom."

Franco and Angela helped pull Maldini into the last boat.

The older man was winded and had swallowed enough water to give his throat a salt burn. "Do you think the apostles had as much trouble with *their* nets?" Franco asked.

"Probably not," Maldini said, still gasping. "But they had Jesus on their side. You're stuck with me."

The boats were lined up and tied together, bobbing in unison to the splashing beat of the waves.

More than seventy-five boys, heads floating above the rising tide, swam on either side of the small crafts. Maldini stood in bare feet, square in the center of the first boat, the edge of a rolled-up fishing net gripped in his hands. Vincenzo, Franco and Angela flanked his sides, each holding the same net, waiting for Maldini to give the order. "The higher we throw it, the farther out it will go," he shouted. "It should float up and out, unfurl like an old flag. Angela, you tell us when."

Angela steadied her feet and tightened her grip. She looked down at the water to make sure none of the boys were close enough to get trapped in its pull. "*Forza, Italia!*" she yelled as she reached up with all her strength and, along with the three others, fell back as they let the net go. They sat in the boat and watched the net float in the air, gently spread out and cover the water as if it were a crisply ironed tablecloth.

"Did we do it?" Franco asked. "Is it out far enough?"

Maldini rubbed the top of the boy's head, both of them watching as the net sank slowly to the bottom of the bay. "You did well, Franco," he said. He turned to face the others. "You all did. But we still have four nets left to throw. And after that comes the hard part. Pulling them up."

"We only have three more nets for the guns," Angela said as she glanced down the side of the boats.

"That's right," Maldini said. "But I asked two of the younger boys to bring out another boat, take it past us to the point and drop their net out there. With what they're going to get they don't need to throw it far or wait very long."

"What are they getting?" she asked.

"I can only pray that they come back with enough fish to feed us all," Maldini said. "We'll have a hungry group on our hands at the end of the day."

"I guess now you could *really* use some help from Jesus," Franco said. "He did some of his best work with fish."

"Jesus never fished in the Bay of Naples," Maldini said. "In our waters, the fish fit a man's net like a well-made pair of shoes."

"Keep the knots in your hand and the rope wrapped around your arm," Vincenzo yelled to four boys swimming around the edges of the boat. "If you lose those, we won't be able to bring the net and the guns to the surface."

"I'm holding it as tight as I can," a cheery-faced seven-year-old said. "And I will pull them up by myself if I have to."

"How could Italy lose a war with a man like you on its side, Lucca?" Vincenzo said.

"Because we always let the ones without heart lead us," Maldini said, leaning over the boat and splashing cool water on his face. "The ones with heart are left to die."

13

IL CAMALDOLI, NAPLES
SEPTEMBER 26, 1943

The bullmastiff led the way down the side of the bluff, walking with delicate ease along its narrow path. Connors followed, one hand holding his rifle belt, the other resting inside his pants pocket. His uniform was sprinkled with dust and blood. He had buried Willis and Taylor at the top of the bluff, overlooking the Bay of Naples, using their helmets and rifles as markers.

They had parked the jeep under an old pine tree, inside a neglected olive grove. There was little wind and the heat was cooling down with the evening shade.

The bullmastiff saw the boys before he did and took a run toward them, barking and kicking up pockets of dust and dirt with his paws. Connors flipped his rifle from his shoulder to his hands and fast-stepped down the path toward the jeep. He stopped between the dog and the four boys sitting in his jeep, rifle at his side. One of the boys had his fingers wrapped around the ignition key. They were thin, dirty and disheveled and none was older than fourteen. Connors looked at each one, getting only frightened stares and nervous shifting in return. The mastiff had his paws on the side of the jeep and was low growling, ready to pounce at any sudden movements.

"Do you speak any English?" he asked.

"We all do," the oldest of the four stammered.

"How is that?" Connors asked. "That you all speak it?"

"We are taught to speak three languages," the boy said. "Neapolitan first. Then Italian and then English."

"Why are you here?" the boy in the front passenger seat asked.

"I was about to ask the same question," Connors said, looking from the boys to the dog. "And since I'm the one with the rifle, I'd like my answer first."

"We're looking for Nazis," the boy said. "See if they're really coming to Naples again. And then report back."

"Report back to who?" Connors asked.

The four shot quick glances at one another and then looked back down at the dog and the soldier. "The others in our group," the one holding the ignition key said.

"Let's say the Nazis are coming back," Connors said. "What happens then?" He walked closer to the jeep, rifle slung once again over his shoulder.

"I guess then we fight," the boy closest to Connors said.

Connors stared at him. The boy's eyes were dark and rich; his face round, sweet and innocent; his hair clipped back and short. "Fight the Nazis?"

"That's what you do," the boy said. "Why can't we?"

"The Nazis have a habit of shooting back," Connors said. "That's one reason to think about."

The boys stayed silent for several seconds, eyes glancing up toward the ridge where the firefight had taken place.

"Does your dog understand Italian?" the boy in the back asked.

"That's *all* he understands," Connors said.

The boy in the back smiled at the dog and snapped his fingers. "*Scendi jou,*" he said in as firm a voice as he could muster. "*E siedati!*"

The bullmastiff lowered his paws, stepped back from the jeep and sat on the dirt, his mouth open, large tongue dangling. Connors looked at the dog and then back to the boy.

"It's good to know he listens to *somebody,*" he said. "Tell you his name if I knew it. But I can tell you mine. It's Connors."

"I am Dante," the boy in the back said. "The boy next to me is Claudio. And the two in front are Gaspare and Pepe."

"How many are there in this group of yours?" Connors asked.

"About two hundred," Dante said, stepping down from the jeep. "Maybe two hundred and fifty."

"All boys?"

"A few girls, but not many," Gaspare said. "Just the ones without any family."

"Any American soldiers down there?" Connors asked, leaning against the side of the jeep, his helmet off and resting on the hood.

"You're the first one any of us have seen," Dante said.

"What about Italian resistance?" Connors said. "Any of them with you?"

"No," Dante said. "They left before the evacuation."

"Are we your prisoners now?" Claudio said, speaking for the first time. He was the youngest, his brown hair touched with streaks of blond, looking nervous and ill at ease in the rear of the jeep.

"Why don't we say that for the time being we're working together," Connors said. "At least until we see how everything in Naples plays out. Just me, the dog and the four of you."

"What is it you want us to do?" Dante asked with a hint of suspicion.

"It's not anything that's going to get you into trouble," Connors said. "If I'm anywhere in this, it's on your side. Understand?"

"*Si*," Dante said, nodding along with the three other boys.

"Good," Connors said, throwing off his pack and wedging it in the back of the jeep between Dante and Claudio. He tapped the younger boy on the knee. "You're going to have to ride on your friend's lap," he told him. "We need to make room for the dog. The same goes for the two of you in front."

Connors waited for the boys to shift seats and then snapped his fingers and watched as the mastiff hoisted himself into the back. "His breath is horrible," Claudio said, cupping a hand in front of his face. "He smells like old feet."

"He's not the cleanest duck in the pond," Connors said, jumping behind the steering wheel. "But he's good company and he smells trouble long before it hits."

"What do you call him?" Claudio asked, moving his hand from his face to the top of the mastiff's head.

"I only knew one Italian name before I ran into you guys," Connors said, shifting into reverse and moving back toward the road. "And that's Benito. So that's who he is. At least to me."

"You named him after Il Duce?" Gaspare said, his olive eyes flushed wide. "In Naples that could get you killed."

"We're not in Naples," Connors said. "Yet."

"You still haven't said what you want us to do," Pepe said, partly hidden under Gaspare's weight.

"Benito understands you a lot better than he does me," Connors said. "Be great if one of you could tell him to stop pissing in the jeep."

14

The four Mark IV tanks were lined up, gun turrets facing the front of the large pink stucco house. German soldiers, armed with machine guns and flame throwers, approached the house from the rear, trampling over grapevines and fig leaves. Von Klaus stood in front of his tank, staring out at what had once been lush gardens and fertile fields. He marveled at the design of the house. The walls were built thick enough to keep out the harshest summer heat and the most chilling winter winds. The marble steps leading to the oak-wood front door were expansive, black iron handrails helping to guide the path. The entryway had the look and feel of a palace hidden in the middle of paradise. A palace he now needed to bring to ruin.

"Has the house search been completed?" Von Klaus asked Kunnalt, standing alongside him.

"Yes, sir," Kunnalt said. "The last of our men should be coming out at any moment."

"And what did they find?"

"It's been pretty much gutted, sir," Kunnalt answered. "A few paintings left on the walls. Some furniture scattered about in the downstairs rooms. Nothing that appears to be of any value."

Von Klaus turned to Kunnalt and smiled. "At least not to us," he said. He walked a few steps closer to the house, gazing up at the windows to each room, every one shiny and clean. "For an abandoned home, it's very free of dust, don't you think?"

"I hadn't noticed, sir," Kunnalt said, in step behind the colonel. "Perhaps it hasn't been left empty very long."

"Have the house searched again," Von Klaus said. "And this time, look beyond what it is the owner wants you to see."

"Looking for what, sir?" Kunnalt asked.

"This is the home of a very rich man," Von Klaus said. "And more than likely a very smart one as well. A man like that would plan ahead. He wouldn't flee from such a place like a crazed peasant with all the valuables he could carry on his back. He would make sure those valuables would be safe, hidden from all eyes. They are in this house, Kunnalt. And I would wager that when you find them, you will also find that man."

Kunnalt snapped his heels, gave the colonel a crisp salute and walked back toward the front entrance to the house, shouting out orders as he moved. Von Klaus reached up and grabbed a tree limb resting just above his head. He snapped off a batch of thin, red grapes and held them in his hands. "I would have preferred wine," he whispered, pulling the grapes from their stems. He leaned back against the side of his tank, eating the grapes one at a time, and waited.

It was just after dusk when the colonel looked up and saw Kunnalt leading an elderly man in a soiled suit out of the house. The man had hair the color of snow and a beard as thick as a farmer's hedge. He was short but stout and moved with the quiet dignity of one bred to wealth. He walked with his head raised, his eyes fueled by an angry fire.

"You were right, sir," Kunnalt said, standing in front of the colonel, the man just off to his right. "There were a number of hidden passageways throughout the house, each of them leading to a series of large underground rooms."

"And what were in these rooms?" Von Klaus asked, gazing over at the man.

"As you expected, sir," Kunnalt said with an air of admiration. "Old portraits in large frames, wooden boxes filled with jewelry and several yellow envelopes sealed and stuffed with money."

"Which room did you find him in?" Von Klaus asked, tilting his head toward the man.

"He was in the subbasement, sir," Kunnalt said. "Hiding in a small closet off the main hall."

"Everything you found belongs to me," the old man said in a hard voice. "And to my family. Anyone else who takes it is nothing more than a thief."

"That's a fine-quality suit you have on," Von Klaus said to him. "And it is a truly beautiful home that you own. In addition, you have all this wealth stored inside of it, enough to feed all that's left of Naples. Every Italian from Rome down has been stripped of all possessions. The only ones left untouched, as you seem to have been, are the Blackshirts. The Fascists. Which would make you a follower of Mussolini. Is that correct?"

"I believe in Il Duce, *si*," the man said, not backing down. "And I always will."

"Loyalty is always admirable, but in your case, it's also foolish," Von Klaus said. "As of today, the Italians want your beloved Mussolini dead, the Americans want him captured and we Germans really don't know what to do with him. We have enough buffoons in our high command as it is. Which leaves you a loyal man with no place to turn."

"He will not abandon those who stay by his side," the man said. "Il Duce will be back and Italy will again belong to him."

"Perhaps," Von Klaus said in a sterner voice. "And if he does return, I hope he rewards your loyalty with a new home and new riches. Because as of this moment, all that you own is the suit you wear. The rest now belongs to Germany."

"This land has been in my family for three generations," the man said. "*No one* can take it from us. Not even Il Duce himself."

"Your family may have owned the land, but they never worked it," Von Klaus said. He gazed at the man, his eyes gleaming and hard. "That's a duty people like yourself reserve for the poor."

"It's not against any laws to employ farmhands," the man said. "And we took good care of them. Treated them as if they were members of my own family."

Von Klaus walked in a small circle around the man. "And where is the poor side of your family now?" he asked.

"Most of them fled," the man said. "A few stayed behind and were killed. They were foolish enough to go against the power of Il Duce."

"Yet you not only stayed, you've managed to survive," Von Klaus said. "With most of your wealth still at your disposal. Seems a poor way for a man to care for members of his family."

"They made their choice," the man said. "And now they have to live or die with the results of that choice."

Von Klaus nodded, the son of a working-class Berlin mill worker about to pass judgment on the landed nobility that stood before him. "And I have made mine," he said. "And *you* will have to live or die with the results of that choice."

"What are you going to do?" the man said, all the confidence and arrogance seeping from his body.

"What I was sent here to do," Von Klaus said, giving the man a last disdainful look. He turned and stepped toward the front of the house. "Empty the house of all its goods," he shouted to his men. "Then blast it down. I don't want even a stone left untouched. Use the flame throwers and torch the surrounding property. All of it, from one end to the other. Once I order the pull out, I want two tanks to stay back and mine the areas around the four sides of the house. I want nothing left standing. Nothing! And I want the smoke to be seen for miles. To be seen and smelled by everyone hiding around us."

"You bastard!" the old man shouted at Von Klaus. "You heartless bastard!"

Von Klaus stared down at the man and smiled. "To a soldier doing his duty, that is considered the highest of compliments," the colonel said.

The old man stood his ground, breath coming out in hard gasps through his open mouth, his hands trembling. He shook when the first blast from a tank shattered the front door of his home and his eyes welled with tears when a second ripped through a third-floor bedroom. The third explosion stripped the man of all judgment. He rushed toward the colonel, standing now a dozen feet away, sanity giving way to suicide.

"I will kill you for this, you Nazi bastard!" he shouted, running at Von Klaus with both arms extended. He had a small revolver gripped in one trembling hand. It had been jammed inside his tobacco pouch, hidden from the soldiers' search.

Colonel Von Klaus watched as he raced toward him, his manner relaxed and indifferent. He didn't flinch as the two soldiers to his left fired three shots into the old man, dropping him face first onto the red dirt that lined the front of the house. Von Klaus walked over to the body, reached down, took the revolver from the man's hand, and put it inside the front pocket of Kunnalt's jacket. "A keepsake," he said to him. "For the time we spent together."

"Do you wish him buried, sir?" Kunnalt asked.

"Leave him for Il Duce," Von Klaus said, walking away from the explosions and fires, back toward the quiet of his tank. "When he returns."

15

PORTO DI SANTA LUCIA, NAPLES
SEPTEMBER 26, 1943

An orange sun was resting on still water in the distance. A line of boys stood along the stone edges of the shore. In the middle of the bay, the four wooden boats lurched to starboard, pulled down by the weight of full nets. Around them, boys and girls bobbed above the waterline like buoys, each holding on to a square of netting or a chord of rope. Vincenzo stood in the center of the rear boat, staring down at the water and at the fishing nets he had helped pull to the surface, each holding thick piles of rifles and handguns. All around him there was a stunned and happy silence, as the boys, on shore and in the water, stared with amazement at their catch of weapons.

"Is this all of it?" Vincenzo asked Maldini. He reached an arm into an open lip of the net, pulled out a lupare and held it firmly in his grip.

"It is all you will need," Maldini said. He was stretched out across three wooden planks, face up to the darkening sky.

"Thank you," Vincenzo said.

Maldini raised his head and looked over at the boys swimming in the water. "Look at them," he said. "They are so happy. They see the guns and believe that now they can fight the Germans. And most of them will die, each with one of those guns in his hands. You should curse me for that, Vincenzo. Not thank me."

Maldini stared at Vincenzo for several moments, seeing in the boy's brooding eyes the same burden of loss that he himself carried. He turned and looked around him at the joyful faces floating in the water and wished they could all be tossed back into another time and place, one that was miles removed from the death they had seen and the destruction that followed. But he knew it to be nothing more than a foolish whim. In time of war, Maldini had learned, life was broken down into a series of moments, each branded into memory. Most of those moments were etched in a horror that would forever be sealed inside the dark reaches of the mind. A few, a very precious few, brought a smile and along with them a sense of once again being alive and filled with hope. Maldini knew as he stared down at the boys and the arsenal of weapons they gleefully embraced that this was such a moment.

"Death will come when it chooses," he said to Vincenzo. "But for today, we are alive, and for that we should celebrate."

Franco looked out at the coastline, at a boat rowing slowly toward them, four small boys struggling with the weight of the oars. "Fresh fish roasted over an open fire would be a perfect way to start," Franco said. "That is, if our little friends managed to catch something other than a chill."

"Have the boys put the guns in the boats and row them to shore," Vincenzo said to Maldini. "I'll swim out and help bring in the fishermen before it turns dark."

"No," Maldini said. "I'll go and help the little ones. You stay. You be the one to tell them to load the guns on board."

"What difference does it make who tells them?" Vincenzo asked.

"The difference is not for now, but for later," Maldini said with a smile. "They need not only to trust you, but listen to what you tell them to do. No matter what happens. The sooner that starts, the better."

Maldini stood, patted Vincenzo on the shoulder and jumped into the cold water. He was halfway out to the lone rowboat when Vincenzo's orders echoed across the waves. He stopped, turned and smiled when he heard the loud cheers from the boys that followed in its wake. He floated in the waves and relished the sight of happy faces and sounds of joyful laughter as the guns were tossed from net to boat.

That would be victory enough for this day.

16

45TH THUNDERBIRD INFANTRY DIVISION HEADQUARTERS, SALERNO. SEPTEMBER 26, 1943

The three officers leaned over the edges of the map and studied the various pieces that were spread across it. Captain Ed Anders reached across the map and moved a tiny wooden tank farther south. "This is where we *should* be by now," he said, frustration and anger edged in his voice. "We haven't moved in over a week. And I still don't have a goddamn idea why."

"Montgomery," Captain Jack Sanders said. He was thirty-five, five years older than Anders, standing off to his left, taller and with thinning blond hair and a thick white mustache. He was a career army man, joining up the day after he finished high school, leaving behind three sisters, a widowed mother and a small grocery store in Gainesville, Florida. "The man won't make a move unless the odds guarantee a victory. He just can't afford to lose a battle."

"The general is doing a slow burn of his own," Captain Frank Carey, the third officer in the tent, said. Carey was in his mid-twenties, stationed with the Thunderbirds' sister division, the Texas, and was viewed by the other officers in both groups as a five-star in the making. His words carried a hint of his Macon County, Georgia, upbringing. "But there isn't all that much he can do about it. Ike said to sit tight until Monty gives the word."

"Any news from your recon team?" Sanders asked Anders.

"Not yet," Anders answered, shaking his head. "But it's still early. The trip down doesn't look like a long one on a map. But the way the Nazis have those roads mined, it's gonna take them a couple of days to get into the city."

"You expecting them to find anything?" Sanders asked.

"Not really," Anders said, standing away from the map. "My guess is the two operatives we had working with the Italians got out before the evacuation. But they can give us a better idea of what's left down there. The Nazis know we're going in there *someday*. My guess is they'll be looking to rip apart everything they can."

"They've been doing that since we got here in July," Carey said, staring at the clear sky outside the tent flap. "You know, my wife always wanted to see Italy. We used to talk about it before the war. Now, it's going to be a lot of years before I can bring her here and give her something to see."

"How much help can we expect from this new guy in power, what's his name again?" Sanders asked.

"Marshal Pietro Badoglio," Anders said. "He's a paper soldier, and if the reports we get are reliable, pretty much an idiot."

"You figure the resistance leaders will listen to him or will they just fire on anybody that drives into the city?" Sanders asked.

"I wouldn't count on much of anything from him or them," Carey said. "The government Badoglio set up collapsed before we even got here. The people out there are on their own again. If you ask me, they've been that way since this war started, and frankly, they're a lot better off."

"We're here to help them," Anders said. "But by the time we're through, we're going to end up doing just as much damage as the Germans."

"I'd end this damn war tomorrow if I could," Frank Carey said. "And get everybody back to wherever the hell it is they belong."

The three officers stepped out of the tent and walked down a narrow road toward their waiting jeeps. They walked in silence, each feeling at loose ends, uncomfortable with the lag in the regular battle patterns they had grown accustomed to as they led their troops through the center of the Italian heartland. They were in a rush to end their days of war and return life to a semblance of what it had once been. It was a dream everyone in and out of uniform hoped to turn into reality.

While they walked the grassy slopes of an Italian town newly conquered, they knew that back home in America, flour, fish, beef and cheese could only be bought with red ration stamps and the sale of sliced bread was banned. In Washington, D.C., the Jefferson Memorial was dedicated in a presidential ceremony and the Pentagon was completed and newly occupied. Movie theaters gave citizens looking for visions of better days Hollywood versions of war with the successful films *Guadalcanal Diary, Watch on the Rhine, Five Graves to Cairo* and Gary Cooper and Ingrid Bergman in *For Whom the Bell Tolls*. Count Fleet won the Kentucky Derby and Duke Ellington had yet another hit with "Do Nothin' Till You Hear from Me." Selman Abraham Waksman, a forty-three-year-old Rutgers University professor of microbiology, introduced the world to antibiotics, while penicillin powder was applied for the first time in the treatment of chronic disease. Race riots scarred Harlem in New York while soft-coal workers threatened to walk off the job, urged on by the president of the United Mine Workers union, John L. Lewis. And the New York Yankees won another World Series.

"I wonder what the winters are like around here," Sanders said, looking to his left as he led the way down the road.

"At the rate Monty and the Brits are moving, we may find out," Carey said.

"He's going to have to move sooner than that," Anders said. "Even his own men are starting to make fun of him. And he has to know that the longer he takes to move into Naples, the more time he gives Patton to move through Italy. To those two, it's never been about wars and men. It's about headlines."

"There is *some* logic to what Monty's doing," Carey said. "Let the

Germans go into Naples and let them go in strong. Once they're in, they've got their backs to the sea. There's no place else for them to go. We come in, close ranks on the roads out of town, and we got them."

"Unless that's what they want us to do," Sanders said. "You guys know as well as I do, the Nazis mined every damn road from Rome to Naples and in between. They mined the bottom of the bay, which can cause our ships a lot of trouble. They mined the walkways and the hillsides. Hell, the bastards even mined their own dead soldiers. The way they have it set up, they can knock off a quarter of our troops without having to fire a single round."

"You think that's what's holding Monty back?" Anders asked. They had reached the base of the road, their backs turned away from the bay. "He's worried about getting through the mine traps?"

"I sure hope that's not the case," Sanders said. "If it is, then we *will* be here all winter, and we'll need Patton to liberate *us*."

"You look around and see the faces of these Italian people," Frank Carey said. "They never wanted any part of this war, no matter whose side they were on. They want to farm, not fight. But when we leave here, they're going to be left with nothing more than holes in the ground and dead bodies to put inside them."

"What makes them so different from us?" Anders asked. "We'll all have bodies to put away once we get home."

"But we'll still have a *home*," Carey said. "Nobody bombed it or ransacked it. Nobody took our clothes and burned our property. It'll all still be there, the way we left it. Might need some touching up, but it'll be standing and our families will still all be there. The people who lived here lost that and I don't know how you ever get something like that back."

"It's not our worry, Frank," Sanders said. "We're soldiers and nobody gives a good damn what we think or how we feel. We're just here to take the land, call it a win and then call it quits. We didn't ask to be here either, anymore than the Italians want us here. Believe me, I'd much rather die with my feet tucked under the sheets of my own bed than in a vineyard on a hill in Italy, no matter how beautiful it is. But I don't worry about that, either. I'm here to fight, not fret."

Carey looked at Sanders and winked at Anders. "I couldn't help but notice that you Florida boys get a little testy when you're standing under the sun too long," he said to Sanders. "You'd think you'd be used to it by now."

"It's the swamp gators I miss," Sanders told him with a smile. "Having those suckers floating along the sides of your boat usually has a soothing effect on a man's tolerance for bullshit."

"I'm going back to my troops," Anders said. "See you guys at tomorrow's briefing. Unless we get an order to move out. In which case, I'll see you on the road to Naples."

"Last division to reach the city gets clean-up duty," Sanders said. "What do you say? You two up to it?"

"I'll be on my third shower by the time you two come rolling in," Carey said. "Count me in on that bet."

"I've never seen the day when my Thunderbirds get bested by the Texas," Anders said to Sanders. "Make sure your boys have plenty of cleaning supplies in their gear."

"Brag all you will, boys," Sanders said, starting to walk from the group. "But we're the ones assigned to follow Monty. Which means we'll be the first Americans in the city."

"You're forgetting something, Jack," Anders said. "A minor detail, but a detail nonetheless."

"What would that be?"

"While we've been up here shooting the shit, one of my recon teams has been heading for Naples," he said. "That's a *Thunderbirds* recon team. By this time tomorrow we'll be the first ones in."

"Looks like you got yourself hit with a sucker punch," Carey said to Sanders. "Don't matter all that much, though. Since you're the unit following Monty, you may never get to see Naples at all."

"That's right," Anders shouted out to them from the base of a ravine. "You know that saying, 'See Naples and Die.' It should really be 'See Naples when *Monty* dies.'"

The loud laughter of the three captains echoed off the silent hills of the Italian coastline.

17

VIA TOLEDO, NAPLES
SEPTEMBER 26, 1943

Connors eased the jeep to a stop, gazing through his windshield at the two boys blocking his path, one of them resting a foot on top of a firm, round ball. They both looked to be about eight years old, wearing threadbare outfits grafted from the torn clothing left behind by adults. The smaller of the two smiled at Connors, his bare foot rolling the ball with the edges of his toes. He had golden brown hair and sea-colored eyes with a dark leather tan covering his mostly bare body.

"*Togliati da mezzo ragazzi*," Dante said from his seat in the rear. "Move out of the way. He's an American. Here to help us."

"Are these two part of your outfit?" Connors asked, keeping his eyes on the smiling boy.

"Yes," Gaspare said. "The big one is Roberto. He doesn't trust *anyone*, not even us, and we are his best friends."

"The other one is Fabrizio," Dante said. "He likes everybody. He loves to play football and is very good at it. He not only looks like a little German, he plays like one, too. He may one day have a chance to play for Team Naples."

"If there ever is a Team Naples again," Claudio said.

Connors jumped from the jeep and stretched out his back and arms. "I didn't even know they played football in Italy," he said. "I always thought it was an American sport."

"It is *all* we play in Italy," Pepe said. "It is the national sport. Every city has a team and from there the best players are picked to represent Italy against all other countries."

"You ever played against a team from America?" Connors asked.

"We have never *seen* a team from America," Gaspare said. "But if there is one, Italy can beat it. You may be better at winning wars, but you can never beat an Italian in football."

"You talking about college ball or professional?" Connors asked, watching as Fabrizio's gaze moved from him to the mastiff, now standing by his side.

"Here, in Italy, a boy plays football from the day he takes his first step," Dante said. "We don't need someone to teach us or show us how. It's just something we all know how to do."

"And he's the best player in your group?" Connors asked, pointing at Fabrizio as he walked toward him.

"No one is better," Claudio said. "He can control the ball and the field. And when he runs, he is like a bird, impossible for anyone to catch."

"That sounds to me like one helluva football player," Connors said, standing across from Fabrizio. "Are you as good as your friends say?"

Fabrizio nodded, eyes shifting from the American to the mastiff and back. "Maybe one day we can play a game," he said in a soft voice.

"That would be fun," Connors said. "All we would need is a little time and a nice place to play. And one of you would need to bring a football."

The boys in the jeep all laughed, while Fabrizio lowered his head and giggled. "The sun has played a *trucco* on your eyes, American," Gaspare said. "The football is right in front of you. There, under Fabrizio's foot."

Fabrizio flipped the round white ball from his foot to his knee and then with his arms spread out, bounced the ball from one leg to the other, his eyes fixed on the bullmastiff, the smile glued to his handsome face. He then lifted the ball skyward with the front of his foot, bouncing it from his forehead to his upper thigh, keeping up the rhythmic beat without ever losing his balance. Connors took a step back and removed his helmet. "He's pretty good," he said to the boys behind him. "With a *beach* ball. How good he is with a football is a whole other question."

"What are you saying, American?" Dante asked. He jumped out of the rear seat of the jeep, caught the ball off Fabrizio's forehead and shoved it at Connors. "This is not a beach ball. It's a football."

"That's not like any football I've ever seen," Connors said, shaking his head. "Maybe what you guys play over here is a whole lot different from what we play back home. You wear pads and helmets when you play?"

"*Cose sono* pads?" Fabrizio asked.

"They protect your shoulders and legs," Connors said.

"From what?" Dante asked, flipping the ball back to Fabrizio, who caught it with the flat of his knee and resumed his bouncing routine.

"So you don't get hurt when you block on the line or tackle a player coming at you on either a run or a pass," Connors said. "It prevents a lot of injuries."

"In football, speed is all you need to stay safe," Gaspare said. "These other things you talk about can only slow a player down."

"What do you like about the football you play, American?" Fabrizio asked, resting the ball against the side of his ankle.

Connors placed a boot on the bumper of the jeep and pulled a cigarette from the front pocket of his uniform. "I like that we play it in the fall," he said, lighting the cigarette and exhaling a drag, thin puffs of smoke clouding his face. "When the weather turns cold and the wind blows down heavy from the hills. I like the smell of the air and the feel of the breeze. I like running on hard ground, the ball held inside my arm, the other fellas rushing in to tackle me and keep me from getting too many yards. In lots of ways, it's not so much the game itself for me. I like baseball a lot more and I'm much better at that. But I love the time of year football is played. People back home always seem happier in the fall, holidays closing in, days getting shorter, sitting around warm fires at night, close to your family, your friends. When you're in the middle of it, you think you have nothing but a lifetime filled with days and nights like that to look forward to. Then a war comes along, shoves you in places you've never been before and you wonder if you'll ever see another fall like the ones you remember."

The boys moved around the sides of the jeep, their feet kicking at dirt and rocks, their heads bowed, an uneasy silence warming its way into their happy moods. "In Italy, football is played every day, no matter what month, no matter the weather," Dante said. "But for all the boys here, the best day to play was Sunday. After mass and before the big family meal."

"All the squares in the city and all the parks would be filled with people watching their children playing football," Gaspare said. "Our mothers would pack baskets with fruit and cheese and wine. Our fathers would stand off together, cheering us on, smoking cigarettes, laughing and talking with their friends."

"The city was so alive, so happy," Claudio said. "I'd look away from the game and find my mother and father in the crowd, always with smiles on their faces. It was everyone's happiest day."

"Now Sunday is just another day," Pepe said.

"Have you ever lost anyone, American?" Dante asked Connors. "Someone close to you?"

"Not the way all of you have," Connors said, shaking his head. "The war hasn't cost me family. The people back home have died the way they were meant to die. But you get close to people when you're in the army, go through training with them, travel across an ocean together, fight a few battles next to one another. Then one day a bullet lands or a bomb explodes and those friends are gone. You have that happen enough times, you pull away. You learn that war isn't the best time to go looking for a new batch of friends."

Fabrizio stepped up to Connors and tugged at the back of his shirt. "I will be your friend," he said to him. "And to your dog, too."

Connors smiled and kneeled down in front of Fabrizio. He picked up the football and held it in his hands. "He's not my dog," Connors said, inching his head toward the bullmastiff. "We just travel together. But I think having you as a friend is something we both would like."

"And I will teach you to play football," Fabrizio said, taking the ball back from Connors. "I will make you the best American player in Naples."

"Then something good might come out of this war after all," Connors said, rubbing the top of Fabrizio's head. He glanced over at Roberto. The boy had kept his head down and his eyes to the ground since Connors first pulled up and had yet to speak a word. "What about you?" he asked. "You going to try and make a football player out of me, too?"

"He doesn't speak," Dante said. "He listens, but never says a word."

"He used to talk all the time," Claudio said. "There were days when we wished he wouldn't talk. But those days are in the past."

"Why won't he talk?" Connors asked.

"His father was anti-Mussolini," Pepe said. "So was most of his family. When the Nazis first came into Naples, the Fascists pointed them out. They were branded as traitors to the cause."

"The next day the Nazis went into their home," Dante said. "Waited until the middle of the night to do it. Woke them from their sleep and killed everyone in the family. All except for Roberto. They left him alone, surrounded by the bodies of his mother, father, grandmother and two sisters. Pepe's father found him there early that morning. From that day to this, he has not made a sound."

"We look out for him," Fabrizio said, putting a hand on the taller boy's shoulder. "He is our friend. Just like you."

Connors put out a hand to touch the boy, thought better of it and then turned and jumped back behind the wheel of the jeep. "Pile in, all of you," he said in a low voice. "I think it's time I got a good look at the rest of your squad."

18

CASTEL DELL'OVO, NAPLES
SEPTEMBER 26, 1943

The wood fires, spread out across the long stone entrance, lit up the cloudless sky. Off in a corner, standing on centuries-old steps, their backs to the sea, three boys sang the words to "Guarda Un Po." Along the farthest side of the castle walkway, stretched out across the length of the path, handguns, rifles and starter's pistols lay in one long row, drying from the heat of the fires and a warm night. Well over a hundred boys and girls were scattered across the open space, sitting around the four full fires, each eating a long meal of fresh fish grilled on wooden sticks and drinking from bottles of wine brought up from the castle basement.

"It's nice to see smiles on their faces again," Nunzia said. She was sitting across from the main fire in the center of the road leading to the castle, a tin cup filled with red wine by her feet, looking at the cluster of boys stretched out around her. "At least for one night."

"A smile goes hand in hand with a stomach full of food," Franco said. "It's been a while since many of them have had both."

"How soon you think before the guns are ready?" Vincenzo asked. He was resting across the cobblestones, his arms folded behind his head, legs crossed.

"Maldini said they should be dry by morning," Franco said. "Then they'll need to be cleaned. If we could find some oil to coat them, it would be even better."

Nunzia looked across the square, at three boys struggling with a wheelbarrow filled with an unexploded bomb. Beyond them, two younger boys bounced a small black ball against the side of a brick wall.

She saw the jeep swing its headlights into the piazza and come to a sharp halt in front of a statue. She watched the soldier get out, a large dog following close behind, and walk into the center of the square, staring out at all the activity around him. He turned to look toward her, their bodies separated by distance and a large bonfire, their eyes meeting for a brief instant.

"The Americans have finally arrived," Nunzia said in a calm voice. "At least one of them."

Connors and the mastiff slowly weaved their way past the scattered children. Their quiet murmurs and soulful singing echoing off the large, barren castle walls, the fires crackling and sparkling high into the air.

Connors stepped over two sleeping boys and turned past the edge of a fire when he saw an older man walking toward him, a small glass in his right hand. "You in charge here?" Connors asked, stepping in the man's path.

The old man shrugged. "They don't even trust me to make coffee," Maldini said.

"Then who?" Connors asked.

Maldini downed the remainder of his drink, wiped his lips with the palm of his right hand and then turned toward the edge of the pier. "The boy in the long-sleeve shirt," he said.

Connors looked past the blaze of flames and down toward the darker end of the pier. "The one next to the girl?" he asked.

"Yes," Maldini said.

"You're kidding, right?" Connors asked. "He's only a kid. Where are the others?"

"What others?" Maldini asked, walking with Connors now toward Vincenzo and Nunzia.

"Anyone else," Connors said. He glanced down at a group of kids drying wet guns and rifles with torn rags. "Resistance fighters. American soldiers. You can't be the only adult here."

"My daughter would give you an argument about how much of an adult I am," Maldini said. "But I'm the only one here old enough to join an army."

"And what's going on with all this?" Connors said, pointing at the kids with the guns and another group wheeling a bomb inside the castle walls. "What're all the guns and bombs for?"

"They're getting ready," Maldini said.

"Ready for what?" Connors asked.

"They think the Nazis might be coming back to Naples," Maldini said.

"They probably are," Connors said. "What's it to these kids?"

"They're going to fight them."

Connors stopped, turned and stared at Maldini. He held the look for several seconds and then smiled. "That's great," he said. "No really. It's a great idea. I don't know who came up with it, you or the kid, but I wish

I had thought of it. In the meantime, I don't suppose you found a radio while you were digging up all these rifles and bombs. The one I got is pretty banged up."

"No," Maldini said, glancing over Connors's shoulder and watching Vincenzo, Franco, Nunzia and Angela come toward them. "There aren't any radios in Naples."

"I have to get word to my command," Connors said. "See if I can get some trucks sent down here and get these kids out."

Connors pulled out a crinkled pack of cigarettes and offered one to Maldini who shook his head. "I have enough bad habits," he said.

"How do you fit into this?" Connors asked. "Or you just somebody else that's eager to die."

"You know me so well and we only just met," Maldini said with a chuckle. "I was drafted, just like you. Except I didn't get a uniform with a fancy patch on the sleeve."

"You even try to talk them out of it?" Connors asked.

"I no longer try to tell people what to do or what to believe," Maldini said.

"Our decision was made before you got here," Vincenzo said, standing behind Connors. "And it won't change, even after you leave."

Connors tossed his cigarette into the fire and turned toward the boy. He glanced over at Nunzia and then focused his attention on Vincenzo. He caught the boy staring at the Thunderbird patch on his sleeve. "We need to talk," Connors said to him. "Just you and me. Quiet and alone."

"We can talk here," Vincenzo said.

"Yes, we could," Connors said, "but we're not." He grabbed the boy by the arm and lead him away from the fire toward the darkness of the silent castle.

They were in an entryway lit by two hanging torches. Connors was pacing, his boots echoing off the stone steps. Vincenzo stood with his back against the cold wall. "Here's how it's going to work," Connors said.

"First thing in the morning, you round these kids up and get them to follow me out of the city. If that doesn't happen, then you and me got ourselves a serious problem."

"What will you do?" Vincenzo asked. "Shoot me if I don't do as you say?"

"I just might," Connors said.

"This is our fight," Vincenzo said. "Not yours."

"What makes you so sure there's even going to be a fight?" Connors asked. "That the Nazis are heading back into the city?"

"Every night their planes dropped leaflets down on us along with the bombs," Vincenzo said. "Told us that tanks would be coming in after the air raids ended, to destroy what was left of the city."

"If that's true, then it's all the more reason to get these kids out of here now," Connors said.

"Everyone we ever trusted has betrayed us," Vincenzo said. "Everyone we believed has lied. Your words don't mean anything to me or to those outside. You're just another uniform marching through the city."

"You got a chance to save those kids," Connors said. "Instead, you're going to let them stay here and, if the Nazis do show up, watch them die."

"What difference does it make where we die?" Vincenzo asked. "In the city fighting or on the road running?"

"The Nazis come back in here, they're not gonna see kids," Connors said. "They'll see targets. Treat you no different than they would me."

"They've treated us in worse ways," Vincenzo said. "They haven't killed your family. They haven't blown up your home. They haven't burned your city."

"I can't let you or these kids be left here to die," Connors said. "You have to understand that."

"You have no choice, American," Vincenzo said. "And you have to understand that."

19

GRAND BALLROOM, VILLA PIGNATELLI, NAPLES
SEPTEMBER 26, 1943

Carlo Petroni lit a hand-rolled cigarette, wooden speckles mixed in with
stale tobacco, and looked around at the barren ornate ballroom that was
often used by the Fascist high command as a place to convene meetings. The villa was once the site of the finest gardens on the Italian
coast, designed by the great Giovanni Bechi himself. Now the grounds
lay scorched, lush green lawns and rose beds turned brown by the constant aerial attacks. Petroni looked away from the flowered patterns lining the walls and turned to the curious faces that surrounded him. He
was eighteen and a convicted felon, sentenced by an Italian court to two
years in the boys' prison at Saint Enfermo. He had been a street orphan
long before the first bombs fell on Naples, left to fend for himself since
early childhood, abandoned by both parents and family. He was in
charge of a small team of thieves who ate the food they stole and sold
their pilfered goods through the black market. Petroni was tall and muscular, dark hair nearly shoulder-length. He had a small scar below his
lower lip and a much longer one running down the length of his right
arm. His war had not been against the Nazis or the Fascists, but had
been fought instead on a daily basis inside the brutal walls of a prison
without rules. Each day was a quest for survival, warding off surprise attacks from vengeful and frustrated guards and other inmates eager to
get a grip on his access to the black marketers working the alleys and
dark rooms of Naples.

When the German evacuation came, the Nazis opened all the prison
doors and sent the convicts back to the street. Most of them did as they
were told and walked out of Naples, under the steady gaze of Nazi
guards. Petroni made sure he and his team of thieves hid and waited.
He saw no profit in fleeing. Nor was there any in fighting, as far as he
could tell. But Petroni did see a potential opportunity opening up in the

next few days. If it all evolved as he envisioned, Petroni would end up with the Germans on one side, the Americans on the other and the Italians, as always, stuck in the middle. It was a golden moment to make some money and begin his postwar life with a pocketful of cash. All he needed to do was play one side against the other and stay alive. And those were talents Carlo Petroni had learned to master since he was a toddler just free of diapers.

"How much longer do we wait?" Piero asked. At thirteen, the youngest thief in the group was quiet and shy, two traits that hid the fact that he was also deadly with a knife and all too willing to prove it.

"Until we see Nazi uniforms," Petroni said. "And then we'll find out if what we heard is true, that some crazy boys are going to try and stop them from doing what they were sent to do. If that happens, then we step in."

"Step in and do what?" another in the group, Aldo, asked. "Fight with the boys against the Nazis?"

Carlo looked at the boy, his same age but much smaller in both stature and girth, and shook his head. "The guards beat on your head a little too much while you were inside," he said. "What are you thinking? We join no one's army. We listened to no one while we were under Mussolini's rule. Why should we listen to anyone, especially those our own age, when there is no one to rule?"

"So what do we do?" Marco asked. He stood apart from the group, staring out through a broken window at the remains of the gardens below. He was shirtless and shoeless and had a small handgun wedged in the back of his brown pants. "You say we're going to step in. What does that mean?"

"It means money in our pockets," Petroni said. "We follow all that goes on between the Germans and the boys. We join with both groups and tell each what they need to hear. Tell the Nazis where the boys are hiding. Tell the boys where the traps are set. Stay back and watch as they all kill each other."

"I haven't heard anything about money yet," Piero said, still not convinced Petroni's plan was worth his time or energy.

"The Germans will see us for what we are and they will pay for the information we give," Petroni said, stomping out the last of his cigarette with the heel of his foot.

"The Germans have money they can give us, maybe even some food," Marco said. "But the boys have nothing to give. So why bother with them?"

"Everyone has something," Petroni said, standing and walking between the small gathering of boys. "If these street fighters can't give us money or food, we'll take their weapons or clothes. But we're looking for more than that from them. The Nazis won't stay long. They'll set the city on fire and leave, head back to Rome and then to the north. That leaves Naples to whoever's left, and that will be us."

"They'll know we're convicts," Aldo said. "And they'll know not to trust us. Why would they take us in?"

"Because we can fight," Petroni said. "Probably better than anyone in their ranks. They sit around fires at night and talk like brave men. But none of them has been in fights like we have, none has killed to survive. They'll want us because they'll need us. They won't be happy about it, they've been warned all their lives to stay away from boys like us. But the people who were so quick to warn them away are dead, and we are still here. Ready to help them."

"How many are there?" Piero asked.

"Does it matter?" Petroni asked with a shrug. "A hundred, maybe two hundred. Even if there's a thousand, what difference does it make? Each one in our group is worth fifty of theirs. It's a match made in hell and hell is where we live."

"And if we're found out?" The question came from a large boy sitting on the one chair left in the room, his long legs stretched out before him, arms folded across his chest, his dark eyes rimmed red from infection. "Or even if a few of them suspect us of dealing with the Nazis. What then?"

Petroni walked toward the boy, arms spread wide, a bemused look on his face. "You're the last one I'd expect to hear such a question from, Bruno," he said with mock surprise. "You know the answer to that better than I do. In fact, you know it better than anyone in this room."

"I just want to hear it come out of your mouth," Bruno said, raising his eyes up to Petroni. "Have you say it to me and everyone else here. It's a decision that needs to be made now. *Before* it starts. And once you make it, you have to keep to it."

"There is no problem with this, Bruno," Petroni said. "Not for you, me or anyone who's spent a day inside that prison together. If our plans are found out or even if you *suspect* someone of knowing what we're up to, then that person must die. Whether he is a German soldier or an Italian boy. The same punishment applies."

Bruno Repello pulled up his legs and stood. He was several inches taller than Petroni and, at twenty, the oldest of the group; he was also its most violent member. He was born into a family of Camorristas that held the city in its grip much like a hawk would hold a squealing mouse. Mussolini's reign had tempered their control, but not enough to wash the taste of power from their mouths. Repello knew that eventually Naples would be returned to its people, a war would end, Germans and Americans would go back to their own lands, savoring a victory or over-coming a defeat. And once again, the Camorra would control the streets. He wanted to be at the controls when that happened. "Then we have talked enough," he said to Petroni. "Let's go out and meet our new friends and give them all the help they need."

20

16TH PANZER DIVISION, FORTY MILES OUTSIDE OF NAPLES
SEPTEMBER 26, 1943

Colonel Von Klaus stood in the center of the railroad tracks, looking down at the large electrical circuit box by his feet. "Are these the main power feeds?" he asked.

"Yes, sir," Kunnalt said. Ernst Kunnalt was tall, with a thick head of red hair buried under his large pith helmet and a relaxed sense of humor he very seldom exhibited around his more serious-minded fellow soldiers. He relished his role as Von Klaus's aide-de-camp and made sure that all his assigned missions were completed promptly, no matter how uncomfortable they might be. "These go in to all the railroad connections. The men discovered another one a half-mile farther down the road that leads into the city."

"Destroy them both," Von Klaus said. "I don't want anything to be able to get in or out of Naples. Also, cut any electricity that may be feeding into the city. There is to be no power of any kind at any time."

"Most of the current was cut off by the evacuating team," Kunnalt said. "From the looks of it, they were pretty thorough."

"Not thorough enough," Von Klaus said. His voice was hoarse, aggravated by a rash of allergies from which there was no relief. Physically, Von Klaus was more suited to the hard-rock terrain and subzero temperatures of the Russian front than to the sun-drenched and dusty roads of southern Italy. "These last few miles, we've passed a number of overhead lines. One or two might still be active. Send a team of men and two tanks to backtrack and cut down any wires they find. Also blast apart the poles and any boxes that may contain electrical wiring. I don't want anything left that has even the remote possibility of being reconnected."

"And where would you like the mines placed, sir?" Kunnalt asked. "We've already buried fifty of them under the tracks. Any train that happens to come through won't make it into the city."

"I want them everywhere you can place them," Von Klaus said. "Side roads, dirt roads, main roads. I want it so no one can follow us into or out of Naples. I also want bombs on timers set on all perimeters, covering railroad tracks and the main highways."

"Timed to go off when, sir?" Kunnalt asked.

"Give them the maximum time," Von Klaus said. "Give it enough so all the tanks are a safe distance away. And keep the bombs clear of the mines so one doesn't set off the other. Once that is completed, we can move into Naples."

"Do you anticipate any resistance?" Kunnalt asked.

"Who is there left to resist?" Von Klaus asked. "The advance scouts reported little movement throughout the city. Children and the elderly mostly, neither of whom should pose a problem. We have more than enough to handle whatever there is. It shouldn't take us more than two, three days on the outside to complete the mission."

"I've never been sent to destroy a city," Kunnalt said, gazing up at the bright sky. "I guess it's not something you think about when you go off to fight a war."

"Losers destroy," Von Klaus said. "Winners conquer. You just happen to be on the wrong side, Kunnalt. If you were with Patton, you'd have sat next to him as he rode through the streets of Sicily, mobbed and cheered by its people. Instead, you will be by my side, riding into an empty city to bomb and burn whatever is left. To the losers fall the unpleasant chores."

Kunnalt stood next to Von Klaus, each relishing the silence that surrounded them. "There are farmlands and houses on either side of the tracks," Kunnalt said after several moments. "Shall I have them searched?"

"There's no need," Von Klaus said, shaking his head. "Split the division and have the farmlands torched and the houses destroyed. We're to leave nothing behind but burnt ground. Let them have their victory, but let it come at a price. I may be out here on a loser's mission, Kunnalt, but I guarantee you, I'll make it a successful one."

21

VIA VICARIA VECCHIA, FORCELLA, NAPLES
SEPTEMBER 26, 1943

Angela cut a thin slab of cheese off a week-old hunk of provolone and handed it with the tip of the knife blade to her cousin, Tino. Crowding beside her in the small olive grove, the boy grabbed the cheese with dirty fingers and jammed it into a corner of his mouth. "Chew slowly," she warned him. "This is the last of the food."

"Are you going to have some?" Tino asked. He was seven, the only relative she had left. He was rail skinny and had severe asthma, his attacks coming on without warning and often lasting for hours. With medicine in short supply, Angela felt he was only a frightened breath away from death.

"I had mine for lunch," she said.

"Thank you for taking me here," Tino said. "It's been a while since I got to see them. I was worried the bombs had moved the graves."

"I told you they wouldn't leave you, didn't I?" Angela said, gazing down at the simply marked graves of her aunt Carmella and uncle Francesco. Tino's parents had been killed during a morning bombing raid.

"Yes, you did," Tino said.

"I'll leave you alone with them," Angela said. "I'll wait for you over by the olive trees."

Tino nodded. "I'm going to tell Mama and Papa I caught a fish and that I helped clean it and grill it. I think they will be happy to hear that."

Angela kissed the top of his head. "Don't forget to tell them yours was the biggest fish in the net. And you were the youngest one in the boat."

"I'll also tell them you have been taking good care of me," he said. "So they don't worry so much about me."

"And then tell them you'll be the one taking care of me when I am old and ugly and too fat to move off a chair." Angela began walking up toward the olive grove. "And no one else can stand to even look at me. But you will be there, Tino, with your smile, a large basket of fruit by your feet and your arms filled with new dresses."

"Every day," Tino said in a low voice. "I promise."

Angela leaned against a thin olive tree. She used to love this time of day, cooking smells blending with the odor of wood burning in stone fireplaces, signaling that the afternoon meal was coming to a full boil. Shoeless children crammed the alleys and halls leading into their crowded apartments, the echoes of youthful laughter bouncing off hard walls. Elderly women, dressed in widow's black, sat on straw chairs, an arm's reach from the kitchen entrance, peeling skin off fresh vegetables.

Angela was born in Forcella and had lived in the tough neighborhood all her life. She knew full well what the rest of the city thought of the people who prowled its streets; there was hatred in the stares and venom in the whispered comments whenever she ventured out of her part of town. Her people were feared and despised, written off as thieves and ruffians, quick to snatch a purse or take advantage of a wayward tourist. She was old enough to understand that many of those feelings sprang from truth, that the high incidents of crime and the large enclave of criminals who lived on Forcella's darkened streets had earned it the right to be called the most dangerous area in Italy.

But she also knew it was the poorest and most neglected neighborhood in Naples. The men were the last hired for jobs and the first to be laid off when factory work was in decline. Many of the women, her mother included, married after they were pregnant, and were often abandoned after several difficult and violent years, left to tend to the needs of small broods of hungry children. Kitchen pantries were as bare as a poor man's pockets, and the black market thrived on the streets of Forcella years before war brought their trucks into even the richest areas. The days were filled with struggle and the night hours were held hostage to the whims of despair on these five ragged city blocks that no one in Italy wanted to know about. Forcella was Harlem, Watts, East St. Louis and Appalachia all jammed inside a small pocket of a city in decay, with no chance for either rescue or redemption.

But Angela Rummerta never saw Forcella as a neighborhood in turmoil. It was her home and she had long ago learned to love the odors of the fruit and fish carts that rambled past her bedroom window in that quiet hour before the sun began to share its light. She knew the words to the soulful ballads sung by women young and old as they hung morning wash on clotheslines too weak to bear their wet burden. She saw smiles and knowing nods where strangers were timid witnesses to hard looks and shifting glances. She could navigate herself into and out of every secret alleyway in the neighborhood's tight streets and could travel blindfolded the hidden passages that linked one stone tenement to another. Now, standing with her back to a burnt-out olive grove, looking down at a little boy crying over the graves of his parents, she longed for the sights and smells of her old neighborhood as much as she did for the family she left buried in its ruin. Angela knew all that was now a part of her past, to be revisited only in memory.

She took a deep breath, closed her eyes and rested her head against the base of the tree, its bark singed from the heat of the bombs.

She heard the snap of the twig but didn't move.

She steadied herself and waited, listening for the weight of the next step to tell her what she needed to know. She held her breath and looked across the dirt path and spotted Tino, clearing debris from his parents' grave. A childhood spent on the hard streets of Forcella had taught Angela how to distinguish between the simple rustling of an early evening breeze and the slow, deliberate movements of lurking danger. She turned her head to the right as soon as she heard the small stone roll against the side of a tree. She spread her feet, took one more look down at Tino, and then jumped to her right.

She stood, her arms by her side, her dark shoes firmly planted on brown soil, staring at the thin end of a German soldier's rifle. The soldier was young, in his early twenties at most, tall and gaunt, his uniform suited to a much larger man, hanging loose across the sleeves and trouser legs. He motioned with his rifle for her to raise her arms and move back against the tree. Angela moved with careful steps, praying that Tino would not call up to her, shielding him from the German's flat eyes with her body. The soldier dragged his feet several steps forward, the heels of his boots kicking up pockets of dirt, staring at Angela, a brown-tooth smile spread across his face. He said something in German she did not understand, then lowered his rifle and rested it against the side of her dress. He held the smile as he used the rifle to search her body for weapons, running it slowly around her waist and against the sides of her neck, then down her hips, stopping at her ankles. Angela swallowed hard but held his gaze and didn't flinch when he brought the rifle against her inner thighs and began to move it slowly up. She nodded at the soldier and smiled, lowering her arms slightly, bringing them down to the edge of her blue blouse, her fingers skimming the length of her long, brown hair. The soldier's eyes widened as he held the rifle butt inches below the front of Angela's panty, swaying it gently from side to side. The soldier stepped closer, keeping one hand on the rifle, stroking her face and neck with the other. She ran her tongue across her dry lips and rested a hand on top of his, rubbing the tips of his fingers. *"Bella,"* the soldier said, using all the Italian he knew, leaning toward Angela's face, their lips only inches apart, rifle now hanging down against his leg. The arid heat of his breath warmed the side of the girl's cheek and neck and a dirt-smeared hand ran its way around the edges of her small breasts, squeezing and pinching them through her thin layers of clothes. He brought his mouth down hard against hers, the pressure of his cracked lips forcing Angela's eyes shut and pushing her head up against the thin tree. The soldier let the rifle fall to the ground, both his arms now wrapped around the back and waist of his Italian catch.

Angela rested one arm around his shoulders and rubbed the top of one of her legs against the soldier's knee. She moved her free hand down beneath her hair and under the top of her blouse. She gently unclipped the snap on the knife strap she kept around her neck, held in place by a brown leather wrap given to her by a grandmother keen on the ways of wayward men. She gripped the handle on the sharp, slender blade and brought it out of its sheath, still holding the soldier's kiss, feeling him unbutton her blouse and move his hands onto her flesh. Angela tossed off the soldier's helmet and grabbed the back of his head, pressing her lips tighter against the force of his kiss. She tasted his saliva, bit at his tongue and then let the power of the knife take its course.

She plunged the sharp end of the blade deep into the soft part of his chest, finding an opening between uniform and skin. She went in hard, held it in place for several seconds, feeling the soldier bite down on her tongue, both of them tasting the blood. His eyes were open now, wide and filled with fright, and his legs began to sag. Angela lifted the knife up, tugging it through nerve endings and soft bone, and then brought it down with a force that went against her age, slicing a curved path toward the soldier's navel. His head slid from her mouth to her neck and his body lay limp. Angela gave the knife one final shove and then pulled it out. She moved away from the tree and watched the soldier fall to her feet, facedown and dead.

Angela stood there, her body running with sweat, breath coming in slow spurts, the soldier's blood covering the front of her blouse and skirt. The knife was in her right hand, small rivers of blood washed down her fingers and off its tip onto the dry dirt at her feet. Angela turned her head and saw Tino standing there, staring up at her with quiet eyes. The boy walked toward her with outstretched arms, then embraced her, holding her tight around the waist. Angela hugged him back, finding comfort in the warmth of someone she loved. She lowered her head against the top of his and rested it there, tears quietly streaming down the sides of her unlined face.

"We should leave," Angela said, afraid to let the boy go, holding on to his sides as if he were a life protector.

Tino nodded and began to walk with her, one arm still around Angela, his fingers held tight against the side of her blood-soaked blouse. They moved down the hill and away from the scorched olive grove.

22

16TH PANZER DIVISION HEADQUARTERS
FIFTEEN MILES OUTSIDE OF NAPLES. SEPTEMBER 26, 1943

Colonel Von Klaus sat on a soft folding chair, feet stretched out, the heels of his boots resting on top of an empty wine crate. He was reading a two-week-old newspaper, its pages crammed with stories that regaled the German people with tales of victorious battles that never happened and the panicked attempts by the Allies to halt Hitler in his tracks. There was no mention of the thousands of bodies lying dead, frozen victims of the Russian winter and an army that thrived under brutal conditions. There were no columns devoted to the advances made by the British and American forces throughout Italy, as they eased their way into reclaiming the country from German hands. Nothing was written of England's resolve not to cave to the pressure of the German assault, its people hanging on to their country despite a pounding that would have caused others to easily raise high the flag of surrender.

German tanks and trucks were short on fuel and in need of fresh tires to continue to mount their massive dual campaigns. Army morale was at its lowest point since the start of the war and the supply runs of food and water had slowed to a trickle. The once-feared Luftwaffe, the centerpiece of Hitler's war machine, was running on low throttle, its pilots flying off into battle with engines in drastic need of repair, their weapon hatches filled as much with propaganda leaflets as with bombs. Von Klaus folded the newspaper in half and tossed it to the ground, weary of the lies that had replaced the reality of Germany's fate.

Von Klaus leaned his head against the back of the chair and closed his eyes, anxious for this current mission to come to a close and curious as to what the future held in store for both him and his family. He knew his life in the military would soon be at an end. A postwar defeated Germany would be a poor home for a career soldier, even if a fraction of the atrocities he had heard about were proven true. He was too poor to pursue a life of leisure and ill-suited for much else beyond a battlefield campaign. He was a man grounded in the ways of a soldier, comfortable in command, at ease with the orders dispatched by unseen faces. In all likelihood, Von Klaus reasoned, his future would be mapped out by events out of his control, his choices and his new way of life, if there was even to be one, left to the whim of strangers.

Von Klaus opened his eyes when he heard the footsteps.

He stared at the disheveled boy standing in front of him, Kunnalt by his side. "Who is your new friend?" he asked.

"A former prisoner of the juvenile jail in Naples," Kunnalt said. "He was freed during the evacuation. He walked into camp a short while ago, said he had information we could use before we move our tanks into Naples."

Von Klaus looked across at the boy. He appeared more rugged in manner than many of the other children he had seen wandering the side roads, lost and adrift. His eyes were harder, his demeanor harsh, his gaze cold and steady. "Why would you want to help us?" Von Klaus asked him, speaking again in Italian.

"I want the war to end," the boy answered. "Helping you will make that happen faster."

"What's your name?" Von Klaus asked, lowering his feet and sitting up in the chair.

"Carlo Petroni," the boy said. "I lived in Piazza Mercato with my family before the war."

"Why were you sent to prison?" Von Klaus asked.

"I was guilty of the crime of hunger," Carlo said with a shrug. "I had no food and there was no money, so I took what I needed from those who had it. I don't apologize for what I did and I wasn't the only one in Naples to steal what I ate."

"I don't like thieves," Von Klaus said. "They not only steal, they lie. Which will put into doubt anything you tell me."

"You'll kill me if I lie," Carlo said. "And being found dead is not part of my plan."

"I can easily have the information beaten out of you," Von Klaus said. "That usually saves time and guarantees that what I hear will be the truth."

"I wasn't dragged here," Carlo said. "I walked in and chose to tell you what I know, not the Americans and not any of the resistance fighters."

"And why are we your chosen ones?" Von Klaus asked, voice dripping sarcasm.

"I stand a better chance to make a profit working with you," Carlo said. "The Americans don't care to pay for information and the resistance fighters expect it for free."

"And what makes you think I'll be so free with my money?" Von Klaus asked.

"What I have to say is worth more to you than to the others," Carlo said. "You and your men are the ones in danger and, if you care about them, you'll pay to save their lives."

Von Klaus walked over to the boy, the two exchanging hard glances, then turned to Kunnalt. "I know he's not to be trusted," he said in German. "What I don't know is if he can be believed."

"He's a criminal, sir," Kunnalt says. "If it is hidden and a danger, he would be the first to hear of it. Especially given the current condition of the city."

Von Klaus nodded and rested a hand on Carlo's shoulder. "I'll pay for your information," he said. "And you'll pay if it turns out to be wrong. And the price I extract will be much higher. Are we clear?"

"Only a fool would refuse such an offer," Carlo said.

Von Klaus glared at Carlo for several moments then turned his back, staring down a grassy ravine toward the city. "Tell me what you think is so vital for me to know," he said.

Carlo took a deep breath, wiped at his brow with the sleeve of his torn wool shirt. He had been living on the streets long enough to be aware that he was about to take a huge risk. The German had not yet extended any payment, let alone told him how much he would receive. There was no guarantee that he would even pay. It would be easy for the colonel to listen to what Carlo had to say and then have him shot, dumping his body along the deserted road. On the other hand, if he said nothing, the German would shoot him just for wasting his time. Carlo was more at home doing business with thieves his own age or older members of the Camorra. While he could never run the risk of trusting them, he had seldom walked away from a deal with the short end of the bargain. But this was his first business transaction with a German officer. He knew how little respect the Nazis had for the people of Naples, branding them all as liars and cheats. Nazi bombs and guns had cost 400,000 Neapolitans their lives. One dead street thief wouldn't be much cause for concern.

"The streets of Naples are not as empty as you think," Carlo said, taking a hard swallow. "You could be taking your tanks into trouble. Not enough to cost you your mission, but enough to cost you some men."

"Who is there to cause us any trouble?" Von Klaus asked, turning back to the boy. "The reports from the advance teams speak of nothing other than smatterings of elderly and children running loose."

"Some of those boys are staying behind to fight," Carlo said. "They may be armed. They'll be fighting you on streets they know well, and they can find places to hide where even your best men will get lost searching them out."

"How many boys and how heavily armed?" Von Klaus asked.

"Last I heard there were about two hundred," Carlo said. "By the time your tanks come into Naples, that number could go up."

"And their weapons?"

"Hunting rifles, mostly," Carlo said, jamming his hands into his trouser pockets, sensing the colonel's interest and growing in confidence that he had made the right choice. "A few handguns and enough bullets to keep both going for a few days."

Von Klaus walked over to the boy, a determined manner in each step, a glint of anger flashing across his tanned face. "Why aren't you with them?" he asked. "Why aren't you getting ready to fight me?"

"I've never been with them," Carlo said with icy detachment. "They're young and listen to those who ask them to fight for stupid reasons. Reasons that will get them killed. I fight for myself and only if the price is right."

"And what price have you placed on your betrayal?" Von Klaus asked.

"Five thousand lira," Carlo said. "That will be enough to help me and my friends buy our way out of Naples. And for three rifles and three ammo belts, protection against anyone who tries to stop us."

"What if the ones trying to stop you are wearing German uniforms?" Von Klaus asked. "Will you kill them, too?"

Carlo smiled and shook his head, quick to sense the colonel's unease. He was having a difficult time measuring Von Klaus. He was used to dealing with men who let the rush of their emotions rule their power to reason. They would also have very little interest in him, keeping their focus mainly on what he knew that might help them. But Von Klaus wanted both. He was looking to wrest free what Carlo could tell him, but he also wanted to walk away knowing the full weight of the motives behind the sale of such information. It was, Carlo decided, what separated the soldier from the criminal.

"There would be no need for me to kill them," Carlo finally said. "Not after I told them that we were friends."

"It would be a lie," Von Klaus said.

"But one that would help keep me alive."

"Perhaps. That's all that matters to people like you in time of war, isn't it? Staying alive."

"It's all that matters at any time," Carlo said. "In battle or out. Staying alive is always the final goal."

"Then you have achieved your goal," Von Klaus told him. "At least for today. My aide will pay you your money. It's a large sum, enough for you to buy your rifles and ammo from someone other than me. You'll take the same path out of my camp you took in and there'll be no need for any further contact."

"What if I hear of something you might want to know?" Carlo asked, pushing past the limit of his luck. "I can get word to you in less than a day."

"Look at me!" Von Klaus commanded in a voice loud enough to catch the attention of the soldiers milling about the surrounding tanks. "Take a good look and remember it. If I ever see you again, it will only be to kill you."

Von Klaus turned and walked up a hill, toward a makeshift tent resting alongside his tank. He glanced over his shoulder and watched as the late afternoon sun spread its warmth across the edge of the Bay of Naples.

23

CATACOMBE DI SAN GENNARO, NAPLES
SEPTEMBER 26, 1943

Steve Connors walked quietly inside the centuries-old tomb of the pa-tron saint of Naples, marveling at the large two-story web of galleries, which also housed the remains of countless bishops. He stared up at the mosaics and frescoes, impressed with their beauty and intricate design. He rested his pack and rifle against a corner wall and ran a hand against the cold stone, which had not crumbled despite the many years that passed and the thousands of bombs that fell. The weight of his footsteps echoed against the stillness of the empty chamber as he made his way through the shrouded darkness, inching slowly across the grounds Neapolitans held as sacred. He settled on a cool corner step, his back chilled against the smooth carvings of angels and saints.

He had wandered in, looking for a silent place to clear his head and plan his moves. He was now in the middle of a different mission than the one Captain Anders had sent him on and he needed time alone. The search and find would turn up empty, that he knew to be true. Any Americans operating in Naples were now either dead or heading toward the safety net of Allied lines. He realized that the minute he met the four boys sitting in his jeep. He knew not just from what they said, but from the way they looked at him and the manner in which they stared at his uniform, at the grenade patches on his sleeve and at the Native American Thunderbird etched on his shoulder. So, as far as Connors was concerned, that door was sealed.

But now he was stuck with an even bigger issue. What they wanted to do went beyond logic and common sense and strayed into the rougher terrain of passion. Those boys wanted to fight not because some officer higher up the ranks had ordered them to. They wanted to fight because the Nazis had left them stripped raw and vulnerable and frightened. They were cornered innocents, holding rusty guns and

makeshift bombs, the pain they carried in their hearts their most valuable ammunition. But Connors knew that no matter how valiant the
cause, theirs was a hopeless dream whose reality would end with bodies
left to rot on empty streets.

Connors had no proof the Nazis were coming back to Naples. The
leaflets that had been dropped could easily have been a ruse to frighten
any strays out of the city. From his eyes, there simply was no reason for
them to return. The city was desolate, huge chunks of it destroyed, no
water or power was available for miles and no one patrolled its borders
but a straggle of wanna-be soldiers. In all likelihood the only troops who
would come marching back into Naples would be members of his own
unit, fast on the heels of Montgomery's British forces.

His initial instinct had been to motor up to Salerno, get a couple of
trucks in tow, come back, round up the boys and bring them to safety.
But that idea involved risk. He could face a delay at headquarters, or
even worse, not be given authority to bring in the trucks and the drivers
to rescue abandoned street kids. And besides, by the time he drove back
into Naples, the boys would be scattered and hidden in places where no
one would find them. He looked around at the dark figures staring down
at him and knew he was on a fool's mission.

"Most of what's written on the plaques is not true."

It was the voice of the young woman he had met by the pier, fresh
and soft, standing off to his left, half-hidden by the shadows.

"Such as?" Connors asked.

"The body of San Gennaro is not buried here, like the signs say." Her
English was choppy, but easy to understand. "Only his head. It's upstairs, in the rear chapel, up against a back wall."

"What about this business about the flowing blood?" Connors asked.
"That's not on the level, either?"

"Depends on who you ask," the woman said. "My grandmother
swore on it to the very day she died. My father scoffs and laughs and
says it is nothing more than the crazy rantings of a silly religion."

"Which side do you fall on?" Connors asked, charmed by her voice,
eager to see the face and body behind it.

"When I was little, I'd go with my grandmother to church on the three days of the year when San Gennaro's blood would flow," she said. "I never saw anything, but the old people acted as if they did. It made them happy. I guess that's all that really matters."

"It says on one of these that he's the protector of your city," Connors said. "Even I know that's a lie."

"He's a saint," the woman said. "Not a savior."

"And what about you?" Connors asked. "What do you do when you're not giving out history lessons?"

The girl stepped out of the shadows and walked closer to Connors, the wooden heels of her clogs clapping against the stone floor. She was tall and thin and as beautiful as any woman he had ever seen. It was a pure beauty, untouched and untamed, refusing to surrender an inch to the poverty and madness that thrived around her. She wore a pale blue dress, and her hair hung thick and loose, resting easily on top of her shoulders. Her lips were full and rich. But it was her eyes that locked Connors in. They were at once sweet and sexual, shining like candles in a darkened harbor. "I can help you," she said.

"What's your name?"

"Nunzia." The young woman fleshed out the smile and offered him a hand to shake.

Connors reached for her hand, gently wrapping his fingers around her soft skin. He held her until Nunzia slowly pulled her hand free. "I was named after my father's mother," she said. "She was one of the first women in Naples to run her own business. It was a large bakery just outside the city limits. She took it over after my grandfather died and kept it going until the war started."

"My grandmother had her own business, too, back home," Connors said. "My family never liked to talk about it all that much, but I was always proud of her for doing what she did."

"What kind of business was it?"

"My grandma Helen was a bootlegger," Connors said. "She made illegal whiskey up in the Kentucky hills, sold it to the farmhands and factory workers in the area. She used her sons, my father one of them, as the runners. My dad used to hand out the jars and pick up the cash. She did well, too. Made a lot of money in her time. Most of which she used to put her boys through school."

"Your grandma would have done well in Naples," Nunzia said. "Here, the men are the ones who give out the commands, but it is the women who enforce the rules."

"Where does that leave those kids?" he asked, standing close enough to smell a sweet mixture of black market soap mingled with natural beads of sweat.

"What do you expect them to do?" Nunzia asked, taking a few steps closer toward the stone walls. "Why should they listen to you? Every uniform they've ever seen, including the Italian, has only caused them loss and pain. It helps make their choice a clear one. Some will flee and hide, wait to be rescued. But most will stay behind and fight if there is someone to fight."

"I can't let that happen," Connors said, in a firm voice.

"I don't know your name," she said, her voice soothing and warm in the stillness of the dark room.

"Connors," he said. "Steve Connors."

"And why do you care so much, Steve Connors?" Nunzia asked. "We mean nothing to you. We're just another city in another country for you to march through with your tanks and your flag."

"They're just kids," Connors said. "They're not soldiers, no matter how many old rifles you put in their hands. And if the Nazis come, they will die. All that's going to be left for you to do, then, will be to find fresh ground to bury them in."

"They are close to dead, already," Nunzia said. "You look into their eyes and you can see it. If there is a battle, it will be more than a chance for them to die. It will be a chance for them to live. I won't help you take that from them. They have paid the price for that right."

Connors stared at Nunzia and shook his head, running a bare hand across the back of his neck. "How would your patron saint feel about all of this?" he asked.

"If you believe in San Gennaro, you believe in miracles," Nunzia said.

STAZIONE ZOOLOGICA E ACQUARIO, NAPLES
SEPTEMBER 26, 1943

The zoo and the aquarium, once considered the most beautiful and prestigious in all Europe, stood in near ruin, their frescoes and underwater world blasted into mounds of cracked cement and dust piles by the bombing raids. Rivers of dirty water flowed down the sides of the walls and flooded into the main hall of the aquarium, serving as a haven for rats and human waste. The structure had been funded in 1872 by Anton Dohrn, a young German with a love of nature, and constructed by A. von Hildebrandt to be a home to species that swam only within the cool waters of the Gulf of Naples. Prior to the war, it was a place of pride for Neapolitans and a favorite visiting place for school children out on a day trip.

Four Nazi soldiers were sitting in a circle on the cold bare cement floor of a darkened tunnel. They had moved into the city earlier that day, coming down from the hills, one of the heavily armed advance teams sent in by Colonel Von Klaus to assess any trouble brewing on the streets of Naples. The units were to set themselves up in choice locations that would allow them to inflict the most amount of damage in the least amount of time. They were each equipped with three cases of dynamite, six dozen high-impact grenades, scope rifles, two flame throwers and a bazooka.

"We could look for a drier place to hide," one of the soldiers, Hans Zimmler, said. He glanced behind him, at the water building up and the large rats swimming in debris. Zimmler, like many of the soldiers under Von Klaus, was a young but experienced fighter. He had served with the colonel since the early days of the campaign, when Nazi victory was considered a divine right. "That water level keeps rising, it could pose a problem for us."

"That's why no one will look for us here," a second soldier, Eric Tippler, said. "From this stairwell alone we can cover both the entrance and the exit. Plus we have a clear view of the streets below. We can target anyone in our sites up to three hundred yards." Tippler was in his mid-twenties, the long scar running down the right side of his face the result not of a wound but of a botched birth. He was the sort of man who thrived in wartime, finding solace in the eye of a rifle scope, pleasure from the pull of the trigger and the death of an enemy.

The other two soldiers, equally as young, as experienced and as deadly with a weapon, remained silent, content to let Tippler and Zimmler argue over the mundane issues of position. They sat with their backs against a stone wall, rifles resting across their laps, helmets tilted over their eyes, indifferent to the conversation around them. They were there to cause harm to the enemy. Anything else was merely a distraction.

"Our weapons are of no use to us if we can't keep them dry," Zimmler said. "It's better to move now than to wait until we're in the middle of a fight."

Tippler shrugged. "The water is from a busted pipe. It should rise another inch, maybe two at the most, and we can use it to our advantage. We can hear as well as see anyone coming at us from behind. And if the rats are a concern, we can always just shoot them. This is the best place for us and where we should stay until the Colonel has completed his task."

Zimmler thought about it for a few silent moments, then nodded. "I'll look for a ground-level place to set up the flame thrower. We'll move the bazooka to the highest point we can find. The grenades we should scatter throughout the middle. This way we can attack from all levels."

Tippler patted Zimmler on the shoulder and smiled as he saw that the other two soldiers were now sound alseep. "You and I go to the roof," he said. "We leave our two lazy friends down here to catch up on their sleep and keep the rats company. We'll set up our target scopes and find the best places to rest our rifles."

"Same wager?" Zimmler asked. "One cigarette to a kill."

"I'll leave that up to you." Tippler grabbed his rifle, gear, three large packets of shells and headed up the dark hallway. "Just remember our last bet. You were so far behind, you had to borrow smokes to pay me."

"I had the sun, you had the shade," Zimmler said. "It's not an excuse. Just a fact."

"It won't matter who has the sun side this time," Tippler said as he and Zimmler walked up the dark hall together, their heavy gear clanging against the sides of the stone walls. "From the looks of this city when we came in, I think the only targets we'll be aiming at will be statues and rocks."

The two boys stood in the darkness and watched the soldiers walk past. They slipped out of the emptiness of the large tank, once a watery home to rare species of fish. Their bare feet slid on the gelled surface as they braced themselves against deadened leaves and shrubs. The two had been living in the barren aquarium for three weeks, finding it a safe refuge from the nightly bombing assaults and a convenient place to store their stolen food and meager items of clothing. Giovanni Malatesta, fifteen, and Frederico Lo Manto, fourteen, had been living on the Naples streets since the early spring.

Giovanni was the only son of a grocer and his seamstress wife. His father, emotional and politically driven, had embraced Mussolini's vision for a new Italy from the very start, hearing in the dictator's words an escape route to respectability for Naples. He proudly wore his Fascist black shirt every day, working behind the counter of his small store, its shelves crammed with the freshest produce, oils, cheese and olives in the neighborhood. His wife, much less political than her husband but just as eager to step up to the better end of life, was given more work than she could handle by the men of the regime, trusting her steady hand to alter and adjust their pants, shirts and dresses. As the Fascist dream of domination gave way to the reality of an inevitable loss, Giovanni's parents were among those singled out as traitors to Italy. One quiet spring afternoon, while their son was at school, their home was broken into by partisan rebels and both were shot dead in the middle of a late lunch of lentil and pasta soup.

Frederico had lived with his grandmother since he was an infant, left behind by a father who died in a bar fight and a mother who succumbed to lung cancer. There was little food and even less money for the old woman and young boy to share, but they managed to survive, finding comfort in each other's company. They did their best to live as normal a life as possible, given the rapidly changing events. Frederico went to school each day and was the evening altar boy for the seven o'clock mass at San Lorenzo Maggiore. There, at any point in the service, he could look up and see his grandmother seated in a straw chair, partly hidden by a marble column, black rosary beads wrapped around her frail fingers. His grandmother, hobbled by arthritic legs and poor circulation, searched the stores and black market alleys for scraps of food and unwanted items she could take home and convert into a meal. It was an existence neither felt would get better and both feared would only grow worse. Their joint prophecy proved true when on her way back to their second-floor, one-room apartment, Giovanni's grandmother was felled by a massive heart attack. She died with her back on the wet cobblestone streets, her pale blue eyes staring up at a cloudless sky.

Giovanni could see the stretched-out legs of the two sleeping soldiers, an open crate of grenades by their feet. The main floor of the aquarium was steeped in shadows, the voices of the other two soldiers echoing down from the upper floors. "They sleep like the dead," he whispered to Frederico. "We can take some of their grenades. They won't even know we were here."

"We need food," Frederico said, his voice barely audible. "Not bombs."

Giovanni brushed away the sweaty strands of black hair that ran across his forehead and put a hand on Frederico's thin shoulder. "Those bombs are worth more than food," he said. "Now stay quiet, grab as many as you can hold and then come back to the tank. If they should wake, you make a run toward the entrance."

"They'll fire on us," Frederico said.

"Just run close to the water and as fast as you can," Giovanni said.

"And never look behind you. By the time they steady their aim, we should be outside."

"What about the other two?"

"They're too far up to be of any concern," Giovanni said.

"We can't stay here now that the Germans have moved in," Frederico said. "With or without grenades."

"We'll move down deeper," Giovanni said. "Back into the zoo. We can hide inside the old lions' caves. From there, we can keep our eyes on the Nazis."

"Should we try to grab their rifles, too?" Frederico asked. He stretched his head forward and saw one of the rifles hanging down loose off one of the soldier's legs.

"Just the grenades," Giovanni said. "Only take what they won't miss."

Giovanni was flat on his stomach, inches from the sleeping German soldier, his right hand inside the open crate of grenades, his left palm down and gripping onto the ridges of the curved step. The soldier was moaning softly, deep into his first restful sleep in weeks, as Giovanni slid past the heel of his boot and pulled out two grenades from the crate. He held the bombs at the thick end and began to inch his way back toward safety. Frederico stood across from Giovanni, keeping an eye on both soldiers, making sure neither stirred. He bent his knees and reached a hand into the open crate, careful not to slide on the wet step. He also pulled out two grenades, held one in each hand and moved slowly back toward the ruin of the aquarium. On his fifth step, his right foot gave way and he fell forward, landing with a low grunt on the base of the stairwell, the darkness his only shield. He held the grenades above his head and stared up at Giovanni. His friend reached over and took the grenades from his hands and then stepped back. Frederico looked down behind him, saw the soldiers still asleep, eased himself to his feet and moved back into his hiding place. "You did well," Giovanni said to him, trying to keep the more excitable boy calm.

"We were lucky," Frederico said. "I think one of these grenades would have to go off to wake those two."

"We could make another run at more," Giovanni said. "We have four. Eight would be even better."

"We've used up enough luck for one day," Frederico said.

Giovanni looked over at his friend and nodded. "Do you think the lions' caves will smell as bad as the fish tanks?"

"They smelled bad when the lions lived there," Frederico said. "I don't think they've changed that much."

They walked out of the rear of the broken aquarium exhibit and up toward the barren cages of a once-vibrant zoo. Each held the grenades carefully in hand, moving free of sound, turning only to give a wayward glance at the sleeping soldiers behind them.

25

VIA MONTE DI DIO, NAPLES
SEPTEMBER 26, 1943

The woman sat huddled in a corner of the villa entrance, her back arched to the street. She was wearing a short-sleeved black dress, a thin pair of sandals and a black ribbon held her thick brown hair in place. Maldini sat down next to her, lit a cigarette and blew a clear line of smoke up into the evening sky. He stared out at the blighted street, once lined with palatial villas and palazzi, and now reduced to a long row of shelled-out buildings. The stretch of street ended with the Gran Quartiere di Pizzofalcone, the barracks that had been built in the seventeenth century to house the Spanish troops who then ruled the city. "I would climb the walls to the top of the *caserma* when I was a boy," Maldini said, as much to himself as to the woman. "All my friends, too. It was so important to us in those days. Now, it sounds like such a silly thing to want to do."

The woman turned away from the door and looked over her shoulder at Maldini, her clear, oval face smeared with dirt and tears. "What do you want?" she asked, her voice soft and dry.

"A place to sit," Maldini said.

"Why here?"

"I love this street," Maldini said. "I walked it all the time, both as a boy and as a young man. I asked my wife to marry me in a rainstorm in front of the Palazzo Serra di Cassano. We stood there, facing that beautiful building, holding each other, both of us soaking wet and crying. There were only happy tears, back then."

"I was born on this street," the woman said. "My family lived at the Palazzo Carafa di Noja. It used to be down farther on the right-hand side."

"I know the building well," Maldini said. "Passed it many times over the years. You were lucky to have lived in such a beautiful place."

"It belonged to my grandmother," the woman said. "And she let me have the biggest room on the top floor."

Maldini leaned over and offered the woman a cigarette. She reached up and took one from his pack with thin, trembling fingers. "Where do you live now?" he asked, striking a match and lighting the burnt tobacco.

"Where I can," the woman said.

"And your family?" Maldini asked.

"My mother and father left with the Germans," she said, fighting back the urge to shed more tears. "My two brothers are in the army. It's been months since we've had any word from them."

"But you stayed behind," Maldini said. "Why?"

"My father didn't want me to go with them. I had disgraced him and our family and I deserved to be punished. He said I had lost the right to die alongside an Italian."

The woman put her head down. Maldini slid over closer and rested a hand on her back. "What is your name?" he asked.

"Carmella," the woman struggled to say, her face still hidden by the fingers of her hands.

"And what was it, Carmella, that you did, that your father thought was so terrible?"

Carmella raised her head and looked at Maldini. "You will hate me, too. Once you know."

Maldini leaned his head back against the hard wood of the villa's front door. He ran a hand through the stubble on his chin and shook his head. "I have no more hate to give away," he said. "I keep what I have for myself."

Carmella waited until she could speak without the rush of tears. The night air around them was still quiet, the bombing attacks less than an hour away. "I spent two nights during the evacuation in the company of German soldiers," she blurted out. "At one of the hotels near Lungo-mare."

Maldini looked at her but remained silent. He had long ago resigned himself to the price of war. He learned that it extracts a fee from every-one it touches. The cost varies from one person to the next. But what-ever the cost, it is often too high to bear. He had heard too many cries of anguish screamed out into the empty night to believe otherwise. In his case, the cost was most of his family and any semblance of a happy life. To the boys he had left back at the pier, their bellies filled with fish and wine, the war had won their youth, stripping them bare of the right to be free and foolish. And to the young woman he now stared at, who sur-rendered her passions to enemy arms, it had ripped from her the pure, innocent joy that such a night, under vastly different circumstances, would once have brought. Maldini knew all too well that you didn't need to die in order to lose your life in a war.

"We do many things we shouldn't do in the course of a life," Maldini said. "It doesn't make them right or wrong, just a part of who we are. In times like these, it becomes too much of a chore to judge others."

"I took money from them," she said in a soft whisper, her throaty voice childlike and wounded.

"And what do you think that makes you?" Maldini asked. "A prosti-tute?"

"That's what my father said I was. A *vergonia* to our family. He said he would rather think of me dead than think of me as a whore."

"Fathers are often cruelest to the ones they most love." Maldini stared away from Carmella and down the slope of the empty street. "I once told my boys that real men are the ones who go into battle in defense of a cause. Now they're both dead and I've lived to see the stupidity and ugliness behind my once cherished cause. I made them feel as if I was disappointed in who they were, that I didn't think of them as men, only as boys. I should have loved them for what they were. *My sons.*"

"I don't know what will happen to me now," Carmella said. "I don't know where to go, what to do."

"We can live only in the moment," Maldini told her. "It's the only choice that has been left to us. And you must fight with all the strength you have to make it through to the next moment. That means for now, for tonight, you will come with me to the train station. We'll hide there, along with the others, until the sun comes up and the bombs stop falling."

"And then what?"

"Those are tomorrow's worries," Maldini said. He got to his feet and reached a hand down for Carmella.

She took his hand, stood, straightened her hair and her dress and slid an arm under his as they both began a slow walk to the main railroad tunnels in the center of the city, both looking to survive another night of war.

26

LA STAZIONE CENTRALE, PIAZZA GARIBALDI, NAPLES
SEPTEMBER 27, 1943

The glare of the bright orange sun mixed with the thick plumes of white smoke, leftover evidence of the predawn damage, as Naples woke to a new day. The squinting eyes of the city's survivors began to emerge from the cavernous railroad tunnels that led into and out of the city. The youngest of the children took the lead, running across empty tracks, kicking a soccer ball back and forth, heading toward the main terminals. Soap and clean water were at a premium, making the trickling fountains of the central station a prime gathering place for the tunnel dwellers. Breakfast had long ago become a forgotten meal; the best that could be expected was a small tin of weak coffee and a hard chunk of stale bread. Fresh eggs were a commodity and were fed to those in the group most in need of nutrition. Hunger was now an accepted part of their daily way of life, mingling comfortably alongside the filth and ravaged conditions of a city long past the point of hope.

Connors had parked his jeep under a tree, a short distance from the tunnels and clear of the aerial assault. He slept curled in the backseat, his pith helmet flat over his face, his rifle within easy reach. The mastiff was stretched out on the ground next to the jeep, one large paw covering his brow. The sound of thin soles running over hard ground caused them both to stir awake. Connors lifted his helmet and stared up at Maldini, the morning sun blocking out half the older man's face. Maldini was short of breath, his face and neck coated with sweat. "What is it?" Connors said, sitting up in the backseat.

"There's a ship," Maldini said. "You can see it from the port or from the top of the tunnels. It's heading toward the piers."

"Ours or theirs?" Connors asked. He jumped from the back of the jeep, reached for his binoculars and followed Maldini up the side of a steep hill.

"It was too far out for me to see which flag it flew," Maldini said. "But I know it's not Italian. Any ships we have are underwater."

Connors reached the top of the hill and perched himself over the side of a damaged stone wall, lying on his chest, elbows digging into dark dirt, staring through the binoculars out toward the horizon. "It's not a ship, it's a Nazi tanker," Connors said, moving his head slowly from left to right. "You can tell by the design. She's running pretty slow, which means she's loaded. I figure she's about a day out of port, maybe a little longer."

"Loaded with what?"

Connors rested his binoculars on the ground and looked up at Maldini. "Fuel," he said in a low voice. "Tank fuel most likely. Those leaflets the kids got were right. The Nazis are coming back. They're coming back for the fuel."

"How can you be sure?" Maldini asked.

"They're not wind-up toys," Connors said, getting to his feet. "Between my guys and the Brits, we got the Panzers spread out pretty thin. They're gonna need all that tanker can hold to get them back up north to Rome."

"The fuel belongs to them," Maldini said. "They can take it and do what they want with it. But the leaflets also said they would destroy what's left of the city. Will that happen, too?"

Connors stared at Maldini and didn't answer. He slowly brushed past him and headed back down the hill toward his jeep.

Vincenzo, Franco, Fabrizio and Gaspare made up one team. Pepe, Dante, Claudio and Angela made up the other. Another boy, Angelo, a fourteen-year-old with an awkward gait and an easy smile, functioned as the referee. They were playing in the large cobblestone square just across from the main railroad terminal, morning sun at their backs, relishing in the joys of their national game.

"Do you know in America, they play football with their hands?" Fabrizio said, bouncing a soccer ball off his right knee and passing it to Franco. "With a ball that looks like an egg and with pads on their shoulders and legs."

"How can you play that way?" Angela said, stepping forward to block Fabrizio's forward progress.

"It's a different game," Vincenzo said, moving down the right side, dodging past Claudio and waiting for a leg pass. "I don't know why they call it football, because it isn't. The only time they use their feet is to start the game."

"It's nice to know there's at least one thing the Americans can never beat us at," Gaspare said.

Vincenzo aimed a floater pass up toward Franco, who quickly booted it to Fabrizio. They stood back and watched as Fabrizio did a spin move, lunged to his left, the ball a blur as it veered from one foot to the other, and then skidded to a stop in the center of the square. He kept his eyes on the open space designated as the goal markers and lofted a soft shot above Dante's outstretched arms for the game's first score. Fabrizio raised his hands and fell to his knees, his small head tilted toward the cloudless sky, a beaming smile spread across his face.

Connors pulled the jeep into the square and inched up slowly toward where the kids were playing. "Look how simple the world would be if left to children," Maldini said, pointing at the ongoing game. "A ball, some boys and a sunny day. Nothing more is needed."

Connors sat in the jeep and followed the action for several minutes. His mind was on the tanker. If it was close, so were the Nazi tanks, which meant the roads out of Naples would be a danger to travel across. The safer move might now be to keep the boys in the city and hidden, than out and running as a group. But that, too, came packed with many risks, the least of which was the near impossible task of keeping more than two hundred children clear of Nazi eyes. Connors looked away from the game and watched as Nunzia walked toward the jeep, two cups in her hands. "I thought you both could use some morning coffee," she said, handing them each a cup. "I hope you like it without sugar, Connors. Since we don't have any."

"This is fine, thanks," Connors said, taking one cup and passing the other to Maldini. The older man looked at the soldier, reached for his coffee and smiled. "I see you've met my daughter," he said to him.

Connors sipped his coffee and nodded. "We talked about religion," he said.

Connors stepped out of the jeep and walked closer toward the game. Nunzia and Maldini followed behind, both feeling relaxed and at ease in his company. Angela and Vincenzo glanced up, indifferent to their impending arrival, focusing their attention on the give and take of a soccer match.

"Do you play football?" Maldini asked him.

"Apparently not," Connors said, drinking the last of the bitter coffee.

He stopped short and followed the soccer ball bouncing along the cobblestones. He stared at the chipped stones, the feet of the children running hard across their damaged surface. Connors tossed his cup to the ground and ran toward the kids. "Stop moving!" he shouted. "All of you, stop! Stay still!"

Vincenzo kicked the ball to Franco and turned to look at Connors. "Keep playing," he told them. "Just ignore what he says."

Connors ran closer to the group, reaching for the pistol clipped to his holster. "I said stay still, dammit!" he screamed.

"What we do and what we don't do are none of your business, American," Vincenzo said, running down the center of the piazza, angling for Fabrizio's return pass. "Let us just play our game."

Connors pulled his gun from the holster, aimed it toward the sky and fired off two rounds. The shots brought all action to a halt. Angela and the boys, breathing heavy from the steady running, turned and stared at him. Fabrizio held the ball with his foot, frozen in place. Nunzia and Maldini stood next to the soldier, both curious and frightened by his behavior.

"You're playing it on a mine field," Connors said.

Connors was on his knees, his hands filled with a small mound of pebbles. He threw one pebble at a time against the cobblestones, watching intently as they landed. "What are you doing?" Vincenzo asked him, lines of sweat streaking his face.

Connors spoke in a calm, soothing voice, eyes focused on the cobblestones. "Mines are laid down in patterns," he said. "Circular or up and down. Once you figure out the pattern, you at least can tell where they are."

"Is that hard?" Franco asked from across the piazza.

"That's the easy part," Connors said.

Connors tossed four more pebbles onto the piazza ground before he heard the clanging sound he needed. The noise came just to the left of

Dante's foot, the boy swallowing hard, not knowing what to think or feel. "There's one," Connors said.

He crouched down and tossed out a half dozen more pebbles, all of them close to where Dante stood. The air was summer warm and the singular breeze humid and stilted. There was no sound other than that of rock against steel. Connors stood as soon as a pebble had found its second target, this time close to Angela. "I'll dig that one out," he told the group as he stepped gingerly around them. "Then work my way across until I can dig up enough of them to get you out."

"Is that part hard?" Franco asked, panic seeping into his voice.

"Yes," Connors said.

A large number of boys had gathered in the piazza, mingling alongside Nunzia and Maldini. "Keep everyone as far back as you can," Connors said to Nunzia, catching her eye for a brief second. "Just in case."

Connors leaned down on the cobblestones, his face inches from the partially buried mine. Vincenzo crawled up alongside him, a small knife in his hand. "I'm starting to think that none of you really does understand English," Connors said.

"You're going to need help," Vincenzo said. "It may as well be from me."

Connors glared at the boy and then looked down at the knife in his hand. "I'll lift off the cobblestones," he said. "You scrape the dust away from the edges. But stay away from the top or bottom of the mine. And be gentle. It doesn't take much to set them off."

Vincenzo inched closer toward the stones, wiped his hand across the front of his shirt and then began to clear away the dirt around the mine, watching as the soldier rested the broken cobblestones off to the side. "We'll need a place to keep them," Connors said. "Away from the Germans and away from the kids."

"I know a place," Maldini said, standing over both Connors and Vincenzo.

Connors stared at the hovering shadow and shook his head. "Might as well get a parade going," he said.

"Where?" Vincenzo asked.

"In Parco Virgiliano," Maldini said. "You've all run and played on the grounds there. There are hundreds of pine trees spread around the property. It would be easy to transport the mines and keep them there out of sight."

"Have you or any of your friends ever transported a mine?" Connors asked, raising his voice above the early morning din. His only greeting was silence and bowed heads. "Did you spend a lot of time after school digging them up and moving them to a park?"

"We never had to before," Vincenzo said, welled-up anger filtering through his voice. "Now we do."

"How?" Maldini asked.

"By cart," Vincenzo said.

Vincenzo looked down at Connors's right hand, the one that was now reaching for the base of the mine and saw the tremble, the twitching up to his wrist. "Is it nerves that makes that happen?" he asked.

"No," Connors said with a wry smile. "And it's not coffee, either. It's fear."

"Look behind you," Maldini told them, pointing to the determined faces of the silent boys of Naples. There were close to two hundred now jamming the piazza, each eager for Vincenzo and the American to complete their task. "You cannot fail them."

"If I make a mistake, we'll all die," Connors said, his voice dry and hoarse from the heat and the dirt. "Just thought it was something I should mention."

"Don't worry about who lives or who dies," Maldini said. "Worry about yourself and what you need to do. If you can do that, then no one needs to die. At least not on this morning."

Vincenzo took a deep breath and made the sign of the cross. He watched Connors place both his hands under the base, his fingers searching with great care for any trip wire or mechanism. "It feels clean," he said. "The wire's buried right under the lid."

"What else is left to do?" Vincenzo asked.

"Nothing," Connors said, "except lift it out."

"Should we say a prayer first?" Vincenzo asked.

"A silent one," Maldini said. "But if the Lord above doesn't know by now we need his help, I doubt he ever will."

Connors gripped the base of the mine, shut his eyes and gave the mine a tug, lifting it out of the ground. He heard nothing but silence. He rested his head on the ground and took a deep breath. "*Grazia a Dio*," he heard Vincenzo whisper.

Vincenzo and Maldini helped Connors to his feet, the mine clutched against the soldier's chest, a warm breeze helping to dry the sweat on their faces. "How many of these you think are planted?" Connors asked them.

"Three, four hundred maybe," Vincenzo said. "They put them everywhere they could think of."

"So can we," Connors said.

"Dig them up and use against the Nazis?" Vincenzo asked.

"If you really want a shot at them," Connors said. "You take everything they gave you and use it against them."

The gathering of boys had stepped in closer to their circle, eager to see what had been accomplished. "Show them what you've done," Maldini encouraged. "Both of you."

Connors and Vincenzo took three steps forward and, with great care, raised the mine up, holding it aloft as if it were a soccer trophy. The group raised their arms in unison and, for the first time in many summers, the sound of cheers engulfed the city of Naples.

27

PIAZZA DEI MARTIRI, NAPLES
SEPTEMBER 27, 1943

Connors wheeled the jeep past Via dei Mille and made a sharp right turn at Via Chiaia, heading for the high end of the city, hoping to get a gauge on how far away the Nazi tanks were. He stopped in front of the Monument to the Martyrs, its base taken up by the hulking stone statues of four large lions, each blanketed by the warm rays of a late-morning sun. He glanced over at Nunzia, sitting casually in the front seat, hands folded across her lap, her beauty given an extra highlight by the evaporating mists. "I've never seen a city like this before," he said, staring with respectful wonder at the vast sixteenth-century marble archways. "Even with all the hits, all the buildings destroyed, it's still the most beautiful place I'll ever see."

"It's a stubborn city," Nunzia said, shielding her eyes and glancing over at him. "Like its people."

"Stubborn I can understand," Connors said. "People from my home town run in that same direction. They're nice folks, friendly for the most part, but you can only push them so far."

"It was much different here before the war," Nunzia said. "Every morning, I would hear my *nonna* sing her old songs while she hung out the wash, my mother singing along with her from the kitchen. Our small house was filled with the smells of fresh coffee and baked bread, and through the open windows you could hear children cry and laugh, adults shout and argue. Now all we hear is silence and all we smell is the dust from the bombs."

"You think you'll stay here after the war?" Connors asked.

"I'll go wherever my papa goes," Nunzia said, shaking her head slowly. "It's difficult to plan past the next few hours. And even then, there seems no point. You, at least, have a place to go back to, a home that you know and remember. None of us here have that. All that remains is what's left of our city."

"What do you want to do?" he asked, removing his helmet and wiping at the thin line of sweat forming across his forehead. "You know, if you could pick something to work at, what would it be?"

She shrugged her thin shoulders, a degree of shyness creeping into her otherwise determined veneer. "I love children," she said. "Love to be around them, hear them laugh, argue, shed tears when they can't get their way. Would be nice to spend my days listening to those sounds. It might help take the place of all the other sounds I've had to hear these past few years."

"You'd be good at that," Connors told her, a warm smile on his face. "I'd let you work with my kids any day of the week."

"You have children?" she asked, a surprised tone to her voice.

"I should have said, if and when I have them," Connors said with a quick shake of his head. "No, I don't have any kids or a wife or for that matter anyone close to one."

"What will you do?" she asked. "When you get back to your home?"

"I was going to be a lawyer before this started," he said. "Now, I don't really know. It's going to be hard to look at words in a law book after you've seen what a war does to those laws."

"You don't look much like a lawyer," she said, shaking her head in a teasing way. "Not the kind I've seen, anyway."

"What kind is that?"

"You have an honest face," Nunzia said, shifting her weight and looking at Connors with eyes that caused him to blush. "Most of the lawyers that prowled around Naples while Mussolini was in power did not."

"I wouldn't make much of a lawyer, anyway," Connors said with a shrug. "Honest face or not. Truth is, I don't really know what I'm going to do if I make it back home. I haven't thought past having a couple of beers and going to a baseball game."

"It sounds like a good place to start," Nunzia said.

Connors looked up and saw a boy standing across from his windshield, a small shearing knife clutched in the palm of his right hand. He had on a pair of worn black shorts, no shirt and no shoes. He was rail thin, with hazel eyes and a head full of floppy light brown hair. He trembled where he stood, his soot-stained feet digging into the parched dirt. He held the point of the knife out, his arm stretched and aimed at Connors.

"*Cose e, piccino?*" Nunzia asked him.

"*Devo pagare per quello che a fatto,*" the boy said, his teeth clenched, frail body matted in sweat.

"E cosa a fatto?" Nunzia asked, leaning one leg out of the jeep.

"Mi a mattzatto la mamma," the boy said, tears starting to fall down the sides of his face.

"What's he saying?" Connors asked Nunzia, her face now a blanket of sadness.

"His mother was killed," she said, her eyes on the boy. "He thinks you did it. He just sees a soldier in uniform. He's too young to know the difference between a Nazi and an American."

"And he wants to get even," Connors said. "So would I."

"Questo signor non a mattzatto a nessuno," Nunzia said, stepping out of the jeep and walking toward the boy. *"E venuto per ci aiutare."*

Connors jumped out of the jeep and saw the fear rise in the boy's eyes. He kept his hands at his side as he moved. He stopped when he was inches away from the dull blade of the knife, looking directly into the boy's smeared face. He raised his hand slowly and rested it on the boy's arm, giving it a gentle squeeze. With his other hand, Connors moved aside the boy's wet hair and brushed away the dirt and tears. He bent down on both knees and was eye-level with the boy, each staring at the other. Behind them, Nunzia clasped her hands across her mouth and stifled an urge to cry. Connors moved his hands away from the boy and left them back at his side, his eyes moist, locked onto the small, pained face in front of him. The boy, still trembling, his nose running and his cheeks flushed red and glowing, dropped the knife and let it fall to the dirt by his feet. Connors stayed on his knees, the air around him still and silent, allowing the moment to decide the next move. He heard Nunzia sob openly, while he held his own in check. All that mattered now was the shivering boy in front of him, who only moments earlier had been willing to kill in order to relieve the burden of his pain.

The boy took a slow, careful step forward. Then, after a slight pause, another. He was now inches away from Connors, close enough to smell the stale sweat and rumpled odor of his uniform. The boy took a quick glance at the Thunderbird patch on the sleeve of Connors's shirt and then rushed forward, his arms wrapped around the soldier's neck, his head buried in his chest. Connors reached out and held the boy close to him, letting him cry and wail, letting the suffering and longing he was much too young to endure rush to the surface.

28

16TH PANZER DIVISION HEADQUARTERS
FIFTEEN MILES OUTSIDE OF NAPLES. SEPTEMBER 27, 1943

Colonel Von Klaus walked alone, head down, shoulders sagging, along an empty stretch of burnt grass. He was a man who liked to avoid conversation or mingling with his soldiers in the hours before a mission was to begin, even one so outwardly simple as his current assignment. He sought, instead, to find solace in his own thoughts, going over a plan in detail, giving weight to the repercussions of each proposed maneuver. He still felt a slight tinge of unease over the Naples mission. He had been in far too many battles, seen too many of his men fall to enemy fire, to allow his emotions to surrender to the notion of no resistance from a virtually abandoned city.

His short meeting with young Carlo Petroni had done nothing but amplify his concerns. Perhaps it was nothing beyond the nonsensical ramblings of a boy out to make a profit. Or maybe the thief spoke the truth, that there was a mobilization going on in Naples, gearing up to take on his tanks as soon as they set foot on Neapolitan soil. He had followed the tenets of his duty and had sent word of the meeting back to high command, alerting them to the possibility of a minor counterattack taking shape. He reenforced what he knew they wanted to hear, that no force, regardless of how large or small, would prevent the successful completion of his mission.

Von Klaus never doubted his victory. He only fretted now over the manner in which he should battle a force that would clearly be small, young, poorly armed and hidden. Their only visible advantage was that they would be more familiar with the terrain than his troops. But even granting them such a minor concession could not make up for the amount of experience and skill his men brought onto a field of battle. The resistors would, in their best moments, amount to little more than an annoyance that needed to be swatted aside. Nonetheless, Von Klaus would be sending his men into a fight against children, and that was a thought that did not sit comfortably on his mind. It was the one ingredient missing from his arsenal of experience, and one he preferred not to add. His mind flashed briefly on his son, living in safety in a city that seemed destined to be bombed, and wondered how he would react if put in a similar position as the boys waiting for him down on the streets of Naples. He rubbed at the corners of his eyes, finding himself fatigued for the first time by the very thought of armed conflict. He stared out at the barren fields around him, at what had once been lush olive groves and vineyards, now left in ruin and decay. Soldiers never get to see a country at its best. They are always present when conditions are at their bleakest, people their most desperate. Every stretch of land he had seen in his military career had been charred and every foreign face belonged to that of an enemy.

Now, for the first time, those faces would be those of children.

"A telegram for you, sir." Kunnalt's voice boomed out from behind him, breaking into his moments of silence. "From command headquarters."

"Is it marked for my eyes only?" Von Klaus asked, still with his back to his young aide.

"No, sir."

"Then read it to me. Let me hear what great wisdom they have to share."

Von Klaus lit a cigarette as Kunnalt rustled open the sheaf of white paper, careful not to tear it as he did. "Well?" he asked, finally turning to face him, catching the loss of color from his face, shaken by the typed words he held in his hand. "What do they have to say for themselves?"

"It's their response to our notification of a potential conflict in

Naples from some of the children who remained behind," Kunnalt said, his voice a few octaves lower than normal.

"I can't wait," Von Klaus said, cigarette squeezed between his teeth.

"They have scrapped plans for one more night of heavy bombing prior to our arrival tomorrow," Kunnalt said. "But they will send one plane over the city."

Von Klaus walked closer toward Kunnalt, his eyes catching the tremble in his hands and his ears tuned to the cracking of his voice. "For what purpose?" he asked.

"They will be dropping 100,000 pieces of candy onto the city streets, sir," Kunnalt said slowly. "Each one wrapped and laced with poison."

Von Klaus dragged on his cigarette and lowered his eyes to the ground. He reached a hand out and took the sheet of paper from Kunnalt's trembling fingers. "Don't speak of this to any of the men," he told him in hushed tones. "I don't want my soldiers to feel shame while they fight for their country."

"Why would they give such an order, sir?"

Von Klaus rested the lit end of his cigarette against the thin sheet of paper and watched it catch fire. He held it, his eyes following the path of the flames as they burned the orders into black crisps, floating gently upwards into the air. "They do it because they are evil, Kunnalt," Von Klaus said. "And they know no other way. But don't ever lie to yourself. Not one of us, officer or soldier, is immune to that evil. In fact, we are very much a part of it. After all, we are the ones who lead its army."

"What time do you wish us to break camp, sir?" Kunnalt asked, still visibly shaken.

"An hour before dawn," Von Klaus said, turning to walk down the path of a once proud garden. "Have the lead and rear tanks fly high the Nazi flag. Raise the flag on the trucks as well. I want anyone who's left in the city to be able to see it from a distance. Might help put a dent in their courage and weaken their will to fight. The fewer dead we leave behind, the better we'll all feel."

"Is there any message you would like me to relay to the men, sir?"

Kunnalt asked, the weight of the colonel's despair measured in his own deliberate tones.

Von Klaus turned and gave him a sad smile. "Yes," he said. "Tell them not to accept any candy from strangers."

29

PARCO VIRGILIANO, NAPLES
SEPTEMBER 27, 1943

Vincenzo escorted the wooden cart through the wrought-iron gates, his hold on the mule's rein firm but gentle. Franco manned the stirrups, guiding the cart with great care over the cobblestone streets, the slab rear of the wagon filled with unearthed mines wrapped in children's clothing. The sides of the wagon were weighted down with heavy rocks, helping to give it a smoother ride.

"Is this the last of it?" Vincenzo asked, gazing up at Franco.

Franco tied the leather stirrups around the wooden stump and jumped to the ground, landing in front of Vincenzo. "I counted about thirty in all," he said. "But there must be at least several hundred more, scattered throughout the main streets."

"We've been lucky so far, but there's no reason to push it," Vincenzo said. "What we have now will have to be enough."

Franco put an arm on Vincenzo's shoulder and looked at his best friend. "I thought you were wrong for coming back here," he said. "Then this morning in the piazza, when I saw smiles on faces that hadn't smiled in years, I saw that it was the right thing to do."

Vincenzo stared into the cart, the mines laid out in a careful order. "I don't know if it's wrong or right," he said. "If a battle starts, those smiles will disappear and many of our own will die. We've all felt the bite of war, but none of us has ever fought in one. I don't know what that will be like or how many of us will have the courage to endure it."

"How much more courage do we need than what we've already shown?" Franco asked. "We live without a home, food or clean water. None of us will ever see our parents again. What's on these streets, what's left here, is all the family and home we might ever know. You were right to want to return to that."

Vincenzo looked around at the vast grounds of the park that housed the tomb of Virgil, many of the thick trees and gardens spared the wrath of the bombs. "My father used to bring my mother here for their Sunday walk," Vincenzo said. "I was just a baby, my sisters not even born. They would hold hands and laugh and talk, stopping under a tree to share a piece of fruit and watch me run across the grass. I always remember her smile, standing there, head resting on the shoulder of the man she loved. I would look back at her and laugh, making her smile even brighter. I don't know what will happen to us, Franco. But I know we won't laugh or smile that way again."

The two of them stood next to the cart, letting the warm breeze and a welcome silence engulf them. They were two teenagers forced to abandon all joy and folly to tackle the decisions of grown men cast into armed conflict. It was a challenge both grasped with tender hands.

"We'll laugh again, Vincenzo," Franco said with a slight shrug. "We have no choice. We're Neapolitans. It's in our blood."

30

STRADA VICINALE PALAZZIELLO, NAPLES
SEPTEMBER 27, 1943

Connors and Nunzia stood on the edge of a hill and looked down at the main road leading into Naples. There, spread out before them across a two-mile span, was the full force of the German 16th Panzer Division. Eighty Mark IV tanks paved the way for more than five hundred well-armed and well-trained soldiers. Behind them, sand jeeps pulled anti-aircraft artillery and two dozen mules ambled along, packed down with bombs and flame throwers. Connors turned away from the convoy and looked at Nunzia. "They're heading toward the main road," he said. "That'll lead them to the center of the city and from there to the piers."

"Will they ever just leave us alone?" she said in a low voice. "They've taken everything and still aren't satisfied. I don't think they'll ever be satisfied until we're all dead."

"We should get back," Connors said, his eyes still on her. "Help get those boys ready for a fight."

"Do you hate them?" she asked, staring down at the convoy.

"Who?"

"The Nazis," Nunzia said.

"Most of the time," Connors said. "A lot of those soldiers are no different from me or the guys in my unit. Same age, pretty much. Same background. Drafted into the army, taken to some country and told to fight and kill the guy on the other side of the field. At least you start out thinking that way. Then one night you're sitting in camp, having coffee and a smoke with some G.I. from the same part of the country as you, sharing a laugh and some memories. Then a bullet goes in his head and he ends up flat on the ground right in front of you. See that happen often enough, you don't think the guy on the other side is like you at all. And all you want to do is kill him."

"Have you killed many?" she asked.

"Yes," Connors said. "But no matter how many of them you kill, it doesn't erase the image of a guy in the same uniform as you, bleeding in your arms, just lying there, waiting to die. It's different from losing family, but it stays with you just as long and just as hard. It turns you into another kind of person. Or maybe just the kind of person you were all along."

"You're a good man, Connors," Nunzia said, her warm eyes staring at him from under the shade of the tree. "Put in the middle of a horrible war."

"I'm a good soldier," Connors said. "That's different from being a good man."

31

CASTEL DELL'OVO, NAPLES
SEPTEMBER 27, 1943

Connors stood in the center of a candlelit room and stared down at a crudely drawn map of Naples. The paper was torn and soiled, the etchings colored in pencil and charcoal. "You guys run out of crayons when you drew this up?" he asked, trying to read the street indicators.

"It has everything we need," Vincenzo said.

"And I need to see and hear everything you know," Connors said, looking up at the boy. "The sooner the better. We don't have much time."

"The Nazis know our streets and roads almost as well as we do," Maldini said. "They've spent enough time here."

"But they don't know how many of us are here," Connors said. "And we need to make that work in our favor. And we need to do something else."

"What?" Vincenzo asked.

"We strip those tanks of fuel," Connors said, walking around the small table, his eyes on everyone in the crowded room. "We strip them of power. We have to blow up that tanker."

Vincenzo and Franco exchanged a furtive glance. "How many explosives will that take?" Franco asked.

"It's not a question of how many," Connors said. "It's how close we can get the explosion to the tanker. The gas will take care of the rest."

"When?" Vincenzo asked.

"Tomorrow night," Connors said. "It has to be hit before the tanks can get to it."

"And what do we do until the tanker arrives?" Angela asked.

"Get ready for war," Connors said.

They worked through the night.

On the side streets that led into the main piazzas in the center of the city, a small squadron of boys raised barricades made from stone and rock and rested empty rifles on top of them. Maldini led the youngest of the boys through the sewers of Naples, giving each a marked post in the underground passage from which they could view the street above and be able to place objects under the wheels of passing tanks without fear of detection. Connors, Nunzia and Franco worked on the small arsenal of unexploded bombs that had been collected, separating the explosives from the shafts and positioning them at posts throughout the city, to be tossed at the enemy. Several dozen boys were placed on various rooftops and church steeples, given the best rifles and the most ammo, free to take aim at the German soldiers who would eventually pass below. Angela and little Tino found all the kerosene that had been stored in anticipation of winter's arrival and placed the liquid into empty wine bottles, corking them with torn shreds of clothing. They left the bottles in church and building entryways, large lit votive candles beside them. Minor roadblocks were set up using old carts and discarded furniture. The strongest of the boys were sent out to lug large pots filled with seawater up to the highest buildings and rest them on top of thick piles of old wood. When the Germans arrived, the wood fires would bring the water to a boil and the water would be tossed down on the passing soldiers. "How'd you come up with that idea?" Connors asked Vincenzo.

"*The Hunchback of Notre Dame*," Vincenzo said. "Only he had oil and much bigger pots."

"His fires didn't burn the building down, either," Connors said. They walked together along the darkened city streets, their eyes focused on all the activity around them. "You like the movie better or the book?"

"I like them both," Vincenzo said.

"You get to go to many movies?" Connors asked.

"Before the war, I would go every week," Vincenzo said. "To the *pi-docchietto*."

"What's that?"

"You see the movie outside," Vincenzo said.

"I get it," Connors said. "Like a drive-in."

"Yes," Vincenzo said. "Except in Naples, no cars. Only feet."

"Do you get yourself popcorn and a Coke when you watch a movie over here?" Connors asked. "Like we do."

"I love Coca-Cola," Vincenzo said with a sweet smile. "But I don't know about popcorn. Is it a candy?"

"No, not really," Connors said, walking past a row of bombed-out buildings. "It's hard to explain. It's just something you eat when you watch a movie. Some people even think it makes the movie better."

Vincenzo nodded, and glanced over at two boys placing makeshift bombs down an open sewer. "Do you think any of this will work?" he asked.

"Probably not," Connors said. "Do you?"

"They need to think we're everywhere," Vincenzo said. "For every one of us they see, they must believe hundreds are hidden. They need to think they're up against thousands, not handfuls. It's our only chance."

They walked in silence for several moments, each lost in his own thoughts. They turned when they saw the pudgy boy from the soccer game approach from behind. He was short and squat and had thick brown hair that he gelled down and parted in the center. His face was a youthful mask of innocence, highlighted by a smile and a pair of watery brown eyes. "Is it all true?" he asked, nodding at Connors and patting the top of Vincenzo's arm. "We are getting ready to fight Nazis?"

Vincenzo hesitated and then shook his head. "Yes, Angelo," he said. "It's true."

"I want to help," Angelo said, close to pleading. "I'll do anything. Just tell me what you need."

"For the moment, nothing," Vincenzo said, avoiding Connors's concerned gaze. "But I'll get word to you soon as I have something for you."

"What do I do until then?" Angelo asked.

"Find a good place to hide," Vincenzo said. "A place where no one can see you. Not the Germans and not even any of the other boys."

"What should I wear?" he asked. "In case you need me to fight."

"If that time comes," Vincenzo said, "you dress for battle. But until then, you do nothing except hide."

Angelo smiled, took two steps back and gave them each a salute. "Don't worry, Vincenzo," he said, turning and heading back down the darkened street. "I'll be the best-dressed soldier in your army."

Connors waited until the boy was out of earshot and then looked over at Vincenzo. "I don't want to put a dent in your plans," he said. "But if that's the best you got, you might as well pack your shoes and some cheese and move up to the hills."

"Angelo is different from the others," Vincenzo said. "He means well, but he's slow. His brain is not right. Two years ago, the Fascists beat his parents to death and held him there to watch. Since that day, he has not been the same boy."

"I'm sorry," Connors said, his eyes shifting to the ground. "Should have figured something wasn't right from the way he talked. Will he be okay by himself?"

"He means well and he has a good heart," Vincenzo explained. "That's something neither the Fascists nor the Nazis could take away. And he usually does what he's told. So, if he hides, he should be safe, no matter how the battle turns out."

"Are there any more boys out there like him?" Connors said. "You know, that need looking after?"

"We are all like him, American," Vincenzo said.

32

Connors and Nunzia walked down the large stairwell, the two ground-floor halls spread out in front of them. The building complex had been one of the first monuments to be erected under Mussolini's rule, an early symbol of his vision for a modern Italy. The designers broke ground in 1929 and the work was completed six years later, and despite the heavy aerial bombings, it had remained relatively intact.

"The main telegraph offices are off to the left," Nunzia said, pointing just past a large marble column. "I doubt you'll find any of the machines still in working order. The Germans made a point of cutting off all the lines of communication."

"It's probably true," Connors said. "But we might as well double check. They'll be looking to set up a command center. The harder we make it for them to get word out, the better."

Nunzia held the banister and stopped, looking at Connors on the other end of the marble stairwell. "Thank you for letting them do this," she said. "I know it was not your first choice."

"I've never been thanked for letting boys head off to die," Connors said. "I don't know if what I'm doing is right or not. Don't even know why I'm doing it. It's not the smart move and for sure it's not a soldier's move."

"Then maybe you're more than just a soldier," Nunzia said. "Soldiers follow rules and orders and listen only to what makes the most sense. They choose to ignore what's in their hearts."

"And if I end up seeing a long line of dead kids after tomorrow, I'm going to wish I'd done the same," Connors said.

"They might surprise you. They're a tougher bunch than they look to be. They've seen horrors most children are spared from. Maybe it's not even fair to call them children."

"What about you?" Connors asked. "Are you tougher than you look?"

"It depends on who is looking," Nunzia answered.

Connors stared back at her and nodded. "What happened to all the men in the city?" he asked. "I mean, I can understand it's easier for kids and old people to hide and not have the Germans notice, but why didn't some of the men stay behind to help?"

"They had wives and daughters to worry about," Nunzia said. "A son takes the place of a father."

"Which side does your father fall on?"

"My father is a dreamer," Nunzia said. "Most Italian men are, especially southern ones. And he had no son to leave behind. So it was left to me."

Connors stood and wiped the back of his pants and shook his head. "This could all turn out to be a suicide mission," he said. "I've looked at it from a hundred different angles and they all point that way."

Nunzia walked across the steps and stood facing Connors, her hand on his arm, their eyes on each other. "It's more than that," she said. "You saw them out there, saw for yourself how they went about their tasks, acting more like men than boys. Their faces were bright and alive, as happy as I've ever seen them. Whatever else happens, it will be worth it just to let them have a day like today."

Connors leaned in closer to Nunzia, their faces separated by breath. After several long seconds, he closed his eyes and turned to pick up his gear. "We better finish what we came here to do," he said. "Let's go check on those telegraph machines, see if we can find at least one that's of any use."

"And if we find one," Nunzia said. "What then? Make contact with your soldiers in Salerno?"

Connors started down the marble hall toward the telegraph office. "I'd love to try that," he said over his shoulder, his voice a loud echo across the thick empty walls. "But it'd be too risky. The Nazis might pick it up as easy as my division. But at some point in this, we're going to need to get word out to somebody. All I have to do is figure out how."

"Won't that still be a risk?" she asked, walking toward him, thin leather shoes silent on the hard tile floors.

"Starting tomorrow, Nunzia, taking risks is all that's left for us to do,"

Connors said. He turned and disappeared around a marble column, in
search of a working telegraph machine.

33

45TH THUNDERBIRD INFANTRY DIVISION HEADQUARTERS
SALERNO, ITALY. SEPTEMBER 27, 1943

Captain Anders sucked on a hard cherry candy as he studied the coordinates on the map. He looked across the wooden table at a young officer
standing on the other side and nodded. "The Germans are here," he
said, jabbing a finger on a stencil drawing of the Naples outskirts.
"Should be in the city no later than sunup." He moved his finger to the
north. "Two of my boys were found dead right about here," he said,
"along with a couple of German soldiers. No jeep and no equipment left
behind. So, what's missing from my little puzzle?"

"Corporal Connors," the officer said. "We haven't heard one word
from him since he left on his mission."

"That's right, Carlson," Anders said. "We haven't heard a damn
thing. And how do you read all of that?"

"My hunch is he's either dead or captured, sir," Carlson said with
some assurance. "If not, we would have heard otherwise by now."

Anders shifted away from the map and glared up at Carlson. He was a
sergeant, newly assigned to his division, transferred over to the Thunderbirds to help the unit cope with the massive losses sustained in the beach
landing. He was in his mid-twenties and slight of build, with a thinning
hairline and a warm face, his soft Boston accent in sharp contrast to the
captain's harsher tones. "If we were talking about most soldiers, I would
agree with you," Anders said. "But not Connors. I've seen him in action.
He's not one to let himself be captured and he sure as hell acts like he's
tough to kill. So I'm betting you're wrong on all counts."

"Then where is he, sir?" Carlson asked.

Anders spit out his candy, watching it land on the brown grass by his feet. "He's in that city," the captain said, running the back of his hand against his sticky lips. "And if something's going on there, I'm betting he's right in the middle of it."

"If that's the case, sir, then whoever he's with should have access to a radio of some kind," Carlson said. "Why wouldn't he have made contact?"

"Hell, there isn't anybody left this side of Rome that doesn't know the Germans are right on the city limits," Anders said. "Anything he'd send our way would just as quick be picked up by them."

"If he's really still alive, we could try and send another team to get him out," Carlson said. "It would be dangerous, but worth the effort."

"Not just yet." Anders stepped away from the map and folded his arms across his chest. "Let's give him a little time. Give him a chance to do some damage and get out on his own."

"What sort of damage, sir?" Carlson asked. "As you said, Connors is alone. And all the indications say that if there's going to be any resistance at all to the Panzers, it'll be minimal at best."

"Exactly," Anders said. "The Nazis are going in expecting a little head butt here and there, nothing too serious. Now, if Connors is in there and he's hooked up with anyone looking to cause some trouble, that could change the game. Not enough to beat them back, but enough to hold them a few extra hours more than they planned."

"How soon before we move the Thunderbirds into Naples, sir?" Carlson asked.

Anders snorted out a laugh. "The army is nothing more than a series of jobs," he said, reaching into his shirt pocket for another piece of hard candy. "Mine is to keep the troops rested and battle ready. It's somebody else's to tell me when to move them out. Soon as I know that, so will you."

"I'm not complaining, sir. The men can use the break. The squad's pretty shot up and beat up. Even so, for some of them, waiting to fight is sometimes harder than the fight itself."

"Maybe," Anders said with a shrug. "But it sure as shit won't get them killed, will it? And after all the action this bunch has been through, dying of boredom should be the goal for every one of those grunts."

34

CASTEL SANT'ELMO, NAPLES
SEPTEMBER 27, 1943

Connors stood facing the sea, the silent peaks of Mount Vesuvius off to his right, his foot resting on an embankment made of tufa stone. The castle had been built in 1329, its large enclosed walls designed to ward off any attack on the city. Through the centuries it had been a home to those who wanted to escape enemy detection and then, eventually, it was turned into an elaborate prison. Connors thought it a good place to station a few boys so they could follow the tank movements and positions. Below him, the entire city was spread out, from wide piazzas to narrow alleys, and from such a high vantage point, nothing could move undetected. He turned around when he heard Vincenzo step up beside him and sit on the edge of the embankment. "When the sun is up and the skies are clear," Vincenzo told him, "it's easy to see all the islands that surround Naples. Sometimes you can even see as far as Sardenia. But now with all the smoke and fire, you're lucky if you can see the city."

"Seeing it's the easy part," Connors said, turning his back to the view and leaning against a stone wall.

"What's the hard?"

"How do we get the boys up here to tell us what they see down there? They can't scream it out and we don't have any signal system set up."

"I know a way," Vincenzo said. He shifted his focus to the Thunderbird patch on Connors's sleeve. "I just don't know how well it will work."

"I think now would be a real good time to tell me," Connors said, catching the boy's stare.

"We can use *picciones*," Vincenzo said. "How do you say it in English? They are birds that fly from one place to another and bring you messages."

"Pigeons," Connors said. "You have carrier pigeons?"

"I don't," Vincenzo said. "But Franco does. Not as many as he had before the war, but enough to get word from the boys up here to us down there."

"Have you used them before?"

"He used to race them." Vincenzo pointed toward the darkening sky. "Run them in circles above our homes. Once or twice he would send a bird out with a note from his mamma to a sick old aunt who lived on the other side of the city. She always got the message."

"We put four boys up here, keep them low and in each corner, they get a full view of the battle," Connors said, walking toward the center of the castle roof. "They'll see the tanks before we do. We just have to hope the Germans are too busy with us to take notice of any pigeons."

"I'll pick the boys and give them what they need," Vincenzo said. "Franco will know if we have any in our group who have handled pigeons before. If we do, I'll make sure they're up here."

"You still want to go ahead with all this?" Connors asked. "There's still time to get everybody out."

"We are where we belong," Vincenzo said. "All of us. This is a time for Italians to fight."

Connors stepped closer to Vincenzo and stared down at the boy. "It's *everybody's* fight," he said. "I left behind too many dead Americans on your dirt and beaches to think of it in any other way."

"Is that how you got that patch?" Vincenzo asked. "Fighting here in Italy?"

Connors ran his fingers across the four square points of the Thunderbird. "This is the symbol of my division," he said. "It's a magic bird that American Indians believe in, brings rain, thunder and lightning down on any enemy."

"Do you believe that, too?"

"Only when I have a division behind me," Connors said. "Each of the squares in the patch represents one of the states that make up most of the ranks. New Mexico, Colorado, Arizona and Oklahoma."

"Is that where you're from?" Vincenzo asked, looking closer at the patch.

"No, I got drafted and was put into the division," Connors said. "But a lot of the guys in the troop are from those parts of my country. Quite a few Indian tribes in it as well. There's been a lot of different blood spilled on your land, not just yours."

"It's a patch of honor, then," Vincenzo said, running his fingers along the seams of the design. "You're lucky to have it."

In the distance, the low moaning roar of a plane engine could be heard. Connors looked up but could see nothing beyond a cluster of evening clouds. "That's not a sound you ever get used to hearing," he said.

Vincenzo shook his head. "No," he said. "But you don't fear it as much as you do the first time. You never welcome it, but you always expect it to come."

"I guess we should head for the tunnels." Connors shoved his pith helmet on his head. "Make sure everybody else gets there, too."

Vincenzo walked over to an embankment and pointed down toward the streets, at a small huddle of boys scrambling for cover. "We've done this for a long time," Vincenzo said. "Everyone has their special place to spend the night."

"Where's yours?"

"Most nights, the tunnels," Vincenzo said. "It's an old habit. I always used to beg my father to take me to the train station when I was a child. I loved to see them come in and go out on the different tracks, smoke running out of the stacks, whistles blowing, each filled with people going to or coming from places I'd never seen."

"What about tonight?" Connors asked.

"I think I'll stay here tonight," Vincenzo said.

"Why?"

"It's the last night," Vincenzo said. "I won't ever have the chance again. I want to see with my own eyes what they do to my city."

"You want to do it alone?" Connors asked. "Or would you mind some company?"

Vincenzo looked at Connors and smiled. "It's a big castle," he said. "There's enough room for two."

The two of them walked toward a distant embankment and sat down, shielded by its thick stone walls, and waited for the nightly destruction to begin.

The tiny cellophane packets landed on the ground like hard rain pellets. A Nazi plane flew low over the city, opened its bomb slots and scattered thousands of chocolate caramels on the abandoned streets below. Vincenzo stared up at the moonlit sky, candy falling around him as if in the middle of a winter storm, his arms spread out, speechless at the eerie sight. Connors sat on an embankment, his rifle in both hands, looking down at the assorted candy that now lay littered across the full spread of the museum roof. He didn't move, his eyes frozen on the pieces resting by his boots, his mind awake to a horror he was too frightened to even imagine. "How soon can you get word out to the streets?" he asked Vincenzo.

"They don't need to hear it from me, American," Vincenzo said, turning to look at Connors. "They can see for themselves."

"They can see the candy," Connors said. "But they won't know not to eat it."

"You think they would poison it?" Vincenzo's happiness quickly dissipated into terror.

"You know them better than I do," Connors said.

Vincenzo looked down at the candy spread around his feet, pieces bouncing off the sides of his legs and back. "Are you sure about this?" he asked.

Connors bent down, picked up a caramel and held it out to Vincenzo. "You want to prove me wrong?" he asked.

Vincenzo ran for the door that led down the stairs and out of the castle. "I'll need help," he yelled over his shoulder. "We'll warn the ones hiding in the tunnels first."

"I'll drive," Connors said, running past Vincenzo and down a narrow flight of steps. "You just say where."

"It should take a half hour to spread the word," Vincenzo said. "Maybe less since they're not dropping any bombs."

"What they're dropping is a lot worse than any bomb," Connors said, taking the steps two at a clip. "Remember that now and remember it tomorrow when it really starts to get hot." He stopped as they both entered the large ornate castle hall and grabbed Vincenzo by the shirt. "In fact, if you're half as smart as you act, you'll never forget what you saw tonight. It might help keep you alive."

Vincenzo slowly nodded his head, lines of sweat running down his forehead, his upper body shivering, leg muscles tight and weak. He stood in place, watching as Connors ran past him, heading for the jeep he had left parked in an alley alongside the castle. For the first time in his life, Vincenzo Scolardi had glimpsed the true face of his enemy and was left with a taste of his own fear.

35

PIAZZA BOVIO, NAPLES
SEPTEMBER 27, 1943

Connors and Vincenzo stood in the center of the square, their backs to the Fontana del Nettuno, looking at the small army of children, their hands crammed with the candy that was falling, as if by magic, from the sky above. Across from the gathering were the remains of the Palazzo della Borsa, the heart of the Neapolitan stock exchange. Both Connors and Vincenzo had raced like a crazed pair through the empty city streets, warning all those in hiding not to eat the candy. Instead, they were asked to grab all that they could and bring them to the Piazza Bovio, where the pile was now high enough to fill Neptune's basin.

Many of the children pleaded for just one piece, their empty stomachs immune to the harsh words of warning that were being shouted at them. "How do you know for sure?" one innocent voice pleaded with Vincenzo. "You only think they're poison. You don't really know."

"They want it to look like kindness," Vincenzo explained, still shaken by the night's events. "They know we're hungry and scared. They want us to think they're our friends. But look around. Look at what's happened to our lives, our homes and our families. Those are not the acts of a friend. Only an enemy would do such things."

"Maybe only a few of them are poison," another boy shouted out. "Some of the candies might be good to eat."

"And how will you choose the safe one?" Vincenzo asked.

"So what do we do with all the candy?" a voice from the back of the crowd shouted.

"We leave it here, in the center of the piazza," Vincenzo said, pointing to the fountain at his back. "To remind us of our enemy."

A tall, lean boy in an ill-fitting cotton shirt and torn pants stepped forward, his hands in his pockets, eyes on Vincenzo. "You're wrong," he said in a loud voice that carried through the huge square. "You and the American are afraid of the Nazis, it clouds the way you think. I say the candy is good and is safe to eat. Letting it sit here and go to waste while we walk around with empty stomachs is foolish."

The boy moved toward the mound of candy lying inside the dry fountain dedicated to the glory of Neptune. Connors brought his rifle to his side and held it out toward the boy. "What will you do, American?" he asked. "Shoot me? For wanting some candy? If you do that, then you have us wonder who is the real enemy. The one who drops candy from the skies or the one who kills to stop us from eating it?"

"This is not a good time to turn stupid," Connors said. "Think it through, slow and clear. If you do that and come away still able to tell yourself candy is worth dying for, then don't look for me to stop you. I'm not making it my decision anymore. That call belongs to you now."

Connors lowered his rifle and moved away from the pile. "You can't let them eat the candy," Vincenzo whispered to him.

"I can't shoot them, either," Connors said. "And I don't know any other way to stop it."

The boy stepped forward, past Connors, his eyes fixed only on the sweets spread around him. He bent down, reached into the fountain and picked up a thick piece of caramel. He brought the candy up toward his face, smiled and began to peel off the thin wrapping.

"Don't eat that one!"

Connors and Vincenzo both looked toward the crowd when they heard Maldini's voice. "Have what's left of Roberto's candy. He can't finish what he took."

The boy dropped his caramel and, along with Vincenzo and Connors, turned to watch the crowd part and Maldini walk past. He was carrying the body of a dark-haired, shirtless boy, his head resting against the older man's chest, his loose hand still gripping the candy wrapper. Maldini's face was red from the horror he had seen and the anger he could no longer control.

Maldini stopped in front of the boy, stared deep into his eyes and lowered his head toward the body of the child he held. "Forget the candy," he said in a softer voice. "And come help me bury our friend."

Maldini turned and walked down the darkened streets of Naples, the gathered boys following close behind him, their heads bowed, their voices silenced.

36

SAN DOMENICO MAGGIORE, NAPLES
SEPTEMBER 27, 1943

It was the church where Saint Thomas Aquinas once sat and prayed. On its walls, spread through five ornate chapels, hung some of the richest and most beloved artwork in all of Italy, including Teodoro d'Errico's masterful *Resurrection* and Roberto d'Odorisio's *Maddonna dell'Umilta*. It is a church that houses the body of the first Catholic bishop of New York, who died in Naples within days of his consecration. On a far wall of one of the chapels hangs a reproduction of the *Crucifixion*, the drawing of Christ long-rumored to have spoken to a penitent Saint Thomas. But on this night, it was a church whose floor was filled with boys, their heads bowed in prayer, their hopes for a future clinging to the isolated wishes and the desperate dreams that theirs was a destiny that could bring defeat to an army fueled by hate.

Large votive candles were lit in every corner of the church, bringing forth a warm glow to all the shadows that knelt before the main altar. Through cracks in a ceiling built to withstand the age of centuries but not the force of bombs, a steady rain of poisoned candy fell on the marble floor, their insistent patter ignored by all of those in the church. Maldini knelt in the front row, the body of the dead boy at rest on the top step of the main altar. Nunzia was next to him, one hand thrust under his shaking arm. Next to the body, a thin boy with an oval face sang the words to the "Ave Maria," his voice filled with a passion he would normally have been too young to possess. Connors and Vincenzo knelt on the other side with little Fabrizio gripping the soldier's arm, his eyes frozen on the body of a boy his own age. Next to him, the bullmastiff spread out, his massive girth squeezing them all into a tight row.

They stayed there for as long as they could, finding comfort inside the walls of what had always been a haven, even for those least likely to seek forgiveness.

They knelt, prayed and sang until the sun rose and brought a fresh day to a battle-weary city.

BOOK TWO

Courage is to feel
The daily daggers of relentless steel
And keep on living.

—Douglas Malloch

THE FIRST DAY

1

VIA TOLEDO, NAPLES
SEPTEMBER 28, 1943

The first blast from the tank shattered the weathered walls of a building that had stood since the sixteenth century. The second sent shards of brick, glass and mortar spilling into the clear morning air. Two German soldiers tossed grenades through the cracked windows of an empty storefront, causing the already weakened structure to collapse. A young, lanky junior officer lifted the top lid of his tank, gave a furtive glance down the empty street, and waved on three other tanks that were idling behind the smoldering turrets of his Mark IV.

The tanks motored past and stationed themselves on the right-hand side of the wide boulevard, each surrounded by six armed soldiers, two brandishing flame throwers. The sunny silence was shaken as they fired one destructive shell after another into the facades of the wobbly buildings that remained. The two soldiers armed with flame throwers moved inside the smoldering homes and offices, thick pockets of dust clouds wrapping them in their mist, and torched what little was left. "Leave them with nothing," the young officer shouted to his men above the din, his tank slowly moving past them. "Only when you can see clear through to the next street will you be free to move forward."

The second hand on a clock in the middle of a medieval tower that rose above the area, just two streets north of Via Toledo, slowly inched forward, its bells ringing out the start of a new hour. It was eight o'clock on a warm Tuesday morning and the final destruction of Naples had begun.

Connors and Vincenzo were huddled inside an apartment doorway, a long thin hanging curtain separating them from the edge of the smoky street. Connors parted the curtain with the end of his rifle and stared out at the tanks, firing shell after shell into the gaping holes of the buildings that lined Via Toledo. "Looks like they're splitting the division four tanks to a street," he said.

"How many soldiers?" Vincenzo asked. He was on his knees, an old hunting rifle by his side, holding two wine bottles filled with kerosene and topped with torn rags.

"Thirty-five, maybe forty," Connors said, sliding his head out for a better look. "That's counting the ones inside the tanks."

"Will we have the time we need?" Vincenzo asked, resting the bottles next to the rifle and looking up at Connors.

"It depends on Maldini and Franco," Connors said. "If they get there at the right time and are where they should be, we have a good chance. But right now there's not a sign of them."

"Don't worry," Vincenzo said. "They'll be there. They have no other plans for this morning."

The tanks were now targeting a string of row houses several hundred yards down the wide avenue, flames rising toward the sky, thick plumes of smoke offering a soft blanket of cover. Connors stepped away from the curtain, leaned down and grabbed one of the wine bottles. "You wait here," he said to Vincenzo. "I'm going to try and get closer. Keep your head down and don't make a move until you hear the signal."

"With all these explosions going off I might not be able to hear anything," Vincenzo said. "What then?"

"Look to me," Connors said. "I'll tell you when to move."

Vincenzo nodded as he watched Connors push aside the curtain and head into the dirt, soot and danger of Via Toledo, running with his head down and his body in a crouched position, rifle at the ready. Vincenzo sat with his back against a chipped stone wall, barely hidden by the edges of the curtain. He rested the rifle on his legs and stared out at the carnage being waged on the street. He looked across at the nearby buildings where there was still no sign of either Maldini or Franco, then back down the avenue, peering into the thick smoke, Connors now a shadow amid the debris. He closed his eyes and laid his head against the moist wall.

It was then that he heard the footsteps.

They were thick-soled and heavy, coming down at him from the cobblestones to his rear. Vincenzo stiffened and gripped the rifle with both hands, one finger gently poised on the curve of the trigger. He slid deeper into the doorway, making sure the curtain hid his entire body. He stayed back and watched the blur of the footsteps pass, a breeze slightly unfurling the curtain. He waited until they had moved farther past him and then quietly brushed aside a corner of the hanging drapery. Through the smoke and haze he glanced at the person who seconds earlier had been close enough for him to touch. He rose up to his knees, let the rifle fall to the ground and felt a slow panic set in.

The footsteps belonged to young Angelo.

The boy was dressed in an all-white communion suit and he lit up the dark street like a low-watt bulb. He had his hands folded behind him and a wide smile on his face, his mind unfazed by the sounds and dangers of the loud explosions and the collapsed buildings. He was an open target stepping onto a field of battle and there was little that could be done to stop his advance.

Vincenzo watched the boy walk into the thickness of the brown maze, Nazi tanks positioned to his left, soldiers spread out across the avenue, their focus on the homes and storefronts. He looked for Connors hidden away in a remote hallway and searched the smoky skies for signs of Franco and Maldini. Vincenzo braced himself against a side of the wall, his breath rushed. He wanted to stop Angelo, but didn't know how without risking detection. He should have told the boy to hide and not given him any false hopes of being able to help in their fight. Instead, he had wrongly given Angelo the impression that he was of value to their cause. As a result, a boy who should have been far removed from any danger zones had now stepped into the center of a killing field.

Vincenzo ran along the side of a building, crouched down, his eyes tearing and his throat raw from the influx of smoke. He needed to get to Angelo before the Nazis caught sight of him. He would use the burning mist as an ally, making him invisible to the armed soldiers standing only a short distance away. He reached the far corner of the building, eyes searching through the haze for the slow-thinking boy. There was an eerie silence on the street now, the tank fire quieted, the flame throwers at ease, the sun fighting to break through the thick envelope of smoke that engulfed them all. Vincenzo saw Angelo standing alone in the center of the street, his arms by his side, German soldiers with their backs to him, only a heave of a stone away. Vincenzo ran from the building, moving to his left and stopping against the side of an abandoned cart. He picked up a small rock and threw it toward Angelo, hoping to get the boy's attention. The rock landed just in front of Angelo and caused the boy to turn around, his eyes squinting into the smoke, a wide smile, as always, lighting up his face.

Vincenzo stepped in front of the cart, waved his arms in the air and saw Angelo nod his head in his direction. Vincenzo put a finger to his lips, begging the boy to stay silent, praying that he would simply walk over toward him and safety. "Vincenzo, *sei tu*?" Angelo asked, breaking the silence, his voice an echo off the cracked walls of the nearly ruined street.

The German soldiers turned as one as soon as the words were spoken. They raised their guns and pointed them at the back of the white suit, a perfect target on a sun-drenched morning. "*Alt*," one of them said, his word a dare as much as it was a command. Angelo turned from Vincenzo and looked across the way at the soldier. For the first time, he seemed to notice the Nazi uniform and his smile quickly faded. His battered mind flashed on the fallen bodies of his dying parents, beaten by the butt ends of hard rifles, and he rushed with arms spread out toward the soldier.

The soldier raised his rifle to eye level, took a quick measure of his target, and fired two rounds into the center of Angelo's chest, thick patches of red quickly coating the front of the white suit. Angelo clutched at the wound and fell to his knees, turning his head back toward his best friend.

His bloody hand waved in Vincenzo's direction before the German fired a third time.

The bullet hit Angelo in the neck and sent him sprawling, dead, to the ground.

Vincenzo stared at Angelo's body, trembling, as the return fire came from out of a collapsed building to his right, four bullets taking down two German soldiers, including the one who had killed the boy. From the rooftop above, he heard the church bell ringing, the signal that Maldini, Franco and the rest were in place. The Germans aimed their guns toward the houses and the rooftops and began to fire. Their tanks inched away from the buildings, switched gears and headed down the center of the street, firing shells as they went. One hard blast landed two stories above Vincenzo's head, bricks and concrete crashing down around him. But he didn't move, his body frozen, his eyes looking down at the body of a boy he had promised to protect.

Maldini ran out of a building behind where Vincenzo stood, a wine bottle with a lit fuse in his hand. He tossed the bottle at an approaching trio of soldiers and then made a jump for Vincenzo, grabbing him around the waist and dragging him back into the alleys leading out of Via Toledo. They turned a corner and hid against a cracked stone wall.

Above them, from the remaining rooftops, two dozen street boys stood and let loose a heavy rainstorm of kerosene cocktails and cylinder tops of the unexploded bombs that had been collected, watching them crash and explode on the tanks and soldiers below. Connors came up from the rear and fired two rounds at a German soldier carrying a flame thrower. The soldier landed facedown on the ruined soil of Via Toledo, then Connors unhooked his belt and pack, slung his own rifle over his shoulder, and picked up the flame thrower. He raced toward the tank taking up the rear of the German attack and jumped on its side. He steadied himself, took a quick scan of the action around him, soldiers falling, bottles exploding, cylinders landing with explosive thuds against the base of the tanks and snapped open the lid. He hung the circular head of the flame thrower in the mouth of the tank and set loose its power, torching those inside. Smoke and screams rose out into the sky.

Connors jumped back to the ground and leaned against the seared tank, assessing the damage. He looked up toward the rooftops and spotted Nunzia, circled his hand above his head, the signal for all those above to make their quick retreat. He saw her return the sign and turned his attention back to the street action. A handful of German soldiers were down and two more of the tanks were disabled. A dozen of the soldiers, some wounded, walked slowly along the street, searching for targets that were no longer there. Connors caught a long glimpse of Angelo's body, lowered his head and quietly backed out of the street, picking up as many weapons as he could hold, heading away from the tanks and the soldiers.

His first battle of the morning was at an end.

Maldini grabbed Vincenzo's shoulder and dragged him away from the wall, the German soldiers fast on their heels. "We can't stay here," he told him. "We'll head for one of the rooftops and then make our way to Lungomare. It's the safest way out."

"I didn't want him to die," Vincenzo said, struggling to get to his feet.

"No one wanted him to die," Maldini said. "It's not your fault and it wasn't his. It's a war and the people no one wants to see dead usually die. You, more than anyone, should know that."

They slipped into a darkened hallway as three soldiers ran past, each firing random shots at unseen targets. Maldini pointed to a stairwell on the right and they began the climb up its narrow steps, the older man leading the boy. "Grab one of those bottles," Maldini said, pointing down at a kerosene cocktail resting by a door jam. "Take that candle, too, and use them both when you have to."

When they got to the second-floor landing, they heard the soldiers enter the foyer below. "You go ahead," Vincenzo said. "I'll meet you at Lungomare."

Maldini walked down the two steps that separated them and tightened his grip on Vincenzo's arm. "Are you sure?" he asked. "I'm leaving behind one dead boy. I don't want there to be two."

"I'm sure." Vincenzo stared into Maldini's eyes.

Maldini took a deep breath and nodded. "Wait for them to come up the stairs. Light the fuse, hold it above your shoulder and let it go. And then run up these stairs as fast as you've ever run in your life."

Maldini loosened his grip on Vincenzo's shoulder and disappeared around a bend of steps. Vincenzo watched him leave, hearing the heavy pounding of the German soldiers in the stairwell below. He pulled the cloth out of the wine bottle, draped its rolled up end over the lit edges of the heavy candle. He tossed aside the candle, shoved the cloth back in the neck of the bottle and moved away from the wall, standing a flight above the three armed soldiers. He stared at them for several seconds, watching as they halted their run and positioned their rifles. He held the bottle up, the flame getting closer to the lip, two bullets landing against the wall just above his head.

"*Viva Napoli!*" he shouted.

The explosion shattered parts of a wall and demolished the handrail. Two of the soldiers lay dead, the third, wounded, moaned in pain. Vincenzo ran down the creaky steps, avoiding the large, broken-off shards of wood. He took the rifles and the ammo belts from the dead soldiers and looked down at the third one. Bleeding from the stomach and neck, the soldier struggled to move a bloody hand toward his gun. Vincenzo bent down and ripped the gun out of its holster. He unclipped his ammo belt and reached for his rifle. The German put out a hand and gripped Vincenzo's arm, holding it tight, bringing it down closer to his open wound.

The soldier was trembling, drenched in sweat and blood. He was young, just a few years older than the street boy. Vincenzo tossed the ammo belts and rifles on the steps behind him, sat down and lifted the soldier's head, resting it on his knee. He removed his helmet and threw it down the stairs. The two stared into each other's eyes without speaking. Vincenzo's hand was pressed on the large hole in his stomach, blood gushing through his fingers. The soldier placed his right hand on top of the boy's, both of them holding down tight, looking to relieve some of the pain. The soldier lifted his head slightly and gently rubbed Vincenzo's cheek with his free hand.

"*Grazia*," he whispered, seconds before he drew his last breath.

2

16TH PANZER DIVISION HEADQUARTERS
IL PALAZZO REALE

Von Klaus watched Kunnalt rush to his side, stop and salute, always aware and appreciative of the young officer's eagerness to please. The troubled look on the man's face was enough to tell him that the news to be delivered wasn't good. "Problems already?" he asked, waiting as his aide took a deep breath.

"We've encountered a minor disturbance on Via Toledo," Kunnalt said. "And we took some casualties."

"I never consider casualties to be minor disturbances," Von Klaus said with a note of irritation.

"Sorry, sir. I meant it as a statement of fact. I didn't mean to sound unconcerned."

"What have we lost?" Von Klaus said, brushing aside the apology.

"Nine men are dead," Kunnalt said. "Three are wounded, one critical. And three of the tanks are down."

Von Klaus stared at Kunnalt, his face red, his voice coated with anger. "Who did this?" he asked, each word spoken softly and in a deliberate tone.

"Boys mostly," Kunnalt told him. "They lined the rooftops, armed with rifles and makeshift bombs."

"Boys plan pranks, not battles," Von Klaus said. "Someone is leading them. Who?"

"We're not quite sure yet, sir," Kunnalt said. "But the men reported an exchange of gunfire with an American soldier. He came at them from a rear flank and seemed to be in control of the operation."

"The Americans are firmly entrenched in Salerno," Von Klaus said. "They won't move until Montgomery moves and that's at least a week away. They may have sent a small team down to gauge activity in the city, but no one is sent out alone. The men may have seen one soldier, but there may be others scattered throughout the city. We need to find them, and quickly. I don't want any repeats of what happened this morning. This mission will be a success if I have to personally bring down every building myself."

"If we capture one of the boys, he might lead us to the Americans," Kunnalt said. "They may have been forced into this fight and might be looking to find a way out."

"They weren't forced to be good at it," Von Klaus said. "Nine dead soldiers and three tanks in ruin. This is insane! I want this stopped before it builds. That means today, Kunnalt."

"Our troops were not expecting resistance," Kunnalt said.

"They're soldiers," Von Klaus snapped. "It's time they began to act like it."

"I've alerted all sniper teams to report any movements back to headquarters," Kunnalt said. "In addition to that, do you want me to request aerial assistance from high command?"

Von Klaus shook his head as he looked down at a large map of Naples spread out on a table under a tree. "This is our battle. Unless you want me to inform high command that one of the most elite tank troops in the German army can't face down a group of children led by one soldier."

"Then no changes to the standing orders, sir?"

"The orders hold as given." Von Klaus looked away from the map and toward Kunnalt. "No mercy in any quarters. Not to the buildings and not to anyone left on the streets. And that includes children."

3

Steve Connors sat on a thick stone in the shadows of a dark basement, his hands on the dials of a broken transmitter, the candle by his feet his only direct light. He moved the dials from right to left and tugged at the white button at the base, all to no avail. He slapped at the base of the machine in frustration and then kicked it to the ground. He sat with his back against the wall and looked out into the darkness. "Does that help make it work?" Vincenzo asked.

He stood in a corner of the room, his voice a small echo in the stillness of the basement. He stepped closer to Connors, until the candle flame helped illuminate his face.

"I need to contact my headquarters," Connors said, staring up at Vincenzo. "I have to get us some help."

"How much better would your soldiers have done today?" Vincenzo asked.

"I saw you freeze up out there," Connors said, his anger now at full throttle. "And I saw a kid with no business being in a fight get killed. That wouldn't have happened with soldiers."

"I didn't expect to see Angelo come down the street," Vincenzo said, his head down and his voice low. "And I didn't know how to stop him."

"We got lucky out there," Connors said. "Only one of ours died. And that's not because we were better than the Germans. It's because they weren't expecting us. That's not going to happen anymore, and that means a lot more people are going to die."

"It was my first fight," Vincenzo said almost sheepishly. "And I was afraid. More than I thought I would be."

"All those military books I hear you like to read are filled with stories about great battles and great soldiers," Connors said, looking at Vincenzo. "They talk about strategy and planning, make war sound like a chess game. And they're all wrong. Those books don't tell you anything about war. They don't tell you what it's like to squeeze a trigger and then watch some guy your own age in another uniform fall down dead."

"At first it was like everything was moving in slow motion," Vincenzo said, searching for the words. "And then when I tried to run, it felt like my feet were buried in water. But then a second later, it was all going so fast, I couldn't figure out how to keep up."

"It seems to go that way in every fight," Connors said, his anger dissipating, his manner softer now, more compassionate toward a boy coming to terms with his first taste of fire. "There are days when you can see every bullet fired coming right at you. Other times, all you see is a flash from a gun and the buzz run past your ear. It's different every time out."

"Are you always afraid?" Vincenzo asked, sitting down across from Connors.

"Never more than the first time," Connors said. "There's no training that can prepare you for that first fight. You don't know how you're supposed to feel or how you should act. It gets easier after you've been through a few, but you always get the fear. You just know how to deal with it better."

"I think I'll always be afraid," Vincenzo said. "I don't know if that will help make me a good fighter."

"You're already a good fighter," Connors said. "Just because you're afraid doesn't mean you're not brave. You've seen a lot of blood for a kid your age and that gives you more of an edge, but it doesn't make you battle-ready."

"I might never be," Vincenzo said. "But this morning was not just about me and Angelo. It was about those children on the rooftops who finally had a chance to fight back against tanks and soldiers."

Connors stood and walked toward the steps leading out of the church, stopping in front of a dust-shrouded statue of Saint Jude.

"He's the patron saint of lost causes," Vincenzo said. "Italians pray to him when they have no one else to turn to for help."

"It do them any good?" Connors asked.

"You've been here long enough to know the answer," Vincenzo said. "But Italians never blame the saints. Only themselves. So they pray every day, and once in a while good things happen and they have a saint to thank for it."

"That hold for you, too?" Connors asked. "The prayer part, I mean."

"Not really," Vincenzo said, looking up at Saint Jude, his marbled hands entwined in long rows of cobwebs. "Even if the saints could hear my words, why would they stop just to listen to me?"

"I don't think I've ever prayed," Connors said. "I would go to services back home, but that's just more because I had to than wanted to. And while I was there, I went through all the motions of prayer. But I've never said one where I really meant it."

Vincenzo patted his fingers gently across the statue's bare feet and looked at Connors. "Maybe that will change," he said in a whisper. "For both of us."

They turned and walked up the narrow steps leading out of the church, leaving behind the peaceful silence.

4

PIAZZA DANTE

Three German tanks rumbled around the center of the square, their engines running hot, officers standing in the open pits, gazing out at the abandoned structures. The large, ornate gate in the middle of the massive building was shuttered. It had been built in 1625 and was positioned directly across from Dante's statue. A dozen German soldiers were scattered around the tanks, their eyes searching the rooftops for signs of trouble. The tanks spread out, the officers directing the drivers to designated spots, each facing a front of the hemicycle that had stood since 1588. They were poised and eager to begin their destructive mission.

The center tank fired first.

Its opening salvo sent the gates flying, splitting the lock and bending the iron grate. The officer ignored the smoke that mushroomed around him, tapped on the sides and looked into the square as the tank moved forward. Three of the soldiers walked in behind the tank, crouched and apprehensive. The actions that had been taken earlier in Via Toledo had been radioed to all the units and they were placed on a full alert. The tank moved under the large monument, crushing some of the bars of the fallen gate as it rumbled past, and came to a halt on the other side, the officer's head still shrouded in the shadows of the arch. He turned and saw the other two tanks holding the same position.

"Looks clear to me," he said, speaking into a hand mike. "We'll send the men in first to draw any of them out. Once that's done, we bring it all down."

The soldiers slid into place alongside the tanks. Outside the towers, Dante's sculpture looked up toward the tolling clock.

It was ten A.M.

The three wooden carts were wheeled in and hidden behind Dante's statue. Each cart was loaded with mines and soaked with kerosene. Vincenzo eased past one of the carts, rifle in hand, and crouched down along the stone basin. Franco and Angela stepped in alongside. "The tanks are right where we need them to be," Franco said.

"The American needs a few more minutes to get in position," Vincenzo said. "Then we can make our move."

"What if more Nazis come from behind us?" Angela asked. "What do we do?"

"We turn the carts on them," Vincenzo said. "Which leaves our people in the square out on their own."

"This is a dangerous plan," Franco said.

"I'm open to any plans that aren't dangerous," Vincenzo said. He waited but Franco stayed silent. Vincenzo turned away, his eyes searching out the tanks in front of him, watching the Nazi soldiers move inside grounds that had been designed for leisurely walks, not great battles.

The center tank shifted gears and ground to a halt, the soldiers positioned around it holding their places and their weapons. The tanks on either side also came to a quick stop, the square filled with rising dust and crouched soldiers aiming weapons at the man and boy standing at ease in the center of the piazza. Maldini stood facing three tanks and a dozen Nazis, his arms held out, a smile on his face. Next to him, little Fabrizio bounced a soccer ball against the side of his foot.

The officer in the center tank motioned toward Maldini, signaling him to move closer. "What are you doing here?" he asked in Italian. "You're not allowed within city limits."

Maldini walked forward, his steps slow and calculated, sliding casually across the rough terrain. "I know, sir," he said apologetically. "I was set to leave when the Germans first arrived. But then my son ran away. He was afraid of the guns. Ever since, I have spent all my time looking for him. This morning, with the grace of God, I finally found him. He was hiding in one of the large rooms above us."

Fabrizio looked up at the German officer, moving the soccer ball from one foot to the other. He then lifted his eyes and saw his target, on a stone wall, fifteen meters to the right of the tank. A mine rested in the center of a brick column, directly above four soldiers with cocked machine guns.

"I could have you shot just for being here," the officer snarled.

"I know, sir," Maldini said. "I beg you, please show us your mercy. We're ready now, my son and I, to go anywhere you want us to go."

"Were there any others hiding in those buildings?" the officer asked. "Besides your son."

"None that I saw, sir," Maldini said. "The buildings I searched looked empty, a poor place to hide for adult or child."

"Your son managed to survive," the officer said. "Despite the many bombing raids."

"The Good Lord must have been watching over him, sir," Maldini said. "It's the only answer."

The officer snorted a laugh and looked down at one of his soldiers. "These Italians love to believe that God takes a hand in everything that happens to them. It helps rescue them from any responsibility."

Maldini kept his eyes on the young officer in the tank and ignored the snide laughter that came from the soldiers grouped around its sides.

Next to him, Fabrizio lifted the soccer ball from his foot to his knee, bouncing it in a quiet rhythm, as he stood balanced on one leg. Maldini turned to the little boy and gently rubbed his head. "It's time to play ball," he said to him.

"I'm not afraid," Fabrizio said.

"That's good," Maldini said. "Because I am."

Fabrizio nodded and moved the soccer ball from his knee back to the flat end of his right foot. He began a slow trot, kicking the ball from one foot to the other, his eyes on the soldiers and the tank officer. The Germans lowered their guns as they watched the boy maneuver around the front of the square, flipping the soccer ball over his shoulder and catching it with the front of his chest. Some of them laughed as he kicked the ball with his right heel and dropped to his knees as it landed on his forehead, always keeping the bounce steady. Maldini stood off to the side, his eyes on the mine positioned just to the right of the center tank, his right hand at his back, its fingers wrapped around the hard end of a revolver.

Fabrizio was on his feet, the ball a blur from foot to chest to head to arm, his hands spread out in front of him, enjoying the nods of approval he was receiving from the relaxed soldiers. "Your boy is an excellent player," the officer said to Maldini, his attention focused on Fabrizio. "One of the best I've ever seen."

"Would you care to see him shoot the ball?" Maldini said. "I swear on my mother's very soul that you'll never live to see a shot like his again."

The officer leaned back against the edge of the circular opening and glanced around at the happy faces of his men. He looked back to Maldini and nodded his approval.

Fabrizio turned to Maldini, the ball floating in midair, his cherubic face gleaming with thin lines of sweat. "Score your goal, Fabrizio," Maldini told him.

The boy moved with stutter steps, his small feet a blur as he inched the ball closer toward the soldiers and the tanks. He flipped the ball up to his knees and began to run as he bounced it, looking up to gaze at his

target, taking seconds to weigh the distance and the angle needed to
make the shot. He was within twenty feet of the tank, a short reach away
from a soldier's grip, when he stopped, turned his back, trotted a dozen
steps forward and placed the meat of the ball on the center of his right
foot. He let it rest there for a fraction of a second, spread out his arms
and slid to the hard ground. He extended his leg out, his body resting
flat on the wet stones, and kicked the ball skyward toward the brick wall
next to the main tank.

The ball whizzed off Fabrizio's foot, a white blur moving up and
away from the reach of any soldier. The officer watched it go, the smile
on his face doing a fast fade when he caught sight of the mine positioned to his side. The ball landed square in the center of the mine,
sending large pieces of brick, stone and shredded glass cascading down
on the tank and the soldiers, its loud blast rocking the piazza. A massive
hot blanket of thick brown smoke engulfed Maldini as he ran toward
Fabrizio, clutched the boy in his arms and sprinted toward the rear of
the square and the open door that awaited them both. Bullets zinged
past them as they ran, the boy clutched to Maldini like skin. "Was it a
good shot?" the little boy asked as they headed toward Connors, frantically waving them on.

"It was your best," Maldini managed to say through gasps of breath
as he and Fabrizio rushed past Connors into the immediate safety of the
office building foyer. Connors stared past them, offering cover fire and
assessing the damage made by the exploded mine. The tank in the central archway was shrouded in rubble, the officer bent over the open lid,
seriously wounded. Three ground soldiers lay dead and scattered. The
other two tanks had moved out of the gate entrances and were in the
center of the square, raining waste on the empty buildings surrounding
them. The soldiers had spread out and were firing down at his location,
bullets nicking walls and shattering glass.

Connors looked down at Fabrizio and winked at the little boy, the
mastiff now alongside him, sniffing and licking at the sides of his face. "I
guess you really are a great football player," Connors said.

Fabrizio patted the top of the mastiff's head and smiled back at Connors. "But I won't be able to practice anymore," he said. "That was the only ball I had."

Nunzia came up behind Connors, resting a hand on the soldier's back. "They're ready," she said in a low voice.

A loud explosion rocked the second floor of the building, dropping plywood and cinder chips down on them. "So are they," Connors said, staring out at the approaching tanks.

The two wooden carts were rolled into the shade of the archways, four mines in each, a heavy smell of kerosene coming off the old planks. Vincenzo bent down against the side of a wall and peeked out into the square, heavy gunfire and powerful explosions rocking the foundation of buildings built to last forever. He wiped his forehead with the torn sleeve of his shirt, took several deep breaths and closed his eyes. Next to him, crouched down and waiting with weapons cocked, six boys stood ready to move on his call. On the other end of the square, Franco waited with a similar group, all huddled in the same position. "When will we know to go out there?" one of the boys asked him, speaking in a whisper.

"You'll know," Vincenzo assured him. "And remember, don't use the carts as shelter. They'll be the first to explode."

"I've never fired a rifle before," the boy said, his voice unable to hide the frail nerves. "I hope I shoot something besides myself."

"Aim it at the ones wearing the uniforms," Vincenzo said to him, patting his leg. "And keep pulling on the trigger. After that it's as much luck as skill."

"I've never killed anyone, either," the boy said.

"You weren't supposed to," Vincenzo said, looking into his eyes. "Neither was I and neither were those Germans out there. But if they don't fight, they'll die. And so will we. My grandfather used to tell me that we don't choose our life, we just live it."

The explosion sent them sprawling to the damp ground. It came from the other end of the square, the power of its blast centered in the building where Connors and the others had been positioned, its facade now crumbled, smoke billowing toward the clear sky, flames shooting out the second- and third-floor windows. The force of the hidden bomb had stretched out into the square, leaving four soldiers dead and a tank disabled, the tracks around its rear wheels shattered into pieces.

Vincenzo stood and turned to the others. "It's time," he said. "Let's show the Nazis that Naples is still alive."

They grouped around the back of the cart and pushed it into the open square, aiming it toward the last functioning tank. From the other end, Franco and his team did the same, their target the soldiers collecting themselves from the mine blast. Vincenzo caught Franco's eye and nodded. "Scatter and fire," he shouted to the boys behind him. "Leave the cart to me."

The boys ran from the cover of the cart, firing rifle rounds in the direction of the soldiers. A few threw themselves to the ground, a handful gathered around thin pine trees for shelter, pointing their rifles and blindly emptying their chambers. Vincenzo rolled the cart with all his might, the mines jiggling, the palms of his hands cut and bleeding from the pressure he was putting on the splintered old wood. Bullets zinged at him from all directions, a grenade blast exploding twenty feet to his left. He ducked down and gave the cart one final push, using the full force of his tired body, and then he rolled off toward a patch of grass to his left. Franco released his cart seconds later, diving behind a thick green bush.

The two carts exploded at the same time, sending wood, brick, steel and chunks of concrete through the air. Vincenzo stood in the midst of all the smoke, waving his arms in a frantic motion, signaling the boys out of the square and back into the arches and the safety of the streets. He ran behind them, then turned to check on Franco. The boy was on his knees, a large shard of wood jabbed into the back of his right shoulder. The smoke around them was dense and the few German soldiers who were left were firing in the blind, bullets landing against walls and bouncing off cobblestones. Vincenzo ran toward Franco, lifted him to his feet and put an arm around his waist. "Can you run?" he asked him.

"Faster than you," Franco said.

Vincenzo gripped him tighter and both boys ran at full sprint out of the mangled Piazza Dante, leaving behind three ruined tanks and a dozen dead soldiers and a square erupting in flames. They ran under the archway and out into the clear sunlight, the marble statue of Dante greeting them both, his stiff arms spread out. Vincenzo and Franco stopped to catch their breath and glanced briefly up at the statue. "What better place to leave behind an inferno?" Vincenzo asked Franco.

"That's another book I didn't read," Franco said, between gasps for breath.

Vincenzo laughed as the two then continued their run, quickly disappearing into the empty streets of their city.

5

PANZER DIVISION HEADQUARTERS, IL PALAZZO REALE

Von Klaus tossed the map to the ground in anger. "They are only children!" he shouted. "I am losing men and tanks to children! We've been in Naples less than five hours and I've already lost more men than I did our first morning in North Africa. This is insanity!"

"Our men are like anyone else, sir," Kunnalt said, trying to bring calm to the situation. "When they see a child, they tend to let their guard down."

"They've done more than let their guard down, Kunnalt," Von Klaus said, his steel composure slowly seeping back. "They've allowed themselves to be duped, made fools of by an army of babies."

"Do you want to issue a shoot-on-sight order regarding children, sir?" Kunnalt asked.

Von Klaus looked at the junior officer and held his gaze for several seconds, his breath returning to normal. "No," he said, shaking his head.

"We have yet to reach that point. And, for whatever it matters, I hope we never do."

"They will be difficult to flush out, sir," Kunnalt said. "We have very little intelligence on them, other than what we received from that prison escapee, Petroni. They're scattered and hidden throughout the city. It will take time to roust them out, time that will be taken away from the mission."

"We don't need them all found," Von Klaus said. "One will do. He is the only professional among the group."

"We could make use of Petroni," Kunnalt said. "He's betrayed them once for money. He might be willing to do so again, for even more money."

Von Klaus nodded. "An internal struggle would benefit us," he said. "It might help eliminate the problem without the men having to gun children down in the streets. Find this Petroni and deal with him."

Kunnalt stood next to Von Klaus, both staring down at a map, their hands resting on top of the thin sheet of paper.

"Spread the tanks out and increase the frequency of the attacks," the colonel said. "They might be able to stop one or two tanks, but they can't stop all of them. Despite their efforts, this city will be destroyed."

"Any other change in orders, sir?"

"Free up some of the men," Von Klaus said. "Break them into squads of six and have them work in advance of the tanks. See if they can spot these traps before we drive into them. I also want the attacks to run through the night. The men can go for long stretches without sleep, so it won't hinder their abilities. But I don't want to give these children any break from the battle they've chosen to start."

"If any are found, do you want them taken as prisoners, sir?" Kunnalt asked.

"Yes," Von Klaus said. "House them in one of the castles by the bay."

"And if fired upon, the men are free to return fire at will?" Kunnalt asked.

"An enemy is an enemy, Kunnalt," Von Klaus said. "Regardless of age."

6

SAN GREGORIO ARMENO

The two barefoot boys ran down a steep hill and turned a corner, both soaked in sweat and gulping for fresh air. Two German soldiers, in full gear, followed, fast on their backs, firing bullets that landed on the stone street and dented rock walls in front of them. Two hundred yards farther up the hill, Connors and Nunzia gave chase, hoping to get to the Germans before they reached the boys. As they ran, Connors looked at the old gun in Nunzia's right hand. "You any good with that?" he asked as they both jumped a huge crater in the middle of the street.

"I never had to be," she said. "Before."

The boys were now at the top of a small bridge, heading for the gated entrance to the church of Santa Patrizia, hoping to seek refuge within its halls. "*Forza, Maurizio*," the older of the two shouted to his friend. "The Germans are getting closer."

"You keep running," Maurizio answered, the burn in his chest clutching at his throat. "With or without me. There's no use both of us dying."

The soldiers were less than a hundred yards away, firing bullets at a rapid pace, determined to bring down the two boys. Maurizio, his legs the weight of air and his stomach cramped, came to an abrupt stop just as he crossed the bridge, a short distance removed from the gilded gates of the church. "I can't go anymore," he gasped, waving meekly to the other boy. "Save yourself, Mario. The Nazis will be happy to have caught just one of us."

Mario skidded to a halt, his back to the gate. He saw the Germans come up the hill, one running, his handgun aimed at the slumped-over Maurizio. The other soldier came to rest against an embankment, dropped to one knee and brought his machine gun to chest level. Just behind them, on the far end of the bridge, he could see Nunzia and the American. Mario stared over at Maurizio, their eyes locking, both resigned. The German with the handgun was over the bridge and close enough for the boys to make out his face beneath the shield of his helmet. He stopped, took a breath and aimed his weapon at the older boy's back. Maurizio glanced at him over his shoulder, rows of sweat clouding his vision, his body trembling, his throat holding back the urge to vomit.

Connors and Nunzia reached the bridge. The American stopped and aimed his rifle at the soldier closest to him, the one with the machine gun. "I can only get one of them from here," he said to Nunzia. "And it's going to be the wrong one. The one with the gun is past my range. If I take out his friend on the right, it might be enough to break his balance."

Connors fell to one knee and peered through his scope. Nunzia kept running, honing in closer to the German with the handgun. The boys held their position, frozen in place. The Nazi with the machine gun took aim at Mario, his movements slow and deliberate, confident he had all the time he needed to take out the boy shivering under the hot glare of the sun.

The gate to the church door swung open.

An old woman, short and squat, dressed in a heavy woolen black dress, a knitted shawl wrapped around her shoulders, moved out into the street. Her hands were hidden behind the stained white apron wrapped around her waist. The German soldier lowered his gun as soon as he saw her, waving the butt end at her, a silent warning to stay away. Mario and Maurizio glanced over, watching as she moved past them, her feet covered in wool socks and hand-made wooden house slippers. "*Signora*, no," Mario warned her to no avail. "*Questo posto non e per te.*"

The old woman stopped, her steel gray eyes focused on the soldier with the gun, her jaw clenched tight, the cheeks sagged and wrinkled. She freed her hands from behind the apron and pulled out a twelve-inch butcher's knife, the one Neapolitan women often used to cut thick mounds of fresh provolone cheese. She reared her right arm back, fingers gripping the tip blade of the knife, planted her feet and squared her body. She released the knife with full force and a hard grunt, watching as it whizzed through the air and landed in the center of the soldier's chest. The German dropped his gun, his two hands clutched around the wooden handle of the knife, his eyes opened wide, his mouth spilling blood and foam, his knees buckling. He fell backwards, landing with a quiet thud on the hard street.

The soldier with the machine gun stood and turned his weapon on the old woman. She looked back at him, her elderly face free of fear. The boys gazed beyond her, staring at Connors in the center of the bridge, down on one knee, taking dead aim at the Nazi. The German caught their look and turned his head.

The first shot from Connors winged him in the shoulder and spun him around, the machine gun falling to the ground. The second caught him in the forehead and sent him crumpling against the brown rock embankment, his legs folded off to the side. Mario and Maurizio stared down at the two dead soldiers and then turned away and ran toward the old woman who eagerly returned their warm embrace. "*Grazia mille, Signora,*" Mario muttered. The old woman didn't speak, content to rub the sweaty backs of the two boys with her gnarled fingers.

She smiled at Connors and Nunzia as they approached. Nunzia leaned over and kissed the old woman on the cheek. "Ask her if she wants to come stay with us," Connors said to Nunzia. "We'll make sure to keep her safe."

The old woman looked at the soldier sprawled at the base of the bridge with a knife jutting out of his chest. Then she looked at Connors and smiled a toothless grin. "That's what I was going to ask you," she said.

7

45TH INFANTRY THUNDERBIRD DIVISION HEADQUARTERS
SALERNO

Captain Anders crumpled up the report he had just finished reading for a second time and shook his head, the flat end of a cigar clutched between his teeth. "Looks like there's somebody down there not too happy about having the Nazis back in Naples. And I got me a damn pretty good idea who that somebody is."

"Connors may be involved, sir," Higgins, a young junior officer said. "But he couldn't have done the kind of damage that's in that report by himself."

"No, I suppose that would be too much to ask of anyone," Anders said. "Even a wild match like Connors. But whatever is going on down there, he's smack in the middle of it. That's a damn sure safe bet."

"We could easily send down a few units, sir." He was barely out of his teens, a tall and lanky young man from Arlington, Virginia, with a hard voice and a soft manner. "Even out the odds some. There's a full division down there. Help or not, he's going to run into thick trouble sometime soon."

"The Nazis got in at sunup," Anders said. "It's barely noon and they're already down six tanks and twenty men. Send some units down to beef up the advance teams and have them move closer to the city. I want them to stop any German units heading into or out of Naples."

"Whoever he's with, they're armed and seem to have some idea what to do with the weapons," Higgins said, gazing down at a map spread across a poker table. "But it's not the Italian resistance. They haven't been seen in Naples in weeks."

"Some of the locals around here insist there are a few hundred kids scattered around the city," Anders said. "It's a stretch to think they could be causing all these problems, but until I get a better picture of what's down there, that's my only bet."

"I saw the intelligence on the Sixteenth Panzer Division," Higgins said. "They're the best the Germans have. Why would they waste them on a search-and-destroy mission?"

"That's their worry, not ours," Anders said. "But you're right, it doesn't make much sense. Their tank commander, Von Klaus, is right up there next to Rommel. He can fight in the desert and in the cities. He's strong on strategy and, as far as I've read, he hasn't lost in any field of battle. I'm glad the generals sent him down there on garbage cleanup. I'd rather he aim his tank shells at empty buildings than at our infantry."

"Do you want us to try to get word to Connors?"

Captain Anders relit his cigar and looked across the table at Higgins, a thin line of smoke forcing one of his eyes closed. "If you can track him down, then get a message out," he said. "Meantime, let's figure out what we can do to get him out of there without riling up Monty and the Brits."

8

VIA MEDINA

The boy walked at a brisk pace, two German soldiers on either side, each with a tight grip on his elbows. The street was empty and silent except for a battery of soldiers pounding through doors and shooting stray bullets into abandoned rooms. There was a tank parked at an angle in the distance, five soldiers at rest under its shadow, enjoying a rare break and a canteen meal. The boy slowed his movements, forcing the soldiers to drag him down the center of the street. They had found him nestled under the desk of the bombed-out remains of an old school, the gun in his hand down to its final bullet.

The boy was fifteen and slight of build with long brown hair running down across his eyes. He had a long, choppy scar on the right side of his face, the result of a childhood bite from a horse. His legs were strong and athletic. His parents had been circus performers, high-wire gymnasts, performing their act throughout southern Italy prior to the war. They were killed by Fascist troops during a crowded late afternoon show in Reggio Calabria. He remembered holding his father's head in his hands and the loud, dismissive laughter of the soldiers surrounding them. The tents and the equipment were burned and destroyed.

The soldiers dragged Pietro closer to the tank, both pleased with their first capture. The boy searched the rooftops for any sign of help, any indication that someone was watching. After several futile seconds, he lowered his head, resigned to whatever fate the Nazis had reserved for him. He kept his eyes on the ground, doing his best to ignore the tank and the soldiers, focusing instead on the ancient rocks and stones that made up the familiar street he had played on as a child. He turned his head to the left, caught a glint of the sun on his face and, for the first time in many weeks, allowed himself a smile.

The heavy iron manhole cover was off to his left, about a thirty-yard run from where he was being tugged along by the two soldiers. He saw the lip slide across and a boy's head emerge just above its rim, waving for him to stop, pointing a finger across the street. Pietro glanced to his right and saw another boy wedged inside a small sewer opening, a grenade clutched in his right hand.

Pietro planted his legs on the ground, bringing the two soldiers to a sudden halt. He turned to each and wedged a hand on their shoulders and did a quick three-quarters backward flip, easily breaking their hold. The soldiers fell back, regained their composure and reached for their rifles. Pietro ran toward the now open manhole, prepared to use the skills he had honed since he was an infant. The two soldiers aimed their rifles at his back, ready to fire, when Pietro stopped, turned and faced them, his arms extended out. He crouched to his knees and did a massive flip backwards, landing within an inch of the open manhole. As Pietro lowered himself into the hole, he gave the two soldiers a gentle wave good-bye.

The soldiers raced toward the manhole, watching the lid slide quickly across its open mouth. As they both scampered past the sewer, a grenade came flying out of the small opening, grazing one of them on the shin. They turned, looked down and caught the full force of the blast in their chests. They were sent sprawling to the ground, backs and legs covered in blood. A small boy emerged from the sewer hole, running for the abandoned rifles and gun belts, looking up at the tank soldiers coming his way, firing shots in his direction. He dragged his booty toward the sewer, dropped them all into the hole and slid back down, bullets whizzing past his legs.

"*Forza!*" the boy shouted to a friend waiting for him in the sewer, the rifles and ammo belts clutched in his arms. "Run as fast as you can. They'll throw grenades as soon as they reach the opening." The two boys scattered down the slippery path, lined with broken steam pipes, rotting water and old grease, turned a corner and disappeared. The force of the explosion behind them was enough to hurl them to the floor, rifles and ammo belts scattered by their sides. "*Bravo*, Eduardo," the small boy said, helping up his younger friend. "We have both done well. Now the rest is up to them above us."

"I want you to know I wasn't scared," Eduardo said. Mud and soot covered the seven-year-old from the top of his thick head of hair down to the cuts on his bare feet. "Not for one second."

The boy patted Eduardo on the head and then gave him a playful nudge. "It's good to know that one of us is brave, then," he said, bending down to pick up the guns and the ammo. "I was so scared up there I don't think I'll ever feel my legs again."

Eduardo put an arm around the older boy. "Don't worry, Gio," he said. "You'll always have me to help you."

"Let's go," Gio said, resting a rifle on his shoulder and draping an ammo belt around his neck, his eyes searching the muddy ground. "I'm afraid of rats, too."

The manhole cover slid open again.

Pietro and two other boys emerged from the darkness. The five German soldiers were spread out across the sewer cover, one of them peering down into the smoke-filled opening. "You worry about the tank," the oldest of the three, a light-skinned teenager, said to Pietro. "We'll deal with the soldiers. Once you finish, head up toward Via Diaz. We'll catch up to you later. And whatever you do, don't drop the mine."

Pietro slid out of the manhole and took the mine from the two boys. "Don't look back," one of them whispered. "Just go. You have the more important job."

Pietro nodded, clutched the mine and turned away, walking carefully toward the tank. The two boys in the manhole opening lifted up two

German machine guns and braced them against the concrete edge of the street. They turned to look at Pietro and then back to the soldiers, took deep breaths and opened fire.

Two of the soldiers fell to the ground dead, one with his head jammed in the sewer cavity. A third lay on the ground wounded, his rifle just beyond his reach. The remaining two spread out on the street and returned fire, their bullets clipping at the edges of the rocks and ground cover around the boys. One shot clipped the light-skinned boy in the shoulder, causing him to lose his grip and drop down into the sewer. "Tomasso!" the other boy called out.

"It's my shoulder," Tomasso said, watching the blood flow out of the wound, the sting of the bullet causing his eyes to tear.

"Stay down," the other boy said. "Reload your gun and give it to me. I need to give Pietro more time."

The wounded boy struggled to put in a fresh clip, then patted the other boy on the knee and handed it to him. "Bernardo, how many are left?" he asked, as the boy bent down to take the machine gun.

"There are two," Bernardo said. "Both heading our way. I can handle it. You go and I'll catch up."

"We came together, my cousin," Tomasso said, wiping at the blood flowing down from his wound. "And we leave together."

"Then we'll leave soon," Bernardo said.

He jammed both machine guns into the crook of his arms and climbed back up to the top steps. He fired all his rounds, every bullet aimed in the direction of the German soldiers, not stopping until the clips were emptied. Then, sweat creasing his eyes, smoke littering a pocket of the street, he waited. Five German soldiers lay on the ground in front of him, facedown and dead. Bernardo dropped the hot machine guns on the street and turned to his left. He saw Pietro's body slide under the center of the tank, as he gently placed the mine in its wheel base, turning it into an instant deathtrap for the next team of soldiers. He pulled himself up out of the sewer and walked across the street, taking the weapons and belts off the bodies of the dead Nazis.

He stopped when he saw Pietro whistle toward him and wave and gave a nod as the boy turned and raced around a corner toward safety. Bernardo took a deep breath and looked around him at the familiar buildings and at the coral blue skyline. He took a final look down at the German soldiers.

"Welcome to Naples," he said in a low voice.

Bernardo lowered himself back into the sewer, arms and shoulders bulging with weapons and bullets, and slid the manhole cover across the top, bringing darkness once again to his world.

9

PIAZZA TRIESTE E TRENTO

The room was on the second floor, the blinds drawn, a candle in the corner burned down to a low wick. Franco lay in the small bed, a thin sheet covering him to the waist, his eyes fluttered shut, a blood-soaked bandage wrapped around his wounded shoulder. He heard the floorboards creak and opened his eyes. "Vincenzo," he said. "*Sei tu?*"

The footsteps came closer and Franco could make out the image of a boy about his height and weight sulking toward his side of the bed. The boy sat on the edge of the spring mattress, the small of his back against Franco's feet, resting a warm hand on top of the sheet.

"Who are you?" Franco asked, able to catch glimpses of the boy's face in between tiny flickers of the candle flame.

"My name's Carlo," the boy said in a thick, harsh voice that Franco did not recognize. "And I can be a friend to you."

"How did you find me?" Franco asked, wiping drops of fever sweat from his brow. "No one knows about this place."

"It wasn't hard," Carlo said. "Nothing is if you know who to ask and where to look."

Franco lifted himself higher in the bed, wincing at the sharp pain in his shoulder. The large, jagged wound had been slow to heal with medication being hard to come by and painkillers nonexistent. Connors had yanked the shank out and Nunzia had cleansed the cut, pulling out as many splinters as she could with a hot pair of tweezers. She then rubbed a boiled lemon and ground pepper paste on the edges of the wound and sealed it with a mixture of penicillin and hot wax before wrapping it with the boiled strands of a torn dress. Franco was running a high fever and his lower limbs were cold to the touch. He reached for the glass that was on the end table, next to the candle, and drank down the last drops of wine.

"You can start telling me what you want," Franco said. "I'm not going anywhere for a few hours."

"I want to help you and your friends fight the Nazis," Carlo said. "Nothing more than that. I have a small group up in the hills that will come join me. We're all very good and you're going to need all the good people you can find."

"Why are you waiting until now to help us?" Franco asked, still suspicious, trying to place both the face and the choppy sounds of the boy's harsh dialect.

Carlo slid down the edge of the bed, closer to Franco, leaning across the sweaty sheets with a smile, exposing a mouthful of neglected teeth. "We followed what you all were doing, but from a distance. We wanted to make sure it was going to turn out to be more than just loud talk in empty piazzas. And we didn't think you wanted any help from kids like us."

"You're from the children's prison," Franco said, a hint of recognition taking shape in his fever-fogged mind.

"That's right," Carlo admitted. "Me and everyone from my group. We're the ones your parents always told you to stay away from. But that was before the war started. Now we're the kind you really need."

"Just because you were sent to jail doesn't mean you can fight," Franco said, his eyes on the older boy's hands. "And it doesn't mean we want you fighting with us."

"We've been to prison and survived," Carlo said, voice overrun with confidence. "The Nazis can do nothing to us worse than what's already been done."

"What were you in prison for?" Franco asked.

"That doesn't matter," Carlo said, shaking off the question. "We come in with you or we fight the Nazis out there on our own. I came here thinking that together would be better."

"Why come to me?"

"The others are scattered and on the move," Carlo said. "You're going to be in this bed for a day or two. It just seemed easier."

"You don't need permission to fight the Nazis," Franco said, his shoulder aching, his eyes heavy from the fever and the heat in the stuffy room. "Just go out and disrupt their attack. If you do that, then we'll know you and your friends are with us. Until then, there's very little for us to say to each other."

Carlo nodded, stretched his legs and stood, gazing down at Franco with cold, distant eyes. "You need what we have," he said. "It's something that will take many Nazi lives and help save some of the boys from being killed. To turn your back on it will be foolish."

Franco rested his head against a feather pillow and stared at Carlo. He was tired and in pain and he wished Vincenzo was in the room to help sort through Carlo's words and determine if they were truthful or a trap. "What is it you have?" he asked, his throat parched and raw.

"A tank," Carlo said with genuine glee. "A Panzer tank. And enough shells to deal with an army of problems."

Franco's eyes widened at the news. "How did you get a tank?" he asked, intrigued by the possibilities such a weapon offered the street boys.

"The same way we get everything," Carlo said. "We stole it. Two nights before the Nazis came into Naples."

"You have to be trained to drive it," Franco said.

"If you can drive a car, you can drive a tank. It comes down to the same thing, only without windows."

Franco pulled aside the sheet and jumped from the bed, his movements startling Carlo, who took two slow steps back. He grabbed Carlo by the center of his white woolen shirt and dragged him to his side, leaving him close enough to smell the raw wound and see the blood draining through the bandage. "If you're lying to me, thief," Franco said, the strength back in his voice, his words fueled by the heat of anger, "if one word of what you just said is not true, I'll find you and I will kill you."

"You heal quick," Carlo said, staring deep into Franco's eyes. "That's a good talent to have during a war."

Franco released his grip and pushed Carlo away, the wounded boy walking the room in a tight circle, his fists clenched, his eyes never wavering from the convicted felon in his presence. "Where's this tank now?" he asked.

"It's wherever you want it to be," Carlo said, slowly regaining his bravado. "You name the place and time and I'll make sure it's there."

Franco bowed his head for a few brief moments, quickly glancing out the window at the bare street below. "Can you get it to Via Vicaria Vecchia without being spotted?"

"The Nazis will think it's one of their own," Carlo said. "We're free to move anywhere we want."

"Have it there at noon tomorrow," Franco said. "Park it along one of the alleys in Forcella."

Carlo nodded and headed toward the door. "Noon it is. Who else will be with you?"

"I was going to ask you the same question," Franco said.

"Then we should wait until tomorrow," Carlo said. "This way, we'll both be surprised."

Franco stood in the center of the room, watching as Carlo closed the door behind him, leaving him shrouded in darkness. He ran his fingers along the sides of his bandage, his legs fatigued from the fever and the shock to his body. He grabbed for his pants, curled at the foot of the bed, and put them on. He found a torn shirt in the top drawer of a small bureau and pulled it over his head, wincing as it drew past the cut. Outside, heavy shells pounded at the buildings in a nearby square, the explosions causing puffs of sand to snake up through the floorboards.

Franco took a final look around the room and walked out, once again ready to do battle.

10

The two tanks surrounded the three-story building, soldiers working the stone edges, pouring gasoline on its pink stucco facade. Inside, a dozen street boys huddled in corners, away from any open windows, all with guns and rifles in their hands. Two soldiers wielding heavy stone mallets bashed down the front door and stepped aside as the tank took dead aim at the ornate fireplace in the foyer. Flames rushed through the center hall, blasted out the three front windows and rocked the wooden floor above. Two of the boys began to cry while another stood and tried to leave the room. The oldest among them, Emilio Carbone, the fourteen-year-old son of a stone mason, stood in front of the door and blocked his path. Emilio put an arm around the smaller boy's shoulders and walked him back toward the center of the room. "This isn't a time for us to run," he said in low, comforting tones. "We have to let the Nazis see our true face."

"We'll die in here!" a boy in a far corner shouted out at Emilio, the walls around him trembling from another heavy hit. Below them, the voices of Nazi soldiers screaming out orders ricocheted off the barren stairwell.

"I know," Emilio said. "All of us did, the minute we came running in here. But in the time we have left, let the Nazis feel some of our pain."

The aftershock of a tank shell blew out a back window, thick smoke clogging the room. The crack and sparkle of flames could be heard licking at the walls in the other rooms, the paint around them melting from the heat and sliding down the thin wood panels.

"They'll come storming through any second now," Emilio said, pointing to the thick oak door at his back. "Let's be ready."

They were lined up in a row of twelve, the open windows and glare of the tanks at their backs. Each held either a rifle or handgun, cocked at the front door, brown smoke from the fire below them filtering through the cracked tiles and coating their bare feet. "Use every bullet you have," Emilio instructed them. "There's no reason to save anything for later."

The front door was smashed open by the butt end of two machine guns, the wilting wood easily caving in to the blow. Three soldiers stood across the smashed entryway, their guns at waist level. The dozen street boys braced themselves against the hot walls and fired their weapons. A steady stream of bullets rained on the soldiers, killing three instantly and wounding two others, the ammo escaping through holes in the side panels. The boys then moved forward, six sliding to the burning ground, the other half dozen straddling above them, all firing at will at the attacking soldiers. "When your gun is empty, reach for a Nazi's that's full," Emilio shouted above the buzz of the fire. "Move forward and never let up."

Three boys slid across the now scalding floor and grabbed machine guns and ammo belts from the dead soldiers by the door. One held up a pack of grenades and tossed it over his shoulder to Emilio. "Slide any extra weapons you find behind you," he told them as he rested the grenade pack on his shoulder and continued shooting across the now wide doorway. The small children's brigade kept moving, their hands scorched from the firing, their faces masked with soot and black powder, hair tinged with dust. The heavy flames from the outside of the building had spread inside, the smoke winding its way down the halls and into the rooms like a silent snake. Some of the boys were groggy, their watery eyes tinged with red, their breath coming in hard, difficult gulps. "We need to get to air soon, Emilio," one of the boys said. He was now in the hall and firing his weapon into the stairwell. "We can fight the Nazis but not the smoke."

Emilio broke from the pack and raced through the halls of the eighteenth-century building, flames shooting at him from all sides, bullets zinging past, the floor below him creaking with every step. He turned a corner and went into a room that was near collapse, the ceiling cracked and hanging halfway down to the ground, a large chandelier shattered below it. He dodged the shards of glass and ducked past thick chunks of plaster, reaching an open window in the rear. He looked down on the remains of a once well-tended garden, its flowers wilted and mauled, its

grass blackened by tire treads and the weight of tanks and trampling feet.
Emilio looked from the garden to the heavens above and smiled.

He ran back into the hall, the heat around him like that of an oven,
the smoke making it all but impossible to see to the next step. He found
two of the boys, crouched in a corner, firing the last of their machine-
gun bullets into the fog that held them prisoner. He lowered a hand
down to them and pulled them to their feet. "Run to the back," he ordered. "In the rear of the house, the room with the broken chandelier.
Jump through the open window and run to safety. Do you hear me?"

"*Si*, Emilio," the boys said, disappearing as if ghosts into the blanket
of hell.

Emilio ran for the others, gathering as many of them as he could
find, giving them all the same instructions, watching as they each scram-
bled through clouds of smoke for the room at the end of the hall. He
leaned against a creaky banister, his eyes heavy, his breath coming in
painful spurts, his right foot resting against the body of a Nazi soldier.
Outside, in the misty afternoon sunshine, eleven street boys were jumping from the fire and scrambling their way to freedom. Emilio smiled,
closed his eyes and fell over in a dusty heap, his body coiled against the
top of the landing. His head rested limp over the side.

Seconds later, the once majestic building surrendered its battle to
the smoke and the flames and collapsed, melting into the ground like a
washed-over sand castle.

11

VIA NUOVO TEMPIO

The wrath of the 16th Panzer Division tanks and its soldiers was now
fully unleashed on Naples. The tanks rumbled through the steamy
streets, unloading one barrage after another. Soldiers fired at the first

hint of any movement and the flame throwers were working at full throttle, their potent line of fire raining down on barns, homes and storefronts. Grenades were tossed on rooftops and rapid-stream machine-gun shells echoed off the empty side streets.

In the midst of the smoke and ruin, a young soldier, face soiled by grease and caked dirt, stepped up to the main tank and saluted the officer standing in the open hole.

"There's a small church on the next corner, sir," the young man said, speaking in a rushed manner. "It's sustained quite a bit of damage and there are fires smoldering on the inside, but sections of it still stand. Shall we leave it and move on?"

The officer glared down at the young soldier, his face draped in a cold, hard shell. "No, moving on is not an option," he said in a stern voice. "Moving through is your only choice."

"Yes, sir," the soldier said. "I only thought that since it's a church, we could leave it as it is."

"You thought wrong," the officer said. "Once we've gone, these streets will fall into enemy hands. Our goal is to ensure that they can't find a scrap of a building, church or otherwise, when they come marching in. Not even a spot that offers shade from the sun."

The young soldier quietly nodded and turned away, to return to a cruel task he never envisioned performing back in Hamburg, when he first proudly wore his uniform and posed for photos with his younger brothers and sisters. He walked in the middle of the street, flames, explosion and debris on both sides of the avenue, the sounds of gunfire fading into the background as the tanks moved forward. He stopped when he reached the church, its facade smoking and broken in half, portions of the side walls blown off. He stepped over rubble and cracked stone and walked into the remains of a building that had been erected centuries earlier by skilled laborers who worked as much out of pride of craft as for want of money. He rested his rifle on the back of a broken chair and walked down the center aisle, eyes fixed on the large crucifix that hung down from a main beam in the ceiling. The ceramic floor of the church, once ornate and glimmering, was now blanketed

with brown dust. Statues of saints rested in heaps under darkened archways and the two side altars had been blown apart, each one sent
smashing through stone walls and into the fiery alleys at their back. The
soldier stopped on the lower step of the central altar and bowed his
head, his knees resting on the cold, chipped marble. He blessed himself
and mumbled a soft prayer, his eyes closed, his hands folded at his waist.

He stiffened when he heard the baby cry.

The quiet wail came from his left, inside one of the confessional
booths, shrouded by heavy purple curtains. The soldier stood and
walked toward the sound, one hand held on his holstered pistol. He
stopped in front of the booth and hesitated, listening closely. He
stepped off to the side and parted the curtains, peering into the darkness of the tiny wooden cubicle. He saw the infant first, cuddled in the
arms of a young woman, the child's chest bare, soiled pants covering
the small curled legs. The woman looked back at the soldier, her body
still, her eyes wide and overrun with fear. Her clothes were torn and
frayed, exposing the sides of her legs and shoulders and her hair, dark
and long, shaded the top of her head and the back of her neck. The
woman had one hand clasped tightly across the baby's mouth, muffling
his loud and eager cries for food.

The woman stood and stepped out of the booth on trembling legs.
She walked up to the soldier, the baby now close enough for him to
touch. He stared down at the smeared face and moved his hand away
from the gun. He looked at the mother, neither one making any attempt
to speak. The soldier turned his head and gazed over at a staircase behind the confessional, leading down to a darkened basement. He slowly
looked back at the woman and rested a hand on her arm, sensing her
flinch from the touch. He pointed toward the steps, nudging his head in
their direction, the restless hunger of the baby calmed by the sight of a
stranger. The woman held her place, her eyes focused on the soldier,
her hands clutching the baby tighter in her grip.

The explosion rattled them both, the front wall of the church blasted
aside, smoke and debris racing toward them like a fast-moving train.
The startled baby began to fill the air with his cries. The soldier tight-

ened his grip on the woman's arm and pulled her toward the stairs, giving a quick check to the front door. He looked at the woman, nodded and pointed down, urging her with an assortment of hand gestures to move at a faster pace. The woman stopped on the third step, the baby in her arms shrieking for food, attention and an escape to a quieter, safer place. She moved closer to the soldier, placing her lips near his left ear, partially covered by the edges of his pith helmet. *"Ti ringrazzio,"* the woman whispered. She then softly kissed his cheek and ran her thin fingers across the side of his face. *"Ti ringrazzio tanto."*

She turned and quickly disappeared down the dark stairwell to the hoped-for safety of the church basement, looking to keep her child alive for one more day. The soldier stood silent as he watched her leave, face still warmed by her tender touch. He turned when he saw the two soldiers behind him, rifles drawn, backs to the small confessional.

"Anybody down there?" one asked.

"No," the young soldier said. "Not a soul."

He moved up the steps, past the booth and headed out of the church.

12

PIAZZALE MOLO BEVERELLO

The large oil tanker was moored off the long dock, a series of thick ropes wedged around iron pillars keeping it in place. Two large overhead spotlights, running off a generator, cast a glow across its rusty exterior. The tanker had arrived in port earlier that afternoon, its hulk filled to capacity with thousands of gallons of fuel, enough to keep the Nazi tanks roaming the streets of Naples until their mission was completed. Small rivers of water spewed from three circular openings at its base, the rumble of its loud engines brought down by the crew to a low throttle. There were a dozen guards patrolling its upper railings, submachine guns tucked behind their shoulders, eyes focused on the lapping water beneath them and the dark city streets beyond.

Connors, Maldini and Vincenzo were crouched behind a wooden shack, two hundred feet from the bow of the tanker. Nunzia and two boys were at the other end of the pier, crammed inside a small ticket booth. Connors slid to his chest and crawled along the ship side of the dock, a few feet removed from the glare of the lights, the shadows of the Nazi soldiers on patrol lining the length of the platform. He turned back toward Vincenzo and waved him forward. The boy slid in alongside him, his movements as quiet as falling leaves, makeshift bomb in his hands, Maldini's wristwatch imbedded in the center of the mechanism. "How much time?" Connors asked, his eyes on the bomb.

"Forty-five minutes like you told me," Vincenzo said. "Thirty to get there and strap it to the tanker and fifteen to get away."

"Sounds about right," Connors said, nodding and checking his own watch. "I'll leave you my pack and rifle. I'll lay the bomb down and you help the others do what they need to do."

Vincenzo shook his head and pulled back from Connors. "I'll put it on the ship," he said.

"Maybe we should have worked this out before." Connors's voice was low but his anger apparent. "I wasn't counting on you turning into a jerk. Any idiot with wire, tape and explosives can make a bomb. But you need to have some clue about what you're doing to lay it in there."

"Have you ever done it?" Vincenzo asked. "Stuck a bomb on the side of an oil tanker in the middle of the night?"

"That's not the point," Connors said. "It's a risky move. One mistake and those soldiers will spot it and they'll be on us in seconds."

"That's why I should be the one to go," Vincenzo said. "You can fight the Nazis off better than me. And after that, you can figure out a way to get the others out of the city."

"It does bother me when what you say starts making sense," Connors said, reaching for the rifle slung across his back. "I'll leave Maldini behind to give you some cover."

Vincenzo lowered his head, the bomb held in the palm of his hands, and slithered off toward the cool waters of the bay. Connors turned and crawled back to the side of the shack, Maldini hunched down beside it. He flipped off his pack and handed it to the older man. "I filled it up with grenades," he said to Maldini. "First smell of trouble, scatter them across the upper deck of the ship."

Maldini took the pack and reached inside, pulling out one of the grenades. "I see our general got his way again," he said with a sly grin.

"He should be a lawyer, not a general," Connors said. "The kid could argue his way out of a firing squad."

"He knows those waters and their currents well," Maldini added. "And he moves like a ghost. He's gone before you can hear him coming. Me, I can wake a room just by breathing."

"Nunzia's waiting," Connors said, hands braced against the wood, checking the guards above, eager to make his move.

"She smiles more since you've been around, American," Maldini said.

Connors turned away from the guards to look over at Maldini. "She's going to help me blow up a tank. It's not what I would call a date."

"Do you come from a family with money?" Maldini asked.

"Hardly," Connors said. "My dad works two jobs. My mom works, too, part-time. The house is small, barely big enough to hold our family."

"A house?" Maldini said. "You have a house? That's not poor. Is your bathroom in the house or outside?"

"In the house," Connors said. "Both of them."

Maldini shook his head in wonder. "A house with two bathrooms," he said. "This the Americans call poor. In my *casa*, I have to walk down two flights of stairs to go to the bathroom. Outside. And pray no one else is using it."

"We're not rich," Connors insisted. "We live from paycheck to paycheck. Like millions of other Americans. It's no different."

"Does your family have a car?" Maldini asked.

"Yeah," Connors said. "But it's a used car."

Maldini leaned his back against the side of the shack, closed his eyes and smiled. "A garage, too, I bet," he whispered. "It must be good to be rich."

Connors looked at his watch and then at Maldini. "When I get back, I'll tell you all about paid vacations and sick leave," he said.

Connors hunched down on his knees and scooted off into the darkness. He ran along the edges of the Calata Beverello, heading toward Nunzia and the boys. Maldini rested his head on the edge of the shack, grenade still in his hand. "Only in America do people get paid to be sick," he muttered.

Vincenzo swam along the edges of the large tanker, using his feet and chest muscles, hands holding the device aloft. He swam in next to the rusty hulk, oil-tarnished water splashing into his open mouth. His shoulders bumped against the ragged side of the ship, old paint chips slicing into his skin. He glanced up above him, trying to avoid the glare of the overhead lights, and saw the muzzle of a machine gun at rest against the top rail. He turned and faced the side of the tanker, his nose jammed against it, and placed the bomb at eye level. He squeezed it into the smoothest area he could find and held it there with thick strips of tape.

There were twenty minutes left on the timer, more than enough time for him to get away and for Connors and the others to complete their task. Vincenzo put an ear up to the watch, making sure it was still ticking, even as the grimy water lapped just under the base of the bomb. He gave a final look up at the Nazis standing guard and silently swam away.

Connors poured kerosene on the rear of the tank, drenching the parked vehicle in the flammable liquid. He held the five-gallon drum tight against his chest, moving about with quiet steps, eyes on the lid of the tank. He soaked the rear treads and poured some under the base, Nunzia and the boys hidden in darkness behind him. He left the empty drum under the tank and walked backwards to the spot where he knew the others would be. Nunzia waited for him, another drum filled with kerosene in her hand. "This is the last of it," she whispered.

"The boys know what they need to do?" Connors asked, nodding over at the two silent teens standing beside Nunzia.

"We'll do our job," one of them said, in a voice slightly louder than it should have been. "Don't worry about us."

Connors took the drum from Nunzia and looked into her face, its beauty glimmering even in the dark well of a dangerous night. "I'm American," Connors said. "I worry about everything."

Connors inched back to the tank, uncorked the drum and poured the kerosene out in a straight line, allowing it to follow him as he stepped away from the silent machine. He knew from earlier surveillance that there were only two soldiers inside the tank, both by now asleep. The other three had gone up to the tanker to spend time with those on guard. He paused to look up at the ship, wondering if Vincenzo's handmade bomb would have any impact against such a massive hulk. He was surprised that they were able to get so close to the ship without being spotted, the overconfidence and carelessness of the Nazis playing perfectly into their hands. The Germans should have had guards on the ground as well as on the tanker. They also had enough tanks to position three to guard against any attack, two on the dock and one hidden off on a side street. In the course of any battle, Connors had learned, it's never the better soldier who survives. It's often the one who takes the time and pains to eliminate all elements of surprise. On this first day of fighting at least, the street boys had done all of that to their advantage.

Connors rested the empty drum by his feet, peering down the dark street at the thin line of kerosene he had left behind. He handed his cigarette lighter to the oldest of the two boys. "Check the time on your watch," he told him. "Wait ten minutes and then drop a light right where I'm standing."

The boy nodded, clutching the lighter in the palm of his right hand.

"Then run to the rooftop and send out one of the pigeons with the message for the others," Connors said.

"We know," the boy said impatiently. "Nunzia's told us this a number of times."

Connors turned and glared at him. "And we're going to keep telling you until you can give it to me backwards," he said. "The idea's not just to do it, but to do it and get out alive. Once the Nazis see the light from the flames, they're going to start shooting. And it won't be at me or at Nunzia. It'll be at you."

Nunzia put an arm around the boys. "They're as afraid as we are," she said in softer tones. "They're just trying not to show it."

Connors looked at her for several seconds and then turned to the boys. "Make sure your feet are clear of the gas line," he said, his manner calmer. "Drop the lighter and when you run, make sure to keep your heads down. Run at normal speed, even when you hear the gunfire. You'll conserve energy and get a lot farther if you do it that way. Panic always slows you down."

"What if there are Germans on the path?" the youngest boy asked. He was about twelve, his dark eyes thick as craters, his face freckled and innocent.

"Then you plan as you go," Connors said. "Look for a sewer and jump in. Find a tree and climb it. You have to be able to do something they can't do. That'll keep you safe."

"Maybe I should stay with them," Nunzia said. "You know the streets well enough by now to get around on your own."

Connors looked at the boys and then back at Nunzia. "No," he said. "We hold to the plan."

"The idea is to keep them alive," Nunzia said.

"The idea is to keep everybody alive," Connors said.

"*Ho capito,*" the oldest boy said, gazing up at Nunzia and giving her a big smile. He was fourteen, sleek of build, with short clipped hair and a long row of missing teeth. "The American worries for you," he said.

"All we have to do is drop the lighter and run," the younger boy said, clasping his right hand inside her warm grasp. "Even I can do something that easy. And I have Valerio with me. There's no need to worry."

"If the road is blocked off, make for the hillside," Nunzia said. "It's too dark for them to follow you up there."

"Don't be afraid to use your guns if you have to," Connors told them. "But only if you have to."

Nunzia gave them each a hug and then turned to follow Connors, both fading into the shadows. "Everybody falls in love in Naples," Valerio said, shaking his head. "Even Americans."

Vincenzo, still wet and chilled from his swim and a run up a side road, stood alongside Maldini, watching as Connors and Nunzia approached from a side street on their left. As he ran, Connors looked at his watch and silently ticked down the seconds.

"Now," he whispered.

The tank explosion lit up the harbor below them, a rich bubble of flames hurtling toward a starless sky. A ship alarm sounded and lights were turned on up and down the pier, all working off the single genera- tor the Nazis had activated. "We should have cut off their electrical," Connors said, shaking his head. "Then they wouldn't know which way to look. My mistake."

"A mistake that won't matter, American," Vincenzo said, "soon as the bomb on the tanker goes off."

"It should have gone off already," Connors said. "It was timed to go with the tank. That was two minutes ago."

"Be patient," Maldini said.

A dozen soldiers with machine guns lined the perimeter of the pier, crouched down and waiting to shoot at the slightest movement. Two tanks came rumbling down Via Acton and three others were speeding across Via C. Colombo, all primed to protect the port and the oil tanker. "That bomb doesn't go, we'll never get another shot at that fuel," Connors said.

"The bomb will work," Vincenzo said.

"I'll have an easier time believing that, General, after I hear a loud explosion," Connors said, his voice a mixture of anger and frustration. "But right now, all I see is one tank down and lots of ticked off Nazis."

Maldini sat on a large rock and stared at all the activity on the pier. Off in the distance, they heard the blasts from Nazi tanks and the rum- ble of buildings that fell and crumbled. The streets of Naples were now a series of bonfires as the enemy assault continued into the late-night hours. "No matter what we do to them, they have won," he said. "They have defeated Naples. If they leave on their own or are chased out, they have won."

"You can't defeat a city, Papa, until you defeat its people," Nunzia said. "The Nazis have destroyed Naples, but they have not destroyed us."

"There is no great victory to achieve," Maldini said. "No matter what, those that remain will stand on piles of rubble as we watch the Nazis leave."

Connors stood on a bluff and looked down at the burning streets, his binoculars resting on a knot of grass by his side. "It makes no military sense, what they're doing," he said. "It's not about holding a position or strengthening a defense. None of that comes into play here. It's only anger and hate that fuel their actions. The Nazis don't fight to win. They fight to destroy."

"Get some rest," Nunzia said, "all of you. Futile or not, we have more battles to fight tomorrow."

Vincenzo walked farther down the hill, crouched on his knees and stared at the oil tanker, tears flowing along the sides of his face. In his right hand, he held a small statute of San Gennaro. The saint's arms were spread out and a peaceful smile crossed his face.

The massive force of the blast knocked Maldini off the rock and sent him rolling down a short hill. Nunzia was tossed next to a pile of rocks. Connors jumped to his feet, rifle at the ready. Vincenzo sat on the edge of the hill, his fingers digging into the dirt, the statue of San Gennaro at his side, his face lit from the glow of the blast below.

The oil tanker split and rose halfway out of the water, thick plumes of bright orange flames lighting the harbor clear through to the islands that dotted the shoreline. The round mushroom cloud that rose from the center of the tanker bellowed high into the nighttime sky, casting its glow along the main drag of Lungomare. The explosion sent the tanks alongside the ship hurtling down empty streets, bouncing along the cobblestones like a child's toys.

Vincenzo picked up the statue of San Gennaro and brought it to his lips, giving the patron saint a soft kiss. He stood and raised his arms and then turned to Connors, smiling broadly. "I told you," Vincenzo shouted. "I told you the bomb would work!"

"What the hell took so long?" Connors asked, returning the boy's gleeful smile.

"The watch was set on Naples time," a still sleepy Maldini said. "It went off when it felt like it."

They stood on the edge of the hill, staring down at the destruction they had leveled against the Nazi invaders. Around the city the tanks were now still and silent, the attention of Nazi commanders and soldiers riveted on the flaming lights of the port. But from the tunnels, sewers and empty gardens that dotted the Neapolitan landscape, the sound of happy children echoed along the empty streets.

"We will have our victory," Vincenzo said, looking down with bright eyes at the port he had helped destroy.

THE SECOND DAY

13

THE ROYAL PALACE

Von Klaus stared out an open window, gazing down at the empty streets toward the port where the tanker still smoldered and burned. Behind him Kunnalt paced the marble floor, hands at his back, head bowed. "Do we have enough fuel to do what must be done and still make it to Rome?" Von Klaus asked without moving.

"Only if we reduce the number of tanks we send into the city," Kunnalt said.

Von Klaus turned away from the window and stared at the officer.

"We must complete our mission," he said. "These homes, these churches. They must be destroyed."

"There is a way, sir," Kunnalt said. "It will allow us to do that and still conserve our fuel."

Von Klaus stepped away from the window and walked over toward the map stretched out across the polished oak dining table. "Show me," he ordered.

Kunnalt hovered over the map and repositioned three of the stick figures. "They live and hide in the sewers, most of them in the central part of the city," he said. "This allows them to move from street to street undetected. If we strip them of that, we strip them of their only advantage."

"And how would you do that?" Von Klaus asked, his eyes firmly on the map.

"We need to firebomb the sewers and tunnels," Kunnalt said in matter-of-fact tones. "Burn the city from below instead of from above. That's where they are hiding and that's where they'll die."

Von Klaus looked away from the map and stared at Kunnalt for several seconds. He then lowered his head and walked back to the window. "These children are as much an enemy to us as any we've faced, sir," Kunnalt said. "They must be dealt with."

"In all our years together, Kunnalt, we've yet to have a tainted victory," Von Klaus said, gazing once again at the ruined tanker. "Let's not make this our first."

14

SAN PAOLO MAGGIORE

It was just before dawn, the streets a mixture of dark smoke and light mist. Connors, a machine gun hanging over his right shoulder, walked past downed buildings and smoldering homes, assessing the damage one day's fighting had wrought and anticipating the severity of the Nazi response. Nunzia walked beside him, arms at her sides, her pace relaxed. He looked over at her, the black hair dangling across the front of her face, her eyes bright and alert, her body shapely and athletic, and wondered if he would ever again be so close to someone as beautiful.

She stopped in front of an ornate double flight of steps leading to a two-tier church with large stone columns. She gripped a stone railing and stared across the divide at a statue of a saint, his arms open, head tilted toward the sky.

"It does makes you wonder," Connors said. "All these bombs falling and tanks blasting away. Most of the buildings fall in a heap. But these churches take the hit, catch a couple of dents here and there, but still stand."

"This was our church," Nunzia said, gazing up at the chiseled entryway. "Where my family came to hear mass. And where I came to pray when I needed an extra favor from Mama or Papa."

"It pay off?" Connors asked.

"Only with Papa," Nunzia said. "He was the softer of the two. It took a lot more than a prayer to make Mama do something she didn't want to do."

"It was just the opposite with me," Connors said. "My mom was like butter in the sun. A smile and a hug and she'd pretty much give you anything. It would take a lot more than that to make my dad budge."

"In Naples, the men talk loud enough to be heard," Nunzia said with a shrug. "But it is the women who make the rules."

Connors stepped closer to Nunzia. "That would be all right by me," he said.

Nunzia looked up into his handsome face, her eyes searching beyond the shell of the hardened soldier, looking for the small-town boy many miles from home who missed the warmth of a family as much as she did. She rested a hand on his cheek and he held it there, his fingers rubbing against the tops of hers. He lowered his head, she raised hers and they kissed, the sun behind them rising over the smoldering city. They held the kiss, letting silence and passion rule the moment, drowning the visions of battles and of friends and family members long since gone. For those sweet brief seconds, they were alone and far removed from any war.

"What happens to you after this?" she asked, still only inches from his face. "Do you get to go home?"

Connors shook his head. "Not for a while," he said.

"Do you have a *fidanzata* that waits?" she asked.

Connors smiled. "That mean a girlfriend?" he asked. "If it does, the answer's no."

"It will happen," she said.

"Why are you so sure of that?" he asked.

"You're a good man," Nunzia said with a warm smile. "It's always easy for a good man to find someone to love."

The rush of machine-gun bullets ended their moment of peace.

The bullets pinged against the thick stone wall just beneath the landing where Connors and Nunzia stood. They both tumbled to a higher step, Connors sheltering Nunzia's body with the back of his as he whirled his machine gun from behind his shoulder and into his hands. "Shots are coming from that corner on the left," he said, peering beyond the stairs. "Too soon to make out how many there are."

Nunzia pulled a gun from behind her waistband and cocked it. "Their shots will warn the others," she said. "We need to get them off the streets."

Connors looked up at the curved stone stairwell that led to the church entrance. "You run as fast and as low as you can into that church," he told her. "I'll give you more than enough cover. Just keep moving." He reached for her hand and held it tight. "No matter what, Nunzia. Just keep moving."

"You better do the same," she said to him.

Connors looked over the break in the landing and spotted the end of a machine-gun barrel poised against the side of a wall across from the church. He braced his gun against his arm and turned to Nunzia. "I'll meet you by the altar," he said.

Nunzia ran up the dozen steps, her body crouched down low, gun in hand. Connors was right behind her, firing into the walls of the building across the way. The return fire was heavy, leaving little doubt that there was more than one soldier aiming down at them. They reached the top of the landing, ten feet of open space between them and the front door. Connors stood behind a thick marble column, Nunzia on the ground next to him. He jammed in a fresh ammo clip and pulled a grenade from the back of his belt. "How many can you see?" she asked, wiping soot from her eyes and peering inside the empty church.

"There's at least two," Connors said. "Probably not more than three. It's hard to clip any of them from here. They're just shooting blind, hoping to hit one of us with a stray. I'll have a clearer line on them once we're in the church."

"Let me have the grenade," Nunzia said. "I won't be able to throw it as far, but you can give better cover to me than I can to you."

Connors handed her the grenade and then crouched down, resting the barrel of his gun against the ancient stone of the column. "I'm going to step out into the open," Connors said. "Give them a target to shoot at. When I do, you pull the pin, count to three and let it go."

"This now makes two things I've never done before this morning," Nunzia said, gazing up at Connors and moving to her knees, the fingers of her left hand curled gently around the grenade pin in her right.

"What was the first?" Connors asked, stepping away from the column and looking down at her.

"I had never kissed a man," she said, looking back for a brief second and giving him a warm smile. She then pulled the pin, held the grenade and tossed it toward the row of buildings on the corner. Connors jumped from the shadow of the column and ripped a series of bullets against the hidden Nazis, clipping off shards of stone and sending pockets of dust into the air.

The grenade blast shattered storefront glass and sent cobblestones sprawling toward the sky, a thick white puff of smoke hiding the Nazis in its midst. Connors and Nunzia turned and ran for the cover of the darkened church, bullets hitting the cement and walls around them. They stepped inside, holding hands and moving as one down the center aisle, the sounds of their rushed footsteps echoing off the walls of a building that was first erected in the eighth century.

They dove behind the main altar, checking the ammo supply in their weapons and resting their backs against the thick marble for support. Three German soldiers riddled the front entryway with bullets as they ran into the church, the heavy pounding of their footsteps coming at them from separate directions. Connors peered around the edges of the altar, through the smoke and haze, the shadows from the lit candles tipping him to the enemy position. The Germans, hiding behind wooden chairs and marble columns, fired heavy barrages up into the altar, their bullets zinging off ancient stone and statues, dust and debris raining down on Connors and Nunzia. "There a back way out?" he asked, covering her as best he could.

"To the right," she said. "There's a flight of stairs next to the confessional. It leads to an alley."

Connors checked the distance from the altar to the steps and then looked out at the Nazis. One was on his far left, crouched down behind a statue of the Blessed Mother. The second was flat down on his stomach, his gun poised between two hard-back chairs. The third was closest to the confessional and was the one he most needed to take out. "We're going to make a run at those stairs," Connors said to Nunzia. "I'll lead. You follow. And if I go down, don't stop running."

"I won't leave you here," she said.

"Don't think of it that way," Connors said, shoving an extra ammo clip into his jacket pocket. "You get out, you can get help and bail me out of this jam."

Nunzia clicked the hammer on her gun and held it across her waist. "No," she said. "I won't do it."

"Nunzia, there isn't any time to argue," Connors said, his low voice filled with frustration.

"Then don't waste any," she said, staring into his face.

Connors and Nunzia leaped down from the altar and ran for the confessional and the stairs thirty feet away, bullets coming at them from three sides. Connors paused at the base of the steps and sprayed his fire in three directions, the empty church now reduced to nothing more than a fire zone. Nunzia slipped to her knees and fired two shots down the center aisle, wounding the soldier hidden behind the chairs. Connors emptied his clip at the soldier to his far left, three of the bullets finding their mark, catching him in the chest and neck. He reached down, grabbed Nunzia up with his right hand and they continued their run toward the dark safety of the stairwell. "Don't stop and don't look back," he shouted. "I'll be right behind you."

They reached the top of the stairs, Nunzia two steps down. Connors turned, fresh clip in his machine gun, and fired toward the third Nazi coming at them from the right aisle. He looked to make sure Nunzia was well on her way, peering into the darkness, hearing nothing but the clapping of shoes against stone steps. Connors turned back toward the church, one leg on the top step, and caught the full force of a German soldier landing on top of him, hitting with a thud against his chest, a six-inch knife held tight in his right hand. Connors and the Nazi fell backwards down the long flight of steps, their bodies bouncing off the hard surface, the German frantically trying to lift his knife and plunge it into Connors. The machine gun slipped from the American's grip, falling into the dark well below.

The Nazi, his right arm raised, the knife hovering just above Connors, gazed down at the American soldier, both of them washed in sweat. Connors held the Nazi's elbow, his head hanging down off one of the steps, the weight of the German pressed against his chest. The Nazi broke Connors's hold and plunged the knife deep into his shoulder, the blade ripping through his uniform, digging into skin and muscle. Connors let out a loud and painful grunt that echoed down the empty staircase, his angry eyes glaring up at the smiling Nazi above him, young and eager to finish off his enemy. He could feel the warm flow of blood coming out of the wound, the strength seeping out of his system, his sweat turning cold.

The bullet came up from out of the darkness and landed in the center of the Nazi's forehead.

His body shook slightly, fingers now loose around the hard end of the knife, and a thin line of blood flowed down the center of his face. His head tilted off to the left and fell forward, landing on top of Connors with a soft moan, the top of his pith helmet jammed under the American's chin. His back arched up at an angle as he coughed out his last breath.

Connors reared and tossed the German off his chest and watched the body slide down the steps next to him. He glanced at the wound, the knife still embedded in his shoulder, blood flowing down the front of his jacket and onto his pants. He looked above him and saw Nunzia's face smiling down at him, smoking gun still in her hand. "Why do I waste time giving you orders?" he asked, relieved to see her there.

"You always forget," Nunzia said. "I'm a Neapolitan. We never listen to anybody."

15

VIA DELLA MARINELLA

The small basement room was dark and dank, the foul smell of soiled sheets and musty furniture filling the air. Connors, washed down in sweat and blood, lay on top of a brown mattress, the wound red and swollen, the knife resting on a tiny end table next to him. Maldini and Vincenzo hovered over him, both watching Nunzia cleanse the wound with a mixture of red wine and kerosene. Connors opened his eyes, his vision blurred, and looked up when he felt Maldini's warm hand on top of his own. "I need to close your wound," Maldini said to him in hushed tones. "It's very deep."

"You mean stitch it?" Connors asked, his throat parched and dry and his voice coarse. His gaze was on Nunzia now, the warmth of her look easing the sting of the mixture she was rubbing on his cut.

"That, only a doctor can do," Maldini said shaking his head. "But I can stop the bleeding and prevent it from becoming infected."

Connors kept his eyes on Nunzia. "How?" he asked.

"We drench a cloth in gasoline," Nunzia said. "We place it over your cut and we light it."

"You need to trust us on this," Vincenzo said. "Much as we have trusted you."

Connors lifted his head off the wet pillow and looked up at Maldini. "How many times have you done something like this?" he asked.

"You will be my first patient," Maldini said as he lit a cigarette in the already stuffy room.

Vincenzo stood on top of the bed, hunched over, both his arms wrapped around Connors's chest. Maldini dumped a long strip of cloth, thick at the top and frayed at the bottom, into a coffee tin half-filled with gasoline. He left the cloth to soak, stood and unbuckled his thin leather belt, freed it from its slots and folded it in two. "Put this in your mouth," he said to Connors, resting the belt against his chin. "This way, when you start to scream, you won't swallow your tongue."

Connors let the beads of sweat drip off his eyelids and smiled. "What makes you so sure I'll scream?" he said.

"You might not," Maldini said. "But I'm going to scream and I'm only guessing how painful it's going to be. So it's better to have one scream than two. Less for the Nazis to hear."

"Maybe you should have been a doctor after all," Connors said. "You have such a calm and natural bedside manner."

Maldini nodded and patted the young soldier's hand. "I promise I'll do my best," he said.

He jammed the belt between Connors's clenched teeth, wiped the palm of his hands on the sides of his pants and then blessed himself. "I thought you didn't believe in any of that?" Vincenzo asked.

Maldini shrugged and pointed at Connors. "Maybe God hasn't given up on him the way he has on me," he said.

He pulled the wet cloth out of the coffee can, gasoline dripping on the mattress and the front of Connors's uniform. He took the thick wad and, with one hand, stuffed it into the open wound, letting the strands hang down on the soldier's chest. He saw Connors flinch from the pain and his eyes tear from the burn of gasoline penetrating the raw cut. He looked up at Nunzia. "Take his hands," he told her. "Hold them tight and don't let them go until the flames are out."

Maldini took a deep breath and then placed the lit end of the cigarette against the loose strands of cloth. He watched as they quickly caught, sending thin lines of smoke and fire heading up toward the wound. He leaned over and gently turned Connors's face away from the flames. "Look into my daughter's eyes," he said in a low voice. "And try to forget you are here."

Connors bolted when the fire reached the thick wad of cloth, Vincenzo and Maldini struggling to hold him down, his fingers digging into Nunzia's soft hands. His face was cherry red and his teeth were cutting down into the folded belt, blood flowing off his gums and lower lip. A rich line of red and blue flames shot out from the wound, the drenched cloth quickly turning black, light, crisp shards flowing in the air. The hole around the cut was burned and smoking, the smell of flesh mixing uncomfortably with that of gasoline. Connors spit out the remains of the belt, fluttered his eyes, lowered his head and sank farther down into the mattress.

"I think you killed him," Vincenzo said as he released his grip on the soldier.

Maldini pulled out the remnants of the burnt cloth and glanced down at the wound, brushing aside the thin lines of smoke. He looked up at Nunzia and nodded. "That's the best we can do with what we have," he told her. "It's not going to bleed anymore. It'll be very sore, but he'll be able to move in a few hours."

"Is it okay to bandage it?" she asked.

"First rub some cream around the edges and pour some of that powdered medicine inside the wound," Maldini said. "That should help it heal. And stay with him. I'll go with Vincenzo and check on the others."

Vincenzo jumped off the bed, his eyes on the now sleeping Connors, the heat and smell of the room enough to overwhelm. He reached down for his rifle and stood next to Nunzia. "If I ever get shot and you find me," he told her, "I want you to promise me something."

"What?" Nunzia asked, her eyes glued on Connors.

"You won't let your father anywhere near me," Vincenzo said.

He took a final look at Connors and stepped out of the room.

The room was bathed in darkness, but tiny lines of sun tried to inch their way through the wooden shutters. Nunzia sat on the bed, the curve of her body wedged in alongside Connors, close enough to let the sweat from his uniform stain the back of her dress. She wiped his forehead with the fat end of a rolled-up rag. She stared down at him, the strong, handsome face caked with lines of soot and specks of dried blood, the wound in his shoulder torched and swollen, white circles of foam bubbling around the edges.

Nunzia reached across the bed and picked up a round mound of cloth. She unfurled it and tore off a dozen large strips, resting them on her knees. She dipped two fingers of her right hand into a half-empty jar of petroleum jelly and stroked the sides of the open wound with them, moving with a warm and gentle touch. She then ripped off the top of a powder pack and poured its contents into the cut's hollow center, watching the white dust disappear into the dark pocket. She covered the cut with the large cloth strips, running them around his shoulder, tying the frayed edges into small knots to keep the bandage in its place.

Nunzia rubbed a warm hand against the side of Connors's cold cheek and held it there for several quiet moments. She then reached down and kissed both his forehead and his lips. She gazed down at him a final time, leaned over and blew out the small candle on the side of the end table. She stood, walked to the far side of the bed and lay down next to him, one arm resting on his shoulder, her hand keeping the wound warm.

In the darkness of the room, Connors opened his eyes and smiled.

16

PALAZZO MARIGLIANO

Nazi soldiers crowded into the three-tiered courtyard, skillfully enclosed by cornices and friezes. The soldiers sprayed the lower and upper windows with machine-gun bullets and smoke bombs, looking to force out any street boys hiding behind its walls. Two of the soldiers entered a darkened hallway on the far left side of the palazzo, walking past the floating smoke, their boots crunching down on shattered glass. One of them looked down and through the haze saw two small shadows in silhouette braced against a pile of stones. He clicked the chamber of his gun and turned it toward the shadows.

Dante and Fabrizio held their breath, their fingers gripping the cold rocks, their bodies wedged in as deep as they could go. They closed their eyes when they heard the soldier stop, only inches from where they stood. Dante gently slid a hand across the stone and to the small of his back, his fingers gripping the barrel of an old target pistol. He turned his head and looked at Fabrizio, shivering with fear, his bare feet sliding on the cold mud. He tapped the small boy on the shoulder and pointed toward the far side of the entryway.

Fabrizio looked up at Dante and shook his head, too afraid to move. Dante pulled the gun from the back of his pants, grabbed Fabrizio by the arm and they both came out into the alley, several feet behind the Nazi. "Run!" he shouted to the little boy.

The Nazi swirled around and fired at the two fleeing boys, his bullets landing on dirt and stone. He gave chase, trying to zero in on his zigzagging targets, both heading for a bolted iron door at the end of the dark passage. Behind them a loud whistle blew, alerting other soldiers in the area. Dante was the first to reach the door, but was unable to turn its massive and rusty handle. He turned, saw the Nazi in the distance and grabbed Fabrizio. "Jump up on my shoulders," he told the smaller boy. "And reach for the railing above you. That'll bring you to safety."

"What will you do?" Fabrizio asked, his lower lip trembling.

"I'll stay and fight the soldier," Dante said, jamming the gun back into the flat of his back.

"Put me down," Fabrizio said. "And let me fight with you."

Dante stared into the boy's olive eyes and kissed his cheek. "What kind of an Italian would I be if I let something happen to the best foot-ball player in all Naples?" he asked. "You go, Fabrizio, and let me worry about the Nazi."

He lifted the boy to his shoulders, clutched his ankles and steered him toward the base of the railing, the Nazi's footsteps now a hundred yards away. "Stretch as far as you can," Dante said, looking down into the mist, the tips of the boy's toes digging into the sides of his neck.

Fabrizio's fingers pawed at the bottom of the railing, missing the bars by inches. He then crouched farther down on Dante's shoulders and jumped, grabbing onto the black iron rails with both hands. "I have it," he said, pulling himself up and over the side, his back to a shuttered window.

Dante turned and saw the German soldier standing across from him, the nozzle of the machine gun pointed at his chest.

The boy put his hands at his back, fingers wedged on the handle of the gun. The soldier glanced above him and saw Fabrizio pull up one of the slants on the wooden shutters, struggling to reach the inside handle. The Nazi lifted his gun and aimed it up toward the small boy.

The mastiff came from out of the shadows.

He jumped and caught the soldier at chest level, the force of his weight sending them both to the ground, and throwing the machine gun up against a far wall. The mastiff, his growl loud and full, thick white foam spreading down the sides of his face, clasped his open jaw be-tween the soldier's shoulder and neck, his sharp teeth easily ripping through the collar of the uniform and shredding exposed skin and mus-cle. The soldier lifted his arm to push him off, but couldn't budge the mastiff, who stood on rear paws and shook his powerful grip from side to side, treating the soldier like a large, overstuffed puppet.

Dante ran for the machine gun and tossed it up the railing toward

Fabrizio. The boy caught it with both hands, his back pressed against the shutter slants, his eyes glued to the action ten feet below. "Use the end of the gun like a hammer," Dante said to him. "Once you get inside, run to the front of the building and head for the sewers. They can't reach you there."

"Come with me," Fabrizio said.

"I can't make the jump," Dante said. "There's a fence in the next alley. I'll get to that and make for the tunnels. Don't worry about me."

"What about Benito?" Fabrizio asked.

"Who?" Dante asked.

"The dog, *cretino*," Fabrizio said, frantically pointing down at the mastiff, still gnawing at the Nazi's neck, the soldier slower now to react, the loss of blood heavy, flowing off his uniform and onto the grimy side street. "You have to take him with you and keep him safe."

Dante reached down and gently nudged the mastiff off the dead soldier. "He doesn't look like he needs help from anybody."

17

VIA DEI TRIBUNALI

Maldini and Vincenzo stared up at the long row of silent trams, their overhead electrical wires cut and dismantled. The dark base of the transit cars was tinged with rust and stained from lack of use, and the compartments were filled with dust and debris. Half were missing wheels, either blown off or stolen by black marketers.

"We could use these to block off a few of the alleys," Maldini said. "That would leave the tanks only one way out, and we can block that end with mines."

"They can't move without current," Vincenzo said. "And not even Marconi could get us that."

"We might be able to push them," Maldini said. "Jam the gears into neutral and slide them down the tracks toward the alleys."

"Even if we could do that, how do we get them from the tracks to the alleys?" Vincenzo asked.

Maldini walked around one of the trams, his hand caressing the red-painted side panel. The trams had once been an integral part of the city's life, an inexpensive and comfortable way to travel, connecting rich neighborhood to poor; working-class homes to shops and factories; relatives to one another. He had sat in their straw seats or held on to their iron poles since he was a child, handing his lira to the ticket taker in the rear or, on occasion, sneaking onto the back of a crowded tram curving its way along the Lungomare district. Couples met and fell in love riding the trams, old women caught up on the day's news, men debated local politics. They were as much a part of the Naples scenery as the bay, the train station and the open-air markets and made the city seem a much smaller and friendlier place.

Maldini turned away from the tram and looked across at Vincenzo. "We drag them there," he said. "We have enough boys and we have a jeep. All we need is some rope to toss over the top and pull them down. How hard can that be to find?"

Vincenzo looked away from Maldini and turned toward the long span of trams. "They would make better barricades than the wooden ones we have," he said. "The tanks just run right through them."

"These trams may be old, but they were built well and with care," Maldini said, a hint of pride in his voice. "The tanks can get over them, but it will take extra fuel and a lot of effort. It will also leave their bellies exposed and give the boys time to jam either a mine or a grenade inside the tire rims."

"Even with a jeep and the ropes, it'll be hard to move trams from the tracks to the alleys," Vincenzo said, shaking his head and looking over Maldini's shoulder, across the wide stretch of Lungomare, at the seven dark entrances that led into the heart of the main square. "That's at least a half-mile drag."

"They'll slide better if we grease the side riding on the street," Maldini said. "We'll send some of the boys to scoop up mud and sludge from the edges of the piers and wipe them across the tram. It'll cut down on the friction."

"It has to be done in daylight. We need to be able to see what we're moving and keep an eye out for any tanks coming at us."

"Which of the boys knows the most about engines?" Maldini asked.

"Gaspare, by far. His father owned an auto-body shop and he's been playing with cars and motors since he was in diapers. But I don't know how much help he'll be. Driving a Fiat One Twenty-four down Via Toledo isn't the same as shifting gears on a dead tram."

"Gears are gears," Maldini said. "If he can figure out the engine of a car, he should be able to find which wires to pull on an old bus."

"And if he can't?"

"Then we'll push them along the tracks," Maldini said in a firm voice.

"That's not much of a plan," Vincenzo said.

"We're not much of an army," Maldini said.

Dante and Pepe sat in a corner off one of the alleys, each putting to-gether the parts to a makeshift bomb. Fabrizio and the mastiff stood behind them, their backs resting on a brick wall. The two boys looked up from their work and caught a glimpse of Vincenzo and Maldini walking be-side the trams. "What great plan are they thinking up now?" Pepe asked.

"I don't know," Dante said. "But it better be a good one. We're run-ning low on supplies and there are more Nazis than ever out on the streets."

"Nothing would happen to us," Fabrizio said, "if we had a patch like the American does."

"Is that why you have a picture of a bird on your shirt?" Dante asked. "To keep you safe?"

Fabrizio looked down at a crudely colored charcoal drawing of a Thunderbird on the sleeve of his shirt and nodded. "I only wish it was a real one," he said.

"What difference would a patch make?" Dante asked.

"It's a magic bird," Fabrizio said, crouching down to face the boys, his voice hushed. "I heard Vincenzo and Maldini talk about it. The bird on his sleeve is called a Thunderbird. It can make it rain bullets and can kill soldiers with bolts of lightning and blasts of thunder."

"Maybe it's why the Americans always win their wars," Pepe said with a shrug.

"But now we can have it, too," Fabrizio said. "And none of us need to die."

"Tell that to the Nazis," Dante said.

"There aren't any Thunderbirds in Naples," Pepe said. "Only pigeons. And they have no magic powers."

"It's a nice idea, though," Dante said. "To have a bird who could bring us guns and bullets. That would be a great way to fight."

"You'll see," Fabrizio said, standing now and petting the mastiff. "It's true. We just need to wear the patch and then nothing can harm us."

18

MUSEO ARCHEOLOGICO NAZIONALE

Six Panzer tanks engulfed the square, gun turrets facing the massive two-story red-stone structure. Fifty soldiers were lined along the perimeter, running thin lines of cable from the street to the brick walls and lodging them in place with plastic explosives. Von Klaus stood in the opening of his tank, looking up to the sky, his cap removed, sun washing rays of warmth on his clear face. "If nothing else, I'll miss this Italian weather," he said to Kunnalt, across from him in the next tank.

"Nonetheless, sir, it will be good to get back home," Kunnalt said. "We've been in the field for so long, I forget what it's like not to wake up on hard ground."

"The bed will be warm, even if the temperature outside isn't," Von Klaus said with a smile. "It'll happen soon enough. Once we're finished with the destruction of this city we can return home, to be present at the destruction of our own."

Kunnalt lowered his gaze for several seconds, his mind flashing briefly on images of friends and family all soon to face the brutal intrusion of a war they had for so long managed to keep a safe distance away. Kunnalt had witnessed the ravages of daily battle for the last several years. As a military man, he was prepared, both mentally and physically, to endure the hardships and cope with the death and ruin that a war always leaves in its wake. But those bodies belonged to strangers and the soil they fell on was always foreign. Soon, the faces of the dead would be familiar and the land left in flames would be his own. Kunnalt knew the limits of his makeup. He was a hard soldier, but a soft man and the very thought of such moments left him shaken.

"Once we're finished here," Von Klaus said, snapping the younger soldier back to the present, "I want the main units to work their way toward the center of the city."

"There's nothing left there, sir, but a few empty homes and some churches," Kunnalt said.

"Which mean nothing to us," Von Klaus said. "But they mean a great deal to these waywards killing our soldiers. Those are their homes and their churches, in the center that is the very core of their city. We may not be here long enough to crush their spirit, but we must do all we can to break their hearts."

"Is that our goal, sir?" Kunnalt asked.

"We weren't meant to leave here draped in glory," Von Klaus said. "Blood and dust will be our medals."

A long line of street boys stood along the edges of the museum roof, staring down at the soldiers closing in. Their hands were wrapped in cloth and there were huge pots of boiling water resting by their feet.

"Wait until they get to the steps," one of the boys shouted down the line. "Then lift the pots and drop the water over the side."

A dozen soldiers marched toward the stone steps that led up to the ornate double doors, three of them lugging fuel packs and flame throwers. Above them, the boys struggled with the cumbersome pots, lifting them up to the edge, hot water splashing on their chests and arms. Behind them, two of the younger street boys checked on the pots resting above the smoldering fires in the center of the roof. "Try and hang on a few more seconds," the lead boy said, the bulk of his pot teetering on the edge, his eyes focused on the Nazis moving up the steps. "They're just about where we need them."

"I can't hold it up any longer," another boy moaned. "It's starting to burn through the cloth on my hands."

"Then let's give them a shower," the lead boy ordered. "Keep your feet planted. We only want the water to go over. Not any of us."

The boiling water cascaded down in streams, landing in the center of the walkway, just inches beyond the steps, soaking and scalding the soldiers caught in its wake. The boys turned away from the edge, running toward the other side of the roof where a small row of thick ropes lay curled in a corner, one end tied around the base of the bell tower. The boys unfurled the ropes and jumped off the side of the museum, leaving behind the pots and the smoking fires.

Von Klaus glared up at the rooftop and then turned to look down at his soldiers as they scattered away from the museum entrance. "There are many things from which a soldier should cower, Kunnalt," he said, in a low tone ripe with anger. "Water is not one of them."

Three of the soldiers bent on one knee and aimed their machine guns at the rooftop, their bullets chipping the curved stone. Three others ran back up the stairs, heading for the closed front door that led into the wide marble entryway. Another small unit followed, urged on by the frantic waves of both Kunnalt and Von Klaus. The lead soldier stopped in front of the door and riddled the ancient iron design with bullets. He then reached out for the silver-encrusted handle and yanked it open.

The explosion sent the door flying out toward the steps, a large unguided iron missile, landing across the upper bodies of three soldiers. Four others lay dead, spread out across the smoke-filled entrance. Von Klaus pounded at the side of his tank with a closed fist, more frustrated than angry at the successful street tactics of the boys. "They must all be found, Kunnalt," he said, his military demeanor broken by the site of the dead soldiers spread out before him. "This cannot be allowed to continue."

Claudio and Angela each wrapped a hand around the thin stem of the pine tree, hidden from view by both height and the sharp, thick-hanging leaves around them. Their free hands held a machine gun, pointed down toward the Nazi soldiers and tanks below.

"I'm so afraid of heights," Claudio said, his face squeezed against the side of the tree. "I can't even remember how I climbed up here."

"Getting up was the hard part," Angela said, holding on to her side with just the fingers of her right hand, checking the activity below. "Getting down will be easy."

"How *do* we get down?" Claudio asked. "I didn't even think about that part."

"We cither jump or get shot down," Angela said.

Claudio closed his eyes and rested his head against the side of the tree. "We'll never survive the fall," he said in a low voice.

Angela looked across the wide piazza, at the other street boys hiding in the cover of the dozen pine trees that lined the museum. She turned back to Claudio and gently tapped the side of his hand. "Get ready," she said. "It's almost time."

The young street boy took a deep breath and cocked his German-manufactured machine gun. "How far away can we aim?" he asked.

"I've never used one of these before," she said, holding up her machine gun. "My guess is that it doesn't go as far as a rifle. I would target those closest. There are enough of us in the trees to deal with all the soldiers in the square."

"You don't seem as nervous as I am," Claudio said. "And you're a girl. I'm sorry you got stuck with someone who gets scared so easy."

"You're who I want to be with," Angela said, giving the younger boy a smile. "No one else. In Forcella, it was always the ones who talked tough that never really gave you the good fight and shivered when real trouble started. The scared ones were always the ones with the most courage."

"Then, you're lucky," Claudio said, returning the smile. "Because there's no one out here as scared as I am."

The small garden cemetery was across the piazza from the museum, pine trees giving shade to six rows of headstones, many of whose markings had faded along with the years. A dozen soldiers were marching along the path, heading toward the chaos in the main square, their manner rigid, their machine guns off their shoulders, gazing up at the rooftops for shadows that were no longer there. As they walked past the locked gate of the cemetery, with a short iron fence lined with small bushes and sunflowers, two of the soldiers turned their heads and looked across at the headstones, many of them tilted back toward the sky. They also noticed the short row of freshly dug graves, spare of any markings, dirt piled about six inches high, and stepped closer.

As they approached the gate, the dirt moved and then parted as Vincenzo, Maldini, Pepe and Nunzia jumped out from under the graves, rifles and machine guns in their hands. They aimed and fired at the surprised Nazi unit, caught off guard and with their weapons at their sides. The four separated and kept up their fire, using the surrounding trees and gravestones as cover. Maldini was next to Vincenzo, spread out on the brown dirt, his head against a stone marker. He fired off a string of bullets and watched as the boy pulled the pin on a grenade and tossed it over his shoulder toward the unit. They were covered in dirt, dark patches clinging to their hair and necks. "What book did you get this idea from?" Maldini asked, smiling as he dodged a flurry of bullets.

"*Dracula*," Vincenzo said, returning the fire and the smile. "It's one of my favorites."

Pepe fired a round from his rifle and then stepped back toward the trees, staring out at the square in front of the museum, now a raging firestorm between the street boys and the Nazis. Tanks sent shells hurtling in all directions, soldiers shot up into the trees and the adjoining hills. Flame throwers torched the walls of the buildings in the area, leaving behind scorched rock and fallen bodies. The piazza was a cauldron of fire and debris, the screams of the wounded and dying filling the air along with the smoke and flames. Pepe rested his head against the back of a pine tree and closed his eyes, shuddering from the sight of his first full battle.

Nunzia crawled up alongside him, one hand on her rifle, the other reaching out for the frightened boy. Pepe opened his eyes and looked over at her, warmed by her touch. "I can't watch it anymore," he said.

"None of us can, Pepe," she said, her eyes etched with a sadness that ventured beyond her years. "None of us were meant to see such sights. But it's here now and we can't hide from it."

"I used to come here all the time," Pepe said, flinching from a loud explosion off to his left. "With my teachers and the other kids from school. We'd eat our lunch by the fountain and then spend the afternoon in the museum. The rooms were dark and cool. They were filled with what a boy would want to see. Now I'll never be able to come here again."

"You'll be back, Pepe," Nunzia said, her voice strong, her eyes seeing only the boy, ignoring the smoke and the bullets aimed her way. "And it'll be a place of peace once again. For you and your friends."

"Why are they doing this to us?" Pepe asked, his words weighted down. "Why do they hate us so much?"

"Some people hate without reason." Nunzia glanced up as a quartet of soldiers ran past the cemetery. "Which then gives us all the reasons we need to fight back."

"I'm sorry," Pepe said in a sad, little boy's voice. "I try to be more like Vincenzo and Franco, but it's so hard. They have so much more courage."

"You have a machine gun in your hands and you're fighting Nazis. I don't know how much braver a boy could be."

Pepe turned his head, inched away from the tree and looked out at the square surrounding the museum. Panzer tanks fired heavy shells in all directions, sending parts of buildings toward the morning sky. Grenades flew through the air like windblown leaves, leaving behind a destructive trail of flame, waste and casualties. Bodies lined the piazza, boys in tattered clothes resting next to soldiers in full battle gear. He took a deep breath and turned back to Nunzia and then, lurking over the curve of the graves and the floating lines of smoke, he saw the shadow of the Nazi soldier.

Pepe kept his eyes on Nunzia, fear taking a huge step back to danger, and gripped the arms of the machine gun he held in his hands. The shadow drew closer. Pepe glanced at the end of the cemetery and saw the front half of a black boot and the tilted barrel of a rifle heading their way.

Nunzia saw the soldier's image cross past Pepe's legs. She looked up at the boy and gave him a firm nod. She whirled on the ground, turned from her chest to her back and fired. Pepe jumped to his feet and pumped machine-gun shells into the center of the shadow. The shots drowned out the soldier's low screams and moans. He fell to the ground face forward, his right arm embracing an old headstone, his legs folded at an angle. Nunzia looked up at Pepe, the smoking gun still coiled in his hands, the boy's inner fears intermingling with a determined resolve. She got to her feet, walked over to the soldier and stripped him of rifle and ammo belt. Pepe stood behind her, his tender eyes following her every move. "Are you okay?" he asked.

Nunzia smiled at Pepe and placed an arm around his shoulders. "I've never felt safer," she said.

Dante and Gaspare were pinned in, their backs to the museum wall, three Nazi rifles aimed at their chest. The middle soldier, three stripes running down the sides of his uniform arm, signaled them to drop their weapons. He fired a bullet above their heads to serve as fair warning. "If we drop our weapons," Dante said, "they will kill us."

"They'll kill us no matter what we do," Gaspare said. "Look around. I don't see any prisoners, only bodies."

"We can't take three of them," Dante said, gripping the hunting rifle in his hand, as the soldiers moved in closer.

"We're lucky if we can take one of them. But if you shoot at anyone, make it the one in the center. He seems the most eager to kill us."

"We could run," Dante said, eyeing the alley to his right. "The way we are now, it's just target practice for them."

"They're too close to run away from. But they're getting close enough for us to run at."

"And then what?"

"They won't be expecting us to rush them," Gaspare said. "And if we can just get one or two on the ground, we might be able to get out of this alive."

"Are you sure that's what we should do?" Dante asked.

"It's all I can think of," Gaspare said.

Dante looked over at Gaspare and nodded. He tossed his rifle to the ground by his feet and raised his hands. Gaspare swallowed hard and did the same. Both boys stepped away from the wall, moving forward on wobbly legs. The Nazis lowered their rifles and closed in on them, eyeing them cautiously, one of them smiling, exposing a low line of crooked teeth. "You two are smarter than the others were," the soldier said to them in choppy Italian, arching his head toward the piazza behind him. "You know that you're too young to die."

"Everyone's too young to die," Dante said, lowering his head and bracing his body for the rush.

They were less than ten feet apart when Gaspare and Dante dropped their arms and bolted toward the three soldiers.

Gaspare caught the middle one chest high, the rifle wedged between them, and the two fell backward in a dusty stumble, the soldier slipping on the mangled stone under his feet. Dante pounced on the Nazi to his right, grabbing for the rifle, turning the butt end away from his body and pushing it down toward the ground. The third soldier, free from any of the entanglements surrounding him, put aside his rifle and pulled out a handgun. He pointed it at Dante's back, watching the boy struggle with might and conviction with a man twice his weight and height.

Gaspare was down on the ground, the Nazi's knees keeping his arms pinned, his fingers scraping against rocks and dirt. Two crisp punches landed flush to the side of his face, instantly causing his right eye to swell. He struggled to move, but the bulkier man's body was too difficult to budge. Gaspare looked up, stared into the soldier's hard, shark-gray eyes and turned his head, barely dodging a third blow aimed at his face. He glanced across at Dante, deep in the midst of his own intense fight, his opponent quick to take the advantage that his age and superior strength ensured.

The Nazi grabbed Dante by the throat, thick fingers of a massive hand squeezing the skin below his jaw, turning the boy's face pepper red. He held him out at arm's length and looked at the soldier with the handgun. "Shoot the little bastard," he said.

The soldier nodded and cocked his gun, easing his finger onto the curved trigger. The boy clasped his hands around the Nazi's wrist, trying to pry free from the hold. "Stay still," the soldier said to him, voice dripping with contempt. "And die as you were meant to die. With a bullet to your back."

Dante, the strength sapping from his body, leaned his face closer to the Nazi and sent a stream of spit into his eyes. The lid snapped on the soldier's temper. He threw the boy down to the ground, his head bouncing off the hard cobblestones. He wiped the spittle from his face and picked his rifle up from the ground. He pushed aside the soldier with the handgun and stood towering over the frightened boy. He stomped a heavy boot on his chest and forced open the boy's mouth with the thin end of his rifle. "Cry if you want," the soldier said to Dante. "It won't bother me."

The bullet caught the Nazi at the base of his neck, just below the thin edge of his pith helmet. His eyes opened wide, his mouth flushed out a stream of blood and his hands fell limp at his sides, the rifle tumbling to the ground. The soldier dropped to his knees and his head sank. The soldier on top of Gaspare jumped to his feet and reached for his rifle, looking up to the trees for sight of the shooter. He aimed toward the thick, spiked leaves of the pines and fired off two rounds. The first return shot nicked him in the arm, the second grazed the side of his right leg, catching more cloth than skin.

The third put a dent in his forehead.

The Nazi dropped like a puppet cut free of his strings, his face resting only inches from Gaspare, his eyes swollen shut, blood from his nose and mouth flowing down onto the front of his dirty white shirt. The third soldier looked up to the trees, down to the two fallen soldiers and then at the two boys, one prone and bleeding, the other on his knees with a German rifle in his hands. He aimed the cocked pistol at Gaspare, his grip not as hard, his demeanor no longer as confident as it was mere seconds earlier, before a volley of shots from unseen rifles had brought down two men in his unit. He fired two shots at Gaspare, the boy dodging the wayward bullets, gathering all his remaining strength to turn his body to the side, his battered face falling off the edge of the curb.

Dante gave the trigger a hard squeeze, the force of the rifle causing him to shuffle his feet, his shoulder feeling the bump from the butt end of the recoil. He dropped the rifle as soon as he saw the look on the soldier's face. He was only twelve years old but had seen enough of death in that short span of time to know when its arrival was at hand. He walked away from the soldier, ignored the thud of his fall, stepped over the bodies of the other two dead Nazis and bent down to lift Gaspare's head gently off the hard stones. He wiped at the streams of blood coming down the sides of the boy's face with the palms of his hands, eager to ease his pain. "You did well," Gaspare said to him, speaking slowly through a ripped lower lip, his voice tight and raspy.

Dante nodded and removed his torn shirt, pressing it against the side of Gaspare's face. Up to their right, Angela and Claudio slid down from the top edges of the pine tree and walked toward them. The street girl, machine gun casually slung over her shoulder, glanced at the three dead Nazis stretched across the edge of the square and then turned to the two boys. "Gaspare needs to be moved to one of the tunnels," she said to Dante. "The one near Via Toledo is the closest. Take Claudio with you and use only the side streets. Take all the Nazi guns and ammo belts, too. This way, if you come into trouble, you have what you need to fight back."

"Why don't you come with us?" Dante asked. "There's nothing much more we can do here."

Angela turned and looked around the square, the smoke from burning tanks and the wails of the wounded touching the sky. There were three tanks and a dozen soldiers still battling with Maldini and a handful of street boys scattered through the piazza. "I'll stay until it's over," she said. "You help get them where they need to go."

"We would have died if it wasn't for you," Gaspare said, helped to his feet by Claudio and Dante.

"That's probably true," Angela said, looking down at the dead Nazis.

Dante stripped the soldiers of their weapons, gazing up at Angela to nod his thanks. The girl looked back at him and smiled. Claudio lifted one of Gaspare's arms and wrapped it around his shoulders and they started to walk toward a side street, their backs to the field of fire. "You be careful," Dante said to Angela as he turned to follow them.

"I come from Forcella," Angela said as she held the smile and watched him go. "We're too tough to die."

19

VIA DELLA MARINELLA

Connors, Vincenzo and Franco walked down the quiet street, placing kerosene bottles and grenades behind darkened stairwells and around the bend of the alleys.

"We're running low on these," Vincenzo said, hiding a bottle under a wooden crate next to a smoldering building.

"We're making up for it with the grenades," Connors said. "And they do just as much damage."

"And as long as we don't run out of Nazis," Vincenzo said, "we won't run out of grenades."

"Where do you live?" Franco asked Connors. "In America?"

"A town called Covington," Connors said, checking the street behind him. "It's in Kentucky."

"Is that in New York?" Franco asked.

"Not even close," Connors said. "It's outside Cincinnati."

"And is that in New York?" Franco asked.

Connors looked at the boy and shook his head. "No," he said. "It's not in New York."

"If you ask an Italian what's in America, he will say New York and California," Vincenzo said. "It's all we know."

"Well, Covington isn't anywhere near either one of those places," Connors said, resting down the last of his grenades. "But it is close to Cleveland. And Detroit. And Kansas City. And St. Louis. Have you heard of any of those cities?"

"No," Franco said. "I haven't even heard of a saint named Louis."

"Wait, I know one," Connors said, snapping the fingers of his right hand. "It's not far from Chicago. You must have heard of Chicago."

Vincenzo and Franco looked at one another and laughed. "Chicago?" Vincenzo said. "You have a city in America called Chicago?"

"Yes, we do," Connors said, confused by the laughter. "And it's a pretty big one, too. Bigger than any city you've got here in Italy."

The two boys shook their heads and laughed even harder. "Wait until Maldini hears this one," Vincenzo said.

"Are you going to tell me or not?" Connors asked.

"In Neapolitan, the word 'Chicago' means 'I shit,'" Franco said.

Connors paused for a few seconds and then joined in their laughter. "Really?"

"Yes," Franco said. "Really."

"Well, they do call it the windy city," Connors said.

"With good reason," Vincenzo said.

20

The long-abandoned pier was shuttered and dark, the noon sun unable to crack through the old slabs of wood and thick piles of rock that framed the walls. Carlo Petroni stood in the center of the high-ceilinged room, his shoes resting on the damp floor, his back to the distant sea, his eyes peering into shadow. He turned his head when he heard the heavy footsteps behind him. "A light wouldn't be a bad idea," Carlo said. "I always like to know who I'm talking to."

"It's wartime." It was a male voice, clearly American, standing less than ten feet away. "You can't always get what you want."

"I came like I said I would," Carlo said. "At noon, alone and without a gun."

Connors stepped out of the shadows and stood next to Carlo. "You also made mention of a tank," he said. "And I don't happen to see one here, do you?"

"It would be stupid to bring it here," Carlo said. He maintained his calm manner, carefully taking note of the soldier hovering over him. He caught sight of the dried blood on his jacket and the bandaged wound below it. "It's where we can both get to it. If that's what we decide."

"It would also be stupid of you to lie about it," Connors said. "Franco doesn't trust you. Vincenzo doesn't know you, and from what little I've seen, I don't like you. Which leaves you lots of room to improve your situation."

"I'm a thief," Carlo said with a matter-of-fact shrug. "That makes it easy for you and your friends not to trust me or want to know me or even like me. But if you want to hear the truth, most of the boys you have fighting the Nazis out on those streets are thieves, same as me."

"They stole because they had to," Connors said, stepping closer to Carlo, his wound still stinging. "You and your band did it because you wanted to. To me, that's a big difference."

"But you'd take a tank from me, thief or not," Carlo said, smiling in the darkness. "So it doesn't matter what I am. What matters is what I have."

"Why'd you bother to take the tank in the first place?" Connors asked. "You don't strike me as a kid who'd risk his life to take on the Nazis. And there's nothing left in Naples to steal. So, what's a tank get you?"

"I want the Nazis out of Naples as much as any of your street boys," Carlo said. "Just because I don't cry when I pass a church or have sad stories to share with you doesn't mean I care any less than they do."

"What do you want for it?" Connors asked.

"I can be a help in what you're trying to do," Carlo said. "I can get in to see the Nazi colonel."

He was neither intimidated nor afraid of the precarious route he was attempting to navigate. He was born into a life of crime and could handle the difficult workings of negotiation and survival with the skill of a seasoned professional. In the shadowy darkness of the pier hole, he had seen enough to weigh and measure the intellect and cunning of the soldier hovering above him. He saw Connors as a battle-hardened veteran, dangerous on the field and capable of dealing with the most vicious of enemies. But he also figured him to lack the skills that were needed to live and eat on the streets of a city like Naples, to fend daily for food and to fight off the predators who had marked the dark territories as their own. Carlo knew that in the open trenches of deceit, a criminal always held the upper hand. "And I can get in to see you," he continued, his bravado running in the red zone. "You have no one on your side who can do both."

Connors took a deep breath and then several steps back, turning away from Carlo. "No deal," he said to the boy, his head down, hands by his side. "You can be on our side or theirs, but I'm not going to let you work both. It's a bad game to play, especially in a war. The only one who comes out ahead is you."

"You're making a poor decision and a big mistake," Carlo said, surprised at the savvy the soldier was exhibiting.

"I told him the same thing, but the American is a stubborn man." Vincenzo's voice came from the other side of the pier, hidden deep against a back wall. Carlo turned, his eyes narrowed, one hand holding a pistol pulled from his pants pocket, trying to pinpoint the other boy's location. "I told him there was only one price a traitor is allowed to pay in Naples. But he chose to spare your life in exchange for your tank."

"If I can't have it both ways, then neither can you," Carlo said, aiming the pistol in the direction of Vincenzo's voice. "You get me and the tank or you get nothing. And either way, I'll get to watch you die."

"We already have your tank," Vincenzo said, stepping forward, Franco walking slowly by his side.

Carlo lowered his gun, trying to quickly gauge whether what he had just heard was bluff or truth. "You wouldn't even know where to find it," he said. "I may be a thief, but you're a liar. You don't have anything, especially not my tank."

The doors to the pier swung open and the sun bolted through.

Carlo shielded his eyes from the rays, the tip of his hand braced across his forehead. Vincenzo and Franco stood by his side, all three boys staring out at the German tank parked between the two iron doors, Maldini waving from the open pit. Connors walked past them, heading toward the tank, rifle draped over his shoulder, his pith helmet hanging on the barrel. He turned and stared at Carlo, who was visibly shaken. "I'm just a bystander in all this," Connors said, a sly smile on his face. "But if I had to guess, I'd say you're not the best thief in Naples."

"You should go now," Vincenzo told Carlo, looking at the boy with open scorn. "The colonel will want to know he's lost one of his tanks. It's better if he hears such bad news from a good friend."

Connors leaned against one side of the tank, smoking a cigarette, his rifle and helmet by his feet. He was staring at Dante, sitting by the front of the tank, a piece of charcoal in his right hand, etching a sketch on a flat, thin foil of paper. Maldini watched from the mouth of the tank, his face cupped in the palm of his hand, his eyes filled with admiration.

"Some day, my little friend, your work will hang in galleries," Maldini said. "But for now, it helps us figure a way to go on."

The boy looked up at Connors and pointed to his drawing. "What do you call that in English?" he asked.

"A catapult," Connors said, tossing the cigarette aside and crunching down on his knees next to Dante. "I used to see them in those Robin Hood movies with Errol Flynn. They caused the Sheriff of Nottingham and his troops a ton of trouble."

"It will cause the Nazis even more," Vincenzo said.

"Robin Hood was a great Italian," Claudio said. "The best with a sword. Even better than Zorro."

"There's no way Robin Hood was Italian," Connors said. "He was English. He lived in Sherwood Forest. That's not in Italy. That's in England."

"I saw the movie," Claudio said. "He spoke Italian. His men did, too."

"They change the voice in the movies," Connors said. "They make the actors sound Italian. But they're not."

"How do you know they didn't change the voice in your country?" Dante asked. "To make you think he was English."

"He wasn't Italian and he wasn't English," Vincenzo said. "Neither were his men. They were myths. They didn't exist. Not here and not in England."

"What about Robin Hood's catapult?" Maldini said, smiling down at them from the tank. "We all know from the movies it can stop men. But can it stop a tank?"

"If there was something heavy enough inside," Connors said. "And if you can get your shot off high and at an angle, I suppose it can do some damage. But you're going to need something more than rocks."

"What if there was a bomb in it?" Vincenzo asked, looking from Maldini to Connors. "We collected one hundred and fifty bombs from the squares. So far, we've used about sixty of the cylinders. A few haven't gone off, but most of them have. If we get lucky and put the right bomb inside the catapult, it could destroy a tank."

"And the Nazis won't know which ones are good and which are bad until they hit ground," Maldini said. "Which means no matter what, if they see a bomb coming their way, they have to go the other way."

"We're forgetting something here," Connors said. "We don't have a catapult. Least not one that I've seen."

"You'll see one soon," Maldini said. "We have plenty of wood, rope and wheels and a dozen boys working to put them all together in an old barn behind the Rione Villa. They should be finished by nightfall."

"Those bombs weigh at least four hundred pounds each, if not more," Connors said, noting the quiet confidence of Maldini and the boys. "You're going to need something in the sling that can hold and release that kind of weight."

Maldini jumped down from the tank and stood between Connors and Vincenzo. "The Nazis helped us with that," he said. "The last night of the bombing, they hit the church of Gesù Vecchio and blew out the bell tower. The bells landed in the square, a little dented but in one piece. They're more than heavy enough to center the catapult and release the bomb."

"First, the Nazis went up against our mines, grenades and rifles," Franco said. "Now we add a bomb and a tank. We get stronger as they get weaker."

"Don't get carried away just yet," Connors warned. "Up to now they've been spread out across the city. With the tanker gone, they're going to tighten the units, bring the fight closer to the center of town. They'll try to squeeze us in a circle, force us to stay in one place longer and drag the fight out until it's to their advantage. It's easier to handle them in small groups; you can hit quick and run fast. The bigger the units, the tougher it gets to do damage without losing a lot of boys."

"There is still time to make changes to our plan," Vincenzo said. "Franco has the carrier pigeons all in place. They can get word out in less than an hour."

"We're going to have to move quicker than that," Connors said. "We need to react to what they're doing and we won't know how until we know what they're doing. The plan will have to change on the fly, which means we don't have less than an hour. We have about fifteen minutes."

"We need more than pigeons to get that done," Maldini said.

Connors spread apart his feet and looked down at the manhole cover below. "What we need are these sewers," he said. "We use the pigeons in the air and Angela's little crew of sewer rats underground. That'll be our line of communication and we keep it open all the time. Get a rotation set up and never stop it. All the boys will know exactly what's being done and where, every second of this battle. We keep all the surprises on the Nazi end."

"We can talk to each other and the Nazis will never see it," Vincenzo said. "We'll be above them and below, invisible."

"Franco, how far can your pigeons go with a message and come back with an answer?" Connors asked.

"A hundred miles," Franco said.

"Who do they fly to?"

"They head for the closest coop in the area," Franco said. "From there, it's up to the messenger."

"How far do you need them to go?" Maldini asked.

"Salerno," Connors said.

21

OSPEDALE DEGLI INCURABILI

Two long rows of beds were lined against both sides of the wall. Small wooden tables were positioned between each bed, a burning candle resting on each, bringing light and shadow into the large room on the top floor of the oldest hospital in Naples. The two dozen beds were filled with children, thin white sheets pressed up against their necks. A number of them had IV drips taped to their arms. Yellow signs with a black circle in the center were taped above the beds, a signal that the children had an illness that was beyond cure.

The Nazi officer and three soldiers, each holding a full canister of gasoline, stood with their backs to the thick wood door that led into the room. They had taken the elevator up from the basement, switching on a back-up generator to put the machines in motion. The officer stiffened when he saw the signs and inhaled the acid aroma of disease. He signaled the men forward with a wave of his wrist, careful not to rest his hands on anything in the room. "Burn it down," he said in a husky voice, "and end their misery."

The three soldiers hesitated, their eyes fixed on the sleeping children. "Make sure you coat the walls as well as the floors," the officer ordered them, oblivious to their unease.

"This is a ward for incurables, sir," one said, careful to hide the disdain he felt at the order. "These children will die in a matter of days."

"They will die in a matter of minutes," the officer snarled back. "This entire hospital will be scattered to the ground and left in ashes. It's filled with people who carry contagious disease. Leaving it alone would be a danger to our men. Not even those sent to evacuate this hellish place had the nerve to walk in here. Which leaves it for us to handle. This is our job and you will obey my orders."

"Yes, sir," the soldier said. He nodded his head at the other two men by his side and walked with them down the center aisle toward the rear of the room.

They began to pour gas on the floors and walls. Each soldier carefully avoided looking at the sleeping children; each moved slowly and silently, filled with dread at the notion of waking anyone from his painless rest. The officer stood by the wall closest to the door and surveyed the scene. He put an unfiltered cigarette to his lips and clicked open the top half of a lighter. He put the blue white flame to the dark tobacco, watching his three men working their way toward the center of the room, a thin line of smoke reaching past his eye and up toward the ceiling.

He inhaled, held the smoke and the breath when he felt the cold steel of a gun barrel push against the side of his neck. "I really hope you understand what I have to say," the voice behind him said. "Because if you don't, you're going to die and never really get the chance to know why."

"What do you want?" the officer asked in clear tones of school-taught English.

"It helps to be educated," Connors said. He unclipped the officer's side holster, pulled out his pistol and inched him back deeper against the wall. "Have your boys put down the canisters and slide their weapons and belts toward you. And just in case they don't give a rat's ass whether *you* live or die, let them know there are three rifles pointed at their backs ready to sever their spines if they don't do what they're told."

"There are dozens of soldiers spread all over the hospital," the officer said, trying to glance over his shoulder at Connors. "Once they hear shooting, they'll come running. You won't last a minute."

"I don't know how long I'll last," Connors said. "I guess it all depends on how good a safety vest you turn out to be. I figure between the uniform and your body, I can hold off at least ten, fifteen stray shots before I have to toss you aside."

The officer swallowed hard and moved his head slightly, trying to lessen the pressure on his neck caused by the gun barrel, and shouted out his command. The soldiers looked up, peering into the darkness around them, then lowered the canisters to the wood floor, their hands and the fronts of their uniforms wet with gasoline. They undid the clips around their ammo belts, letting them fall to the ground with a muffled thump, and stepped forward. They held out their rifles and crouched down.

"Tell the tall guy in the center to slide them over to your right, next to the door," Connors said. "Rifles first, then the ammo."

The officer stiffened, the muscles around his back and arms tightening, his eyes fixed on his men. "And if I refuse?" he asked, the cigarette in his mouth burning down to the quick. "You don't have it in you to shoot me, not like this. Unarmed and with my back to you. It goes against everything you Americans believe in."

Connors cocked the gun and pushed the barrel harder against the officer's neck. "If those rifles and packs aren't next to my feet the next time I look down, you're going to be able to smoke through your throat." His words were low and hard. "Right now, that's about all I believe in."

The officer let the remnant of his cigarette slip out of his mouth and ordered the silent soldiers to do as requested. Connors watched as the rifles and ammo packs landed against the wall next to his boots. He then stepped away from the officer and shoved him toward the three soldiers. "Fold your hands and rest them on the back of your heads," Connors ordered. "And don't forget what I told you. There's a rifle scope on your every move."

Vincenzo and Angela came out from behind one of the beds, their clothes reeking of gasoline. "You find a place?" Connors asked.

Vincenzo nodded as he pulled off his shirt and threw it over his shoulder. "The Museo Pignatelli," he said. "On the second floor there's an empty room about this size. The children can be put there and we can leave two of the boys behind to watch over them. Allow them to die in peace."

"Any of them contagious?" Connors asked.

"No," Angela said. "We put up those signs during the evacuation, so the Nazis would leave them alone."

"Let's move it then," Connors said, staring down at the row of beds filled with children wasted away by disease. "We got about ten minutes to get these kids out of here. Do it fast and do it quiet. If anyone spots us, just keep going and leave it to me. You two stay with the kids and keep them covered."

Vincenzo ran toward the closest bed, rested the IV drip on its side next to the sick child, stood behind the iron bar and rolled it over toward Connors and Angela. "The elevator is down the hall and to the left," he said. "It can hold two beds at a time. That makes six trips in all."

"Get moving," Connors said, looking at Angela as she walked closer to the four Nazis in the center of the room. "I'll catch up to you."

Angela walked with deliberate steps, her dark oval eyes focused on the officer in the center, the bottoms of her shoes drenched in gasoline. She held a pistol in her right hand.

"Grab one of those beds and follow Vincenzo," Connors told her. "He's waiting for us."

"What are you going to do about them?" she asked, without turning, her eyes never wavering from the officer.

"What do you want me to do?" Connors asked.

"They were going to burn a room filled with dying children," Angela said, her words rushing out, her anger beyond anyone's grasp. "I think the same punishment should be given to them."

Connors shook his head and rested a hand on Angela's back. "You don't really think that."

Angela turned her face and stared up at Connors. "They're Nazis," she said.

"But you're not," Connors told her.

Angela turned back to the Germans. She stepped up closer to the officer, their eyes locked, each viewing the other with sheer contempt. Angela jammed the pistol in his stomach. "I want so much to kill you," she whispered.

"But you can't," the officer said, his expression fearless and smug. "The American spoke the truth. You're not a Nazi and, in the end, that will be your downfall."

"Angela, get the kids out of here," Connors ordered. He was standing over her, his rifle curled in his hands. "We can't leave Vincenzo waiting too long. He's exposed out there."

Angela lowered her head and pulled the gun away. She turned, walked toward one of the beds and began to roll it to the elevator. The officer watched her leave and then turned to Connors, his eyes brimming with scorn. "You can't win a war if you're not prepared to rid yourself of the enemy," he said. "It's a harsh lesson the Italians are much too weak to learn."

"Would it have bothered you at all to set fire to these kids?" Connors asked. "Letting them die that way?"

"No," the officer answered with a slight smile. "It would only have bothered me not to do it."

Connors glared at him and nodded. "That's good for me to know," he said in a low voice. He took several steps back and waited as three street boys emerged from the shadows, rifles in hand. "Gennaro, you stay and keep an eye on our friends," he ordered the oldest boy. "Claudio, you start moving the beds toward the elevator."

"What about me?" Gaspare asked. His eyes were still red and swollen from his scuffle in the piazza.

"Grab the guns and the ammo belts over by the back door and get them out of here," Connors said. "Don't be afraid to use them if you have to."

The boys moved into position, the wheels of the beds gliding softly along the gas-drenched wooden floor. Connors ran down the hall and toward the elevator door, held open by an impatient Vincenzo. "Start heading down," Connors said, waving him on his way. "I'll take the stairs. If they try to hit you at the door, I can come at them from the side. If that happens, you and Angela fire at them from your end and move the elevator back up."

Vincenzo slid the black iron gates shut and stepped back, careful not to dislodge the IV needle in the arm of the dying boy by his side. He looked across at Angela, squeezed in against the far wall, her eyes staring down at a silent, raven-haired girl in the bed mustering all her strength to give a weak smile. The girl brushed aside her hair and Angela leaned down and kissed her damp forehead. "Where are you taking us?" the child asked, her dry voice pained by every word.

"Away from the Nazis," Angela said.

The elevator landed on the main floor. Vincenzo unlatched the hook and swung open the black gate. He grabbed his rifle and turned to Angela. "Wait," he whispered. "When I wave, move the beds out, one at a time."

Vincenzo stepped into the main hallway at the rear of the hospital, three candles in the middle of a small wooden table the only light available, and looked for moving shadows at both ends. The door to the stairwell next to the open elevator swung open and Connors stepped out. "Get the kids out and then send it right back up," he told Vincenzo. "Claudio and Gennaro will swing in the next two and we just keep the rotation going until we get all twelve down here."

"We'll be moving toward the ramp in the back," Vincenzo said, pointing just past Connors's right shoulder. "Once we get outside, we'll be fine. We can use the alleys and side streets to get to where we need to go."

"There's only five of us," Connors said. "And there's twelve beds that need to be moved through the streets. How you going to make that work?"

"Let me worry about that," Vincenzo said, turning away. "You just worry about the soldiers. There's got to be at least fifty of them in the hospital. And then there's the four tanks covering the front."

"They're here to kill people who can't move," Connors said, his voice dripping with anger and bitterness. "They're not expecting any bullets coming their way."

Vincenzo watched Angela wheel the first of the beds out of the elevator and reached in to pull out the second. "Do you want me to stay with you?" he asked Connors. "In case they come at you from more than one side?"

"You stay with the kids," Connors said, stepping into the elevator, staring down at the sick child. "There's something I need to take care of before I leave."

The tank commander signaled an all-clear and fired the first shell into the center of the hospital. The blast buckled the fourteenth-century structure, sending large stone cinders and thick chunks of glass hurtling to the base of the square below. Smoke and flames shot up the stairwells and engulfed the halls. Connors braced himself against the cold marble of a far wall, his eyes on the four Nazis standing across from him in the now-empty ward. It had taken six silent trips to strip the room of the sick children, bringing them down to the alleys and away from the scope of the Panzer tanks.

"It's still not too late for you to save yourself," the officer said to Connors, his voice now a distant echo. "They fully intend to bring this hospital crashing to the ground. And there's nothing left for you to do to prevent it."

Connors, a rifle in one hand and a cigarette in his mouth, stared down at his feet, the floors and the walls still wet and moist from the heavy splashes of gasoline. "I don't want to prevent it," Connors said, looking back up at the Nazi. Then he pulled the cigarette from his mouth, tossed it on the floor and saw the instant rush of flames lift and spread down the center of the room, chewing up the floorboards and crawling up the walls. "See you in hell," he said.

He walked out of the ward and shut the door behind him.

The beds were held together by belts and rope, moving three to a line, pulled down the barren streets of Naples by Vincenzo, Claudio, Gennaro, Gaspare and Angela. The group walked with heads bowed, all their strength needed to roll the shaky beds along the hard and rocky cobblestones. At their backs, thick plumes of black smoke rose toward the sky, telling them that the destruction of the hospital was under way.

They turned a corner, the wheels on the beds squeaking and vibrating with each hard spin, the loud and fiery explosions heating their backs, the heavy footsteps of Nazis echoing all around them. "We won't be able to get to the museum without running into soldiers," Gennaro said. He looked across his shoulder and down the deserted streets as he lugged the heavy beds toward safety, the skin around his small hands frayed and bleeding. "It will be hard to defend ourselves and keep the children safe."

"If the Nazis come at us," Vincenzo said, "we separate from the beds. Have them aim their fire at us, not at the children."

"We leave the beds out in the open?" Angela asked.

"We have no other choice," Vincenzo said. "You stay with them, duck down between the openings. If they start shooting at them, you fire back. But you keep down until that happens."

Claudio stopped, bucking the force of the rolling beds with his back. Five Nazi soldiers were running up the empty street toward them, rifles perched and ready. From behind them, they heard the pounding footsteps of three more, running at full gallop, each poised to kill. Vincenzo bolted away from the side of the beds, tossed himself to the ground, his elbows scraping the cobblestones, and began to fire his rifle. Gaspare, Gennaro and Claudio split and ran toward the shuttered doorways of an empty produce store for cover, firing their guns in both directions. Angela eased down between the sides of the beds, whispering words of comfort to the frightened children. The slant of the street kept them rolling at a slow pace toward the oncoming Nazis. The three Nazis running toward them from the far end of the street focused their attention on Vincenzo, firing a steady stream at the boy who was spared any cover. Vincenzo turned on his back and emptied his rifle toward the soldiers. He hit one at chest level, bringing him to his knees. Claudio and Gaspare fired machine gun shells at the five Nazis coming at them from above and Gennaro emptied his pistol, each looking to draw the fire away from Angela and the children in the beds. All of their shots missed their marks and they were forced to cower for cover as machine-gun bullets riddled the doorways of the buildings where they crouched.

The two soldiers were thirty feet away from Vincenzo, the boy down to his last two bullets, when Connors stepped out of a bombed-out bakery and aimed a machine gun their way, the volley of bullets taking down both Nazis. "Grab their guns and ammo belts," he shouted to Vincenzo. "Then go and back up Angela. I'll check on the other three."

Connors ran to the corner, gazed across at Angela huddled between the three long rows of beds, the faces of the kids under the sheets warmed by the sun, their eyes too weak even to glance at the firestorm around them. He stared at them for several seconds and then eased a grenade out of his clip and ran toward the three cornered boys. He stopped beside a stone wall, tossed the grenade to Claudio and pulled a second machine gun from behind his shoulder and began firing both at the five Nazis running at him down the empty street. "It's not a gift," he shouted out to Claudio who was staring at the grenade in his hand. "Pull the pin and throw it at them."

Claudio undid the pin and hurled the grenade toward the sky, forcing the Germans to scatter. The bomb landed several feet across from a fountain, the blast hurtling rocks and debris and killing one of the five. Connors fired the last of his rounds into the thick gray smoke, clipping off two more Nazis. He stood next to Claudio, Gennaro and Gaspare, pushing the boys back deeper into the doorway, keeping his eye out for the last of the soldiers.

Connors looked down at the empty machine gun in Gaspare's hands and then up at the boy's battered eyes. "You hit anybody with that yet?" he asked, smiling.

Gaspare shook his head and smiled back. "No," he said. "Unless you count the statues in the square."

"He's getting better," Claudio said. "At least now he's aiming the gun away from us and at the Nazis."

Connors handed one of his machine guns to Gaspare. "Here's a fresh one," he said.

"The last of the soldiers are hidden behind the fountain," Gennaro said, peering through the thinning smoke.

"You stay here and cover Vincenzo and Angela if they start to head that way," Connors said. "I'm going to circle around and see if I can make a move on them without getting spotted."

"Don't worry, American," Gaspare said, gripping the machine gun. "I'll shoot them if you do."

"That's sort of what I was counting on," Connors said, before disappearing around the bend of the building.

Vincenzo and Angela were huddled against the sides of two lumpy mattresses, their rifles wedged between the iron slants of the beds. Vincenzo, his knees bent and curled, watched as Angela wiped the brow of a sallow-faced boy. "*Grazie, signorina,*" the boy whispered.

"*Per niente,*" Angela said, looking down at him with warm, sad eyes.

"What does he have?" Vincenzo asked, checking to make sure the bottled IV continued to drip into the boy's arm.

"He's tubercular," she said, lowering her voice, her face masked by the lines of smoke coming at her from the hospital fire on the streets above. "They all are. It's a long and painful way to die. My brother died from it last year. They kept him in the same ward as these children. We had no money to get him medicine or anything to help with his pain. All that was left for my family to do was sit by his side and watch. Those weeks killed my mother as much as any bomb."

Vincenzo looked up at the remains of the burning hospital and shook his head, one hand gripping the side of the mattress. "Even if your family did have the money, the Blackshirts would have taken it from them," he said. "Before the Nazis, we were surrounded by thieves. Now, we're surrounded by murderers."

"You're wrong," the boy in the bed managed to say, struggling to lift his head, his sunken eyes staring straight at Vincenzo. "You're surrounded by friends."

Vincenzo looked over at the boy, touched by the generosity of his words and the strength it took to say them. He moved up closer to the side of the bed, inches from the boy's sweat-streaked face and kissed him gently on the forehead. The boy smiled and then rested a bony white hand on top of Vincenzo's, its touch cold despite the heat of the day.

The bullet ended their shared silent moment.

It landed between the beds, whizzing past Vincenzo and causing him to fall on top of the boy's frail frame for support. Vincenzo reached for his rifle, turned and stood next to Angela. It was Angela who caught the moving gleam of the rifle scope, bouncing off the rays of the sun. "Sniper!" she shouted, lifting her rifle above Vincenzo's head and shooting toward the rooftop to her left.

"We have to move the beds," Vincenzo ordered.

"We can't move them all." She emptied her rifle and reached into her back pockets for more shells.

Vincenzo left his rifle and a case of shells by her feet. "You keep shooting," he told her. "You need to keep his head down. I'll move the beds into the piazza. I just need to get close enough for our boys to see me. Then we'll have enough hands to move the children to the museum."

"What about the soldiers by the fountain?" Angela asked, spraying the rooftop with gunfire.

"We leave them to the American," Vincenzo said, starting to pull three of the beds. "He'll be in position before I can even get to the center of the square."

Angela braced her back against one of the beds, firing her rifle at the sniper, exposed to any open shot the Nazi could take. "Leave me," Vincenzo said. "Find some cover and keep that soldier's head down. I'll make sure the children are safe."

From the other end of the square, Connors had worked his way to the shaded side of a shuttered printing shop, the two Nazis behind the fountain less than thirty feet away. He glanced past the fountain and saw the three boys holding their position, exchanging heavy fire with the Nazis. Off to the right, he watched as Vincenzo struggled with the twelve beds, pushing them forward, Angela flat down on the ground behind him, shooting up at a German sniper. It was a miracle that none of the kids in the beds had been shot yet, and Connors knew that miracles didn't last very long in a firefight.

Connors jumped out into the open and drew the attention of the two soldiers. He fired and hit one, grazing his shoulder, and ran toward the other, bullets nipping at the dirt around his feet. He threw himself to the ground, rolled and came up on one knee, his machine gun pouring rounds at them both. He stopped when he saw one fall back into the empty fountain and the other flat on his face.

Claudio, Gennaro and Gaspare lowered their guns and with smiles as bright as morning walked out into the open square. Claudio and Gennaro were the first to see Vincenzo and ran to him, grabbing the reins on six of the beds and pulling them forward. Gaspare waved toward Connors who was running toward the boy, his eyes on Angela and the sniper on the roof. "Stay down, Gaspare!" he shouted. "Stay the hell down!"

"I did as you told me, American," the boy said, pumped with pride. "I held the gun and aimed it at the soldiers."

Connors was ten feet away when the shot rang out.

The bullet went through Gaspare's back and opened a small hole in his chest, the boy's smile still holding, a frozen glaze crossing his eyes. A line of blood formed in the corner of his mouth and his legs began to weaken. Connors caught him just as he was about to fall. "I'm sorry, American." Gaspare looked up at the soldier who held him gently and rocked him back and forth. "I wanted you to be proud of me."

"I am proud of you, kid," Connors said.

"Would I have become a good soldier?" Gaspare asked, closing his eyes to the sun, the circle of blood around his chest growing larger.

"You already are," Connors told him. "You're the platoon leader."

Gaspare managed a feeble salute and lowered his head, the boy's long war at an end.

Connors held him tight, his forehead on top of the boy's thick hair, his quiet tears mixing with the pool of blood forming at his waist. He looked up when he saw Vincenzo, Gennaro and Claudio pull up by his side with the dozen beds, each one of them in silent mourning as they stared down at the body of their friend. "Stay with him for a while," Connors said, resting the boy gently on the cobblestones. "I'll be right back."

Connors raced down the center of the square, nodding toward Angela, his machine gun aimed and firing at the rooftop. "Take my gun," he told the girl. "I'm going to smoke him out. When I do, you take him out."

The street girl clutched the machine gun, checked the clip and aimed it at her target. Connors unclipped two grenades and tossed them on opposite sides of the roof. The sniper stood when he saw the grenades land, casting a quick glance down at Connors and Angela. "He's yours," Connors whispered.

Angela emptied the clip into the sniper's chest. She ignored the two grenade blasts and kept squeezing the machine gun's trigger, the empty clicks the only sounds now heard in the silent, dusty square.

Connors walked with Gaspare's body cradled in his arms, an angry Vincenzo by his side. "We don't have time for this, American," he said. "We have to get the kids to the museum before this entire square is surrounded by even more Nazis."

"Then get them there," Connors said, walking at a racer's pace. "I don't remember asking for your help."

"I want to see my friend buried as much as you do," Vincenzo said, trying to soften his tone. "But it's too dangerous a risk to take. You should know that better than any one of us."

Connors stopped and turned to face Vincenzo. Claudio, Gennaro and Angela were several feet behind them, struggling with both the beds and their emotions. "He died like a soldier and he's going to be buried like one," he said. "And I don't know shit. If I did, there wouldn't be so many people dying around me."

"The Nazis will be here soon and they will kill these children and us along with them. Gaspare wouldn't want that to happen and you can't let it."

"Then get the hell out of my way and let me bury him," Connors said.

They buried him in a shallow grave in a grassy patch under the shadows of the museum and several rows of pine trees. Vincenzo, Claudio, Gennaro, Angela and Connors stood around the fresh grave, hands at their sides, their heads bowed, gurneys with the children in a tight circle around them. "One of you should say a prayer for him," Connors whispered.

"I thought you didn't believe in prayer," Vincenzo said in a sarcastic tone.

"I don't," Connors snapped back. "But he did."

Vincenzo looked over at Claudio and nodded. The children, including the sick ones in the beds, blessed themselves, folded their hands and closed their eyes, listening as the street boy sang the haunting words of the "Ave Maria," his voice filling the square with the echoes of his young and powerful sound.

22

PIAZZA MATTEOTTI

Nunzia sat at the small table in the kitchen of the first-floor apartment, a glass of red wine cupped between her hands. Connors sat across from her, loading an ammo clip into his rifle, still simmering from the events of the day. Nunzia studied his face, the unspoken resolve masking the innate sadness at the tragedy that engulfed him, clutching him in its horrid embrace. "None of this is new to us," she said in her customary soft tones. "We've lived with death for too many years, all of us, young and old. Every one of us that you meet has had to bury or leave behind someone we love. It's as much a part of our lives as this glass of wine."

"It's not new to me either." Connors looked up from his gun and gazed into her eyes. "I've seen my share of dying since I put on this uniform, a lot more than most. And it helps to put some steel inside your heart. But that's one soldier against another and, while you never like it, you learn to deal with it. I can't think of anything that gears a man up to stomach what they were going to do in that hospital to those kids. Or for watching an innocent boy, who had no kind of business being in a war, die in front of you. Once you see all that, I don't know how you shake it."

"There are many who can't," Nunzia said.

"You can't think about it," he said, "and you can't bury it. Those are hard rules to follow. I don't know if I have the kind of courage you need to keep moving and not lose hope. The boys have it, so does Angela and your dad. And so do you."

"We've made it hard for you just to be a soldier," Nunzia said, reaching a hand out to touch the top of his. "You've come to mean a lot to us and I think we've come to mean a great deal to you. That makes your job much more difficult. It's easier if you go into a fight not caring about the people who are involved."

Connors wrapped his fingers around her hand and leaned across the table, his face inches from hers. He pulled Nunzia gently toward him and kissed her under the flickering glow of the dwindling candle. She returned the kiss with a fevered passion and they slid slowly to the wooden floor, their arms wrapped tightly around one another, bodies brushing against the sides of the shaky old table. "There's a small cot in the back of the room," she whispered.

Connors covered her face with his hands, gently stroking her cheeks and neck, and nodded. They stood and walked together in silence into the dark emptiness of the room, leaving their guns at rest on the table behind them. They fell on the bed, Connors cradling her in his arms, their weight creasing the sides of the dusty feather mattress, their bodies entwined, the love that was inside both of them free to escape.

23

45TH THUNDERBIRD DIVISION HEADQUARTERS
SALERNO

The young soldier stood at attention, nervous eyes scanning the cramped tent filled with maps, chairs and crumpled papers. He was a relatively fresh recruit, on loan to the 45th to help ease the burden of the heavy losses they had sustained in the beach invasion of Salerno. He had been given little time to acclimate himself to the easy ways of a division that emphasized action over formality. There was no one soldier in Salerno who epitomized that attitude better than the commanding officer who sat across from him.

Captain Anders cast aside his briefing books and looked up from the poker table, a cigar jammed into a corner of his mouth. "All right," he said impatiently. "Let's hear it."

"One of the locals has brought in a pigeon, sir," the soldier said, trying not to stumble over any of the words. "Actually two of them."

"What's he want me to do?" Anders asked, confused. "Eat them?"

"No, sir," the soldier said. "They were carrier pigeons and the messages they were delivering are written in English."

"Did he give you the messages?"

"Yes, sir."

The soldier flipped open the front of his shirt and pulled out two rolled-up slivers of white paper. He handed them to Captain Anders, who snatched the sheets from him in mid-reach, unfurled the papers and read them both. When he looked up again, there was a wide smile across the captain's face.

"When did these come in?" he asked, jamming the sheets into his pants pocket and reaching for a pack of matches.

"Early this morning. It took the man a few hours to get anybody to listen to him, and then awhile longer for the unit to figure out who in command should get them."

"He still around?" Anders asked. "The man with the pigeons?"

"Yes, sir. He's down the hill a ways, waiting for me to return."

"And he's still got the birds with him?"

"Yes, sir. He asked if it was okay to feed them and give them some water while I was up here with you. I told him I didn't think it would be a problem."

"He can give them a steam bath and a shave if that's what they need," Anders said. "Just so long as they're ready to fly back out again in about ten minutes."

Anders sat down at the table and tore off two slips of paper from the bottom of a yellow legal pad. He slowly printed out a long series of words on each and rolled them up like cigarettes. He looked up and handed the papers to the young soldier. "Have him strap these on those pigeons," Anders told him. "And tell him to make sure they find their way back to Naples before dark."

"Do you want me to go with him to make sure he does as told, sir?" the soldier asked as he put the papers in his shirt pocket.

"The man went to a lot of trouble to find us," Anders answered, "when the easy thing could have been to stay home with the birds and toss the messages out. I think that's earned him a little trust. Don't you?"

"Yes, sir. I do."

"Then let's get it done," Anders ordered. "And before you go down to him, patch me through to air command."

"Yes, sir."

Anders stared at the young soldier as he saluted and left the tent. He put a match to his unlit cigar and took several deep puffs, filling the tight quarters with the gray smoke and pungent smell of Italian tobacco. He looked down at the map spread out across the table, small wooden stick figures serving as point markers, and flicked down the one that stood positioned over Naples. "We might end up taking that damn city without even seeing it," he whispered to himself. "And it would serve those Nazi bastards right. They can't let a Thunderbird come into a town and not expect him to give them more than a handful of trouble."

24

STAZIONE ZOOLOGICA E ACQUARIO

Eric Tippler lowered his high-powered rifle and stared down from the tower perch at a group of street boys as they turned a corner and walked in his direction. He pulled a white cotton handkerchief from his back pocket and wiped the dust from his glasses. He then raised the rifle, steadied it against the stone embankment and turned to the soldier next to him. "Pick one," he said.

Hans Zimmler stood behind Tippler, arms folded across his chest, one side of his head resting against the cool stone. "Tall one on the far right," he said.

"Head or heart?" Tippler asked.

"Make it more interesting than that," Zimmler said. "Arm first, then leg, then head."

Tippler looked away from the square and up at Zimmler. "It can't be done," he said. "Two shots are the most I can get off. The others will drag him away before I can get to a third."

"I'll make it worth it for you," Zimmler said. "I'll double our bet. Two cigarettes instead of the one."

Tippler leaned down farther, all but his head and arms resting on the hard rock floor, peering through his scope, targeting the hit. "Make it three," he said. "One for each shot I take."

Zimmler pulled three cigarettes from his shirt pocket and rested them next to the barrel of Tippler's rifle. "They're yours if the boy dies."

Tippler stiffened his body, from the neck down still as a statue, curled his finger around the trigger and squeezed off the first round. "Leg first," he muttered.

From his perch, Zimmler watched the street boy fall to the ground, both hands grasped around his kneecap. Two of the boys reached out for him, their arms stuffed under his, rushing to drag him to the safety of a brick archway. Tippler's second shot was fired less than one second later, bullet landing at the base of the wounded boy's shoulder and sending him reeling backwards, its force tossing one of the other boys face forward into the brown dirt of the square. "Last shot for the gold," the Nazi said as he pulled the trigger on the third and fatal bullet.

Tippler released his grip on the rifle and turned on his back, staring up at Zimmler, reaching behind him for one of the cigarettes he could now claim as his own. "Got a light?" he asked.

Zimmler tossed him a lighter, eyes still focused down on the square. "It seems there'll be no shortage of target practice for you today," he said, leaning forward and pointing at an array of street boys converging on the square from all four angles, each running low, guns and rifles in their hands.

Tippler stood up, cigarette dangling from the center of his mouth, looked out at the square filled with boys partially hidden in corners and against walls and nodded. "Well, we know they're not here to take control of an empty zoo," he said, blowing two thin lines of smoke through his nose. "They must have heard that Panzers are heading into the area. It's the only reason for so many of them to gather here."

"I'll get Zoltan and Glauss from downstairs," Zimmler said, picking up his rifle and moving from the ledge. "We can make better use of the box of grenades they're sitting on from up here than they can from down there."

"I just hope they haven't used them all up killing water rats," Tippler said not bothering to hide the sarcasm.

"Do you want me to bring you anything?" Zimmler asked, walking into the short alcove toward the long row of stone steps.

Tippler looked back out at the square and studied the position of the boys. "As many cigarettes as you can find," he said. "I feel a long and profitable day coming on."

Wilhelm Glaus stretched his arms toward the ceiling and twisted his neck from side to side, right foot resting on a large box of German grenades. The stench of the abandoned aquarium and festering zoo cages had infiltrated his clothes and gear pack, while the endless army of war-starved water rats parading up and down the stairwell had shoved his patience beyond its normal limits. Over the span of the interminably long past several days, Glaus felt as much a prisoner as any of the animals who once lived within the walls of the ancient structure.

Glaus looked up when he heard the echo of Franz Zoltan's steps cascade down the empty halls, his low whistling coming across loud as an aria. Zoltan was a rare breed of soldier, always in a pleasant mood, never troubled by the orders he was given to carry out and content with both his place and position within the pecking order of command. He had been groomed since childhood to be a career soldier and had learned to find solace in being told what to do by others, be they strangers or friends, so long as they wore the same uniform.

Zoltan turned the corner and smiled when he saw Glaus, his chubby face red and his breath coming in spurts. "Lots of activity in the square," he said to Glaus. "It's filling up pretty quickly, boys hiding on all sides. Something big looks like it's about to happen, which answers your question as to why they would want us to sit here and do nothing but wait."

"It's about damn time," Glaus said, turning to reach for his rifle. "If I had to spend one more day in this shit hole, I was going to let the rats have me for breakfast."

A different voice responded. "They're Neapolitan rats," Maldini said, his body shrouded in darkness, a machine gun in his hands. "They might not have the stomach for Nazi blood."

Glaus instinctively turned, aimed his weapon at Maldini's voice and fired twice. The return volley came at him from the side, from deep inside the empty fish tank, three bullets piercing through his arm and the side of his neck. He dropped his rifle and fell over backwards, his head resting on top of the crate of grenades. Zoltan stood frozen in place, his eyes zeroed in on the dead soldier next to his boots. "Turn around," Maldini told the soldier, "and walk up to the tower. We'll be right behind you."

Zoltan glanced to his left and saw Giovanni and Frederico step out from behind the slimy terrain of the fish tank, guns in their hands, walking toward Glaus and the crate of grenades. One of the boys looked back at him and waved. Maldini came out from behind the shadows. "You've done well," he told the boys.

"It wasn't easy," Frederico said, lifting one end of the grenade crate, his head turned away to avoid the dead body perched near it. "These Nazis were no fun to live with. All they did was sleep and talk about the war and the rats."

"And they also made bets about us," Giovanni said, stepping over Glaus and picking up his end of the crate. "A dead boy was worth a cigarette."

Maldini stared down at the boys, each holding a gun in one hand and the side of a grenade crate in the other, then turned to Zoltan. "I don't need cigarettes," he told the soldier. "So I'll kill you for free. Now, let's go to the tower. It's time we met your friends."

Zoltan nodded and began a slow, deliberate walk up the wide stone stairwell. "Strip the dead one of his weapons," Maldini told the boys as he followed the Nazi. "And come up along the dark end of the stairs. Any trouble, just stay hidden. If they've heard any shooting upstairs, let them think it's me. Right now, you two are the strongest in here. You're invisible and you have machine guns and grenades. Not even a Nazi would bet against you."

Connors looked up at the imposing structures surrounding him, at the large spacious square and at the six tanks positioned in a semicircle around the zoo and the archways. He checked the dozens of boys around him, spread and scattered, laying low, guns poised. Von Klaus had, as he had expected, adapted to their continued presence, sending stronger forces into every square, each now prepared to meet a level of resistance and confront it in harshest terms.

But the boys had adjusted in their own way to the ever-shifting course of battle. Combat experience can be achieved in moments, each second of fighting worth a month of training. Connors knew that many of them still weren't fit to be in the middle of such fiery fields. There was among them, however, a core group, led by the examples of Vincenzo and Angela, who seemed to be gaining in confidence. They had learned to adapt to the give and get of a hit-and-run street skirmish, utilizing their own knowledge of the city and its hidden secrets while exploiting the weaker points of their exposed enemy. Connors understood that future battles would only get harder, and that any talk of victory against such a superior force was more a boy's wish than a soldier's reality. But as he looked out across the square, just minutes away from another deadly confrontation, he also knew that rumblings of doubt were now imbedded inside the Nazi camp, chipping away at their veneer of confidence and that, in itself, was cause for hope.

Franco slid up alongside Connors, two machine guns strapped around his neck and a row of grenades clipped across his waist. "It's here," the boy said. "About fifty or so meters behind the other tanks. The signal for them to fire will come from Maldini up in the zoo towers. As of right now, everything that needs to be in place is in place."

Connors nodded, glancing across the square at Nunzia, who was huddled against a stone wall, a machine gun cradled in her hands, four street boys hiding in her shadows. She looked over at him, gave him a wave and a warm smile, her face luminous under the glare of the guns and the dust swirling through the piazza. Franco caught the exchange between the two as he sat down next to Connors, checking the ammo clips on his guns.

"My uncle was a captain in the army," Franco said. "Fought in many battles during the first world war. He told me he was always a good soldier, but when he fell in love with my *zia* Anna, he became an even better one. Maybe the same will be true for you."

Connors looked questioningly at the boy.

Franco checked the tank movements behind Connors before speaking again. "I have eyes and I know where to look. Besides, I had a bet with Maldini. He said you wouldn't ever gather the courage to say anything to her."

"It's not exactly the best time for a romance," Connors said.

"Anytime is a good time," Franco said with a shrug. "Even in a square filled with tanks, soldiers and snipers, you've touched her heart and she's taken yours."

"You should write a book," Connors said, getting ready to step into the square.

"You can't find love in a book," Franco said as he stood and gripped both machine guns.

The tank shell exploded one floor above, shards of brick and glass spraying the ground around them. The force of the blast knocked Connors face forward, machine gun slipping from his hands. Franco dove into the darkened hall of an empty building, a thick cloud of smoke swooping down the corner stairs. German soldiers riddled the area around the two of them with heavy fire, bullets clipping off pieces of stone and sending pockets of dust floating into the air. From the other sides of the square, Nunzia and the street boys answered the barrage with one of their own, bringing down a handful of the soldiers closing in on them, all the while watching the tanks churn in a semicircle and pound at the buildings and houses above them. She looked over toward Connors and, through the pockets of smoke and fumes, could see that he was still on the ground.

The tank attack made movement into the square difficult, the Nazis looking to pin the boys into the craters of the buildings and kill them in clusters. If they did venture into the square, they would be easy targets for the soldiers on the ground and the sniper in the tower. "They're getting too close," Gennaro said to Nunzia, his voice coated by the dust. "And they've made it so we can't advance and can't retreat. And we can't stay here. Which leaves what?"

"Move the children farther back into the buildings," Nunzia said. "But they must keep shooting. We need to hold out until Papa gives the signal."

"We have to stop at least one of those tanks," Gennaro said, gazing down the square at a Panzer firing two shells into a building next to the zoo. "And we can't do that with these guns alone."

Nunzia stepped out into the square, firing her machine gun at a string of soldiers closing in on the burning house Gennaro and the others were using for shelter. "Let me worry about the tank," she shouted over her shoulder. "You keep the children safe. Move only when you hear the signal."

"What if it doesn't come?" Gennaro shouted back at her.

Nunzia never answered, thrust into the middle of a crossfire battle with a quartet of Nazi soldiers, who returned her volleys with an arsenal of their own. She was down to her last few rounds, desperately reaching behind her, looking to pull a fresh clip from her waistband, the Nazis closing in, their bullets raining down on her, each shot missing her by fractions. She tossed herself to the hard ground, firing off the last of her bullets as she rolled, releasing the old clip and jamming in a fresh one. She came up on one knee and fired full force into the small circle of soldiers. Two of them took hits, grunting as they dropped to their knees. A third held his fire for a brief moment, his eyes shifting from Nunzia to the fiery second floor of the small house behind her. She saw his head shake and bounce back, a small bullet wound in his forehead sending him face up to his death. Nunzia gave a quick glance above her and saw Gennaro standing in an open window, light blue flames licking at his back and sides, a hunter's rifle poised in his hands. He lowered the gun, tossed Nunzia a quick kiss and disappeared into the burning room.

The last soldier came at her from behind, towering over her, his shadow covering the bodies of his dead comrades. The Nazi kicked Nunzia to the ground, the bottom of his hard boot landing square in the center of her back, the machine gun in her hand sent skimming along the cobblestones. He walked toward her, watching as she struggled to reach for the gun, gasping for air from the severe force of the kick, and pulled a knife out of the protective sheaf of his ammo belt. The soldier stood above Nunzia, reached down and lifted her up to his chest, holding her by the back of her hair. His eyes narrowed and he gave her a bitter smile as he drew the knife closer to the side of her neck. Nunzia held his arm with both hands, the tip of the blade inching closer to her skin, the weight of the Nazi's body bearing down on her slight frame. She moved her head away and braced her legs against the hard edges of the cobblestones, arching her back, using all her remaining strength to escape the sharp glint of the knife.

The bullet tore through the Nazi's neck and lodged in his throat.

He dropped the knife and fell on top of Nunzia, his eyes quick to lose all signs of life, his head tilted, foam, blood and spittle seeping out of the corners of his mouth. Nunzia inched herself away from his slumped body, casting the soldier aside and jumping to her feet. She took the knife from the Nazi's hand, looked across the square and saw Connors rush toward her, the smoking gun still in his hand. They were less than ten feet apart when she saw the Nazi soldier come out from behind the base of the fountain, aiming his rifle at Connors. "Get down!" she shouted. "Now!"

Connors dropped to the ground, his eyes following Nunzia's, turned on his back and fired three rounds at the German standing to his right. He held the position as he watched the soldier topple over the side of the waterless fountain. Connors then rose to his knees, looked around the square and raced toward Nunzia, catching her in his arms. As they held one another in silence, the six Panzer tanks had positioned themselves on the north and south sides of the smoldering square, their steady barrage bringing finality to the few remaining structures. Connors lifted Nunzia's face, gently holding it with three fingers of his right hand. He stroked each cheek, leaned his head forward and kissed her. For the briefest of moments, they were both able to ignore the fire and destruction around them.

Connors opened his eyes, Nunzia still in his embrace, and looked over her head. The Nazi had his back to them, his rifle raised and aimed at a street boy fleeing from one of the fast approaching tanks. Connors ran his hand down the side of Nunzia's arm and grabbed for the knife she still held in her right hand. He pried it loose from her fingers, moved her aside, took two forceful steps forward and flung it, blade first, toward the soldier. The knife pierced his uniform and severed several main arteries, sending both the rifle and the soldier tumbling to the ground. Connors waved the street boy forward, signaling him to move to higher ground and safety. Nunzia stepped up quietly from behind and handed Connors an ammo pack and a German machine gun. "You're pretty good with a knife," she said.

"It's something I picked up from an old lady I met the other day," Connors said, taking the gun and pack and her hand.

Maldini held the gun to Zoltan's back, standing with the Nazi in the shadows of the stairwell. They both could hear the footsteps coming closer, less than one floor above them. Maldini quickly glanced behind him and saw Giovanni and Frederico hovering in a corner, rifles hanging across the top of the crate of grenades. "Remember this," he whispered into Zoltan's ear. "No matter what happens, I'll make sure you die before I do. *Capito?*"

The Nazi arched his back. He stiffened when he heard Zimmler's voice echo down at them. "Glaus!" he yelled, his voice booming like a stereo in and out of the empty fish tanks. "Zoltan! Time to wake up and join the war. The tanks are in the square. So are some of those boys that have been pestering us. We need you to bring the grenades up."

Zimmler stopped in midstep and Maldini heard the click of his rifle trigger. "Answer him," he whispered to Zoltan. "Tell him you're on your way. And say it loud so he can hear you."

"We're bringing them up," Zoltan shouted in German. "We're just getting our gear ready."

"Can you manage on your own?" Zimmler asked. "Or do you two women need a man's help?"

"Have him come down to you," Maldini said, moving the gun away from Zoltan's back and placing it up against his neck. "Tell him you found some wine, lots of it, and ask what you should do with it."

"Do you want us to bring the wine up as well?" Zoltan asked, wiping at the sweat coming off his brow. "Glaus found a case hidden in one of the tanks earlier today."

Maldini heard the hurried footsteps and turned to the boys behind him, holding up his right hand and signaling them to prepare to fire. Giovanni and Frederico pressed their rifles against the top of the crate, spread out their bodies and took aim at the dark steps above them. Maldini put an arm around Zoltan's waist and the two stepped farther back against the stone walls of the aquarium. Zimmler turned the corner, standing several feet across from the two men, his rifle slung casually over his shoulder, a smoldering cigarette jammed in the center of his mouth. Maldini looked at the two boys and nodded.

Both bullets found their mark, hitting Zimmler at chest level and sending him skidding down the remaining steps. Giovanni and Frederico stood and walked over to where the soldier was stretched out, their rifles aimed down at him, waiting for any movement. "His time with us has passed," Maldini said to them, still holding the gun on Zoltan. "Take his rifle and belt and start heading up. And do it quietly. We still have one more Nazi to deal with."

"What about him?" Frederico asked, pointing his rifle at Zoltan. "You sure it's safe to leave him here alone? He might get loose and shout out. Warn the sniper we're coming his way."

"Don't worry," Maldini said, walking past the boys and the bodies of the two dead Nazis. "He'll be bound and gagged. And he won't be alone. We have an army of rats down here who will keep a very close eye on our friend."

Tippler had one eye squinted shut and focused his other down the trigger line of his high-powered rifle. He had a street boy in his scope, moving from a burning building to the edge of the fountain. The sniper stiffened his upper body, held his breath and squeezed down on the trigger, the recoil bouncing off the top of his shoulder. The boy fell in a heap, his head down as if asleep, crouched in a corner of the square, hidden by the shadows of a long-abandoned basin. "Like sending pigs to the market," the sniper said in a low voice, a half-smile on his lips. He gently brushed the rifle along the edges of the embankment seeking its next target.

Tippler stopped when he saw the American soldier running through the square, a young woman by his side. He pulled a fresh bullet from the pouch on his belt and slid it into the cartridge holder, jamming the casing in place. He wiped the rifle down with a damp cloth he kept next to his cigarettes and double-checked the scope. "There you are," the sniper said. "The ghost of Naples. I wonder how many of his cigarettes Zimmler would wager on your life?"

Tippler stretched out his body, his legs flat against the cold stone floor, his shoulders and arms tight and tense. He gazed through the scope and slid his hands along the dark wood barrel of the rifle, the index finger of his right hand resting on the curve of the trigger. He lifted the butt end of the rifle half an inch higher for better leverage and bore down on his target.

Giovanni and Frederico rested the grenade crate on a lower step and stood with their backs against a wall, inches from the German soldier. The older boy grabbed Frederico's right hand and held it tight, looked across at him and nodded. They came out of the darkness together, throwing their bodies at the flattened Nazi. They landed on his back just as he squeezed the trigger, sending the shot astray and the rifle cascading over the edge of the embankment. Frederico picked up a rock and landed blow after blow at the head and neck of the surprised Tippler, who struggled frantically to regain his focus and turn his body. Giovanni, his hands gripped around the soldier's ammo belt, leaned down and pushed him forward. Tippler's arms hung over the side of the tower, several hundred feet above the battle zone.

Tippler managed to turn his head and caught a numbing blow to the eye from the sharp end of a rock. A thick line of blood spurted out of the large gash, clouding his vision. Frederico tossed aside the rock and moved next to Giovanni, each boy pushing and pulling with all their strength to get the soldier out of the tower. Tippler kicked furiously at them, landing hard, painful blows to their backs and arms. Giovanni ducked one feverish swing of a boot, jumped to his feet and pressed his hands against a stone pillar. He lifted his legs and jammed the thin soles of his shoes against the center of Tippler's crotch. He closed his eyes and pressed down with full force, the muscles and veins on both his arms and neck bulging, his feet shoving the Nazi's body closer to the edge of the tower. Frederico leaned his shoulder against the soldier's back and tugged at his ammo belt with both hands. One final push from both and Tippler slid out of the tower and fell screaming over the side. The two boys stared down after him, watching him land with a loud thump on top of a moving tank.

Giovanni and Frederico, both drenched in sweat, the sides of their arms red with welts, turned away from the embankment and found Maldini standing behind them, the crate of grenades in his hands. "He loved to laugh and make bets with the others," Frederico said. "How many shots it would take to kill one of us. He never lost."

"He did today," Maldini told them.

He rested the crate next to one of the stone pillars and pulled free a grenade. He peered over the side, the tanks venting their wrath against old buildings shrouded in flames and abandoned homes lost under blankets of smoke. In the midst of all that madness, soldiers with machine guns searched for street boys cowering inside the wall of fire or shielding themselves under rocks and stones. In the center of the massive square, wedged in next to a crumbling fountain, he found Connors and Nunzia, fighting back to back, their guns spraying bullets in every possible direction. Maldini checked the time on his wristwatch and then looked up at the two boys. He pulled the pin from the base of the grenade and sent it spiraling down toward a trio of Nazi soldiers. "It's time to join our friends," he said.

Connors aimed his machine gun at an approaching tank and held fire, looking up at the Nazi soldier flying down out of the aquarium tower. He backed up several steps, reaching a hand out for Nunzia and pulling her along with him, as the soldier landed on the other end of the square. "I was expecting a louder signal," Connors said, ducking under a Nazi fusillade of bullets.

Nunzia fired off a half dozen rounds and then glanced up at the tower. She saw her father lean over the edge and toss out a German grenade. "That was just an appetizer," she shouted. "Here comes the meal now."

The blast of the first grenade sent three soldiers hurtling to the ground, facedown and dead. The next dozen grenades caused a break in the Nazi offensive. Within minutes, the square was filled with street boys rising up from the sewers, running out of fiery buildings and jumping down from smoke-filled houses, each firing weapons at the now-surrounded German soldiers. Connors ran toward an open manhole, grabbed a sack of grenades from a street boy and jumped on the back of a Nazi tank. He turned to his right and saw a rainbow of kerosene cocktails rain down on two other tanks swinging away from the buildings to bear down on the boys. Connors ducked under the massive fireball that was quick to follow and then unpinned two of the grenades and tossed them into the open slot above. He jumped off the tank, the explosion hitting while he was in midair.

The three remaining tanks were moving in a tight circle, heavily armed soldiers closing in behind them, looking to shoot their way out of a square that just minutes earlier they could claim as their own. A Panzer tank, its turret loaded and in position, blocked their path. Vincenzo stood in the open hole, a pair of goggles hanging off his neck.

"You think they'll be all right?" Nunzia asked, looking through the haze and smoke at the Panzer tank parked beside the aquarium.

Connors turned to her and nodded. "The Americans have Patton," he said. "The Brits have Montgomery and the Neapolitans have Vincenzo. Not a loser in the bunch."

Vincenzo lowered his head and looked down into the hull of the tank. Dante was pushing buttons and shifting gears, while Claudio and Pepe stood by his side, loading bombs into the hold. Fabrizio was huddled in a corner, the bullmastiff at his feet, trying to find comfort inside the tight space. "What's taking so long?" Vincenzo asked. "Can you drive this tank or not?"

"We got this far, didn't we?" Dante shouted back. "Just give me a few seconds. There's all these buttons and gauges I need to get used to."

"How soon do you want us to fire?" Claudio asked.

"They're closing in," Vincenzo said, staring out at the oncoming Nazi tanks and soldiers. "They'll be on us in less than five minutes unless we attack."

"Do you think they figured out we're not one of theirs?" Pepe asked.

"They're Nazis," Vincenzo said in an irritated tone. "Not morons."

Dante pushed three buttons and moved an iron lever toward him. He took a step back to read the gauges and accidentally stepped on the mastiff's tail. The dog turned his head and snarled. "Why is he in here?" Dante asked Fabrizio, who was calming the dog with a pat on his massive head.

"To protect us," Fabrizio said with a knowing nod.

"Get ready to fire," Vincenzo shouted down. "And move it forward. If you can, shift that turret above ten meters to the left. You'll hit a whole section of soldiers. Once you start, Dante, no matter what happens, don't stop."

Dante was mesmerized by the power of the vehicle he commanded, his eyes staring with amazement at the array of switches, gears and gauges amassed before him. He stood atop a wine crate and looked through the slot hole at the square, smoke and fire billowing in all directions. The Nazis were running toward them, forced out of the square by the bullets and bombs fired and thrown by Connors, Nunzia and the street boys. He turned to Claudio and Pepe and nodded. "Load it," Dante said. "And be careful. We want the bombs to go out, not come in. Wait for the signal from above."

"What do you want me to do?" Fabrizio asked.

"Keep an eye on Vincenzo," Dante told him. "It's going to get really loud soon and I may not be able to hear his commands. You listen for me and make sure that I do."

Vincenzo stared out at the advancing tanks and troops, at a section of a Panzer division fleeing from the weathered guns of the boys and the damage inflicted by their own grenades. "Fire," he shouted into the hole. He wrapped his fingers around the sides of the tank as the first shell came spiraling out of the turret, disappearing in a blur as it exploded against the far side of a building wall, its brutal force sending four Nazi soldiers down to the ground.

The boys in the hole applauded, Claudio pumped a small fist into the dusty air and the mastiff barked his approval. Dante shifted a lever and pressed two buttons, checking the levels on each of the gauges, smiling when the tank jolted forward. Pepe stepped in alongside Claudio, grabbed hold of the two arms of a rotating machine gun. He peered down through the opening, jammed his fingers along the trigger points and opened fire. Claudio shoved a fresh shell into the hole, slammed it shut and waited for the signal to launch.

The street boys had the Nazis bottled inside the square.

From the tower, Maldini launched his grenade attack. From the rear, Connors and Nunzia fired on the soldiers, directing the boys against the tanks, utilizing the flame throwers, mines and kerosene cocktails at their disposal. Angela worked the sewers, moving from opening to opening like a frenzied rabbit, tossing out bags of grenades and fused cylinders, dragging down wounded boys and those low on ammo. Vincenzo and his captured Panzer moved into the square, its fiery turret shelling the three remaining tanks, the battle raging at its fullest and angriest, boys, girls, women and soldiers all fighting for a piece of a now-demolished square.

Connors looked up and saw flames shoot out of the rear tracks of the Nazi tank. Three of its soldiers jumped out of the smoky hole and ran down one of the empty side streets. The few remaining soldiers were now frantically searching for a way out of the inferno they had initiated. Connors turned to Nunzia, put a hand on her shoulder and yelled out, "They've had enough. Call everybody back."

Nunzia jumped to the fountain in the center of the square and fired her gun into the air, waving one arm in a circular pattern. Within minutes, the street boys disappeared as quickly as they had appeared, slipping back into the safety of the sewers, side streets and alleys. The Nazi tanks were abandoned. Dead soldiers lined the large square, many of them as young as the oldest of the boys. Connors walked among them, his head down, his machine gun at rest by his side. "Win or lose," he told Nunzia, now walking next to him, "you always end up with that same empty feeling. Wanting to burn down abandoned buildings and houses isn't a good enough cause to die over."

He and Nunzia turned when they saw the tank approach, Vincenzo and Fabrizio waving at them from the open hull. Fabrizio jumped down from the moving tank, the mastiff fast on his step, and ran toward them. He stopped when he reached Connors, who reached down and picked the boy up. "What the hell were you and the dog doing inside that tank?" he asked.

"I was the second in command," Fabrizio said, smiling. "I would pass Vincenzo's orders down to Claudio. Without me, victory would have been much more difficult."

Vincenzo, Claudio and Pepe stepped out of the tank and stared at the bodies and the fires that filled the square. Maldini, Frederico and Giovanni were fast behind them, coming down from the steps of the demolished aquarium. "The Nazis came here expecting to find Naples," Maldini said, gazing up at the flames and smoke. "And instead they found a pocket of hell."

"Let's go," Nunzia said in a low voice, walking between Connors and Maldini, an arm under each. "We've all seen enough blood for one day."

The mastiff ran ahead of them, stopping in front of a deserted tank, fire billowing out of its back and sides, a German pith helmet resting next to it. The dog began to bark and claw at the ground, trying to wedge his body under the tracks, reaching his head in, his large jaw swinging from side to side. "What the hell's he doing?" Connors asked, running toward the mastiff, his machine gun cocked and ready.

Connors stood above the dog and glanced down. The mastiff had a soldier's hand in his mouth, its fingers curled around a semiautomatic handgun. He heard a low muffled scream coming out from under the tank. Connors reached down and yanked the gun out of the soldier's hand, then dragged him out from under the front end. The mastiff was inches from the Nazi's face, white foam dripping along his jaws, his foul breath hot on the soldier's neck. Connors pulled the German to his feet. He was much younger than Connors and stood shaking and shivering despite the horrid heat. Connors took two steps back and aimed his gun at the German's stomach, the others circling around them, each looking into the face of the enemy.

"You speak English?" Connors asked.

The soldier nodded. "I lived in England for six months." His voice was shaky. "On a student exchange."

"Take a look around," Connors said. "Look at what you did to this place. Then look at the people behind me. This was their home, the place where they lived and played and tried to make a life. You see it?"

The soldier's eyes moved slowly around the burning square and then settled on the faces gathered behind Connors. "Yes," he said, his voice choked by smoke and fumes.

"Maybe you'll remember it then," Connors said. "Unlock your ammo pack and let it drop to the floor. Then turn around and leave this place."

The soldier swallowed hard and undid his belt, stepping aside as it fell on the ground. "If I'm to be shot," the soldier said, "I'd rather be facing the one shooting me."

"You might get that chance someday," Connors said. "But not today. Now get out of my sight, before I let the dog rip you to shreds."

Connors took a step back and watched as the soldier slowly lowered his hands and turned away, then sprinted toward one of the alleys closest to the tank. Connors bent down and patted the top of the mastiff's head, running his hand down along his jawline. The dog lifted his front paws and leaned them on the soldier's chest, his large tongue licking drool across the side of Connors's face. Connors stood up and shook his head, wiping off the spittle with the sleeve of his uniform. "I'll tell you one thing," he said. "This dog is better at finding a Nazi than any of us can ever hope to be."

"Of course he is," Fabrizio said. "He's a street dog. Just like us."

THE THIRD DAY

25

PIAZZA GARIBALDI

Von Klaus slammed his fist down against the center of the map. The blow caused the thin wooden legs of the table to collapse and sent the paper flowing to the ground, the mild breeze setting it adrift along the parched grass. "They're like deadly rodents," he shouted to Kunnalt.

"It's difficult to contain them in battle, sir," Kunnalt said, making a feeble attempt at an explanation. "They come from all directions. They launch their attack, strip our men of their guns and grenades and then scatter. And they've been very good at utilizing the few weapons they have."

"They took one of our *tanks*, Kunnalt," Von Klaus said. "That makes them very good at utilizing one of the weapons *we* have. They're using German bullets and artillery to kill our men. We're not only fighting on their ground, we're fighting on their terms."

"We can alert high command and ask for air cover," Kunnalt said. "The bombings might force them out of their hiding places and then the ground troops can take care of the rest."

Von Klaus stared at Kunnalt, anger and frustration etched in every line of his face. "In its history, the Sixteenth Panzer Division has beaten the British in the deserts of Africa and pounded the Americans in the hills of Italy. It has marched victorious through Poland and eastern Europe and braved the brutality of the Russian front. But now it remains stalled, at the mercy of children in an empty city, in need of airpower to allow it to stake a claim to victory. If we can't win this fight without air support against this kind of army, then we have betrayed the history of this division."

Von Klaus had been convinced that the rebellion would be mild, easily quelled by his far-superior troops. But now an element of uncertainty had begun to creep into his thinking. And he was experienced enough as an officer to know that where there was doubt there lurked the seeds of defeat.

"How much use has our young traitor been to us?" Von Klaus asked.

"He doesn't seem to have made any impact, sir," Kunnalt said. "My guess would be that the Italians trust him about as much as we do."

"Except the Italians didn't pay for his help," Von Klaus said. "We did. And I expect full worth for my money. Can we find him?"

"He's camped in the hills," Kunnalt said. "He claims he offered the street fighters his help and was rebuffed. Now he says he's got enough boys behind him to go in and attack the ones fighting us."

"So, he not only betrays his own kind," Von Klaus said, "he's even willing to kill them."

"Sometime tomorrow is when he plans to make his move, sir," Kunnalt said. "Providing we meet his two requests."

"Which are what?" Von Klaus said, his voice coated with contempt.

"We supply him with the weapons needed to fight and defeat the boys," Kunnalt said. "And we guarantee him safe passage out of Naples after it's done."

"Tell him I've accepted his terms," Von Klaus said. "But also tell him I wish to speak to him prior to his attack. I want to go over his plan. Soldier to soldier."

Kunnalt looked at Von Klaus and nodded. "How soon?"

"Now," Von Klaus said.

26

Connors leaned against the side of a Corinthian column, staring out at the imposing thirteenth-century castle that came complete with a moat, five stone towers and a complex series of archways. "It'd be hard for the tanks to get up here," Connors said, pointing out the black rock structures and the closed-in brick columns. "Most likely they'll decide to fight us out by the grass, leaving their soldiers exposed."

"Unless it can fly," Maldini said, "a tank won't be able to take the castle. Right now, it's probably the safest place in all Naples. But things often change faster than we would like."

"It's like a small city in there," Connors said. "You could hide a battalion behind those walls and no one would have a clue they were in there. The Nazis should have made this one of their early targets or turned it into their headquarters. They should've done whatever they needed to keep it out of our hands."

"The Nazis might have been saving it for last, bring it down on their way out of the city," Maldini said with a shrug. "Just before they left for Rome."

"Maybe." Connors lit a cigarette. "It looks to me like they've spread themselves out too wide. Even when they looked to take the city from the center and then branch out from there, they did it in chunks, not as a whole. The boys have been good fighters, better than I thought. And the plans have been solid, risky enough for the Nazis not to figure them out in advance. But even with all that, it just doesn't feel right."

"You're just like Vincenzo," Maldini said, arching his eyebrows over at Connors. "You both overthink every move and maneuver. You need to have reasons for every action taken. It's because you're a soldier and he wants to be one. You ask military questions and expect military answers. That's not always the right place to stop."

"Explain it to me, then," Connors said. "Tell me why the second most decorated officer in the German command, running with the best tank division they have, can't beat back an army of kids?"

Maldini stared at Connors for several seconds, his arms folded as he stood against a stone wall. "Because the Colonel has a stomach for battle but not for murder," he said. "If these were American troops he was fighting, they would have already tasted the full power of that division. But they're children. He sees it and he knows it. He's a fighter who can't give the order that will ensure his victory."

"But he can't allow himself to lose. He won't be able to live with that either."

"You're right," Maldini said. "That he cannot do. Which means, at some point, he will have to shove aside the concerns of the man and take on the demands of the soldier. Then it will take much more than surprise attacks and street cunning to run him out of Naples."

"If that's going to happen, it's going to be soon. He's not long on time and he's low on fuel. He's got to finish the job here and make a run for the north, ahead of the Brits and my guys."

Maldini checked the sky for signs of an early-rising sun, his face and hair tilted toward the mild breeze. "It will be today, tomorrow at the latest. But for now, the sun still greets the morning as if the world were at peace."

"When I first met you, back in the square," Connors said, "I wasn't expecting much. You seemed more interested in your wine than in the kids."

"Don't be fooled," Maldini said. "I still prefer wine to children."

"I've seen you fight," Connors said. "And I saw how you helped Vincenzo and the others with the plans. That's not something a drunk usually does."

"My father was an engineer," Maldini said. "He helped design many of the tunnels we now use to run from the Nazis. I used to watch him work. I loved to see how a pencil drawing he began on a thin sheet of paper in his little office would end up covering hundreds of miles of a city's streets. And it was how I made my living, too."

"That explains the planning," Connors said. "But you're also good with a gun. Not many engineers are."

"This isn't Italy's first world war," Maldini said. "And it's not mine either."

Connors patted Maldini on the arm and started to walk away. "I'm going to see if the boys need any help."

"Are there any Italians in the rich city where you live?" Maldini asked, nodding his head toward the soldier.

"It's not rich," Connors said. "And there are no Italians. You'd probably have to drive to St. Louis to even find a family that serves anything with a red sauce on it that's not barbecue."

"You don't have pasta as your *primo*?" Maldini's manner was more curious than concerned.

"Only if macaroni and cheese counts. And then it's your only course."

"What do you put on the macaroni and cheese?"

"Salt," Connors said. "Sometimes milk if it's served too hot."

"In Naples, not even a sick infant would put milk on his pasta," Maldini said with pride. "We don't even like to put milk in our coffee. And there, at least, you could understand its function."

Connors snickered and walked toward the older man. "What's your favorite meal, Maldini? The one you would ask for if you could ask for anything?"

"I would begin with a fresh antipasto misto." Maldini leaned his head against one of the columns, his eyes closed, his mind conjuring up favorable images. "A nice bottle of red wine and fresh bread just out of the oven. Then, a large bowl of linguini in a thick red sauce swimming with clams and mussels. After that, a steak pizzaiola with a green salad dressed in olive oil and lemon. Two cups of espresso and a long glass of Fernet Branca and maybe some crunchy biscotti if I still have room."

"That's pretty impressive," Connors said. "Want to hear mine?"

"Will it depress me?"

"Yes," Connors said. "But it won't take as long."

"Already I don't like it. A great meal should take time, both to make and to eat."

"You want me to feel like a king," Connors said, "put me down in front of a large platter of sliced meat loaf swimming in mushroom gravy and ketchup, side helpings of twice-cooked potatoes, fresh corn on the cob and my aunt Jane's oven-fresh rolls. Top it off with a thick slab of peach pie and a double scoop of vanilla ice cream. That's close enough to heaven for me."

Maldini shrugged his shoulders and stared out across the expansive green lawn that separated the castle from the main road. "There should be more than enough room in heaven for both. Do you at least drink wine with such a meal?"

"Afraid not," Connors said with a laugh. "Milk usually or sometimes pop or maybe even a beer."

"I'd rather go hungry than eat a meal without a glass of wine," Maldini said.

"Why are you asking?" Connors asked. "Just curious or are you planning a move to the States?"

"Not me," Maldini said, shaking his head. "Made in Naples, stay in Naples. But I have a daughter who's always wanted to travel. So it's nice to know about a place she might one day visit."

The four boys had slept in the tunnels longer than they should have, running now toward the castle, hoping to get there before the tanks and soldiers arrived. In the distance behind them they heard the drone of the engines and could feel the trembling along the cracks on the street. One of the boys, the tallest and oldest, stopped and turned to look at the barren avenue behind him. "We should be okay," he told the others. "They must be at least half a kilometer behind us. We can make the castle with time to spare."

"Then why are we running?" the youngest of the quartet asked.

"In case I'm wrong," the older one said, picking up his run and moving along at a faster pace.

The four turned a corner, saw the imposing castle on their left, a half-mile farther down the wide road. They turned and gave each other relieved glances and sighs, grateful to be so close to the next chosen sanctuary in their fight. "I told you not to worry," the tall boy said, his breath coming out in hurried rushes. "We should be inside the castle in less than ten minutes."

The youngest slowed his pace, arms folded against his chest, trying to ignore the burning feeling deep in his lungs. "We can walk the rest of the way and still get there before the Germans. And that's what I'm going to do."

"No reason to take any chances." The tall boy held to his run and waved the others to follow. "We can all catch our breath and get some rest once we're inside."

"This wasn't worth the extra twenty minutes of sleep," one of the two silent boys said, his head down, his tired arms dangling against his sides.

They were within the shadows of the castle when the first bullet was fired.

It hit the younger boy in the fleshy part of his shoulder and sent him spiraling to the ground, blood from the wound mixing with scraped skin from the fall. The other three boys skidded to a stop and rushed to their knees to help their injured friend. Their eyes scanned the empty street for any signs of the shooter. "Don't waste your time on me, Antonio," the youngest boy said, his mouth dry, his eyes tearing up from the pain. "Get yourselves inside the castle. Don't leave them any more targets."

"Put your arms around my neck," Antonio ordered him, shoving his own arms under the back and folded legs of the wounded boy. "We're going to get behind those walls together."

A second shot bounced off the edge of the pavement just to the left of the crouching boys, sending tiny fragments of rock bounding toward the sky. "Then we need to find that sniper," one of the quiet boys said.

From the jagged rooftop of the castle, Vincenzo, Franco and Angela looked to their left and saw the advancing line of Nazi tanks and soldiers. It stretched more than a half-mile down the center road, the sea to its left, burning structures to its right. Farther down the road they saw the four street boys running toward the front gates of the castle, led by a tall, lanky teenager.

"That's Antonio Murino and his friends." Angela couldn't hide her frustration. "They've never been on time once since I've known them. They can sleep through anything. If they could, they'd sleep through the rest of the war."

"So would I," Franco said with a shrug, looking across the stone wall at Vincenzo. "It's all about the company you keep."

The three of them jumped back when they heard the shot. They glanced over the edge of the wall, watching the four boys huddle together and Antonio try to lift the wounded one into his arms. Franco pointed across from the castle, down a side street hidden by shadows and ruin. "There's smoke coming from that alley," he said. "It was only one bullet, but I don't think they'd risk a soldier out alone."

Vincenzo braced himself against the side of the wall and waved an arm at Connors and Maldini. "One of the boys is down," he yelled. "They're close enough to make it, but they'll need some help."

"We'll get them in," Connors shouted back. "Meantime, try to spot that shooter and fire down on him when you do. Chances are you won't hit him, but the cover fire will at least keep him clear of us."

Connors checked the clips on his machine guns and looked over at Maldini. "You up for an early-morning run?"

"Only to keep you company," Maldini said as he tossed his rifle across his shoulder. "If it were up to me, I'd sit here, have a coffee and watch the tides rise and fall."

Connors and Maldini were halfway across the grassy field, heading for the open road and the four boys. The morning sun warmed their backs, the Nazi tanks and soldiers were closing in from the streets above. From the rooftop, Franco and Angela fired a stream of gunfire in the direction of the sheltered alley, hitting nothing but rocks and cracked glass.

"He may have pulled back," Vincenzo said, moving along the castle walls, desperate for a better glimpse. "The question is why. He had four open targets and took only one. Why risk the exposure if you're not going to make the move?"

Angela lowered her gun and stood up straight, her eyes betraying her concern. "Maybe it was a mistake," she said.

Vincenzo pointed toward the center of the alley. "Someone ordered him to stop. I think there are tanks down those side streets." He stared into the smoke-filled corners of the streets, his hands resting on the tops of the tower rocks, watching as Connors and Maldini closed in on the four boys. "One of you go and find Nunzia," he said. "She should be in one of the rear rooms on the main floor. Have her get everyone ready. This battle's going to start a little sooner than we thought."

As Connors and Maldini ran toward the four boys, the Nazi tanks were now visible down the road behind them. Antonio was still holding the wounded boy in his arms. "The sniper's off to the right," he told Connors. "He fired twice and then stopped. Maybe he's just waiting for us to run."

Maldini reached over and checked on the wounded boy, lowering the bloody shirt and glancing at the gurgling bullet hole. "What's his name?" he asked Antonio.

"He's my cousin Aldo," Antonio said. "The two behind me are Pietro and Giovanni."

Maldini rubbed the top of Aldo's head and walked over toward Pietro, the young boy shivering in the early-morning sun. He leaned down and wrapped his warm hands around his shoulders. "I need someone strong and brave to protect me when we make our run for the castle," he told him. "Would you do that for me?"

Pietro stared back at him, his lower lip trembling, his olive eyes wide with fright, and nodded. "*Si*," he said. "I will protect you."

"Then I have nothing to fear," Maldini said. He stood, keeping an arm across the boy's shoulder. "For now I have you with me."

"We'll run on the sniper's side of the road," Connors announced. "If he's still there, that'll cut down on the angle of his shots, make it harder to hit any of us." He looked at each of the four boys, the rumblings of the approaching tanks echoing in his ears, and gripped the two machine guns in his hands. "We don't leave behind any of our wounded. If someone gets shot, those closest to him make the grab. Just like Antonio here did. But if one of us gets killed, the rest keep moving. Leave the dead where they fall."

Maldini walked over and stood next to Connors. "Now that the American has put us all in such a happy mood," he said. "What else is there to do but run?"

They moved in a straight line along the edges of the street, crouching low, using the rays of the sun behind them as cover. Connors led the way. Antonio, with Aldo in his arms, was close behind. Maldini took up the rear, his eyes focused on Pietro and Giovanni.

They were less than a quarter of a mile from the castle entrance.

Connors skidded to a stop, guns at his side, when he saw the tank slam out of the front of a burning building. Seven others soon followed, each with a dozen soldiers in its wake, their rifles and machine guns aimed at the two men and four boys. The tanks spread out and blocked off the road to the castle entrance, the soldiers crowding in alongside each one. Connors turned and looked behind him, where a dozen other tanks and more than sixty soldiers were closing in. He took a deep breath and stared over at Maldini. "If you can think of something clever to get us out of this," he said, "now would be the time to tell me."

"As a matter of fact," Maldini said, squeezing Pietro closer to him. "I do have an idea."

"Share it with me."

"We're going to surrender," Maldini said. "And then let them have everything they want. Including the castle."

Connors walked over to Maldini, his eyes to the ground, shaking his head. "That's an insane idea," he said. "Even if it works."

"The insane ones always have a better chance," Maldini said, moving with Pietro toward the waiting Nazi tanks and soldiers.

27

Carlo Petroni walked down the center of the street, making his way toward the Palazzo Reale and a meeting with the colonel. He knew he was short on time. The street boys had dismissed him and taken the tank he had stolen from the Nazis. Von Klaus, who neither liked nor trusted him, had grown impatient and wanted results from the money he invested. Carlo realized his initial plan of playing one side against the other was no longer valid, which left him little choice but to side with the Nazis, gather his small band and do battle against the street boys. It was what he planned to tell Von Klaus at their meeting, attempt to convince the dubious Nazi that he would be a useful ally in the fight to quell the children's uprising. His one other possibility was to run, make his way north and ply his criminal trade on the fresh streets of Rome or Milan until the war was at an end. But it was not in Petroni's nature to flee, regardless of how dangerous or untenable the situation in which he found himself. Carlo also knew enough to understand that whatever the outcome of the battle for Naples, it wouldn't last beyond another day or two. And he was confident he could survive for that short a time, even against a vindictive Nazi. Carlo Petroni was a good thief, but he excelled at surviving.

He was about to turn a corner when he saw the little boy running toward him, a large dog by his side. "Don't go down that street," the boy shouted, his voice barely heard above the loud barks of the dog.

Carlo ignored the boy and continued walking, turning down a side street that would bring him out closer to Nazi headquarters. The boy's footsteps grew louder as did his shouting. "Stay out of there," he yelled. "It's too dangerous."

Carlo was halfway down the street when he turned and faced the little boy and the dog. "What do you want?" he asked.

"You can't go down there," the boy said. "Come back this way. I'll show you a safer way to go."

"Who are you to tell me where to go?" Carlo asked.

"My name is Fabrizio," the boy said.

"Your name means nothing to me," Carlo said. "And your words mean even less. Now go play with your dog and leave me alone."

"The street is mined," Fabrizio told him. "You have to come back this way."

"Did one of the others send you here?" Carlo asked. "To tell me some lie and get me to come back with you?"

"No one sent me," Fabrizio said. "And I never lie."

"You live in Naples long enough, you'll learn that the truth is not your friend," Carlo said with a dismissive wave.

Carlo turned and continued his walk down the dank street. Fabrizio and the mastiff watched him go, the boy stepping back from the shadows.

Fabrizio and the mastiff were halfway up a short incline leading toward the tunnels when the explosion rocked the street behind them. They ran back and stood against a brick wall, staring through the waves of smoke at the ruined body of Carlo Petroni.

28

MASCHIO ANGIOINO

The large window spaces on all sides of the castle were filled with street boys, their rifles and guns hanging over the side. The tank was down in the center of the vast square, a short distance away from the locked front door. The rooftops were a sea of heads and rifles, each poised and aimed at the tanks below. Nunzia now stood next to Vincenzo and Franco, Angela by her side. She looked down at Connors and her father and the four boys huddled around them, tanks and soldiers on either side. "They have no choice. If they're to make it, they must give up their weapons."

"The Nazis aren't interested in prisoners," Vincenzo said. "Only in casualties."

"We can't just stand here and do nothing," Nunzia said. "We have to get them out of there."

Vincenzo turned away from the street. "I don't know how," he said. "If we start shooting, the Nazis will fire on them first before they turn to deal with us. If we don't start shooting, they might also be killed. And they're too boxed in to make a run for the grass, especially with the wounded boy."

"They might be willing to let the others go free," Franco said, "in return for the American. He's probably worth more to them than any of the others."

"I hope that's not true," Vincenzo said. "That would make Maldini and the boys useless to them, which means they'll be killed first."

"The American has to betray us," Angela said. "It's the smartest move he's got and the only one."

"He would never betray us." Nunzia's voice rose in anger. "He'd die before he would do anything like that."

"I know he wouldn't," Angela said, straining her neck in an effort to get a closer look. "That's why I hope Maldini thinks of it first."

Vincenzo whirled around and stared down at the younger girl. "What the hell are you talking about?"

"Down there, they're surrounded by Nazis with no hope for escape," Angela explained. "But if they surrender and offer to lead them to us, then the Nazis would be in our circle. That's how we would do it in Forcella. But since I'm not the general, I'll shut up and leave the thinking to you."

Vincenzo looked from Angela to the array of tanks and soldiers lining the street below, Connors, Maldini and the four boys standing in the middle of it all, their arms raised, their guns tossed to the ground. "Pull the boys away from the windows," he said after several quiet moments.

"Put them on the other side of the castle, facing the inside, laying low and unseen. Move the tank away from the entrance, at least for now."

"It's going to take more than that to get it done," Franco said. "We haven't gone up against that many tanks and soldiers since this started."

"I know it will," Vincenzo agreed. "While Nunzia gets the boys in position, we'll line the area around the front of the castle with mines, on both sides of the wall. And find Gennaro. Tell him to hide over by the drawbridge, down by the moat. Once the tanks are in and through, have him burn apart the chains that hold the bridge down."

"Why do that?" Angela asked.

"Once they're in, I want them to stay in. If they give us too much of a fight, the boys and everyone else can leave by the windows and down the walls. The soldiers can follow us, but the tanks have only two ways in or out. We take those away, they're stuck here."

"What about the bronze door?" Franco asked. "It's strong but the tanks can smash their way right through it."

"It will take them some effort," Vincenzo said. "Even more if we barricade it with our own tank."

"What about the tanks and soldiers outside the castle?" Angela wanted to know. "They won't all come into the courtyard."

"We'll split our forces," Vincenzo said. "Front and back, we fight them from both sides of the castle."

Nunzia put her hand on Vincenzo's arm. "You think the Nazis will fall for it?"

"That all depends," Vincenzo said, picking up his rifle, "on how good a traitor your father can be."

Maldini, his hands high above his head, looked at the young German officer and turned away from Connors. "I can give you the castle," he said. "All I want is for the boys to be safe and the wounded boy to be cared for."

"And what of the American?" the officer asked. "Do you wish for his safety as well?"

"The American can look out for himself," Maldini said, in a dismissive manner.

The tanks and soldiers were spread out on both ends of the road, hot wheels smoking, turrets fully loaded, men staring with impassive expressions. The officer, his hands folded behind his back, glanced down at the wounded street boy, now resting on the ground, his head leaning against Antonio's leg. "How many are in the castle?" he asked Maldini. His Italian was choppy but clear. "And where?"

"About a hundred boys," Maldini told him without hesitating. "All armed and ready to fight. But with the American out of the way I can get them to put down their weapons and surrender. They'll listen to what I have to say. And more important than any of my words, they'll see your tanks and soldiers inside the castle walls. They've grown tired of the battle and their spirit is already weak. With my help, you can take them with few if any shots fired."

Connors glared over at Maldini and shook his head in anger. "You have no idea what you're doing," he shouted. "They'll take the castle and then kill every kid in there. I knew you were a drunk, Maldini. I didn't know you were a coward and a fool."

Maldini motioned back and forth between Connors and the officer. "You two still have your war to fight," he told them. "Ours is at its end. Let us walk away from it alive."

The officer stared at Maldini and weighed his options, glancing across his shoulder at the wide expanse of the medieval structure. He believed in the skills of his men and the strength of his force; he could take the castle from the outside. But the Italians would be armed and ready for a struggle. Both men and tanks would be lost. They had the advantage of height, able to shoot down on his troops from the brick safety of their enclosure, while he held the upper hand in firepower and military expertise. It would, he realized, be easier and less costly to take control of the castle from within, enabling his men to surround the Italians and bring the fight to them on more advantageous terrain. That left open the question of trust. He didn't fully believe the older man's instant conversion from street fighter to war-weary savior, but he'd seen enough battles on this front to appreciate the Italian penchant for switching sides when the road before them grew difficult. It would be within the old man's nature to cast aside the American. Their alliance was tenuous under the best of circumstances. But the Italian hatred for the Nazis and all that had been done to their people and country was beyond borders and the officer needed to weigh such feelings in his final decision.

"Kill the American," he said to one of his soldiers. "Then have the old man and the boys lead us into the castle. We'll do what needs to be done once we're inside."

Maldini stepped in between Connors and the soldier, looking over at the officer and shaking his head. "Understand, I don't care whether the American lives or dies," Maldini said. "In fact, if you wish, I'll kill him myself. But we need to let him live for a few minutes longer. Until we're inside the walls of the castle."

"Just out of curiosity," the officer said, "tell me why."

"He still has many who follow him hidden behind those stone windows. If we kill him here, on the road, in full view, they'll attack us. They won't care whether you hold prisoners or not. But if you let him walk in with us and he happens to die during a moment of battle, then he will be a casualty of war instead of a martyr."

The officer stepped up to Maldini and stared down at him, their faces inches apart. "I warn you, old man," the officer snarled. "If any of this is a ruse, it'll be your head my bullets will be aimed toward."

"I'd have it no other way," Maldini said.

Vincenzo stared down at Connors, Maldini and the four boys leading the convoy of tanks and soldiers toward the front gates of the castle. "Let them in," he told Franco. "As many as can fit inside the walls. And make sure Gennaro stays low and out of sight."

"What about the boys?" Nunzia asked. "And Connors and Papa? How do we keep them safe once the shooting starts?"

"I'll be down there with them," Vincenzo said. "Somebody needs to greet our guests, why not me?"

"You'll just be another target," Angela said. "They won't let you walk in there with any guns in your hand."

"I won't need a gun in my hands," Vincenzo said, turning to leave.

Angela and Franco followed him out, but stopped at one of the darkened landings to look down at the street. It was filled with soldiers and tanks heading toward the castle. Connors and Maldini were each followed by a Nazi holding a machine gun. Angela heard the locks to the large, bronze front door click and then saw it swing open, flooding the darkened entrance with sunlight. "This could be a big mistake," she said to Franco. "Once they're in, they can kill as many of ours as we can of theirs."

"How much time before they come through the doors?" Franco asked, stepping away from the window, the approaching Nazi brigade masking half his body in shadows.

"Ten minutes, maybe more if they move the tanks in before the troops."

"That should be more than enough for what we need to do," Franco said.

"Which is what?" she asked.

"Mine those doors. It won't be enough to keep all the soldiers out, but it should at least slow their first wave."

"We don't have enough mines left to block off every door. But we can have some of the boys soak down the ones we can't mine and put somebody with a kerosene bottle close enough to each to set it off."

Franco looked over at her. "There was some grumbling among the boys when you joined the group," he said. "It never was anything personal. You're a girl and it was hard for some of them to get over that. They thought it wasn't your place to be fighting next to an army of boys."

"Were you one of them?"

"Yes."

"And how do you feel about it now?"

"The same way I felt about it after that first day I watched you lay down some of the mines," he said. "You were the only one of us not to break into a sweat. You've saved a lot of lives being with us and I'm glad that you are."

Angela picked up her machine gun and began to walk toward a door in the rear of the corridor. "You should be," she said. She walked past Franco and out toward an unlit staircase.

Vincenzo stepped into the courtyard through a side door, watching the influx of tanks and soldiers crowd the scenic square. He had a long row of grenades and thin bomb cylinders strapped around his waist, the wires jutting out from each connected to a small device with a red button he held in his right hand. He walked with a quiet purpose toward the young Nazi officer who stood facing Connors and Maldini, and he gave a knowing nod to both men as he approached. The officer caught the look in their eyes, turned his head and saw Vincenzo give him a wave, ignoring the three Nazi rifles aimed in his direction. The officer studied the wired mechanism around the boy's waist and raised a hand slightly to hold his men at bay. "It won't work," he told Vincenzo, watching as the boy positioned himself next to a tank, his hand at his side, finger pressed on the red button linked to the wires. "I don't think those bombs are for real and, even if they were, I don't believe you have the courage it takes to set them off. It's one thing to kill soldiers hidden behind a wall. It's quite another to willingly take your own life along with that of mine and my men."

"That's not something you'll know until I let go of this button," Vincenzo said, his voice maintaining a calm, reasonable tone, the flutter in one of his eyes the only sign of internal distress. "It'd be a waste of many lives if you were wrong."

The officer reached an arm out for Maldini and dragged the older man closer to him. "Do you know this boy?" he asked.

"I first met him several days ago," Maldini said, looking from the Nazi to Vincenzo. "I wanted to keep the boys who remained in Naples safe and I was told to turn to him for help."

"Why him?" the officer asked.

"They pointed him out as their leader. He was the one most eager to kill the Nazis when they came into the city."

"How eager?"

"Eager enough to die doing it," Maldini said.

The officer pushed Maldini aside and glared at Connors. "What about you?" he asked in English. "Do you know this boy as well?"

Connors shrugged. "Dirty shirt, torn pants, dark hair, dark eyes," he said. "You spend enough time around here and they all start to blend into one another. Everywhere you turn it feels as if you're looking at the same kid."

The square was now filled with twenty tanks, with another fifteen lining the outer perimeter of the castle. One hundred soldiers were inside the square, guns at their sides, their eyes focused on the large open windows above them. Except for the four prisoners in the middle of the square and Vincenzo standing in front of the tank, none of the other street boys were visible.

The square was silent.

"Do you think the boy speaks the truth?" the officer, sweat now lining the dark collar of his uniform, asked Maldini. "About the bombs strapped to his body?"

"I don't know," Maldini said, shaking his head and eyeing the Nazi carefully, trying to weigh his resolve. "And I'm relieved not to have the burden of such a decision placed on my shoulders."

The officer stepped away from Connors and Maldini and approached Vincenzo. The boy had been watching the positioning of the tanks and the deployment of the troops, one squad assigned to each of the interior buildings, the contingent of soldiers outside the castle walls placed on the edges of the grass, fifty meters beyond the front entrance. The plan in place did not take into account such a large number of tanks and soldiers beyond the walls, which now meant the fleeing boys would be making their drop down the side of the castle under the glare of Nazi rifles. He glanced over at Connors, catching his eye, and saw the same look of concern across his face. Vincenzo had read enough military history to know even the greatest plan always contains one essential flaw. Overcoming that unexpected error is what often separated a great victory from a monstrous blunder. Vincenzo had left himself only a matter of minutes with which to come up with that solution.

The officer stood ten feet away from the boy, legs spread slightly apart, a cocked pistol in his hand. "What is it you want?" he asked.

"Let the prisoners go free." Vincenzo tried to bury his nervous fear deep enough so that it would not be noticeable in his voice. "The other two as well. None of them means anything to you. The castle is your prize and that you already have."

"But if I don't do as you ask, you'll kill them as well as yourself once you set off your bomb," the officer said. "That doesn't seem a wise move on your part."

"I never said I was wise," Vincenzo said, stepping away from the tank and curling the wires in his left hand. "But I do prefer dying at my own hand, not yours. And I think your prisoners feel the same way."

"Why only these boys?" the officer asked. "Why not free the others hiding behind those walls above me as well?"

"I only ask for what I think I can get," Vincenzo said. "The boys above us are not here as anyone's prisoners. They're here to fight."

The officer stood in place for several moments, his eyes shifting from the castle walls to Maldini, who was doing his best to act indifferent, to Vincenzo, who was all outer calm and inner turmoil. "The lives of just one of my soldiers is more important to me than half a dozen Italians and a vagabond American," he finally said. "You can go and take the rest of them along with you. You may escape death today, but it will come soon enough for you. And you can well expect it to be by the hand of a German."

Vincenzo stared back at the officer, his warm eyes glaring at the man's youthful face. The two were no more than four years apart in age, but the gulf between them was canyon-wide, its boundaries unbroachable due to the blood lust that had been fueled by the words and actions of those who were strangers to both. And because of it, one of them would die soon.

Antonio and Aldo were the first to be released, followed by Pietro and Giovanni. Vincenzo and Connors walked in silence beside one another, several feet behind Maldini and the young officer. The Nazi stopped at the front gate and signaled his soldiers to allow the others through. "I'll see you again," he said to Vincenzo, his jaw muscles twitching, the fury of his anger seeping through the calm veneer he had clearly spent so much time perfecting.

"I hope so," Vincenzo said. "And next time, I won't bring a bomb with me. Only a gun."

Connors waited until they were well out of earshot of the officer before he spoke. "That's not real, is it?" he asked Vincenzo, pointing toward the bomb wrapped around the boy's waist.

"Neapolitans would rather die than commit suicide," Vincenzo said. "The wires aren't even connected to any of the grenades. There was only time enough to make it look real. I found this meter lying next to the boiler in the basement. Without that it wouldn't have worked."

"How soon before they make their move?" Connors asked.

"We have five minutes to be clear of the gates. The moat gate will be dropped and the doors will be closed. The Nazis within the walls will have no choice but to hold their position."

"What about our boys?" Maldini asked. "How will they get out?"

"They've been told to climb out the front windows then to get across the lawn and head down the road to Lungomare." Vincenzo tried to avoid the hard stares of the Nazi soldiers surrounding them. "But I didn't count on so many soldiers and tanks stationed outside the walls. I didn't think he'd split his force."

"No shit, you didn't think," Connors said, angry and frustrated. "Some general. You didn't even think he'd use the most damn basic strategy in the world."

"I was busy." Vincenzo's words were equally angry. "I was trying to figure out a way to save your life."

"And while you were burning up brain cells doing that," Connors said, raising his voice, ignoring the glares of the Nazi soldiers, "you left a hole in your plan wide enough to wipe out half the kids in the castle."

"We need to think of another way to get the boys out," Maldini interrupted. "We have some time. The battle inside will keep them occupied."

"Why don't we take a look at each of our hands and figure out what we don't have," Connors said, his anger now coated with sarcasm. "Guns would be the first thing that jumps to my mind."

"I have six grenades around my waist," Vincenzo said. "We can start with those and take our weapons off the wounded the way we usually do."

"Not this time," Connors said. "We may clip off a couple with those grenades, but the return fire'll be too heavy for us to get close enough to rip a machine gun off a dead soldier. We need a plan B, Chief, and we needed it five minutes ago."

Maldini stopped and looked down at his feet. He was inches from the lid of a manhole cover. He gazed over at Connors and Vincenzo. "The two of you can go on like an old married couple," he said. "It makes a man lose any desire to think things through. One of the benefits of being a drunk, I learned long ago to drown out the chatter I don't want to hear."

"What?" Connors said, his frustration way past the level of reason. "Is there a point to all this? Because if there isn't, I'm not in any mood for a long-winded Neapolitan folk tale."

Maldini patted Connors on the side of his shoulder and smiled. "I have your Plan B," he said.

The tanks were placed in a circular pattern, their turrets primed and ready to bring down the castle walls, when the first of the ignited wine bottles came crashing down on them. Within seconds, the morning sky around the castle was obscured by a heavy rain of gas cocktails and hand grenades. Soldiers rushed toward the sealed doors of the interior buildings only to be blown back by the mines attached to each knob by long, thin wires. The doors that were mine-free had been soaked with gasoline. The instant a soldier stepped in the shadow of those doorways, a streak of blue-white flame erupted, set off by a street boy in a dark corner. Boys stood in the wells of open windows, firing down into the crowded court, wounding and killing the Nazis who were now squeezed against the sides of the tanks, the only cover available to them. The tanks shelled the front of the buildings and the soldiers riddled the upper walls with machine-gun spray, attempting to ward off the attack that had turned the peaceful landscape into a cauldron of black smoke and trampled bodies.

Outside the castle walls, the Nazi tanks were placed in a straight line to fire fierce volleys against the thick hide of the structure, hoping to bring down the buildings and kill the street boys hidden deep in its hold. In the center of the action, the young officer ran along the perimeter of the battle, one of his sleeves streaked with blood, shouting out his commands, hoping to be heard and seen above the din of battle and through the fire-enhanced colors of war.

Nunzia fired off the last rounds in her chamber, clicked in a new ammo clip and turned away from the open window, her eyes singed red by the heavy smoke. "The front walls are weakening," she said to Gennaro. "We have to get the boys out soon."

"We need to wait a few minutes longer," Gennaro said. "If we have them climb out the windows now, they'll be nothing but targets to the soldiers outside."

"Wait for what? They've held them off, now it's time to get them out."

"Our tank should be in place by now, blocking the front entrance," Gennaro said. "The Nazis need to shoot at it and set off the bombs inside. The cover smoke from that should be enough to get some of the boys down unharmed."

"We don't need to wait for the Nazis," Nunzia said. "We can set off the tank ourselves."

Nunzia and Gennaro ran to the other side of the building, each carrying a half dozen grenades in a tied-up woolen shirt. As they turned a dark corner, two Nazi soldiers came up the stairs, guns firing in their direction. Nunzia pushed Gennaro to the ground, braced her legs and back against a wall and fired back. She lowered her smoking machine gun when she heard the soldiers fall down the flight of steps. "Let's go," she ordered Gennaro.

Together they ran toward the open window that stood directly above the tank that barricaded the front entryway to the castle. They rested their hands on the chipped ledge and stared down at the empty tank. Nunzia looked out across the lawn, toward the long line of tanks firing their heavy shells at the base of the castle, an attempt to topple it from the bottom. Soldiers ran around the edges of the property, shooting up at the boys, thick circles of rope bound to grappling hooks hanging across their shoulders, anxious to get close enough to jam the hooks into the open crevices of the castle. "There are so many on both sides," Gennaro said. The panic that was starting to creep into his voice matched the anguished look on his face. "We set a trap for them and we're the ones who end up trapped."

"Let me have your grenades," Nunzia said, reaching out for the boy's knotted up pack. "Then make your way down the halls and tell the boys to get ready."

Gennaro stood and stared out the window, his dark eyes roaming past the tanks and the soldiers, looking beyond the smoldering fields and ruined fountains and statues. "What are they doing?" he asked, pointing out across the large boulevard to an area just beyond the reach of the shell fire.

"Who?" Nunzia peered through the smoke, trying to identify the three stick figures in the distance. Her eyes came alive when she realized who it was huddled over what looked to be an opening in the ground. She turned toward Gennaro and saw the look of awe and respect on his face. "Maybe," she told him, "we're not as trapped as we think."

"Whatever they're planning to do," Gennaro said, feeling the heat of the flames at his back and the tremble of the building each time a shell found its mark, "I hope they do it soon."

"Let's make sure we do our part," Nunzia said. She pulled the pin on one of the grenades, shoved it back inside the folded garment and dropped it down into the open lip of the empty tank. She grabbed Gennaro's arm and ran with him, away from the window and down the stairs. As they turned around the curved landing, stepping over the bodies of the two dead soldiers, the explosion lifted the building off its base, a missilelike plume of smoke shooting up toward the front of the castle, masking it in clouds of darkness. Below them, the tank had shattered into sharp and deadly pieces, which now flew at bullet speed through each end of the courtyard. The bronze doorway, a cannonball from another century embedded in its center, landed against one end of a tank, crushing three soldiers in its path. In the center of all the destruction, the young German officer leaned with his back against the side of a tank, his legs folded under his chin, tears now lining the sides of his face. The intensity of the battle had taken hold of him, stripped him of his bravado and weakened his desire to fight. He sat there, holding an empty gun in one hand, his body shivering in the warmth of the madness that had engulfed his troops, surrendering to a soldier's deadliest enemy.

The overwhelming power of fear.

Vincenzo stood inside the mouth of the open sewer, reaching a hand up for Maldini. Connors was already down below, racing several hundred yards ahead of them, searching out any weapons and bombs that had been hidden there by the street boys in the days before the start of the battle. "Follow the line of water," Maldini shouted out to him. "It will lead you right under the castle."

Connors stopped, bent over and picked up two kerosene-filled wine bottles resting in a corner next to a rusty, old fuse box.

"You should find another half dozen or so before we reach the walls," Maldini said, catching up to him.

"How many of these did you lay down?"

"We're low on everything in Naples," Maldini said across his shoulder, "except wine bottles."

"You two move ahead, get Nunzia and those kids out of the castle," Connors said. "I'll trail back and try to do some damage with whatever I find down here."

"There shouldn't be more than two sewer lids between here and the castle," Maldini said. "And be careful. If you're seen, they'll figure out a way to stop us before we can get to the boys."

The three ran down the dark corridors, Maldini leading the way, moving with subtle grace through the oily darkness of the dank and muddy path. He stopped when they reached the first sewer cover. "They're right above us," he said to Connors. "Grip your fingers through the holes and slide it across. Makes less noise that way. Light those bombs and toss them, close the lid and keep moving."

"Which way, Columbus?" Connors asked. "And don't tell me to follow the water again. There's water everywhere down here."

"You run in a straight line to the second sewer," Maldini said. "From there take the bend to the right. The walls will start to close in around you. That should put you right under the subbasement. From there it's a straight run to the water tunnels and the sea. We'll meet you there."

"We'll be swimming along the shore and to the west," Vincenzo said. "This way we move with the speed of the current. That gets us away from the Nazis faster."

"What about the ones who can't swim?" Connors asked. "How do you plan on getting them through?"

"These boys have been playing in the waters of the bay since they were infants," Maldini said. "If there's one thing they know how to do, it's swim."

"There might be one who can't," Connors said, averting Vincenzo's gaze, his fingers wrapped around the openings of the sewer cover. "What do you do with him? Pray he doesn't drown?"

"We won't let you drown, American," Vincenzo said with a chuckle. "At least not in front of Nunzia."

"I guess there isn't a bay in your rich town either," Maldini said, shaking his head and moving down the slippery path toward the base of the castle, Vincenzo trailing just behind.

"Just the Ohio River," Connors mumbled to himself. "And nobody swims in that. Not even fish."

The front wall of the castle fell in a fiery heap, thick dust and heavy smoke branched out across the charred lawn like a large gray blanket. The bodies of boys and soldiers mixed with one another as the rubble fell on the packed soil below. The Nazi tanks now unleashed the full vent of their assault. Shell after shell ripped away at the stone-hard fortress, grenades and bullets flew through the coarse air. Death and destruction marched in the shadows of their path. It was an inferno with no end, the massive fuel of the battle reaching out a bloody hand to squeeze and whither any and all who crossed its path.

Nunzia was in the next tower; Gennaro and Franco cowered by her side. "We must get to the subbasement," she said. "It's our only chance to escape."

"What about the others?" Gennaro asked. "Can we get to them before the castle collapses?"

"No one will be left behind," Nunzia said in a loud, firm voice as she led the two boys away from the shaking corridor. "Angela is getting the children out of the towers on the water side. We'll work our way down and meet up with them underground."

The three turned a corner, flames licking the sides of the walls, smoke flowing through every opening. They skidded to a stop and stared down at a large crater at the edge of their feet where there had once been a stone floor. The rocks had been blown away by three salvos from a tank stationed across the path. Nunzia looked into the dark void, the eyes of the two boys focused on the fire raging at their back. "We need to jump," she said, reaching for their hands. "It's just one floor down. We can make it."

"What if the next floor collapses from our weight?" Gennaro asked, his voice cracking.

"It's a chance we have to take," Nunzia said. "If we stay here, we'll be dead inside of five minutes."

"I don't want to go first," Gennaro said.

"I'll go," Franco said, stepping in front of Nunzia and Gennaro, his feet poised on the edge of the splintered floor. "And then the two of you follow me down one after the other."

"Aim for the center," Nunzia told him, "and keep your legs bent, it'll help brace your fall."

Franco turned to Gennaro and nodded. "I'll be down there waiting for you," he told him seconds before his jump.

Nunzia closed her eyes and waited through what seemed like end-less moments until she heard the hard landing and Franco's soft voice. "The floor here is solid," he yelled up through the haze of smoke. His voice was a faint echo that mixed with the booming sounds of the Nazi tanks. "But the walls sound like they're going to break apart any minute."

"Hurry, Gennaro," Nunzia urged, placing a hand on the frightened boy's sweaty back. "You have to jump now. There isn't any more time."

Gennaro turned and looked behind him at the fast approaching flames. He could sense the melting of the stone walls around him and his lungs filled with the acrid mix of fire and dust. He gazed up at Nun-zia, her beauty untouched even in the center of a cauldron, and placed a warm hand on her face. "*Un baccio, per buona fortuna*," he said to her.

Nunzia nodded and bent down and kissed the boy gently, her lips soft against the blushed tones of his cheeks. "*Grazie mille*," Gennaro said.

He then stepped back and pushed her over the edge and down to the floor below. He heard her shout out his name as she fell into the empty cavity, landing with a soft thud alongside Franco. She screamed up to him and, along with Franco, yelled for him to make the leap to safety. But Gennaro could no longer move. His small, quivering body and his gentle soul had surrendered to the long war.

"*Grazie mille*," Gennaro said again, in a soft, foggy whisper, disap-pearing behind a collapsing wall and an angry rush of flames.

Connors slid the manhole cover halfway across the opening and lifted his head just above the lip. He stared out at a raging field of heavy heat and thick smoke, dead soldiers, exploding tanks and bullets zipping past at every conceivable angle. Two of the tanks were off to his left, toppled over and smoldering, their iron shells melting into the parched earth.

The remaining soldiers were grouped in tiny clusters, some spread out chest to the ground, others bent on one knee, all firing the last of their ammo toward the open windows above them. Connors stared up at the castle, its thick walls withering and crumbling, huge pockets of fire rising into the sky, black smoke covering the wide interior like a cape. Stranded across the vast breach of such horrible decay were the strewn bodies of soldiers and boys, enemies now linked only in death.

Connors closed his eyes then took a deep breath, his lungs filling with the vile taste of battle. He clicked open his cigarette lighter, brushed the flame against the three strips of cheesecloth jammed inside the tip of kerosene-filled wine bottles, and tossed them out of the sewer. He watched the bottles crash and land in the center of a quartet of merging soldiers. The instantaneous blast sent them all tumbling, their bodies ripped apart. He reached down, turning his head away from the action above, and picked up two more bottles, the cigarette lighter still clutched in his right hand.

Connors never saw the soldier.

The Nazi was on his knees, a thin piece of rope wrapped around the palms of his hands, waiting for the American to lift his head out of the sewer opening. He made a diving lunge toward Connors, flexing the rope twice around his throat with deadly speed and precision. Connors's head snapped back far enough for him to look up into the Nazi's eyes, his hands dropped the bottles and instinctively reached toward his neck in an attempt to ease the pressure. The Nazi pushed down harder on the rope, his eyes bulging from the effort, his jaw muscles clenched, his lower lip bit and bleeding. Connors reached a hand up and tried to swing the Nazi down into the open hole. He pressed his weight against the hard end of the sewer and forced his head to turn, the chord cutting through his skin, a long gash opening just above his neck line and instantly filling with blood and dirt and frayed rope. Connors brought his right hand up, fingers curled into a hard fist and landed a stinging blow flush to the center of the soldier's nose. It stunned him and his grip momentarily loosened. Air once again ran freely through Connors's windpipe. He threw two more punches, one glancing off the Nazi's helmet, the other finding its mark on the right side of the soldier's cheek. Connors then lowered his aim, fought off the urge to give in to the pain, ignored the weightlessness of his legs, and directed his hardest punch at the Nazi's Adam's apple. The sting of the punch sent the Nazi reeling to his left, inches away from Connors's face, the rope now hanging loose around his neck. Connors took a quick glance around and then pulled the Nazi's head toward him, resting it against the base of the sewer. He coiled his arm around the young soldier's neck, pushed it back farther and then snapped it down and held it until he heard the final crack of bone against muscle.

He pushed the Nazi away from the sewer and stepped down slowly back into its darkness. He touched the gash across his neck, saw the front of his shirt sopped through with blood and gave a final sad and tired look at the collapsing walls of the castle. He lowered his head and slid the sewer lid closed, its rusty edges skimming the sleeves of the Nazi soldier's uniform. He climbed down the thin steps and stepped into the center of the unlit corridor, running toward the sewage tunnels at the farthest end, a dust storm raining down on his head from the heated battle above.

Maldini stood with his arms inside the round end of the sewage tunnel, his legs immersed in the cold waters of the bay. The tunnel jutted out a dozen feet past the rear of the castle, its thin corroded cover overrun with grass, dirt and moss. The water was at low tide and the current was pulling gently to the west as Maldini reached up and helped ease the first boy out of the tunnel. "Keep your head low," he said as he placed him in the water. "Walk while you can and then swim when you must. And rest if you get tired. So long as you hug the shore, it'll be difficult for the Nazis to see you."

The boy nodded and began his slow move downstream as Maldini turned back to the tunnel. Inside, the shaft was crammed with two long rows of soot-stained boys, some wounded, others shaken and frightened, all of them overwhelmed by the intense level of fighting they had just endured. Vincenzo and Nunzia crawled along the length of the tunnel, keeping the boys in line, tending to wounds and calming fears. Franco was down at the rear end, directing the ones who were still fleeing the burning castle. Maldini did a rough head count. There were less than fifty boys waiting to pounce into the bay. It meant that at least twenty-five lives had been lost in the fight.

He helped each boy out of the tunnel, his hands red with the blood from their wounds. Maldini prodded them on their way, offering meaningless words of courage and support, watching as they floated in the waters of the bay. He eased the last of the boys into the water then jumped back up into the tunnel, running up to join Vincenzo and Nunzia. In the distance, he could make out the shadowy forms of Franco and Angela. "Call them down," he said. "It's time for them to go. Then you two follow. I'll stay back and string together the line of grenades and swim out to meet you as soon as that's done."

"What about Connors?" Nunzia asked. "We don't leave without him."

"Yes, you will," Maldini said firmly. "Both of you will. It's going to take me a few minutes to string the line and get the grenades in place. He'll be here by then."

"What if he isn't, Papa?" Nunzia asked.

Maldini could hear the desperation in her voice. He gently gripped his daughter's arms in his hands. "It won't take the Nazis long to figure out our escape route," he said. "Once they do, if those boys aren't out of the water they will die. They are in this fight because of us. Many have been killed thanks to the plans we put in place. I'm not going to let anyone, even a man I've grown to care about and respect, allow that to happen. In my place he would do the same."

"Your papa is right, Nunzia," Vincenzo said quietly. "We wait until the grenade lines are strung. It's the best we can do."

Nunzia's black eyes were red temper hot and her cheeks were flushed with anger. Her hands balled into tight fists. "He would never leave any of us," she said, spitting out each word. "He would fight until he was dead. If either one of you leaves this place without him, without knowing if he's alive or dead, you'll have betrayed a friend."

Maldini looked back at his only daughter and nodded. "Get Franco and Angela," he said. "The four of you go out there and make sure the children get to safety. We've left enough of our dead behind for one morning."

"And the American?" Nunzia asked.

"I'll get him out of the castle," Maldini said. "I promise you. It's the least I can do for the man my daughter loves so much."

Nunzia embraced her father and held him tight in her arms. "*Ti amo, Papa mio,*" she whispered.

"*Anche io ti amo,*" Maldini said back to her. "*Con tutto il mio cuore.*"

Vincenzo held Nunzia's hand, waiting as Franco and Angela ran up next to them, both crouched down to keep their heads from hitting the ragged top of the tunnel. "Let's go," he told her. "The children are waiting."

Maldini waved them off as he watched each one dive into the cold water and disappear around the bend of the sewage tunnel, swimming their way downstream. He found a soggy cigarette in his torn shirt pocket and tried to light it with a damp match. It caught on the third try and he smiled when he heard the crackling of the brown tobacco. He took a deep drag and blew the smoke up toward the tin ceiling. He then turned away from the water's edge and walked back into the mouth of the storm.

Maldini found Connors in a rear corridor, hunched down on his knees, hiding from the shadows of two passing Nazis, the handle of a long knife palmed in his right hand. Maldini inched in toward him, walking gingerly on the slippery subbasement floor strewn with water, dust and debris. He gave Connors a quick nod and pulled a pistol from his waistband, waiting with his back pressed to a redbrick wall for the Nazi soldiers to cross his path.

When the two soldiers were five feet away, standing on opposite ends of the subbasement, Connors moved first. He leaped to his feet, grabbed one Nazi from behind, and shoved the knife deep into the center of his back. The second Nazi turned when he heard the scuffle but Maldini stepped out of his nook and fired three shots, sending the soldier sprawling to the muddy floor. Maldini ran toward Connors, stopping only to retrieve the Nazi's machine gun. He was quick to notice the rope cut across the American's throat and the blood flowing freely down the front of his chest. "I knew you wouldn't be able to find your way alone," he said to Connors. "I should have left you a compass."

"It wouldn't have helped," Connors said. "I have no sense of direction."

An explosion just above their heads caused the ground to tremble and the walls to crack and splinter. "Then follow me close," Maldini said, starting to run down the back end of the subbasement. "I won't come back for you a second time."

"I'm right on you," Connors said.

He followed Maldini out of the subbasement, into the sewage tunnel. Above them, they both could hear the heavy footsteps of Nazi soldiers, searching through rubble and flames for any hidden boys or escape routes.

Maldini led the way around tight corners and through dusty crawl spaces, navigating each turn with an agility and skill that belied his years. He scampered like a child in search of a favorite, secret place. As he ran, rushing to keep up with the older man, Connors realized that while Vincenzo and the others knew their way around the streets of Naples, Maldini could take them into places no Nazi could ever find. He was their one guide to the underground, moving through tunnels and sewers with relaxed precision and a confident step.

They were both out of breath when they reached the last loop of the sewage tunnel. Maldini wiped at his brow with the corners of an old handkerchief. "The water's up ahead," he said between gulps of breath. "Jump in and turn to your right. The current will then take you where you need to go."

"I'll go in when you go in," Connors said. "You don't have the time to put up that grenade line by yourself. The Germans will figure out a way to get down here, it's only a matter of minutes."

"You don't need to know how to swim," Maldini said with a knowing smile. "The bay is kind to all, even Americans. And I'll be right behind you. It won't take me long to get the line ready."

"I think you told me once you weren't cut out to be a hero," Connors said.

Maldini shrugged his shoulders. "I'm from Naples," he said. "We lie a lot."

He walked to a corner of the dark tunnel and picked up a rolled-up row of tin wire, a dozen grenades strung through its loops. He turned and looked up at Connors. "My daughter's waiting for you," he said. "And Neapolitan women hate to be kept waiting. Especially the foolish ones who think they're in love."

Connors gave him a warm look and an easy nod. "She's waiting for her father, too," he said. "I'll see you in the water."

As Connors's heavy boots sent a vibrant echo against the slate sewer walls, Maldini started to unspool the long row of wire, walking backwards, carefully laying each line down in a wide zigzag pattern. There were enough grenades on the roll to send a fireball hurtling down the central sewage line and back through the gaping holes in the castle structure. It would be enough to bring down the remains of the building and all who stood inside.

Maldini had unfurled half the line when he heard the familiar sounds of Nazi boots and machine-gun fire coming down the far end of the corridor toward him. He picked up his pace, releasing the wire as he did, placing the last of the grenades down in the center of the sewage tunnel. He slipped to his knees, reached a hand out for a loose grenade, gazed up at the soldiers, who were shooting and shouting as they closed in and quietly pulled the pin as he dropped the bomb. He got to his feet, bullets zinging past him, landing with loud echoes against the sides of the tunnel roof and walls, and ran for the open hole twenty feet away. His run gave way to a slide as he slipped on a strip of oily surface, waving frantically for Connors to stand away from the tunnel exit. "Worry about my daughter," Maldini shouted. "Not about me."

"Stay low and keep running," Connors yelled back, watching Maldini get on his feet and run toward him. "I hate traveling alone."

The first bullet ripped into Maldini's shoulder and sent him sprawling to the ground, his face laying flat inside a mud puddle. He lifted himself up to his knees and wiped the brown water from the sides of his face. He looked over at Connors, less than a dozen feet away, and pressed his right hand across his heart. "Take care of my daughter," he said to him.

The second bullet hit Maldini in the square of his back but he never felt its sting. The loud explosion of the grenade line and the loud mushroom fireball that followed in its path drowned out all his pain. Connors saw Maldini's head tilt back and his eyes close seconds before the fatal blast. He saw the line of flames come zooming in his direction and threw himself under the lapping waves of the bay, the ferocious anger of the fire above warming the murky water. He stayed under, kicking his feet and flapping his arms, as he awkwardly moved several feet away, hugging the shoreline and coming up for air under the shade of a hanging tree and a mound of wilted grass. He saw the mouth of the fire rush back toward the castle walls. He stood up in the shallow water, the salty waves washing and stinging his wound, and stared at the lip of the tunnel, expecting somehow to see Maldini miraculously emerge from inside the firestorm.

The bright morning sky had turned into early afternoon rust, fire and smoke high enough and thick enough to cover miles of the empty city. Steve Connors wiped the dripping beads of water from his face and walked back toward the open end of the sewage tunnel. He stood in front of the lip, the flames now down to thick, crisp curls of blue and white smoke, inside walls the color of coal. He removed his battered pith helmet and rested it inside the tunnel. He then took several steps back and saluted.

He held the salute for several silent moments, in memory of the man who had just given him the only gift that would ever matter.

His life.

29

PIAZZA GARIBALDI

Von Klaus stared down at the thin map spread out across the front end of his tank. Kunnalt held it down with both hands. The colonel then grabbed the map, tore it in half and tossed it to the ground. "One hundred men dead!" he shouted. "More than twenty tanks destroyed! Another fifteen more with barely enough fuel to make it out of the city. It's a disaster and one that should never have happened."

"The Italians have also sustained a significant number of casualties, sir," Kunnalt said, defensively.

"This Third Reich of ours was to have lasted a thousand years, Kunnalt," Von Klaus said. "Each one shrouded in glory. And now, we can't even defeat an army of children."

Von Klaus walked toward the well of his tank and pulled out a bottle of red wine. "There is no honor in fighting such a battle," he said. He poured the wine into a tin cup and handed the bottle to Kunnalt. "Not like this. Not against children. There will be no victory for us here. No matter the final outcome."

30

VIA DON BOSCO

Nunzia sat huddled with her head down, a black sweater draped across her shoulders. Connors leaned against the side of a pine tree, staring out at the clear sea that overlooked the bluff. A contingent of street boys had gathered around them, building a small fire, boiling small tins of watered-down coffee, breaking off pieces of stale bread, their weapons at rest by their sides. They moved about silently, respectfully mourning one of their own. Vincenzo walked over and handed Nunzia a tin of coffee, waited as she took it and watched as she nodded her thanks. He moved several feet to her left and sat down between her and Connors, his legs bent against his chest, his eyes focused on the patch of dirt by his feet. The mastiff was in front of them, his thick paws stretched out, his head curled to one side.

"We all should try to get some rest," Connors said in a low voice. "Both sides have had enough fight for one day."

"We sent all the boys up into the hills for the night," Vincenzo said. "They can take care of their wounds up there and get a night's sleep without any worry."

"Did Dante and Pepe come back with anything we can use?" Connors was talking to Vincenzo but his eyes zeroed in on Nunzia, wishing he could will away her sorrow or take the burden of her grief.

"The news isn't good," Vincenzo said.

"Let me hear it anyway," Connors said.

"Half the city's been destroyed." Vincenzo stared back down at the ground, his voice tired and hoarse, arms and face still soiled from the day's heated combat. "Von Klaus is moving his remaining tanks and troops toward the railroad tunnels and then into the center, into the middle of what we call *Spaccanapoli*. It's the core of our city. If he's successful at burning down both, his mission will not be a total failure."

"How many tanks does he have left?" Connors asked.

"Dante counted thirty," Vincenzo answered. "He was a distance away, so he might be off by one or two either way."

"And soldiers?"

"About two hundred. Subtracting the wounded."

"Where are they going to start? City or tunnel?"

"Pepe saw an advance team moving toward the tunnels," Vincenzo said. "Which makes sense. It's the easier of the two targets. And it's a short distance between both areas, so they could move quickly from one to the other."

"So will we," Connors said. He stepped away from the tree, walked past Vincenzo and the silent Nunzia to bend down over the small sparkling fire. "It all ends tomorrow," he said with his back to them, eyes peering into the crisp flames.

"There are less than a hundred boys left," Vincenzo said, taking slow sips from his coffee tin. "About a dozen are wounded, but not enough to keep them out of the fight."

"Leave the wounded ones in the hills," Connors said. "And let them have enough guns and ammo in case some Nazis make their way up there."

Connors stood and walked to Nunzia. He knelt down in front of her, reaching out a hand to caress the side of her smeared face. "You might want to sit this one out," he said. "Stay up in the hills and help take care of the wounded kids."

She looked at him, her eyes hard but warm, and shook her head, holding on to his hand with the edge of her fingers. "This is where I belong," she said. "It's where we all belong."

He stared at her for several quiet seconds, then took a deep breath and nodded. "Stay here with Vincenzo," he told her. "You both need to get some sleep. Have all the boys ready just before dawn and be down by the tunnels. I'll meet you there."

"Where are you going now?" she asked.

"I've never ridden on a tram before." Connors leaned down and kissed her on the cheek and forehead, holding her close to him, losing himself in her warmth and sweetness. "I think it's about time I did."

31

VIA FRANCESCO PETARCA

Connors stared up at the six large, rusty trams. Their severed overhead wires cut them off from all current, the sides of their bodies were greased and oiled. Thick ropes were wrapped around their top rows, snaking down past the cracked windows and curling up under their base. He turned away and took in the wide mouths of the street alleys behind him, less than five hundred feet of hard cobblestones standing between the openings and the trams. He walked toward his jeep, where Dante, Pepe, Claudio and Angela were sitting inside. The mastiff stood next to the vehicle, his head jammed against Fabrizio, who was by his side. He took the keys out of his pants pocket and flipped them toward Dante. The boy caught them with his right hand. "You always wanted to drive it," he said.

Behind them, the sun was starting to set, leaving them less than an hour of clear daylight. The surrounding area was barren, buildings torched and crumbled up and down the wide boulevard. "We probably won't finish before dark," Connors said. "If we don't, we'll build some fires along the alley entrances so we can see where we're going. One more fire in this town isn't going to attract any attention."

"Where do you want me to drive?" Dante asked, anxious and eager, but also nervous.

"In front of that first tram, for now," Connors said. "Stop it about six inches past the front end. Then grab the ropes from underneath and above the trams and tie them down hard to the back of the jeep. Anywhere would be good, except the wheel base."

"You're going to have the jeep pull the trams?" Angela asked.

"That was Maldini's plan," Connors said. "Unless you think you can do it on your own, I'm going to go with it."

"It will work," Fabrizio said, stepping up alongside Connors, the dog fast by his side. "If Maldini said so."

"Then there's nothing else to do but get to it," Connors said.

They began their work at dusk.

First they moved the silent trams across their tracks, the rear wheels of the jeep kicking up thick pockets of dust and hurtling small rocks into the air as it burned off strips of rubber. Its engine cranked and all cylinders were churning as Dante switched gears with the poise of a safe-cracker. Connors and Angela moved from tram to tram, making sure the gears stayed in neutral. They soaked the insides with kerosene, so they could soon be used as weapons against the remaining Nazi tanks.

Once they were across from the mouth of the alleys, on the back road leading into *Spaccanapoli*, Connors and Angela shifted the gears of the trams into park and slammed down on the emergency brake. Dante jumped the jeep into reverse and backed up into the front of the first tram. He jammed on his brake, helping to ease their stop. Behind him, Pepe and Claudio quickly undid the ropes.

Dante then circled the jeep around and eased it in front of the center of the first tram. "We're going to have to drag each one across the mouth of that alley," Connors told him, pointing at the five hundred feet distance they needed to travel. "You tie the ropes from under and above the tram back onto the jeep and you run that engine as hard as it can run. Even if it starts to smoke, don't stop giving it gas. The rest of you come with me. We'll push it from the other side. Use your back, your hands, I don't care what, you have to get it to the ground."

"The dog, too?" Fabrizio asked.

"I can't think of a better time to have him around," Connors said.

Angela stared up at the imposing old structures, long abandoned and decayed. "I don't think there's enough of us to do what you want."

Connors looked away from the concerned gaze of the young street girl and up beyond her shoulders. He nodded his head toward the near distance and smiled. "There is now," he said.

They all turned to see Nunzia and Vincenzo walking down the center of the boulevard, followed by the remaining street boys. They moved in tight formation, numbering less than a hundred, each carrying weapons by their sides or strapped loose across their backs. Their bodies had been scarred by war and marred by loss as they marched through the streets of their city. Connors walked closer to meet them, followed by Fabrizio and the mastiff. "I should have learned by now to give up on giving you people any kind of an order," he said to Nunzia and Vincenzo.

Nunzia embraced Connors, silently holding him in her arms. Vincenzo turned to wave on the ones behind him toward the ropes and the trams. "I promise you, American," he said. "When you give us the right order, we'll follow it."

It took them most of the night.

They pushed and tugged at each tram, twenty boys linked to one long thick strand of rope, Dante straining the gears and wheels of the jeep, ripping through the skin of their hands and the thread of its tires, all in the effort to topple the old steel dinosaurs. As each tram collapsed on its side it filled the air with mounds of dust and sent chunks of broken cobblestones and glass hurtling in all directions. The boys dropped the ropes and scurried away, waved clear from the massive hulks by Nunzia and Angela. After each takedown, the boys would stand in a semicircle and pump their small fists toward the sky, wiping drops of sweat and blood against the sides of their arms, eager to move on to the next tram in the line.

Once the half-dozen trams were resting on their sides like tired, old animals, the frayed ropes were double-looped around their tops and bottoms and then dragged, one by one along the bumpy, cobblestone streets, toward the wide end of the alleys.

"What if Maldini was wrong?" Vincenzo asked Connors. "What if the tanks won't risk going over the trams?"

"They won't be able to help it," Connors answered with assurance. "A tank officer's biggest weakness is that he thinks there's nothing he can't run over. And these trams are so old and beat up, those Panzers should be able to jump them without any problem. That's why it's important to have the mines and grenades rigged on the inside. I don't want anything but flames coming out of those alleys."

Vincenzo looked over at Connors and stared into the soldier's clear, confident eyes. His uniform was reduced to brown smudges, blood smears and black soot marks, but the patch of the Thunderbird Division was still clean and visible. "Will it be enough to give us a victory?" he asked.

"You won your fight back on the very first day," Connors said. "Just by staying here and standing up to the Nazis. But now you want more than that. Now you want to beat them. That's going to be a little harder."

"I'm glad you stayed with us," Vincenzo said. "I don't know if the boys would have held together without a soldier on their side."

"You would have thought of something, General," Connors said, walking down toward the alleys and the trams. "I'd bet my life on it."

32

45TH THUNDERBIRD INFANTRY DIVISION HEADQUARTERS SALERNO

Captain Anders folded the paper in half and slipped it into an envelope. He held it in his hands and stared out the open flap of his tent. He had written so many of these letters in such a short period of time. He had grown weary of trying to explain to mothers and fathers why their sons would never come home again, their bodies lost in the fight for control of foreign soil. He glanced down at the box of dog tags resting next to his foot and tossed the envelope on top of the pile.

Anders looked up when he saw Higgins walk into the tent. "I only want good news," he said to him. "And that's an order."

"Air command has agreed to send a plane to Naples, sir," Higgins said. "A B-24. It should be there sometime today."

"Just one?"

"It's all they could spare, sir," Higgins said. "They need the rest up north against the Nazis and down the coast to protect the Fifth Army."

"One might be enough to do the job," Anders said. "At the very least it'll give us some idea of what we're looking at down there."

Anders walked over to the table in the center of the tent and gazed down at the large map. "Looks like Patton's making his move," he said.

"You can always count on him to rattle the cages and get things rolling. This'll force Monty's hand. There's no way he lets Patton get too far down that coast. He'll want to make sure he can share in the glory and the headlines. Which means it won't be long before we're on the move, too."

"Every city from Rome on up is in chaos," Higgins said. "It's a dog-fight anywhere you go. The Allies against the Germans with the Italians stuck in the middle. All our reports indicate that the Nazis are making the Italians pay a heavy price for switching over to our side. You can't go a block on any street without finding a body."

Anders looked away from the map and down at the box of dog tags next to his desk. "Everybody's paid a heavy price," he said.

THE FOURTH DAY

33

STAZIONE CENTRALE

Nazi soldiers walked in small groups along the empty tracks, following in the dusty wake of their tanks. They kept their eyes on the wooden slants in front of them, ever mindful of the mines that had been placed under the dark shiny rocks. Kunnalt was in the center tank, standing tall in the open mouth, his binoculars focused on the four wide entrances to the tunnels. "Fire into them," he shouted to the tank commanders on either side of him. "If those boys are in there, I don't just want them blocked in. I want them killed."

It was eight o'clock in the morning, the first day of October in 1943 when the first of the Nazi shells exploded inside the train tunnels of Naples.

The dozen tanks moved in a semicircle, unleashing an arsenal of weapons inside the gaping mouths that once connected Naples to its sister cities in the north. The thick old brick sides of the ornate archways collapsed under the assault, landing in front and inside the tunnels, sending mounds of dust and rock cascading in all directions, falling at the fiery feet of the flames.

Kunnalt turned and waved his soldiers in ahead of the tanks, watching as they riddled the dark tunnels with machine-gun fire and the oppressive power of the flame throwers, some stopping to launch grenades deep into the misty craters. Kunnalt surveyed the scene and nodded his approval.

Kunnalt's men stopped at the tunnel entrance. Their guns were poised, their flame throwers were in idle. The tanks were at their backs, turrets smoking and at rest, engulfed by dust and flames and specs of debris as the soldiers waited for any sound of life.

"Check for bodies, then seal the tunnels," Kunnalt ordered the junior officer. "Then double back and meet up with us at the next location."

"What of the wounded, sir?" the officer asked.

"There won't be any wounded," Kunnalt said. "At least none that you can find. Have I made myself understood?"

The junior officer snapped a salute, nodded and turned to watch as Kunnalt's tank veered to its right, circling away from the tunnels and toward its next destination.

That was when they saw the catapults.

They were two hundred feet away, three of them lined up twenty feet apart. Cracked tower bells were jammed in the center of their mouths, large unexploded bombs planted inside their bases. They were built of rotting planks of wood, burned bricks and rusty chains, held in place by rods and gears pulled off the bodies of dead tanks. Vincenzo and Nunzia stood behind the catapults, heavy wooden mallets in their hands. Two boys were assigned to each one, looking to Vincenzo for the signal to fire. "Be patient," Vincenzo told them. "Wait for the American and the boys to get in place and then for the Nazi to make his move."

"What if he fires on us before we get a shot off?" one of the boys asked.

"Then you pray he misses," Vincenzo said, his eyes looking beyond the boys and past the tanks and soldiers, into the mouth of the smoking tunnels.

They were crouched down inside the rodent-infested sewers under the train tunnels, fifty boys squeezed in a space suitable for half that number. The walls shook and dust came down at them like ocean waves. They could feel the heat of the fire and the collapse of the rooftop shingles crashing down on the tracks. Most of them had their eyes closed and their hands flat against the sides of their ears. "How much longer do we need to wait?" Dante asked Connors, his small body jammed in next to the soldier's brawn.

"You'll know before I will," Connors said to the frightened boy. "So when you give the signal, that's when we'll move."

"How will I know what to look for?" Dante asked.

"You won't need to look. You'll hear it."

The shelling had stopped and the soldiers had ceased their fire. The dust around them had settled and the crackling fires, only inches from their heads, were burning on their own. Dante looked up at Connors and shrugged his small shoulders. "Now?" he asked.

"Great call, Sergeant." Connors patted the boy on the head and then clicked the chambers on his two machine guns.

Connors popped open the sewer cover and slid it across the grimy rails of the tunnel. He jumped out of the dark hole, checking the front and rear entrances. The Nazi soldiers were all on his left side, their focus on Vincenzo and the catapults. The tunnel was dark and blanketed from floor to ceiling in smoke and fire, giving the boys a difficult but perfect cover to walk through. Its farthest end was blocked off by the presence of a silent Nazi tank. "Let's go," Connors whispered down into the hole. "Cover your nose and mouth for as long as you can. Hold your breath if you have to. You're going to make it through. Don't worry. We'll be coming up onto the soldiers who are on the outside end, with their backs to us."

The line of boys streamed out of the tight sewer openings, emerging from both sides of the tunnel, each one slowly adjusting to the heavy veil of smoke, the crumbled mounds of stone and the thick burning wood that surrounded them. They held their rifles by their sides, feeling their way through the murkiness, occasionally pressing a hand against a scorched wall for guidance. Connors walked down the center of the tunnel, keeping an eye both on the line of boys and on the Nazi activity close to the entrance. The soldiers had by now retreated back to the cover of their tanks, firing heavy volleys in the direction of the catapults.

Connors stood by the tunnel entrance, the air clearer, the boys grouped behind him alongside each wall, his back to the Nazis less than fifty feet away. "Dante, you and your group move to the right," he whispered, waving the boys out of the tunnel. "Claudio, you take your boys and move to the left. Stay low and don't fire until you see me move out and wave to Vincenzo. And let's hope they don't see us first."

"What if they do?" Claudio asked, talking in hushed tones.

"Shoot at them until you run out of bullets," Connors said. "And after that, just run."

"Your plans are much easier to follow than the ones Vincenzo thinks up," Claudio said, too frightened even to venture a smile.

"I like to keep things simple," Connors told him.

Connors stayed behind, his machine guns poised at the Nazi soldiers, watching as the boys made their way out of the tunnel and along the tracks, quietly closing ranks on the enemy. He looked to his left and to his right and signaled both Dante and Claudio to stop and hold their positions. The Nazis were moving forward, looking to get closer to Vincenzo and the catapults, the shells of their tanks falling short of their intended mark by a good fifty yards. Connors looked up at the clear sky and the sun drifting toward its center.

It was a horrible waste of a beautiful day.

He stepped toward the middle of the tracks, waved his hand, and then he and the boys opened fire. Nazi soldiers fell in a heap, caught unaware by the rear attack. Connors wrapped the two machine guns around his shoulders, yanked two grenades off his belt, pulled the pins out with his teeth and threw them toward the tanks and soldiers. He rolled to the ground, swung the guns back into his hands and resumed firing, targeting the Nazis closest to the tanks and leaving the easier targets for the boys on his flanks.

"Okay, Vincenzo," he said to himself. "It's time to ring those bells."

Vincenzo and Nunzia were on their knees in front of the first catapult, legs scraping against sharp rocks wedged between the tracks, debris from the exploding tank shells dancing in the air around them. Each held a mallet and looked out past the tanks and soldiers at Connors and the street boys as they exchanged heavy fire with the Nazis outside the railroad tunnels. Vincenzo rubbed the sides of the old tower bell strapped to the center of the catapult and got to his feet, the mallet raised high above his head. He pounded down two blows to the left side as Nunzia did the same to the right and then both stepped back. The chain holding the bell in place snapped and released both the bell and the bomb it held in its well. They watched as the bomb arched high toward the sky, then sank down toward a Nazi tank, its engine revving hard, the driver anxiously shifting gears to avoid its impact.

The explosion rocked the terminal and flung the tank ten feet off the ground.

It bounced across the tracks, crushing several soldiers in its wake, and came to a fiery halt on the rocky slope near a concrete platform. Vincenzo pumped his fist. Nunzia and the boys jumped in the air and cheered with delight. The boys rushed toward the two remaining catapults, pounding down on the chains holding the bombs and bells, eager to release their havoc on the Nazis. "You did it, Vincenzo," Nunzia said. "You really made it work."

"It wasn't me," Vincenzo said, touching the side of her face and walking toward the others. "It was your father. If we win anything at all today, it will be because of what he did and what he showed us could be done."

"He would have been pleased to hear that," Nunzia managed to say.

Vincenzo turned and looked back at her and smiled. "I don't think so," he said. "It's more likely he would have come up with something to be angry about."

The Nazis were trapped.

Connors and the boys bore down on them, firing their rounds, tossing their grenades and cocktails. Vincenzo and Nunzia sent their heavy artillery hurtling, demolishing two tanks at a clip. Kunnalt surveyed the fiery scene and ordered his tanks and soldiers to swing to the right, leave the main station and head for the center of the city. There was one unobstructed road open to them and they moved straight for it, firing wildly at the boys at both ends of the tracks.

"All right," Connors screamed out, "everybody move back. Take the wounded and put them in the tunnels. The rest of you get up those hills and out of sight."

Dante stepped up next to Connors and stared at the retreating tanks and soldiers. Blood ran down the side of his face from a gash above his eye. "They should be coming up to the spot any second now. Unless we placed them wrong."

"We'll know soon enough," Connors said. "How'd we do on casualties?"

"We lost four boys," Dante said. "Six others are wounded. One of them could use a doctor."

"Have Nunzia look at him," Connors said. "See if she can patch him up and keep him together for a couple of days. We should have some help in here by then."

Dante took a cigarette from out of his pants pocket and put it to his mouth. He snapped off a match and was close to lighting it when Connors reached over, pulled the cigarette from Dante's lips and put it up to his own. He then lifted the boy's hand that was holding the match, lit the cigarette with it and took in a deep drag. He shook Dante's arm and put out the match. "That was the only one I had left," Dante said.

"Good to hear," Connors said, walking along the tracks, watching the Nazi tanks near the narrow road taking them out of the main station. "You're not a sergeant just yet. When you are, then you can smoke."

The loud series of explosions knocked both of them off their feet. The Nazi tanks had driven across the mine field set by the street boys. Dante's machine gun bounced along the edges of the track. The heavy continuous blasts sent German soldiers sprawling and strewing armor parts in all directions. Connors got to his knees, watching the destruction taking place at the far end of the station as he wiped a hand across the reopened wound around his neck. He turned to check on Dante. The boy was on his hands and knees, his eyes lost in the massive spectacle that was unfolding. "How many did you and Franco lay down?" Connors asked.

"All that we had left," Dante said in hushed tones. "There were about a dozen and we laid them in under the rocks about ten feet apart, just like you told us to do."

"That should be enough to wipe out at least half those tanks," Connors said. "And if more than twenty soldiers come out of that alive, I'd be surprised."

"So I did a good job?" Dante asked.

"Yes," Connors said to him, slowly getting to his feet and retrieving his weapons. "You did a very good job."

"Now can I have a cigarette?" Dante asked, running to catch up to Connors.

"Wait until after the war," Connors said, looking over his shoulder.

Nunzia poured red wine over her hands and dried them on a clean dishrag. She looked down at the wounded boy and smiled, moving a row of damp, thick strands of hair away from his eyes. They were inside one of the four tunnels, the boy resting on a soiled thin mattress, his head propped up on three folded shirts. There were a half dozen lit candles around them and in the shadows of the semidarkness, Nunzia could see the severity of the boy's stomach wounds.

"*Come ti ciami?*" she asked the boy.

"Maurizio," he said.

He was close to twelve, thin, with a sweet angular face and deep, rich black eyes. His hands rested quietly at his side and he moaned slightly with each sharp jolt of pain. He looked into her face and nodded. "*Non che niente da fare,*" he said in a low voice.

Nunzia rested two fingers across his lips and rubbed her hand along the sides of his face. She reached behind her and pulled out a sopping wet cloth from a small pot filled with brown water. She squeezed the water from the cloth and rested it on top of Maurizio's warm forehead. Nunzia turned when she saw the shadow approach, pulling a pistol from her waistband. She lowered the gun when she spotted the familiar face.

"Thought you could use some help," Connors said.

"The shrapnel wound is very deep," she said. "I think I can stop the bleeding and bandage it up. But I don't know what to do about the two bullets in his stomach."

Connors looked down at the boy and then back up to Nunzia. "He's losing too much blood. Those bullets need to come out."

"I don't know how," Nunzia said.

"Please," Maurizio said, running his tongue across dry lips, his words coming out in slow spurts. "Don't touch them. I know you want to help. But I can't take the pain. Just stay with me. Both of you. Don't let me die alone."

Nunzia wiped at the corners of her eyes and leaned in closer to the dying boy, holding on tight to both his hands. Maurizio stared up at Connors, his breath coming in tight hushes. Connors yanked his canteen off his hip and poured some water into his hand. He dipped two fingers into his wet palm and brushed them against Maurizio's cracked lips.

"My rosary beads," the boy whispered, moving his fingers along his pants. "They're in my pocket."

Connors dug a hand into the boy's pocket and eased out a string of black beads, the bottom row wrapped around a silver crucifix. He gently pried open Maurizio's palm and placed the beads in the middle, then closed the hand and held it to his chest for several seconds. He rocked on his heels and watched as the boy brought the crucifix up to his lips. "*Grazia*," he said, his eyes once again shining.

The boy began to shiver and shake, the blood gushing from the open wound, his thin legs trembling under the torn cotton pants. He held out his arms and awkwardly lifted his head. "Be with me," he said to Connors and Nunzia. "I'm too afraid to die alone."

Connors and Nunzia stretched out in the middle of the empty tracks, resting their heads on Maurizio's thin shoulders, their arms wrapped around his bloody body. They closed their eyes, listening as the boy said a soft and gentle prayer.

They stayed and held him until he died.

Connors waited for Nunzia outside the tunnel entrance, his uniform drenched in Maurizio's blood, a moist cigarette smoldering in his right hand. His face was flushed red and he pounded against the hard brick wall with his fists. All soldiers reach a point, as do most men, when the reality of death overwhelms them. It can happen on a battlefield or in a mess hall. With some, it can occur decades after the last bloody body was seen, thousands of miles removed from the painful memory. But the moment always finds its place. For Steve Connors, that place was in the middle of an empty train tunnel in an Italian city torn to shreds, listening to a frail boy taking his last breath.

Nunzia stepped up behind him and placed a hand on his shoulder. Connors kept his head down, eyes staring holes through the grimy side of the wall, his hands pressed against the still-hot bricks. "I cleaned his wound and found a shirt in the back pile that fit him," she whispered. "And I folded the rosary beads around his fingers."

"They try to teach you to keep it all buried, from day one of boot camp," Connors said, the top of his head pressed against the wall. "To act as if you can't see any of the horrible things that happen around you. To keep your focus on the enemy and not on some guy you just left bleeding back in the middle of a mud field, whose last name you're not even sure you can remember. But how can you not see it?"

"No one really survives a war," Nunzia said. "There are never any winners or losers. There are just those who bury their memories and those who live with them every day."

Connors turned around and slammed his back against the wall, his eyes bitter and red. "He was twelve and he got shot in a battle over train tracks," he said. "And he died braver than any soldier I've ever seen in the field. He looked right into my eyes and there was no anger there, no hatred. There was just a quiet peace. That little boy understood more about living and dying than I ever will."

She walked over to him and rested her head against his shoulders, her arms wrapped around his waist. "Death and war is all that most of these boys have known," she whispered. "What happy times they've had in their lives are so far in the past, it's difficult to even imagine. They now live day to day. Just like me and just like you."

Connors clasped his hands around hers and held on to them tight, his head still crammed with images he knew would linger for the rest of his life. "The other boys are waiting," he said finally. "We need to be with them."

"They wait for you," she said. "Vincenzo is their heart and my father was their soul. But you're the one who lifts their courage, who makes them believe they belong on the same field with the Nazis."

"It doesn't sound like I'm doing them any favors," Connors said.

"You give them hope," Nunzia said. "That's something they haven't had since the war started and it's something no boy should be without."

Connors lifted Nunzia's face, his arms around her waist. "Is that what I give you?" he asked. "Hope?"

"Yes," she said with a gentle nod of her head. "That and much love."

"I'll look for you when the dust settles," Connors told her.

"I know you will."

He brought her back up to him and kissed her one last time.

34

SPACCANAPOLI

The final battle for the streets of Naples began at two in the afternoon on a sunny first day of October.

The sky was as clear as a pane of glass and the sun burned down on the large piazza that was dominated by bombed-out houses and dark, imposing office buildings, their windows blown out. In the center of the square was a large church, its three-tiered steeples grasping for the heavens, its curved stone steps leading to the shuttered iron doors. Seven wide alleys led into and out of the square, a dim route to another area of the city. *Spaccanapoli* sat on Naples like a giant squid, it's large tentacles spread in all directions.

Four boys were positioned in each of the alleys, hidden against the sides of walls, guns and cocktails in their hands. Vincenzo peeked out from behind a large mound of rubble off one of the main alleys. He saw fifteen Nazi tanks move up and down the square and into the side streets, a large contingent of soldiers following in their wake. Von Klaus stood in the well of a tank in the center of the square, his eyes on the empty buildings, binoculars at rest, his body calm and at ease. Vincenzo leaned back down, head and shoulders resting on the sharp piles of brick and stone, wishing that somehow he could make the peaceful morning last forever.

Von Klaus surveyed the positions of his tanks and the placement of his soldiers. He took a deep breath and tapped against the side of his vehicle. The men in the well below him slammed in the first shell, braced themselves against the tank walls and fired. The first shot of the final battle landed in the middle of an abandoned pharmacy and sent it crumbling to the ground.

Vincenzo lit the fuse end of his kerosene bottle and hurled it over his head, watching it land against the rear of a Nazi tank. The hidden street boys jumped from their posts along the nooks and crevices of the alleys and fired at the soldiers that were stationed at the base of the square. The Nazis whirled at the sound of the shells landing at their feet and returned the shots with a furious volley of their own. The boys emptied their guns and began to back into the alleys, tossing rocks at the soldiers who were following them in, a tank trailing each small group. Vincenzo monitored the action, running down the center alley, sliding through the front door of the collapsed tram blocking his path, and emerging from the other end. He moved from one alley to the next, gazing over the tops of the trams, watching the boys lead the tanks and soldiers down the narrow strips. The Nazi soldiers were in aggressive pursuit, stepping over the bodies of fallen boys and firing down on those who scampered toward the trams. "Remember to jump in the driver's side," Vincenzo shouted. "It's the only place not mined."

He watched one boy slip and tumble across the dark cobblestones and then quickly get back to his feet, his body one long strip of welts, bruises and open cuts. He turned, threw his last rock at a rushing Nazi and looked across the tram at Vincenzo. "What if the tanks don't even try to go over these?" he asked.

"We've left them no choice," Vincenzo reassured the boy. "A tank never backs up. Especially if it sees its enemy waiting on the other side."

"I only pray you're right," the boy said. He dove head first into the driver's side door.

"So do I," Vincenzo said in a low voice, his eyes on the Nazi tank less than twenty feet away.

Nunzia, Franco, Claudio, Pepe and Dante were running across the far end of the square, pursued by six Nazi soldiers, both groups firing at each other. The children circled and dove behind the edges of a large, empty fountain next to a pink stucco two-story building. Angela bolted out the shattered front door, tossed a lit kerosene bottle toward the soldiers, then jumped in beside the others behind the base of the fountain. The explosion killed two of the soldiers, sending debris down across their backs and heads. The children braced against the sides of the fountain and checked the ammo on their guns, the soldiers' footsteps a rock-toss away. "They're coming at us from both sides," Angela said, glancing above the clipped wing of an urchin. "We can't let them trap us in here."

Dante secured his last clip into the chamber of his machine gun. "I'm tired of running," he said. "I'm tired of everything. I think we all are."

Nunzia looked at each of the children, holding them down, away from enemy range. "We just need to go a little farther," she pleaded. "Once I get you out of the square, then you can rest."

"No," Dante said, his warm eyes sad, his lips pursed and determined. "We came here to fight, not to run."

Nunzia watched as, one by one, they nodded their heads in agreement, then checked their rifles, machine guns and pistols, prepared to step into the teeth of the fight. "The Nazis have seen our backs for three days," Angela told her. "It's time for them to see our faces. See who it is they're fighting."

Nunzia looked above the rim of the fountain, a dozen soldiers easing in closer to them, crouched down low, machine guns at the ready. She turned back to the children around her. "Spread out across the base," she said, "and fire until your guns are empty. If you need to run, head for the side alleys above us. And God be with you all."

They rose as one, firing the last of their bullets at the surrounding troops.

The return volleys were heavy, landing against the sides of the fountain and in the pink stucco wall behind them. Pepe rotated his machine gun from left to right, taking down two Nazi soldiers before the sting of a shoulder wound sent him sprawling to the dirt. Angela fired her rifle from waist level, scatter shooting and landing with a sniper's precision. She tossed aside the empty gun and pulled the blade from the crook of her neck and flung it into the chest of a leaping soldier, his reach a mere inches from her face. Nunzia emptied her pistol and jumped under Franco and Claudio's fierce fire, reaching for the machine gun of a fallen soldier. She came up on one knee, ripping bullets into the fronts and backs of the oncoming Nazis.

Beyond them, the piazza had exploded into a vast killing field, the fire on both sides heavy and often hitting its mark. The tanks rained down their anger on both brick and body, rumbling through the side streets and over collapsed and burning structures, seeking out their human targets. Von Klaus worked one end of the square, shouting out orders, directing his scattered troops to wreak their havoc on an enemy he never envisioned being as resilient or as dangerous as the street boys. Kunnalt, his shoulder bleeding from a wound sustained in the tunnel battle, was keyed in on the other end, his tanks firing at the array of silent buildings and the wild scampering of the children. Plumes of thick smoke, haze and blood filled a square that had once been the pride of all Neapolitans.

Connors was on the steps of the church, in the center of a small arsenal of machine guns, flame throwers, kerosene bottles and grenades, six boys spread out to his left and right, firing down on the Nazis with the final remnants of their rage. He tossed aside an empty machine gun and reached down for another, looked up across the square and saw Nunzia lead Angela and the boys on their valiant charge. He signaled the boys around him to seek shelter and keep firing as he inched his way forward, separated from the woman he loved by the enemy he loathed.

Vincenzo stood across the road, surrounded by a kneeling and wounded cluster of street boys, their weapons strewn by their sides, each watching as the tanks made their move onto the toppled trams. The front ends of the tanks squeezed down on the rusty hulks of the ancient buses, the sound of bending steel and breaking glass vibrating out of the dark, smoky alleys. The treads on the tracks churned as they eased themselves into the soft well of the hunkered vehicles. Fabrizio stood behind Vincenzo, the mastiff at his side. "Don't worry," Vincenzo said in a voice loud enough to be heard above the din of the tanks. "Maldini will not let us down."

The tank in the middle alley went first.

The mines buried inside the tram gave off a violent and angry shudder, then the force split the tank and the body of the bus in two. The front end of the tank flew out from the mouth of the alley, trailing a long thin line of flame and smoke. It flipped end over end and skidded to a halt along the edge of the rail tracks. The tram let loose a large gulp of fire up the alley walls, torching what remained of the convoy of soldiers before forcing its flames into the open square.

The next three explosions shook the foundation of the piazza and sent the facade of many buildings and homes tumbling to the ground in scattered heaps. Soldiers and boys fell, carts and statues were toppled, shattered glass came down from on high, slicing its way through flesh and bone.

Von Klaus looked at the fires coming out of the alleys, shaken by the blasts, his face tinged a heavy shade of red from the intensity of the four-edged cauldron, knowing that within the confines of those tight dank corridors he had lost four tanks and twenty brave men. He slammed his fist against the side of his tank, as much in frustration as in anger, losing the tight leash he kept on his emotions, finally allowing the hardness of the street soldier to overcome the frailties of the man. He ordered his tank to circle around toward the mouth of the empty alleys and fire a volley of shells as it moved. The treads ran over and crushed rocks, glass and bodies. He saw Kunnalt, wounded and fighting on in a corner of the square, his soldiers firing at a woman and a line of street boys. "You win," he shouted across the space between them. "You'll finally get your wish."

"Which wish is that, sir?" Kunnalt shouted back.

"To see them all dead," Von Klaus said.

His tank moved forward, his eyes still on the bleeding young officer, the fires and explosions around them growing louder with each passing second.

The B-24 flew above the demolishing landscape, its experienced crew looking down at the inferno that engulfed *Spaccanapoli* with silent dismay. "Hold off on dropping any bombs," the pilot instructed through his mouthpiece. "They're too bunched up. We'll end up wiping out the whole plaza. I think it's best to bring it around again and see if we can get some gunfire in there without hitting somebody other than Nazis."

"You get us close enough, we might be able to knock off some of them tanks," a gunner in the bubble, Sharky, said. "Help give those boys a little bit of a break."

"Anybody make out that guy from the Thunderbirds in the crowd?" the pilot asked.

"Hard to see through all the smoke, but it looks like there's a G.I. cornered over by that church to your right," another voice answered.

"Whatever we do, let's make sure we don't hit any of those kids." The pilot glanced over at the lieutenant to his right. "They're dealing with enough shit without having to worry about us on their ass."

"If you can get close to the north end of the square," Sharky said, "I can get in a good swipe at those tanks and soldiers jammed in beside those alleys."

"There are kids coming at them from the other end," the pilot said. "By the time I swing around, they'll be there."

"Might just be enough for those tanks to know we're here," the rear gunner said. "Make them take a step back, knowing we're closing in."

"Let's all just be patient," the pilot said. "I'm going to keep moving around until one of you finds an opening. When you see enough clearance, then take your shots and make them count. Make the tanks a priority. The kids are too close to the soldiers for us to risk a swoop."

"Do you want to keep the tanks contained in the square?" one of the gunners asked. "Or do you want them back out on the road?"

"Let it play itself out," the pilot said, swinging the front end of the B-24 high to the left and away from the piazza. "In the square or out, be nice if we leave behind some burning tanks. There's some pretty intense fighting going on down there. Which means that more sooner than later, one side's going to have to move back. That's when we go in."

"Those kids look to be pretty much holding their own," Sharky said. "Be nice if we can give them a hand."

"They know we're here," the pilot said, gently easing the B-24 clear of the battle zone. "And they know we'll be back. For now, that's all we can give them."

"Comfort first," Sharky said, surveying the scene behind him, "bombs and bullets later."

Vincenzo placed the wounded boy under the shade of a large pine tree, resting his head on top of a mound of torn clothing. He turned around and put both hands on Fabrizio's slender arms. "I want you and the dog to stay here and keep an eye on the wounded," he told him. "I need someone I can trust to keep them safe."

Fabrizio nodded several times, his eyes wide and filled with confidence. "I won't let anything happen to them," he said.

"You should all be safe here," Vincenzo said, the fires of the alley glowing at his back. "This street is not on a route the Nazis will want to take."

"Where will you be?" Fabrizio asked, staring at Vincenzo and the dozen street boys standing behind him.

"Where I belong," Vincenzo said.

He turned away from the boy and ran toward the fire in the alleys, the rest of the street boys trailing close behind, three of them holding thin blankets under their arms. "Jump right through the flames and you'll be okay," Vincenzo shouted, picking up his pace. "If the fire gets to your clothes, don't worry. Someone will get to you before it can get to your skin."

"Why are we going in this way?" one of the boys yelled out. "Some of the other alleys are wide open and clear."

"There are soldiers and tanks waiting in the mouths of those alleys," Vincenzo said. "They expect us to make a run at them from there. They're not counting on us running through fire. Remember to have your guns ready to shoot as soon as you cross the flames. We'll only be a surprise to them for a few seconds."

"I hate surprises," one of the boys said as he picked up his pace and passed Vincenzo and the others, several feet away from the arching flames.

"So do the Nazis," Vincenzo said.

Nunzia, Angela and the boys stood in front of the fountain, firing the last bullets in their guns, the bodies of half a dozen soldiers strewn about their feet. A shot fired by Kunnalt, standing in the well of his tank, his uniform smeared in blood, clipped Claudio in the shoulder and sent him sprawling, one side of his head landing on top of a chipped piece of stone. Nunzia and Pepe pulled the boy behind the fountain, both still firing guns with their free hands. As she emptied the bullets in her chamber, Nunzia looked past the smoke and the heavy return fire and saw Connors running across the square toward her, two blazing guns in his hands. "Nunzia, get down!" Franco shouted, shoving her to her knees.

She broke away from him and turned to catch a rifle tossed to her by Angela. She gave a quick glance at those around her. Franco bled from his leg and arm, holding a machine gun in the crook of his good shoulder. Pepe was shooting from a sitting position, a large bloody gash open on his forehead. Claudio was throwing rocks and stones, trying to get to a fallen soldier's gun, his arm washed in blood. Angela, the front of her shirt soaked the color of beets, stood her ground and fought with both a gun and a knife.

Nunzia clicked the trigger on the rifle and turned to aim it at Kunnalt, now out of his tank and coming at her, less than ten feet away. Connors was in the middle of the firefight, ramming the backs of Nazis with the butt end of his guns, shooting them as they went down, inching his way toward her. She turned her head and quickly looked his way, catching his eye and holding the gaze for the briefest of seconds.

Kunnalt's first shot hit her flush in the stomach, knocking her backwards, the gun flying from her hands.

The second one landed just below her neckline, its force turning her around and away from him, her right hand curled just above the edge of the fountain. Angela and the boys held their fire, eyes frozen on Nunzia's fallen body. Connors ripped through the Nazi line, in a frenzy, killing all that stood between him and the woman he loved. He rushed to her side, watching as Kunnalt drifted away, enveloped in a veil of smoke. He dropped to his knees and turned her face toward his, desperately aware that the wounds were deep and fatal. "No," he mumbled, in between broken breaths and muffled sobs. "Don't do this. I'm begging you, please, don't die. I'll get you out. We all will. Just please. Hang on for me. Please."

She placed a hand across his quivering mouth, her warm eyes calm and peaceful. Connors heard and saw nothing else but her, alone in the center of a brutal storm. "A good man always finds love," she said to him. "You found it with me, even here, even now."

"Yes," Connors said, "I did find it."

"And you will again, my American."

Connors held her closer, kissing the top of her head, her blood oozing onto his shirt. "*Ti amo, Nunzia,*" he told her. "*Ti amo.*"

She looked at him and smiled. "Who taught you to say that?" The coldness reached her waist, her body giving in to the power of the bullets.

"Your father," Connors said. "He told me if I said it twice, the love will last forever."

"I think he made that part up," she said.

"I believed it," Connors said, rocking her gently back and forth. "I still believe it."

Her hand slipped away from his face and her eyes slowly closed. Connors held her for several minutes, running his fingers through the strands of her hair, the tears falling from his eyes and mixing with the blood on his shirt. He then rested her head back on the ground and turned to the silent, stunned street boys around him. In the far corner of the square, he saw Kunnalt running back to his tank. He stood, reached for Nunzia's rifle and handed it to Angela. He then looked at each of the children. "I want you to stay with her," he told them. "Don't leave her alone for any reason. If anyone goes near her, make them very dead."

He picked up a machine gun and ran out into the smoke and haze of the square, in search of Kunnalt.

Vincenzo and the street boys jumped through the thick flames of the exploding trams, side-stepping the destroyed tank, and came out the other end of the fire shooting at the Nazis grouped at the far side of the alley. The soldiers turned, quickly got to their knees and began to return fire. Several feet behind the soldiers, Von Klaus swung his tank into position, looking to ensure that the boys' charge would be a futile one. Vincenzo and the boys moved forward. Bullets bounced off the sides of the walls and the hard pavement, but many also found their mark and boys tumbled to the ground. In the center of the alley, Vincenzo lifted his right arm. At the signal, the boys dropped their guns and pulled two grenades each from the back waistbands of their pants. They pulled the pins.

"Let them taste it," Vincenzo shouted out and watched the arched path of the grenades reach the fleeing Nazi soldiers.

The explosions rocked the alley and sent them all to the ground. Vincenzo landed with a thud against a sharp piece of rock, which sliced a deep cut across his cheek and just below his eye. He crawled to his feet, glared out past the rushing smoke, the alley now empty except for Von Klaus and the mouth of his tank. Vincenzo stood on shaky knees, a small pistol clutched in his right hand, watching as the tank eased its way into his end of the alley. White fumes embraced Von Klaus as he looked down at the boy from inside the open well. The tank inched forward and came to a stop, twenty feet away from Vincenzo and the street boys. "I will not allow you a victory," Von Klaus shouted down at him. "Not today and not ever."

"It is still our flag that flies here," Vincenzo said, holding his ground, gripping the trigger of the pistol, his mind fogged by the blow to the head and the blood that flowed down the side of his face. "Not yours."

"That flag will be the last thing you will live to see," Von Klaus said, poised to give the order to fire. "Your adventure ends with honor, but in death."

"There's no honor in fighting a Nazi," Vincenzo said. "Or dying at his hand."

"Then you'll die like an Italian," Von Klaus said. "Free of both honor or victory."

The shot came from an open window just to the right of Von Klaus.

It caught the colonel flush in the square of his side, forcing him to clutch and double up. Vincenzo looked up and saw a stunned Fabrizio standing in the window. The boy stared at the rifle in his hands. "I'm sorry I didn't do what you told me to do," he said. "But I didn't want any more of my friends to die."

Behind Vincenzo, two of the street boys had slid open a sewer cover and had begun to scamper into the open hole. Von Klaus lifted his head and looked at Vincenzo, a pistol in his right hand. He squeezed off two shaky rounds, one missing the boy, the other grazing his right leg, sending him down to one knee. Above them, a B-24 hovered in the skies.

Vincenzo fired back as he retreated, his shots ricocheting off the sides of the tank. Two street boys rushed up and grabbed him, dragging him, legs first, into the sewer hole. Vincenzo and Von Klaus held the hard look between them until the very second the leader of the street boys disappeared under the cover of a tunnel, the hot shell from the tank turret exploding just above his head.

As Vincenzo and the boys raced along the edges of the tunnel runway, they could hear the heavy fire from the B-24 shell Von Klaus and his tank. Vincenzo, his arm wrapped around the shoulders of an older street boy whose name he didn't even know, looked up at the shaking, dusty curved lid of the tunnel. "Enjoy the rest of your time in Naples, Colonel," he said.

Connors and Kunnalt exchanged gunfire as they both ran. Connors emptied the last bullets in his machine gun, the final blasts missing the fleeing Nazi. He tossed the empty gun to the ground and closed in on his target. Kunnalt turned, a pistol aimed toward Connors, but was caught at chest level by the soldier's leap before he could get off another shot. They crashed through the large front window of a long-abandoned storefront, the weight of the American knocking the wind from the Nazi, the force of the fall reopening Connors's shoulder wound. They rolled on the marble floor, over rocks and debris, kicking aside thin slants of old wood and discarded cardboard boxes. Kunnalt pushed back Connors's head and jabbed several punches into the now bleeding wound, blood rushing out in thick spasms. Connors lifted his right knee and shoved Kunnalt off him. He hit him twice in the face and once in the chest, sending the Nazi sprawling along the dusty floor, flat on his back.

Kunnalt stretched out his left hand and wrapped it around a thick hunk of stone. Connors was on his knees and coming up toward the officer when he caught the blow against the side of his face. A second punch hit him at the back of his neck and sent him skidding toward the side of an old fireplace, ashes still piled high in the redbrick center. Kunnalt hovered over him, yanked Connors by the hair at the back of his head and rubbed his face and eyes in the pile of ashes. Connors struggled to lift his head, feeling along the marble floor for leverage, looking to push back at the Nazi. The tips of his fingers rubbed against the end of a sharp, rusty old iron poker. Connors pushed his head back several inches, his mouth filled with the taste of ash and slid his body down until he could grasp the poker in his right hand.

Kunnalt straddled the American, grabbing the back of his wet shirt and lifting him to his knees. "A soldier should not have to die this way," Kunnalt said, a knife held tight in his right hand. "Not for a bunch of children."

Connors whirled around, broke the hold and got to his feet. He reached back and jammed the poker deep into Kunnalt's stomach, watching the Nazi's eyes widen and hearing the knife fall to the floor. He held it there for several seconds, Kunnalt growing weaker, his left hand gripped around the end of the poker, the blood flowing out of his midsection, the life ebbing from his face. Connors stood above Kunnalt and felt the breath of death flow from his open mouth. He slammed his boot against the end of the poker, ramming it deeper into the Nazi's body. Connors stepped back and let the Nazi fall facedown against the cold marble floor, the tip of the poker rising out of the center of his back.

Connors looked down at Kunnalt and then walked slowly out of the store.

The square was a thick mask of smoke.

Four Nazi tanks fired at what was left of the buildings and fleeing children. Connors walked toward the fountain, Angela and the boys still hovering over Nunzia's body. Vincenzo, Fabrizio and the mastiff were now with them. Connors stepped between the boys, bent down and gathered Nunzia's body in his arms. He held her close to his chest, his eyes staring at her peaceful face. He turned and placed her gently inside the fountain, lining a series of thick rocks around the edges of her body. Vincenzo moved in alongside him and rested a hand on top of hers. "You had her love," Vincenzo said to him.

Connors looked away from Nunzia and stared at the boy, his face and leg bleeding, a machine gun in his left hand. "Sometimes that's just not enough," he said in a low voice.

The shell exploded just above their heads, chunks of pink stucco flying down at them, the Nazi tank bearing in on the small group, firing bullets in their direction. "Up the church steps," Vincenzo yelled, pointing to his right, waving the group away. "Grab some weapons and hurry. We'll let the tank come to us."

The group ran toward the dozen steps of the large church, the last building in the square untouched by Nazi bombs, stopping only to pick up guns and grenades from the side of the fallen. Vincenzo followed, firing his gun at the approaching tank as he moved. Connors, his back to the oncoming vehicle, bullets spitting at the dirt around him, held his place above Nunzia's body. "You, too, American," Vincenzo said. "You're not going to do her any favors by dying. Get to the church and help the others. They need you there."

Connors whirled and glared at Vincenzo. "If you don't mind, General," he said. "I'm not in the mood for taking orders."

Vincenzo turned from the tank to the soldier, his voice softer. "It's not an order," he said. "It's a favor. Help us finish what we started."

Connors and Vincenzo held their look for several seconds, ignoring the guns and the shells exploding around them. The soldier looked down at Nunzia one more time, then picked up two machine guns and a row of hand grenades and followed Vincenzo toward the steps of the church.

They stood with their backs against the bronze doors of a medieval structure built for prayer, the tank inching its way up the stone steps, firing an angry volley of bullets as it lumbered toward them. The ragged army held its place and fired back. Connors and Vincenzo rained machine-gun fire against the steel of the tank. Angela, Franco, Claudio, Dante and Pepe tossed grenades at the handful of soldiers hidden by the shadows of the vehicle. Fabrizio threw as many rocks and stones as he could find, the bullmastiff barking angrily by his side. Three other Nazi tanks circled the square and headed in their direction.

The tank bounced from one step to the next, close enough now for the boys to reach out and touch. Angela tossed out her last grenade and ran down the steps, trying to reach an abandoned machine gun. A Nazi soldier leaped out from behind the tank and fired, hitting her in the knee. She fell, grabbed for the machine gun and threw it to Franco. The boy caught it on the run, then he, Connors and Vincenzo jumped on top of the tank and crawled their way toward the lid.

The boys snapped open the lid of the tank and jumped off, Franco fired at the soldiers huddled behind the vehicle, giving the wounded Vincenzo the cover he needed. As they all scooted up the stairs, Vincenzo pulling Angela along with them, they watched Connors jam his guns inside the lid of the tank and fire until his bullets were spent. The tank creaked to a halt, a mere inches from the front doors of the shuttered church.

Connors cast aside his guns and unpinned his last grenade, tossing it at the soldiers firing from behind the tank. He jumped off the front end just as the explosion hit, sending three more Nazis tumbling to their deaths. He ran up the steps and grabbed Fabrizio, shielding the boy with his body.

"We only have a few guns left to fight with," Vincenzo told him. "They still have three tanks, all heading here."

"And we're short of bullets and grenades," Franco said.

Connors looked up and down the line, each one of them either too spent or too wounded to move. The steps leading up to the church were speckled with blood and bodies. The entire square was a bright blaze of flame and horror, bodies crumpled alongside buildings, tanks over-turned and shedding oil and smoke, fires raging in all corners.

The three tanks rumbled along the sides of the square, closing in on the church, looking to take aim and end the final stand of Connors and the street boys. "You can run," Connors said. "They'll get some of you, but not all. It makes no sense for everybody to die."

"Send Fabrizio and the dog," Angela said. "The rest of us will stay."

Fabrizio stepped out from behind Connors. "I will never leave my friends," the youngest of them said.

Connors reached down and lifted the small boy into his arms, hold-ing him against the flowing blood of his upper body. He kissed Fabrizio on the cheek and stared into his gentle eyes.

"It was a miracle we took it this far," Franco said. "I thought we would all be dead the first time we tried to fight the Nazis."

"We were just one miracle short," Connors said, looking down at the circling tanks. "That is, if you believe in those things."

They heard the plane before they saw it.

The B-24 came from out of the smoke and the clouds to bear down on the Nazi tanks. Vincenzo stepped away from the door and looked up at the American plane, firing at the now-fleeing tanks, chasing them into the alleys at the far end of the square. He turned and glanced over at Connors and shrugged, half his face covered in blood. "It's getting harder not to believe in miracles," he said.

The B-24's machine-gun turrets riddled the last remaining Nazi sol-diers in the square, then circled back, giving the Panzers time to clear away from the area. It swooped down one final time and dropped three hundred pounds of bomb on top of the three tanks, sending each to its final destiny.

The streets of Naples were free of Nazi rule.

Connors, Vincenzo and the others walked down the steps of the church, out into the burning square. They moved together silently through the smoke and haze, staring at the bodies of the children and soldiers that filled the piazza. They stopped in front of the fountain and Nunzia's body. "I want to bury her," Connors said to Vincenzo. "Do you know a place she would have liked?"

"Nunzia was like her father," Vincenzo said. "She loved the sea and the city. There are places along Piazza Trento e Trieste where she can see both."

"Take us there," Connors said.

The American turned and lifted Nunzia's body into his arms and walked with her slowly past each remaining street boy. One by one, they gently kissed her folded hands. Connors followed Vincenzo out of the square and into the darkness of a quiet alley. The rest of the group inched in behind them, their wounds still open and bleeding, their hands finally free of guns, the Italian sun warming their backs.

They kept their heads bowed in silent prayer as they went off to bury one more of their dead.

35

LUNGOMARE

The bonfires lit the night sky.

The group sat around the warm flames, drinking from tin cups filled with red wine, their wounds bandaged as well as possible, staring out at the quiet sea and up toward a blanket of stars. Fabrizio rested his head against the side of the sitting mastiff, both of them gently drifting off to sleep. Connors lit a cigarette and offered one to Dante. "I'm not a sergeant yet," the boy said, shaking his head.

"You fight like one," Connors said, sliding the pack back into his pocket.

"No planes, no tanks and no soldiers," Vincenzo said. "It's been years since that was true."

"What happens to us now?" Angela asked, her leg wrapped in cloth, blood still seeping through.

"The Americans should be here in a day or two," Connors said. "Some medical units as well. They'll try to find anyone who's left from your families and put you together with them."

"We won't have to worry about getting killed," Franco said. "But now we have to figure out how to live."

"That's always going to be harder," Connors told him. "No matter what side of the war you're on."

"What about you?" Claudio asked. "Where will you go?"

"I'll stay here until my unit comes in," Connors said.

"The Thunderbirds," Vincenzo said, eyeing the patch once again.

"Right." Connors gave him a knowing nod. "Then, wherever they go, I'll go with them."

"Will you get into trouble for helping us?" Vincenzo asked.

"They don't ever get too mad at you for killing the enemy." Connors tossed the last of his cigarette into the fire. "Whatever they come down with, I can handle."

"I'm happy you stayed with us, American," Vincenzo said. "We all are. It's your victory as much as ours."

"Was it worth it?" Connors asked, staring at him from across the fire.

"Yes," Vincenzo said without hesitation.

"Just for you or for everybody?"

"It means as much to the ones who died as it does to the ones who live," Vincenzo said, standing now and facing the fire. "This fight wasn't for us. It was for Naples."

Franco and Dante threw more wood on the fire, watching it grow bigger, giving the night an afternoon's warmth and glow. The group sat closer to the fire. Connors looked past them toward the quiet lapping of the bay. He closed his eyes and smiled when he heard them begin to sing the first words to their favorite Neapolitan love ballad.

They stayed until early morning, singing the slow and sad lyrical words to "Parla Mi D'Amore, Mariu." Their faces were warm and their cheeks red, their wounded bodies aching from the weight of battle.

They lifted their eyes toward the sky and sang out in full voice as they held one another.

They were all that remained of a battered army of children, determined to die for the sake of their freedom.

And now they had finally found peace.

On the streets of a ruined city they could once again claim as their own.

EPILOGUE

Without victory, there is no survival.

—Winston Churchill

Vincenzo stood on the crowded platform looking up at the train. His shirt and pants pockets were crammed with official-looking documents, all stamped by both the American forces now in place in Naples and members of a provisional government that had been installed to oversee the rebuilding of the city.

Much had happened since the end of their battle against the Nazi tanks. The Americans had come in several days later and taken control of Naples. The boys were given medical aid and attention. Connors came by each day to check on their status. He eventually moved out with the rest of his Thunderbird division, heading up north toward Amalfi and the coast.

"Will you ever come back to Naples?" Vincenzo had asked the last time he saw the American.

"Why wouldn't I?" Connors said to him. "I have a lot of friends here."

Once their wounds were healed, Angela and the boys were put in temporary quarters as soldiers and city officials sought any surviving members of their families. One by one, each member of the group was sent to live in a place he or she would call home. There, they could once again be children, instead of soldiers.

Vincenzo picked up the valise by his side, packed with clothes given him by soldiers, and walked toward the steps of the train.

An American officer blocked his path.

Vincenzo stared up at him and saw that he wore the same patch as

Connors on the side of his shirt. He put down his valise and waited for the American to speak.

"Are you Vincenzo?" the officer asked.

"Yes," the boy said.

"My name's Anders. Do you have a couple of minutes for me?"

"The train doesn't leave for another twenty minutes," Vincenzo said.

"How about we sit on that bench over there?" Anders pointed to a stone slab just off to the right. "You want some coffee or anything?"

"No," Vincenzo said, walking to the bench and sitting down. "I have all I need."

"Where's the train taking you?" he asked. The captain sat down next to the boy and put an unlit cigar into a corner of his mouth.

"Milano," Vincenzo said. "My aunt lives there. My father's sister. She's going to take me in."

Anders nodded his head, both hands flat across the tops of his knees. "You and your boys gave those Nazis one helluva run," he said.

"Why are you here?" Vincenzo asked.

Anders gave the boy a slight smile. "Connors told me you didn't have much patience for bullshit," the captain said. "As usual, he wasn't lying."

Anders reached a beefy hand inside his uniform jacket, pulled out a thin yellow envelope and handed it to Vincenzo. The boy took the envelope and held it on his lap.

"After Naples, I sent Connors and some of my Thunderbirds up the coast," the captain said. "They teamed up with the Texas Division and some of the Brits and went against the Nazis who were fighting their way down from Rome. Some of those battles got pretty hot and not all of them went our way."

"What happened to Connors?" Vincenzo asked, fearing he already knew the answer.

"I lost a lot of good men in those fights," Captain Anders said, staring down hard at the boy by his side. "Steve Connors was one of them."

The two sat silently for several minutes, gazing out as passengers rushed to catch the waiting train. "Before he went out," Anders continued, "he asked me to give you that envelope, just in case anything happened. I don't know what he put in it, but he said whatever it was, you had earned it."

Vincenzo took a deep breath and wrapped his fingers around the yellow envelope, his throat dry, his lower lip trembling.

"He respected you, kid," Anders said. "He respected all of you."

"And one of us he loved," Vincenzo said in a low voice. "Nunzia."

"For what it's worth," Anders added, "we checked on that Panzer colonel. Von Klaus. He was pretty banged up but he got out of Naples alive. He probably wished he hadn't. When he got back home, he walked into his house and found his family shot dead and the SS waiting in his dining room."

"He was only a soldier," Vincenzo said.

Captain Anders took a deep breath and stood up, then placed his hands on the boy's shoulders. "I would wish you luck, son," he said. "But that would be nothing but a waste of time. You know that better than I do. We just try to live while we can and make the best of it. So you just be well and stay well."

Vincenzo gripped the envelope tighter and watched as Captain Anders turned and disappeared into the crowd.

Vincenzo sat in a seat next to a large window. He felt the train inch its way forward, easing away from the platform and out of the station, the puffs of white smoke from its front stack cascading down around the tracks. He took a deep breath and tore open one side of the yellow envelope. He reached inside and pulled out the Thunderbird patch Connors had worn on his sleeve. He stared at it for several seconds, his moist eyes blurring his vision. He brought the patch up to his chest, lowered his head and cried silent tears.

The train was now chugging along its path, engine running at full throttle, heading north. Vincenzo lifted his head and looked out at the passing scenery, a maze of battered homes, blocked-off roads and military convoys. He caught his reflection in the thick glass and wiped the sides of his face with the palm of his hand.

Outside, white smoke billowed from the front of the train, sending thick clouds streaming through the air.

It was a day of peace in a time of war.

PRESENT TENSE

Present Tense

A Radiohead Compendium

Edited by Barney Hoskyns

CONSTABLE

CONSTABLE

First published in Great Britain in 2019 by Constable

1 3 5 7 9 10 8 6 4 2

Copyright © Rock's Backpages, 2019

The moral right of the author has been asserted.

All rights reserved.

A CIP catalogue record for this book is available from the British Library.

ISBN: 978-1-47212-944-4 (hardback)
ISBN: 978-1-47212-943-7 (trade paperback)

Typeset in Minion Pro by SX Composing DTP, Rayleigh, Essex SS6 7EF

Printed and bound in Great Britain by Clays Ltd, Elcograf S.p.A.

Papers used by Constable are from well-managed forests
and other responsible sources.

Constable
An imprint of
Little, Brown Book Group
Carmelite House
50 Victoria Embankment
London EC4Y 0DZ

An Hachette UK Company
www.hachette.co.uk

www.littlebrown.co.uk

Contents

Introduction

In the fine essay included here on Radiohead's 2000 album *Kid A*, Simon Reynolds asks why we shouldn't consider its predecessor – 1997's *OK Computer* – to be the best British rock album ever made.

It's a more than legitimate question. I've regularly listened to *OK Computer* for over twenty years and can't see too many rivals to such a crown: not *Revolver*, not even *Exile on Main St.*; certainly not *Sgt. Pepper* or *London Calling* or *The Stone Roses*. Yet in the *Observer*'s 'One Hundred Greatest British Albums' listicle of June 2004, *OK Computer* polled no higher than 24 – a reflection, one might suggest, of the residual suspicion towards Radiohead's seriousness, their emotional grandeur, their willingness to risk pretension and complexity in their playing. The UK's rock-critic consensus never quite abandons its dim view of the 'progressive' tendency in pop music.

To get from the neo-Nirvana abjection of 1993's breakthrough hit 'Creep' to the anguished six-and-a-half-minute prog epic that was *OK Computer*'s 'Paranoid Android' in the space of just three albums remains astounding. Few listeners who bought the group's debut album *Pablo Honey* (1993) would have given Radiohead much chance of evolving beyond what John Harris called the 'angst-ridden paroxysms' of their early sub-grunge emoting.

Second album *The Bends* was, of course, a key transitional work. Within minutes of the opening 'Planet Telex' it was clear they'd taken a giant stride forward from 'Creep' and the sour 'Anyone Can Play Guitar'. Yet the suspicion around them remained and even grew, rooted in an inverse snobbery towards middle-class boys from Oxford in the era of Britpop. For what were Radiohead if not, inadvertently, the anti-Oasis – a band with scant interest in being big for the sake of it, public schoolboys bored of the hoary trappings of rock stardom. They wanted to take rock beyond the stale conventions of the mid-'90s and had a number of attributes to help them: principally the musical gifts of Thom Yorke's singing and Jonny Greenwood's brilliance as a guitar player and all-round sonic architect – but also the con-siderable contributions of their colleagues Colin Greenwood (bass and older brother of Jonny), Phil Selway (drums), Ed O'Brien (guitar) and, not least, exemplary engineer-turned-producer Nigel Godrich.

Radiohead were also willing to stare humanity's dystopian hi-tech future in the face and question where we were all heading. In time, this convinced the group to leave traditional rock elements behind them – at least temporarily – and embrace the textures and signifiers of electronica as they moved into the new millennium. Yet they never entirely abandoned the beauty of their melodies, and even when Yorke's lyrics were at their most elliptically irritating he could move you to tears with the seraphic yearning of his vocal lines.

INTRODUCTION

While *OK Computer* remains a musical Matterhorn that neither they nor anyone else are likely to top, Radiohead have consistently delivered music which confirms their stature as the most daring of major rock bands. Are there any more intoxicating bursts of popular music than '2+2=5' or 'Burn the Witch', any Smiths-inflected anthems more drivingly potent than 'Knives Out' or 'There There', any ballads or downtempo lamentations more beautiful than 'Nude' or 'Pyramid Song' or 'Sail to the Moon' or 'Give up the Ghost'? Other contemporary acts may have had their great phases (PJ Harvey, Joanna Newsom, Feist, Arcade Fire, Interpol, Grizzly Bear, Queens of the Stone Age), but few have amazed and surprised us for so long.

It's been a genuine pleasure assembling the reviews and interviews for *Present Tense*: to travel from Ronan Munro's prescient early reports about On A Friday (what a relief they dropped *that* name) to the exceptional reportage, portraiture and commentary of writers such as Reynolds and Will Self, Ann Powers and Adam Thorpe, John Harris and Pat Blashill, Will Hermes and R. J. Smith – and of Mark Greif, whose towering essay in *n+1*, 'Radiohead, or the Philosophy of Pop' may be the most extraordinary thing ever written about the group.

Do Radiohead, by virtue of their radical intelligence and engagement with our terrifying times, elicit more intelligent critical writing than Oasis? And is it rock snobbery to suggest as much? Judge for yourself as you read *Present Tense* and follow the band's twenty-eight-year journey to the tense present day of 2019.

Barney Hoskyns, Rock's Backpages, April 2018

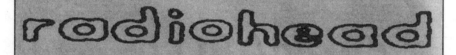

PLEASE NOTE

ON A FRIDAY
HAVE CHANGED THEIR NAME
TO

radiohead

FIRST E.P. OUT IN APRIL

One: Friday On My Mind

1

Review of On A Friday at the Jericho Tavern, Oxford

Ronan Munro, *Curfew*[1], September 1991

I spend the entire set tonight desperately trying to think what exactly On A Friday remind me of. Not so much the music as the vocals. The next day it hits me: Kirk Brandon! Yes, he of Spear of Destiny and silly haircut fame.

Now, On A Friday's singer Thom hasn't got a silly haircut (in fact, he's hardly got enough hair to have any kind of a cut), but he does possess a voice very reminiscent of Brandon – the way he elongates every syllable and almost howls rather than sings – and it's the way it's so at odds with the rest of the band that's so intriguing.

I'm sceptical after the first couple of numbers, which come a little too close to that Manchester sound for comfort, but delve a little deeper into On A Friday and a whole new angle on them opens up. While the drums and bass (with a little help from the keyboard player) do evoke an indie-dance groove thang, there's

---

1 Local Oxford music magazine, since retitled *Nightshift*.

an almost country and western feel to the band at times, more R.E.M. than Kenny Rogers though, fortunately.

Confusing? Not if you see them live for yourselves (which you all will when they inevitably become extremely famous and you swear you were here at the beginning). In my book it's a good thing when you can't easily place what you're hearing, and when you can dance to it as well then even better.

There's an impressive turnout tonight, justifying the early buzz surrounding the band (they've already been recommended by the Candyskins); certainly their sound is well tuned to what's going on at the moment and it shouldn't be long before they're attracting major label attention.

Just a couple of questions, though: doesn't the bass player, Colin, look like Christopher Walken from *The Deer Hunter*? And what's with the subliminal backing vocals? They make the inside of your head go all funny, like.

2

The First Demo Review

Ronan Munro, *Curfew*, November 1991

Currently my favourite local band, On A Friday here prove just why they are with a highly impressive – albeit old – two-track demo. 'What Is That You Say?' is what good commercial indie guitar music should be about and shows you don't have to sell out to break out.

On A Friday are a well-polished band with highly imaginative songwriting ideas and are possessed of an unusually talented lead singer who would appear to have a pitch-bend lever inserted in his throat. How he manages to retain control as he switches from the low to high notes in the way he does, I don't know. The band also manage to make proper use of a backing vocalist, which is something that too many bands never get the hang of.

'Stop Whispering' sees another storming vocal performance while the guitars hover dangerously in the background. Halfway through, the song begins to deliberately break down before a scream brings it all rushing back with a weird organ sound fighting with a very Velvet-Underground-sounding guitar for supremacy. Lovely.

On A Friday are due in the studio this month to record with Slowdive's producer and the result should be with us in November. Until such time try and see them live if you can – you'd be a fool not to.

3

On A Friday: an Interview

Ronan Munro, *Curfew*, November 1991

At the end of October, Oxford's thinnest band (the Wild Poppies split up ages ago), On A Friday, played the Jericho Tavern to a good-sized crowd and there was a man from EMI there.

A mere two weeks later they are playing the Tavern again and the place is heaving. There are twenty-five record-company A&R men there and, what's more, they have all paid to get in. To put it bluntly, On A Friday are happening.

It's a good job, then, that we've chosen this month to put them on the front cover. If we'd waited any longer, they'd be splashed all over the nationals and we'd be left with egg all over our faces.

The first time I saw On A Friday, I was so drunk I couldn't remember a single thing about them. The second time I saw them I thought they were really rather good, if a little weird. Ironically, I finally realised what a great pop group they were at a pathetically-attended gig at the Poly, with crap sound and a ludicrously curtailed set.

While On A Friday's music is lively, catchy, intense and easily good enough to stand up on its own, what makes them just that much better is singer Thom's voice. He is possessed of that rare and special thing: a naturally musical singing voice. How many bands have you seen ruined by a bad or boring singer? I lost count many years ago. Thom doesn't just deliver his lyrics; he uses his voice to interact with the other instruments, almost as if it were one itself. This often makes the words hard to comprehend. What are the songs about?

Thom: 'Erm . . . well, "Nothing Touches Me" is based on an artist who was imprisoned for abusing children and spent the rest of his life in a cell, painting, but the song is about isolating yourself so much that one day you realise you haven't got any friends anymore and no one talks to you.'

Sounds pretty miserable – but your music is quite happy, isn't it?

'Yeah, I'm just aggressive and sick.'

Twenty minutes later, Thom reveals that he doesn't really know what the songs are about.

On a Friday, far from being a singer and his backing band, are a collective of five individuals, each with a strong input into the band's music. All stamp their individual influences and tastes on the music, and this means that the end product doesn't really sound like anyone else. Thom, Phil (drums), Colin (bass), Ed (guitar) and John (guitar and organ) find common ground in bands like the Buzzcocks, R.E.M., the Fall and (ahem) Peter Paul and Mary (this could be a wind-up), but beyond this they go for anything from Curve to Bootsy Collins to techno. They also seem to argue lots.

They've just been into Courtyard Studios with Chris Hufford, producer of Slowdive's album.

Colin: 'He heard about us through a mutual friend and came to see us at the Jericho. Afterwards he was almost shaking. He said we were the best group he'd seen in three years and invited us to record with him at the Courtyard. We see it as an investment.'

And the investment seems to be about to pay off sooner than they expected. The five songs they recorded show a massive leap in depth and professionalism from their last demo, impressive though it was. The new tape should be available from Manic Hedgehog by the time you read this and it's well worth forking out three pounds for. In short, it's a stormer.

All five members of the band are Oxford-born and bred and all have returned to their home town after time away at college. How much influence has Oxford had on their songs?

Thom: 'Loads. "Jerusalem" is all about Oxford. So is "Everybody Lies Through Their Teeth". It's such a weird place and it's very important to my writing.'

It's the subject of Oxford – in particular, music in Oxford – which provokes the arguments. Wildly differing views are thrown out as to why Oxford has, or hasn't, got a decent music scene . . .

' . . . if the Tavern closed, there wouldn't be any scene at all.'

'No? What about the Dolly and the Venue?'

'And the Old Fire Station? I know it's crap, but there are a lot of towns the size of Oxford haven't got a venue like that. Oxford has got a lot more soul than, say, Cambridge, but it comes from places like Cowley rather than the university. Students come here for three years and leave without contributing anything.'

'I don't think it's all the students' fault. It's the people who run the university who are the problem. They control everything in Oxford from their corridors of power. They have a say in all the licensing of clubs. That's why we get terrible places like the Park

End Club. Oxford is crying out for a couple of decent nightclubs. And it's the dons who say that bands can't play in the colleges, not the students . . .'

The argument continues with no real agreement or fixed conclusions. Everyone agrees that things could be better, but they could be a lot worse.

'There are a hell of a lot of bands in Oxford for its size, and the Dolly and the Venue and especially the Tavern are good venues. The Old Fire Station looks like it was designed by the people who build Little Chefs. The stage is almost an afterthought, you feel like you're playing on a salad bar.'

On A Friday also say some very complimentary things about *Curfew*, which makes me feel like my life isn't totally wasted. And indeed, if this humble and overworked editor's gushing opinions can help On A Friday towards the mega-success they are due for, then *Curfew* will have achieved at least one useful thing in its time. And successful On A Friday will be. No ifs and buts with this lot. This time next year they will have outgrown all the venues they talk about, and for once I think I may just have got it right. Are they ready to be stars?

Thom: 'People sometimes say we take things too seriously, but it's the only way you'll get anywhere. We're not going to sit around and wait and just be happy if something turns up. We are ambitious. You have to be.'

4

Review of On A Friday at the Venue, Oxford

John Harris, *Melody Maker*, 22 February 1992

Terrible name. Apt for beer-gutted pub rockers, perhaps, but ill-suited to the astonishing intensity of this bunch.

On A Friday swing between uneasy calm and crazed desperation, hinting at extremes that belie the just-got-paid/let's-get-pissed overtones of their moniker. Like Kingmaker, they've opted for the rock-as-catharsis principle, exorcising demons at a rate of knots and steering well clear of anything approaching frivolity.

Their angst-ridden paroxysms frequently depend on their sheer volume – without warning, piercing screams will fly from the stage while the band pound their instruments. Within seconds, they'll revert to a disciplined, razor-edged mode, revealing a schizophrenia that gives songs like 'Stop Whispering' a frightening volatility, furthered by the frantic movements of their singer: a diminutive, close-cropped young man whose jerky demeanour sums up On A Friday's screwed-up appeal.

They leave us with a speeding hymn to megalomania entitled 'Nothing Touches Me' – a perfect example of their manic-but-melodic charms, and an indication of credible self-confidence. 'Promising' seems something of an understatement.

Two: Pop Is Dead

1

Review of Radiohead at the Richmond, Brighton

Paul Moody, *New Musical Express,*
27 February 1993

We couldn't have waited much longer, really, could we? What with Suede so colossal, and the likes of the Auteurs and Kinky Machine still rubbing their eyes and blinking in the spotlight, *somebody* had to come along and remind us what greatness looks like.

So, thank God it's Radiohead. In the depths of the Richmond (sold out and cluttered with gawky, grinning boys and swaying, dreamy-eyed girls) they manage to take pop music – forget 'indie', *please* – and coat it in a glitter-dust not seen since Suede at Central London Poly and T. Rex, oh, anywhere. You can tell they're going to be dazzling from the moment Thom – even more scrawny and whey-faced than usual – bawls 'I wish something would happen!' during 'You' and mop-haired lead guitarist Johnny answers with these skyrocket, glam-chord progressions that sidle up to you and then scream in your ear.

It's their vulnerability that makes Radiohead so compelling. Thom may belt his guitar and glare stone-faced at us from deep behind his fringe, but look a little closer and cracks open up a mile wide and the whole thing suddenly crumbles into sand. 'Creep' is the obvious example. The song Pulp's Jarvis Cocker could never give up playing Twister long enough to write, it sets the controls on slow burn and then bursts into flames the moment he screams '*I wish I was special – You're so special!*', like the furious little brother of Ian Brown circa 'I Wanna Be Adored'.

'Lurgee', too, is more medicine for the soul – a chilling, chiming thing that could give 'Back to the Old House' a bear hug if it saw it in the street. It marks the moment at which the girls at the front fall in love with Thom and the entire Richmond gulps audibly in recognition.

There are lesser moments, sure, when you gather your senses and realise that third guitarist Ed has got his shirt wide open and is busying himself with the Bernard-from-Suede Guide to Rock Posture, and that anybody with three guitars must by law have something in common with the Family Cat, but that's about it.

Besides, next single 'Pop Is Dead', with its crashing death-rattle snare and '*It's no great loss*' refrain lets you know that Radiohead are fully aware of how ridiculous the notion of being in a pop group really is; that young males should have something better to do than stare glassy-eyed at motorway junctions through transit van windows and eat overpriced meals in late-night service stations.

The whole thing finally implodes with the appropriately named 'Blow Out', which applies the basic principles of foot-on-monitor theory (find riff and attack savagely), finds all the newly lovestruck girls dancing wildly and Thom grinning beatifically

– until, that is, his final 'See you again!' when the soundman applies a ridiculous stadium-rock reverb which leaves his words hanging in the air.

It's so un-Radiohead it's unbelievable, and when Thom pulls a spastic face and skulks off as a result, he becomes the most misunderstood and put-upon peroxide singer in a rock'n'roll group ever.

For this week, at least.

2

Review of *Pablo Honey*

Simon Price, *Melody Maker*,
20 February 1993

<hr>

They say we're repressed, us Brits, don't they? So the cliché goes – brilliantly personified by the encounter between Basil and Mme Peignoir in the 'Wedding' episode of *Fawlty Towers*. We bottle up all our passions behind a reserved exterior, until one day we get arrested for marching stark naked down the high street.

You want another cliché? Boys Don't Cry. In this respect, Radiohead's promisingly imperfect *Pablo Honey* is as British and Boyish as they come. Thom Yorke spends most of the time expressing himself in the most hackneyed – and therefore meaningless – language possible, the language of the emotionally mute (*'You are the sun and the moon and the stars are you'*, is the album's first line) and then he'll suddenly crack, take a fall (as in Albert Camus' *La Chute*, or Thom's own line *'You're free until you drop . . . without a ripcord'*), strip himself stark naked and emote in the most extreme terms: *'I wish I was special, you're so fucking special/But I'm a creep, I'm a weirdo/What the hell am I doing here?'*, or *'I'm better off dead'*.

Radiohead aren't the new Suede (despite guitarist Jon's frantic glam poses), but if Suede are the New Smiths and if we must play these games (this *is* the music press, so I suppose we must), I'd hesitantly put Radiohead down as the New Jam.

Much of *Pablo Honey* is very *Setting Sons*. (Historical note: The Jam, a classic Boys' Band, sang about the UK's decay and The Unbearable Shiteness Of Being with mixed emotions of fury and fondness. Every kid at school thought they were gods. The atmosphere when 'Going Underground' went straight in at No. 1 was a million times more intense than anything surrounding 'Teen Spirit'. They were fucking MASSIVE.)

Sometimes Radiohead err too far on the side of Boy-Rock. 'Ripcord', with its muscular, slashed chord progression, recalls Steve Jones on the Pistols' 'Stepping Stone', while 'How Do You?' is all 'Into the Valley' heroics, Thom's voice occasionally breaking into the strained, declarative holler that Bono left behind when he finally realised the absurdity of it all. And, strangest of all, 'Blow Out' starts exactly like Dire Straits' 'Sultans Of Swing'.

'Anyone Can Play Guitar' is either a hilarious parody of Carter USM's 'Do Re Mi So Far So Good' or it's a case of simple melodic plagiarism. A lyric like *'And if London burns, I'll be standing on the beach with my guitar/I wanna be in a band when I get to Heaven/Wanna grow my hair, wanna be Jim Morrison'*, suggests the former. So does the song that precedes it, 'Thinking About You' (*'Your records are here, your eyes are on my wall/Your teeth are over there, but I'm still no one and you're now a star/I still see you in bed, but I'm playing with myself'*). Coupled together, the songs form a believer's/cynic's dialogue on Pop Stardom. Then again, what if Radiohead really do just wanna be Mega City Four? It's a close thing sometimes.

The thing that tips the balance in their favour is Jon Greenwood's guitar. When he makes that grotesque crunchy noise in 'Creep', just after the words '*so fucking special*', it sounds like the prison door being slammed and locked on a man's entire hopes and aspirations. Why do I keep coming back to this song? Not just because it was one of *the* songs of 1992 (inexplicably absent from our critics' chart – you had, by law, to be American or Suede) but because it seems to have touched a nerve among you (witness the extraordinary devotion on the faces of the kids who recited every fucking word of every song when Radiohead played my club at ULU last month). And it will, let's face it, be the main reason you'll buy *Pablo Honey*.

So fucking special . . .

3

'Creep' Stumbles Onto Fame

Jim Sullivan, *Boston Globe*,
8 October 1993

It's barely noon, but Radiohead's Thom Yorke has been awake for a very un-rock'n'roll-like four hours. This certainly can't be one of the perks of nascent stardom. He's been in his hotel room staring at the TV, getting rudely acquainted with US televangelists' custom of begging for dollars. He's feeling sorry for all those people dialling in to pledge.

But why did the young Englishman rise with the roosters in Norfolk, Virginia, anyway? Yorke, on the phone, mutters something about being tossed off the tour bus at an ungodly hour but adds, with a laugh, 'I don't quite know why. I don't have complete control of my fate at the moment.'

Success will do that and, at the moment, the young band is in a very enviable position: the group's debut album, *Pablo Honey*, just turned gold, signifying sales of 500,000 copies. 'Creep', the first single, has become a from-out-of-left-field hit.

Sings a fragile, envious Yorke: '*I wish I was special/You're so* [expletive] *special/But I'm a creep/I'm a weirdo/What the hell am*

I doing here?/I don't belong here.' Jonny Greenwood's scraping, stuttering guitar licks explode into a full-throttle frenzy as Ed O'Brien and Yorke join him. It's an anthem for anyone who has ever felt left out of the mix or cast aside. Hurt, but verging on hostile.

'Creep' first found a home on alternative radio, but it has crossed over to the pop charts (up to No. 29) and album-oriented rock stations. When played on the latter format, its delicate chords, nervous arrangement and self-loathing viewpoint provide a rather sharp contrast to the strutting, testosterone-prone fist-waving bands that dominate.

'Actually,' says Yorke with a laugh, 'live, there are elements of that strutting stuff in us. But still, at the same time, [we're] fully aware of it. I have a real problem being a man in the '90s, anyway. Any man with any sensitivity or conscience toward the opposite sex would have a problem. To actually assert yourself in a masculine way without looking like you're in a [hard-]rock band is a very difficult thing to do . . . It comes back to the music we write, which is not effeminate, but it's not brutal in its arrogance. It's one of the things I'm always trying: to assert a sexual persona and on the other hand trying desperately to negate it.'

'Creep' is a most inadvertent hit. Bostonians Paul Q. Kolderie and Sean Slade were in England, producing *Pablo Honey* with Radiohead. The band ran through the song in the studio to allow the engineers to set the proper levels. It was an old song, explains Yorke. There was no plan to even record it until Kolderie and Slade said they thought Radiohead had something there. And they had the tape rolling.

'It was just a song we were doing that hadn't worked very well in rehearsals,' says Yorke. 'We didn't really have an angle on it.

And then we discovered we didn't need an angle on it, except maybe Jonny's guitar . . . "Creep" just grabbed people by the throat. It wasn't intentional.'

The inspiration, Yorke suggests, came from the fact that Radiohead was an untested entry in this vast 'alternative' rock field. Did the five belong? 'It was at a crossing point in my songwriting,' Yorke says, 'because I'd gone from writing songs in my bedroom to being somebody who had huge [record company] figures over my shoulders listening to me.' In other words, he was a potential commodity.

Fans of 'Creep' are no doubt pleased that it's not the only worthy song on *Pablo Honey*. And fans of *Pablo Honey* may be pleased to hear that, in concert, Radiohead has improved over its early recording days: more fury, more clamour, more hypnotic guitar bliss. 'That's simply a question of [the fact that] since we started we must have done 400 gigs and you learn quite fast what works and doesn't work,' says Yorke.

Radiohead's 'Stop Whispering' is moving up the alternative charts. All this success – the band co-headlines with pals Belly – has forced the band members to reconsider their relationship to the music industry.

'There's very much the British feeling of "I'm not worthy, why am I here?"' says Yorke. 'Certainly, there's an implicit neurosis about how the press is going to treat you . . . And when we signed with our record company there were a lot of weird political things going on. It's learning to actually isolate yourself from relying on people around you. I'm kind of a kid about things like that. It stresses me out. I'd like to go back and play with my building blocks and just let my parents worry about the record.'

4

From the Bedroom
to the Universe

Paul Lester, *Melody Maker*,
23 October 1993

I've heard screaming before, but nothing quite like that. At once exhilarated and anguished, it is the scream of a girl on the verge of a nervous breakdown.

'I love you, Thom!'

The scream is four syllables long, very sharp and extraordinarily loud, somehow managing to pierce the commotion of the Providence, Rhode Island, crowd and the noise blasting out of Radiohead's enormous PA.

'I love you, Thom!'

There it goes again, sharper and louder now, a terrifying mix of frightened child, ecstatic weenie, and wailing banshee. Of course, I have no trouble hearing the scream – everyone in club Lupo's (Jesus, everyone in Providence) can hear the yell-from-hell; it's just that I don't seem to be able to work out where the fuck it's coming from.

'I love you Thom!'

That does it, I've got to find out who on earth is responsible for this orgiastic-moan-cum-death-rattle. So, as Radiohead build towards the climax of their finale 'Pop Is Dead', I wade into the fray, a claustrophobic crush of pretty preppies, frat-house freaks, cropped jocks, sweaty crowd-surfers and all-round psychos. And there she is again, squashed between the 'Beavis-and-Buttheads', the tiny kid with the giant voice.

'Hey! Look at this!' the drenched (new) waif calls out, instantly recognising me from the hotel where Radiohead and the *Maker* have been staying and on whose doorstep she has been camping out over the last few days in the vain hope of catching a glimpse of her heroes. The girl – Sharon, twenty-one, from Massachusetts – is shivering, not from cold, but like she's just seen a ghost or Christ or the ghost of Christ.

'Oh my God,' she sighs, 'that was the best thing I've ever seen. They are just awesome.' Suddenly, Sharon starts pulling up her sweatshirt to reveal her midriff. It is purple. So determined was she to get close to Thom E. Yorke – Radiohead's singer, guitarist and reluctant messiah – that she braves the mêlée, risking, in the process, such irrelevancies as life and limb.

I guess that's the kind of thing you do when you're in love.

'He is sooo gorgeous,' swoons Sharon, prodding at her equally bruised thighs and grinning, oblivious to the gawping hordes, oblivious to the *pain*. Clearly, she can't feel a thing. Obviously, she would do it all again.

''Course I would!' she beams. 'Anyway, it doesn't hurt a bit.'

Brett who?

———

I've seen bigger bands. I've seen better bands. I've seen U2 in Germany, New Order at Reading, Public Enemy at Wembley and Barry White in Manchester. So, no, you can't possibly blame me for assuming I'd seen everything. And I have, in a sense. But I've never seen five undernourished ex-college boys from the home counties inspire such reckless enthusiasm, such devotion, such *love*. I've never seen a fan letter for an 'indie' band from a man in death row before. I've never seen a bunch, tagged 'ugly losers' by hacks in their home country, make so many luscious teenies (male and female) on the other side of the Atlantic quiver and shake. And I've never seen a group of hicks from the sticks make some poor bastard stuck in a wheelchair at the back of a concert hall smile so hard he could cry.

I see all of this and more in America with Radiohead.

Yeah, *that* Radiohead. The Radiohead we all used to studiously ignore when they were called On A Friday. The Radiohead we sort of began to notice when their monument of misery, 'Creep', crawled out of Parlophone last September. The Radiohead we begrudgingly gave press space to when their next slabs of caustic plastic, 'Anyone Can Play Guitar' and 'Pop Is Dead', scraped the charts (respectively Nos. 32 and 42) and their debut album, *Pablo Honey*, reached the Top 30. The very same Radiohead we pushed aside in our rush to sanctify Suede and who we're now being forced to (re-)assess in the light of the 'Creep' re-issue (No. 7 with loads of bullets) and the band's impressive Stateside success – the LP has shifted upwards of half a million units, while estimates suggest it will have sold a cool million by the end of the year.

Yes, indeed. *That* Radiohead.

Embarrassed? *Nous?*

No. Not us. Never. We know no shame and have even less

pride. Besides, Radiohead, we now realise, are worth every cringing second of the shameless *volte-face* it takes to be granted an audience with them. Certainly Thom E. Yorke – a man who seems to have taken Elvis Costello's early 'revenge and guilt' persona and multiplied it several-fold – is becoming a fascinating figure at the centre of British pop. If the sensitivity, irritability, suspicion, rage and anxiety displayed in Yorke's words are anything to go by, he should be a chap with a chip the size of a small banana republic on his shoulder. And if the savage riffing and thrillingly conventional ('Music for lapsed rock fans' is how I describe Radiohead later, to the band's assent) attack of the players is any measure, then Jonny Greenwood (lead guitar), Ed O'Brien (rhythm guitar), Colin Greenwood (bass) and Phil Selway (drums) will be bullish and brash, defensive and aggressive, in the mould of the young Joe Strummer and Paul Weller.

Wrong! Radiohead are disarmingly charming, articulate on every subject from representative democracy to *fin de siècle* Muggletonian asceticism, erudite from morning till night and educated to the max. Their received pronunciation has more in common with royalty than rockers. And they could probably knock out the odd authoritative political column for the *Guardian* in their spare time. I can't help wondering, as I watch Thom leave the Providence gig, head towards the tour bus and reduce a startled female to a trembling wreck (Sharon!) and the Greenwood brothers get swamped by autograph hunters, whether these strange (banal?) pop rituals are beneath them. And I can't help wondering just who are these pale young men whose songs and sounds, eyes and skin are exciting thousands of music lovers thousands of miles from home.

———

'He's great, but what is his problem?' asked Steve Mack of That Petrol Emotion when he first saw Thom E. Yorke at a Radiohead gig last year. The crusty kitten-hunk had a point. Yorke may well be as much of a gentleman as the others in the band; it's just that he's rather more prone to bouts of moodiness. And don't forget that the enigmatic singer is the man responsible for this little litany of lacerating self-loathing: *'I'm better off dead'* ('Prove Yourself'); *'I failed in life'* ('Stupid Car'); *'What do you care when all the other men are far, far better?'* ('Thinking About You'); *'All my friends said bye-bye'* ('Faithless The Wonder Boy') and, of course, *'I wish I was special'* ('Creep').

Back in the Providence hotel bar and bearing in mind his reputation for sporadic fits of pique, even black periods of nihilistic despair, I approach Thom cautiously and repeat that Petrol enquiry: what *is* his problem? Nursing a bottle of Beck's in the corner, he reasons that 'I'm a lot of different people when I write.'

I hear you've been in a steady, happy relationship for three years. How come you sound so haunted and hurt, fierce and fucked-off/up in your songs? 'You can feel those things in any relationship,' he explains, eyeing me from beneath his Cobain-ish blonde fringe, apparently unaware of the fact that Sharon (again!) is spying on him, à la *Fatal Attraction*, from a nearby table.

'Am I for real?' he repeats. 'Good question. I am sincere about what I do.'

How about that line from 'Faithless': *'I can't put the needle in'* – have you ever been tempted, in one of your more downer moments, to try hard drugs? Or were you just flirting with heroin imagery?

'I wouldn't be that pretentious to play the Kurt Cobain,' he winces. 'That phrase is more about trying to get back at people, get nasty.'

Tonight, you introduced 'Yes I Am' (the B-side of 'Creep') by saying, 'This is for all the people who shat on us.' What made you say that?

'That was just . . . I wrote that song about the sensation of being the underdog for so long and how suddenly everyone's nice to you. And it's like, "Fuck you",' he snarls, offering a glimpse of the human behind the hysteria.

More glimpses: Thom was born in Scotland twenty-five years ago (it's his birthday on the day of this bar confessional. Ed and Colin present him with a book by leading dissident intellectual Noah Chomsky), moving to Oxford when he was seven. His childhood was all right, but he hated his public school ('It was purgatory,' he says. 'It nurtured all the worst aspects of the British middle-class: snobbery, lack of tolerance and right-wing stupidity.').

After a tortuous failed romance ('Have you ever seen *Who's Afraid of Virginia Woolf?* It was like that for a year and a half, lots of fighting in public'), Thom went to Exeter University, where he studied English and fine art, shaved his head, started DJing and discovered he had a dangerous taste for drink ('I almost died from alcohol poisoning once,' he shudders at the memory. 'I lost it for a bit.').

Thom doesn't say whether or not things got so bad he ever thought about ending it all ('Might have done, might not have done,' he half-laughs), but he does agree with my theory that 'Creep' is the exact inverse of the Stone Roses' 'I Wanna Be Adored': the former is fuelled by self-pity, the latter by arrogance – both by egocentricity bordering on narcissism.

'Creep' is saying 'I Wanna Be Abhorred', isn't it?

'Yeah, definitely.' Thom is quick to agree but slow to disclose any more. 'It's about [pause] . . . it's about sympathy [longer pause] This is all very hard. If, erm . . . Yeah, I s'pose. Mmmm [very long pause]. As soon as I say this, everyone will take the piss. It's just, I think [pause for several centuries] . . . part of me is always looking for someone to turn around, buy me a drink, give me a hug and say it's all right,' he says at last, breaking the painful silence. 'Because I just go off on one. For days I can't talk to people. And it shocks me because I'm still doing it. I want to be alone and I want people to notice me – both at the same time. I can't help it. There's this book, *The Famished Road*, where the main character has these forces following him around and pulling him about – I feel like that.'

Thom continues to bare his soul and disprove the idea that commercial reward + public acclaim = emotional stability. 'It sounds really tossy, this. If I was a painter, it would be like, "Wow! That's wonderful!" But this is pop and in pop you're not meant to say things like this.'

————

You are if you're Radiohead. You are if you're Thom E. Yorke. And you are if you're one of the dandy Greenwood duo.

Jonny is twenty-one, Colin is twenty-five. Their father died when they were young, leaving their mother to worry about her two wayward sons. 'She thought Jonny was being dragged away by the forces of evil,' confides Colin the day after the Rhode Island gig, chain-smoking Camel cigarettes inside the tour bus now parked outside the Avalon – the venue for tonight's Boston show. 'She got a bit better when she saw us on *Top of the Pops*.

Mind you, she thinks everyone on that programme's a drug-taking lunatic. Actually, she's not happy unless she's worrying. Very Radiohead, that. We're all worriers, you know. Even when there's nothing left to worry about.'

Jonny, who left Oxford Polytechnic after one term to concentrate on the band, is Radiohead's resident musical genius, the Bernard Butler to Thom's Brett Anderson. Something of a prodigy at school, he played viola for the Thames Valley orchestra, then began hanging around with Colin and co. as soon as the group started. Pretty soon, all five members were sharing a house in Oxford, just like the Monkees.

'No, *Banana Splits*,' corrects Jonny, joining me in the scorching Indian summer heat on the pavement – sorry, sidewalk – outside the Avalon.

'Which of us was the father figure? No patriarchs! We were all mothers.'

I ask Jonny whether he thinks Radiohead have achieved success in the States rather quicker than Suede because the latter are more of a tease and Americans mistrust any ambiguity of any kind.

'Are we more boyish? Ooh, no,' he grimaces, genuinely peeved at my proposal. Jonny later admits to being more than slightly repulsed by a nipple ring given to him by a female fan who appeared stark naked at his hotel door a few nights ago and asks me, at the end of our chat, not to mention the gender of his partner back home. Meanwhile, Jonny's staring at the sun, telling me this: 'We get fans of both sexes. Groupies? That's a terrible word. How seventies. No, we don't get offers. We're not the Manic Street Preachers. We're a testosterone-free band. We didn't form this group to unleash our libidos on the general public.'

Colin, who has a degree in English from Cambridge University, spent his formative years in the kitchen at parties with Thom, wearing black body-stockings and garish mauve and green shirts and generally, as you do, trying to halt the hegemony of goth. Another one of Colin's favourite pastimes was outraging the boys at school (Radiohead attended the same school, although – apart from Colin and Thom – they were all in different years) by getting off with their male friends. Then he went to college and really let his hair down.

'We all pretty much shot our load at college in terms of drinking and drugs,' admits the most candid member of the band, squinting at the sun coming through the bus window and closing the blinds as scores of Radiohead's new American fans mill about on the street below, waiting for their bass-playing idol to emerge. 'It was nothing extreme,' he adds, sounding for all the world like an Oxbridge don with an epicurean bent. 'Nothing more than speed or dope. Smack? No! People can't afford that indulgence in terms of time and money these days.

'I remember at college,' he goes on, furiously inhaling and exhaling, 'there was this chemist on the corner – it was the local methadone-dispensing clinic. I used to walk past and see all these junkies queuing up. Then I'd walk round the corner and they'd be shooting up, which wasn't very nice . . . '

Colin has already informed me that Brett Anderson's celebrated remark – 'I'm a bisexual who's yet to have a homosexual experience' – was lifted from the notorious slacker manual *Generation X*. What about those early gay encounters of yours, Colin?

'Yeah, well. Yeah, well. Yeah!' he laughs, momentarily embarrassed before divulging: 'Well, yeah, I had a couple of flings at college with some guys. But my girlfriend knows about them, so it's all right. She doesn't like me hanging out with her gay friends in London too much, just in case I get tempted! I'll show you a photo of her if you want. She's a biker. She's more rock'n'roll than me. She's a biker woman. She got three bikes on our holiday in Greece. You know, I was the only guy in Greece on the back of a bike with a woman on the front!' he chuckles, leaping up to dig a photograph of Madeleine, his crazy biker-chick girlfriend, out of his travel bag.

Ed is the only member of Radiohead who doesn't have a partner back home. There are advantages to this. For one, he has more money than the others. (A homesick, love-struck Colin has spent about £600 ringing Madeleine every night. Drummer Phil doesn't disclose a precise amount for his nocturnal calls to girlfriend Kate, but he does tell me that he wishes he'd bought shares in British Telecom.) For another, he gets to flirt with women on the road. Like Tanya Donnelly of Belly, for example, who – take note, True Stories fans – has just broken off her engagement with her US rocker boyfriend. Even as we speak, Radiohead's playmate Tanya is jumping down the steps of Belly's astrodome of a tour bus and interrupting my chat with Ed as we sit in the shade outside the Avalon.

'Sorry!' Tanya squeals in my general direction after bounding towards Ed to plant a big kiss on his cheek, that legendary 'shark-with-lipstick' smile forming on her face. 'I thought you were just some college geek doing an interview.' (Memo to 4AD: you can forget about any more Belly front covers.)

Ed's parents split up when he was ten, although he moved back in with his father in Oxford five years ago – he's twenty-six now, but his dad, a Happy Mondays fan, is pretty cool. After a regular adolescence ('I used to think girls hated me,' he says. 'I couldn't speak to girls till I was seventeen'), Ed went to Manchester University, then 'did his Jack Kerouac bit', taking a Greyhound bus around America, exorcising most of his Bacchanalian tendencies.

'Someone held a party for us the other night and none of us went,' laughs the handsome, blue-eyed, six-foot five-inch guitarist. 'Drinking just depresses me nowadays. Until recently I was drinking very heavily and I loved it. But then it started to act as a depressant. I like to smoke dope a lot, but that's about it. Crack and coke? We've been offered it. I *am* intrigued, but . . . the same goes for girls – there's a hidden rule that no one goes with groupies. I hate that side of things, it's so dirty and seedy. It might be all right in a Guns N' Roses video, but it's not for us. We're quite a moral band, you know.'

———

I don't speak to Phil Selway – who only last night was stopped outside the band's tour bus by a girl and asked whether he was 'the roadie or just a hanger-on? Oh, and can you get me Thom's autograph?' – until after Radiohead's storming appearance in front of three thousand devotees at New York's Roseland Ballroom. I know it was storming because Thom's skinny-rib black jumper is hanging over a heater pipe in the band's dressing-room after the gig and it is dripping with sweat. Really. Drip, drip, drip.

I also know it was storming because all sorts of record company and MTV types are schmoozing and salivating and generally declaring Radiohead to be the best new band since whoever, the cure to all known diseases, etc. etc. You wouldn't know it was storming to look at Ed, who, after a puff or twenty-seven of, well, puff, has got what he calls 'the fear'. And you definitely wouldn't know it to look at Thom E. Yorke. Evidently, schmoozing with record-company and MTV types comes just below verruca removal on his list of likes.

Fearing the onset of one of Thom's 'moods', I drag Phil into a corridor and ask him why he thinks Radiohead have Made It Big in the United States, as opposed to – just to pick a name at random – Suede. (Interesting fact: Suede immediately faxed their congratulations on hearing that *Pablo Honey* had gone gold.)

'Americans like our Englishness,' says the drummer, Liverpool Poly graduate and former Nightline counsellor (true!), leaning against a drab grey wall. 'It's a far more abrupt kind of Englishness than Suede's – more energetic, more frenetic and direct.'

Just as Phil is starting to get into his stride, a rude American strides over to where we're standing and starts listening to our conversation. Surreally enough, it turns out to be Michael O'Neil, production assistant on MTV, better known as the voice behind America's latest lobotomised cartoon cult Beavis,[1] of *Beavis and Butthead* infamy.

'Radiohead rock, man!,' O'Neil/Beavis announces unprompted, as Phil and I exchange looks of the 'An Uzi, an Uzi, my kingdom for an Uzi' variety. 'Are they gonna be big? Let's quote-unquote: "Bigger than U2!" Definitely. They know how to write songs, they know how to sing and they know how to play. They're cred. They've got attitude. They're alternative crossover! They're like

---

1 Editor's note: the man who *actually* did the Beavis voice – and Butthead's too – was, of course, their creator Mike Judge. Exactly why Michael O'Neil claimed he voiced the snickering, sexually frustrated thoughts of Beavis must remain a mystery.

Jim-Morrison-meets-Jimi-Hendrix. MTV love them. They're rockin' the country!'

Huh-huh, huh-huh. Only this time, the joker's not joking. Radiohead's acid anthems and simply twisted pop are just what Europe, America, the world ordered.

One million people can't be wrong. Can they?

Three: Round *The Bends*

1

Review of *The Bends*

Ted Drozdowski, *Rolling Stone*,
18 May 1995

L uck and lyrics that capped the zeitgeist's ass made Radiohead's 'Creep' the summer radio hit of 1993.

The song initially stiffed in the band's native England, where the pained introspection of its *'I'm a creep/I'm a weirdo'* refrain collided with the glib irony of [the London] Suede and other codifiers of pop taste. Even Radiohead guitarist Jonny Greenwood hated the tune, and his sputtering guitar – a neural misfire signalling the final explosion of singer Thom E. Yorke's constipated synapses – was attempted murder. Nonetheless, 'Creep', which buoyed the otherwise unspectacular debut *Pablo Honey*, bulls-eyed our national inferiority complex and left Radiohead and James the last great UK hopes for America's brass ring.

Radiohead's reach may fall short with *The Bends*, a sonically ambitious album that offers no easy hits. It's a guitar field day, blending acoustic strumming with twitches of fuzzy tremolo and eruptions of amplified paranoia. Only Catherine Wheel's riptide of swollen six strings approximates the crosscurrents of chittering noise that slither through these dozen numbers. And as with Catherine Wheel, Greenwood and co-guitarist Ed O'Brien's devout allegiance to pop steers them clear of the wall of bombast that Sonic Youth perfected and that countless bands have flogged into cliché.

Yet pop allure also trips up *The Bends*. Yorke is so enamoured of singing honeyed melodies that he dilutes the sting of his acid tongue. In 'High and Dry', whose title is spun into one of the album's best hooks, Yorke gently sashays through the lines *'Drying up in conversation/You will be the one who cannot talk/All your insides fall to pieces/You just sit there wishing you could still make love'*. There's no hint in his presentation of the poison such abject isolation secretes. Elsewhere, oblique lyrics – an English inclination – erode the power of Yorke's decayed emotions, especially in a song like 'Bones', whose big riffs and swaying bass otherwise bellow for airplay.

'Creep' whacked Americans because its message was unfiltered. That's what we've come to expect of our contemporary rock heroes, from Kurt and Courtney to Tori Amos. Which doesn't mean *The Bends* won't grab that brass ring. But it'll be a difficult stretch.

2

World Class: How Radiohead Gave Us *The Bends*

Wyndham Wallace, *The Quietus*,
3 March 2015

You see that figure over there with the fuzzy ponytail poking out from under a Greek fisherman's cap, his jeans torn at the knees, his ankle-length grey raincoat rescued from a charity shop's neglected racks? That's me, the music editor of Exeter University's *The Third Degree* magazine, an expensively educated former private schoolboy desperately looking for a way in life that won't lead him to join the army, like his father, or to work in the city, like many of the people around him plan to.

See that guy, seated with me at the same wobbly coffee table, scanning the Student Guild coffee shop, from beneath a wild mop of bleached hair, for an excuse to stand up and leave? That's Thom Yorke, who's too well brought up simply to walk away. He's already living my dream, I'm sure, but he's not especially happy. It isn't my fault: his band's first record has been delayed by a couple of weeks. His label has forgotten to 'sell it in', the name given to the process of persuading shops to take stock of forthcoming releases. His gripes seem wholly justifiable.

It's May 1992 – just under three years before Radiohead will release *The Bends*. The *Drill* EP, which is currently languishing in EMI's warehouses, is the group's debut release, though they've been knocking around since 1985, when they formed – under the unpromising name of On A Friday – within the centuries-old grounds of Abingdon school, outside Oxford, where Yorke and his bandmates were boarders. I studied three and a half miles down the road at an even grander establishment – or at least that's how many of its staff and pupils haughtily thought of it – but this isn't something we've discussed. We've not discussed much, in fact: I barely know the man.

By now, Yorke has left Exeter University and returned to live in Oxford. I, meanwhile, still have over a year left to go. Nonetheless, we share a couple of friends. There's Paul, whose hair showers down his back to his beltline and who books shows for the students, generously ensuring I'm on the guest list any time I want. In later life he'll teach special needs kids and any of his wilder tendencies will be indulged instead on a vintage motorbike. Then there's Shack, the dreadlocked individual behind technology-loving duo Flicker Noise. He'll go on to enjoy a career as a musician and DJ – under various names, including Lunatic Calm and Elite Force – but he and Yorke used to play in Headless Chickens, an indie punk act featuring Thom on guitar and backing vocals. You can hear Thom on their only recorded track, 'I Don't Want to Go to Woodstock', part of a showcase seven-inch for local label Hometown Atrocities. It features two other woefully-named acts, Jackson Penis and Beaver Patrol, alongside the rather more prosaic Mad At The Sun. If you really care enough, copies are available these days for about £75.

I try to placate Yorke's concerns about their debut, informing him I've given it a great review, like I expect him to care what I think. I've described it as 'a storming opener to their career, a noisy guitar affair reminiscent of the Catherine Wheel', but I don't tell him I've given Kitchens Of Distinction's 'Breathing Fear' and Suede's 'The Drowners' joint Single Of The Month status. Nonetheless, I'm excited to see the band perform and I'm particularly keen to see if he can replicate that fifteen-second wail at the end of 'Prove Yourself', the lead track, though I don't articulate that last thought out loud. I'm actually far too nervous: Yorke's the first person I've ever met whose band has signed a deal.

As a student music critic I've met other musicians, of course, but they were already with a label by the time our paths met. Yorke, on the other hand, was a DJ at the university venue, the Lemon Grove, up till the end of last summer, and Paul reckons he's probably the best they've ever worked with. Yorke would entertain my friends and me on Friday nights as we sank Snakebites and Black until our limbs were loose enough to dance. Sometimes I'd make requests – the Stone Roses, the KLF, maybe Happy Mondays – and I far preferred Yorke's indie playlists to the club-fixated Saturday nights, which were hosted by Felix Buxton, later of Basement Jaxx. Back then, Exeter's Oxbridge rejects were far more privileged than they could ever have guessed, for many more reasons than they ever realised.

This encounter is the first time Yorke and I have talked for more than a moment or two over the record decks. Despite not really knowing him, I've still got this nagging feeling. He seems focused and self-aware, his bearing suggestive of a man confident that his choices will prove worthwhile. The music I've heard has helped: the *Drill* EP isn't an exactly stellar start to their career, but it's a convincing debut. It sounds like it was recorded in a budget-priced, provincial studio by a band excited at the possibilities newly available to them: the vocals distorted and artfully buried in the mix, the guitars raw and fluid, the bass lines imaginative, the snare drums tightly tuned. In the flesh, too, Yorke is just like a budding rock star should be and, though his mildly aloof demeanour makes me feel a little uncomfortable, it's something I can't resent, the existence of our mutual acquaintances making me feel quietly loyal to him. In years to come, I like to think, I'll be able to tell people I used to have coffee with Radiohead's Thom E. Yorke.

Six months or so later, I'm behaving like the worst kind of student, shitfaced, most likely stoned and, more worryingly, high on a sense of my own importance. A white label of 'Creep' landed on my doorstep only a few weeks earlier, and it's the most exciting thing I've heard in a while. This time I honour Radiohead with a Single Of The Month – 'This has to be one of the best pieces of rock since Everest,' I write, oblivious to how this will make me wince in my future – and now they're playing at the university. I get to hang in the dressing room for a little while with a couple of friends, enjoying what I like to think of as Thom's victorious homecoming. These companions include one of my more glamorous associates, who, with admirable premonition, swiftly displays a fondness for Jonny Greenwood's prominent cheekbones. He, inevitably, behaves like a gentleman.

His brother, Colin, is similarly polite, and there's no sense coming from any of the band that this represents the fulfilment of a long-held rock'n'roll fantasy: there's no hurried necking of beers, no backstage shenanigans, no foolish conduct of any sort. Life spent on the road with Radiohead is no Valhalla.

I talk to them eagerly about the brilliance of 'Creep' and they seem neither uninterested nor unusually responsive. Naturally, no one's rude, so I stay there a while, albeit driven by my enthusiasm for their music and my solidarity with their cause rather than any sense of intimacy. But while no one would notice if I weren't there, I never once feel as though they wished I were someone or somewhere else. I'm simply a face to whom there's no need to be impolite, and they're really only concerned with the job they've come here to do. Still, I have this feeling that I, alone with the few, have recognised untapped potential, that I'm – though the phrase has yet to be coined – an early adopter. I'm convinced that 'Creep' is such an unmistakable anthem that there's no way it can be overlooked. I'm just one of the lucky ones who knows this because I've got one of the first copies. It's obvious others will soon agree.

Fifteen sheets to the wind, however, isn't a good place to be when you're in the mood to show off. Soon after the band start playing their new single, I edge my way to the front of a sparse crowd and, as Jonny Greenwood crushes out those iconic chords, I throw my arms into a crucifix and bellow along with the lyrics, directly beneath Thom's microphone stand. Worse still, I do so with my back to Thom, taking on the responsibility of cheerleading with an uninhibited passion. My hands rise and fall as I exhort others to sing along with me. They stumble back, embarrassed, leaving me isolated in front of the singer. I carry on regardless: I am Radiohead's champion. I am a complete disaster as well, but soon enough everyone else will look stupid for not having been down there with me.

Another few months pass and I drive three-plus hours from Exeter to north London on a rainy Sunday afternoon in March 1993. Belly are headlining the Town and Country Club in Kentish Town, and the Cranberries – currently seducing the British music media on the back of their debut single 'Linger' – are on first. Former Throwing Muse Tanya Donnelly's stab at mainstream stardom is all the rage and I know I should be excited to see both bands, but really it's the middle act, Radiohead, that are the main reason for my trip. By now, 'Creep' is a hit Stateside and it's infiltrating the UK too, having been recognised as a Single Of The Year by a number of publications. Their debut album, *Pablo Honey*, meanwhile, has been on the shelves for two weeks, stirring up what I describe in *The Third Degree* as a buzz as big as Suede's the previous year. 'That was quite some buzz,' I add, not as droll as I think I am.

I remember little of the show, sadly, aside from being excited at the chance to say 'Hello' to their tour manager and consequently ingratiate myself backstage. I find my way to their dressing room, but they've already got their fair share of hangers-on, so – having briefly said 'Hello' to the four of them I can find – I ask where I might find their frontman. There's a nonplussed reaction, a collective shrug of the shoulders. Sandwiches wilt under mirrored lights. Stepping outside into a concrete corridor, I can hear laughter coming from Belly's dressing room, out of which people are spilling into the passageway to my left. To my right, some dozen feet away, steps lead down towards the stage, and I hear a shuffling sound, or maybe a cough, emanating from a hunched, gnomish figure lurking at the top. It's Thom and he's alone. I hesitate, then shamble over. We exchange pleasantries but conversation stalls and Thom begins to look increasingly gloomy. It's time to get me coat.

Fast-forward another twelve months to 27 May 1994. It's almost two years since Thom and I shared that awkward coffee on the eve of Radiohead's debut. That's me again, clinging to the balcony railing of London's Astoria club. What's happening in front, from the moment Radiohead tear into 'You', is an almighty revelation. Whatever I may have thought of them in the past, there's an unprecedented urgency to their performance that nonetheless refuses to diminish the fluency of their playing, the ragged sketches they'd drawn on *Pablo Honey* delivered as sculpted, muscular beasts, elegantly wild yet mature. In a sign of their growing confidence, they drop the unfamiliar 'Bones' second song in and 'Black Star' follows after a furious 'Ripcord', Yorke introducing it with a pre-emptive, self-deprecatory apology for performing another new track.

It's far from the last, too: soon we get 'The Bends', 'Fake Plastic Trees' and 'Just', Yorke, in his Hawaii '81 T-shirt, bug-eyed and snarling, jerking his head convulsively to one side like Ewen Bremner in Mike Leigh's *Naked*. To his left, Greenwood Jr, his own shirt several sizes too small for him, handles his guitar like he's trying to tame it, while his brother lurks in the shadows, calmly bobbing his bobtailed head as he uncurls ingenious basslines. At the other end of the stage, Ed O'Brien – dressed like he's auditioning for Mandy Patinkin's role as Inigo Montoya in *The Princess Bride* – wrangles unforeseen chords from his instrument, slapping meat back onto the bones of their songs as though he'd previously underestimated his capabilities. Behind them, calm and unobtrusive, Phil Selway holds things together. I'm slack-jawed, wide-eyed and bowled over.

They return for an encore, playing 'Street Spirit (Fade Out)' for possibly the first time in public, revealing a sensitivity that 'Creep' only hinted at, its understated beauty seductive and spellbinding. Afterwards, I'm unusually speechless and, when the band appear in the Keith Moon bar later on, while I'm sinking dirty pints at an adrenalin-fuelled pace, I'm far too over-excited to even consider saying 'Hello'. I'd realised during 'My Iron Lung', unveiled almost half an hour into the show, that I'd never talk to them again. The way that barrage of explosions from Jonny Greenwood's guitar blew apart Yorke's artless melody, tearing it violently from the cotton wool of the song's coiling guitar lines and consciously dragging bassline, ripped a hole in the world around me. This faultless exhibition of sustained tension and release confirmed that Radiohead had become what I'd always hoped they'd be. Within little more than a year, the world would at last agree.

————

So what does *The Bends* mean, two decades on from its March 1995 release? Personally, it represents the end of a rite of passage: in the three years since Yorke and I had shared a coffee, I'd graduated from university, worked briefly in a record store and then moved to London, where I worked as a publicist for a variety of American acts. I took my job seriously: however late I stayed out partying, I was always behind my desk by 10 a.m. in an office above a piss-stinking alleyway a few metres off central London's Oxford Street. I'd left behind my comfortable upbringing to live in a shabby Soho flat – built for two, if shared by four – which provided a base for adventures I'd never expected to enjoy: I'd got drunk with Guided By Voices, barred Liam Gallagher from the Afghan Whigs' dressing room and smoked Snoop Dogg's weed at *The Word*.

It wasn't always easy being posh in the world of indie rock: I was gullible and over-sensitive, unsure of my place in – and unfamiliar with the customs of – London's thriving music industry. But I felt like I'd come of age and, when I first heard *The Bends*, it seemed to me that both Radiohead and I had reached the end of a crucial portion of an ongoing, thrilling journey. We'd shared similar backgrounds, had pursued comparable trails and had even crossed paths along the way. In my mind, their triumph was emblematic of what I too had achieved: the fulfilment of my long-held dream of an alternative existence in the music business.

To empathise with this far-fetched sentiment, there's something you need to understand: despite all the opportunities fee-paying schools might offer, they're not designed to propel people along such a path. (They weren't back then, anyway.) A 1980s middle-class upbringing hardly groomed one for success outside the traditional professional establishments, and though there were rebels – the smokers, the tokers, the drinkers, the thinkers – for most of them it was a stance, an opportunity to enjoy freedom before they settled down in the home counties with a well-spoken partner, a couple of precocious kids, a favourite seat on the London train and an inflated nostalgia for their misspent youth. 'Just like your dad, you'll never change . . . '

Having left university, I knew that my parents wished the time I was spending writing uncommissioned reviews for *Melody Maker* and *NME* was instead being spent preparing applications for jobs in more respectable fields. They weren't unsupportive, but this wasn't what they'd had in mind when they'd put my name down at birth for a fiercely competitive place at a prestigious educational establishment. Still, if private schools insisted on one thing back then, it was instilling in their pupils a sense of responsibility. My own headmaster called this one of 'the right habits for life', as important as keeping your fingernails clean and your hands out of your pockets when talking to staff. Whatever route was undertaken, you learned, you were to apply yourself fully to the task in hand. It's one of the few things I grasped during those ten bleak years away from home that has ever proved useful at all.

It's not too far-fetched to suppose that, like me, Yorke and his colleagues were reasonably cautious before they decided that music was a valuable pursuit. When families spend tens of thousands of pounds educating their children, only a few of their offspring dare reject the expectations that have built up around them. Even Jonny Greenwood, one imagines, spent a few sleepless nights at Oxford Brookes University before he walked out three weeks into his music and psychology degree to sign the band's deal with EMI's Parlophone imprint.

Not that such a background makes things harder than it is for those from state schools. Far from it, obviously: the familial financial cushion that most privately educated school-leavers have is unquestionably a significant reassurance for the ones willing to take a risk. But you can hear in Radiohead's *Drill* EP a need to be taken seriously; to – as the song said – 'prove' themselves. Its songs are lean and considered, balanced by a rough-and-ready sound that suggests they're scrupulously self-aware, uncommonly determined and attentive to where they want to sit in the grander scheme of things. You can bet that their teachers soon claimed a part in the band's global success.

But what does *The Bends* mean beyond my own narrow existence? It emerged on the back of an era in which music's tectonic plates had been shifting violently. Shoegaze had roared, then whimpered; the baggy movement had collapsed in a comatose haze of its making; Britpop had gorged itself upon its own noxious legend and, by the time *The Bends* was finally released, even grunge's poster boy Kurt Cobain had been dead for a year.

Judging from Thom Yorke's DJ sets at Exeter University, the band would have been familiar with all of these movements, shifting from the predominant domestic British sounds of their school days to explore noisier sounds coming in from the US, their common thread a sense of independence and a distaste for the status quo. This kaleidoscopic amalgam of potential inspiration informed everything Radiohead did in those early days, even if it was yet to be distilled to its essence.

The *Drill* EP is, inevitably, stamped with the indie production tropes of its time. Truth be told, it doesn't sit entirely uncomfortably alongside the likes of Kingmaker and Cud. But, by the time *The Bends* hit stores, Jonny Greenwood would be seen on Sunset Strip billboards wearing a T-shirt he'd bought at a show by Cell, a New York band championed by Sonic Youth. One member still recalls with pleasure how Thom Yorke once told him – after a show headlined by Radiohead – that Radiohead should have opened for them.

The quintet embraced influences that felt disorientating, smudging familiar genre boundaries and pursuing avenues that dismayed as many as they excited, albeit on a smaller scale than the band would later attempt. But it wasn't just critics that were confused about where they fitted in. Despite their efforts, Radiohead barely knew where they stood either. Everyone was scrambling for a new Seattle, a new Britpop, and times were becoming so desperate that, within months of *The Bends'* delivery, the media would be championing 'Romo'. Wherever you tried to place them, Radiohead failed to conform. This wasn't what was expected of them.

If *The Bends* came from anywhere, it was from a desire to comprehend this confusion of influences. After all, the members of Radiohead, one senses, didn't become a band because they wanted to make a noise, but because they wanted to make music and, crucially, knew how to make it. Some groups form because of a need for camaraderie or rebellion or escape, but none of these reasons seem relevant to Radiohead. Working together was simply the smartest option available to them: collectively, they could carry one another to their goal. They became a band, just as they've since become what they now are, because they embraced the duty of being Radiohead.

Becoming Radiohead took time, too: there was much to digest, so much to learn, before they could understand just what this responsibility meant. *The Bends* is consequently the sound of five men fighting their way out of a tangled web of conflicting convictions and prejudices with an uncommon earnestness, reconciling their tastes and their ambitions, sifting through the Pixies and the Smiths and Dinosaur Jr and the Beatles and Talking Heads and Happy Mondays and Elvis Costello and Tim Buckley. It's the sound of five men taking an exploratory dive into deep waters, finding themselves lost, and still somehow redrawing the map of where it is they should resurface. It wasn't called *The Bends* for nothing.

Before that, though, there was 'Creep'. Love it or loathe it, it represents a critical juncture for Radiohead in their development, just as it embodies for me the night before the morning I realised in what an undignified way alcohol could make me behave. It's common knowledge that the band has leaned towards a negative sentiment for this song for years: even Greenwood's first, extraordinary interjection of noise apparently stemmed from his attempt to mess up a song that he thought was far too fey. (One might say he had a point.) But, in drawing upon what was happening on both sides of the Atlantic, 'Creep' combined a grumbling Englishman's indie sensitivity with the sometimes nihilist, always principled spirit of the US guitar underground. Predictably, with Cool Britannia approaching its zenith, it was left to America to be first to 'get' it: in the UK, the track peaked upon its first release at No. 78 in the charts. But after it became a hit Stateside, the band conceded to a UK reissue that made it into the Top 10. They'd just adopted their albatross.

Listening to 'Creep' now, it's understandable that they were unenthusiastic about its British re-release and why they soon found it so unbearable that it failed to make it onto their set lists for most of the 2000s. The appeal of such lyrical transparency soon dwindles when you're forced to stand in front of crowds repeatedly denouncing your significance. What once appeared honest is rendered almost ridiculous by virtue of its repetition – for both the singer and the audience. No wonder Yorke looked so genuinely nonplussed in 1997 as he sang the song at Glastonbury: *'What the hell am I doing here? I don't belong here . . . '*

Feasibly, there may be yet another dimension to their uncomfortable relationship with the song. By virtue of their upbringings, these well-bred boys were most likely indoctrinated with the conviction that such declarations of self-pity were hardly becoming when uttered from beneath a stiff upper lip. To sit about whining and whingeing is decidedly non-U – *infra dignitatem*, you might say – if you came from the kind of establishment they did (though God help anyone who tried). These may not have been conscious beliefs, but they probably coloured their growing distaste for a track that had been very good to them. Still, whether or not this is correct, the truth is that 'Creep' contains none of the complexity of the music they were soon writing and, even amid other songs they were already playing, it seemed a little . . . trite. To some, their subsequent decision to bench it may seem precious or at least disrespectful to fans, but honestly: imagine yourself, night after night, in front of increasingly huge audiences, having to pretend, in a tremulous voice, that you're still the same jerk you were on that lonely night you first wrote the song. You'd soon start feeling sorry for yourself too.

In the year between 'Creep''s two deliveries, Radiohead released two other singles. 'Anyone Can Play Guitar' was the first and coincided with the release of their patchwork debut album, *Pablo Honey*, in February 1993. It ridiculed the idea of pop stardom with unusually acerbic bitterness, something that perhaps contributed to its commercial failure: *'Anyone can play guitar/And they won't be a nothing anymore'*, Yorke growled, adding wickedly, *'Grow my hair, grow my hair/ I am Jim Morrison . . . '* 'Anyone Can Play Guitar' appeared to be a reaction to the spotlight that 'Creep' had attracted and, a year later, 'Pop Is Dead' – which, tellingly, never made it onto an album – was even more alienating for the media, as well as the general public and, presumably, the band's record label too. *'Oh no, pop is dead, long live pop/It died an ugly death by back-catalogue'*, Yorke sang, echoing Morrissey's line from 'Paint A Vulgar Picture' – 'Reissue, repackage, repackage! Re-evaluate the songs' – in an ill-advised video that found him carried in a glass coffin, heavily made up like a dead fop.

Furthermore, Yorke wasn't finished. *'We raised the dead but they won't stand up,'* he went on, *'And radio has salmonella/And now you know you're gonna die,'* before he concluded, ahead of a whirring squawl of guitars, that *'pop is dead, long live pop/One final line of coke to jack him off/He left this message for us.'* If the song's meaning wasn't clear enough, though, Yorke would elaborate on it at the band's London Astoria show in 1994 with the words, 'Dedicated to members of the press, as it always has been,' altering the lyrics to *'one final cap of speed to jack him off'*, then muttering, 'fucking bunch of losers'. 'Pop Is Dead' appeared so contemptuous that it was hard even for Radiohead's biggest fans to like.

Fortunately, *Pablo Honey* itself contained enough notable moments to maintain belief in their explorations. Admittedly, almost half of its songs were already available – the whole of the *Drill* EP was included, for one thing – but, if one accepted that the best songs were indeed the ones that were most fresh, it indicated that the band were developing at a pace. Sure, they still struggled to stand far above many of the other acts that were scoring 7/10 reviews in the music press: 'Vegetable' was merely lovable if one really wanted to love it, for instance, and 'How Do You?' could only just summon up enough bile to satisfy a sweaty teenage audience too young for the Sex Pistols. But in its two closing tracks it provided a signpost towards where they were moving. 'Lurgee''s quiet compassion and 'Blow Out''s lysergic drama displayed a mature aplomb that would prosper on *The Bends*, their willingness to let the music define them an overdue replacement for the record-company styling to which they seemed to have fallen victim: the red-and-white striped trousers, the dubious haircuts, the 'received wisdom' that seemed to inform many of their visual decisions. '*You do it to yourself, you do, and that's what really hurts . . .*'

These intriguing fumblings, with moments of generous inspiration scattered amid them, were a tentative reconnaissance, a preliminary warm-up, a necessary step in Radiohead's evolution. In fact, *Pablo Honey* was an application letter, one might say. *The Bends*, of course, would be the interview.

First, though, in October 1994, there was a stopgap EP, *My Iron Lung*, its opener in fact lifted directly from the tapes of the band's monumental Astoria show, with only Yorke's vocals newly tracked. '*This is our new song,*' he wailed, '*Just like the last one/A total waste of time/ My iron lung*' and, every time I heard this, I'd remember that disconsolate Yorke at the top of the steps at the Town and Country Club in '93. They still loved making music, while playing live could be satisfying and they probably enjoyed each other's company too, but already Radiohead were learning that they didn't like being in a band: all the rigmarole that came with it seemed only to inspire revulsion. Maybe this was less true for the rest of them, but Yorke in particular seemed to be struggling to come to terms with the games that they'd been led to believe needed to be played.

The Bends was made as Radiohead first stepped on the treadmill, and already they wanted off. It was, one suspects, a record upon which they knew they'd stand or fall, informed by everything that preceded it. In many ways, it feels more like a debut album than *Pablo Honey* – with its mixed bag of strengths – ever did, as though it were the culmination of a lifetime's work. Second albums are notoriously difficult to make and, by all accounts, *The Bends* suffered a more than troubled gestation, yet it still comes out sounding fully formed, defining them in a way that *Pablo Honey* by and large failed to do. The privileges and the prejudices, the accolades and the rebukes, their pasts and their presents: all of these and more converged as one, crashing and grinding into each other until they found their place, only to soar off on a new, graceful trajectory. It was the end of a rite of passage.

The songs themselves only need to be recollected here because *The Bends* became so omnipresent and inescapable, so much a part of the sound of summer and winter 1995 that its over-familiarity bred a certain degree of fatigue. At the time of its release, however – in the wake of *Definitely Maybe* and *Parklife* the previous year – it appeared unusually literate and accomplished, and, in some people's minds, towered above everything championed by an over-excitable press for years.

If they'd been little more than the sum of their influences on *Pablo Honey*, now Radiohead were like no one else at all – like no one apart from Radiohead, that is. Even this was a concept that would soon be demolished: each new record from the band would swerve passionately away from where they'd last paused. They'd reinvent themselves repeatedly, first reshaping alternative rock, then dragging intelligent techno and electronica into the mainstream, before exploiting their well-earned, hard-won independence by at least attempting to disrupt conditions precipitated by the arrival of the internet.

That was to come, though: in March 1995, they staked their first real claim to greatness with a forty-nine-minute collection of accessibly timeless, visionary songs that may have gathered a little dust since but which stand up remarkably well. Admittedly, *The Bends* was only quietly revolutionary: there were no heroics, no ill-suited bursts of attention-grabbing histrionics, merely layer upon layer of intriguing arrangements that demanded repeated plays to unravel. But that mysterious sound of empty space being filled by shimmering guitars at the start of opening track 'Planet Telex' now seems prescient: Radiohead were taking up camp in territory few people seemed interested in investigating. This worked because *The Bends*' lyrics were more elliptical and the songs more intelligent, than anything they'd previously tried. Indeed, they were smarter than almost anyone in mainstream 'alternative' music was trying to be, a far cry from the wilful idiocy and tabloid realms in which direction every other band seemed to be drunkenly heading.

The sonics of the album, too, were polished, yet rarely drew attention to themselves. Yorke's voice, meanwhile, still seemed to slur from note to note in his quieter moments – though he continued to rage bitterly at other times – but he seemed to be inhabiting the songs rather than testing out a role, whether amid the crunching guitars of the title track or the tender acoustic strums of the heartbreakingly puzzling 'Fake Plastic Trees'. On 'Just', the band might have given in to their American influences, but they still packed the song with colourful fireworks and 'Bullet Proof . . . I Wish I Was' boasted a haunting, peculiarly English desolation. Then there was the lilting grace of 'Nice Dream''s strings and Yorke's impressively feminine falsetto, which gave way to an impressively dramatic flurry of squealing guitars while, in 'High and Dry' and 'Street Spirit (Fade Out)', they mapped out a terrain towards which a pack of other songwriters would soon rush: anthemic, gutsy, mid-paced songs of unapologetic but never over-egged sentiment. Few would ever do it as well.

Radiohead, of course, would soon leave these copycats trailing and many of us would travel with them, leaving *The Bends* behind. In fact, in a sense – especially in the light of what came after – *The Bends* nowadays sounds a little gauche, as if it's tied to a period of Radiohead's lives, and indeed our own, whose ideals have long since withered. Since then, we have grown wiser with experience, and the cultivated excesses of *OK Computer* and the stubborn experimentalism of *Kid A* and *Amnesiac* have underlined the band's insistence that great musicians have a responsibility never to stand still, a reminder of an older generation who challenged themselves to constantly refine their talent and explore new domains with each and every release.

The Bends, therefore, is attached to the 'old' Radiohead, a band who, for a while, were compromised by major label practices but who, in overcoming their distaste and disenchantment with the institutions into whose beds they'd unwittingly climbed, surpassed the promise others saw in them. It may exude an awkward, sometimes unwelcome nostalgia, but remember that it once offered far, far more than that. Without *The Bends*, one imagines, Radiohead might never have become what they are.

So – you see that man up on stage, his arms twitching spasmodically, his voice like an angel's, his colleagues filling up arenas with ever-restless inventiveness? That's Thom E. Yorke, lead singer of Radiohead, one of the greatest groups to have emerged in our tiny little lifetimes, and it all started with *The Bends*. Now, you see that fellow buried deep in the crowd, his balding pate lit up beneath the moon, still struggling with ghosts from his entitled youth but determined to leave them behind? Yeah, you guessed it: that's me, once again.

Did I tell you I knew them when I was younger? They couldn't give a damn, of course, but I'll be proud till the day I die.

3

Don't Call 'Em Britpop

Clare Kleinedler, *Addicted To Noise*,
May 1996

Britpop. It's all over the place all of a sudden. There's Oasis, the Beatles rip-offs trying to emulate the Rolling Stones' drug-taking, groupie-filled past. Then there's Blur, the self-described 'middle-class' darlings of the UK music scene who just can't seem to make a dent in America. Don't forget Elastica, Pulp, Supergrass and Echobelly. But whatever you do, please, please do not include Radiohead in the list of Britpop bands.

The only thing Radiohead have in common with the above-mentioned bands is that, yes, they are from England. What makes them different from their fellow UK musician brothers and sisters is that Radiohead do not limit themselves to playing recycled '60s music and they do not engage in public spats with other bands. Nor do they spend their free time bragging about how 'fookin' great' they are. They don't have to talk the talk. Radiohead's songs and live performances speak loud enough for themselves.

Radiohead's current album, *The Bends*, alone made 1995 a year of great music. Every single song on the record is amazing;

from the breathtakingly beautiful melody of 'Street Spirit' to the ear-piercing, guitar-wailing 'Just'. And after over fifty weeks on the charts, people are finally beginning to take notice. The album is currently bobbing in and out of the Top 10 in Britain and is enjoying its first break into the Top 100 here in the states. MTV can't get enough of the band's video for the single 'High and Dry', and virtually every other music critic in the US and the UK voted the album as one of their Top 10 for last year.

Not too shabby for a band that used to play to a crowd of about, um, two people at parties ten years ago when they first started out. Having met at an all-boys private school in Abingdon, England, singer/guitarist Thom Yorke, guitarists Jonny Greenwood and Ed O'Brien, bassist Colin Greenwood and drummer Phil Selway formed the band out of sheer boredom. The group put the band on hold to attend college (except for youngest member Jonny, who stayed behind at school) but rehearsed during breaks and holidays. By the summer of 1991, the lads re-grouped and decided to take this whole music thing seriously.

They called themselves On A Friday and started gigging around their home town of Oxford. Though in retrospect Yorke says that 'we were pretty crap', their appearance at Oxford's Jericho Tavern in October of 1991 attracted about 25–30 A&R guys and inspired a journalist from a local zine to write: 'And successful On A Friday will be. No ifs and buts with this lot. This time next year they will have outgrown all the venues they talk about and for once I think I may just have got it right.'

The journalist was right. The band changed their name from On A Friday, a name that proved confusing on flyers if they played a gig, for example, on a Thursday, to Radiohead and scored themselves a record deal with Parlophone. The band recorded their debut album *Pablo Honey* in three weeks and released it to minimum hype and enthusiasm. In 1993, the band's single 'Creep' was re-released and the rest is history.

'Creep' was probably the best and worst thing that has ever happened to Radiohead. While the single propelled *Pablo Honey* into gold album status in the states, the song became somewhat of an anthem for the band, especially singer Yorke. Much to the band's dismay, Radiohead became 'that "Creep" band' and Yorke became the weirdo of all weirdoes, the misunderstood, reluctant poster boy for a generation that identified with the agonising lyrics *'I wish I was special/You're so fucking special/ But I'm a creep!'*

MTV picked up a heavy rotation of the video and even invited the band to play to a crowd of bikini babes and frat boys at the channel's Beach House. Seeing the video of that performance proves how undiscriminating the whole 'Creep' obsession was; frat boys banging their heads to Radiohead? Creepy.

Although many bands dream of having a hit single early on, the men of Radiohead loathed the idea. The band was immediately pressured to come out with another 'Creep' and the recording of their follow-up album became a nightmare. Yorke and co. 'crawled' around the studio with producer John Leckie (Stone Roses, Ride) for three months, driving Leckie and each other crazy. According to the group, it was a major low point for the band, a time that saw each member go through bouts of self-doubt and depression. Finally, Leckie ordered everyone to go home, with the exception of Yorke, and made him go to work. The band went back out on the road for a bit, came back and in two weeks *The Bends* was finished.

Since the release of the album in March of 1995, Radiohead has been a non-stop touring machine. The band has done several headlining club tours around the globe and supported R.E.M. last year in America, giving them the opportunity to play arena-size venues. While touring is very much a part of the rock'n'roll lifestyle, off time is spent in a very un-rock'n'roll manner. The members of Radiohead prefer books over parties and each keeps a fairly low profile in the public, choosing to stay in Oxford rather than join the Britpop masses in London or Manchester. Often referred to as 'the most polite band in music', the guys are pleasant, with the exception of an occasional stress-induced outburst from Yorke.

I've personally experienced both aspects of the band. The first interview I'd ever done was on the phone with bassist Colin Greenwood. As fate would have it, during the interview my computer crashed, as did my tape recorder. Of course, I didn't realise until after I'd hung up with Greenwood that my tape was blank. In fear of losing my job, I frantically called Greenwood back, explaining through tears what had happened.

'No problem,' he replied calmly. 'Call me back in two hours and we'll do it on my lunch break.' A gesture I will never forget.

On a heavier note, I had a run-in with Yorke on a bad day last year during the KOME Almost Acoustic Christmas Show in San Jose, California. 'I just got here! Leave me alone!' he shouted as I approached him for an interview. Completely shattered and feeling like a worm, I crawled into the corner, and wondered if I had chosen the right career path.

So it is that dreadful memory that's weighing heavily on my mind as I arrive at the Phoenix hotel in San Francisco for my interview with Yorke and guitarist Jonny Greenwood. My heart pounds and my palms begin to sweat as tour manager Tim walks me over to meet Yorke.

'Hi. Have we met before? You look familiar,' says Yorke, pleasant as can be.

'Um, yeah,' I stammer. 'We definitely have.' I wait until later to let him know the when, where and how. Yorke and I have a seat on some plastic lawn furniture next to the pool. His hair is a blinding orange today, contrasting sharply with the oversized black-black sunglasses on his face. Seems he is nursing quite a hangover but is in good spirits nonetheless. Jonny bounds over, shakes my hand and slides into a chair. The reluctant girl-magnet of the group, he's got 'cheekbones that could start a war' (according to my friend Cat) and a bob of shiny black hair that hangs carelessly into his eyes. Noticing a painful-looking shaving cut on his chin, I inform him that he is bleeding.

'Oh, I know . . . I enjoy it, though,' he says, pressing his hand against the cut. Staring at the splotch of blood on his hand, he looks surprised. 'Cool! Should I go and mop?'

'No. Bleed on the table,' says Thom, sarcastically.

The two of them could be brothers. They don't look anything alike, but they do weird things like finish each other's sentences and repeat every other word the other is saying. Jonny's real-life brother is Colin but, after hanging out with these two, I'm beginning to wonder if they were related in a previous life. They even play-fight over who will answer what question, constantly cutting each other off, competing to see who can be cleverer. But it is all in fun. No Liam/Noel-esque punch-outs here in Camp Radiohead.

Addicted to Noise: How is the tour going so far?
Thom Yorke: Pretty good. It's quite exciting, but I've got to stop drinking.

72

ATN: Better than the last tour?

Thom: Yeah, it's sort of . . . yeah. I think so. And they've all sold out, which is pretty amazing.

ATN: **Did you ever retrieve any of the stolen equipment from the Soul Asylum tour? (The band awoke one morning in Denver to find their entire truck, filled with all of their gear, had been stolen right out of their hotel parking lot.)**

Jonny Greenwood: Nothing at all. Not a musical sausage.

Thom: Not a bleeding sausage.

ATN: **Let's start from the beginning. You all met at school . . .**

Jonny: It was a dark, moonlit night . . .

Thom: A dark, moonlit night . . .

Jonny: We should make it more romantic than it was. It was a boring afternoon at school, probably.

Thom: I'm still fond of Jonny coming in and playing every instrument that he could possibly think of to get into the band . . .

Jonny: Yeah, turning up with gel horns.

Thom: Yeah. He started with the harmonica and we weren't into that.

ATN: **Is it true that none of you knew how to play your instruments when you first started the band?**

Thom: It's all relative, but I would say it was true . . .

Jonny: [To Thom] Really?

Thom: Well, you were quite good.

Jonny: Well, we just didn't play in public. I don't think we were as bad as most bands . . . we just sort of . . . we didn't think we were very good.

Thom: It was more a low opinion of oneself, you know, but justified low opinion, I think.

ATN: **You all seem to have different musical influences: jazz, Scott Walker, XTC, Magazine, various trip-hop groups . . . How do you all write music together?**

Thom: Well, it's not like you go to a recording studio or rehearsal going, 'Well, we're gonna make it sound like this.' It's pretty bad if we do anything like that, because there would be no point. I think, like, if you were a painter, you wouldn't, like, argue about who to copy, you know. You presume you get over that. It's not really an issue. If we were all into the Pixies and nothing else, then it would be pretty obvious what the band would sound like. I think it's the same with any band, really. I mean, if you talk to R.E.M., their influences are pretty disparate . . . about as disparate as you can get, really. Anyway [looks at Jonny], he's got me into jazz now. Bastard.

ATN: **So finally *The Bends* is getting some recognition. Why do you think it took so long?**

Thom: Well, the nicest thing is that *Billboard* thing. They have three journalists with their faces going [makes a fake grin] and we were No. 1 in two of them and three in the third, I think.

Jonny: It's weird. It's been kind of a reversal from *Pablo Honey*. We had an album that sold a lot but wasn't taken much notice of and now we've become that horrible thing of a bands' band or a critics' band.

Thom: Frightening.

Jonny: Which is kind of a big reversal for us . . .

Thom: Because they're even more fickle than the public.

Jonny: It's a nice change from the first album.

ATN: **Is this kind of what you wanted from the beginning, to slowly climb up the charts?**

Jonny: Yeah. At least now, when journalists miss the point and reviewers miss the point, then we can sort of disagree with them. But when reviewers are saying bad things about the first album, we just sort of half-agree with them. [Thom lets out an enormous laugh.] There's some truth to what they're saying. If they say [*The Bends*] is rubbish and no one has said that, so it makes sense, really.

Thom: It makes us a little nervous.

ATN: **What are your inspirations for your songs?**

Thom: [They] change all the time. Mostly books about politics at the moment.

ATN: **Speaking of politics, do you plan on pursuing a career in it, since you're involved in the Rock the Vote UK and you have a new song called 'Electioneering'?**

Thom: Oh yeah. I think I wanna become a politician. Well, I wanna actually get into the arms trade first and make my money there. Pop stardom, arms trade, have it all.

ATN: **What has been the highlight of your career thus far?**

Jonny: Career? You sound like my mother . . . she says that. 'When are you going to get a career?'

Thom: Yeah. 'Why have you chosen this career?' A career is going in the army.

Jonny: Career suggests long . . .

Thom: Longevity . . .

Jonny: . . . and planning. There's something quite depressing when you hear a band say, 'We want to make music together for another 20–30 years'.

ATN: (jokingly) **You don't want to do that?**

Jonny: I don't know what I want to do, really. Music. That would be good, but you know, I don't plan on anything, really.

Thom: Peter Buck, he said . . . we were at this bar, and these two girls came up and tried to pick a fight with us. They started on me by saying something like . . . Oh . . . there was a Vancouver show where I walked onstage and said, 'We've been all over the world and you're the rudest fucking audience we've ever met' [laughs] and a fight ensued [laughs harder] and she sort of tried to pick a fight with me about that and that didn't work. Then she turns to Peter Buck and says, 'R.E.M. guy' and started pushing him and stuff. It was really fucking weird! We both just stood there, and he said, 'Well, you gotta sort of cultivate a healthy sense of the absurd,' which I thought was pretty cool. Then I said, 'Yeah, it's all gonna mean shit diddly when you're dead.' And he said, 'No, no, it will mean nothing well before that.' So, that resounded in my head.

ATN: **So what have been the highlights in being in Radiohead?**

Jonny: I heard one of our songs used by the BBC for a trailer for *Match of the Day*.

ATN: **What's that?**

Jonny: Oh, you know, sort of [announcement] on BBC1 tonight. [Mimicking the announcer] 'We'll be showing the Everton match.' And they'll play a Radiohead song to it. It's usually something like Tears for Fears or something . . . [Thom making drum noises in the background.] It's surreal, yes.

ATN: How about lowlights?

Thom and Jonny: Lowlights?

Thom: Is that code?

ATN: **Highlights, lowlights . . .**

Thom: Oh, lowlights. Oh sorry. I thought it was a type of milk or something. Lowpoints. Soul Asylum was pretty fucking low, I think.

Jonny: Yeah, that was pretty bad.

Thom: That was pretty low [laughs]. Just having one's gear stolen, then having to carry on with the tour. It wasn't much fun. Especially since we just came off R.E.M., so you couldn't really go down further. Couldn't really get much more let down. Handy link to a song. [One of Radiohead's new songs is called 'Let Down']

ATN: **You all seem to stay away from the Britpop party scene. Why is that?**

Thom: There is one at the moment, apparently. We don't really like cocaine that much.

Jonny: We're from the wrong city, as well . . . Oxford.

Thom: Yeah, deliberately. They don't let us out.

ATN: **So much of what is written about you in the press tends to focus on your volatile personality. Why do you think the papers are so obsessed with that aspect of Thom Yorke?**

Thom: Because most people in my position have learnt to behave and I haven't and I'm just not very good at behaving . . .

Jonny: I think people like their pop stars easy.

Thom: Like film stars, really. You can't be temperamental; you're basically a distraction.

Jonny: I think they want 'Pop Star Lite', really. L-I-T-E.

Thom: Someone from R.E.M. was saying to me the other night, 'Get nervous when you realise you can do it. When you can go through a whole evening having talked to fifty people and not remember a fucking word of any of it. Then you really are in trouble.'

ATN: **I've read somewhere that you've been writing down happy thoughts for the next album. Have you written anything down so far?**

Thom: Nearest I got was writing about the colour of the sky in LA.

ATN: **That's happy?**

Thom: Yeah, because that particular day it had rained the night before and you could actually see the sky. That's as happy as it's got, so far.

ATN: **That's all?**

Thom: Yeah, that's it. [Both laugh]

ATN: **What can we expect from the next album? Do you plan to put some of your current B-sides on it?**

Thom: There's been talk of doing a B-sides album at some point.

Jonny: Yeah, they are rather good and do get lost . . .

Thom: But then that's sort of cool. Otherwise we'd be getting into Prince territory and release three albums a year and there would be no quality control and people would see through it, wouldn't they, really, frankly?
Oh . . . Um . . . [to Jonny] what can we expect from this next album? Jon? It'll be analogue.

Jonny: Um, it will be, yes, sort of western.

Thom: Analogue.

ATN: **Western?**

Thom: Western analogue. Communist.

Jonny: Post-techno-gothic.

ATN: **Will it be somewhat experimental like the B-side remix of 'Planet Telex'?**

Jonny: I think we'll do more stuff that will be experimental, but again, it will be as unlike 'Planet Telex' as . . . [it will be] weirder than anything else.

Thom: The best indication of what we're going to do is that we're building our own studio, we're producing it ourselves and it's going to be a fucking mess.

ATN: **Why are you going to produce it yourself this time?**

Jonny: Because we sort of always wanted to and we were used to it when we were recording in bedrooms and it's not really that much different . . .

Thom: Yeah, we just really want to get that bedroom mentality of not giving a fuck and not worrying about it being a record.

ATN: **Where are you building your studio?**

Jonny: That's a secret.

ATN: **I don't mean the address! Where, like [the] city, [the] place . .**

Jonny: [laughing] 17 Turnpike . . . No, it's a sort of old apple storage place or banana storage place . . .

Thom: Lots and lots of upside-down trees.

ATN: **Do you think that is going to be good for you to be out in the middle of nowhere?**

Thom: Oh, very good. There's no toilet . . .

Jonny: Chi . . . good for the vibes.

Thom: [To Jonny] The chi? Is that as in tai chi?

Jonny: It flows up through the ground. Farms nearby. I mean, we've always been the kind of band . . .

Thom: [cuts him off] Is that what chi is?

Jonny: Yeah [trying to finish his sentence] That's recorded . . .

Thom: Does that come up through the ground?

Jonny: Yeah [continuing the story]. That's why . . .

Thom: [again, cuts Jonny off] I thought that was sewage.

Jonny: No. That's why [it's good to] be barefoot and not wear shoes.

Thom: Really?

Jonny: Yeah. So anyhow . . .

Thom: [Cuts Jonny off again] Fucking hell, I didn't know that!

Jonny: So, yes. We're recording there. We've always been the kind of band who records in picturesque village holes rather than in city youth centres, so yeah, that's probably a good thing. I don't know.

ATN: **Can you talk about some of the songs that you've already written for the album?**

Thom: OK, what can we say about the . . . I don't know if they're any good, really.

ATN: **I heard 'Electioneering' is excellent.**

Thom: Yeah, it's all right. I don't know. I don't like any of it, really. Some days I like all of it, some days I don't like any of it. What do you think, Jonny?

Jonny: Yeeess. Sometimes all of our songs don't sound good, sometimes they all sound great.

ATN: **How are they sounding like today?**

Jonny: People keep telling us we sort of sound like Queen, uh . . . Pink Floyd. Someone said we sounded like a skiffle band last night . . .

ATN: **A skittle band?**

Thom: You know, skiffle. Rockabilly . . .

Jonny: So it's anybody's guess. Sort of skiffle-Pink Floyd that sounds like Queen. Yeah, that's us. Easy to categorise, as you can tell. That cliché, that old pigeonhole that we fit into so well.

ATN: **A lot of bands like Garbage, R.E.M. and even k.d. lang refer to Radiohead as their favourite band. How does it feel to be admired by fellow musicians?**

Thom: I don't get it. Well, we're not that good. You know . . .

Jonny: I don't know. I feel their band is better than ours.

Thom: A lot better than ours.

Jonny: We always have a feeling that we can do better. There's always acres and acres of room for improvement. Just about everything we do, from every interview to every song we record, every concert. But maybe that's what keeps us going. Imagine being satisfied with something.

Thom: Satisfied is when you get fat and, like, go home.

Jonny: And have so much confidence in yourself that you don't worry . . .

Thom: Try to find more satisfaction by eating more . . . that's what I do. So that's why I come on the road.

ATN: **If you weren't in Radiohead, what would you all be doing?**

Jonny: We'd be asking k.d. lang, or Garbage, or R.E.M. for jobs. I don't know, what would we do?

Thom: I would be um . . . I'd be a politician!

ATN: **No, really.**

Thom: I would!

Jonny: I'd stick with college, really. And I'd be graduating this

year and have an honorary doctorate degree in
something . . .

ATN: **Where did you all go to school? Thom, you went to Exeter, right?**

Thom: Yes, I went to Exeter and I did English literature and fine art.

ATN: **[to Jonny] And you were in college when the band got signed?**

Jonny: Yes. I did four weeks or something like that.

Thom: Then your tutor said, 'Leave!'

Jonny: [laughing] Then they turned up in a white van and dragged me up to some concert somewhere.

ATN: **What about the others?**

Jonny: Colin went to Cambridge.

Thom: [in royal-esque accent] Cambridge! English literature!

Jonny: [also doing accent] Philip probably went to Liverpool . . .

Thom: [accent] We can't remember what he did!

Jonny: Edward did politics in Manchester [laughing].

Thom: [accent] Politics and economics . . . mostly politics! Northern Irish politics!

ATN: **Then he can be your campaign manager.**

Thom: Oh yes!

ATN: **Tell me about your songwriting process. How does it all come together?**

Jonny: It's quite defecatory.

Thom: Yes, it's very defecatory and it's a friggin' mess and, um, often you'll have a song for a year, which you won't know what to do with, and then Jonny will change one note and it'll all fall into place. And some songs are completely automatic, like 'Lucky', where there was absolutely no thought process or anything involved. We just played it one day and that was it. I played the chords once around and everyone joined in and that was the song [laughs]. It was just frightening, frankly.

ATN: **Tell me some interesting fan encounters.**

Thom: Mostly people trying to convert me to God.

Jonny: There's some people who follow him around and say, 'You should use that power you have to spread the word of our lord Jesus Christ!'

Thom: And I say, 'I'll spread something else instead.' I had someone come knocking at my door in Oxford. And I was forced to slam it in her face. Because that was the line that was drawn and she went across it . . . [laughing . . . trying to have a sense of humour about it]

Jonny: Someone grabbed me when I was onstage at a Canadian show and said, 'Quick, write your name on my arm.' Which wasn't a first, but they showed up at the next show, which was like three hundred miles away, which was quite strange. But stranger still was that my name was sort of, very roughly . . . didn't even look like my name . . . they had it tattooed on . . . permanently.

Thom: There's a lesson there. Always write neatly.

Jonny: Yes, that's a good lesson.

ATN: **Did that freak you out?**

Jonny: Nooo . . . I just wish they would've asked Thom to draw something. It's better than an anchor or a lion's head.

ATN: **So you just signed 'Jonny'?**

Jonny: Well, it was more like Jeremy, actually . . . [laughing]

ATN: **Do any of you have tattoos?**

Thom: No. I get a transfer occasionally. I find [tattoos] very sexy. Hmmmm.

ATN: **But you don't want to get one?**

Thom: Well, not on me.

Jonny: Yeah, standing in the mirror admiring your own tattoo . . .

Thom: And getting off on it. Anyway, ohh . . . that could get really messy.

ATN: **OK . . . I have some questions that have been emailed to me by the members of the Radiohead emailing list. Some of them are very strange.**

Thom: Yes, let's answer those.

ATN: **First question. Thom, why are there so many car references in your songs like 'Killer Cars', 'An Airbag Saved My Life', 'Stupid Car' . . .**

Thom: First of all, where did you get the title 'An Airbag Saved My Life'?

ATN: **Everyone on the Radiohead emailing list is talking about it.**

Thom: Oh fuck! Never mind.

Jonny: That was quick!

Thom: Yeah . . .

Jonny: It hasn't been recorded or filmed live yet . . .

Thom: Or done anything at all . . .

ATN: **Someone already has it on tape.**

Thom: Ah fuck! London!

Jonny: How? When did we do it?

Thom: We did it in London for XFM.

Jonny: Oh yeah. We did it well, though, so that's all right.

Thom: No, we did it dreadfully.

Jonny: No, it wasn't.

Thom: Really?

Jonny: No, it was good.

Thom: Oh, OK. Why are there so many references to cars? Well, I'll tell you why. It's because when I was younger my parents moved to this house, which was a long, long way from Oxford and I was just at the age where I wanted to go out the whole time. I used to have this one car, and I very nearly killed myself in it one morning, and I gave my girlfriend at the time really bad whiplash in an accident. I was seventeen. Hadn't slept the night before. Anyway, eventually, my dad bought me another car, a Morris Minor, you know, and when you drove around corners in it, the driver door used to fly open. And I'd only do fifty miles an hour and on the road that went from my house to Oxford, there were fucking maniacs all the time, people who would drive a hundred miles an hour to work and I was in the Morris Minor and it was like standing in the middle of the road with no protection at all. So I just gradually became emotionally tied up in this whole thing.

ATN: **What are your feelings on vegetarianism?**

Thom: I think we were right and the rest of the world's wrong [referring to mad cow disease]. Yeah . . . we were right . . . nah, nah, nah . . . so there.

Jonny: I find it increasingly hard to do, because you discover with horror that your favourite chocolate sweets have gelatine in them . . .

Thom: And cheese, when they put the rennet in . . . that's the most disgusting thing imaginable! I think, basically, that it's the responsibility of the supermarkets to fucking get themselves sorted out, you know. Because basically people rely on supermarket chains and they're really the ones that should be endorsing vegetarianism. 'Cos if they don't, then it'll never happen, you know.

ATN: **What do you want fans to see in your work?**

Thom: The word of God!

Jonny: Yes.

Thom: [Notices my silence, waiting for him to finish] That was pretty good, I thought! [laughs] Um, if people get it, they wouldn't think it's depressing. When people sort of say, um . . . all that fucking annoying thing about, 'Oh your work's so depressing, na, na, na . . .' Well, it's not because those are just the words. The point is I put the words to music which I think is incredibly uplifting, otherwise, there would be no point to doing it at all.

ATN: **Several people on the list want to know this: Jonny, do you have a girlfriend?**

Jonny: I have hundreds, yeah. A different one every day. No, no, I'm not interested in women or sex or anything . . .

Thom: No. Messy, smelly . . .

ATN: **How do you feel about the whole promotion aspect of the US?**

Thom: I sort of envision myself in a sort of a Billy Graham role, you know . . . shake hands and spread the word of God and fuck off and take the money and run . . .

Jonny: We have money?

Thom: Apparently. Apparently, it comes later. We haven't seen any money yet.

ATN: **What do you do in your off time?**

Thom: Off time? Don't have any. Try and sit still. Can't do it.

Jonny: We usually sit around and think about what we're going to do with our on-time, sadly.

Thom: Yeah. It's really, really, really pathetic. In fact, we all need to get hobbies.

ATN: **You told me last time we talked that you were going to travel to Japan for vacation. Did you go?**

Thom: No, I was going to. The reason I didn't was because it's so fucking expensive and we haven't seen any money yet.

Jonny: The Japanese are the most . . . I think the most stylish nation on the earth.

Thom: Yeah . . . it's embarrassing. Makes the rest of us look like ill-dressed spazzes.

ATN: **So I take it you like touring Japan?**

Thom: Yeah. Any opportunity to go back will be gladly received [laughs]. We keep trying but they say they don't want us.

ATN: **That's not true. My sister just called from Tokyo this morning and asked when you're coming.**

Jonny: The official line, allegedly, is that we're going to go back when we can sort of . . .

Thom: . . . sell something new.

Jonny: No, when there are clubs that have room for about a thousand people. And after that it's like 15–20,000 people . . .

Thom: Oh, right. So we don't go back 'til then? [sarcastic]. Oh, yeah. That really makes sense. I think someone's lost the plot [reaches up in the air as if trying to grasp Jonny's meaning].

Jonny: We hope we can play Budokan and we'll go back when we can sort of . . .

Thom: What is the Budokan?

Jonny: It's a horribly big, scary place.

ATN: **Didn't the Beatles play there?**

Jonny: Blur played there too.

ATN: **Well, if Blur can sell it out, you should be able to . . .**

Jonny: Well, this is what we're vaguely trying to hope, yes.

Thom: How big is it?

Jonny: It's like Wembley Arena.

Thom: Oh, fuck that. I'm sorry, but people are losing the plot here, thank you very much. That's not my idea of a good night out. At all.

Jonny: Hmmm. We'll see.

Thom: [Back to the previous question] Um, as I said, trying to sit still, which was something I tried to do over Christmas. Sit in front of the television for more than twenty minutes without just shouting at it and getting up and moving out again. And I find it very, very, very, very difficult indeed. Other than that, I play with my Macintosh. All day long. Very sadly.

ATN: **Games?**

Thom: No, I don't play games. I do sort of art work, but it's actually usually related to the band. I always find that I'll do this image and put Radiohead above [it] and I'll go, 'Fuck, I'm doing it again! Shit!' Yeah . . . so I think we all need to get hobbies.

Jonny: Macramé. It was very big in the '70s. It's like crochet, I believe. It's made of crochet material.

ATN: **Do you weave them?**

Jonny: I think so. I'll let you know next time I see you. I'll take it up.

ATN: **Are you going to make me a pot-holder?**

Jonny: I'll make you a tea cosy.

Thom: How about shoelaces? And decorate my house.

ATN: **In pot-holders and tea cosies.**

Jonny: Do you want to get married?

ATN: **Excuse me?**

Thom: [waving his hand in front of Jonny's face] No, that was my gag!

Jonny: Because I can legally marry you now.

ATN: **What?**

Thom: Well, I could actually . . . [trying to cut in]

Jonny: [cutting Thom off] No, we're reverends . . .

Thom: [cutting Jonny off] Oh, yeah, we're reverends . . . we're all reverends.

Jonny: We started our own church.

Thom: The Holy Church of Waste.

Jonny: Well, we can legally marry people and bury people in thirteen American states, including California.

Thom: So if anybody needs, you know, to get married, we can do it for them now. [To Jonny] How much did it cost us? Twenty dollars?

Jonny: Ten dollars or something. So we are going to conduct a mass community-style wedding at our LA show, that's tomorrow.

Thom: Waste packaging is going to be the next thing.

ATN: **Your fan club and newsletter are called** *W.A.S.T.E.* **. . . what's the obsession with waste?**

Thom: Waste? Well, um, just waste, really. You know,

everything about it. Waste, waste, you know . . . it really fucking does my head in, man! It does, honestly. I sound like a real idiot, but it's true. Think about it, when you go to the supermarket and you come home and you have your vegetables and they're in cling-film . . . and what do you do with it? You put it in the bin, and where's it go?

ATN: **Recycle.**

Thom: Well, not in our country it doesn't.

ATN: **You guys don't have a recycling programme?**

Thom: They do not have anything like that in Britain. Britain is so backward, it's frightening.

Jonny: They put a little curly thing [on packaging] where they sort of have a little recycle sign, and you think 'great' then you look at it a little closer and it says 'recyclable'. Instead of 'recycle'.

ATN: **But there's nowhere to recycle?**

Thom/Jonny: Yeah.

Thom: I think the most important thing for anyone to do at the moment is that, really. That's why I'm becoming a politician, so I can find a way to get rid of my rubbish.

Jonny: I think if you drive far enough, you can get your paper recycled. That's about it, you know.

Thom: [But] you cannot recycle plastic in Oxford or London. So where the fuck does it go? And it's not like it even costs that much to do it! Anyway, that's far more important than Radiohead. That's why we formed a company called Waste.

ATN: **Can't you just bring your own bags and put produce in that?**

Thom: Can't do that in Britain. You can do this thing where there's this farm and you get a big hamper of food every weekend and they come deliver it, and that's your food for the week. And that's what we're going to be doing when we get back. But I mean, if you need to dash out and stuff, you come back with bananas in cling-film . . . and you put them in a bin, and it's like . . . and that's why we formed the Holy Church of Waste.

ATN: **To start the recycling programme going on in Britain?**

Thom: Yeah.

Jonny: And marry people.

Thom: And marry people.

Jonny: And bury people.

Thom: We can christen people . . .

Jonny: . . . into the Church of Waste. I mean, there's nothing derogatory about the idea. There are a lot of people in the public in England, like the Reverend Ian Paisley, who actually have no qualification . . .

Thom: Yeah. He woke up one morning and decided that he wanted to be a reverend.

Jonny: And people tend to use titles like that to get people to throw their money. It's quite easy to get master's degrees and doctorates . . .

ATN: **It is?**

Thom: Oh yeah. It's a piece of piss! I actually got one for being mad from Oxford!

ATN: **Oh, like the honorary ones?**

Jonny: No, no, actual ones. Where they send you booklets, and you have to answer . . .

ATN: **Oh, mail order ones.**

Jonny: Yeah, but they're all legal. You can get mail order anything. You can be a rabbi if you wanted to. It's very, very disrespectful.

Thom: Never leave your house. It'll all turn up in big packaging and bits of foam and cardboard, which you'll then put in the attic . . .

Jonny: [yells over to a roadie] Cline!! Clare, can Cline be in our photo shoot?

Thom: No! He doesn't go with any of our clothes . . .

[Jonny and Thom are both distracted for a minute]

Thom: Sorry, we're not behaving. I'm sorry about the KOME thing . . . I'm really sorry about the KOME . . .

ATN: **It's OK, don't worry about it. Any last thoughts?**

Jonny: Yes, lots. Why do Americans express the word 'say' with the word 'like'? Like, he's, like, let's do this and he's, like, let's do that . . .

ATN: **[Tries to explain] I don't know where it started . . . maybe with the whole Valley Girl thing in the '80s . . .**

Thom: Valley Girl? Valley Girl? That's an interesting phrase.

ATN: **I can't get out of it either and English isn't even my first language . . .**

Jonny: What is your first language?

ATN: **Japanese.**

Jonny: All right!

ATN: **But I've forgotten it all . . .**

Jonny: Nooo! I know pidgin Japanese . . . *Phil-san wa, doco desu ka.*

ATN: **You're better at speaking Japanese than I am.**

Jonny: Nooo! *Jonny no* Radiohead *desu.* Can you remember how to count? [Jonny and I count in Japanese together]

Thom: [waving disc player] All the new songs are on this. It's a mini-disc-Walkman-recording-thing.

ATN: **You can record onto a disk?**

Thom: Yeah. And you can name them as well, which is the cool bit. So when every track comes up, it's got a different name on it . . . Three hundred pounds it cost me, but it's amazing. You can make records on that. It's like a DAT, you know . . . but it's easier to use. You can use it as a data input-and-output thing using the optical line in . . . so it can be like a hard disk if you want it. It's got, like, instant access to each track as well . . . just go [pushes the button] and it's there . . . it's not like rewinding a tape or anything . . . So, I'm giving it the hard sell.

ATN: **Well, that's all for now.**

Jonny: *Domo arigato.* (Thank you very much)

ATN: *Doitashimashite.* **(You're welcome)**

Jonny: *Hai. Dewa mata.* (See you again)

Four: Neurotics Anonymous

1

Party On!

Tom Doyle, Q,
June 1997

Brightly early most weekday mornings before 9 a.m., when other rock stars still have at least a good six hours of kip ahead of them – or have yet in fact to go to bed following another night of drunken or chemically-induced shenanigans – Radiohead's curiously angular guitarist Jonny Greenwood can usually be found in the middle of a field in the quiet Oxfordshire countryside, flying his kite.

If the widescreen possibilities of this undeniably evocative scene have a touch of Pink Floyd-like imagery about it, then that perhaps is no coincidence, since the soundtrack on the rake-thin twenty-five-year-old man's personal stereo is *Meddle*, an album released in 1971, the year he was born. This evidence alone may not be enough to suggest that Radiohead are slowly, surely mutating into the New Pink Floyd. But then there are other factors which have to be taken into consideration. Not least the fact that singer Thom Yorke warmly recalls recording parts of their self-produced third album, *OK Computer*, at their recently acquired studio farmhouse while, outside the window, herds of Jersey cattle lumbered lazily through sunny fields. In the background, an industrial chimney belched acrid smoke into the sky. 'It was the Floyd,' he enthuses before – perhaps typically – feigning vomiting in self-disgust at having been forced to draw this seemingly unthinkable parallel himself.

Bassist Colin Greenwood has his own thoughts about his brother's kite-flying plot to turn Radiohead into a progressive rock ensemble. 'Jonny made us all watch *Pink Floyd Live in Pompeii* and said, "Now this is how we should do videos",' he offers, grinning, his already frighteningly voluminous eyes widening in mock disbelief. 'I just remember seeing Dave Gilmour sitting on his arse playing guitar, and Roger Waters – with long greasy hair, sandals and dusty flares – staggers over and picks up this big beater and whacks this gong. Ridiculous.'

Nevertheless, there is no getting away from it: Radiohead's keenly-awaited third album is a sprawling, hugely experimental affair that cannot be described without using the words 'out' and 'there'. The return single, 'Paranoid Android', by way of indication, is a six-and-a-half-minute epic in three movements. Jonny Greenwood admits that, during the making of the record, he had found himself becoming involved in a brave but perhaps futile pursuit: trying to unearth half-decent prog rock albums.

'It's been very disappointing because most of it is *awful*,' he softly admits in his engagingly posh way. 'I've got it into my head that prog rock albums must be good because they attracted a lot of fans. So far, I've just trawled through fairly tedious Genesis albums.'

Aside from all of this, there has also been the suggestion that Radiohead have been gradually morphing into R.E.M. since the Oxford quintet's extended supporting sojourn on the Monster tour in the summer of 1995. Certainly Thom Yorke's friendship with Michael Stipe – who made the onstage pronouncement that 'Radiohead are so good, they scare me' – has been well-documented. In fact, Yorke and Jonny Greenwood have just returned to Oxford from London, where they were collaborating with Stipe on tracks for *Velvet Goldmine*, the glam-rock-scrutinising film that Stipe is currently producing. Notably, on *OK Computer*, there is evidence that Yorke's approach to lyric-writing has taken on a distinctly more oblique, Stipe-like bent.

Whatever comparisons are being made, it's clear that Radiohead have gone through something of a transitional period. It seems reasonable to declare that toying around with groundbreaking studio techniques and constructing wildly ambitious musical atmospheres now figure heavily in their collective imaginations. Queen for the '90s, anyone?

'I've been building up my chest just now so that it looks good in a white vest,' warns the small and slight-framed Yorke, with his characteristic level of sarcasm. 'Christ, you should've seen the 'tache I had last week.'

———

After coming down from such a high as Radiohead experienced when R.E.M. took them under their wing and nursed them through the crucial period when they learned how to get their music across to stadium-proportioned crowds (Yorke claims that his most deep-rooted nightmare is to become Jim Kerr at his worthiest), the band were given carte blanche to record and self-produce their next album. As a consequence, *OK Computer* unarguably finds them breaking into new territory, from the looped-up, all-fronts assault of 'Airbag' through the searingly anthemic 'Electioneering' to the soothingly effective 'Exit Music (For a Film)', ostensibly 'She's Leaving Home' retold with a pan-icky edge.

Preliminary sessions began – in a stroke of magnificent indul-gence, at actress Jane Seymour's mansion near Bath – in the spring of last year, the very same place where the Cure initially developed the commercially disastrous *Wild Mood Swings*. The previous summer, Johnny Cash had rented the house before an appearance at Glastonbury. The flowing-locked English rose could be reas-sured that Radiohead were rather less of a rock'n'roll proposition. Although they did rearrange the furniture.

'We recorded in her library,' Jonny Greenwood explains. 'It was wonderful going somewhere that wasn't designed for recording. Recording studios now tend to be quite scientific and clinical. You can't really impose yourself without getting over the fact that there are fag burns in the carpet and gold discs all around. It's good to go and decide that we'll turn this beautifully furnished sitting-room into whatever.'

While they are a five-strong band of self-confessed 'neurotics anonymous', the fact that Radiohead are so keen to guard the rural location of their studio farm headquarters, where the album was completed, is indicative of their growing status as the archetypal art-school-grounded English rock band afforded the Imperial-Leather-like luxury of creative freedom. This, it would seem, is a direct result of the fact that, throughout their five-year existence – while everyone's heads were turned in the directions of (initially) Blur, then Suede and now Oasis – Radiohead have quietly grown into a formidably successful act. Their second album, *The Bends*, has now achieved platinum status in Britain, a trend more or less followed in most record-buying nations.

When, at the beginning of 1996, Parlophone Records released 'Street Spirit (Fade Out)', the fourth, campaign-closing single from *The Bends*, its hypnotically languid tone rendered it too dark and sombre to be playlisted on Radio 1. It still debuted with a one-fingered salute at No. 5. On the release of War Child's *Help* album the previous September, Radiohead's magnificently moody contribution, 'Lucky' (oddly included on *OK Computer*), proved to be the stand-out – although the band had been forced to complete the track in an intensive five-hour period to meet the required deadline, after a day spent posing for a War Child camera crew dispatched to film them *pretending* to record. 'They were waiting for us to record the song and we were waiting for them to go,' smiles the unnaturally lofty Ed O'Brien, credited on the group's sleeves for supplying 'polite guitar', as opposed to Jonny Greenwood's 'abusive guitar'. Of the video footage depicting casualties of the Bosnian conflict that was subsequently set to the track, Yorke – never one to understate his emotional reactions – simply says, 'It had me in tears.'

Today the five members of Radiohead, fresh from tramping through the fields of rape for their *Q* photo session, mill around the management offices close to their recording studio, seemingly a relaxed and quietly polite bunch who enjoy a laugh of wry and knowing variety. O'Brien, lightly stoned this afternoon, since this is effectively a day off for the band – although pockets of them will frequently disappear into the adjoining recording room to continue work on B-sides – is charming and affable and has earned a reputation as the band member renowned for his on-stage acts of over-exuberance. The band gleefully recall the guitarist once disappearing over the lip of the stage at a theatre gig in North Carolina, tumbling into the orchestra pit and then struggling for ages to clamber back out.

Groomed drummer and, impressively, ex-Samaritan Phil Selway proves suitably genial for someone who has had a Japanese fan club – Phil Is Great – set up in his honour. Another of the Phil Is Great club's meetings is planned for the following week, when Radiohead make a promotional trip to the Pacific Rim.

The Greenwood brothers, who share no distinctive physical resemblance, are polar opposites. Jonny rarely touches alcohol; Colin can regularly be located in a pub after frenzied searches five minutes before the band are due on stage. Jonny is silent unless coaxed; Colin is effusive when engaged in the topics of books, records and other bands. Jonny was likely described as 'a dreamer' by his teachers, his head seemingly operating at some cloud-high altitude; Colin is sharp and wary and likely the cornerstone of Radiohead. When together, both share an inscrutable look if questioned on any subject. Colin admits to feeling guilty of acting a touch cruelly to his colour-blind younger brother when they were growing up: he would mix up the crayons, which the guitarist claims 'retarded me'.

'We share the same gene pool,' states the elder, directing another meaningful look towards his sibling.

'But I got the shallow end,' adds his toothily blessed younger brother, without any detectable hesitation.

Meanwhile, the boyishly-proportioned Thom Yorke pads around barefoot in blue canvas jeans, Radiohead fan club T-shirt and Gaultier shades, his short, spiky hair dyed black after extended periods as peroxide blond and retina-damaging orange. Quietly intense, he is a man possessed of a bitingly sharp sense of humour, although an air of brow-beaten cynicism can be detected in his every utterance. The others simply describe Yorke as 'a bit of a worrier', but it would seem that his enduring reputation as a troubled and overly angsty individual is reasonably well-deserved, despite his claims to having recently 'learned to relax a little'. He talks with his head bowed and eyes closed, covering his face with his hands and peering through his fingers, sometimes curling his limbs up into a tight ball, as if he is under physical attack. The prospect of Radiohead performing this summer to forty thousand people in Ireland as well as headlining a major festival (interestingly, on the same weekend as the strategically unannounced Glastonbury bill) seems to fill him with dread.

'I can't see why we're doing these big gigs,' he shrugs. 'Thing is, whoever it is up there, it's not the person sitting here. It's a completely different state of mind that you have to spend a long time getting into. I can't switch it on and off. When even the logistics of these big gigs are discussed, I just fucking freeze up. It's not something I'm emotionally capable of dealing with yet. Hopefully I'll get back into a different frame of mind where it won't worry me.'

While there is a certain fragile quality to Yorke, the two sides to Radiohead's chief songwriter are exemplified in those moments when his distinctive singing voice swoops down from a choirboy falsetto to a low, anguished snarl. Similarly, in conversation he can suddenly cop an attitude, turning shirty and argumentative. O'Brien remembers his first impression of the young Yorke when the two were involved in a play – the former acting, the latter providing musical accompaniment – at the Oxford school where Radiohead first met as teenagers.

'There was this tense dress rehearsal,' O'Brien remembers, 'and Thom and this other fella were jamming freeform cod-jazz throughout it. The director stopped the play and shouted up to this scaffold tower thing they were playing on, trying to find out what the hell was going on. Thom shouted down, "I don't know what the fuck we're supposed to be playing." And this was to a teacher.'

———

Born with one eye closed on 7 October 1968, the infant Thom Yorke had already endured five major operations on his paralysed eyelid by the time he was six. Made to wear an eye-patch during his early school years, he was cruelly mocked by his schoolmates. He half-bitterly brushes off suggestions that this may have caused him to have a slight chip on his shoulder.

'Oh no,' he states, sharply. 'I was sweet and lovely and nothing ever happened to me. [Cagily] When I was younger I was in the music room most of the time, anyway. It was great. No one came down there and there were these tiny rooms with sound-proofed cubicles. I suppose I'm quite an aggressive person. I was a fighter at school, but I never won. I was into the idea of fighting [laughs hysterically]. I've had to calm down a bit, otherwise I'd go nuts.' Yorke recalls the moment in his younger life when he realised that he was not perhaps quite as handy with his fists as he'd imagined. 'In first year at college, I went through this phase where I was into this granddad hat and coat I had,' he quietly explains. 'They were immaculate and I was into dressing like an old man. But I went out one night and there were these blokes, townie guys, waiting to beat someone up and they found me. They said something, I turned around, blew them a kiss and that was it. They beat the living shit out of me. One was kicking me, one had a stick and the other was smashing me in the face. That put me off fighting a bit.'

Back in mid-'80s Oxford, where Radiohead first bonded and began rehearsing, essentially as the school band, they called themselves On A Friday. Selway was in the sixth form, O'Brien in the fifth year, Yorke and Colin Greenwood in the fourth and Jonny Greenwood – the last to join – in the third. 'We're still in our same classes and years, really,' the elder Greenwood grimly decides. 'The thing about having been together for such a long period is that there are some heinously embarrassing group shots from ten years ago when we were in adolescence with varying styles of haircut and demeanour which would now be openly laughed at in the street.'

During this era, of course, the quiff was king ('You'd literally take a photograph of Morrissey to the barber and say, "I want it like that"') and if On A Friday resembled the Smiths visually, they had yet to find a foothold musically. The four others remember tapes of Thom Yorke's early compositions as being 'schizophrenic'. 'One track, "Rattlesnake", just had a drum loop that Thom did himself at home on a tape recorder with bad scratching over the top and kind of Prince vocals,' Jonny Greenwood remembers. '"The Chains" had viola and was meant to sound like the Waterboys. "What is That You See" was a feedback frenzy. After hearing it, I knew Thom was writing great songs and I knew what I wanted to do.' Nevertheless, the younger Greenwood's ambitions were thwarted by the group's reluctance to let him join. Described to them as 'a precocious talent' who would whip through an assortment of instruments in an attempt to impress his potential bandmates, Jonny sat onstage, in Phil Selway's words, 'with a harmonica, waiting for his big moment' at On A Friday's first gig at Oxford's Jericho Tavern in 1987.

As each member wandered off to college or university, rehearsals would take place only during their lengthy summer breaks as students. But On A Friday were improving by leagues and, by the summer of 1991, when their first real demo went into circulation (released as the *Drill* EP in 1992), there were suddenly legions of A&R men cramming into the Jericho Tavern. Within weeks, On A Friday signed to Parlophone and, out of 'sheer embarrassment', changed their name to Radiohead.

————

As imageless as a police identity parade and embodying such extremes of stature and build that Ed O'Brien probably towers a whole foot above Thom Yorke, Radiohead initially found it difficult to attract attention during the lifespan of their debut album *Pablo Honey* when other, more fashion-conscious outfits were hogging the limelight. On its initial release in the UK, the second, self-hating single, the possibly classic 'Creep', stiffed. As with the Fixx before them and Bush afterwards, Radiohead suffered the indignity of being rejected by their motherland and embraced by America when 'Creep' became a slacker anthem after an extended period of over-exposure on college radio. By the time Radiohead arrived in America for their first tour, 'Creep' was already in the *Billboard* Top 40 and for the summer of 1993 its mutant guitar crunch and soaring melody spilled out from car radios and apartment windows all over America. Its follow-up, the bracing 'Stop Whispering', failed to maintain the momentum and the band found themselves performing to capacity audiences interested in hearing one song. For a time, Yorke re-christened the song 'Crap'.

'At that time the whole so-called alternative rock thing happened there,' remembers Yorke, 'populated by sad programmers from the '80s who didn't have a clue what they were putting on and "Creep" suffered from that. It was a good song, but afterwards it was, "Well, let's have more like that please because the pro-grammers understand it," and it's like "No, sorry."'

'We didn't know what was normal in America,' Jonny Green-wood muses. 'We went over there and we'd turn on MTV and "Creep" would be on again. We thought, Oh, that's good.'

'People were being very nice to us over there because "Creep" was doing so well,' adds Selway. '"Stop Whispering" didn't do quite so well, so that opened us up to the more cynical side of it.'

'We were hysterical,' decides O'Brien. 'One moment we'd be giggling, the next we'd be really down. Our reactions were extreme.' Regretfully, it was around this time that Radiohead, under pressure to visually reinvent themselves, became the tightly-trousered, big-haired rock band they felt America expected of them. Jonny Greenwood and Yorke even accepted modelling assignments for American fashion magazines, the latter sporting a hellish tangle of hair extensions atop his cranium.

'I *was* rock,' winces the frontman with an embarrassed laugh. 'There were so many elements to that period, but the hair was the worst. It was such a weird trip anyway, because suddenly we were seen as this big investment and there was money being thrown at us. It didn't last long enough to mess us up, but then I suppose, for a while, it probably did.'

The most positive knock-on effect of 'Creep''s US success was that on its re-release in the UK, it reached No. 7. On the negative side, Radiohead were in danger of looking like a one-trick pony. Immediately they set to work on *The Bends*, titled after the dramatic side-effects of emerging from the depths too rapidly. Cutting between *Zooropa*-fashioned loop collages ('Planet Telex'), folk rock ('Fake Plastic Trees') and hushed atmospherics ('Bulletproof'), the record managed to distract the listener for long enough to forget that 'Creep' existed. Of course, America couldn't get its head round it.

'There's this assumption, especially over here, that Radiohead are big in America,' O'Brien offers. 'Radiohead are not big in America. We had "Fake Plastic Trees" as a single and it was played on a radio station. They did a survey of their listeners – 18-to-25-year-old males who drive four-wheel-drive jeeps – and it came bottom of the list. The thing with Radiohead and America is that we had one pop hit there.'

'And they don't remember it anyway because they've got the attention span of insects,' Yorke mutters darkly. 'Our so-called success in America was that it allowed us to do lots of things, but it also meant that somehow we owed somebody something. But I couldn't work out who and I couldn't work out how much.'

———

Flying in the face of the drug-hoovering, groupie-rogering rock band image, Radiohead present themselves as Evian-sipping abstainers, content to play a hand of bridge on their tour bus, thank you very much. Nevertheless, the punishing eighteen-month touring schedule that followed was not without casualties.

There is an undercurrent of obsessiveness within the group, a matter most evident when they play live. Jonny Greenwood plays his guitar with such teeth-grindingly frantic force that he unknowingly lacerates his fingers. Recently, he has taken to strapping on an arm brace, which could be seen as a unique guitar-hero affectation. However, Greenwood insists he's been ordered to wear it since it was diagnosed that his playing style was causing repetitive strain injury. Similarly, he is keen to point out that the bulky headphones he sported throughout the latter half of the Bends tour are industrial ear shields he was advised to wear after suffering from a dangerously leaky lughole.

'My ear was ringing and bleeding for two weeks on the American tour,' he reveals, with strangely calm detachment. 'There was this terrifying gig in Cleveland, where I was nearly fainting. I was taken to hospital at three in the morning and the doctor said the situation was really grim. I'd love to do without both of them, but the arm brace I'm still going to need. It's conceited to deny there's any affectation but, having said that, I enjoy putting on the arm brace before I play. It's like taping up your fingers before a boxing match. It's a ritual.'

The most memorably grim incident of the tour, however, occurred in Munich, when Yorke blacked out and collapsed on stage. 'That had been building up,' he mumbles while wriggling uncomfortably in his seat, head in his hands. 'There'd been an incident in America where I'd really been as sick as fuck. This cold had got to my throat and whacked me out. It turned into laryngitis. The promoter takes you to the doctor, that's the normal standard thing, and the doctor says, "Oh, no, you're fine to play." You argue with them. They say, "No, take these drugs and you'll be fine." Then you realise the promoter is paying the doctor. It got bad again in Germany because we were sleeping on a cold damp tour bus in the middle of winter. This doctor turns up – usual thing, paid by the promoter – with this huge bag of drugs. All sorts of shit, man. He offered to inject me with steroids, which I refused. I didn't take anything because I thought I could get through it. We did the soundcheck, and I was like, "Oh shit, this is really bad." My voice was not there at all. By that point, it's too late, you can't cancel. I go on and third song in, I lost it. I remember hitting the floor and then I wasn't there.' He pauses and his face contorts into a perverse smile. 'It was great, actually.'

Most things about Thom Yorke's burgeoning rock-star status seem to trouble him deeply. The word he uses most frequently is 'doomed'. While he claims not to suffer from an acute fear of fame ('it's just that I have no respect for it'), he admits that his growing friendship with Michael Stipe has involved the R.E.M. singer offering guidance on how Yorke should deal with his concerns, although the Radiohead frontman is protective of their relationship. 'If you don't have any semblance of a normal life, then you won't be able to write,' he muses, 'and if you can't write, then you won't be there. He's helped me deal with most things I couldn't deal with. The rest is not anyone else's business and that's what's great about it. Anyway. Whatever. It sounds like I've been touched by an evangelist or something.'

Why still bother making music, then?

'Because I can be very drunk in a club in Oxford on a Monday night and some guy comes up to you and buys you a drink and says that the last record you made changed his life. That means something. It makes you chill about it.'

As a result of the anguished nature of your lyrics, are Radiohead fans obsessive individuals as a whole?

'They were. In the letters they can be, yeah. But when you meet people it's a different thing. People put pen to paper for different reasons, some of them quite weird. It was set up like that from the first record because of "Creep" and all the hyperbole around that, but actually we lost most of that debris when we brought out *The Bends*. Murderers have stopped writing to me to say how much they relate to "Creep", so that's cool. Now it's just people who're into what we're doing and there's respect on both sides.'

So your motivation is purely and simply the music you make and the reaction you'll get from it?

'[Sarcastically] I know it sounds awful, but, yes. [Changes mood] But y'know, that's probably lies as well . . . '

You do seem to eat yourself up about everything.

'I'm not eating myself up,' he continues defensively. 'It's just that if I read that last statement, I would think, "Wanker". Because whoever's said it isn't being honest.'

There was a certain point at which Nirvana had to pull back because they felt they were getting too big and they couldn't handle it. Can you see yourself doing the same if you get *really* famous?

'Yeah, I've got the pull-back button ready. You have to have. That hotline back to the President.'

How would you do that? Release a few seventeen-minute singles?

'No . . . no, there's other ways to do it. There's other shadows you can find. You can still be there. That was the thing I've had to learn recently. But it still gets to me.'

Do you ever fear for the ill-effects of increased success on your mental health?

'Oh, yes,' he exclaims, his mood strangely and suddenly lifting. 'Thank you, yes.'

Later that afternoon, as the light begins to fail, Thom Yorke appears to have returned to a more balanced state and almost rhetorically enquires, 'I don't think that this has been about moaning, do you?' Pulling an 'urgh' face when his band mates invite him down to the beer garden of a local pub for some light tea-time refreshment, he wanders off instead in the direction of the studio to continue work on the B-sides for 'Paranoid Android'.

As the others wend their way through the winding country lanes on the way to the hostelry, the talk turns to the fact that their frontman seems to be bearing so much intolerable weight on his shoulders.

'It's weird to see the public representation of Thom,' ventures Jonny Greenwood after a time, 'because it's quite different. I find Thom to be very affectionate and child-like.'

'Yeah,' his brother adds, 'but we don't draw the curtains of our bedrooms at night when we're going to sleep and see all these people staring up at the window. We don't have to deal with that. It's different graduations of stress, I suppose. What's important to him is that if he can have two different personas it's a way of protecting himself.'

'Well, I shared a room with him for four years,' Selway laughs, before tellingly adding, 'and that's not the man in the interviews.'

Deeply weird bunch, Radiohead. Insular, posh, irrationally paranoid, yet capable of creating achingly beautiful songs resplendent with mind-warping sonic tricks. They might just have the potential to re-chisel the granite face of rock music if their new-found prog-rock edge doesn't devour them or they don't disintegrate in the process. God help them if they ever get into proper drugs.

'Us on hard drugs? That would be horrible,' Thom Yorke had stated earlier, in a lighter mood. 'We'd probably end up sounding like Bryan Adams.'

2

Review of OK Computer

Nick Kent, *MOJO*,
July 1997

———

Because it's so damnably hard to pigeonhole effectively, you'll probably be seeing the new Radiohead album described in all manner of half-hearted ways over the next few weeks.

Some will glance at titles like 'Paranoid Android', hear what sounds a bit like a Mellotron (but probably isn't) swelling up on two or three tracks, note the strange song structures throughout and lazily conclude that the Oxford quintet have decided to come over all prog rock, like some late '90s manifestation of early King Crimson. Others will hear the spacey mix and all those freaky guitars buzzing around and immediately think, This must be their 'psychedelic' record. But I can only imagine someone listening to it on hallucinogenic drugs having a pretty grim time. It's not punk rock, lad rock, Britpop or grunge, either, and you can forget about 'easy listening' right now. There's little that's 'easy' about this record, little sugar-coating on the pill this time, no temporary oasis of perfect pop escapism and calm to bury yourself in while you try to come to terms with the trickier stuff.

Thom Yorke may be big mates with the lofty likes of Michael Stipe these days and he may accept the odd prestigious music-industry award standing alongside Brian Eno but, on this record, fame and success haven't removed the considerable chip still weighing on his shoulders.

From the very outset of their career, Yorke and Radiohead have always taken a pride in their perceived status as rock's rank outsiders. They've never belonged within any cosy community-minded groups, while their best-known song – 'Creep' – is as close to a definitive anthem for outsiders as has been written in the last twenty years. Now they've been allowed to produce themselves – and it can't be over-emphasised: the fact is, they've done a great job – Yorke and co. have finally created their own little sonic galaxy, part enchanted planet, part outsiders' club, with Yorke the ultimate anti-glamour rock star, sneering and seething – often with tongue not altogether out of cheek – while his co-workers content themselves by performing some of the most ingeniously arranged guitar-bass-drums-with-a-bit-of-synth-based music ever made.

'Airbag' has a stately but slightly tortured 'lost-in-space' feel, a bit like early Pink Floyd but more melancholy. The mix is alive with flanged guitars weaving among each other like snakes; '*I am born again,*' sings Yorke, but the abjectly mournful tone his voice elicits would lead one to feel this could be a curse and not a blessing. Next up, 'Paranoid Android' is the frankly audacious choice for first single, so you've doubtless already been confronted with its deeply eccentric, plaintive-acoustic-ditty to paranoid-screaming-electric-noise-and-back navigations, topped off with a sequence that sounds not unlike a bunch of pissed monks chanting in an abbey somewhere in the depths of Czechoslovakia.

'Subterranean Homesick Alien' counters 'Android's giddy changes by being a slow, beautifully languid piece led by a jazzy electric piano that features one of Yorke's most beguiling vocals to date, as he sends out a touching message of comfort and sympathy to alien life-forms trapped discontentedly on this planet. It helps to know that 'Exit Music' was written for the close of Hollywood's recent grunge re-styling of *Romeo and Juliet*. Lyrically, *all hell* is about to break loose, the song's heroine is having trouble with her breathing and yet the music moves at such an eerily calm pace it feels as if everyone – singer and musicians – are on the verge of losing consciousness.

'Let Down' is the album's one potential anthem-rocker, full of luscious chiming guitars and a haunting melody that could easily charm its way into the higher regions of the international singles chart. Then things swiftly turn weird and ugly again with the arrival of the vindictive 'Karma Police'. *'That's what you get/When you mess with us,'* Yorke snarls/sings by way of a chorus, but the slightly turgid rhythm makes you wonder whether he's being malicious or just ironic. Echoes of *White Album* John Lennon are well evident here, specifically the somnambulist lurch of 'I'm So Tired' and certain of the chord changes of 'Sexy Sadie'.

'Electioneering' is the full-tilt anarchic rock bash-up and sounds a bit like a splendidly warped deconstruction of dear old Alice Cooper's 'School's Out'. On the edgy 'Climbing Up the Walls', Yorke takes a detour onto Tricky's turf with a claustrophobic trip-hop vibe and distorted vocals before bringing in the rest of the group to return the sonic thrust closer to the guitar-based heart of Radioheadland. 'No Surprises' is the other potential hit here: an enchanting guitar ballad – somewhat in the vein of the

Velvets' 'Sunday Morning' – this could ultimately turn out to be Radiohead's very own 'Losing My Religion'. 'Lucky' you probably heard on the *H.E.L.P.* benefit album a couple of years ago. As haunting as ever, it fits in here perfectly as an extended melancholy farewell alongside 'The Tourist', the remarkable last track. Deep, slow, deeply soulful – just beautiful.

What does it all add up to? Certainly a record to which the adjectives 'dour' and 'dense' seem particularly appropriate when hearing it the first few times. Because there's so much going on here it can get a bit hairy at the beginning. It opens up quickly enough, though, and once you've been hooked, it never stops growing on you. Better than *The Bends?* Probably. Record of the year? Conceivably. Others may end up selling more, but in twenty years' time I'm betting *OK Computer* will be seen as the key record of 1997, the one to take rock forward instead of artfully revamping images and song-structures from an earlier era.

3

Radioheadline

Adam Sweeting, *Esquire,*
September 1997

A couple of hours earlier, Radiohead's Thom Yorke had looked like a bedraggled refugee who'd hitchhiked all the way to California from Sarajevo, slouching about in floppy striped trousers and a black leather jacket so worn out it was beginning to disintegrate. Even with four-inch-thick soles on his scruffy trainers, he seemed shrunken and stunted. You'd never imagine he was a rock star. You'd be more inclined to buy him a bowl of soup.

Yet now, here he was on stage at the Troubadour on Santa Monica Boulevard, looking like he was about to murder somebody by sheer willpower. Radiohead were in the midst of playing 'Talk Show Host'. As they stoked the song to a climax, Yorke became Robovocalist, strutting across the stage like a starship trooper ruthlessly subjugating some unsuspecting new planet, thrashing manically at his guitar. As the tension seethed upwards and began to verge on the unbearable, with Yorke and guitarist Ed O'Brien combining in a cyclone of whiplashed chords and ear-popping reverb, Yorke's eyes narrowed to a squint and his lower lip began to jut out obscenely.

He advanced to the edge of the stage, and his gaze fixed on a hapless onlooker in the front row. For what felt like hours, with the band raging around him, he glared pitilessly down at his target with an expression of concentrated hatred. It seemed that, at any moment, steam would come out of his victim's ears, his eyeballs would melt and his head must surely explode. Then suddenly the song was over. Yorke spun contemptuously on his heel, and the spell was broken. I made a mental note never to stand in the front row at a Radiohead show.

Yorke is the grand enigma of Radiohead, the central mystery of a band that a few sceptics still claim are merely English pomp-rock revisited, perhaps because their background recalls the arty educatedness of veteran progressive groups such as Genesis and Pink Floyd. It's as if they were created to be the polar opposite of the professional yobbishness of Oasis's Gallagher brothers. The quintet are articulate and cerebral and all live in Oxford, determined to steer clear of the backstabbing ferment of London. Where Oasis play primitive meat-and-potatoes rock with stubble and underarm hair, Radiohead's new album – their third, *OK Computer* – is fifty-three minutes of complex, allusive music, often unbearably emotional and as intricate as classical music or jazz. The band's growing confidence in their own abilities and judgement was written all over the disc's first single, 'Paranoid Android'. As if to cock a snook at frothy trivia such as the Spice Girls or Hanson, it was a six-minute micro-symphony in four movements, complete with a 'destabilising' passage in 7/8 time.

'There was this popular conception that we were all set up to do the big third crossover album,' reflects lead guitarist Jonny Greenwood. 'I think people who know *The Bends* [their second] will like it, but I'm not sure it's going to cross over into middle-American kids.'

'I don't think it's quite as people imagined it would be,' adds Yorke, with a twisted smile. 'A lot of people have experienced a nasty shock.'

It's possible that, without Yorke, Radiohead would be too technical for their own good. With him, they've grown into a formidable combination of expertise and musical ambition, given focus by Yorke's eerily affecting voice and the howls of rage, anguish and disgust that teem through his lyrics. 'At the end of the day, the vocal is the most important thing,' says O'Brien. 'It's more important than any guitar textures or rhythms or anything. The vocal is the thing that pulls you into the song.'

At the soundcheck before the Troubadour show, Yorke put the group briskly through their paces, trying out most of the songs they would play during the set later on. There was an absolute minimum of time wasting, though during pauses to fiddle about with drum mics or O'Brien's amplifier, Jonny Greenwood squatted down on stage to speed-read the last few pages of a Paul Theroux book.

'Let's do "The Bends",' said Yorke sharply, so they did. He cut them off after a couple of choruses. 'Let's do "Planet Telex".' Thirty seconds in, Yorke waved his arms impatiently to signal a halt. He had a problem with his guitar. The others didn't notice and kept playing, so Yorke scrubbed grumpily at his Telecaster to shut them up. Everybody jumped smartly to attention.

But Radiohead are intelligent and adult enough to accommodate everybody's personality foibles, small or large. The quintet have known each other, and played music together, since they all attended Abingdon boys' school. All of them read music to some extent and four of them have degrees. Jonny Greenwood is the exception, although you'd hardly call him the thick one. With his long, gangling frame, thick flop of black hair and dramatically angular bone structure, Jonny could have stepped out from an early Pink Floyd album sleeve, especially when he wears bell-bottom jeans and skinny T-shirts. Being the youngest, Jonny had to quit his psychology and music course to stick with his graduate fellow-musicians as they sought to turn the band into a serious professional enterprise.

Bassist Colin Greenwood, Jonny's smaller but less shy elder brother, has an English degree from Peterhouse College, Cambridge, and is usually reluctantly cited as Radiohead's leading intellectual. Top of his hit-list are modern American poetry and English Renaissance literature. If he wasn't in a band, he murmurs, he wouldn't have minded having a go at writing. Between them, the Greenwood brothers bring an aura of dreaming-spired bohemianism to Radiohead. It's the sort of thing that makes some music critics spiteful about the band's intellectual middle-classness. Radiohead try not to take any notice.

'We've never hidden it,' shrugs O'Brien, rolling himself some Golden Virginia while slouched beside the swimming pool at the pseudo-Camelot of Hollywood's Chateau Marmont hotel. An inflatable shark and a baby dinosaur bob in the blue water, perhaps subliminal reminders of the prevailing Los Angeles business ethos and the monstrous success of Steven Spielberg's *The Lost World: Jurassic Park*, at that moment devouring the nation's box offices. O'Brien is as personable and gregarious as you could wish, and makes such a marked contrast to the furtive, twitchy Yorke that they could be a comedy writer's idea of the perfectly mismatched couple.

'I was amazed to hear that Joe Strummer went to public school,' O'Brien reflects languidly. 'Well, we're not very good actors. We haven't paid our dues. We went to college and stuff like that and that's all part of the make-up of the band. It's very important for us. We carried the band on during college, but we were able to go off and do different things. Thankfully, we didn't get a recording contract when we were eighteen [although they did have a demo tape rejected by Island Records] and the fact that we signed when we were twenty-two or twenty-three meant we didn't need to seek out the rock'n'roll lifestyle. Our student days were fairly wild and we got it out of our system to a certain extent.'

Yorke's view is angrier and more melodramatic. 'The middle-class thing has never been relevant. We live in Oxford and in Oxford we're fucking lower-class. The place is full of the most obnoxious, self-indulgent, self-righteous oiks on the fucking planet, and for us to be called middle-class . . . Well, no, actually. Be around on May Day when they all reel out of the pubs at five in the morning puking up in the streets and going "Haw haw haw" and trying to hassle your girlfriend. It's all relative.' And that's not all. 'The thing that winds me up about the middle-class question is the presumption that a middle-class upbringing is a balanced environment when, in fact, domestic situations are not relevant to class,' he hisses. 'A bad domestic situation is a bad domestic situation. It's just such a fucking warped perspective on things.'

Calm is restored by drummer Phil Selway, the oldest member at thirty. He briefly held down a 'real' job as a desk editor with a medical publishing firm in Oxford. O'Brien remembers how the others recruited Selway when they were still at school and he'd already left, lending the sticksman an aura of experienced adulthood. A summit meeting was arranged in a local pub and they all pussyfooted gingerly round the subject of his recruitment so nobody should lose face. It's rare, I suggest to Selway, for a band to have stuck together as long as Radiohead without a single personnel change. Not even a Spinal Tap-style exploding drummer.

'It's odd in some ways, because on some levels you feel you're still stuck at that stage of your life and you've never actually left school,' says Selway drily. 'I think the original feeling about the band and the loyalty to each other and the friendships are still very much intact. You have to allow each other a lot of scope for development, especially when you're working so closely together, and I think we've managed that.' Selway is aghast that the press has discovered he used to be a Samaritan. 'God knows how this ever got out in the first place,' he winces. 'It's hideously embarrassing, because it's supposed to be confidential and you're supposed to remain anonymous. I'm sure any other Samaritans who read that are thinking: "jumped-up little tosser, putting himself across as some kind of saint".'

On the other hand, it could be very useful to have a practised sympathetic ear inside the pressure-cooker of a hard-working rock band. The stresses of touring have driven apparently well-balanced musicians round the twist, let alone a character as volatile as Thom Yorke. Some of his morbid, isolated lyrics on their last album *The Bends*, as well as the band's self-hating 1993 hit 'Creep', have drawn assorted freaks, emotional cripples and even convicted murderers to the band. R.E.M.'s Michael Stipe, a Radiohead admirer who is accustomed to having meanings he never intended foisted on his own lyrics, suggested that Yorke could do himself a favour by masking the bleeding edge of his emotions. *OK Computer* thus finds our small but feisty hero making a conscious effort to look outside himself.

For all its bleak, psycho-medical imagery, Yorke reckons *The Bends* did him a power of good. 'I realised afterwards there were a lot of things that had been sorted out in my head. I've always used music to sort myself out, because that's what it's there for. At the end of *The Bends*, I felt charged by external things and I wasn't internalising everything. Everything became much less of a personal trauma, which is why it was a bit of a strain to read that that is still the way people see us.'

But transforming the public perception of Radiohead will take time, particularly when *OK Computer*, for all its subtleties and melodic grace, is frequently as jocular as a midnight coach ride through Transylvania. While to some extent the band only have themselves to blame for starting the 'miserablism' bandwagon rolling, episodes such as the notorious *Melody Maker* article which lined up Yorke as the man most likely to follow Kurt Cobain into DIY oblivion still rankle. 'It was awful for the rest of us, seeing a friend go through that,' says O'Brien. 'I wanted to go down to the *Melody Maker* offices and say, "Do you know what you're doing? The impact your writing has on someone's character?" It's really irresponsible.'

The extent to which listeners' responses can be brainlessly pre-programmed is astonishing. One American journalist automatically assumed that 'Exit Music (For A Film)', despite its painstakingly literal title, must be about suicide. In fact, it was written to play over the end credits of Baz Luhrmann's movie of *William Shakespeare's Romeo + Juliet*.

'I think it's got to the stage of, fuck it, you can't be responsible for people being screwed up and unstable,' reckons O'Brien. 'When you have people writing in from Death Row, it's quite a heavy burden on young shoulders, to put it mildly. Patti Smith said something about a song capturing a time, and that's it, you can't be responsible six months later if people take it differently. I think people have seen over the last year that Thom is not the tortured artist, and he's really enjoying being able to look outside himself.'

'I've always seen our songs as being quite positive, really,' Selway argues. 'They confront very painful topics but at some time there's always a sense that there's a struggle with them and an attempt to overcome them, so I don't think there's anything in there that would intentionally incite people to do anything. You can't censor yourself overly, can you? You would just get a very half-baked second-guessing album. I think we are quite direct, both musically and lyrically, and long may that continue.'

Radiohead have a perverse streak which makes them kick against expectations, and they're deeply suspicious of doing the obvious. *The Bends*, from 1995, was a majestically brooding piece of work whose gleaming production and string of powerfully melodic songs made it feel suspiciously like a mainstream American rock album. The new disc, by contrast, is exactly what your average FM radio programmer would not have ordered. You have to figure that Thom Yorke is the ringmaster, the *éminence grise*. The group seem to need Yorke's edginess and unpredictability to keep goading them forwards. One moment he'll be sunny, charming and glad to talk. Then he'll be withdrawn and tetchy and will growl at you if you ask him a question. It's as if he lacks a protective layer between his emotions and the outside world. He's like a sheet of emotional blotting paper. If he feels angry, he'll bleed hot, red anger. If he feels frustrated, his pinched face and clenched body-language scream 'frustration'.

'It all comes from Thom, really, and they all sort of gather round and support him,' according to John Leckie, who produced *The Bends*. (The band didn't use him on *OK Computer* because they say they no longer needed a 'father figure' in the studio.) 'It's a good chemistry because Jonny's pretty wild, you never really know what he's going to do. When they're in the studio, they jump around the same way they do on stage and knock things over, and Thom rolls on the floor just doing a guide track. It's pretty exciting.'

Anything else? 'They're drug-free, as you probably know. The occasional little puff or something with me . . . it's not so much that it's frowned upon, it's just something they don't connect with. And they do the *Guardian* crossword every day. That's the most important thing, I'd say. Things like that, which set them apart from the usual lads' kind of thing.' Leckie also recalls that debates about such topics as which song should be the next single would go on for weeks, with nobody able to take a final decision, but Yorke thinks the band have become more outspoken in their dealings with each other.

'I think we're much more used to shouting at each other now, which is good. There used to be a lot of serious in-fighting under the guise of reasonable discussion and now it's lots of shouting and eventually we'll decide, so that's kind of cool. It's sort of like a marriage, when you learn to shout at somebody and that it's a good thing. I could very easily walk in and say we're going to do this, this and this, but it won't work because it's going to sound flat. I think the most exciting thing is when everyone in the band feels they can try things out, but there's a point where you have to say, "No, we've got it." I think it's a case of recognising when you've got it; that's the difficult bit, because you can go on for ever otherwise.'

Their record company expects *OK Computer* to be a landslide victory and the band took their promotional duties so seriously that they even swallowed their pride and played for half an hour at the annual Weenie Roast event organised by radio station KROQ, at the Irvine Meadows open-air amphitheatre south of Los Angeles. The station wields such influence in the L.A. area that bands daren't refuse to participate, even though they don't get paid. This prompted the bizarre spectacle of Oasis and Blur on the same bill, alongside the Foo Fighters, the Wallflowers, the Cure and many more representatives of what the Americans call 'modern rock'.

I tagged myself on to the Radiohead convoy as they trundled down highway 405, aiming to arrive in plenty of time for their mid-afternoon slot. Despite rumours that Radiohead are 'big in America', their lowly position on the Weenie Roast bill was proof that they aren't yet. Once through the aggressive security cordon, we found ourselves in a glum backstage wilderness of Portaloos and tiny mobile dressing-rooms barely large enough for a medium-sized solo artist, let alone a quintet featuring two very tall guitarists. 'Welcome to hell,' said Colin Greenwood, gazing around him in saucer-eyed horror. With some difficulty, tour manager Tim Greaves had acquired canteen meal-tickets for the band, but the food was a digestion-challenging mix of polystyrene burgers and the kind of salad probably best suited to mopping up oil in your garage. Jonny Greenwood gazed down sceptically at his plate. Yorke, nursing a hangover, propped his head on his fist and glowered.

Television evidence would later prove that Radiohead were there, but their spirit wasn't. Yorke spent the afternoon in a state of sullen misery and spat and snarled at the audience even though they were trying to respond favourably. 'Are there any screaming little pigs in the audience?' he demanded, squinting malevolently at the half-full auditorium. Some girls shrieked back at him obligingly. 'This song's for you,' said Yorke, and they launched into 'Paranoid Android'. Colin wasn't needed on bass for a time and sauntered about beside his amplifier with his hands in his pockets, like a man waiting for a lift home. Then they played 'Exit Music', which seemed to go over rather well, but Yorke had convinced himself that he was at war with the crowd. 'You fucking loved that, didn't you?' he sneered, then cued Radiohead vengefully into 'The Bends'. Afterwards, the band admitted sheepishly that it hadn't been their finest hour. At least it was evidence that the group haven't succumbed to brain-dead crowd pleasing with all their performances running as predictably as a piece of computer software. You often hear that they're due to become 'the new U2', but it isn't something they seem to want. After all, it would mean making an album every four years and only playing in football stadiums.

In the end, when all the psychoanalysing and brainstorming and earnest debate is over, Radiohead still love to crank it up, rock out and hit the audience between the eyes. Maybe they should do it more often. Consider that legendary power chord that kicks off 'The Bends'.

'Oh, it's better every night live,' Yorke enthuses, suddenly animated and sitting up in his chair. 'It's always a let-down when you hear it on tape, because when you're standing in the room with all the amps on, you just remember why you want to play electric guitar. In America, I often walk on stage and go, "Hello, this is the chord of D" – BLAAAAAM! That's what it is, y'know? There's a song attached to it, but basically it's just BRRRAAAAANNNGGG!!!'

Band of the Year: Radiohead

Pat Blashill, *Spin*,
January 1998

The pupils of Thom Yorke's eyes zip from side to side like nervous insects. We're on the Eurostar train from Paris to London and Radiohead's singer is compulsively looking out the window at a pastoral French landscape. He doesn't see the sheep and the farms – he is keenly aware that those things out there will disappear very soon and then we will enter a tunnel and be deep, deep underneath the sea. This is significant for a man who once wrote an album called *The Bends*.

When we go under, I ask Yorke if he's claustrophobic.

'Yes,' he says matter-of-factly. 'Er, increasingly so, actually.'

A couple of days on the road have taught me that even when Thom Yorke isn't suffering from one of his various phobias, he's still more than a touch intense. He moves like a shattered little prince. He laughs a sudden, explosive, truncated laugh. His hair is short, black, and spiky. His lazy eye flutters and droops, a handicap as well as the punctuation point of his fractured charm. When he was a kid, they used to tease him about it. That may be why he's so worried that people occasionally mistake him for an arrogant prick.

Life has been like this for Yorke: his problems have become his strengths, his obsessions have fed his repulsions and his fears have inspired his music. We're on this train because Yorke hates to fly and he's positively terrified of cars. Just yesterday, someone asked him why he has written so many songs about car crashes. This was Yorke's answer: 'I just think that people get up too early to leave houses where they don't want to live, to drive to jobs where they don't want to be, in one of the most dangerous forms of transport on Earth. I've just never gotten used to that.'

Of course, because of his job, Yorke has to ride around in cars all the time. He even got inside one with a remote-control driver to shoot the video for Radiohead's latest single, 'Karma Police'. And as he sat in the backseat, lip-synching, something went wrong, and carbon monoxide fumes began pouring into the car. Yorke was terrified. And as he started to feel faint, he thought, 'This is my life . . . '

———

Radiohead may be the most uptight paranoid art-rock band presently operating on the planet. But even as such, they've been pretty lucky bastards. The group – Yorke, bassist Colin Greenwood, guitarists Jonny Greenwood and Ed O'Brien and drummer Phil Selway – began their career with a smash-hit song about being worthless. They weren't even sure they liked 'Creep' or the 1992 album it came from, *Pablo Honey* – especially after the song became a slack-rock anthem, the kind of timely hit that a band can come to regret, like a tattoo of your last girlfriend's name. So in 1995, they made a much better, much weirder second album (*The Bends*) and a bunch of very cool videos that evoked nothing so much as the finest Pink Floyd album covers. It wasn't a miracle that rock critics started loving Radiohead – it was a miracle that fourteen-year-old girls didn't stop.

'I was surprised to see what the music meant to people,' Yorke says. 'We went from being a novelty band to being the band that everyone quoted in the *NME* and *Melody Maker* "Musicians wanted" columns. After a hit like "Creep", bands don't normally survive. It can kill you. But it didn't.'

Radiohead toured behind *The Bends* for a year and a half. When Yorke returned to the band's semi-sleepy hometown of Oxford, he was full of new causes for alarm. He'd always been pretty familiar with the scary things inside his own head, but international touring had bestowed upon him a whole new world of inspirational hobgoblins. Now he knew he had to write songs about all sorts of horrible things. Domestic violence. Politicians. Cars. Bacon.

So Yorke and Radiohead went to work on an album about global hideousness. He fussed and fretted and became annoying to everyone he knew, but in the end it was all worth it. Because *OK Computer* is a gorgeous and haunting record. It's full of spindly guitars and freaked-out noise, poppy songs with Beatles in-jokes, and other numbers that ramble on for minutes before they actually become songs and it's especially full of mystery. Nothing is explained, everything is suggested. *OK Computer* is rife with terror and cynicism, but it's not particularly ironic or self-conscious. Apparently, the only thing that doesn't make Thom Yorke uncomfortable is the idea of making something quite beautiful and sincerely creepy.

'I think people feel sick when they hear *OK Computer*,' Yorke tells me. 'Nausea was part of what we were trying to create. *The Bends* was a record of consolation. But this one was sad. And I didn't know why.'

The album debuted on the *Billboard* charts at No. 21 and, fortunately for Yorke, lots of people have been eager to explain the meaning of *OK Computer*. An online correspondent for *Addicted to Noise* divined that *OK Computer* was based on Philip K. Dick's *V.A.L.I.S.*, a book that Yorke had not read. Other less excitable critics pounced on the record's title and songs like 'Paranoid Android', the bizarre first single, and decided the album was about Radiohead's fear of technology – they were unaware that Yorke and Jonny are actually quite avid Mac fans. Yorke himself didn't explain much, except to insist that 'Paranoid Android' is about the Fall of the Roman Empire.

The band showcased most of the songs on the album in two sold-out, high-profile concerts in Los Angeles and New York. In attendance were Liv Tyler, Madonna, Marilyn Manson, Courtney Love, R.E.M.'s Michael Stipe and Mike Mills, Mike D. of the Beastie Boys, three mysteriously unnamed supermodels, and, apparently, Liam Gallagher. Gallagher alone remained unimpressed, and felt the need to point out, in these pages no less, that Radiohead are 'fooking stoodents' or, in plainer English, college graduates. At least that was mostly true.

Meanwhile, MTV, a long-time supporter of the band, anointed the unsettling animated video for 'Paranoid Android' a Buzz Clip. In June, Yorke met Jonathan Glazer, the director responsible for their earlier clip 'Street Spirit (Fade Out)', on a deserted lane three hours from London, to shoot the chilling, Orwellian video for *OK Computer*'s second single, 'Karma Police'. In late

September, 'Karma Police' debuted on the music channel in heavy rotation, despite the fact that the video features lots of fire, the same element that got Beavis and Butthead into so much trouble a few years ago. It would seem that for MTV, Radiohead are above the law. The truth is weirder: the folks at the network like Radiohead videos because they don't exactly make sense.

'All their videos are intriguing,' explains Lewis Largent, MTV vice-president of music. 'Everybody has a different interpretation of them. The videos aren't cut and dried – like their video for "Just" [from *The Bends*], when the guy dies – that sort of mystery makes them watchable time and time again. You can watch "Paranoid Android" a hundred times and not figure it all out.'

For his part, Glazer thinks 'Karma Police' is about retribution, but he's not sure if that even matters. 'Radiohead are all about subtexts, about underbellies,' he says. 'Thom thinks about music in the same way that I think about film – he thinks it's a dialogue. That's why in the video he just sings the choruses – because the verses mean whatever we want them to mean.'

In fact, when Radiohead recorded *OK Computer*, Yorke was trying to make each song sound like reportage from inside twelve different brains. The record is a collection of fictions that might be true. It isn't about soul-baring or venting and it's not really about Thom Yorke either, which is just one of the things that sets Radiohead apart, not just from the last few years of alternative rock, but from our entire culture of confession.

'I just can't stand endless self-revelation,' Yorke says. 'Honesty is kind of a bullshit quality, really. Yeeaaaaaaaahh. There's honesty and there's *honesty*. Honesty about being dishonest is more healthy than professing to be honest.'

For better or worse, Radiohead arrive at a time when most

guitar bands are still labouring under the legacy of hardcore punk and Amer-indie rock and are therefore as concerned with 'realness' as most rap stars. But Radiohead aren't afraid to be a little pretentious: they make grand, sweeping rock music because they believe rock music can still be a transcendent thing. Even though their songs sometimes seem as shambling as, say, Pavement's, or as odd as Tortoise's, they more certainly conjure up the epic paranoias of Pink Floyd or the baroque grandeur of Queen. Like those bands, Radiohead really believe that they can fly. They may not have gotten around to acting like rock stars yet, but *OK Computer* is definitely a Rock Star album.

———

In Paris, I meet Radiohead for dinner at a Swiss restaurant. Afterward, we spill out onto the cobblestone streets and head for the band's van.

'Paris is unbelievable, isn't it?' Jonny Greenwood asks, as we glance around at the darkening seventeenth-century block.

Yes it is, I say. And now you get to go do an interview at something called Fun Radio.

'Which means it will be everything but,' Jonny says with a smirk. Jonny is the youngest and prettiest member of Radiohead. He's the one with the cheekbones. He can tell you all about the experimental music John Cage composed for shortwave radios. When he was a kid, his older sister forced him to listen to English art-punk bands like Magazine, and the first instrument he played was violin. On *OK Computer*, Jonny plays viola, keyboards and guitar. Onstage, he wears a wrist brace (a souvenir from years of smacking around his guitar), and sometimes he plays a transistor radio.

Is there a conceptual artist inside you struggling to get out? I ask Jonny.

'I would never admit to that,' he says with a frozen smile.

———

The next morning, as the Eurostar finally rockets out of the darkness and back into the English sunlight, Yorke stops squirming in his seat. But only a bit. We are, after all, still talking about *OK Computer*. The band began recording the first bits of the album during the summer of '96 in their rehearsal studios, a converted apple shed. In September, Radiohead rented actress Jane Seymour's mansion, St Catherine's Court, moved in all their equipment, and began recording there. Things went well. At first.

'It was heaven and hell,' Yorke says. 'Our first two weeks there we basically recorded the whole album. The hell came after that. The house was . . . ' Yorke pauses for a quarter of a minute: 'oppressive. To begin with, it was curious about us. Then it got bored with us. And it started making things difficult. It started doing things like turning the studio tape machines on and off, rewinding them.'

The house was haunted?

'Yeah. It was great. Plus it was in a valley on the outskirts of Bath, in the middle of nowhere. So when we actually stopped playing music, there was just this pure silence. Open the window: nothing. A completely unnatural silence – not even birds singing. It was fucking horrible. I could never sleep.'

Radiohead finally finished recording and mastering in February of 1997. After they got some distance from the record, they were a little startled by it. 'At the eleventh hour, when we realised what we had done,' Yorke admits, 'we had qualms about the fact that we had created this thing that was quite revolting.' The people at Capitol Records felt the same way at first, especially since they didn't hear anything on *OK Computer* that sounded even remotely like a single, let alone like 'Creep'. But now, everyone's settled down a bit. Capitol's president Gary Gersh, when asked about Radiohead, has even said this: 'We won't let up until they are the biggest band in the world.' Actually, the only folks who are still worried about Radiohead are their fans. These days, Yorke gets a lot of concerned letters. Some suggest that maybe he should take a long vacation.

'I need to get a life of some description, at some point,' he says quietly. 'I mean, when your fans are writing to tell you to get a life, you know you need to listen.'

Do you think there's reason for people to be concerned about you when they hear *OK Computer*?

'I reckon.'

Yorke pauses for a second, and then laughs a slightly warmer laugh, one that suggests he's actually going to be just fine.

———

On the final night of the Radiohead tour, the band played a seaside arena in Brighton. They veered between moments of delicate, spacey psychedelia and shrieking, cut-up guitar flurries, from the anthemic chords of 'The Bends' to the elegant schizophrenia of 'Karma Police'.

Thom Yorke held his arms out like some sort of cubist Christ figure and occasionally made small requests of the audience. The second thing he said into the mic was, 'Don't do that thing where you move side to side, because people go under and this is not a fucking football match.' The third thing he said was, 'Please don't do that crowd-surfing shit either.' And the audience quite cheerfully obliged him. They were, by and large, boys with glasses and girls making passes. 'Stoodents.' The cute library couple next to me went into a clinch every time Radiohead played something slow, but when I tried to talk to them they just giggled nervously and discovered they could not speak.

After the show, I found myself standing on the beach under a full moon, laughing idiotically and throwing stones at the Atlantic Ocean with a couple of Radiohead fans I met backstage. One of them was Michael Stipe, and the Brighton show was the third Radiohead gig he'd seen in the last week. 'They played Reading on Friday night and a band can't really lose on a Friday, because for everyone there, it's fuck-or-fight,' he told me, 'but they were really great on top of that. When we toured with them two years ago, they played "Creep" every night. But now, they've taken that song back from the fans and they've made it really beautiful.'

Stipe was referring to *that* song, the one with the guitar that sounds like the Concorde. The big hit that made everyone think that Radiohead were a flash in the pan five years ago. And he's right: 'Creep' was great that night. It was delicious and slow and sore all over. Yorke even improvised a little. To be precise, he changed the words of the chorus from *'I'm a weirdo'* to *'I'm a winner'*.

Five: The Earnestness of Being Important

1

Karma Police

Barney Hoskyns, *GQ*,
October 2000

The posters on the ancient streets of Arles give little away. Sting is playing soon in Marseille. Upcoming is a 'Super Big Reggae Party' with U Roy and Alpha Blondy. A bullfight will take place next week in the town's ancient Roman amphitheatre. Even as one approaches the equally ancient Theatre Antique, built during the reign of the Emperor Augustus, there's scant indication that the most acclaimed group on Planet Pop is here, in Provence, to play its first live show in eighteen months. On one side of the open-air auditorium the evening sky is charcoal grey; from the other, bright golden light streams across crumbling columns and arches.

But now the old men promenading with their tiny dachshunds pause in their post-prandial tracks. For covering the railings encircling the theatre are sheets of black plastic; towering over the old brickwork is scaffolding that supports chunky klieg lights. Clustered about the theatre's back entrance is a throng of polyglot youths. A shiver of excitement ripples through the boys and girls as a slight, dark figure emerges from the doorway. No satin or sunglasses on display here; not even a tattoo. Just a guy in grey New Balance sneakers, bag slung over shoulder and head tilted into a mobile phone. Voices – French, German, Dutch, English – yap at Colin Greenwood, bass player with Radiohead, as he follows the band's producer Nigel Godrich into the sharp light. Soundcheck over, they're heading for the band's huge, lime-green tour bus to eat dinner.

Blinking and squinting behind them comes Thom Yorke, the group's tortured frontboy with his dabchick hair and wonky, lopsided eyes. Radiohead's eighteen-date summer tour of Europe hasn't even started, and already this most alternative of pinups looks vaguely defeated.

'Thom, Thom!'

'Thom, here, Thom!'

One particularly persistent German *madchen* monopolises Yorke as he tries to beat a path to the bus. He stops, poses patiently as the boys and girls capture him with tiny cameras.

And then the Creep who could be God slinks off, alone, into the sultry evening.

————

Radiohead are once again setting their controls for the heart of the rock machine, heavy weights on their slender shoulders. The weight is especially heavy on Thomas Edward Yorke, thirty-one, whose songs and lyrics and singing have made him – possibly against his own better instincts – a near superstar.

According to Colin Greenwood, 'excessive praise' for the group's third album *OK Computer* 'did Thom's head in'. Now Radiohead must follow the record up, knowing that almost anything they do may disappoint profoundly. Tonight, in Arles, the world will hear the first fruits of the band's long labours in studios in Paris, Copenhagen and England.

To understand what's expected of Radiohead is to acknowledge just how bankrupt 'rock music' has become at the dawn of the twenty-first century – as a sound, as a movement, as a pseudo-religion. ('*Oh no, pop is dead, long live pop,*' Yorke bleated back in 1993. '*It died an ugly death by back catalogue.*') Post-Cobain, R.O.C.K. has withered on the vine, discredited as a cultural force, toppled by teen pop and hip hop and even by what passes these days for 'country' music. In America, Pearl Jam struggle to stay relevant; in Britain, the embers of Ladrock barely flicker as Oasis go through their death throes.

Shining like a beacon in the midst of this morass is 1997's shimmering, densely-textured *OK Computer*, a masterpiece that took the moribund rock genre and resurrected it in thirteen astonishing tracks built around Yorke's soaring voice and melodies and the (multi) instrumental genius of Colin Greenwood's kid brother Jonny. At a point when Britrock was being shored up by lumpen cool and microwaved Beatles riffs, Radiohead dared to attempt something big and brainy and unabashedly beautiful.

In so doing they kept alive a continuum that ran from U2 through R.E.M. – the ideal of polite, slightly anguished boys reaching for meaning and anthemic transcendence through guitars and amplifiers. Radiohead revived rock's passion, its *urban hymnody*, recalling nothing so much as that post-punk period of *rockism returned* (U2, Echo & the Bunnymen, Simple Minds). Yet they also forged insistently forward, staring hard into a dystopian, over-technologised future, uninterested in peddling stadium clichés.

Significantly, the long time-lag between *OK Computer* and its successor – *Kid A* – has created a gap, a lacuna quickly filled by a spate of post-Britpop faux-Radioheads: Witness, Muse, Six By Seven, Coldplay, JJ72, Motorhomes and more. There's a quintessential Britishness about the whole crop: the self-doubt and introversion of university-educated boys called James and Dominic hand-wringing over liquid guitars. How wonderfully earnest they are, lost in dreams of Thom Yorke's ugly-duckling deity and Jeff Buckley's ecstatic grace.

Like Radiohead itself, these bands are part of a growing resistance to the paralysing pop-culture irony that's undone rock as we used to know it. Asked why people were getting so excited by his band, Coldplay singer Chris Martin offered a disarmingly simple explanation: 'It's not because of our politics or any agenda – it's because people are looking for what's important in music again.'

Yet right now the question is less whether the Muses and Coldplays will have any relevance once the masters return. The question is: are Radiohead themselves interested in trying to top the musical Matterhorn that is *OK Computer*, or are they turning defiantly away from the role of rock saviours that the world wants them to assume?

———

A Thom Yorke mix tape sends subterranean shockwaves through the lichen-covered granite of the Theatre Antique. (As a student, the singer was a revered turntablist at Exeter's Lemon Grove club.) The local *jeunesse dorée* munch on baguettes as an evening church bell peals over mangled dance beats.

The distorted digital grooves aside, the setting for tonight's show recalls nothing so much as *Pink Floyd Live at Pompeii* – or even the Grateful Dead playing the pyramids, man. Indeed, those who decry Radiohead as ersatz prog-rockers – as too earnest, too studenty, too middle-class – will have a field day mocking the choice of unorthodox venues (piazzas, more Roman theatres) on this low-key jaunt around Europe and the Mediterranean.

Swifts and swallows dart through the heavy air as, with uncanny synchronicity, the Yorke tape gives way to the Inkspots singing 'When the Swallows Come Back to San Juan Capistrano'. At 9.30 p.m., the gathering clouds burst and rain falls from a great height onto the huddled crowd.

For a cataclysmic half-hour it looks as though we may not be hearing Radiohead after all.

An image, frozen in pop time (or at least the early summer of 1993): a quintet of limp-haired youths unloading their 'gear' from a battered van outside a venue in Clapham Junction, south London. An unmistakable pre-gig anxiety written on their support-band faces as they heave amps through the emergency exit door. One runty little dude with big peroxide-blond locks and a glowering stringbean boy like something out of *Deliverance*.

The image comes to mind because Radiohead at this point were just A. N. Other post-grunge band, and a band who most decidedly *hadn't* been embraced by that summer's mushrooming Britpop hype. Five university-educated boys from Oxford playing sub-U2 'rock' with none of the swooning panache of Suede, Radiohead got short shrift in the cruel UK music press. At least some of the animosity came down to the entrenched anti-middle-class bias of weeklies like the *NME* and *Melody Maker*. 'Anyone Can Play Guitar', Yorke sneered on Radiohead's debut album.

But in Britain only the underprivileged are taken seriously as avatars of modern youth.

Somewhat drab as the debut [*Pablo Honey*] was, it did feature a song that put them on the map and very nearly became the albatross that finished them. A postscript to the dark abjection of grunge and its slacker offspring losercore, 'Creep' was a startling slice of self-flagellation sung in Yorke's most putrifyingly miserablist style. '*I'm a creep/I'm a weirdo,*' Thommy-boy yelped; '*What the hell am I doing here?*' When you saw him singing it – all spluttering rage and convulsion – the self-hate was toxic. This was a Kurt Cobain from the dank corridors of provincial English boarding schools.

That 'Creep' took off in, of all places, America was a double helping of irony, especially when Radiohead found themselves playing 'modern rock' radio beach parties and weenie roasts. 'When "Creep" went through the roof, Capitol Records just wanted to milk it,' *Pablo Honey*'s co-producer Paul Q. Kolderie says. 'They were doing "I'm a creep" contests and placing ads that said, "Beavis and Butthead say Radiohead don't suck".' Although a reissued 'Creep' reached the UK Top 10 in the fall of 1993, American success made the British press still more suspicious of Radiohead. It also set the terms for the band's uneasy relationship with America. On the one hand, like U2 and the Police before them, they were prepared to work hard at cracking the US market, taking several support slots on tours. On the other, Thom Yorke balked strongly at the schmoozing that was expected of him. The thorny issue of how an intelligent band retains its credibility whilst hawking its wares around the world's pre-eminent music market is one that continues to dog Radiohead (not to mention Capitol Records) as they embark on the promotion of *Kid A*.

———

'Bonsoir, tout le monde!'

Yorke's first words immediately endear him to the dripping Arles audience as it wrings out its T-shirts. (Would Liam Gallagher have bothered with such a gesture?) Eighteen months after the group bid *adieu* at the Stade de Bercy in Paris, Radiohead is once again a real live entity, not simply an aggregation of website rumours. Launching into 'Talk Show Host', a B-side favourite of fans-in-the-know, the band quickly makes its case. Jonny Greenwood's keyboards swirl around drummer Phil Selway's circular groove and rhythm guitarist Ed O'Brien's chopped funk-rock chords as Yorke lets rip. *'You want me?'* he bawls in the song's most transparent line. *'Fuckin' well come and find me!'*

The applause soaked up, the group turns to 'Bones', a track from their breakthrough second album *The Bends*. *'Now I can't climb the stairs,'* Yorke howls over the churning boogie riffs. *'Pieces missing everywhere/Prozac painkillers . . .'* Jonny G. is on guitar now and he's stabbing at the strings, pulling out notes that shriek and quiver in the air.

We feel it in our dampened bones. Radiohead rocks.

———

The Bends (1995) changed everything. Recorded in a state of semi-crisis, a point when the unavoidable tensions of sustaining a band had boiled over, it steamrollered the slovenly Britpop competition of the time.

'*The Bends* was neither an English album nor an American album,' said Paul Kolderie, who mixed the album after John Leckie (Magazine, Stone Roses et al.) had produced it. 'It really had that feel of, "We don't live anywhere and we don't belong anywhere.'"

Sonically, *The Bends* was a far richer proposition than *Pablo Honey*. Here was an art-rock band unafraid of being musos. The sheer range of textures was dazzling and came with a host of other vaguely proggy signifiers: sudden time changes, string parts written by prodigy Jonny, fractured, oblique lyrics about alienation and disease. Mix Pink Floyd with Nirvana and Jeff Buckley (who blew Radiohead away when they saw him live in London in April 1994) and you get both angst rock ('Just', 'The Bends', 'Black Star') and plangent lamentation ('High and Dry', 'Nice Dream', 'Fake Plastic Trees'). More than anything, this is where Yorke finds his voice – a voice suddenly outgrowing its Bono/Ian McCulloch origins as it built from tremulous softness to soaring intensity, supported by superhuman lungs. '[Radiohead] possess the great lyric singer of his time,' says Scott Walker, for whom the group adjusted their schedule to play the Meltdown festival in London this summer.

Radiohead weren't the only British band shooting for something more than indie cool – both the Verve and the Manic Street Preachers wanted to make big, ecstatic music – but it was *The Bends* that most mocked the Blur/Oasis spat that blew up around Britpop in 1995. 'The Britpop movement was wrong for us because it was so awash with this knowing irony,' remarked Jonny Greenwood. 'In some ways it wasn't about . . . being serious about being in a band.'

By year's end, *The Bends* had put Radiohead on the world's stage and earned them the friendship of their heroes R.E.M. When Michael Stipe took Yorke under his wing, offering pointers on how to handle success, it was as though the older band was passing on the mantle. By 1996, when they started work on *OK Computer*, Radiohead had accepted that being in a rock band didn't mean they had to behave like rock stars. 'I think what happened within the band,' John Leckie told journalist Mac Randall, 'is that they had this kind of paranoia about being polite, straight, from Oxford, never getting into any trouble or scandal, very clean, not rock'n'roll at all. That's the way they are, and yet at the time they were worried about that, about taking on a rock'n'roll career and not being rock'n'rollers. They had to learn to be themselves and to be comfortable with that.'

As they set about recording *OK Computer*, Radiohead became an entity unto itself, removed from the British music scene. Unlike the majority of groups who 'make it' in the UK, Radiohead did not up sticks and move to London. They remained in and around Oxford, where they'd all grown up, and knuckled down to work in their own rehearsal space near the village of Sutton Courtenay. Opting to produce the new album themselves with the help of *Bends* engineer Nigel Godrich, Radiohead adopted a looser, more experimental approach to their third opus. 'We weren't listening to guitar bands; we were thoroughly ashamed of being a guitar band,' Thom Yorke admitted. 'So we bought loads of keyboards and learned how to use them and when we got bored we went back to guitars.'

The bulk of *OK Computer* was recorded in a spooky Elizabethan mansion belonging to ageless actress Jane Seymour. St Catherine's Court, outside Bath, offered the right ambience for the band's bold new sound – an enveloping, almost symphonic montage of guitars and machines, loops and chorales. Into this big, open sound was poured all of Yorke's obsessions with the way technology ate into people's souls, his vocal performances comprising a single long lament for human feeling in a hyper-mediated universe. Songs like 'Paranoid Android' and 'Subterranean Homesick Alien' alternately expressed separation from society and yearning for connection.

For some, the result was a '90s *Dark Side of the Moon*; for others, it was a masterpiece that blended the Byrds and the Beatles with Can and Miles Davis, a work that gave new validity to the term 'concept album'. For Capitol, it came as something of a shock. Convinced they had the new U2 on their hands, the West Coast label had assumed Radiohead's third album would be *The Joshua Tree* to *The Bends*' *Unforgettable Fire*. Capitol hadn't reckoned with Radiohead's own growing suspicion of the crude brushstrokes that stadium rock required. Even *OK Computer*'s most overtly commercial track, the sublime 'Let Down', was all about the distrust of apparent sincerity. 'We're bombarded with sentiment, people emoting,' Yorke complained. 'That's the letdown. Feeling every emotion is fake.'

If Yorke's postmodern malaise was a spanner in the pop works, Capitol sounded bullish after the first drooling reviews appeared. 'There's nothing I've seen in any country in the world that's excited me as much,' the label's then-president Gary Gersh told me. 'Our job is just to take them as a left-of-centre band and bring the centre to them. That's our focus, and we won't let up until they're the biggest band in the world.'

But did such a hoary notion mean anything anymore? Not to Radiohead, who in an earlier era might have been Pink Floyd or even the Beatles but who'd surfaced at a *zeit* when the *geist* was all about questioning and subverting the fake plastic pillars that supported the rock mythos. In her book *I'm a Man: Sex, Gods and Rock'n'Roll*, poet Ruth Padel calls rock 'a theatrical dream of being male . . . full of male teenage selfishness, contradiction, violence, misogyny, narcissism, supremacism, resentment, anger, darkness and fantasies of omnipotence'. For Radiohead, as for R.E.M. before them, rock has become an exhausted cartoon, an arena of empty exhibitionism.

Shattered by the *OK Computer* tour, which took them through to the end of 1998, Radiohead finally regrouped to begin work on a new record at the beginning of 1999. As with *The Bends* and *OK Computer,* painful false starts – this time in studios in Paris and Copenhagen – were the order of the day. Ed O'Brien's often painfully honest 'diary' on the band's website radiohead.com kept fans abreast of the maddeningly uncertain process by which they were writing new material. At the root of the band's uncertainty was a central loss of faith: the faith in rock itself.

————

'This is a new song . . . '

Here are the words we've been waiting Thom Yorke to say all day, and now he's said them. Tomorrow they'll be on the net and rock's global villagers will be e-gabbling about 'the new songs'. Radiohead play seven new songs at the Theatre Antique and most of them leave the crowd looking bemused. Are they songs at all? Or are they mere experiments, fragments worked up to resemble finished pieces?

'Optimistic' is moody and muted, as is the warmer 'Morning Bell', sung mainly in falsetto and arranged in 5/4 time. Neither appears to possess a chorus, and both suggest Yorke is aiming for the shapeless, post-triphop sound of 'Rabbit in Your Headlights', his mesmerising cameo on U.N.K.L.E.'s *Psyence Fiction* album. 'Dollars and Cents' is more spacious, opening out into long vocal lines on its chorus, but it's hardly 'The Tourist'. Later comes the monochordal grunge-fuzz of 'Everyone – The National Anthem', with Jonny Greenwood miking the 'found sound' of a transistor radio and the others grinding away over Phil Selway's pounding sixteenths. 'In Limbo' is formless but pleasingly dreamy, with Ed O'Brien at the keyboard and Selway playing splashy jazz fills, but 'Everything In Its Right Place' – based around electric piano chords that sounded like old Steely Dan or Stevie Wonder out-takes – is nothing more than an ascending motif masquerading as a song. Doubtless it's a precautionary measure to make the last new number, 'Knives Out', the most accessible. With Yorke strumming an acoustic and O'Brien harmonising nicely, this Smithsy item could almost be Travis.

What stirs the youth of Arles, of course, is the majestic megaballads ('Lucky', 'Exit Music', 'No Surprises', 'Climbing up the Walls') and the post-grunge blasts of angst ('Bones', 'Just', 'My Iron Lung'). 'Oh, you know this one,' Yorke says as he introduces 'Street Spirit', then adds, *'Phew!'* 'Thank you for being so nice on our first gig back,' he grunts after penultimate encore 'Nice Dream'.

What chance a backlash when *Kid A* is released next month? Already knives have glinted in the British press. 'Why would a band with such a rare gift for combining sonic invention with memorable, emotive songs give up half its winning formula?' asked the *Observer*. 'Prog rock for dullards,' sneered the *Guardian* of Radiohead's Meltdown appearance in July.

On the eve of the Meltdown show, Thom Yorke posts a typically cryptic note on radiohead.com. It's a direct quote from Malcolm

Lowry's *Under the Volcano* and begins thus: 'Or is it because there is a path, as Blake well knew, and though I may not take it, sometimes lately in dreams I have been able to see it? . . . I seem to see now, between mescals, this path, and beyond it strange vistas, like visions of a new life together we might somewhere lead.'

With *Kid A*, Radiohead are taking the road less travelled, a winding track that makes a sharp exit off rock's superhighway. Modern music may be about to experience its most dramatic rebirth.

2

Kid A:
Revolution in the Head

Simon Reynolds, *Uncut*,
November 2000

What went wrong with British rock? Surveying the current panorama of mediocrity, it's hard to recall a more barren time. The last four years' output of UK guitar-based music makes the early '70s – that fabled hiatus of stalled stagnation between '60s supernova and punk renewal – seem like a period of astonishing abundance and diversity. (Which it actually was, if you think about it: the official rock history gets it wrong, as it so often does.)

What happened to the culture that produced bands like Roxy Music, Joy Division, the Fall, the Banshees, the Specials, the Associates, the Human League, the Smiths, My Bloody Valentine (and this to-name-just-a-few litany includes neither obvious greats nor the mavericks that brighten the corners of Brit rock's pantheon)? Bands who each created their own aesthetic universes and singular pop languages. Now steel yourself and scrutinise the standard-bearers of recent years: Gomez, with their amiable pastiches of bygone Americana: Manic Street Preachers, the People's Choice after years of dogged slog, peddling overwrought new wave melodrama alarmingly redolent of the Boomtown Rats; Catatonia, Stereophonics, Gay Dad and other inkie cover faves offering what apparently passes for star quality, singing and songcraft in this blighted isle. The sense of doldrums, of living through undistinguished times, is completed by the steady drizzle of solo albums and post-break-up projects from the debris of Madchester and Britpop – Butler, Squire, Brown, Coxon, Ashcroft.

Why does British rock continue to come up empty? Obviously, Britpop shoulders much blame – for its jingoism and nostalgic flight from contemporary multiculture; for sanctioning derivativeness and grave-robbing necrophilia; for its anorexic, anachronistic fetish for the snappy three-minute ditty (as if the seven-inch single was still the culture's prime format). Most pernicious of all is the damage done to the ideal of independent music by Britpop's Make It Big At All Costs ethos, which made the pursuit of innovation for its own sake unfashionable, even faintly ludicrous. If the Stone Roses started this tendency (citing only the most obvious influences, like the Beatles, as mark of their ambition and self-regard) and the Manics turned it into ideology (so that having obscure influences or experimental impulses became the sign of defeatism and elitism), it was Oasis who made it orthodoxy. Their sole *raison d'être* was to be big, to create a sense of size that we could all bask in. And so empty boasts about seeing no reason why this band shouldn't be as big as the Beatles became compulsory for the kind of groups that exist to fill up one-page features in the weekly music papers.

Since major labels alone have the clout to make bands that big, the result was a massive withdrawal of energy and interest from the independent sector. Look at the indie charts now and you'll find a motley coalition of drum'n'bass and techno records, death metal albums and other micro-genre niche-markets and pop stars who happen to go through independent distribution. The kind of diverse but unified independent music culture that in 1988 could sustain an AR Kane album at No. 1 for four weeks doesn't exist anymore.

By now, though, there should have been the backlash, seeds of regeneration budding if not blooming. Britpop's bubble burst quite a while back (*This Is Hardcore*'s unexpected shortfall, the bloat and crapulence of *Be Here Now*) and the gold-rush A&R blunders have issued their dismal debuts and in many cases already been downsized from the rosters. But apart from the odd cult-figure-in-waiting (your Badly Drawn Boys) and veteran shape-shifters (your Primal Screams, Saint Etiennes and so on) this unprecedented inspiration-drought continues.

Why?

Dance culture done it. Dance culture was the worst thing that ever happened to British rock. Not just because its unparalleled enticements permanently hijacked the greater portion of rock's potential audience (even in its lamest, most edge-less form – trance and hard house – clubbing beats gigging by an unbeatable margin). But because the electronic arena has sucked up a good ninety per cent of the musical intellect available, Brit rock ails because this country's sharpest musical minds are dedicated to making instrumental, non-band music. Why should the Eno-style inspired non-musicians bother with all the friction and hassle of being in a band when they can implement their ideas quickly via compliant, near infinitely flexible machines? Dance culture and its home-listening-oriented adjuncts even hold out the possibility of making a few bob. As a result, rock has been left to people with the worst motivations: fame, exhibitionism, the desire to make music like they did in the good old days (the '60s, punk/new wave). Or it's left rock to people with something to 'say': the quote machines, the would-be poets. 'All mouth, no trousers' has been Brit rock's cardinal liability since the post-punk era, when attitude, self-salesmanship and music paper-friendly gift of the gab became more valued than instrumental skill or sonic vision.

For most of the '90s, the ferment of post-rave music made the mounting failure of Brit rock easy to ignore. So why not just dispense with rock and be done with it? Because dance has its own downside – what you might call 'all trousers, no mouth'. The problem with funktional ravefloor fodder and *Wire* magazine-type abstraction alike is that it is so sheerly sonic, about the materiality of rhythm and texture and nothing else. Whereas the genius of British pop has always been the way that sonics and discourse, music and ideas about music, have meshed and cross-catalysed each other. It's not that dance music is meaningless. It can even 'say' stuff about the world outside the club's walls, through vocal samples, rhythmic tension, bass pressure, atmospherics. But the feelings dance music communicates tend to come in primary colours, without shading or ambivalence. Mostly, it has the vicarious quality of the drug experiences it's generally designed to enhance: blasts of euphoria, impersonal force-fields of energy that you can plug into. It can be hard to connect the weekend's sensation rides and artificial highs with everyday life.

Which is why the late '90s saw lots of people who'd been through the rave adventure suddenly feeling stranded in an emotional void. I really noticed it in 1997: friends hitherto exclusively of the electronic persuasion were suddenly listening to albums by bands like the Verve and Spiritualized. Above all, they were listening to *OK Computer*. That album had the ravishing textural splendour required to seduce ears used to electronica's lavish sonic palette, but it also contained the complicated emotions, spiritual nourishment and solace that rock at its best has always provided.

In a sense, dance music has been Britpop's accomplice, its partner-in-crime – together they have created a fatal split in British pop culture, separating musical innovation from all the other stuff that the UK has always excelled at (stylisation, attitude, arty pretentiousness) and without which music is 'just' music. A great British rock record in the Y2K would have to fuse the severed halves, reconnect sound and significance, get the balance right between trousers and mouth. A great, fully contemporary rock record would have to rival the vivid colours, spatial weirdness and rhythmic compulsion routinely available in the realm of electronic music but combine them with the kind of interiority and potential for individualised response that surface-and-sensation oriented, collective-high-inducing dance rarely reaches.

Kid A is such a record. On 'Everything in its Right Place', the lead vocal is just one strand in a shimmering tapestry of multi-tracked and treated Thom Yorke voice-goo, whose pulse-riffs and rippling patterns simultaneously recall Robert Wyatt's *Rock Bottom* and contemporary avant-electronica outfits like Curd Duca. On 'Kid A', a drastically processed and illegible Yorke vocal nestles amid a honeycomb of tweeting'n'cooing space-critters and enchanting music-box critters – again, the track would be right at home in the world of 'glitch techno' labels like Mille Plateaux or Mega. The jack-knifing two-step beat that powers 'Idioteque' explicitly nods towards contemporary dance, but leeches the joy out à la PiL's 'Memories' or Joy Division's 'She's Lost Control' – call it death garage. At the opposite extreme, the beat-less 'Treefingers' – a miasma of glistening vapours and twinkling haze – could be an eerie dronescape from Aphex Twin's *Selected Ambient Works Vol II* or Eno's *On Land*. Now you too can own your own miniature of eternity.

Elsewhere on the album, the coordinates are less electronica and more the remotest extremities of the rock tradition. All wincing and waning atmospherics, 'How to Disappear Completely' is the missing link between Scott Walker's desolate orchestral grandeur and the swoonily amorphous ballads on My Bloody Valentine's *Isn't Anything*. The grind-and-surge bass-riff, cymbal-splashy *motorik* drums and asteroid-belt-debris guitars of 'The National Anthem' initially recall Faust or Loop at their most *kosmische*, until the free-blowing entrance of the Art Ensemble of Chicago-style horns takes the song to another outer zone altogether. 'Optimistic' combines the noble pure-rock drive of the Bunnymen circa *Heaven Up Here* with the gnarly, swarf-spitting graunch of Gang of Four. 'In Limbo' would be *Kid A*'s most old-fashioned sounding song (imagine a fey, fatalistic castaway from Eno's solo albums trapped in the treadmill churn of Led Zep's 'Four Sticks') if not for its dazzling sound: a shimmer-swirl of dense overdubs, as if the song's swathed in a cloud of hummingbirds.

Kid A's sound is astounding throughout: warm, smudgy, the instruments seeming to bleed through and mingle with each other uncannily. Colin Greenwood's bass is a particularly powerful presence, often seeming to throb from inside your own body, hip hop-style. On 'Morning Bell', it's like the rest of the music is the outer crust or husk of the monstrously swollen but tender bass-pulse.

Revealing fact: most Radiohead websites provide 'guitar tabs' so that fans can copy the three guitarists' every last fret fingering, chord progression and tone-bend. Something tells me there won't be too many tabs transcribed from *Kid A*, though. (Tabs ingested, Christ yeah!) The use of effects like sustain and delay, in tandem with the signal-processing and disorientating spatial potential of the mixing desk, is frequently so drastic that the guitars function as texture-generators rather than riff-machines. They're just another means of sound-synthesis. Indeed, it's often impossible to tell where a sound originated – it could be from guitars, keyboards/synths, orchestral/acoustic instruments or from digital effects/samples/mixing board malarkey.

Kid A is the return-with-a-vengeance of a phenomenon that had seemingly petered out: post-rock. This highly contested genre dates back to 1993–94, when various smart operators began to notice the glaring and ever-widening gap in sonic vividness between guitar-based music and 'sampladelia' (the whole area of digital music that encompasses dance, atmospheric electronica and hip hop). The result was a loosely connected network of artists engaged in closing that innovation gap, a semi-movement I had the temerity to christen 'post-rock'. At its utmost, post-rock delivered an aggregation of psychedelias: the original psychedelic cosmonauts (especially the Krautrock contingent), the Jamaican psychedelia of dub, the neo-psych resurrection of the late '80s (Spacemen 3, Sonic Youth, MBV and so on), the digital psychedelia of '90s electronic dance. What all these phases had in common was their partial or total abandonment of live performance as the model for recording: the willingness for music to be unrealistic, anti-naturalistic, a studio-spun figment.

Despite its early promise, though, the reality of post-rock rarely lived up to the dream. Too much post-rock failed to supply what people get from trad rock (the singer's charisma/neurosis, big riffs, something to look at onstage, tunes you can hum in the bath, the whole apparatus of identification and catharsis), without ever really rivalling what full-on dance offers either (groove power, surrogate drug-sensations, the rush). What you got was mood music – not necessarily emotionless but tending to elicit admiration rather than involvement. I always thought post-rock would languish on the hipster margins until an Established Band took on its ideas – an R.E.M., Pearl Jam, U2 (who came close, and nearly whittled away their superstardom in the process). Now Radiohead have embraced post-rock (if not the concept, then certainly its techniques and its intent) but brilliantly merged it with all that indispensable trad-rock stuff like Emotion and Meaning.

Kid A is the kind of record that makes you want to curl up in a foetal ball inside your headphones, immerse yourself utterly – not just to catch all the loving sonic details, but because it's a record for wallowing. Yorke may resent the hack stereotype of himself as 'tortured artist', but his words and delivery do little to resist it. The song-moods run the gamut of dismal D-words: despondency, dis-association, dejection, discomfort, and (on the Floyd *Animals*-redolent 'Optimistic') broader cultural themes of decline and de-evolution. Ian McCulloch hyped his first solo album back in 1989 by saying that it was time for 'some bleak' (the context being Madchester's Day-Glo positivity). Against a similar backdrop of vacant, boom-time optimism, Radiohead bring the bleak in a thousand shades of lustrous grey.

What's striking about *Kid A* is how perfectly the colours of Yorke-as-instrument fit with the band's palette. Sometimes he gets a little help from technology – effects lend a wincing toothache edge to his voice on the solar-wind howl of 'The National Anthem', while on 'Everything in its Right Place' and 'Kid A' Yorke offers himself up as raw material to be slice'n'diced, played backwards. On 'In Limbo', the chorus (either '*in a fantasy*' or '*your inner fancy*': diction is deliberately imprecise throughout, adding to the sense of Yorke as an ensemble player rather than frontman) crumbles and disappears into the band's wall of sound.

You can learn a lot about bands through their fans: one of the top Radiohead websites has a section called Song Interpretations, where fans email in their own private and widely divergent readings of lyrics that are either opaque or so indistinctly enunciated they enter ''*Scuse-Me-While-I-Kiss-This-Guy*' territory. As with any classic rock band, Radiohead's music musters the aura of gravity that puts fans into this interpretive mode – a sensation of deep-and-meaningful that's as important as any actual statements being made. Although this kind of approach can be reactionary in that perennial sixth form/undergraduate/music paper-reader middlebrow way, it has a certain oppositional value at this precise moment because it goes against the grain of the pop culture – teen pop's ascendance, dance at its most complacent and non-utopian (trance, garage, R&B, all basically accept reality as it is). Radiohead's re-invocation of art-rock seriousness, at a time of compulsory triviality and pseudo-camp cynicism, is a reminder that people once believed music could change minds, could have profound, life-shaking impact.

This earnestness of being important is one reason why the Pink Floyd comparison dogs Radiohead, although Joy Division would be just as appropriate. *Kid A* is the kind of record that would have come out on Harvest or Virgin in the early '70s, on Factory or 4AD in the early '80s. Today, if this was an unknown band's debut, you'd have to say Domino or Kranky. (Often the record sounds like lo-fi on a *Dark Side of the Moon* budget, lo-fi for audiophiles.)

Kid A is also an album in the bygone sense of the word. The immaculate aesthetic logic of the track sequencing (something of an obsession for Radiohead) lends *Kid A* the sort of shape and trajectory that lingers in your mind. Rather than reprogramming the CD into micro-albums of favourite bits, people will want to play and replay it in its entirety. Smart, too, of Radiohead to resist the temptation to release a double or even use the CD's full capacity, and instead go for a 50-minute duration, just a little longer than the classic vinyl elpee.

How groundbreaking is *Kid A* really? Committed margin-walkers will argue that if you like the title track, you'll find more wildly warped and deranging stuff on tiny glitch-techno labels out of Cologne or will claim that freaks in Japan or New Zealand are unleashing more out-there space-rock jams than 'The National Anthem'. They might be right (I couldn't tell you). But the fact is, in pop music context is everything. It matters that this is Radiohead, who didn't have to go out on such a limb, but did. Radiohead are shoving all this strangeness, hitherto the preserve of hipster snobs, down the earholes of the *Q* readership – not exactly a vanguard of listeners. And the fact that the band's slightly middlebrow following will, out of sheer loyalty, learn to love it, is exciting. (*Q* readers are often mocked for picking *OK*

Computer as the Greatest Album of all Time – but why not? Who says the Best LP Ever couldn't occur in rock's fourth decade rather than its first?)

Context is everything and it makes a mighty difference that this is an awaited record. There's a momentousness that – unjustly, inevitably – will never pertain to the next effort by Labradford or Mouse on Mars. The sense of a Major Band on a Journey that is exceeding expectations recalls the giant steps made with each successive album by the Beatles or the way that certain art-rock luminaries progressed by taking the weirdest elements of their previous record and making them the blueprint for their next (for example, the sequence that climaxed with Talking Heads's *Remain in Light*) or just springboarded into a strange beyond of their own imagining (for example, Kate Bush's *The Dreaming*). Radiohead could have easily, profitably, remade *OK Computer*. But instead they've made a record where every track sounds 1) unlike each other and 2) unlike anything they've done before, yet still 1) works as a glorious whole and 2) has a distinct Radiohead signature.

Saviours of Brit rock? Don't know about that, but *Kid A* is a shining example and stinging reproach to the rest of the Brit rock pack for their low horizons and underachievement.

3

'Kid A's . . . Alright'

John Harris, *Select*,
November 2000

***

The band are in a big top, the burger van is admirably non-corporate, the new songs are . . . well, new. And the audience is utterly bewildered: Radiohead, it would appear, are back.

'This is for the band,' says Thom Yorke, just before Radiohead play a song called 'I Might Be Wrong', the recorded version of which will not appear until summer 2001 (at least). ''Cos we had the bloody stupid idea of playing in a tent.'

In all fairness, the idea seems sane enough. As a gig venue, the tent easily passes muster: Radiohead promised an upgrade in sound quality vis-à-vis the run-of-the-mill outdoor event, and they have delivered. The visuals are a little rudimentary and the three lasers outside that beam a pyramid into the night sky are a bit Pink Floyd, but that's a relative trifle. Most importantly, the tent is a 'non-branded environment'. That, more than a love of fresh air and a wish to see unremarkable fields on the outskirts of British cities, is why everyone is standing in the mud-strewn grounds of Tredegar House, Newport, Gwent. Naomi Klein's anti-capitalist bible *No Logo* is Radiohead's *livre du jour*; the tent means they are doing their bit.

In a corner of tonight's field, just along from Ultimate Burger and to the left of the admirably non-corporate toastie van, there is the only beer outlet: a compact and bijou version of your average festival bar. Its queues are about ten people deep. It takes twenty minutes to get a drink. 'It's bloody Radiohead, though, isn't it?' groans one wag. 'You're not meant to have a good time.'

The wait, however, is not the main issue. The bar, as it turns out, is selling nothing other than Budweiser. (Actually, you can also get Virgin alcopops, but that's hardly the point.) The beer is served from the can into big red cups – and the cups, of course, are branded. With a dirty Budweiser logo. *Select* doesn't want to be picky or anything, but this really doesn't seem right. So, if only for the sake of conversational sport, we sidle up to Ed O'Brien at the brief after-show soirée. It's being held in an old farm outhouse that rather suggests the kind of room where you once had breakfast on a geography field trip. Everyone, incidentally, is drinking bottled Kronenbourg.

So, Ed. Why are Budweiser doing all the beer?

[Genuinely shocked] 'Are they?'

Oh, yes.

'Isn't it the Workers Co-op? [i.e. the Workers Beer Company]?'

No, you can only get a Budweiser. In a branded beer cup.

'Beer cup? OK. We'll sort that out. That'll change. I didn't know that. You carry on learning. [In humorous voice] We haven't changed the beer cups! We've failed!'

Enough about 'branding'. The key reason for the current clamour around Radiohead is the imminent appearance of *Kid A*, aka Radiohead's Unfathomably Experimental Electronica

Album, aka The Record That Will Save British Rock as a Viable Creative Force. Naturally, it is neither of these things. Ed O'Brien calmly informs *Select* that *Kid A* is 'just a collection of songs that fit well together on a record, that we made in the last year and a half.' The description fits Radiohead's ironically blank aesthetic to perfection – their video collection, let us not forget, was called *Seven TV Commercials*; the passes on their last tour were labelled 'Generic Sticky Pass'. Perhaps *Just a Collection of Songs that Fit Well Together on a Record that We Made in The Last Year and a Half* would have made the ideal title.

Radiohead, after all, are currently in the business of deflating expectations. Though Ed O'Brien's internet diaries initially looked like a simple matter of fan-friendly warmth and admirable spontaneity, they also shed enough light on Radiohead's travails to show that they were merely a five-piece group having problems with their fourth album. And the fact that they quietly began touring a good three months ago speaks volumes: the intention is obviously to avoid the grisly fate documented in the tour film *Meeting People is Easy*. The problem was simple: walking to the world's stages after thousands of publications had claimed that *OK Computer* was a work of twenty-four-carat genius. 'A few people write in specific magazines that are really influential,' Thom told *Select* in December 1997, 'and everyone just reiterates it again and again and again. And whatever the sentiment was in the original review turns into this garbled echo . . . Expectations got really high. I had a real crisis. We all did.'

'This feels very different from *OK Computer*,' says Ed. 'It feels more like *Bends*-era in terms of our attitude onstage and where our heads are. There's just not that big cloud over our heads that we had doing *OK Computer*. There are expectations, but it's like,

"We're going to do this on our terms." Round the time of touring *OK Computer* was dark. And there were little things, like the fact that it rained the whole time we toured. Which you might not think makes a difference, but actually . . . And that was a heavy record. And this isn't.'

Long-term, Radiohead want to avoid the 'Here we are with our brand-new album' scenario completely. Colin Greenwood has talked about his dislike of 'having this massive dump every two-and-a-half years, with fanfares and clarion calls'. Fortunately, technology is on their side: more visionary minds within the music business know that the hour[ish]-long CD is as transient a notion as the forty-five-minute LP and online distribution will eventually kill it. Groups will release two songs here, five songs there and eighteen songs when the fancy takes them. Their subscribers will pay on a track-by-track basis and everyone will be much happier. Simple.

For now, however, Radiohead are stuck with the stone-age ritual of promoting their new album via a spurt of British tour dates. In the light of their recent pronouncements, the whole enterprise feels distinctly transitional, a little uncomfortable even. There is also the fact that the gig doesn't mutate into your usual frenzied exorcism – thanks to Radiohead's timing, this is an altogether cagier affair. Out of the twenty-three songs they play tonight, ten have only been heard by band insiders and – thanks to leaks on the web – hard-bitten internet apostles. Just to make things even more interesting, three of those ['You and Whose Army', 'Dollars and Cents', 'I Might Be Wrong'] aren't even on *Kid A*. You begin to suspect, in fact, that the new album won't make complete, coherent sense until its sister record – which the band have hinted will be released pretty quickly – sees the light of day.

Rather inevitably, the audience flits between loud abandon and a mixture of curiosity, nodding appreciation and where's-the-bar bafflement. Radiohead begin with 'The National Anthem', one of the album's more adrenalised songs, and then play 'Bones'. That, in turn, is followed by the altogether more obtuse, pared-down 'Morning Bell'. And so the pattern is repeated: 'My Iron Lung' is succeeded by 'You and Whose Army'; 'No Surprises' by 'Idioteque', 'Airbag' by 'Everything in its Right Place' – for the most part, just Thom and his electric piano. As with most of *Kid A*, it lies several light years from strait-laced, four-four rock.

There is something deeply ill-at-ease about a world in which 'alternative' music is recurrently played to forty thousand people and used to soundtrack the goals of the week. Blur discovered it when they played the entirety of *13* to nonplussed festival audiences in the summer of 1998. 'This is not the idea at all,' you could hear the crowd's mind thinking. 'Stop it now! Get the Stereophonics on!' Needless to say, the spectacle of Radiohead playing their new material in front of eight thousand people in a huge tent explodes the contradiction completely. Most of the new songs singularly fail to suit their surroundings. They'd be much better off in a place about a third of the size. And maybe, just maybe, that's the whole point.

'When you're playing to eight thousand people,' says Ed O'Brien, 'there are going to be people who just want you to play out-and-out rock, but people hopefully know us better now, know that we won't do that. We might do a little bit: we played "The Bends" tonight, which we haven't played for two years . . .'

'People going to the bar during the new stuff?' muses Jonny Greenwood. 'I don't know about that. I'm not sure. Were they leaving? [Fatalistically] Oh, well. Maybe that happens.'

It's now 11 o'clock. Radiohead have long since played their last song, the distinctly anti-climactic 'Motion Picture Soundtrack'. Phil Selway, Colin and Jonny Greenwood and Ed O'Brien are bouncing around the aforementioned after-show gathering. (Thom, in keeping with his own brand values, is nowhere to be seen.) Things have obviously gone pretty well; they give off a relaxed aura no doubt heightened by the fact that there is no gargantuan world tour looming. This trek lasts a mere five weeks, after that they'll decide on their next step. Naturally, all conversations quickly hurtle towards the new record: its obtuseness, its disdain for orthodoxy, the fact that even the most slavish Radiohead disciple will initially get a headache trying to understand it. Have they played it to their friends? What do they think?

'Well,' says Ed O'Brien, 'I played it to my old man. For me, he's always the benchmark. 'Cos he hated *Pablo Honey* – "Couple of good tracks on there, 'Creep' and 'Blow Up' and that's about it." And he was right, I think. And when I gave him *The Bends*, I didn't hear anything for a couple of days and he loved it. Played him *OK Computer*, didn't hear from him for a week and he came back and said, "I think it's amazing." This is a Pink Floyd fan from the '70s! And with this one, he came back and said, "I don't know whether I understand some of the sounds, but I think it's got a quality that someone who's fifty-five can understand." But, generally, he thinks it's more for our generation – ours and sort of sixteen-year-olds. The sounds are a bit too perverse for him.'

About eighteen months ago, when the album's creative hind legs were dragging, it seems that Radiohead came perilously close to splitting up. This was around the time that Ed's diaries took on a tone of something approaching despair and when he asked the

170

not-at-all-rhetorical question, 'Are we moving into Stone Roses territory?'

So – how close was a split?

'I don't know. I mean . . . basically, the questions will always be asked, "Are we still enjoying it? Are we actually doing something different? Are we gaining from doing this?" If we're going over old ground, there's no point doing it. We're obviously not doing it to maintain some kind of lifestyle, because we don't have those kind of lifestyles. You've got to keep learning. And the other thing is, you've got to enjoy it. It was like, "Fucking hell – you get to thirty-two years old, and if you're not enjoying it . . . "'

When Colin Greenwood's problems with the bi-yearly 'dump' are mentioned, Ed's eyes light up. He talks about online opportunities with the kind of visionary zeal that's usually the preserve of internet entrepreneurs. He has seen the future, it seems. It's best described with a rather prosaic word, but that doesn't diminish the excitement. 'Subscription, mate,' Ed froths. 'Subscription. Things are going to change. I think there's an analogy between what's happened with football and what's happened with music. I'm not having a go – you make a good living doing this – but basically bands get screwed by record companies. That's a fact. And that's all going to change: with the onset of online distribution, the whole way that music is made will change. Seventy-eights dictated the way music was made, then 45s, then 33s, then CDs – it's all changed. Now, wouldn't it be great to do a track a month, and do it on subscription and people could download it? And two years down the line, you could do a compilation for those who wanted one. So, ten years down the line, bands could be in the same place that footballers are now – your Coldplays could be on forty grand a week.'

Jonny Greenwood, by contrast, isn't quite so messianic about the whole subject: 'I'm not sure about that. It'd be nice to get things out really quickly, release them as we do them, but where does the specialness go? I remember getting Smiths albums and the whole package, the whole idea, being really amazing. So I'm in two minds about all that.'

Now, of course, we are standing in a completely brand-free environment, finally free from even Ultimate Burger and the toastie van. With no less enthusiasm, Ed is happily manoeuvred towards his fondness for anti-corporate bible *No Logo*. It obviously got to him . . .

'Oh, very much so. It put into words what I was feeling. And I liked the way there was some optimism at the end; the fact that she talks about this growing global mood.'

You reportedly went on a demo recently . . .

'The May Day one. The one in London where they daubed the cenotaph with paint.'

Did you, er, see any action?

'Not really. I remember standing underneath Churchill, with the green Mohican. Was it scary? No. It was a little bit hairy up the front, I suppose.'

The crowd in the outhouse slowly thins out, as the fridge runs dry and their taxis arrive. The youth (and middle-youth) of Newport have long since departed, to either excitedly await the arrival of *Kid A* or quietly wonder what on earth has happened to the group who wrote 'Fake Plastic Trees'.

At around midnight, a diminutive figure scuttles through the dregs of the party. It's Thom Yorke, wearing a mischievous smile. 'Alright?' he says.

'Alright?' replies *Select*.

And then he disappears, leaving his guests to pick their way home, through thousands of Budweiser cups.

Six: Whose Army?

Review of *Amnesiac*

R. J. Smith, *Village Voice*,
26 June 2001

The prop plane circled the ballpark, trailing the type of banner you might also see at the beach. The message, though, was not what you usually see at LA's Dodger Stadium. 'Radiohead *Amnesiac*' it read, orbiting lazily in the afternoon heat. The guy beside me looked up and pondered. 'I wonder who they think their audience is,' he said.

'You and what army,' I should have answered.

A quick summary before the plane runs out of fuel: in 1997 Radiohead issued *OK Computer*, a panoramic wall of datapanik that critiqued new tech through dazzling use of some very old technology – electric guitars. They sold about 1.5 million US copies, influenced indie rockers and turntablists and a few brave rappers, made a documentary where they begged the world to go away like they were vampires melting in the sunlight. And then they really freaked out. Last year they released *Kid A*, which, besides having really bad cover art, freaked out Radiohead's *fans* – with basically no guitars, no science-fiction narratives, and plenty of emergency-room blips that sounded creepy, downsized, evasive. Radiohead came back from success by basically turning into another band.

The whole record arrived as a statement about what they were not (rockers or pop stars) and what they would not do (tour, advertise, do interviews, shoot videos, enjoy themselves). *Kid A* confused everyone and sold about 800,000 US copies. Most important, with Thom Yorke ready to spontaneously combust, *Kid A* chewed out some negative space, turned down the buzz, and let them get on with making music. The shock is that what the reaction to *Kid A* gave them the courage to do after all – besides reach out to their audience with interviews, videos and airplanes – was release a better *Kid A*. Or maybe that should be said another way. *Kid A* introduced us to their new intentions and what a year ago seemed like a gesture now sounds like – hey! – music.

Amnesiac's songs are taken from the very same sessions that produced *Kid A* and the basic outline is the same: verse-chorus song structures only when the mood hits, texture as important as melody and all over the place the same electronic poptones – the sound of dead brain cells bouncing down an incandescent hospital stairway. Where *Kid A* couldn't help but be seen as a reaction to fame and intense scrutiny, *Amnesiac* illuminates what Radiohead are now and will likely be for a long time: an evasive, wilfully experimental rock band who feel uncomfortable in their own skins.

Which isn't to say that there aren't some subtle distinctions between the two records. If *Kid A*'s songs seem rooted in a pitched battle over the future, *Amnesiac*'s feel recorded the moment after. The songs are obsessed with achieving a sense of peace, a release from a world that's power-mad, polluted and obsessed with technology. *Amnesiac* feels like the first post-WTO record, its anti-globalism so deep at the core of the music that it feels intuitive. This should be no surprise from a band that has plugged Naomi Klein's *No Logo* from the stage, and a singer who has spoken out for third-world-debt forgiveness.

Where the end-of-the-world dread was once framed in slightly corny sci-fi narratives, it now just *is*. Events have conspired to make this music mean more – events and symbols, like the black-clad messengers marching down urban centres all over the world, trashing McDonald's and questioning globalism. And the music has changed too and I bet will continue to change for records to come. They are wrestling with a sound that eschews tension and release and instead mimics processes – decay, disruption, memory.

Yorke is a particularly English sort of social critic: even when he's singing about the end of the world, his words are modestly few. '*While you make pretty speeches/I'm being cut to shreds,*' he croons on 'Like Spinning Plates' and that's about as direct as he gets; he doesn't trust pols ('You and Whose Army' has been described as a slap at Tony Blair), but even less does he trust the confessional mode. So how he conveys his themes ends up a little round-the-way, a strange strategy when your subjects include the heat-death of the universe. Except maybe it's not a strategy after all. It's just him.

He's stubborn in a passive kind of way. Last year he drove journalists crazy by refusing to answer questions except through odd, shattered online dispatches; the truly twisted thing about this was that driving journalists crazy didn't even seem to provide much pleasure. Thom doesn't know from fun. He doesn't seem to get pleasure, either, from telling Radiohead fans in 'Knives Out' that guitars are never to fully return. '*I want you to know/He's not coming back/He's bloated and frozen*', he sings at half the tempo the band is playing. But then: '*Still there's no point in letting it go to waste.*'

And the rest of the band? They hang with him. Yorke once described his relations with his bandmates as akin to the UN, where he's the United States. He's a behemoth more equal than others, but if the other guys have strong feelings about that, they hide them well. They hide themselves well, too, when the music requires it – drummer Phil Selway replaced by a hard drive in one cut, re-emerging on 'Pyramid Song' with a head-bobbing full trap set flourish. These UN delegates craft a sound that takes in the stubbornly passive techno of the Warp label and folk-rock as embraced by R.E.M. and Sigur Rós, a sound that wants to embrace '60s big-band jazz but doesn't quite know how – 'Life in a Glass House' is like Mingus produced by George Martin, a great way to end the record.

They must have voted as a bloc to come up with 'I Might Be Wrong', which sports a fat blues guitar line lodged like a mote in God's eye. Here they are a band in the pre-industrial sense: you know, with guitars and a drummer and stuff. But then they flip the script and the chip skips and they become a symphony or a hard drive.

It might get a little random, without the ten-ton prude at the microphone. But as long as Thom Yorke sings with a disengaged voice that seeps out of the muck like swamp gas and as long as his lyrics continue in their current clipped mode, he and Radiohead might just remain brilliant, strong-willed and down-right clammy. The kind of people who will smash a Starbucks and then embarrassedly excuse themselves and withdraw into the dust.

2

How Radiohead Learned to Loathe the Bomb

Peter Murphy, *Hot Press*,
11 October 2001

In the days following the terrorist attacks on New York, the Pentagon and Pittsburgh on September 11 2001, Radiohead were not the kind of band anyone wanted to listen to. As news networks broadcast raw hand-held footage shot by bystanders – film that probably cost a couple of dollars to process but looked like scenes out of *Independence Day* – and as surrealist montage and reportage fused into one, this writer had to force himself to play their last three albums. Too emotional. Too paranoid. Too aware.

Thom Yorke, a singer plagued by '*unborn chicken voices*' – the Chicken Licken of rock'n'roll, in fact – might've wondered if it wasn't an acorn that hit him on the head but a piece of the sky, a chunk of American Airlines Flight 11 from Boston, slicing through a stitch in time. As far back as *OK Computer*, you could find eerie pre-echoes in songs like 'Airbag' ('*In the next world war/In a jack-knifed juggernaut/I am born again*'), which might've been written by Jeff Bridges' character in *Fearless*, a guy who walks away untouched from an air accident with delusions of immortality. In 'Idioteque' off *Kid A*, stray lines escape the cold Kubrick surfaces of the music like interplanetary SOS signals: '*Ice age comin', ice age comin'* . . . *We're not scare mongering* . . . *This is really happening* . . . '

Of course, Radiohead couldn't have predicted any of this, but sometimes the arts have an uneasy relationship to ESP. We've all heard about the cover art of hip hop act the Coup's *Party Music* and its eerie resemblance to the mutilated Twin Towers. Primal Scream have been playing a new song called 'Bomb the Pentagon' all summer. New York resident David Bowie posted a message on his website saying no one could've imagined what happened on 9/11, seemingly forgetting his own doomsday soothsayings on 'Five Years' and *Diamond Dogs*. Mere days after the disaster, Martin Amis wrote that 'the temperature of planetary fear has been lifted toward the feverish; "the world hum", in Don DeLillo's phrase, is now as audible as tinnitus.'

Your reporter didn't want to be catching a train to Belfast; he wanted to be under the table in the nearest tavern. If the purpose of terrorism is to inflict terror, then I didn't want to give the perpetrators the pleasure. I wanted to be frivolous. I wanted to forget.

But Radiohead wouldn't let me.

———

When the world goes to war, the weird turn pro. Throughout the last century, creative minds of every discipline have attempted to make sense of war by making war on sense. The responses to the social traumas of the times – not just international conflict but industrial revolution, racial tension, technological convulsions – took the form of a whole prism of isms: cubism, surrealism, dadaism, modernism, post-modernism, abstract expressionism, vorticism. After World War I, representational art couldn't hack it as a means of conveying The Horror. Strapping young boys went into battle and came back in cubist bits and pieces. T. S. Eliot's *The Waste Land* was one of the first of the strange new twenti-eth-century visions, a panorama of echoes with its texts edited – or rather, cut up – by father of modernism Ezra Pound. Joyce and Beckett followed. Sergei Eisenstein's *Battleship Potemkin* found its image in Francis Bacon. Fritz Lang's *Metropolis*, Charlie Chaplin's *Modern Times* and Lorca's *Poet in New York* dwelled on the dehumanising forces at work in urban societies.

Elsewhere, Schoenberg and Stravinsky punched holes in classical music for Stockhausen, Cage and Riley to peer through and even folk tunes like 'I Wish I Was a Mole in the Ground', a strange ditty recorded by Bascom Lamar Lunsford in the late 1920s, corresponded with Breton and Buñuel's surrealist manifestos. A decade later, milestones such as Picasso's *Guernica* and Dali's *Autumn Cannibalism* refracted the ravages of the Spanish Civil War. After bearing witness to the slaughter of innocents, neither painter could ever see the human form in the same way again. Similarly, in 1939, Billie Holiday recorded Abel Meeropol's 'Strange Fruit', written about lynchings in the deep south, a song full of strange and grotesque images of bodies hanging like fruit for the crows to pluck and the wind to suck.

Rock'n'roll itself was born in the shadow of the bomb: that crazy cowboy riding the missile in *Dr Strangelove* could've been Sam Phillips or Jack Clement. Ginsberg, Kerouac, Burroughs,

Pollock and Charlie Parker tried to expel through their work the dread that entered the species' nervous system at Hiroshima–Nagasaki, 1945. Thirty years after World War II, Captain Beefheart's 'Dachau Blues' from *Trout Mask Replica* attempted to translate the unspeakable truths of the death camps – the 'Bluebeard's castles of our century' in the words of critic George Steiner – through dada blues and spasmodic jazz.

The 1960s brought their own shit-storms. Bob Dylan wrote 'A Hard Rain's a-Gonna Fall' in '63 as a spooked response to the Cuban missile crisis. It was, in the words of biographer and folk expert Robert Shelton, a 'poetic cosmos whose extremes of horror and lost tenderness somehow match the hells and heavens of modern reality'. At Woodstock 1969, at the height of the Vietnam war, Jimi Hendrix made a napalm painting out of the 'Star Spangled Banner'.

Neil Young reprised this act with Crazy Horse in 1991, taking Sonic Youth on tour during the Gulf War and saturating songs like 'Blowin' in the Wind', 'Powderfinger' and 'Cortez The Killer' with white-hot hails of feedback. U2 hauled their Zoo TV extravaganza across America soon after, parodying the madness of a conflict that for many seemed to exist only in the hysterical nightmare mind of CNN.

And in the last years of the century, Radiohead perfected their own form of comic-paranoiac expressionism, a sound that encapsulated, in the word of one writer, 'what it's like to feel terrified by the times'. In September 2001, in the wake of those attacks on a no-longer-impregnable Fortress America, Radiohead were the last band you'd want to see live, but maybe the one that mattered most. The night of the eleventh, they were on stage in Berlin, Thom Yorke dedicating 'You and Whose

Army' to US President George Bush. As the world entered a period of queasiness on a par with the Bay of Pigs, the band journeyed on to Belfast, opening that show with 'The National Anthem' and sounding like – well, there's no other metaphor for it – a war machine being cranked into life. The pre-show tape selection of crooned ballads and doo-wop tunes only added to the eerie 1930s' atmosphere. Over two hours and ten minutes, Radiohead played a taut set, with songs like 'Morning Bell', 'Paranoid Android', 'Pyramid Song' and 'Exit Music (For a Film)' all taking on chilling new meanings, until eventually the tension dissipated into 'How To Disappear Completely' and everyone left the building feeling no better but perhaps a little less alone.

———

Anybody want a drink before the war? Champagne in a plastic tumbler, in a too-bright room. It's an hour or so after that show in Belfast's Odyssey Arena and I've just been asking Radiohead guitarist Jonny Greenwood if there'd been any talk of how to approach the night's set in the light – or darkness – of the week's events.

'No, none at all,' he says. 'I think everyone in the room had gone through the same week. You lose the will to be upbeat, obviously.'

Was he tuned into the resonances in songs like 'Airbag' and 'Idioteque' on stage?

'Yeah, obviously, but that happens all the time, I suppose, resonances with what's going on. Although, let's face it, the last week was the biggest event of the century.'

He's picking listlessly at the subject rather than getting his teeth into it. I take it to be the infamous Radiohead reticence or a guitarist's prerogative. Only later do I hear that his wife can't get a flight out of Israel. As Jonny's bassist brother Colin enters the room, I'm talking about how the *Kid A* and *Amnesiac* albums reminded me of the consparanoia TV shows that prevailed from the late '70s to the mid-'80s, as unease in the Middle East infected another generation of post-bomb babies. I'm thinking of *Quatermass, Edge of Darkness* . . .

'*Threads*,' remembers Colin, referring to the documentary style projection of a nuclear winter that put the fear of God into every schoolchild old enough to understand its implications.

Jonny: 'I remember going into primary school and everyone saying, "There's going to be a nuclear war today."'

'The paranoia,' continues Colin, 'and *Day of the Triffids*. It's weird playing these shows at the moment. You play some of the songs and it just feels too much. But playing Berlin was really good two nights ago, Tuesday night. Eleven thousand people had bought tickets and they all came and there were like forty walk-ups.'

Earlier, as Thom jerked like a wired-up rag doll to his band's relentless *motorik* during 'Idioteque', singing '*Women and children first*' in a shrill, panicked voice, I kept thinking of Martin Amis's nuclear war essays, written under the influence of terrified new-fatherhood in the mid-'80s. Some men find in the role of parent new survival mechanisms, reasons to be cheerful parts one, two and three. Others become susceptible to all manner of survival phobias. A week after the Twin Towers, Amis was reprising those essays in a *Guardian* feature entitled 'The First Circle of Hell'. 'The illusion is this,' he wrote. 'Mothers and fathers need to feel that they can protect their children. They can't, of course, and never could, but they need to feel that they can. What once seemed more or less impossible – their protection – now seems obviously and palpably inconceivable. So from now on we will have to get by without that need to feel.'

Thom Yorke became a father some months ago – one wonders how it affected him?

'I think with him it's definitely the former rather than the latter,' Colin says. 'It's really interesting, 'cos it's obviously been so good for him as an experience. I think now with Noah he definitely has that pragmatism of having a child and that's what's important. I was talking to him about it in Berlin. If you're not gonna be with your kid, then you might as well make sure it's worthwhile being away. And that's been great, I think. He's been less obsessing about the potential perils of the future and more thinking about making the moment worth it and making time matter. It's fucking great, 'cos all you wanna do is see everyone happy that you've been working with for fifteen years. And you can see with Thom and Phil, they're really enjoying making this work *because* they want to be home as well.'

Jonny: 'I think it makes you aware of what's important about making music and what's not worth wasting – all that pain and the unproductive side gets avoided.'

Flashback to another moment from the Belfast show: the refrain of 'You and Whose Army' struck a chord with the crowd for obvious reasons, but was offset by the rather amusing premise of Yorke inviting *'the Holy Roman Empire'* outside for a scrap. On the night, it sounds like a guy arguing both ends of the sectarian divide in one song.

'It's a good example of what I love about his lyrics,' observes Colin, 'that combination of direct involvement and aggro and that sublimation at the end of it, taking it somewhere else and elevating it at the end. That's a mark of his great gift as a songwriter, to make you feel things viscerally and transport you from that point to somewhere else.'

Of course, the inverse of that is 'Exit Music (For a Film)', the tale of two lovers fleeing from peril, ending with the softly sung line *'We hope that you choke'*.

'That's true,' Colin concedes, 'his voice always jars for me at the end, when he's singing that and people are singing along with it as well, but in a good way, it's a good dissonance.'

One thing about Radiohead in 2001 – they've become almost an amorphous organism. Anyone who saw the grim documentary *Meeting People is Easy* will understand exactly why the musicians and Yorke in particular have grown so wary of the kind of Best Band in the World hoopla that accumulated around them between *The Bends* and *OK Computer*. These days, they infiltrate the culture in more insidious ways. In an interview last year, Brad Pitt compared them to Beckett. There's a veiled reference to 'Exit Music (For a Film)' early in Chuck Palahniuk's novel *Choke*. Neil Jordan wanted to use their music in *In Dreams* but couldn't because he feared the sounds would overpower the visuals. Strange bedfellows until you consider the inevitable connections between the work of all concerned and recent events. Pitt starred in the film of Palahniuk's *Fight Club*, whose premise centred on the notion of domestic lo-tech terrorism. Palahniuk's novel *Survivor* is a tale narrated into the black box recorder of a crashing plane by Tender Branson, the last living member of the Creedish Death Cult. Neil Jordan, for his part, explored the doomsday atmospheres of the Cuban missile crisis in his adaptation of Patrick McCabe's *The Butcher Boy*.

Mind you, all this is news to Jonny Greenwood – he still has trouble getting his head around hearing Radiohead's music disseminated through mass media. 'You see it on trailers for television shows, from football to documentaries about Concorde,' he marvels. 'It's strange how it seeps through and doesn't get heard that often in other ways. The first time you hear your music on the radio, it's really weird that it's coming out of a box where nothing's moving. I still can't get over the shock of it. And most times people don't know that it's Radiohead, in a way.'

The Radiohead on stage tonight are the end product of a process of deconstruction that began shortly after the *OK Computer* campaign. When the quintet reconvened to record a follow-up to that album in Paris and Copenhagen at the start of 1999, they were a band of blind men holding different parts of the elephant. Yorke, the group's benevolent dictator (he once likened Radiohead to the UN, with himself as America), seemed to be fighting shy of melody, choruses, even lyric. Under the influence of Krautrock and the Warp label back catalogue, his strategies were radical to the point of advocating that the players abandon their chosen instruments. Guitarist Ed O' Brien, on the other hand, figured they should record an album of straight-ahead three-minute tunes. Jonny Greenwood didn't necessarily agree with either, being in thrall to composers like Olivier Messiaen – one of the pioneers of the ondes Martenot, an instrument that would feature largely on the new sounds alongside a whole battery of black boxes and analogue synthesisers – and Charles Mingus.

Jonny: 'The Mingus thing started with the excitement of discovering those big-band records that weren't how big bands are normally perceived. Suddenly there's this chaotic, dark, really vicious music. But then we had to obviously hire in a brass section and try and get them to play like that, and me and Thom were in the room trying to conduct and there's not many gestures you can do! But they were amazing, and really young as well.'

————

The *Kid A* sessions were strained affairs as the band groped to find common reference points. There were echoes of U2's *Achtung Baby* and R.E.M.'s *Monster* traumas: different configurations of personnel fighting to reconcile melody with experimentalism.

'It's also the relationship between all the people involved as well,' Colin reflects. 'It's like a mid-life crisis, whether you still like each other or are you happy making compromises and stuff like that. We were trying to find another way of doing what we do without ending up in a similar sort of space as *OK Computer*, where there was this feeling that you were being fast-tracked into being processed as the next R.E.M. or U2 type thing. I'm not slagging them off, but in terms of how they're perceived by people. But I think it was also just a fear of putting a record into a shop. I think we had to definitely rethink a lot of things. They were studio albums as well, which was the first time we'd done that in a way, because before we'd always recorded music we'd played live, like *OK Computer* and *The Bends*.'

When *Kid A* was released in October 2000, its abandoning of guitar-based song structures was received with some incomprehension by not just the band's critics, but many of their peers. The album got guardedly positive reviews, but one often suspected this was because the writers were too chicken-hearted to admit they didn't get it. In retrospect, *Kid A* was as misunderstood as *OK Computer* was overrated. It wasn't even that much of a departure, especially if you figured the intervening *Airbag/How Am I Driving?* extended EP into the equation.

'It's very interesting, that whole diffusing a sticky situation,' Colin says. 'Nick Hornby wrote that thing in the *New Yorker* where he thought we were terrible because we'd sort of betrayed the faith that people had after *The Bends*, that sort of nostalgic way of writing. But I think that record is really fantastic, and *Amnesiac* is more a sort of echo of what we'd done with *Kid A*. It was a fine line of wanting to do something that was creative and also wanting to try and back away from all the media nonsense. And I think it's a sideways thing; looking back on it, *Kid A* was really strong, it wasn't just avoiding people who wanted us to do another *OK Computer.*'

I put it to Jonny that a lot of the *Kid A* criticism was like football commentary, as in 'they're not fielding their best players' or 'they're not playing to their strengths': Thom's tunes and Jonny's guitar.

'It's as though lots of people who really liked us heard a few bands coming out who sounded similar,' he considers, 'and they were thinking, "Oh, Radiohead are going to show us how to do it!" They wanted us to sound like the bands who sound like us, but better!'

'It was spurned-lover stuff,' adds Colin. 'I think it was a real fight in the studio as well. There was that conflict between wanting to do something that was good, but also wanting to do something that was unexpected. That was the big tension. You have to deal with the concept that you have to put a record out into the public arena and if you read the papers you're obviously aware of where other people want you to go. And if that's not where Thom is comfortable, it causes a lot of tension and it can impact upon the creativity as well. You feel that the tools you have to do your music have been taken away from you and sort of appropriated and debased.'

Jonny: 'I remember a version of "Motion Picture Soundtrack" that we recorded that had the kick and the snare and it just had no magic to it and the other version was far better. The point is, we played both versions to our managers and they said, "Yeah, it's better but it's not going to sell as much!"' Of course, the version without the backbeat made the final cut. But interestingly enough, American audiences, long ridiculed for their conservatism, welcomed *Kid A* and its sister album *Amnesiac* with open arms.

'We've had the most support in the world from America on the last two records,' Colin says. 'And this last touring that we've done in America, playing those open-air concerts, the references we always like to make are bands like the Grateful Dead, some concerts like Phish did, Neil Young I guess, a sort of roaming festival, open air, recording bootlegs vibe. And it was really a privilege to be able to play open-air in Chicago or in Seattle or Liberty Park right next to the Trade Towers for two nights; it was the most beautiful setting. What we mean in America is completely different to anywhere else in the world. You can lose a lot of baggage halfway across the Atlantic and you can go to America and take them on their terms, not English press terms. And we've definitely relished that.'

So what next for Radiohead? Contrary as ever, they seem freed up and optimistic in a world that feels anything but. The forthcoming *I Might Be Wrong* mini-album will showcase the band's robust live arrangements of material from the last two albums. After that, Colin talks about a return to premiering new songs live before re-entering the studio.

'I think we're in a very similar situation now as we were going into *OK Computer*,' he suggests. 'I think we had to do two records and take time out to get back to that point, 'cos definitely, by the end of touring *OK Computer*, you felt you were being *propelled*. And because a lot of the structures on *Kid A* and *Amnesiac* were a lot looser, you have to improvise and make up things a tiny bit, so there's more room for random accidents. Whereas with *OK Computer* we'd honed it to this stadium-fulfilling thing, every song had the same thing played every night and it stopped being musical and became more about repetition and less about performance. It's very interesting, the body language of people on stage. [With Thom] it's all from his body. His dad was a boxer and he taught Thom how to do some boxing when he was a kid and you can see that sort of physical, brawling, punching quality. He's got such amazing, rhythmic. intuitive drive.'

———

After the show, Thom's not doing press but he *is* hanging out in hospitality. Wearing a scrub of beard, he looks, as ever, like a man on leave from the Carter Family's country noir classic 'Worried Man Blues', the story of a guy who lays down to sleep by a river and wakes up in chains. A couple of hours earlier, he'd dedicated 'Street Spirit' to 'all the Americans who can't get home' and I was reminded of what it must have felt like watching Neil and Crazy Horse on that Gulf war campaign. Elsewhere in the show, as I scouted for a line that might make sense amidst images of a traumatised fireman breaking off from digging in the Manhattan ruins to speak to a priest, or of exhausted medics cutting themselves and putting salt on the wounds to stay awake, the refrain from 'Lucky' seemed to hang in the air long after it was uttered.

'Pull me out of the air crash . . . we are standing on the edge.'

<u>3</u>

Review of *I Might Be Wrong* – *Live Recordings*

Stephen Dalton, *Uncut*,
December 2001

Drawing a line under *Kid A* and *Amnesiac*, this eight-track mini-album performs an efficient job of reminding us that Radiohead remain powerful live performers.

The duty of concert recordings to re-invent studio blueprints is conscientiously applied, with off-kilter arrangements, extraneous noise and frothing psycho-jabber galore. Thus 'The National Anthem' is a brutalist riot of dirty scuzz-bass and radio static, 'Idioteque' a ragged post-junglist meltdown, 'Everything in its Right Place' a chattering menagerie of self-sampling vocal fragments on an infinite fractal loop. Rock'n'-frugging-roll, dude.

Thom Yorke builds to a fiery freak-out in almost every song, spitting death-rattle bile in 'I Might Be Wrong' and 'Dollars and Cents'. But there are moments of pure, unforced beauty, too, notably the queasy piano reading of 'Like Spinning Plates' and a debut airing of the lusty, much-bootlegged acoustic rarity 'True

Love Waits'. Anyone still hammering the flagrantly untrue 'no tunes' argument against Radiohead should start their re-education here.

All the same, a vague air of missed opportunity hangs over this frustratingly short snapshot. Many stand-outs from the live shows have been overlooked: the luminous 'You and Whose Army', say, or the exquisitely sour 'Knives Out'. The pointed lack of material from before *Kid A* also seems perverse, denying the historical and sonic framework that these incendiary concerts provided. The scaling-down of ambition which some dissenters detected in these albums is thus reinforced, when actually their live presentation proved the opposite.

But for all their self-imposed limitations, at least Radiohead prove here that they can conjure blazing intensity, visceral physicality and raging rock dynamics from even wilfully opaque jazzoid chuffing. No surprises, then, but some grandly fucked-up old friends.

Seven: The Most Gigantic Lying Mouth of All Time

<u>1</u>

Review of
Hail to the Thief

Will Hermes, *Spin*,
26 June 2003

I t's all right – you can admit it. When the bedroom lights are
out and all you can see are the shooting stars on your screen
saver, you've heard yourself whisper: 'It's so not OK, computer.
You mediate our work, our play, even our sex lives. Do you have
to mess with our rock bands, too?'

It's an understandable response to the dystopian blip pop of
Radiohead's 2000–01 tag team, *Kid A* and *Amnesiac*. But it's a
misguided one. Electronic music has informed the band's
approach ever since singer Thom Yorke was a club DJ in college
during the early '90s. And anyone who's caught them in concert
during the last few years – or heard 2001's *I Might Be Wrong: Live
Recordings* – has felt how bone-shaking those two albums are at
their core. If anything, *Kid A* and *Amnesiac* have improved with
time; if they don't rival the passive-aggressive guitar grandeur of
OK Computer, they're logical extensions of it.

Anyway, *Hail to the Thief* obscures the are-we-rock-or-not? debate from the get-go. '2+2=5' opens with an electronic sputter that turns out to be the crackle of a guitar amp, not a laptop. A sly digital beatbox gives way to drummer Phil Selway's very human pounding; the song itself is a schiz-out that mixes the tantrums of the Pixies with the sad dreamscapes of Sigur Rós, two of Yorke's most beloved bands. From track to track, *Thief* seesaws between the chill of sequencers and the warmth of fingers on strings and keys, like roommates having a stereo war. Yet the tension somehow holds things together – when the piano rises from the loop quicksand of 'Backdrifts' or jostles with the clipped beats of 'Sit Down. Stand Up', it feels more like a band playing to a multitude of strengths than the formal wrestling of *Kid A*.

But like all their records, *Hail to the Thief* is driven by psychic stress – in this case, the strain placed on people of conscience by a world in which so-called democracies bum-rush the electoral process and attack nations in lieu of practising diplomacy. Beginning with its title (a common Bush-dissing protest-poster slogan), the record is filled with war-haunted narrators ready to sandbag and hide ('2+2=5') or lie down in a bunker ('I Will'). Some of them imagine walking amid bullets ('Scatterbrain') and dragging out their dead ('A Wolf at the Door'); others want to suck your blood or eat you alive. And naysayers are powerless. *'We tried, but there was nothing we could do,'* croons Yorke on 'Backdrifts', a conspiracy blues riding antsy digital beats. *'All tapes have been erased.'* The record's most lacerating track, 'Myxomatosis' – named after a virus used to curb rabbit populations in Europe – asserts that even those brave enough to speak out are *'edited, fucked up, strangled, beaten up'* by a news media whose gatekeeping policy Yorke nails: '*No one likes a smart-ass/But we all like stars*'. (Word to Michael Moore.)

But *Hail to the Thief* is too impressionistic to be reduced to a political screed. Like even Radiohead's most abstract work, it's strewn with the burnished, elongated melodies that have made them the most diversely covered band since the Beatles: see classical pianist Christopher O'Riley (*True Love Waits*), jazzman Brad Mehldau ('Exit Music (For a Film)'), the Flaming Lips ('Knives Out'), and the surprisingly hot *Strung Out on OK Computer: The String Quartet Tribute to Radiohead*.

It's also a reminder of the group's key paradox: no other band makes fear and sorrow seem so empowering. 'We're not an indie band,' Yorke once insisted; Radiohead refuse to disappear up their aesthetic arses. Instead, they pitch a big – if strangely decorated – tent and invite a crowd, on their own terms. Because as grim as things may get, there's still strength in numbers.

2

Make Rock Not War!
An Interview with Thom Yorke

Will Self, *GQ*,
July 2003

n the medieval trench that's Turl Street in Oxford, Thom Yorke, the city's most famously and aggressively diffident son, rocks back and forth in his blue-and-white basketball shoes, howling with derision.

'Oh no!' he yelps, 'I can't stand this stuff! I used to walk past this window and see if I could pick out just one thing – one thing I could wear.'

He moves on from the dummies wearing waxed jackets, grey flannels and tweeds, to the shoe shop next door. 'These aren't so bad,' I say. 'Couldn't you cope with at least a pair of shoes?' He scrutinises the rows of Church's handmade boots and brogues with some care, before conceding that if he had to, he'd be prepared to don 'those up there'. And what were they, the proverbial glass slippers that the Cinderella of rock would be bespoken for? Why, suede loafers, of course.

Yorke was looking both suede-coloured and a loafer when I'd found him in the coffee lounge of the Randolph hotel an hour or so earlier. The Randolph is the kind of four-square hotel you'd expect to find in the centre of Oxford. It has an air of solid eighteenth century prosperity about it: a few bewigged burghers wouldn't look out of place, stuffing their faces with boiled beef before climbing into their broughams for a drive round this immemorial seat of learning. Yorke was drinking black coffee from a half-plunged cafetiere and glancing at the headlines of that morning's *Guardian*. His state of modish *deshabillé* – open-necked blue-and-white striped shirt, flared jeans and a curious, round-necked nylon zip-up waistcoat – combined with a couple of days' gingery stubble and mussed hair, to give him an anachronistic feel: twenty-first-century bedsit-boy cut and pasted on to the coaching house's sepia interior.

Yorke began talking politics without any preamble, and so our encounter was immediately and incontrovertibly datelined: 25.4.03. The fall of Baghdad happened only sixteen days previously and its shattered brick and mortar was on his mind more than other kinds of rock. Yorke has been drifting into more and more explicitly political waters for the past three years. Together with Bob Geldof and Bono, he took up cudgels on behalf of the Jubilee 2000 campaign to 'drop the debt' of the developing world and, while he hasn't exactly taken the hypocritical step of embracing the anti-capitalist movement, he's been making quite a few noises-off about greed and rapaciousness. On the first Sunday of the Anglo-American attack on Iraq, both of us had attended the demonstration at RAF Fairford in Gloucestershire, the airbase from which the B52 bombers set off with their bunker-busters, daisy-cutters and all the other horrible exploded euphemisms of warfare.

And now there was *Hail to the Thief*, Radiohead's first album in three years, and surely its title alone was a provocative tilt at the government of George W. Bush? Certainly, Yorke was concerned to put his seriously bitter credentials on the coffee table. 'Did you hear John Humphrys interviewing Geoff Hoon on the radio this morning?' he asked me. 'He was pushing Hoon hard on the issue of weapons of mass destruction and basically Hoon didn't have an answer for any of it, couldn't justify why it is that they won't let the UN weapons inspectors back in.'

I asked him if he was politicised when he was at Exeter University and Yorke displayed his trademark diffidence. 'On and off. I didn't like all the factionalism and the language you have to adopt. But I was involved a bit, we managed to ban some of the Young Conservatives from the student union and I was proud of that.'

His time at university wasn't exactly formative for Yorke; instead I think it probably confirmed him as a stayer more than a goer. In previous interviews he's waxed disconsolately about his discombobulated childhood, the frequent changes of school and the bullying at those schools because of his paralysed eye (a congenital defect that's left him with an oddly profound monocular stare). But to me he seemed emotionally grounded and secure. He conceded – albeit uneasily – that his had been a happy – if profoundly unmusical – family. 'My parents didn't even have a hi-fi until I got one, they had one of those radio-cassette things.'

His father, a salesman for a company that made mass spectrometers and other equipment used in the nuclear industry 'spent the 1960s walking around with a test tube of plutonium in his hand'. There was Thom and his younger brother, who ended up attending Oxford University. 'He was at Hertford College.

I hung around a bit with his friends. What I remember most was that, however trashed the place got the night before, these people would come and clear it all up in the morning.'

Yorke was a musical prodigy of sorts, and by the age of thirteen he was strumming a guitar and composing lyrics. A half-generation too young for punk, his early influences – he confessed with a wry smile – included naff Japan ('I loved David Sylvian's voice') and the predictable R.E.M..

Yorke's earliest musical forays were deconstructive. 'You always have that "I can do better than that" impulse and more specifically you want to find out a way of doing it.' But pretty soon he was gigging at weekends, with the support of his parents. 'They heard the music all the time coming from above their TV, because that's where my room was. But they were pretty good – they could've been a lot worse. They bought me amps and shit.'

I asked him if he got a major buzz out of that early gigging, but he seemed nonplussed. 'It's difficult to remember what it was like before we made records, but I do remember being surprised that people liked it. When you're on stage you feel you've got something, but you're not sure that it will last. I get much higher off of it now that I'm better at it.'

My Struggle wouldn't be a good title for Thom Yorke's autobiography. Far from being forced to hump their equipment around the small club circuit, Yorke and his boyhood jamming friends – then tentatively named On A Friday – had a record deal within months of going at it full time. These were the very same geezers who kept returning to Oxford at regular intervals throughout their various college careers to rehearse. In fact, the reason why I think Yorke is so grounded is that he's always stayed so decisively put, either geographically in Oxford or emotionally within the same cliques of friends and colleagues. Twelve years on, he's still playing with the same band of brothers and he's still with the partner he met at college in Exeter.

Rachel was one of the group of friends Yorke met at the art college where he did the fine art half of his degree. Another friend from this era does the artwork for Radiohead's albums and he told me that he was still in touch with the rest of the art students he hung out with at that time. Long-lasting relationships with friends and his lover, regular contact with his parents – particularly now that Yorke has given them a grandson, Noah – and a rootedness in Oxford that's reminiscent of his friend Michael Stipe's commitment to Athens, Georgia. None of this speaks of a particularly tortured soul and, while I don't doubt that his much-flagged breakdown after the worldwide success of *OK Computer* was traumatic, Yorke seems to have come through the psychic proving ground of rock stardom with his head screwed on both tight and right.

Still, there was a hint of paranoia as we walked out into the slightly gloomy noontime in the rain-splattered heart of England.

Reaching the junction of Broad Street, the Cornmarket and George Street – the very commercial hub of the city – Yorke pointed to a row of bars and said, 'That's where they herd everyone on a Saturday night now. The police post patrols at both ends of the street, and if it all goes off they shut the place down. Oxford can be pretty heavy on a Saturday night.'

Next off it's the surveillance cameras – which are mocked up to look like old fashioned street lamps – that claim his attention. Later in our ramble, Yorke talks about the aggro on the train up from London (a case of *KO Commuter*?). And when I call his attention to how preoccupied he appears by random acts of senseless violence, he admits that he was involved in a fight as recently as two years ago. 'This guy said something as I went by, he obviously recognised me and stupidly I followed after him and asked him to repeat it. Next thing I know he's swinging on me, kicking me and all these people are just walking past, totally ignoring it.'

A slight, five-foot seven-inch man, it's easy to see why Yorke's boyhood sense of vulnerability has been carried forward into adulthood, preserved in the aspic of fame and emolument. Yorke obviously hated the notoriety that went with the massive commercial success of *OK Computer,* and to me he said that 'I don't want to do that stadium-rock thing'. He said that he was no longer recognised in the street and that Stipe had taught him how to make himself 'invisible', just by assuming the correct and confident mental attitude as he walks down a street. I dare say I must've been queering Yorke's incognito – with our disparity in heights and our obviously purposeless trawl about the teeming streets we must've appeared an odd couple – but during the three hours I spent with him he was recognised four times and asked for autographs. By the time we were walking back across the centre of town he suggested we avoid the busiest streets, clearly fed up with being spotted.

Earlier, propped on the high wall of one of the college gardens, we looked down on the immaculate lawns surrounding the Radcliffe Camera, one of those domed Renaissance Oxford buildings which give the city an almost oriental air. Yorke pointed to one of the alcoves let into the Camera and said, 'That's where we did a lot of drinking when we were teenagers.' A remark that led us inevitably on to the subject of drugs and intoxication in general. 'I was always advised not to do acid,' Yorke said. 'My friends thought that what with everything that was going on in my head already it wouldn't be a good idea.' I observed that I hadn't ever read or heard him make any comment on intoxication, whether in connection with his own creativity or simple hedonism. 'I've never wanted it to colour the music,' he said, 'that's why I leave it open.' When I pressed him he said, 'Obviously it's important not to stay like this' – he swept a hand over his sober mien – 'all the time. You get it with music anyway, but alcohol is grotesquely inappropriate for making the required change . . .'

'And what would be better?' I pressed him again.

'Oh, I dunno, something prescribed, I s'pose.'

'What, Prozac?' I quipped, but this was as far as Yorke would go on the matter.

He doesn't go much further down the road to rock excess in any other direction either.

A long-time vegetarian, he 'gave up meat in the early '90s; touring was playing havoc with my digestion'. Smoking roll-ups also had to go. 'It was destroying my voice, I'd make it halfway through a gig and then it'd crack.' But Yorke was happy to confess to getting badly snake-bitten in the past. 'The first time I drank them I had to go to the doctor the next day because I was still seeing double and he told me that I had alcohol poisoning.' But he conceded that this kind of heavy drinking had also been jettisoned. Yorke seems to have entered the detached house of common sense through practising this kind of restraint, rather than pressing on to the illusory palace of wisdom offered by class As.

Achingly sensible chap.

As we walked down the passageway that leads between Merton

and Corpus Christi Colleges and out on to the green expanse of Christ Church meadow, I began to feel a little like the decadent Sebastian Flyte in Evelyn Waugh's *Brideshead Revisited*. Yorke was coming on so cuddly and sexless that he could've been Flyte's teddy-bear Aloysius. What about groupies? I wheedled. Wasn't it part of your perception of rock stardom when you were plonking away on your guitar in your bedroom? Yorke laughed raucously. 'Ha-ha, yeah, man, it never happened. I'm just too bloody-minded; if I see other people doing it, then I just don't want to do it. It's as simple as that. I remember being at the Brits one time and Oasis were doing their Oasis thing and it was all very amusing and everyone was very amused in their tolerant manner. It made me want to do the exact fucking opposite. That's just me.'

This English reticence extended into Yorke's money talk. Presumably, I pointed out, he had cartloads of wonga? 'Probably not as much as you'd think, but yeah, it's all right.'

But d'you live an expensive lifestyle or what?

'I consider it to be slightly too expensive, yeah. But that's mostly wrapped up in the two houses that I've bought.'

You're not into larging it, are you, you're not that kind of person?

'I'm almost pathologically the opposite. I ring up my bank manager to ask him if it's all right for me to buy a Mini.'

And does he laugh?

'Yeah.'

Do you give it away?

'What?'

The money.

'What, *charity*?' Yorke affected a twee tone.

Yeah. Will you be divvying it up for Iraq?

'Well, I keep cutting out those Red Cross ads, so I guess I'll do that, but fucking hell, the Americans should be forking out for that.'

This was a rare flash of contentiousness and, when the two of us sat down for lunch at a Thai restaurant just off the High Street, Yorke's remarks about the very meat of *Hail to the Thief* were as vegetarian as his pak krua noodles. 'I'm not quite sure how we arrived at that title, we had lots and lots of ideas kicking around, and that was the one where everybody said "Yes" . . . but I don't think it's highly antagonistic, because out of this week's current context it sounds to me something from a fairy tale. I think the reason the others were into it was because it fitted the way the record sounded. The political stuff is only there because of the lyrics and the lyrics are only written that way because that's the way they came out. It wasn't like I sat down to write something political, but my mindset is more immersed in that than it was four or five years ago. There are a lot of reasons for that: a lot of it comes from listening to the radio compulsively because it coincides with my son's eating times.'

But the political climate in the States had definitely been hardening to opponents of the war and so I was interested in whether Yorke thought the album's title would affect its reception in America. Would Radiohead be touring? 'Oh yeah – well, hopefully.'

I've only done one American interview, but the interesting thing is that it really isn't as bad as you might assume.

'Obviously this is something we've been talking to our press people over there about, and they say, don't worry about it, it doesn't mean shit. This debate is throughout the whole country, it's not like you see it from the other side of the river. The whole thing is kicking off so badly in America, even in *The New York*

Times every day of the week now. I brought it up four times with the band and said, look, this may kick off, but they were confident that it wouldn't happen and that it wasn't the main point.'

Even if the US reaction isn't as anodyne as Yorke expects, he's got his creative get-out formulated: 'When something works, it works and you just have to leave it. With this, when I was typing up the lyrics at the end, it suddenly dawned on me that this was like – oh, shit! But I hadn't had that at all while making it, it was only at the end when it was too late to do anything about it . . . that's the point at which it's not yours anymore anyway.'

Can you let go of your work once it's finished?

'This one was really fucking hard, we had massive arguments about how it was put together and mixed. Making it was a piece of piss; for the first time it was really good fun to make a record . . . but we finished it and nobody could let go of it. 'Cause there was a long sustained period during which we lived with it but it wasn't completely finished, so you get attached to versions and we had big rows about it.'

Was it very emotionally draining?

'For me it was the last straw.'

But if this makes Yorke out to be po-faced about his own creative process, at other times in our conversation he was bizarrely irreverent and self-deprecatory. Of *OK Computer* he said that 'even when we were making that record it was quite a weird thing for us, because we were thinking, "They're going to fucking hate this" . . . Everything was one big wind-up, especially for the press, because we wanted to make what we thought was a really over-the-top record and I remember feeling like we were taking the piss and they swallowed it whole. It was actually a good record, so that was fine, but it was a real shock. "Paranoid

Android", I just thought it was really funny, but everybody was talking about it, hmm, like a serious song, and I was, "C'mon, it's a fucking joke!" Anyway . . . ' And he lapsed into noodling.

There was also a certain mildly schizoid cast to Yorke's peregrinations. On the one hand he conceded to 'becoming the CEO of a major company' every time Radiohead brought an album out and having – especially with *Kid A* – taken a fanatical interest in the minutiae of sales and marketing, but at the same time he inveighed against the way the major record labels were vertically integrating production and distribution, with the end result that they 'put out shit'. He'd told me he was through with the big gigs and yet he also admitted that he was doing a big-venue tour for the new album. He told me that he never ever read his own reviews, and yet once the tape was off he gave a trenchant and impassioned critique of how low pay in the music press meant that critics had to review albums on the first play.

I suspect that I met Yorke in that feel-good zone before the public reception of *Hail to the Thief* got under way, and that were I to be allowed time with him after a blip in the steadily-mounting acclaim his music has received over the past decade, then I'd see a distinctly more paranoid android.

Still, why complain? Yorke proved a thoughtful and grounded companion for a saunter around the dreaming spires. With his literary references ranging from e.e. cummings to Philip Larkin to Dante, and his musical from Charlie Mingus to Thelonious Monk to Bruckner (as we'd dallied in a college chapel he suggested we might thieve an antique spinnet), he's cultured, but not oppressively so.

I also don't think his demitasse radicalism is anything but the truth as he sees it. I asked him why, unlike Robert del Naja of

Massive Attack and Damon Albarn of Blur, he hadn't been a more vocal opponent of the Iraq war. 'I totally bought it. I thought that if this [the existence of weapons of mass destruction] is true then we obviously have to do something about it. I was trying not to believe that our glorious leader is misguided in his political allegiance but, as time went on, the way the current American administration was behaving made it so fucking obvious that it was nothing to do with anything except what they wanted.'

Yorke emphatically rejects the role of being a spokesman for a generation. 'It's fucking tits!' he spat when I tried the hat on him, but with his vague environmentalism and hazy anti-establishment pronouncements he seems tailor-made for the job, or at any rate he would be if he could just get it together to visit a decent tailor. He had conceded – as I'd forced him to contemplate the suiting and booting in Turl Street – that he'd recently bought a handmade pair of Chelsea boots from a shoe shop in Jermyn Street, but then he spoiled even this excessive act by saying: 'But you'd have to have a proper suit to wear with them and I haven't, so they're just sitting in my cupboard.'

Back outside the Randolph hotel, Yorke and I parted and he shuffled off to rehearse with his band. He'd admitted that Oxford could sometimes seem a little on the small side and that, while he couldn't face the sleeplessness that the metropolis engendered in him, he might like to live in a city where there was a bit more of a scene, like Bristol. But watching the back of his khaki jacket recede down Beaumont Street, it occurred to me that he'd be a fool to move anywhere but another university town. Because despite his multi-platinum album sales and his thirty-seven years and his alleged prickliness, Yorke faded into the afternoon throng with nary a ripple, just another student type with a CND lapel badge to prove it.

3

The Story of Tchocky

Ian Gittins, Q, summer 2003

O n 27 February 2002, Radiohead designer Stanley Donwood mounted the stage at the Staples Center, Los Angeles, to receive a Grammy for Best Recording Package for his work on the curious, book-like sleeve on their *Amnesiac* album. With him was his closest colleague and creative sidekick, Tchocky. One of the worst-kept secrets in Radiohead circles was thus blown wide open: Tchocky was none other than Thom Yorke.

Possessed of a strong interest in the visual arts and graphic design, Yorke has adopted the Tchocky alter ago to work alongside his former college friend Donwood on the band's striking sleeve art ever since 1995's *The Bends*. With his name extended to the even more whimsical Dr Tchock, he also scores a co-credit for 'cartography' for the complex map of abstract symbols that accompanies new album *Hail to the Thief*. Donwood has long been acknowledged as the prime creator of the abstruse, tangential cover art that complements Radiohead's equally cerebral music, but Tchocky's role is somewhat more nebulous. How did this bizarre persona originate? Yorke, typically contrarily, declines to elucidate, but the character is clearly closely derived from *Chocky*, a 1968 sci-fi novel by *Day of the Triffids* author John Wyndham.

The Wyndham book tells the story of Matthew, an ingenuous eleven-year-old who is 'possessed' by the spirit of Chocky, a missionary sent from a distant, declining galaxy to investigate the potentialities of Earth. It's easy to imagine this tome appealing to an adolescent Yorke, particularly as it pre-empts a staple Radiohead lyrical theme: think, for example of the '*Aliens [who] hover, making home movies for the folks back home*' from *OK Computer*'s 'Subterranean Homesick Alien'.

Yorke's notorious control-freak tendencies lead him to habitually insert several digits in every area of Radiohead's singular pie, and Donwood himself freely admits the singer's extremely hands-on role in the band's artwork. 'Dr Tchock does pretty much everything while I drink Martinis in the cocktail lounge,' he sarcastically told one questioner in a rare webchat interview two years ago. In truth, the pair work in close tandem on a host of creative ventures.

Donwood's first Radiohead project was the sleeve for *The Bends*. Its abstracted, jagged images and plaintive slogans ('It's so beautiful up here . . . I don't ever want it to end') appear relatively primitive next to the complexities of the artwork on the later albums, and Tchocky doesn't receive a credit. However, it was on the artwork of 1997's seismic *OK Computer* that Donwood really came into his own.

Donwood decamped to actress Jane Seymour's palatial mansion outside Bath with the band as they made the album, and Yorke would frequently leave recording sessions to pore over a laptop with the designer as the pair attempted to create visuals which reflected the fractured, abstracted music that Radiohead were crafting.

'There was a lot of time spent in the vast library, a computer in a corner and an old armchair in front of it,' Donwood told Q two years ago. 'Someone was screaming into a microphone outside at night. For me, everything was about being erased, like taking snapshots then scraping away the surface to reveal the bones.'

'We were both obsessed by the idea of noise,' concurred Yorke. 'Background noise. Everything is background noise. Our whole lives, how our minds work. And the whole album is about that – levels of mental chatter.'

The resultant sleeve was a masterpiece of modern urban paranoia akin to T. S. Eliot's *The Waste Land*, with dislocated, random phrases of varying levels of profundity and banality emerging at angles from striking graphics. 'Jump out of bed as soon as you hear the alarm clock!' one motto ordered. 'Authorities here are alert,' proclaimed another. 'When we were finished, I was incredibly happy with it,' reflected Donwood. 'But then I had grave doubts.'

This was beguiling and provocative sleeve art, though, and inevitably websites sprang up dedicated solely to deciphering the quantum mass of cryptic, gnomic symbols. Fans on www.followmearound.com pointed out phrases in Hebrew and Esperanto; somebody translated a Greek motto: 'Don't throw unnecessary objects in the sea.' 'The lyrics for "Airbag" are shaped just like a tank,' mused one dogged seeker after truth. 'Perhaps it has to do with the line *"In the next world war"*.'

As *OK Computer* revived the great lost *Sgt. Pepper* art of stoned students theorising over the meaning of album sleeves, Donwood and Tchocky raised the bar again with 2000's *Kid A*. Where *OK*

Computer's cover was blanched and erased ('bound up with the idea of white noise,' as Yorke had it), *Kid A*'s was rich, febrile and utterly compelling. As Radiohead's querulous, questing music spiralled off into more freeform and esoteric terrain, Donwood ensured the graphics were equally far-out. *Kid A*'s cover depicted what looked like an Alpine landscape from a distant galaxy. Inside, geometric shapes loomed over blasted vistas: a nuclear family stared into a glacial abyss. A sheet of tracing paper carried detailed sketches of what looked like a viaduct caught in a dinosaur's mouth and Radiohead's trademark cartoon bears danced on a mountain top. The effect was of a saturated, overloaded collage: the credit ran 'Landscapes, knives and glue by Stanley & Tchock'.

It's standard critical practice to bracket *Kid A* and 2001's *Amnesiac* together as the two constituent parts of Radiohead's headstrong, musically wilfully 'difficult' phrase. This has always been a dubious critical device: as Yorke once despairingly noted, 'If *Kid A* is "difficult", there really is no fucking hope for us.' Nevertheless, whatever the musical similarities, the Donwood/Tchocky-generated library book that housed the album represented a quantum leap for Radiohead's visuals. Donwood regarded it as vastly different from its predecessor. '*Amnesiac* was in close-up and *Kid A* was wide-angle,' he explained. 'Same goes for the artwork – *Kid A* was rural, and *Amnesiac* urban. There was a break between making the two sleeves and I had *Amnesiac* on a CD player all the time we were doing the pictures. It's a headfuck, really – if the music is intense and constant, then the accompanying artwork is sort of automatic.'

Inside a red, hardback cover depicting a sobbing cartoon figure, a riot of images proliferated. Radiohead's talismanic bear dissolved into tears: stern letters over a modern cityscape declared 'The Decline and Fall of the Roman Empire Volume II'. A sketched drawing depicted the presidents of AOL and Time Warner hugging as their monolithic corporations merged, while ghostly trees appeared to mourn the death of the planet. The aggregation of semi-captured, glancing images of waste and decay seemed to combine in a nightmare depiction of a world living on borrowed time. The degree of detail and the intensity of the apocalyptic imagery were stunning – an idea shared, in early 2002, by the Grammy Awards committee.

Unsurprisingly, Donwood and Tchocky failed to use the stage of the Staples Center to gush effusive thanks to their A&R men and corporate paymasters. 'I felt pretty stupid,' claimed Donwood afterwards. 'Awards ceremonies are simply corporate occasions that exist to raise the profile of various products, though the limos were nice – and the champagne and the hotel. All that stuff was a lot of fun, but the Grammy thing itself was in the Staples Center, which exists because Mr and Mrs Staple sold a fuck of a lot of office supplies. Go figure, as they say in the States.'

The most recent manifestation of Donwood and Tchocky's visual creative juices was the sleeve to *Hail to the Thief*, with its puzzling, intricate map of phrases and slogans ('Plague Pit', 'Dog Lashes', 'Succubus') that will have geeks and computer techies across the planet pondering and decoding for decades. Is it really a 'non-alphabetical index to honeycomb roadmap, labyrinthine catacombs, &c'? Or is it just a series of portentous modern buzzwords, artfully arranged? 'We just do what we do,' offers a deadpan Donwood. 'They make songs and I draw pictures.'

Yet Donwood and Tchocky's creative collaborations stretch well beyond Radiohead's sleeve art. Yorke's alter ego is a frequent contributor to the designer's website, www.slowlydownward. com, an intriguing collection of abstract art, short stories and impressionistic nuggets of prose. Tchocky and Donwood are currently offering visitors the chance to take part in their slyly satirical NO DATA survey.

Definitively Yorke-like, the survey, 'covering consumer life-styles, personal habits, sexual preferences, looming terrors and crushing humiliations' invites readers to supply information to NO DATA, 'a division of Anonymous Industries, which in turn is part of a huge transnational corporation that you don't need to know about, apart from the fact that it's more powerful than a Government, but less accountable, unelected and possibly even unscrupulous.' There follows a range of statements with which you are invited to agree to disagree:

All participation is a myth
I have been manipulated and permanently distorted
There is no justice in road accidents
I am being paid to act weirdly

Once the reader has woven his way through this maze of provocative statements, s/he is thanked for their co-operation and told: 'The information has been stored on our database. Your secrets are our secrets.' You can almost hear Yorke's sardonic, reedy laugh as you read the words.

Anybody seeking a fantastic visualisation of Radiohead's ascetic, troubled ethos is also pointed towards Radiohead TV, Donwood and Tchocky's recent innovation on the band's official website, www.radiohead.com. Subtitled 'The Most Gigantic Lying Mouth of All Time', the arch, beautifully designed programming consists of snatches of tracks, videos, blipverts and subliminal sloganeering and a handful of faultlessly arty mini-movies by Donwood, Dr Tchock and collaborators. The staple themes of alienation, paranoia and creeping globalisation are, you won't be surprised to hear, all present and correct.

'Would I still do art for Radiohead if they became shit? Not only that, but I'd become shit too, in solidarity,' Donwood commented recently in interview, and there is no doubt that his status as the visual realisation of Radiohead's muse outstrips that of any other band and designer: only Joy Division/New Order and Peter Saville really come to mind. His graphics are as intrinsic an element of Radiohead as Yorke's existential howl or Ed O'Brien's plangent guitar arabesques.

In John Wyndham's novel, Chocky exits his corporeal home when he is discovered and probed by scientists. His privacy is crucial. By contrast, Yorke uses Tchocky as a means of communicating with the band's fans. Journalists and band followers can lob questions towards Radiohead at their spin-off website, www.spinwithagrin.com; most answers, when they sporadically appear, are credited to Tchocky. 'We are not little rag dolls you play with but say nothing and go back in the box when your [sic] finished with us,' he recently indignantly told a hack who mildly questioned the band's ideals.

Finally, Tchocky also makes sporadic appearances on fan websites, verbally sparring with delighted disciples who unexpectedly suddenly find themselves debating with their hero. An afternoon visit to Radiohead's official chatroom, the oddly-monikered The Byzantine Ziggurat, finds devotees in full flow deconstructing the minutiae of the *Hail to the Thief* sleeve. Tchocky is not in attendance.

'He hardly ever comes in,' explains a chatter by the rather prosaic name of Sock. 'He's like the rest of the band. They only really log on nowadays and come in here when they're drunk. Have I ever spoken to Tchocky? Yes, just once. It was on Christmas Day. There were only three of us in here, then suddenly Tchocky came in to talk to us.'

And what did he say?

'He said, "Merry Christmas, you fucking cunts."'

4

Radiohead, or the Philosophy of Pop

Mark Greif, *n+1*,
autumn 2005

've wondered why there's so little philosophy of popular music.
Critics of pop do reviews and interviews; they write appreciation and biography. Their criticism takes many things for granted
and doesn't ask the questions I want answered.

Everyone repeats the received idea that music is revolutionary.
Well, is it? Does pop music support revolution? We say pop is of
its time and can date the music by ear with surprising precision,
to 1966 or 1969 or 1972 or 1978 or 1984. Well, is it? Is pop truly
of its time, in the sense that it represents some aspect of exterior
history apart from the path of its internal development? I know
pop does something to me; everyone says the same. So what
does it do? Does it really influence my beliefs or actions in my
deep life, where I think I feel it most, or does it just insinuate a
certain fluctuation of mood or evanescent pleasure or impulse
to move?

The answers are difficult not because thinking is hard on the subject of pop, but because of an acute sense of embarrassment. Popular music is the most living art form today. Condemned to a desert island, contemporary people would grab their records first; we have the concept of desert-island discs because we could do without most other art forms before we would give up songs. Songs are what we consume in greatest quantity; they're what we store most of in our heads. But even as we can insist on the seriousness of *value* of pop music, we don't believe enough in its seriousness of *meaning* outside the realm of music, or most of us don't or we can't talk about it or sound idiotic when we do.

And all of us lovers of music, with ears tuned precisely to a certain kind of sublimity in pop, are quick to detect pretension, overstatement and cant about pop – in any attempt at a wider criticism – precisely because we feel the gap between the effectiveness of the music and the impotence and superfluity of analysis. This means we don't know about our major art form what we ought to know. We don't even agree about how the interconnection of pop music and lyrics, rather than the words spoken alone, accomplishes an utterly different task of representation, more scattershot and overwhelming and much less careful and dignified than poetry – and bad critics show their ignorance when they persist in treating pop like poetry, as in the still-growing critical effluence around Bob Dylan.

If you *were* to develop a philosophy of pop, you would have to clear the field of many obstacles. You would need to focus on a single artist or band, to let people know you had not floated into generalities and to let them test your declarations. You'd have to announce at the outset that the musicians were figures of real importance, but not the 'most' anything – not the most avant-garde, most perfect, most exemplary. This would pre-empt the hostile comparison and sophistication that passes for criticism among aficionados. Then you should have some breathing room. If you said once that you liked the band's music, there would be no more need of appreciation; and if it was a group whose music enough people listened to, there would be no need of biography or bare description.

So let the band be Radiohead, for the sake of argument, and let me be fool enough to embark on this. And if I insist that Radiohead are 'more' anything than some other pop musicians – as fans will make claims for the superiority of the bands they love – let it be that this band was more able, at the turn of the millennium, to pose a single question: how should it really ever be possible for pop music to incarnate a particular historical situation?

Radiohead belongs to 'rock' and, if rock has a characteristic subject, as country music's is small pleasures in hard times (getting by) and rap's is success in competition (getting over), that subject must be freedom from constraint (getting free). Yet the first notable quality of their music is that even though their topic may still be freedom, their technique involves the evocation, not of the feeling of freedom, but of unending low-level fear.

The dread in the songs is so detailed and so pervasive that it seems built into each line of lyrics and into the black or starry sky of music that domes it. It is environing fear, not antagonism emanating from a single object or authority. It is atmospheric rather than explosive. This menace doesn't surprise anyone. Outside there are listeners-in, watchers, abandoned wrecks with deployed air bags, killer cars, lights going out and coming on. 'They' are waiting, without a proper name: ghost voices, clicks of tapped phones, grooves of ended records, sounds of processing and anonymity.

An event is imminent or has just happened but is blocked from our senses: '*Something big is gonna happen/Over my dead body.*' Or else it is impossible that anything more will happen and yet it does: '*I used to think/There is no future left at all/I used to think.*' Something has gone wrong with the way we know events and the error leaks back to occurrences themselves. Life transpires in its representations, in the common medium of a machine language. ('*Arrest this man/He talks in maths/he buzzes like a fridge/He's like a detuned radio.*') A fissure has opened between occurrence and depiction, and the dam bursts between the technical and the natural. These are not meant to be statements of thoughts *about* their songs or even about the lyrics, which look banal on the printed page; this is what happens *in* their songs. The technical artifacts are in the music, sit behind our lips and slide out when we open our mouths – as chemical and medical words effortlessly make it into the lyrics ('polystyrene', 'myxomatosis', 'polyethylene').

Beside the artificial world is an iconography in their lyrics that comes from dark children's books: swamps, rivers, animals, arks and rowboats riding ambiguous tracks of light to the moon. Within these lyrics – and also in the musical counterpoint of chimes, strings, lullaby – an old personal view is opened, a desperate wish for small, safe spaces. It promises sanctuary, a bit of quiet in which to think.

Such a pretty house
and such a pretty garden. No alarms and no surprises . . .

But when the songs try to defend the small and safe, the effort comes hand in hand with grandiose assertions of power and violence which mimic the voice of overwhelming authority that should be behind our dread-filled contemporary universe but never speaks – or else the words speak, somehow, for us.

> *This is what you get*
> *when you mess with us.*

It just isn't clear whether this voice is a sympathetic voice or a voice outside – whether it is for us or against us. The band's task, as I understand it, is to try to hold on to the will, to ask if there is any part of it left that would be worth holding on to, or to find out where that force has gone. Thom Yorke, the singer, seems always in danger of destruction and then he is either channelling the Philistines or, Samson-like, preparing to take the temple down with him. So we hear pained and beautiful reassurances, austere, crystalline, and delicate – then violent denunciations and threats of titanic destruction – until they seem to be answering each other, as though the outside violence were being drawn inside:

> *Breathe, keep breathing.*
> *We hope that you choke,*
> *that you choke.*

And the consequence? Here you reach the best-known Radiohead lyrics, again banal on the page, and with them the hardest mood in their music to describe – captured in multiple repeated little phrases, stock talk, as words lose their meanings and regain them. 'How to Disappear Completely', as a song title puts it – for the words seem to speak a wish for negation of the self, nothingness and nonbeing:

> *For a minute there*
> *I lost myself, I lost myself.*

> *I'm not here. This isn't happening.*

A description of the condition of the late 1990s could go like this: at the turn of the millennium, each individual sat at a meeting point of shouted orders and appeals, the TV, the radio, the phone and mobile or cell, the billboard, the airport screen, the inbox, paper junk mail. Each person discovered that he lived at one knot of a network, existing without his consent, which connected him to any number of recorded voices, written messages, means of broadcast, channels of entertainment and avenues of choice. It was a culture of broadcast: an indiscriminate seeding, which needed to reach only a very few, covering vast tracts of our consciousness. To make a profit, only one message in ten thousand needed to take root; therefore messages were strewn everywhere. To live in this network felt like something, but surprisingly little in the culture of broadcast itself tried to capture what it felt like. Instead, it kept bringing pictures of an unencumbered, luxurious life, songs of ease and freedom and technological marvels, which did not feel like the life we lived.

And if you noticed you were not represented? It felt as if one of the few unanimous aspects of this culture was that it forbade you to complain, since if you complained, you were a trivial human, a small person, who misunderstood the generosity and benignity of the message system. It existed to help you. Now, if you accepted the constant promiscuous broadcasts as normalcy, there were messages in them to inflate and pet and flatter you. If you simply said this chatter was altering your life, killing your privacy or ending the ability to think in silence, there were alternative messages that whispered of humiliation, craziness, vanishing. What sort of crank needs silence? What could be more harmless than a few words of advice? The messages did not come from *somewhere*; they were not central, organised, intelligent, intentional. It was up to you to change the channel, not answer the phone, stop your ears, shut your eyes, dig a hole for yourself and get in it. Really, it was your responsibility. The metaphors in which people tried to complain about these developments, by ordinary law and custom, were pollution (as in 'noise pollution') and theft (as in 'stealing our time'). But we all knew the intrusions felt like violence. Physical violence, with no way to strike back.

And if this feeling of violent intrusion persisted? Then it added a new dimension of constant, nervous triviality to our lives. It linked, irrationally, in our moods and secret thoughts, these tiny private annoyances to the constant televised violence we saw. Those who objected embarrassed themselves, because they likened nuisances to tragedies – and yet we felt the likeness, though it became unsayable. Perhaps this was because our nerves have a limited palette for painting dread. Or because the network fulfilled its debt of civic responsibility by bringing us twenty-four-hour news of flaming airplanes and twisted cars and blood-soaked, screaming casualties, globally acquired, which it was supposedly our civic duty to watch – and, adding commercials, put this mixture of messages and horrors up on screens wherever a TV could only be introduced on grounds of 'responsibility to know', in the airport, the subway, the doctor's office and any waiting room. But to object was demeaning – who, really, meant us any harm? And didn't we truly have a responsibility to know?

Thus the large mass of people huddled in the path of every broadcast – who really did not speak but were spoken for, who received and couldn't send, were made responsible for the new Babel. Most of us who lived in this culture were primarily sufferers or patients of it and not, as the word had it, 'consumers'. Yet we had no other words besides 'consumption' or 'consumerism' to condemn a world of violent intrusions of insubstantial messages, no new way at least to name this culture or describe the feeling of being inside it.

So a certain kind of pop music could offer a representative vision of this world while still being one of its omnipresent products. A certain kind of musician might reflect this new world's vague smiling threat of hostile action, its latent violence done by no one in particular; a certain kind of musician, angry and critical rather than complacent and blithe, might depict the intrusive experience, though the music would be painfully intrusive itself, and it would be brought to us by and share the same avenues of mass intrusion that broadcast everything else. Pop music had the good fortune of being both a singularly unembarrassed art and a relatively low-capital medium in its creation – made by just a composer or writer or two, or four or six members of a band, with little outside intrusion, until money was poured into its recording and distribution and advertising. So, compromised as it was, music could still become a form of unembarrassed and otherwise inarticulable complaint, capturing what one could not say in reasonable debate and coming from far enough inside the broadcast culture that it could depict it with its own tools.

A historical paradox of rock has been that the pop genre most devoted to the idea of rebellion against authority has adopted increasingly more brutal and authoritarian music to denounce forms of authoritarianism. A genre that celebrated individual liberation required increasing regimentation and coordination. The development could be seen most starkly in hard rock, metal, hardcore, rap metal – but it was latent all along.

Throughout the early twentieth century, folk musics had been a traditional alternative to forms of musical authority. But amplification alone, it seems, so drastically changed the situation of music, opening possibilities in the realm of dynamics and the mimesis of other sounds, that it created avenues for the musical representation of liberation that had nothing to do with folk music's traditional lyrical content or the concern with instrumental skill and purism. Specifically, it gave pop ways to emulate the evils that liberation would be fighting against. Pop could become Goliath while it was cheering David. One aspect of amplification by the late 1960s stands out above all others: it opened up the possibility, for the first time, that a musician might choose to actually hurt an audience with noise. The relationship of audience to rock musician came to be based on a new kind of primitive trust. This was the trust of listeners facing a direct threat of real pain and permanent damage that bands would voluntarily restrain – just barely. An artist for the first time had his hands on a means of real violence and colluded with his audience to test its possibilities. You hear it in the Who, the Doors, Jimi Hendrix. In the 1960s, of course, this testing occurred against a rising background of violence, usually held in monopoly by 'the authorities', but being manifested with increasing frequency in civil unrest and police reaction as well as in war overseas. All of which is sometimes taken as an explanation. But once the nation was back in peacetime, it turned out that the formal violence of rock did not depend on the overt violence of bloodshed, and rock continued to metamorphose. The extremity of its dynamics developed toward heavy metal during the 1970s – and some connected this to industrial collapse and economic misery. Later it was refined in punk and post-punk, in periods of political defeat – and some connected the music's new lyrical alternations of hatred of authority with hatred of the self to the political, economic and social outlook.

Maybe they were right. But this is perhaps to give too much automatic credence to the idea that pop music depicts history almost without trying – which is precisely what is in question.

To leap all the way into the affective world of our own moment, of course, might require something else: electronic sounds. To reproduce a new universe, or to spur a desire to carve out a life in its midst, a band might need a limited quantity of beeps, repetitions, sampled loops, drum machines, noises and beats. 'Electronica', as a contemporary genre name, speaks of the tools of production as well as their output. Laptops, Pro Tools, sequencers, and samplers, the found sounds and sped-up breaks and pure frequencies, provided an apparently unanchored environment and a weird soundscape that, though foreshadowed in studios in Cologne or at the Columbia-Princeton Electronic Music Center, didn't automatically fit with the traditions of guitars and drums that pop knew. But the electronic blips the music used turned out to be already emotionally available to us by a different route than the avant-gardism of Stockhausen or Cage. All of us born after 1965 had been setting nonsense syllables and private songs to machine noise and then computer noise, since the new sounds reached our cradles. Just as we want to make tick and tock out of the even movement of a clock, we wanted to know how to hear a language and a song of noises, air compressors and washer surges, alarm sirens and warning bells. We hear communication in the refined contemporary spectrum of beeps: the squall of a microwave, the chime of a timer, the fat gulp of a register, the chirrups of cell phones, the ping of seat belt alerts and clicks of indicators, not to mention the argot of debonair beeps from the computers on which we type.

Radiohead, up until the late 1990s, had not been good at spelling out what bothered them in narrative songs. They attempted it in their early work. One well-known and well-loved but clumsy song sang about the replacement of a natural and domestic world by plastic replicas ('Fake Plastic Trees'). That account was inches away from folk cliché – something like Malvina Reynolds's 'Little Boxes'. Its only salvation may have been the effect observed rather than the situation denounced: '*It wears you out*', describing the fatigue human beings feel in the company of the ever-replaceable. *The Bends,* the last album produced before their major period, had this steady but awkward awareness, as the title implies, of being dragged through incompatible atmospheres in the requirements of daily life. But the band didn't yet seem to know that the subjective, symptomatic evocation of these many whiplashing states of feeling – not overt, narrative complaint about them – would prove to be their talent.

On the first mature album, *OK Computer,* a risk of cliché lingered in a song of a computer voice intoning '*Fitter, happier, more productive*' – as if the dream of conformist self-improvement would turn us artificial. But the automated voice's oddly human character saved the effect. It seemed automated things, too, could be seduced by a dream of perfection equally delusory for them. Then the new commensurability of natural and artificial wasn't a simple loss but produced a hybrid vulnerability when you had thought things were most stark and steely. The band was also, at that time, mastering a game of voices, the interfiling of inhuman speech and machine sounds with the keening, vulnerable human singing of Thom Yorke.

Their music had started as guitar rock, but with the albums *Kid A* and *Amnesiac* the keyboard asserted itself. The piano dominated; the guitars developed a quality of an organ. The drums, emerging altered and processed, came to fill in spaces in rhythms already set by the front-line instruments. Orchestration added brittle washes of strings, a synthetic choir, chimes, an unknown shimmer or bleated horns. The new songs were built on verse-chorus structure in only a rudimentary way, as songs developed from one block of music to the next, not turning back. And, of course – as is better known, and more widely discussed – on the new albums the band, by now extremely popular and multimillion-selling, 'embraced' electronica. But what precisely did that mean? It didn't seem in their case like opportunism, as in keeping up with the new thing; nor did it entirely take over what they did in their songs; nor were they particularly noteworthy as electronic artists. It is crucial that they were not innovators; nor did they ever take it further than halfway – if that. They were *not* an avant-garde. The political problem of an artistic avant-garde, especially when it deals with any new technology of representation, has always been that the simply novel elements may be mistaken for some form of meanings of 'revolutionary' – one, forming an advance in formal technique; the other, contributing to social cataclysm – are often confused, usually to the artist's benefit, and technology has a way of becoming infatuated with its own existence.

Radiohead's success lay in their ability to represent the feeling of our age; they did not insist on being too much advanced in the 'advanced' music they acquired. The beeps and buzzes never seemed like the source of their energy; rather, they were a means they'd stumbled upon of finally communicating the feelings they had always held. They had felt, so to speak, electronic on *OK Computer* with much less actual electronica. And they did something very rudimentary and basic with the new technologies. They tilted artificial noises against the weight of the human voice and human sounds.

Their new kind of song, in both words and music, announced that anyone might have to become partly inhuman to accommodate the experience of the new era.

Thom Yorke's voice is the unity on which all the musical aggregations and complexes pivot. You have to imagine the music drawing a series of outlines around him – a house, a tank, the stars of space or an architecture of almost abstract pipes and tubes, cogs and wheels, ivy and thorns, servers and boards, beams and voids. The music has the feeling of a biomorphic machine in which the voice is alternately trapped and protected.

Yorke's voice conjures the human in extremis. Sometimes it comes to us from an extreme of fear, sometimes an extreme of transcendence. We recognise it as a naked voice in the process of rising up to beauty – the reassurance we've alluded to in the lyrics – or being broken up and lost in the chatter of broadcasts, the destroying fear. In the same song that features a whole sung melody, the vocals will also be broken into bits and made the pulsing wallpaper against which the vulnerable, pale voice of the singer stands out. Only a few other popular artists build so much of their music from sampled voice rather than sampled beats, instrumental tones, or noises. The syllables are cut and repeated. A 'wordless' background will come from mashed phonemes. Then the pure human voice will reassert itself.[1]

A surprising amount of this music seems to draw on church music. One biographical fact is relevant here: they come from Oxford, England, grew up there, met in high school and live, compose and rehearse there. Their hometown is like their music. That bifurcated English city, split between concrete downtown and green environs, has its unspoiled centre and grey periphery of modest houses and a disused automobile factory. Its spots of natural beauty exist because of the nearby huge institutions of the university, and if you stand in the remaining fields and parks you always know you are in a momentary breathing space, already encroached upon. But for the musically minded, the significant feature of Oxford is its Church of England chapels, one in each college and others outside – places of imperial authority, home to another kind of hidden song. The purity of Yorke's falsetto belongs in a boys' choir at evensong. And then Yorke does sing of angels, amid harps, chimes, and bells: *'Black-eyed angels swam with me/. . ./ And we all went to heaven in a little row boat / There was nothing to fear and nothing to doubt.'*

---

1 Stanley Cavell used to say that the first impulse opera evokes is to wonder where in the physical singer the immaterial song can be located. In live performance, the striking thing about Thom Yorke is how small a person he is. Not only is his voice excessive, beyond human averageness, it is moored to a smaller-than-average body and onstage persona that seem to dramatise the question, in his music, of where voices come from – from individual people or the techniques that surround and overmaster them.

And yet the religion in the music is not about salvation – it's about the authority of voices, the wish to submit and the discovery of a consequent resistance in oneself. It is anti-religious, though attuned to transcendence. The organ in a church can be the repository of sublime power: a bundling of human throats in its brass pipes or all the instruments known to man in its stops. You can hear your own small voice responding, within something so big that it manifests a threat of your voice merely being played mechanically and absorbed into a totality. To sing with an organ (as Yorke does at the end of *Kid A*) can be to discover one's own inner voice in distinction to it and at the same time to wish to be lost, absorbed, overwhelmed within it. A certain kind of person will refuse the church. But even one who refuses the church will not forget the overwhelming feeling.

Sublime experience, the philosophical tradition says, depends on a relation to something that threatens. Classically it depended on observing from a point of safety a power like a storm, cataract or high sea, that could crush the observer if he were nearer. (By compassing the encompassable power in inner representation, it was even suggested, you could be reminded of the interior power of the moral faculty, the human source of a comparable strength.) Radiohead observe the storm from within it. Their music can remind you of the inner overcoming voice, it's true. But then the result is no simple access of power. This sublime acknowledges a different kind of internalisation, the drawing of the inhuman into yourself and also a loss of your own feelings and words and voice to an outer order that has come to possess them.

The way Yorke sings guarantees that you often don't know what the lyrics are; they emerge into sense and drop out – and certain phrases attain clarity while others remain behind. This de-enunciation has been a tool of pop for a long time. Concentrating, you can make out nearly all the lyrics; listening idly, you hear a smaller set of particular lines, which you sing along to and remember. It is a way of focusing inattention as well as attention.

The most important grammatical tic in Radiohead lyrics, unlike the habitual lyrical 'I' and apostrophic 'you' of pop, is the 'we'. '*We ride*', '*We escape*', '*We're damaged goods*', '*Bring down the government/. . ./They don't speak for us*'. But also: '*We suck young blood*', '*We can wipe you out/. . ./Anytime*'. The pronoun doesn't point to any existing collectivity; the songs aren't about a national group or even the generic audience for rock. So who is 'we'?

There is the scared individual, lying to say he's not alone – like the child who says, 'We're coming in there!' so imagined monsters won't know he's by himself. There's the 'we' you might wish for, the imagined collectivity that could resist or threaten, and this may shade into the thought of all the other listeners besides you, in their rooms or cars alone, singing these same bits of lyrics. There's the 'we', as I've suggested, of the violent power that you are not: the voice of the tyrant, the thug, the terrifying parent, the bad cop. You take him inside you and his voice spreads over all the others who – somewhere singing these words for just a moment – are like you. You experience a release at last, so satisfying does it feel to sing the unspoken orders out loud to yourself, as if at last they came from you. You are the one willing the destruction – like Brecht and Weill's Pirate Jenny, the barmaid, washing dishes and taking orders, who knows that soon a Black Ship will come for her town, bristling with cannons. And when its crew asks their queen whom they should kill, she will answer: '*Alle!*' So the characteristic

Radiohead song turns into an alternation, in exactly the same repeated words, between the forces that would defy intrusive power and the intrusive power itself, between hopeful individuals and the tyrant ventriloquised.

It has to be admitted that other memorable lyrics sing phrases of self-help. Plenty of these important lines are junk slogans from the culture and of course part of the oddity of pop is that junk phrases can be made so moving; they do their work again. In a desperate voice: '*You can try the best you can/If you try the best you can/The best you can is good enough.*' Or: '*Breathe, keep breathing/Don't lose your nerve.*' Or: '*Everyone/Everyone around here/Everyone is so near/It's holding on.*' On the page, these lyrics aren't impressive, unless you can hear them in memory, in the framing of the song. Again, one has to distinguish between poetry and pop. The most important lines in pop are rarely poetically notable; frequently they are quite deliberately and necessarily words that are the most frank, melodramatic, and unredeemable. And yet they do get redeemed. The question becomes why certain settings in music and a certain playing of simple against more complex lyrics, can remake debased language and restore the innocence of emotional expression. (Opera listeners know this, in the ariose transformations of '*Un bel dì*' ('One fine day') or '*O mio babbino caro*' ('Oh, my dear papa'). But then opera criticism, too, has a long-standing problem with lyrics.) In the midst of all else the music and lyrics are doing, the phrases of self-help may be the minimal words of will or nerve that you need to hear.

The more I try to categorise why Radiohead's music works as it does, and by extension how pop works, the more it seems clear that the effect of pop on our beliefs and actions is not really to create either one. Pop does, though, I think, allow you to retain certain things you've already thought, without your necessarily having been able to articulate them, and to preserve certain feelings you have only intermittent access to, in a different form, music with lyrics, in which the cognitive and emotional are less divided. I think songs allow you to steel yourself or loosen yourself into certain kinds of actions, though they don't start anything. And the particular songs and bands you like dictate the beliefs you can preserve and reactivate, and the actions you can prepare – and which songs and careers will shape your inchoate private experience depends on an alchemy of your experience and the art itself. Pop is neither a mirror nor a Rorschach blot, into which you look and see only yourself; nor is it a lecture, an interpretable poem, or an act of simply determinate speech. It teaches something, but only by stimulating and preserving things that you must have had inaugurated elsewhere. Or it prepares the ground for these discoveries elsewhere – often knowledge you might never otherwise have really 'known', except as it could be rehearsed by you, then repeatedly reactivated for you, in this medium.

But is the knowledge that's preserved a spur to revolution? There is no logical sense in which pop music is revolutionary. That follows from the conclusion that pop does not start beliefs or instil principles or create action *ex nihilo*. It couldn't over-turn an order. When so much pop declares itself to be revolutionary, however, I think it correctly points to something else that is significant but more limited and complicated. There is indeed an antisocial or countercultural tendency of pop that does follow logically from what it does. That is to say, there is a characteristic affect that follows from a medium that allows you to retain and reactivate forms of knowledge and experience that you are 'supposed to' forget or that are 'supposed to' disappear by themselves – and 'supposed to' here isn't nefarious, it simply means that social forms, convention, conformity, and just plain intelligent speech don't allow you to speak of these things, or make them embarrassing when you do. Pop encourages you to hold on to and reactivate hints of personal feeling that society should have extinguished. Of course, this winds up taking in all classes of fragile personal knowledge: things that are inarticulable in social speech because they are too delicate or ideologically out of step, and things that should not be articulated because they are selfish, thoughtless, destructive and stupid. That helps explain how these claims for 'What I learned from pop' can go so quickly from the sublime to the ridiculous and back to the sublime. It explains why we are right to feel that so much of what's promised for pop is not worth our credulity. But, again, risking ridiculousness, I think the thing that pop can prepare you for, the essential thing, is *defiance*. Defiance, at its bare minimum, is the insistence on finding ways to retain the thoughts and feelings that a larger power should have extinguished.

The difference between revolution and defiance is the difference between an overthrow of the existing order and one person's shaken fist. When the former isn't possible, you still have to hold on to the latter, if only so as to remember you're human. Defiance is the insistence on individual power confronting the overwhelming force that it cannot undo. You know you cannot strike the colossus. But you can defy it with words or signs. In the assertion that you can fight a superior power, the declaration that you will, this absurd overstatement gains dignity by exposing you, however uselessly, to risk. Unable to stop it in its tracks, you dare the crushing power to begin its devastation with you.

Power comes in many forms for human beings and defiance meets it where it can. The simplest defiance confronts nature's power and necessity. In the teeth of a storm that would kill him, a man will curse the wind and rain. He declares, like Nikos Kazantzakis's peasant Zorba, 'You won't get into my little hut, brother; I shan't open the door to you. You won't put my fire out; you won't tip my hut over!' This will is not Promethean, simply human.

In all forms of defiance, a little contingent being, the imperilled man or woman, hangs on to his will – which may be all he has left – by making a deliberate error about his will's jurisdiction. Because the defiant person has no power to win a struggle, he preserves his will through representations: he shakes his fist, announces his name, shouts a threat and above all makes the statements 'I am', 'We are'. This becomes even more necessary and risky when the cruel power is not natural, will-less itself, but belongs to other men. Barthes gives the words of the French revolutionist Guadet, arrested and condemned to death: 'Yes, I am Guadet. Executioner, do your duty. Go take my head to the tyrants of my country. It has always turned them pale; once severed, it will turn them paler still.' He gives the order, not the tyrant, commanding necessity in his own name – defying the false necessity of human force that has usurped nature's power – even if he can only command it to destroy him.

The situation we confront now is a new necessity, not blameless like wind or water and yet not fatal as from a tyrant or executioner. The nature we face is a billowing atmospheric second nature made by man. It is the distant soft tyranny of other men, wafting in diffuse messages, in the abdication of authority to technology, in the dissembling of responsibility under cover of responsibility and with the excuse of help – gutless, irresponsible, servile, showing no naked force, only a smiling or a pious face. The 'they' are cowardly friends. They are here to help you be happy and make fruitful choices. ('*We can wipe you out anytime.*')

At its best, Radiohead's music reactivates the moods in which you once noticed you ought to refuse. It can abet an *impersonal* defiance. This is not a doctrine the band advances, but an effect of the aesthetic. It doesn't name a single enemy. It doesn't propose revolution. It doesn't call you to overthrow an order that you couldn't take hold of anyway at any single point, not without scapegoating a portion and missing the whole. This defiance – it might be the one thing we can manage and better than sinking beneath the waves. It requires the retention of a private voice.

One of the songs on *Hail to the Thief* has a peculiar counter-slogan:

> *Just 'cause you feel it*
> *Doesn't mean it's there.*

To sense the perversity of the appearance of these words in a pop song, you have to remember that they occur inside an art form monomaniacally devoted to the production of strong feelings. Pop music *always* tells its listeners that their feelings are real. Yet here is a chorus that denies any reference to reality in the elation and melancholy and chills that this chorus, in fact, elicits. Yorke delivers the lines with an upnote on 'feel' as he repeats them, and if anything in the song makes your hair stand on end, that will be the moment. He makes you feel, that is, the emotion he's warning you against. Next he sings a warning not to make too much of his own singing: '*There's always a siren/Singing you to shipwreck.*' And this song, titled 'There There', was the first single released off the album, pressed in many millions of copies; it was played endlessly on radio and MTV.

The purpose of the warning is not to stop feelings but to stop you from believing they always refer to something, or deserve reality or should lead to actions or choices or beliefs – which is, of course, what the messages you hear by broadcast like you to make of them. The feelings evoked by a pop song may be false, as the feelings evoked by all the other messages brought to you by the same media as pop songs may be false. You must judge. If leading you to disbelieve in broadcast also leads you to disbelieve in pop, so be it; maybe you believed in pop in the wrong way. You must distinguish. The broadcast messages are impersonal in one fashion. They pretend to care about you when actually they don't know or care that you, as a single person, exist. Impersonal defiance is impersonal in another way; it encourages you to withdraw, no longer to believe that there is any human obligation owed to the sources of messages – except when they remind you, truly, of what you already have subtly sensed and already know.

You can see a closed space at the heart of many of Radiohead's songs. To draw out one of their own images, it may be something like a glass house. You live continuously in the glare of inspection and with the threat of intrusion. The attempt to cast stones at an outer world of enemies would shatter your own shelter. So you settle for the protection of this house, with watchers on the outside, as a place you can still live, a way to preserve the vestige of closure – a barrier, however glassy and fragile, against the outside. In English terms, a glass house is also a glasshouse, which we call a greenhouse. It is the artificial construction that allows botanical life to thrive in winter.

Radiohead's songs suggest that you should erect a barrier, even of repeated minimal words, or the assertion of a 'we', to protect yourself – and then there proves to be a place in each song to which you, too, can't be admitted, because the singer has something within him closed to interference, just as every one of us does, or should. We'll all have to find the last dwellings within ourselves that are closed to intrusion and begin from there. The politics of the next age, if we are to survive, will include a politics of the re-creation of privacy.

4

Thom Yorke, Free Agent

Ann Powers, *Los Angeles Times,*
28 June 2006

L ast year, Thom Yorke was supposed to unwind. Radiohead, the
band whose decade-long ascent has turned the singer into
pop's definitive reluctant visionary, was on hiatus after a pro-
tracted cycle of recording and touring.

Yorke was savouring the retreat from what he wryly calls
'making RECORDS, in big capital letters' and the chance to
reacquaint himself with his Oxford home, his longtime partner
Rachel Owen and two young children. But instead of clearing a
space for calm, Yorke found himself up to his neck in new
thoughts.

'At my house, there's a room about this size,' Yorke said,
gesturing at the spacious suite in San Francisco's Clift hotel where
he sat discussing *The Eraser,* the album he's releasing on 10 July.
'The entire room was just covered – the whole floor, with notes
and scraps of paper. A friend of mine came by just before we
started recording and he was just looking through it, laughing
his head off, saying, "How are you going to piece this together?"'

Yorke's workroom mess, mirrored by the sonic 'bits and bobs and shreds of all sorts of random chaos' on his laptop, gave him a sense of freedom he'd momentarily lost within Radiohead, which lands in LA for two nights at the Greek Theatre starting Thursday. In league with two long-time collaborators, the visual artist Stanley Donwood and producer Nigel Godrich, Yorke enclosed himself amid these fragments, shutting out other influences. 'That's how you get that thing where a project has its own universe,' he explained. 'You say, well, everything in this room, that's all there is, that's all I've got.'

The fruitful little island of disarray contrasted radically with the high-stakes mood surrounding Radiohead's most recent chart-topper, 2003's *Hail to the Thief*, which left the band seriously in need of some elbow room. Made quickly, during a time when Yorke was becoming deeply involved with the environmentalist group Friends of the Earth, *The Eraser* is a return to focus for Yorke, whose energy had flagged under the weight of his band's outsized reputation. 'It was done in the context of Radiohead,' he said, adding that he initially dreaded telling his bandmates he'd embarked on the effort. 'The best thing about it was that it wasn't a problem. Of course it was fine. Why wouldn't it be?' That the band dynamic 'is a liquid thing is very important'.

On its current tour, Radiohead is playing a wide swath of favourites plus some exciting new material, perhaps enriched by the confidence Yorke says he's regained by making *The Eraser*, which will be released on the super-hip independent label XL. Radiohead is one of pop's highest-profile free agents, having parted with EMI, the conglomerate that released its previous seven albums. *The Eraser* could be viewed as part of a larger move toward independence.

Asked whether Radiohead would consider distributing its next album independently, Yorke unhesitatingly said yes. 'We have two or three options and that's one,' he said. 'Once we finish whatever we think is good enough to put out, then we'll start thinking about it. We haven't discussed it a great deal. I would love for us to drop a chemical weapon within the music industry. But I don't see it as our responsibility, either.'

In the meantime, there's *The Eraser* – a project the label-resistant Yorke hates to label 'solo'. What began as a side trip into the abstract electronic music he loves became, to the singer's surprise, forty minutes of remarkably powerful and direct music. Sure to be one of the year's critical and cult favourites, *The Eraser* is an evocative portrait of life made slippery by urban sprawl, murky political alliances and global warming – and given hope through individual and communal resistance – with the blips and bleeps of Yorke's laptop excursions coalescing into soulful, politically charged songs.

'It started out with loads and loads of beats and la la la,' Yorke said, mocking his own obscurantist tendencies. 'It was pretty intense and very, very heavy.' Yorke's busman's holiday gave his producer a chance to highlight Yorke's poignant tenor and melodic sense. 'In the midst of it all there were two or three things that made Nigel and me go, "Ooh, there's something really direct here. Someone might even understand it the first time around."'

'In the band he's always finding ways to bury himself,' Godrich said in a phone interview. 'Being a big fan of his voice and his songs, I wanted to push that. It would have been sad if he'd just made an oblique record. But because it was predominantly electronic, I had a really good excuse to make his voice dry and loud.'

The leap beyond the band context might easily have led Yorke into murky territory. A fan of experimental electronica, the singer first came up with a collection of tracks that didn't really reach out. 'It made complete sense to me, but there wasn't enough there for anybody else,' he said of these early efforts. But the desire to meld his voice with the computer's led to unexpected intimacies. 'The music, no matter what way you look at it, is coming out of a box,' said Yorke, noting that even the acoustic sounds of piano, guitar and bass samples on *The Eraser* are computer-processed, and he cites Bjork's 1997 electro-torch suite *Homogenic* as a primary reference point. 'It has its own space. We consciously decided to not expand it beyond that. The vocals are exactly the same, right there in the speakers. The record was built to be listened to in an isolated space – on headphones or stuck in traffic.'

The traffic reference is no casual one for Yorke, whose concern about the environment nearly caused him, at one point, to 'flip my lid'. Its songs send up warning flares that are cosmic in scope, yet movingly personal – the sonic equivalent of a hand held up to a tidal wave. That's an image Donwood included in *London Views*, the 'apocalyptic panorama' inspired by *The Eraser* that makes up the album's cover art. One of the linotype's most powerful segments depicts King Canute, the legendary English monarch who proved the limits of kingly power by trying and failing to command the ocean. The tale inspired Yorke's flood of lyrics too.

'In the paper one day, Jonathan Porritt was basically dismissing any commitment that the working government has toward addressing global warming, saying that their gestures were like King Canute trying to stop the tide,' Yorke said of the British environmentalist. 'And that just went "ker-ching" in my head. It's not political, really, but that's exactly what I feel is happening.

We're all King Canutes, holding our hands out, saying, "It'll go away. I can make it stop." No, you can't.'

Such 'not really political' talk has become tough for Yorke to resist, despite his desire to stay in the artist's traditional spot above the fray. *The Eraser*'s most controversial song is 'Harrowdown Hill', named after the Oxfordshire neighbourhood where authorities found the body of Dr David Kelly, a whistleblower who allegedly committed suicide after telling a reporter that Tony Blair's government had falsely identified biological weapons in Iraq.

'I called it "Harrowdown Hill" because it was a really poetic title,' he said. 'To me it sounded like some sort of battle, some civil-war-type thing. Finishing the song, I was thinking about the 1990 poll tax riots – another of England's finest moments, when they beat . . . protesters, and you know, there were old ladies there and kids with families. I didn't expect that many people to realise that Harrowdown Hill was where Dr Kelly died. I'm not saying the reference isn't there, but there's more to it.'

'Harrowdown Hill' makes its point through startling sounds and shards of emotionally charged speech; it's as political as a private – even secret – moment can be. Its startling beauty is typical of *The Eraser* – which, like all of Yorke's best work, finds its strength in the spaces where words and music dissolve, only to form something new. Literary types might call it poetics. For Yorke, it's all about hearing the world through the individual voice.

'I have friends who were involved in the tsunami,' he said. 'Talking to them, you realise that no matter how huge or terrifying an event is, you're not going to grasp it from the newspaper; it doesn't even matter if you see the wave on television. The only way you can actually relate to it is when someone explains their experience, one to one.'

Eight: Present Tense

1

OK Computer:
Why the Record Industry is
Terrified of Radiohead's
New Album

Andy Gill, *Independent*,
5 October 2007

E ver since a cadre of politicised hippies tore down the fence at
the 1970 Isle of Wight Festival, the more anarchically-inclined
of rock fans have demanded that music be 'free', contending that
pop's position under the entertainment-industry umbrella fatally
compromises its aesthetic and political freedom. Now, as Radiohead offer their album *In Rainbows* to the world potentially for as
little as a penny apiece, that revolutionary ambition is upon us.

Ironically, it has been triggered not by penniless hippies in
some inner-city squat, nor by indie-label firebrands, but by one
of the biggest bands in the world, whose rise occurred under the
stewardship of EMI, the UK's bastion of corporate entertainment

for over three-quarters of a century. And, piling irony upon irony, far from having their aesthetic and political freedom compromised by the relationship, Radiohead have actually grown more artistically adventurous with each successive album and remain one of the industry's most politically engaged acts.

Under the new set-up, fans will be offered the chance to buy the band's album for whatever they deem appropriate. Most will pay between one pound and five pounds, which seems reasonable. Those desperate for a more physical artefact are offered a high-quality vinyl double-album package, with lavish artwork and an extra CD of otherwise unavailable tracks, for forty pounds – and even at that price, the band will sell shedloads. The CD version of the downloads, it's reported, will creep out sometime next year.

The move has been widely viewed as the inevitable corollary of the rise of digital downloading, which in less than a decade has all but demolished the old retail sector. It's shocking to consider that Napster, the website that established the notion of free access to music via file-sharing, was only started in 1999 but, by 2001, had a worldwide user base of more than twenty-six million fans, all looting whatever music they could find. The mainstream industry, unable or unwilling to see beyond the hardware forms – vinyl, CD, cassette – that were the backbone of their business, was blindsided by the file-sharing boom, and instead of seeking some form of accommodation with downloaders, initially reacted by trying to criminalise them: acts such as Metallica and Dr Dre instigated legal action against Napster in 2000, and the following year A&M Records sought an injunction preventing its copy-righted recordings from being offered via the website.

The RIAA (Recording Industry Association of America) began suing individual alleged file-sharers, an aggressive policy that backfired somewhat when the organisation appeared to be bully-ing victims including a twelve-year-old girl, a sixty-six-year-old woman allegedly downloading gangsta rap, and, in 2005, a woman who had died the previous year, aged eighty-three. To date, they have instigated over twenty thousand cases.

But not everyone believed Napster was entirely damaging to a record's sales potential. Some felt the opposite was true in many cases – that the exposure afforded by file-sharing could stimulate sales. This was proven in 2000 when tracks from Radiohead's *Kid A* appeared on Napster three months before the album's official release. An unflinchingly experimental album, significantly differ-ent in style from *OK Computer* and featuring no obvious singles, it was a challenging work, yet despite the millions of free downloads, it still became the band's first American chart-topper. Previously, their best placing had been the lowly 21 achieved by *OK Computer*. Clearly, Napster had not harmed its prospects, and it could be argued to have provided invaluable promotional assistance.

The industry came to realise that the larger war was lost and started developing relationships with 'legal' download services such as Apple's iTunes, belatedly tapping into the revenue stream facilitated by the popularity of the iPod. The effect on retailers, however, has been catastrophic. The big chains, such as Virgin, struck deals allowing them to sell CDs at a more competitive price, but the smaller-volume operators – the independent shops that sustained the indie fringe – have been unable to compete and are disappearing. Record labels, meanwhile, are struggling to find a new role within the industry, with many forced into the current, seemingly endless, round of mergers.

Radiohead are not the only act to embark on this strategy – their announcement was followed by a similar offer from Alan

McGee on behalf of the Charlatans' next album – but they are the biggest. In recent years, however, their sales have declined; after *Kid A*, the *Amnesiac* and *Hail to the Thief* albums could only manage gold certification in America, which has led some to speculate that the new strategy may be a means for the band to compensate for declining popularity by keeping a larger proportion – indeed, one hundred per cent – of sales revenue, rather than the small share previously offered by Parlophone.

The band, originally called On A Friday, signed a six-album deal with Parlophone in 1991 after a chance meeting between the label's Keith Wozencroft and guitarist Jonny Greenwood in the Oxford record shop where the latter worked. They changed their name to Radiohead (after a track on Talking Heads' *True Stories*) and began recording their debut album *Pablo Honey*. Their first single, 'Creep', a double-edged exercise in ironic self-deprecation, reflected the band's admiration of the Pixies, but was poorly received on its first release; Radio 1 considered it 'too depressing' to play. But the song built a following in America, where its smouldering dynamic and cathartic chorus slotted neatly into the prevailing grunge aesthetic. It remains their biggest hit and helped hoist *Pablo Honey* to a respectable chart position, just outside the Top 30.

But as their American promotional tour stretched into its second year, the band grew bored with playing the songs they had written years before and almost broke up. Keen to distance themselves from 'Creep', their follow-up album *The Bends* featured the kind of artistic volte-face that sends chills down label bosses' spines, with the band re-establishing themselves as an arena-rock outfit with the ability to inject powerful emotional content into complex musical structures. 'When *The Bends* came out,' drummer Phil

Selway later said, 'everyone went on about how uncommercial it was. Twelve months later, it was hailed as a pop classic. The record company were worried there wasn't a single on it, and we ended up with five Top 30 hits from it.'

The Bends might have scared their label, but its unprecedented blend of melodic prog-rock and soul would serve as the template for a generation of lesser talents, most notably Coldplay. Their stature was also rising among their peers, with R.E.M.'s Michael Stipe – whose idealism and idiosyncratic appearance made him an obvious role model for singer Thom Yorke – admitting that he was scared by how good they were. 'Thom Yorke, with "My Iron Lung", that's just an amazing metaphor to put into a song,' Stipe gushed to me in 2001. 'Stuff like that just makes me want to work harder and write another song that's as good as that.'

The reception accorded *OK Computer* in 1997 suggested that Stipe's admiration was shared by millions, as this complex work became their most popular album. Yorke admitted he was surprised at the reception, saying that 'what really blew my head off was the fact that people got all the things, all the textures and the sounds and the atmospheres we were trying to create'. The subsequent world tour was filmed for a fly-on-the-wall documentary, *Meeting People is Easy*, a film that revealed the band's growing distaste for the music business as they laboured through a gruelling year of concerts. In the year after the tour's conclusion, their only public appearances would be at a couple of benefit concerts for Amnesty International and the Tibetan Freedom Movement, indications of the growing political engagement of Yorke.

Since then, Yorke has used his rock-star profile to bring good causes to his fans' attention, advising them to read books such as

Naomi Klein's anti-corporate tract *No Logo* and Alastair McIntosh's *Soil and Soul: People Versus Corporate Power*, an account of the author's campaigns to prevent industrial despoliation of Scotland's Western Isles. More recently, the singer has bitten the bullet avoided by most stadium-rockers, criticising the 'ridiculous' amount of energy needed to fuel large-scale concert events – even threatening to cease touring the more far-flung destinations unless steps were taken to reduce carbon emissions.

After *OK Computer*, Radiohead came close to splitting up. Yorke suffered severe depression, which led to writer's block, and the members' different ideas as to their future direction seemed to presage solo careers. But again they reinvented themselves, turning from guitar-based rock and creating music heavily influenced by jazz, electronics and the avant-garde. The sessions furnished two of the most unusual albums ever to top the album charts, 2000's *Kid A* and, a year later, *Amnesiac*. Sales were understandably lower than those of *OK Computer*, but the return of their familiar, crowd-pleasing guitar-rock style alongside the more recent electronic passages and experimental developments on 2003's *Hail to the Thief* restored a certain equilibrium to their progress.

Hail to the Thief was the final album delivered under Radiohead's original Parlophone contract, and more cynical observers saw its restoration of relative sonic normalcy as an attempt to bolster the band's commercial appeal to suitors, which for a gold-chip act like Radiohead would include virtually every major label. But as the years passed, no deal was done. The band was clearly in no hurry to get into bed with the corporate world again, as Yorke and Greenwood took time out to make solo albums. Then, suddenly, the announcement that *In Rainbows* would be sold directly by the band, cutting out the various middlemen and the cosy industry practices weighted so heavily in the labels' favour. And one can only imagine the trauma wrought in record-label boardrooms by their decision to charge whatever purchasers deemed appropriate.

Radiohead's decision is only the latest, if the most damaging, nail in the coffin of the mainstream music business. Not that the labels' clients will be wasting their tears; for decades, artists have complained about the inequity of contracts, with their in-built skimming of ten per cent to cover 'returns' of damaged copies (even on supposedly indestructible CDs), and the way that instead of receiving the same percentage of revenue from the higher-priced CD as from vinyl, artists were routinely offered the same sum. And for decades, all but the most powerful artists were unable to do anything about it. At the other end of the scale, naive young bands who accepted huge advances would discover, when they were less successful than expected, that they were heavily in debt to their label and prevented from releasing material elsewhere until it was paid off.

A spendthrift, short-term culture prevailed at many labels, in which vast sums were expended promoting singles acts who would never recoup it in album sales, while longer-term prospects were deprived of the support that might help their careers blossom. Back in the '60s, even a lower-division journeyman rock band like Budgie got to make a handful of albums before they were dumped; by the '90s, successful indie acts with hit singles were being cut adrift prematurely, often because label bosses were 'slimming down' the artist roster to just a few stars and steady sellers to make their company more attractive to potential purchasers.

It was a climate that bred waves of artist disaffection. When the likes of Prince and George Michael declared themselves little more than 'slaves', the general reaction was one of incredulity; but if stars of that magnitude felt hard done by, just imagine how demoralised and crushed the ranks of lesser earners must have felt. And when artists such as Bob Dylan, Paul McCartney and most recently Joni Mitchell would rather do business with a company like Starbucks than with the established labels, something is drastically rotten in the state of Denmark Street.

Digital downloading has turned the entire industry on its head. Facing sharp falls in album sales, established acts have re-thought their approach. Until recently, a band would tour primarily to encourage sales of their album. Now, the Stones, for instance, make vastly more money out of concert tickets and merchandising than from record sales. For Prince, it's well worth giving away his new album to promote his profitable run of shows at the O2 Centre.

But Radiohead's decision to, in effect, give away their album hoists the whole issue on to a much higher level, prompting a slew of thus-far-unanswerable questions. Such as: won't fans expect to get all music for free, even that made by penniless acts? How does a small act establish and develop itself, without sales income or label assistance? Indeed, why bother making records at all, when the promotional effect on club gigs results in such low returns? What happens to the staff laid off when record shops close? And doesn't this simply establish a new class division, between those who are able to own and operate computers and those who are denied access – how do they get to enjoy *In Rainbows*?

I've no idea but, for the moment at least, the pay-what-you-like strategy affords punters the opportunity to make sharp critical assessments where they really hurt: right there in the musicians' pockets. So: shrewd or stupid? You be the judge.

2

Review of *In Rainbows*

Robert Sandall, *Daily Telegraph*,
9 October 2007

Not since 1998, when Oasis delivered *Be Here Now*, their fever-ishly anticipated sequel to *What's the Story (Morning Glory)?*, has a rock album generated as much heat ahead of its release as Radiohead's *In Rainbows*.

The fuss over the past week has centred on the band's decision to offer it, in the first instance, as an MP3 download from their own website for which fans can choose to pay whatever they like. But this was only the last drama in a saga which has rumbled on for the best part of three years. Out of contract with their old label Parlophone in 2003 after finishing *Hail to the Thief*, and with only themselves now to please, Radiohead have dallied over *In Rainbows* like no other record in their sixteen-year career. On the face of it, this is not good news. Extended, unsupervised periods in the recording studio are notoriously bad for rock bands and tend to result in overblown stillborns like Fleetwood Mac's cocaine opus *Tusk* and the inconsequential doodlings that dominate the Stone Roses' sadly mistitled *Second Coming*.

But in Radiohead's case, the delays and the false starts have had a happy ending. Maybe it was a good thing that Jonny Greenwood, who was appointed the BBC Concert Orchestra's composer in residence in 2004, was distracted by his first commission ('Super Het Receiver') when the band began work on their seventh album in early 2005. Thom Yorke's abrupt departure later that year to work on a solo album clearly didn't do any harm either. Perhaps it was the very fact that their two most restlessly experimental members have been able to let off steam away from Radiohead meant that when the band finally reconvened last year they set about recording their most straightforwardly enjoyable album since *OK Computer*.

Here, back at last, is the magic ingredient that has been lacking, or at least hiding, on Radiohead records ever since a highly-disgruntled Thom Yorke came off the road exhausted in 1999 and announced that he had 'had it with melody'. What a sad day that was, coming from the man who dreamed up 'Fake Plastic Trees' and 'Karma Police', to name but two of the sublimely original tunes that turned Radiohead into a much-loved, multi-million selling global draw. Say what you like about *Kid A*, *Amnesiac* and *Hail to the Thief* – and there is much that can be said, for and against – none of the group's twenty-first-century offerings boasts a melody that can hold a candle, let alone a lofted cigarette lighter, to the best of Radiohead in the 1990s.

Though *In Rainbows* puts that to rights, it takes its time to show its full hand. The opening track 'Step 15' finds Yorke doing his impersonation of a ghostly choirboy over a mildly autistic, *Kid-A*-flavoured hip-hop beat. 'Bodysnatchers' continues in a vein familiar to fans of the band's recent work, with a fuzzed guitar riff having a fight with a competing time signature from the rhythm section while Yorke wails over the top. Everything changes with track three, 'Nude', a song that sounds like a classic old soul ballad with some slightly strange sonic edges. This reminds you instantly of the widescreen, emotionally coloured splendour that Radiohead used to evoke on a regular basis before the urge to unsettle listeners usurped the desire to offer them something more cathartic.

In Rainbows doesn't really put a foot wrong from then on in. The band can't resist a dash of dissonance and random distortion here and there, but then again they wouldn't still be Radiohead if they had edited that out of the mix; and for every nod to weirdness for its own sake there is a string arrangement that's more up George Martin's street than Messiaen's.

Likewise, a few of Thom Yorke's lines still retain that truculently tetchy undergraduate air, particularly when he starts bemoaning the 'collapsing infrastructure' on 'House of Cards'; but Yorke has never written a more direct love song than the bell-strewn 'All I Need', or penned a catchier singalong anthem than 'Jigsaw Falling into Place'. Radiohead aren't obviously trying to reclaim ground they surrendered after their world conquest with *OK Computer*: their guitar arrangements here tend to favour acoustic strums and delicate arpeggios rather than the thunderous twang of old.

They've done epic, for the time being anyway. For all that, their seventh album sits far closer to their third than it does to their sixth. With a less unconventional outfit, you would have to call *In Rainbows* a return to form. With Radiohead it feels more like the band have finally solved a problem that only they would ever have thought needed solving in the first place.

3

Review of Phil Selway's
Familial

Wyndham Wallace, bbc.co.uk,
August 2010

Guaranteed worldwide coverage because of his day job as Radiohead's drummer and signed to Bella Union, a UK indie label currently at the top of its game, Phil Selway is in an enviable position.

It's hard not to wonder what his fate might be were he not part of one of the world's most successful rock bands, however. Singer-songwriters serving up softly spoken whimsy aren't exactly in short supply, after all, and *Familial* certainly breaks few boundaries. In fact, even the most fervent of Radiohead fans might lack the patience to get excited about this humble collection. But therein lies its charm.

Distancing himself as much from the oblique lyrical tendencies favoured by Thom Yorke as from Radiohead's complex approach to alternative, occasionally experimental rock, Selway here restricts himself mainly to acoustic guitars, barely perceptible rhythm tracks and whispered sincerity. Indeed, the most striking aspect of its production is his modesty: rather than gathering together famous friends, he turned to Lisa Germano, an artist whose profile has dwindled so far since her 1994 4AD debut that she barely qualifies for cult status, and to Wilco's Glen Kotche and Patrick Sansone.

Instead of Nigel Godrich's expansive studio techniques, Selway hired engineer Ian Davenport and recorded in his management company's studios. Forsaking oblique angst at the world's injustices, moreover, he writes as a man in his mid-forties about, as the title suggests, domestic matters, inspired by the 2006 death of his mother. Consequently *Familial* initially seems timid, even half-hearted, but persistence reveals an album full of sweet sentiment and honest meditations. Opener 'By Some Reflection' dwells in hushed tones on the familiar artistic problem of depression, 'The Ties That Bind Us' is full of references to '*the family man*' and his desire to '*shield*' his son '*from my mistakes*', and 'Broken Promises' addresses the loss of his mother in universal, touching terms.

Whether this understated, almost folksy collection is easily distinguished from the endless stream of sensitive types pouring out their hearts onto tape, however, is hard to say. But 'Don't Look Down', with its subtle background drone, is as soothing as chamomile tea, and 'A Simple Life' boasts a startling, haunting brass arrangement.

If Selway's fame can help encourage people to explore the more refined subtleties of music like this, then he's served himself and his fellow songwriters well.

Review of
The King of Limbs

Mike Diver, bbc.co.uk,
February 2011

R adiohead's sense of timing is quite something. Just when it looks like Arcade Fire, on a high after victory at the Grammy and Brit awards, are set to become The Biggest Band In The World, the Oxford five-piece confirm that their eighth album isn't only done, but yours for a few bucks in mere seconds – no need to get dressed, let alone leave the house.

When it looks like teenage hip hop crew Odd Future are going to send Twitter into meltdown on the back of an alarming video, these old-timers position their own promo clip online, sit back and watch social networks collapse under the weight of a million thumbs-in-a-frenzy sorts expressing their adoration.

Their grasp of timing, in an arrangements-versus-attention sense, is equally remarkable. Just as 2007's *In Rainbows* shaved several minutes from the run-time of the preceding *Hail to the Thief*, so *The King of Limbs* cuts their full-length form down to a concise eight tracks and thirty-seven minutes. It's the band's shortest ever album, perfectly tuned to the listener of the twenty-first-century – perhaps more likely to listen to music on the way in or out of work, on a commute, than at their leisure with a nice glass of red. Of course, the digital distribution of the band's previous LP was so successful that this set was sure to follow a similar release pattern – something tangible will follow in March – but this is a remarkably neat and tidy package. Perhaps it wasn't sequenced with succinctness in mind; but that it does its job in a short space of time is important.

Because if *The King of Limbs* dragged its limbs for too much longer, the impression left might be very different. For five tracks this album unfolds in a manner very similar to *In Rainbows'* memorable array of electro-chirrups and synth-sweeps, all glitches and groans where, a decade previous, Radiohead were very much A Guitar Band. The staggering, off-kilter step of opener 'Bloom' might not click with those holding a candle for The Return of the Gallagher a week from this record's release, but to anyone with even half an ear tuned to *In Rainbows* it'll seem very (although not over-) familiar indeed.

'Morning Mr Magpie' plucks its way into a Foals-ian spin, the masters seemingly taking on board a few tips from their hometown pupils. 'Lotus Flower' – the source of #thomdance Twitter activity once its video was unveiled – is another piece that looks backwards rather than projecting into bold, new sonic territories. It flails and flaps, but in a manner entirely in keeping with its makers' predilection for the metronomic; to the wrong ears, it's five minutes of the same beat, utterly unremarkable.

But that's the beauty of Radiohead – they've never, certainly not since the breakthrough days of 'Creep', been a band for the people. They're too idiosyncratic for that, and even though there are moments aplenty here that suggest the band hasn't furthered their vision, subtle differences to a tested formula ensure *The King of Limbs* is another great album from Britain's most consistently brilliant band. And come 'Codex', it truly strikes the listener dumb. Like 'Motion Picture Soundtrack', 'Street Spirit', 'Sail to the Moon', 'Nude' – insert your own favourite slow-paced Radiohead number here – it's a piece of rarefied beauty. Thom says something about dragonflies, something else about nobody getting hurt; the words blur and blend, though, as beneath them the simplest, most strikingly gorgeous piano motif bores its way into the heart.

And it's here, not any of your limited-character blogging or video-sharing sites, that Radiohead trump all comers, again.

5

Jonny Greenwood:
'What do I do? I just generally
worry about things . . . '

Rob Young, *Uncut*,
April 2011

————

The car pulls into the courtyard of a small complex of offices in the middle of a housing estate on the fringes of Didcot, an Oxfordshire railway town. There are two doors into this unit and we take the right-hand one at first, which leads, like the proverbial rabbit hole, into a warren of cramped rooms.

Here's a drum kit, now a stack of guitar amps and, finally, as the air becomes muggier, even slightly fetid, we reach the control room, a windowless space piled high with effects racks, keyboards, a crumpled black leather sofa and mixing desk. This is where Jonny Greenwood has been lurking, putting the finishing touches this damp January morning to his soundtrack for Lynne Ramsay's adaptation of Lionel Shriver's *We Need to Talk about Kevin*, made for BBC Films and starring Tilda Swinton and John C. Reilly.

Despite being enthused by the outcome – mainly music played by Jean Kelly on a seven-string Irish harp – Greenwood seems eager to get out of this lightless place and, after manager Bryce Edge hands him a plastic bag of victuals from the local Waitrose, suggests we retire to the awards-lined lounge of his management's offices up the left-hand staircase. Looking at the shiny discs, trophies and statuettes Radiohead have picked up for *OK Computer*, *Kid A* and others over the years, one can't help but wonder: how is work progressing on the follow-up to 2007's *In Rainbows*?

'It seems to be slow, but there's lots of work going on,' Greenwood explains. 'We've been with each other an awful lot. It's more about working out which is the right path to go down for each of the songs and ideas. I don't think people appreciate what a mess most bands' records are until they're finalised, the songs are in order and you've left the right ones off and put the right ones on and suddenly it has something. We're quite incompetent, I think, and always have been.'

Right now, Greenwood is representing his parallel side, his composerly career which has run alongside (and fed into) Radiohead for several years. This month his music – introspective orchestral stuff – graces the soundtrack of Tran Anh Hung's *Norwegian Wood*, a stately, melancholy, period-detail-soaked adaptation of Haruki Murakami's coming-of-age novel. At just over two hours, the film's hazy, atmospheric evocation of late-'60s' Tokyo is strangely static and for much of the first hour the only music that's heard is a sprinkling of early Can tracks.

'I told him about Can,' claims Greenwood, 'because originally, he had lots of Doors, and I had the Oliver Stone heebie-jeebies about "This is the '60s", Jimi Hendrix and so on. I thought, Can, they had a Japanese singer, it sort of fits . . .'

Greenwood's music for films began in 2003 with *Bodysong*, a wordless documentary about human motion and activity with antecedents in films like *Koyaanisqatsi*.

'Jonny always wanted to go against the grain, mess with expectations,' recalls *Bodysong*'s director, Simon Pummell. 'At one point he was looking into the possibilities of soundscapes of extinct languages. The way the percussion in the "Violence" section slowly shifts into a more synchronised, obsessional beat – and moves from excitement to something oppressive, as the images escalate from brawling to genocidal brutality – is an example of the music really telling the story together with the images.'

He moved from art-house to mainstream theatres with Paul Thomas Anderson's *There Will Be Blood* in 2007, with a harsh catgut accompaniment – 'music about the characters and the landscape', he says – that scaled the movie's epic peaks and troughs with atonal introspection and wide-horizon scrape. Partly derived from a stand-alone commission he'd written for the BBC Concert Orchestra called 'Popcorn Superhet Receiver', it was a musical language of understatement.

'It's recurring textures,' explains Robert Ziegler, who conducted the orchestra on both soundtrack recordings. 'Certain clusters that he used, especially in *There Will Be Blood*, just nailed the quality of the film. And some of the new music he wrote – propulsive, rhythmic things – worked out wonderfully. He got that menace; on one of the most brilliant cues, "Open Spaces", he played the ondes Martenot [an eerie-sounding early electronic instrument] and the whole conception of it was perfect. Those huge Texas landscapes and it was just this little cue, but it lifted the whole film.'

I ask Greenwood whether he needs something visual as a starting point. 'Yeah,' he replies, 'I enjoy having something to write the music for that's concrete, but at the same time the luxury of it not being that concrete, more an excuse to write music. My most exciting days ever are the morning of recording a quartet or an orchestra or a harp player, and knowing they're coming, and setting up the stands and mics and putting music out for them. And then after four hours it's all over and you've got something. I've had a real soft ride. Traditionally film composers are way below the make-up people in the pecking order. It's not seen as important, unless you find enthusiastic directors. And I've been lucky three times in a row.'

Is that excitement greater than coming out on stage in front of thousands at a Radiohead gig? 'Yeah, I think it is,' he says. 'Because you've got weeks of preparation, and it's just on paper and wondering what is going to happen. These great musicians are coming in and you can hand them something that's fairly lifeless and they can make it very musical. That's been a big discovery for me: you realise how much they put into it . . . they can make things sound musical even if it's just a C major chord. It can sound far more exciting than you thought it was going to. It's a big secret, but you don't realise how much input comes from these people. "I can do this four or five different ways – which way would you like it?" Or "You can get this kind of effect from the strings" and so on.'

Robert Ziegler is in no doubt of Greenwood's talents as a composer, citing Polish modernist Penderecki as an antecedent. 'Obviously he's got the same attraction to masses of sound and big clusters of orchestral sound. As a film composer you have to be careful not to "frighten the horses" and the producers . . . '

There Will Be Blood led directly to Greenwood's next commission, as Tran Anh Hung used some of it as guide music on early cuts of *Norwegian Wood*. 'When I saw *There Will Be Blood*,' says Hung, 'I was completely seduced by Jonny's music. It was a "new sound" with a profoundness that I have not heard elsewhere in films. The emotions coming from his music were so . . . right, so mysterious and yet so obvious. No doubt for me that Jonny's music would give a dark, deep beauty that *Norwegian Wood* needed.' Eventually Greenwood adapted another piece, 'Doghouse', for the finished film. 'Doghouse' is a triple concerto for violin, viola and cello, inspired by thoughts of Wally Stott's scores for Scott Walker songs like 'It's Raining Today' and 'Rosemary' languishing in the BBC library. On a structural level, 'As a toddler l was once shown that the note D on a piano is between the two black notes, and that's D because it is in a kennel, and that piece is written with this symmetrical pattern that started on that note,' Greenwood explains.

———

The hands-on business of composing music might seem diametrically opposed to rock's spontaneity. But since 2000's *Kid A*, Radiohead have been moving away from the sound of five men in a room playing live to a more laboriously constructed, digitally processed approach. The forces of group and orchestra were combined on the group's most recent offering, 'Harry Patch (In Memory Of)', a tribute to the last surviving WWI veteran (who died in 2009, aged 111).

How does Greenwood, who trained on the viola at school, see these two methods complementing each other? 'There have always been bits of orchestration in Radiohead,' he acknowledges.

'It's always been good to have the knowledge of music theory and I've used it all the time. A big part of what we've always done is slightly scientifically tried to copy something which we can't. It's always been like that, whether it was bits of *OK Computer* that in our heads we wanted to be like *Bitches Brew* – and the fact that none of us could play the trumpet, or jazz, didn't bother us. Which sounds like arrogance, but it's more that you aim and miss and don't let it bother you. And a lot of this film stuff is trying to do something I don't really know how to do, so I'm scrabbling around and getting a little lost and unsure, but it's been a nice way of working.'

In person, Greenwood is reserved and modest. But all the same, he becomes enthusiastic when discussing the more exciting aspects of his job. Here is a man, it seems, who even uses his down-time constructively in the pursuit of making music.

'Touring's been good for working on classical stuff,' he explains. 'I've had hours and hours in hotel rooms. The silence . . . '

So is there such a thing as a typical day for him at present, and what does he do when he's not working?

'I play the piano a lot at the moment,' he says after a pause. 'I don't know, I'm a bit low on hobbies. I used to do lots of photography . . . I don't know. What do I do? What do you do? I just generally worry about things, I think? And daydream ideas for programming.' That puts him back in his stride. 'The programming is really fun at the moment, very satisfying. I spend half my time writing music software, computer-based sound generators for Radiohead. Trying to bypass other people's ideas of what music software should do and how it should sound, going back a step. It's like building wonky drum machines, not using pre-sets, basically. It's like Mouse Trap, you construct things.'

Has he got a mathematical mind, then?

'I like a lot of popular science writing – John Gribbin and stuff. Lots of nerdy science and linguistics books. Yeah, I'm a bit trainspottery, let's not deny it.'

'As a guitar player he's extraordinary: a virtuoso, frenetic and full of personality,' testifies Bernard Butler, who views Greenwood as one of a quartet of players with distinctive styles who emerged at roughly the same moment, including himself, John Squire and Graham Coxon. 'We're all very emotional and slightly deranged guitar players and have an overwrought and melodic sensibility. I can't think of any guitar players with those qualities at the moment. It's a most un-Radiohead thing to do, but he probably did meet a devil at a crossroads somewhere, along the A1 probably.'

How, I ask Greenwood, would he like to be remembered, as a composer or as a respected guitarist?

'God, not as a "guitar stylist"!' he bursts out. 'Helping to write some very good songs, playing on them and recording them with this amazing band is like nothing else. As to what people think years from now . . . You see our record winning top album of the last whatever years, but then you see shocking albums winning the same thing twenty, thirty years ago and you think, it's nice but . . . all that really matters is what we do next, really.'

Such a comment naturally leads to more gentle probing about forthcoming plans for the Radiohead crew.

'We've been recording and working,' he allows. 'We're in the frame of mind of wanting to finish things and then decide what to do next. The old-fashioned way of thinking, when we had a record label, was: "You need to book the tour today, even though you're only halfway through the record." And we can't do that anymore. We just want to finish something and be satisfied.'

Leaving EMI to go it alone has meant, not surprisingly, 'you lose the structure, but then you are a bit freer. None of us are very nostalgic for those days of waiting for somebody's approval of your recording. But I've always said [that] at EMI we had a good relationship compared with some people.'

But in the age of digital distribution and the increasingly invisible presence of music on the high street, and given that *In Rainbows* was launched with its radical pay-what-you-like policy – plus an extraordinary, free, televised late-night gig at east London's Rough Trade store – chances are, however the next record ends up, there'll be something of a fanfare.

'I don't like how music dribbles out,' he announces as we wrap things up. 'I like events. That's the only thing, really.'

6

Review of
Atoms For Peace's *Amok*

Wyndham Wallace, bbc.co.uk,
February 2013

A supergroup they may ostensibly be, but it's hard to shake the impression that – despite the presence of Radiohead producer Nigel Godrich, Red Hot Chilli Peppers bassist Flea, regular Beck drummer Joey Waronker and Brazilian percussionist Mauro Refosco – in reality *Amok* is the second chapter in Thom Yorke's solo career.

It's hard, too, to avoid comparing *Amok* with Radiohead, given Yorke's distinctive voice and talent for an unusual tune, both of which remain central to his new project. Here, however, he immerses himself fully in the glitchy electronica that's inspired him since working on *Kid A*. Though there are traits familiar from recent 'head albums – *The King of Limbs*' 'Feral', for instance – *Amok* has its own restless, simultaneously sophisticated and gauche personality.

In fact, it displays the same twitchy rhythms and occasionally genial sincerity that Yorke displays with his onstage dancing. Built from three days of studio jamming around existing laptop sketches, its intent is to lend electronica a sense of songcraft, to create a world where digital and analogue blur, and frequently it succeeds. Yorke's ghostly falsetto traces an easily followed line through the agitated percussion and nebulous textures of 'Before Your Very Eyes . . . ' and 'Unless', while 'Stuck Together Pieces''s defining features are a rolling bassline and rippling guitar that drift amidst the muted clatter of programmed beats.

'Judge, Jury and Executioner', meanwhile, buries acoustic guitars in a cloudy chorus of incorporeal vocals, its slightness deceptive thanks to a weirdly infectious melody, and there's a sense of claustrophobia inherent in 'Ingenue''s befuddled atmosphere and oddly tropical backdrop. But the more one delves into *Amok*'s spasmodic content, the more one perceives the characteristics that make Radiohead so special: the unexpected breakdown, the unforeseen musical diversion. Here, though, divorced from his band's familiar expressive delivery, their genesis as abstract ideas generated in solitude is occasionally too conspicuous.

Nonetheless, while *Amok* – like *The Eraser* – is unlikely to arouse the same passions as, for instance, *In Rainbows*, it's an often fulfilling and fascinating indulgence. Yorke remains consistently inventive, whatever company he keeps.

7

In a Room with Radiohead

Adam Thorpe, *Times Literary Supplement*,
18 May 2016

C olin has contacted me to say he'll be recording with his band 'nearish you', outside Saint-Rémy-de-Provence. We would have most of the morning to chat, as recording is usually between midday and the early hours. I have never before seen a band at work in the studio, and the band in question – Radiohead – is notoriously secretive about its methods. Would I get a glimpse?

The route keeps to the ancient Via Domitia between olive groves and ripe vineyards: joining the road just metres away from our flat in central Nîmes, I leave it an hour later for a country lane, down which the studios are reached between two stone pillars. La Fabrique was once a nineteenth-century mill where madder root was crushed into red dye and artist's pigment. In 1889, Van Gogh voluntarily entered the asylum in Saint-Rémy, producing dozens of paintings; perhaps he paid the mill a visit.

At any rate, his spirit would be a suitable presiding genius for the band's sojourn here: what I have understood through Colin is that Radiohead achieve their music through a kind of obsessional persistence, much of it by trial and error. Years ago, Colin played me the taped result of a week or so's exploration in their Oxford studios; it was a mere sketch and I wondered how on earth those basic rhythms and chords could become one of the intricate, haunting and eccentrically original numbers, streaked by Thom Yorke's bright voice (frequently ranging into a crystalline falsetto), that have turned Radiohead from a sixth-form band into the world's most inventive.

I park in the front courtyard and Colin appears in a dark blue jersey, jeans and white trainers, greeting me warmly. The plan is to start with breakfast as the rest of the band trickle in. I haven't seen them since they played the huge Roman arena in Nîmes three years before. Colin was nervous at the time: over supper in our flat, he reminded us that this gig was their first since the tragic accident in Toronto, when the lighting rig collapsed onto the stage and the tour's drum technician, Scott Johnson, was killed. The Nîmes concert was remarkable, ending with multiple images of Scott. Backstage afterwards there was a palpable sense of relief.

The old mill, a three-storey edifice of vast length and many glassed-in arches, sits in two hectares of parkland and is famous for its varied acoustics: the likes of Morrissey and Nick Cave have recorded here. After coffee and croissants in the cosy dining room, Colin takes me on a tour, from the music library holding the biggest vinyl collection in the world to a gargantuan grain storehouse now full of dusty film canisters and boxes containing unplayable digital tapes (an early misstep in the march of progress).

The studio itself is strange: a sunlit suite of rooms with antique rugs, ornate fireplaces and elegant period furniture, lined with books in wooden cabinets and invaded by recording equipment, as if the teenage scion of a stately home has taken advantage of his parents' absence. A whiteboard shows only a list of tracks in black marker pen, starting with 'Daydreaming' and ending with 'Burn the Witch'. The rejected James Bond film tune, 'Spectre', floats in the middle, slightly separate. Colin points to the main console, a vast sweep of knobs, buttons and faders. 'This is a Neve 88 R, seventy-two channels, made in Burnley. Worth about a hundred thousand. It's analogue, like this reel-to-reel Studer, but we also use digital. It's all about looping and layering.' In the older, vaulted section, part of the floor is stone, with a giant hieroglyph chiselled out. 'Probably Roman,' he explains, 'where the millstone went.'

This is all layers as well, a *mille feuille* of epochs and moments and seems perfectly attuned to Radiohead's methods. We wander out into the grounds: tree-surrounded lawns, large swimming pool, further courtyards and barns, decayed cottages and a softly roaring mill-race. In one of the larger *granges*, numerous canvases display abstract explosions of colour. The barn's speakers are wired up to the recording studios: the band's resident artist Stanley Donwood reacts in acrylic to what he hears, the results to be modified and manipulated on computer for the LP's cover.

Colin is discreet about his role, playing the straight man to his charismatic younger brother Jonny, whose gaunt good looks seem forever obscured behind loops of lamp-black hair. Colin once told me, half-jokingly, that he reckoned he was 'rubbish' at playing, that he really had to concentrate on the complex rhythms, the bass line often holding everything together: in concert he keeps his back to the audience, bowed over the guitar, with a little rhythm-marking jump now and again, as if over an invisible rope. It's at moments like these that I sense the band dissolving back into its sixth-form origins: as if my own distant memories of tootling on a sax in a cellar to my school friends' blasts of guitar and drums might just have ended up in a similar place, being roared at by hundreds of thousands of fans. I once asked Colin what that was like. 'You focus down on the stage, which becomes your own intimate space. You're just playing in your room with friends.'

Phil the drummer greets us in one of the courtyards. I tell him that my grown-up children watched him perform solo recently in Victoria Park in London and they thought he was the best. 'Oh, blimey,' he says, touchingly pleased. 'I looked around and realised I was the oldest participant, apart from Patti Smith.' The five members of Radiohead have been worrying about their age for some time: dining with the band one evening in an Arles square thirteen years ago, I heard Thom Yorke announce that he would quit rock music when he was forty. He didn't want to be a Mick Jagger, still prancing about in his withered old age. Fifty now looms, but when he appears crossing a lawn in a kind of Flaubertian dressing gown and towel turban, cool behind reflective shades, he could be twenty, aside from his salt-and-pepper stubble. He agrees that the last Nîmes concert was 'pretty emotional'. Knowing he has another long day of intense creating in front of him, we leave him be.

Colin and I catch up on personal things at the table on the gravel sweep between mill and garden, with a view of clipped box shrubs in ornamental vases, and brawny Ed, the genial six-foot-three guitarist, basking shirtless a few yards along. I ask Colin if he's pleased with the recording so far: expectations are high after five years. 'I can't talk about it much, as Nigel [the producer] is really secretive about our ways. But I like a lot of it. It's beautifully lyrical in places. There's one with a straight chord sequence, so that can go next to the cold spy one. The fluffy puppy next to the warthog!' I ask if the band are perfectionists. 'Oh, I don't know. I suppose we can't be or we'd never release anything. And we all have different likes.'

Back in the studio, the youthful technicians are checking things over. Jonny, ever restless, is in a brass-studded leather chair crouched over his home-made sound machine (little hammers hitting various objects) and its accompanying laptop, and Ed is listening to him in front of his long row of guitars. Jonny establishes a rhythm, part-calypso, part-reggae, with his yoghurt cartons, tubs, bells and mini-tambourine. 'Sounds a bit like Marvin Gaye,' Ed comments.

For all the priceless equipment, we have indeed come back to lads tinkering in their rooms: perhaps this is the heart of all this fertile imagining, its idiosyncrasies not so far from a poet's manner. Colin ushers me gently out, the secret ceremony about to begin. I mention Freelance [a regular column in the *Times Literary Supplement*]; he's a *TLS* fan (he read English at Cambridge). 'That'd be cool. It might be the only one, we're not commissioning anything. A literary piece, written by a poet! Just make sure you call me the more handsome of the Greenwood brothers,' he adds, grinning, and I drive out of the gates into the ordinary world.

Contributors

Pat Blashill wrote about rock and pop for *Rolling Stone, SPIN* and *Details* from 1987 to 2003. He grew up in Texas, consuming a steady diet of Butthole Surfers records and Ed Wood movies. He now lives in Vienna, Austria, and still writes about stuff for the Munich newspaper *Sueddeutsche Zeitung*.

Stephen Dalton began his career on the *NME* at the dawn of the 1990s, surviving acid house, Madchester, grunge, Britpop, electroclash, New Grave, New Rave, and at least four 1980s synth-pop revivals. Over the last 20 years he has also been a regular contributor to *The Times, Uncut, Electronic Sound, Classic Rock, Hollywood Reporter* and various other publications.

Tom Doyle is an acclaimed music journalist, author, and long-standing contributor to *MOJO* and *Q*. His work has also appeared in *Billboard*, the *Guardian*, *The Times*, and *Sound on Sound*. He is the author of *The Glamour Chase: The Maverick Life of Billy MacKenzie*, which has attained the status of a classic rock biography since its original publication, and biographies of Paul McCartney and Elton John. He lives in London, England.

Ted Drozdowski is a freelance journalist and musician living in Boston, Massachusetts. His work has appeared internationally in a wide variety of publications including *Tracks, Rolling Stone* and *Musician*. Before freelancing, he was associate arts editor at the *Boston Phoenix* and an editor at *Musician*.

Andy Gill has written for *NME, Q, MOJO*, the *Independent* and numerous other publications. He is the author of, among other books, *Don't Think Twice, It's Alright: Bob Dylan, the Early Years* (Carlton).

Ian Gittins is a music writer for the *Guardian*, formerly of *Melody Maker* and *Q*. He was co-author with Nikki Sixx of Mötley Crüe of the *New York Times* bestseller *The Heroin Diaries,* and with David Essex of his *Sunday Times* No. 1 bestselling autobiography *Over the Moon.* He is the also the author of *A Perfect Dream*, a 2018 biography of the Cure, and is currently writing a book with Billy Connolly.

Mark Greif is an author, educator and cultural critic. His most recent book is *Against Everything.* One of the co-founders of *n+1*, he is a frequent contributor to the magazine and writes for numerous other publications. Greif teaches literature at Stanford University.

John Harris is the author of *The Last Party: Britpop, Blair and the Demise of English Rock* (2003), *So Now Who Do We Vote For?* which examined the 2005 UK general election, a 2006 behind-the-scenes look at the production of Pink Floyd's *The Dark Side of the Moon*, and *Hail! Hail! Rock'n'Roll* (2009). He now writes about music for *MOJO* and *Q*, while devoting most of his working time to reporting, commentary and video journalism at the *Guardian*. He was named Political Commentator of the Year at the UK Press Awards for 2017.

Will Hermes is the author of *Love Goes To Buildings On Fire: Five Years in New York That Changed Music Forever* (Farrar, Straus & Giroux, 2011), an acclaimed history of the New York City music scene in the 1970s. A contributing editor for *Rolling Stone* and a long-time contributor to NPR's *All Things Considered*, his work appears periodically in *The New York Times*; he has also written for the *Village Voice*, *Spin*, *Slate*, *Salon*, *The Believer*, *GQ* and other publications. He co-edited *SPIN: 20 Years of Alternative Music* (Crown/Three Rivers, 2006), and his writing has been included in the *Da Capo Best Music Writing* series.

Barney Hoskyns began writing for *NME* in the early '80s and is a former contributing editor at British *Vogue* and US correspondent for *MOJO*. He is the author of the bestselling *Hotel California* (2006), the Tom Waits biography *Lowside of the Road* (2009), and *Trampled Under Foot* (2012), an oral history of Led Zeppelin. He has written for the *Guardian*, *Uncut*, *Spin*, *Rolling Stone* and *GQ*. *Small Town Talk*, his history of the music scene in and around Woodstock, New York, was published in 2016.

Nick Kent was one of the most important and influential music journalists of the 1970s and remains a hugely respected commentator to this day. He wrote for *New Musical Express* and *The Face* and is the author of *The Dark Stuff*, a collection of his journalism.

Nick has written for numerous publications and lives in Paris with his partner, Laurence Romance, and their son. His memoir *Apathy for the Devil* was published by Faber in 2010.

Clare Kleinedler began her career at groundbreaking online zine *Addicted to Noise* in the mid-'90s. She went on to serve as the music editor for *WIRED* magazine in early 2000. Her work has been published in numerous publications including the *Los Angeles Times*, the *San Francisco Chronicle*, *BAM*, *Paper* and *XLR8R* among others.

Paul Lester was Features Editor of *Melody Maker* and Deputy Editor of *Uncut*. Since then he has written books on Gang Of Four and Wire, and interviewed over a thousand musicians for the *Guardian*, the *Sunday Times* Culture section, *Telegraph* Arts & Books, *MOJO*, *Classic Rock*, *Classic Pop* and *Prog*. He is currently the editor of *Record Collector* magazine.

Paul Moody is a writer and musician. His first band, The Studio 68!, recorded an album called *Portobellohello* in 1992. He later joined the *NME* and then toured the world in psychedelic renegades Regular Fries. More recently he co-wrote a book called *Looking For The Moon Under Water*, based on George Orwell's description's of his perfect pub (published by Orion). He now lives in Hastings, England, and dreams of the perfect wave.

Ronan Munro is the editor of Oxford music monthly *Nightshift*, originally *Curfew*, and was the first journalist to write about and interview On A Friday, the five-piece band that became Radiohead.

Peter Murphy is a writer, spoken-word performer, journalist, musician and actor. He has published two novels, *John the Revelator* and *Shall We Gather at the River* (Faber), while his non-fiction work has appeared in *Rolling Stone*, the *Guardian* and *Hot Press*, and he has released two albums with the Revelator Orchestra. He is a regular contributor to the *Irish Times* and RTE's arts show *Arena*, and currently performs and records under the name Cursed Murphy.

Ann Powers is a critic for NPR and a contributor at the *Los Angeles Times*, where she was previously chief pop critic. She has also served as pop critic on *The New York Times* and an editor at the *Village Voice*. Powers is the author of *Weird Like Us: My Bohemian America*, a memoir; *Good Booty: Love and Sex, Black & White, Body and Soul in American Music*, on eroticism in American pop music; and *Piece by Piece*, co-authored with Tori Amos.

Simon Price is an award-winning British music critic. His three-decades-plus career includes nine years at *Melody Maker* magazine and twelve at the *Independent on Sunday* newspaper, during which time he was voted Live Reviews Writer of the Year on three consecutive occasions at the Record of the Day Awards. He currently contributes to publications including *Q* magazine, the *Guardian*, *Metro* and *The Quietus*. Price currently lectures in Music Journalism at the BIMM Institute in Brighton.

Simon Reynolds is the author of eight books about pop culture, including *Shock and Awe: Glam Rock and its Legacy* (2016), *Retromania: Pop Culture's Addiction to Its Own Past* (2011), *Rip It Up and Start Again: Postpunk 1978–84* (2005), and *Energy Flash:*

A Journey Through Rave Music and Dance Culture (1998). He started his career as a music critic at *Melody Maker*, where he was a staff writer from 1986 to 1990. Since then he has freelanced for magazines including *The New York Times*, the *Village Voice*, the *Guardian*, *Pitchfork*, and *The Wire*. Reynolds operates a number of blogs centred around the hub Blissblog http://blissout.blogspot.com/. Born in London, a resident of New York during much of the 1990s and 2000s, he currently lives in Los Angeles.

Robert Sandall wrote for *Q*, *Rolling Stone*, *The Word* and *GQ* magazines. He was the chief rock critic for the *Sunday Times* from 1988 and later wrote regularly for the *Daily Telegraph*. He was best known for presenting, with Mark Russell, BBC Radio 3's *Mixing It* programme from 1990 until 2007. After ending on Radio 3 the show moved to Resonance FM in London, where it continued under the name *Where's the Skill in That?* for a further two years. Sandall also presented editions of the BBC's *Late Junction* and contributed to BBC Radio 4's *Front Row*. He died in July 2010.

Will Self is the author of ten novels, five collections of shorter fiction, three novellas, and five collections of non-fiction writing. His work has been translated into 22 languages; his 2002 novel *Dorian, an Imitation* was longlisted for the Booker Prize, and his novel *Umbrella* was shortlisted for the Man Booker Prize. His fiction is known for being satirical, grotesque, and fantastical, and is predominantly set within his home city of London. His subject matter often includes mental illness, illegal drugs and psychiatry. He is a regular contributor to publications including the *Guardian*, the *New Statesman*, *The New York Times* and the *London Review of Books*.

R.J. Smith has been a senior editor at *Los Angeles* magazine, a contributor to *Blender*, a columnist for the *Village Voice*, a staff writer for *Spin*, and has written for *GQ*, the *New York Times Magazine*, and *Men's Vogue*. He is the author of *The Great Black Way*, the James Brown biography *The One*, and *American Witness: the Art and Life of Robert Frank*. He lives in Cincinnati.

Jim Sullivan began writing freelance music reviews and features for the *Boston Globe* in 1979. He also wrote for such national music publications as *The Record, Creem* and *Music-Sound Output*. He joined the staff of the *Boston Globe* in 1988, specialising in pop music and culture until 2005. He also freelanced for the *Boston Phoenix* and the *Christian Science Monitor* and currently does the same for Boston public radio station WBUR's arts website, the ARTery, the *Cape Cod Times* and Best Classic Bands. He also hosts a podcast/video show called Boston Rock/Talk.

Adam Sweeting was the features editor of *Melody Maker* and was rock critic for the *Guardian* as well as contributing to *Q, Uncut, GQ* and *Esquire*. He has written regularly for the *Daily Telegraph* and *The Times Saturday Magazine* and is a prolific obituarist for the *Guardian*. He is a co-founder of, and regular contributor to, the arts website theartsdesk.com.

Adam Thorpe is a Franco-British poet and novelist whose works also include short stories, translations, radio dramas and documentaries. He is a frequent contributor of reviews and articles to various newspapers, journals and magazines, including the *Guardian*, the *Poetry Review* and the *Times Literary Supplement*. His most recent book is *Notes from the Cévennes: Half a Lifetime in Provincial France*.

Wyndham Wallace's first book *Lee, Myself & I* (about his friendship with Lee Hazlewood) was published in 2015 by Jawbone Press. He writes regularly for *Uncut* and *Classic Pop*, as well as contributing to other publications including the *Guardian* and *The Quietus*. He's also the co-editor of Norwegian guide-book series *The Poor Man's Connoisseur*, translates German films for English speakers, and can be seen in *Almost Fashionable: A Film About Travis*.

Rob Young is a Contributing Editor of *The Wire* and also writes for *Uncut, Sight & Sound*, the *Guardian, Frieze* and *Artforum*. His books include *All Gates Open: The Story of Can* (Faber and Faber, 2018), *Electric Eden: Unearthing Britain's Visionary Music* (2010), *Rough Trade* (2006) and *Warp* (2005). He lives in Oslo.

Index